Karen Chamberlain is a late bloomer in her writing, producing this first book after having worked with the Health Department during a stressful time over the last few years. Karen now lives in Victoria with her border collie and cat.

Karen Chamberlain

IMAGINE

AUSTIN MACAULEY PUBLISHERS
LONDON * CAMBRIDGE * NEW YORK * SHARJAH

Copyright © Karen Chamberlain 2023

The right of Karen Chamberlain to be identified as author of this work has been asserted by the author in accordance with sections 77 and 78 of the Copyright, Designs and Patents Act 1988.

All rights reserved. No part of this publication may be reproduced, stored in a retrieval system, or transmitted in any form or by any means, electronic, mechanical, photocopying, recording, or otherwise, without the prior permission of the publishers.

Any person who commits any unauthorised act in relation to this publication may be liable to criminal prosecution and civil claims for damages.

This is a work of fiction. Names, characters, businesses, places, events, locales, and incidents are either the products of the author's imagination or used in a fictitious manner. Any resemblance to actual persons, living or dead, or actual events is purely coincidental.

A CIP catalogue record for this title is available from the British Library.

ISBN 9781035823178 (Paperback)
ISBN 9781035823185 (ePub e-book)

www.austinmacauley.com

First Published 2023
Austin Macauley Publishers Ltd®
1 Canada Square
Canary Wharf
London
E14 5AA

To my mother and my father who showed me the magic of books. Also, to my girls, thank you for your help and support with this book.

Chapter 1

It was Saturday morning and I was tidying up and passing the time to go to meditation eventually, when I started thinking about what to do with myself for the future, as time was ticking on and I was getting older.

I heard a little voice in my head (which wasn't unusual as I often spoke to ghosts, especially when I was younger and no, I'm not going nuts) *'what if everything you had been taught or told was wrong.'* I smiled to myself. *'I've often thought I was on the wrong time line; nothing has turned up yet and I'm not getting any younger. I think I gave up those thoughts a long time ago.'*

That also made me think of my parents, who had passed away a couple of months ago, feeling sad at their passing, but I felt as though I didn't really know them.

I went and sat on the sofa turning up the radio, as I loved this song coming on, with the sounds of John Lennon singing his song 'Imagine' in his dreamy English-Liverpool voice, full of hope. While I hummed away to the song it sent me into one of my daydreams; I have always been a daydreamer and always loved this song while I went into my daydream.

I started to drift back, almost like watching a movie in my head, to when we lived in New Zealand in a small town called Puku, when my mum first said I was 'weird'. I think I was around 7 or 8 having lots of dreams of different places and cultures that I had never been to. Talking with relatives, especially grandparents that had passed, going to tell my mum with her calling me, 'Weird' which brought out my temper, stomping my feet and going off down the street with distant sounds of thunder. I would find a bush area near the river to sit in with my dog (you can do that in NZ no snakes or spiders), to calm myself as I loved being outdoors. I would sit in the bush talking to my dog or would sit there listening to the sounds of nature around me.

Some of the most vivid dreams I had were of flying on a dragon out in the cool New Zealand air at night, excited and squealing but then waking up in my bed, only to be told it was a dream by my mother, feeling disappointed.

I would ask her what she thought they meant but all she did was end up getting angry at me, "If you don't stop having these dreams, we will have to take you to a 'special doctor' to see why this is happening. Now stop it!"

I hated doctors who were always trying to recommend some sort of medication to Mum, just as much as school; so, I stopped telling her about my dreams after that. I just kept them to myself or talked to my cat or dog, which I always had one around.

My dog would wander off sometimes and find someone who was walking by, to get their attention. A few times it was a man with dark hair who had a silver streak in the front, that I wasn't scared of for some reason, but I would have to grab her and tell him to bugger off!

My temper grew as I became a teenager finding other teenage girls really horrible. I had a close group of friends who knew me and tolerated my tempers, especially one girl who had a terrible stutter called Prudence Priddle.

That was just too much for the bullies, Prudence Priddle from Puku, to let go. We became good friends, because I was called either a weirdo, witch or just a plain dumb blonde. The dumb blonde jokes always wound me up bringing out my temper and getting me into trouble with the teachers.

Prue and I ended up giving ourselves nicknames from the Flintstones of Wilma for me and Betty for her, Wilma's sidekick. I smiled at the thought of us going around school together, wondering how she was going.

As I hit puberty, my temper became worse. I had always had poems or rhymes coming into my head of things I would like to happen. As I reached puberty, I learned to say those poems to myself and point at the person picking on me, with something usually happening. My favourite one was making chairs and tables collapse, giving Prue and I time to make our escape, giggling as we did.

If we got picked on in the corridors, things would happen like the school alarm bells ringing for no reason at all.

Prue would always encourage me with her laughter and positive ways, even though she was being picked on as well.

The teachers were always calling out my name when something mysterious happened, hearing my class mates laugh. I enjoyed making people laugh, so I became the class clown, doing more pranks just for the sake of it. Unfortunately, this also got me sent to the head master's office, getting to the point that I spent more time, there than I did in the classroom.

I was always picky on my food but as my temper grew this made me worse cutting down on a lot of things, angering my mother again. She would try to encourage me to cook so that I would eat more, but I hated it.

My mother would get annoyed, "No one will marry a woman who can't cook, has a bad temper and is skinny."

I would just go off in a huff, for another walk saying, "I don't care, I'm never getting married and if I do, he'll have to cook."

My teachers would constantly give me bad reports commenting on the pranks and if I wasn't doing pranks, I was always looking out the window daydreaming and not concentrating.

I did enjoy one subject in school and that was history. That subject also had a great teacher Mrs Armitage, who made history exciting, delving into why people did things and how they lived.

I asked Mum one time about the history of our family and all I got was her mother's side came from Norway and her father's side came from Germany and that she didn't know anything else other than they immigrated to New Zealand. Dad's side was a bit more transparent mainly coming from England.

I didn't get much relief when I got home from school either. My brothers Christian and Robert, who were older, were also horrible to me. Christian was worse calling me weird, especially if he heard me talking to Mum about my dreams in the past. He would think it funny if he could lock me in a cupboard when Mum and Dad went out, hearing me screaming and kicking. Robert ended up letting me out in the end telling me to stop being a baby.

I also learned to talk to ghosts around these times, feeling they were the only ones that would listen to me and not pick on me.

It was the 70s and the Star Wars era, so everyone had visions of "having the force with them." Mum caught me one day mimicking the Star Wars Jedi with powers saying to my dog, "You are in my power and you will do as I command you" with my dog sitting there starry eyed. All I heard was, "Hannah you stop that now!" It just made me angry again and I stormed off.

We might have been mother and daughter but Mum was from a small town where girls didn't worry about careers or anything, got married and had children. This was also evident in the treatment of my brothers who were allowed to do anything they wanted and weren't expected to do anything around the house. This just made me argue more with my parents. Some people would joke with me saying I was the milkman's daughter, because I was so different from everyone else in the family.

Mum and Dad decided to encourage me to get into some sport, as Dad especially, found that helped him when he was younger. So, I joined the school basketball team first, but kept falling over on the court or would get pushed by the other team, making my temper flare with a poem coming into my head and they would mysteriously fall over, hurting themselves. I decided this wasn't my thing, so I quit that.

I tried the school hockey team next and found that more to my liking, having a stick in my hand, being able to belt something down the field, which also helped stem my temper. They tried me out on the wings first, but I hated running, not being able to get my breathing right, so I was put in the backs.

The first time I played in the backs, I went very pale because we were playing a team with strong Māori girls in it. They would come running down the field with murderous looks on their faces smashing the hockey sticks of anyone who tried to get the ball off them, flicking mud up from their boots, like steam rollers. They would swipe at you even if you weren't going for the ball, causing me to learn to jump very quickly or take off, always finding a huge puddle to skid into.

I would recite the poems in my head again, which usually helped making the opposition team fall over, so we could get the ball off them. I would always take myself to hockey games jumping on my bike, because no one else in my family was interested and wouldn't take me to the games. I always came home with mud splattered everywhere, split lips and bruises all over my legs, but I felt satisfied.

With summer coming up, Mum had a friend who had a marching team (not the American Batton type) deciding this would be a good sport to keep me out of trouble as well as giving me some discipline during summer. I wasn't really interested at first, but I found out Prue was involved in the team, so I reluctantly rode my bike to a practice session, thinking I'd give it a go.

I didn't think much of it at first but Prue encouraged me to stick with it. I did end up enjoying the technical side of it as well as the travelling away for competitions. This gave me my 'wanderlust' and also gave me my freedom from home and my horrible brothers.

Prue and I would get up to mischief without getting caught, which was even better. Our favourite pass time when we were away was getting out the Ouija board bringing ghosts out and scaring the other team mates.

A church group came to the school one day, teaching about spiritual awareness and growth; so, I decided to check out a Sunday school session one time. Mum thought it was a good idea, but didn't want to come nor did anyone else in my family; so off I went again on my bike to go to Sunday school.

I didn't like it, but on the way, home I found a poster on a lamppost about yoga and meditation in an old church in the city. I decided that sounded more like what I wanted. I went to a session telling my mother I was going to a different church that met on a Wednesday evening, hiding my leotard in my bag. She thought it was strange but was pleased. I wasn't annoying her to go with me.

I got there a bit nervous, changing into my leotard (it was the 70s) which always managed to climb up my bum, walking into a hushed room with bare feet, by myself. There were other people there with friends talking quietly, watching as I walked in, hearing the old wooden floor boards squeak as I walked. I stopped, trying to find a board that didn't squeak, but it just didn't happen, getting annoyed and just walking to a spot hearing squeak-squeak-squeak all the way.

We did yoga first, going into all sorts of different positions thinking I was going to snap in some of them. The teacher then turned all the lights down and lit a candle in the middle of the floor. We had to look at the candle then put it in our heads to shut down any thoughts from the day. I smiled at myself, *'That's easy, I'm always doing that.'*

The teacher took us through a series of exercises while we did, feeling great. I continued to go to the classes feeling happy for the first time in my life, that I was on the right path and it was also helping me with my dreams and visions.

I knew I couldn't share these with anyone, but I did enjoy the trip while doing meditation, feeling released. It was even better when I was able to drive there getting into the church to change, walking into the room trying to act like a hippy or just to be cool (I was a teenager it depended on my mood).

My teacher also introduced me to crystals and herbs, loving the feel of crystals in my hand feeling a little buzz come off them when I handled them.

It wasn't until I was due to leave school that Mum found out I was going to a yoga and meditation class but by that time I was well practiced at going into a deep meditation with visions of flying again, coming back to me stronger than ever. I would just ignore her and go off to my bedroom and play loud music, while she ranted at me through the door.

My brothers also tried to get at me, threatening to tell Mum and Dad that I was being weird, saying that Mum and Dad would have me committed in a psych hospital. I was getting a lot more cunning now putting things in their beds hearing them squeal or hiding some of their things. I usually got in trouble in the end though or they would shove me in a cupboard listening to me scream.

I did other things, like go to ballroom dancing classes in the evenings. I always managed to get guys who had two left feet, standing on mine constantly. I had one guy who was quite nice looking; I think he might have been German or something, who stood on my feet constantly apologising. I didn't see him again after that thank goodness, I don't think my feet would have survived. Mind you I got a short Italian guy the next time who had just been eating garlic; so I don't know what was worse.

I also did other country kid things like ride horses, which I really enjoyed with Prue.

She was a great horse rider. Going out to a local farm to exercise them because they didn't have time. We would race out on the paddocks flicking up mud, because it was usually raining or windy, coming home filthy with Mum getting angry again. She would growl at me, "you should have been a boy."

At around 16, we started going to the pubs to listen to music (yes, I was supposed to be 18 but we got in with a bit of makeup on). While we drank, we didn't get too drunk preferring to enjoy the dancing and the music as it was another outlet for my anger.

One night I did get a little tipsier than planned after yet another argument with a guy I was seeing, going to the toilet swaying all the way, when a security guard came over, "Hannah, I think you've had too much to drink."

I went up to him swaying close to his face sneering, "Who are you, my husband? No, you're not."

He smirked, "Not yet."

This just made me angry. I said, "In your dreams," and stormed off.

I finally got to the age where I could leave school graduating with a pass in typing (not sure how I did that) and history. I managed to get a job in a stuffy little office moving out of home, but only lasting a year because I started to daydream again, looking out the windows, wanting to be free.

Prue got in touch with me one day saying she was moving to Sydney; did I want to go with her? I was off like a shot ready to experience a big new world. Unfortunately, my brothers also moved to Sydney, but I didn't have to have anything to do with them.

I felt free at last managing to get an office job still, but I was able to save up and start travelling. As soon as I had enough money, I would be off going around Australia first then off to the UK and Europe; loving all the history and sometimes talking to ghosts.

When I went to Germany an old guy came up to me speaking German not knowing what he was saying. I did speak basic German to get me out of trouble, saying to him, "Kein Deutsch sprechen (no speak German)" with the tour guide helping me explain to him.

He apologised in English saying, "Oh you looked like a family that was from here."

The tour guide smiled at me, "Maybe it's just your colouring, you do look a little German I guess."

I shrugged, "Who knows."

I was just walking away from the old guy when I spotted a man standing there watching us, who looked familiar with black hair and a silver streak through the front of it. I stood there looking at him, when he noticed me doing this, walking off in the opposite direction.

Mum and Dad had also followed us over to Sydney in the end. I would go and see them from time to time, but generally I hung around Prue and a couple of other friends I had made in Sydney. It was nice not to have people picking on me because of what I liked doing.

I would still get poems, as I called them in my head, especially when I was angry, which didn't happen as much these days. I had found a doctor who recommended an implant to keep my hormones and hopefully my tempers under control a bit. It worked well for a while.

Prue and I were still living together dating guys, but a few of them were cruel with her stutter and me with my temper, so they didn't hang around very long.

Every time I went to see my parents they would ask if there was any nice guy in my life. I would just laugh at them, "I'm having too much fun." My mother would get annoyed with me looking at her watch, "Time is ticking Hannah."

I would just get angry and walk out.

I ended up meeting a guy who tolerated my temper and cooked, when he felt like it. We ended up getting married too quickly, which pleased my mother. We had two lovely girls but it didn't last, especially when my temper returned.

I started to take swings at him not actually touching him, but I appeared to have a force behind me, that threw him up against the wall a couple of times. He had had enough after the third time, walking out and leaving me with the girls.

While I preferred being with my girls by myself, it was hard making ends meet, along with trying to be there for my girls. Mum and Dad would come and see the girls or would look after them and help out financially sometimes; but otherwise, our relationship had just gone back to the way it was before.

This breakup just made me shut down again with the responsibility of bringing up two girls on my own. To take my mind off things I had started to do some research into my mother's side finding only what Mum had said, that they were from Norway and Germany but one interesting thing, was that the women I had found kept their family surname, Dragĕ.

Once the divorce had gone through, I decided that is what I was going to be known as and changed it by deed poll, more to annoy my mother and causing a rift between us again.

When my parents passed away, I found out that my eldest brother, Christian was in charge of the estate. I was left a little bit of money and also a book that was wrapped in an old dusty cloth.

Christian sneered, "It's probably a photo album or something. I couldn't open it, so you're welcome to it."

I put it away forgetting about it for now, getting over the sudden death of my parents. The money did help me pay some of my mortgage off, which I thought would help me with my retirement at least.

My younger brother Robert just took his share and disappeared, not bothering to keep in touch with either of us.

Chapter 2

My alarm went off on my phone, reminding me that I had a meditation class to go to in a couple of hours, snapping out of my daydream. I smiled to myself, '*I always set an alarm because of my daydreaming.*'

Wow that was a big trip down memory lane. I hadn't had a big daydream like that for a long time. I felt a little disappointed at what I hadn't done in my life not even doing some of the things off my bucket list.

I sighed thinking, '*Well I still had a bit of time before I went to the meditation class,*' so I decided to get the book my mother had given me, which came up in the daydream.

I had moved into this unit at Cronulla, which is one of the old red brick ones, when my girls went their own way. It is a cute little one-bedroom place, that I redecorated when I moved in, with a balcony that had views of the sea. I was lucky to buy it just before the prices went mad in Sydney, only having a small mortgage on it.

I eventually found the book wrapped in a cloth with a string around it. I sat on my bed with Kimba, my lovely white cat, coming up to see what I was doing, purring around my arm, annoying me.

I looked at it wondering what it could be, undoing the string which was knotted, struggling to get it undone at first. I didn't want to cut it as it looked really old and wanted to preserve it.

I almost felt like an explorer going into a hidden treasure, but then I chuckled to myself and Kimba, it's probably just a photo album or something like Christian said. I finally got the string undone opening up the cloth which was dusty and smelt old, but noticing when I opened it, the inside was clean and had designs on it of a shield with a dragon—like a coat of arms. I was intrigued. Thinking it might be the Dragĕ family coat of arms.

I opened the cloth fully exposing the book that had a thick brown leather binding on it with swirls engraved through it, which looked similar to old Norse designs, I had seen in my history lessons.

It just had the name 'Dragĕ' in the middle, in black old script writing. I opened the cover to find a little note in there, unfolding it recognising my mother's distinct handwriting saying, "*Dear Hannah, I tried to stop the magic in our family, but it didn't work with you.*

Love Mum."

I sat there dumbfounded, '*What does she mean by that?*' I put it down on the bed looking back at the book, finding a family tree on the first page, with my name at the bottom then my girls names, Amelia and Charlotte underneath mine.

Above my name was Mum with a symbol next to that, not sure what it meant; then above hers was grandma Matilda's and grandpa Bram with a different symbol who I hadn't met in person, but had as a ghost. Above her was grandma Elese with the same symbol as grandma Matilda, but after that the tree had faded out. I flipped some of the other pages but there was nothing on them, sitting back feeling confused by Mum's note, as well as this.

It was getting close to the time to go to my meditation group, which wasn't too far away, so I decided to put the book away and have a look when I came back.

I closed the book putting Mum's note in there, covering it with the cloth, then started to tie the string back up, when some words came into my head and for some reason, I needed to say them, as I was tying the string up, saying them out loud, '*tie it up, tie it strong don't let anyone else come along to take it away, this book is for my eyes only and here to stay.*' To my surprise, a white light went along the string then I heard a click sound like a lock in the room.

I took a deep breath thinking, I guess that has locked it or was it my imagination—who knows! I put it back in the box and then back in the cupboard just in case. It was time to get changed into something comfortable (no leotards now it's the 2000s) and go.

As I drove to the class, which wasn't far away, I was thinking about that daydream and the book, along with my mother's note.

Deep down inside me I felt that I am going to be in for a disappointment with regard to Mum's note. I guess I will find out sooner or later why I am getting that feeling. I know I am a little disappointed with some of my life choices as well, but unfortunately you can't turn back time, smiling at the thought of Cher's song coming into my mind, 'If I Could Turn Back Time' when it came on the radio, as I drove up to the meditation centre singing it.

I found a park, still thinking about the book and Mum's note, going into the centre taking my shoes off and finding a spot; not really paying attention to anyone around me; which is quite normal for me, as I still go alone to these types of things, with no one else interested in it.

I put my mat down straightening it out and standing on the corners, still deep in thought when Miranda, a petite woman who wore no makeup, had fine chiselled cheek bones and auburn hair that was always pushed back in a tight bun, came into the room who was taking the meditation this afternoon.

She clapped her hands asking us all to get comfortable on the wooden floor either sitting or lying. My hips don't do very well on any floor, especially a wooden floor, so I always allowed plenty of time to get down and up at the end of the session. I was just about to do my usual process of going down, when Miranda came over to me with a curious look on her face, "It's Hannah, isn't it?"

I was already starting to get into the zone with the smell of the dragon's blood incense being burned, looking up, surprised to see Miranda there. I smiled briefly not really interested, "Yes that's right, Miranda, is there something wrong?"

She appeared a little flustered, "Oh no, Hannah, I just couldn't quite remember your name. What is your surname?"

I stretched my arms out a little and my legs getting ready to go down to the floor, "Dragĕ."

She put out her hand to shake mine like a posh lady, holding her hand close to her body, thinking to myself, this is odd, so I took hers shaking it quickly with a little buzz briefly exchanging between us, when we touched.

I heard someone coughing in the background wanting to get started, making Miranda smile again, "Come and see me after the session Hannah, I'd like to talk to you."

I nodded not really interested, "Sure." Miranda moved away looking at me then changing her focus back onto the class.

I shook my head, "It's going to be a strange day, I think."

I had a two-stage lowering strategy to get down onto the floor and with Miranda's interruption it was going to have to be quicker than I would normally do.

I started my manoeuvre, which was slowly bending my knees down to the floor, sit briefly on my heels, put my hands on the floor and slowly lower myself down. I felt like I had eyes watching me, but I ignored them as I really didn't care what they thought, getting to the age of being like that.

I finally managed to get down just as Miranda was starting the CD she used for our meditation, which was similar to mine, as I had bought mine from here. I tried to put the book and Mum's note out of my head, to keep it clear for the meditation.

I got comfortable relaxing myself with my breathing ready for the meditation, starting to go into the visualisation of being in a boat on a river, with water gently lapping at it while it floated along. I could hear birds singing and insects flying along the banks of the river. The sun was warm on me as I lay in the boat, which was always a Nordic boat, just gently floating along.

The boat stopped unexpectedly and I couldn't hear the CD any more. This wasn't unusual as I sometimes got visions this way.

I sat up to see why the boat had stopped feeling peaceful and calm, looking around at a green field. I got the urge to get out of the boat stepping on the shore looking around. I could smell the grass that was beneath my feet as I stepped on it, hearing the sound of crisp grass crunch under my feet. I looked to the left and then the right not seeing anything but a field and bush, so I went forward towards a big tree.

As I got closer to the tree, I could see an elderly woman standing there who I recognised, smiling as I got closer. It was Matilda my grandma. I smiled at her giving her a hug which she returned. She pulled away from me without saying anything taking my hand, turning it palm up, putting her palm into mine sending a white light pulse through me.

I looked confused at her, "Why have you done that, grandma?"

She smiled softly at me, stroking my face gently on the cheek, "It is time Hannah for you to learn the family book."

I felt tears coming to my eyes as she wiped them, "Your mother didn't want to continue the magic from the family. She thought it would be better and safer for you. Please don't be angry at her."

I could hear Miranda calling us back now, turning to give grandma a hug and a kiss, "I'll try, grandma."

I walked back to the boat wiping away the tears getting in and floating hearing my breathing come into focus and the smell of the incense hitting my senses.

I lay there breathing feeling the tears roll down from my eyes, quickly wiping them away so no one could see them. Miranda always liked us to do some stretches before we got up, bringing our knees into our chest and then rolling onto our sides.

Being on my side helped me with my plan of getting up as well, starting by going on my knees and then slowly pushing myself up, putting my hand on one knee. As I was about to do that one of the men in our group came over with his hand out, "Can I help you?"

I really didn't want to have any help in case my eyes looked moist still or my makeup had run, shaking my head, not wanting to look at him, "No I am ok, thank you."

I put my hand on my knee to push myself up, but it slipped off, as I stumbled, seeing a hand reach forward to take my hand with a warm glow being felt between us, as I looked up at him. I wanly smiled, "Thank you."

He held onto my hand a bit longer than expected, as I said, while looking at him, "Do I know you from somewhere?" He let go of my hand, "I've been here a couple of times, maybe you remember me from that."

I nodded, "Yes that is probably it. Thanks again."

He walked away, as I thought about his hair, which looked familiar. It was black with a silver streak in the front of it; I'm sure I've seen someone like that before.

Miranda clapped her hands breaking me out of my thoughts, "Ok everyone form a circle so we can send everyone off with good vibes."

We did as she asked, forming a circle, feeling a little buzz between us as we sang a song *"thank you mother, thank you father for this day and bless us all as we go our separate ways without negativity to come our way"* moving around gently in the circle singing it three times. We then stopped and clapped our hands.

I gathered up my things and went over to Miranda, hoping to get going so I could have a nice glass of wine and have a look at the book again.

Miranda was talking to someone else, so I thought, I'll just leave it and talk to her next time. She saw me about to go, coming over, said, "Hannah please come with me, I would just like to see how your meditation went?"

I hesitated thinking, '*I've been coming to this group for a while and although I was friendly with her and a few of the others here, I wasn't socially friendly; but now all of a sudden she is interested in my meditation.*'

Miranda stopped to see me hesitate, waving for me to follow her, to a quieter area of the room, which was hard, because it was basically a box room with gear all around it from different classes held there.

I followed reluctantly trying to be nice, putting on a smile, going over to the corner of the room that had windows looking out over another building, with a late afternoon sun shining through it.

I squinted a little with the sun hitting my eyes trying to look at her, as Miranda put her hands together almost in prayer, "I was curious how your meditation was going Hannah? Do you get a lot of visions coming through?"

I sighed, "Yes Miranda, I usually get some sort of vision through my meditation. I did tell you that once before, but you weren't interested. Why are you wanting to know now?"

Miranda put a shocked look on her face, "Oh did you? I'm so sorry I must have been distracted or something; we all have those moments—don't we? If you want, I would like to recommend you to go and see a woman who can help you with your visions and send you to a better group. I mean, you're welcome to stay here if you like, but there are other groups that could help you better. What do you think?"

I wanted to get going, "Yes alright tell me her number and I will give her a ring." She got her phone out reciting the number to me as I put it in my phone, with the woman's name being Suzannah Keller.

I put it in, "Ok, thanks Miranda. If I don't ring her, I'll just come back here."

Miranda looked a little disappointed, "Well I hope you do Hannah, but otherwise I will see you back here."

I went out feeling a little annoyed for some reason, putting my things in the car and walking over to the supermarket, which wasn't far away in the mall at Cronulla. I still hated cooking, so picked up some microwave meals, some fruit and some cat food. I bumped into the guy who helped me up in the meditation session, "Oh hi, Hannah, isn't it?"

I thought, 'Yep strange day.' "Yes, that's right. What's your name?"

He didn't answer looking at my basket full of microwave meals, "Do they taste alright, those meals; I haven't tried them?"

I looked down at them, "Yes, these ones are ok. I'm vegetarian so they're not as bad as the ones with meat in them."

His phone went, "Sorry I have to answer this, I'll see you at meditation." He walked off, talking on the phone.

I watched him as he walked away, getting a good look at him this time, in case I "bumped" into him again.

He was a well-built guy but not really muscley, a little taller than me with jet black hair and a silver streak in the front, that was long and pushed back off his face, as I thought, I know I've seen that before somewhere.

He was dressed in jeans and a t-shirt with odd black shoes. He was quite pale for living in Australia, but had nice eyes, that look dark one minute then a hint of yellow, which was a bit strange.

He was clean shaven with a square determined jaw. He reminded me of the actor Pierce Brosnan in some ways. As he walked away from me, I thought, *'Nice bum.'* I sighed time to go home and get away from these strange people.

On the way to the car, I picked up some hashbrowns from Nulla Café who knew me now, with the young girl behind the counter joking with me, "Ah, Hashbrown, Hannah."

I smiled paying for the hashbrowns, "Thanks Cecilia, I'm not feeling very hungry as usual, but these always fill the gap."

I joked with her, "I don't even feel like cooking my microwave meals."

She laughed back, "Well you're always welcome to our hashbrowns. We do have other food here as well you know?"

I nodded, "Yes, you keep telling me Cecilia, see you next time."

I smiled to myself thinking my mother would be horrified. I nibbled on one of the hashbrowns on the way back to the car, noticing that guy I saw in the supermarket, still on the phone near Nulla Nulla Café now, as he waved to me still talking. I did a little wave carrying on pleased to go home.

I got back home, parking the car around the back of the building under the carport, climbing upstairs going into my little sanctuary again, opening the balcony doors to let the sea air float in, then giving Kimba some food.

It was still quite cool outside, but I just felt like sitting on the balcony while I ate the other hashbrown, having a glass of wine. I thought about Miranda giving me that woman's number, not sure whether I will ring her or not.

I finished my glass of wine with a bit of courage in me now, thinking it was time to look at this family book, getting it out of the cupboard. I turned on the lamp and shut the curtains going to sit on the bed to have a look at it.

I thought of some of the times I had dabbled in, what I had considered were magic chants, rather than poems, which I thought they were at first, when I was in my 20s and 30s away from Mum's critical eye, especially here in Sydney.

They were simple ones, but usually worked, but this felt a lot bigger. I am in my 50s as well, having life and people push all those dreams and thoughts down so deep, I wasn't sure if I could bring them back again, even with grandma Matilda's help.

I was glad I had been to meditation first as it had calmed me to a degree and opened me up. I looked at the hand that Matilda had touched, bringing my hands together closing my eyes and breathing deep, feeling the pulse within me, which started to grow sending pulses all through my body. I opened my eyes looking down at my hands that were glowing, pulling them apart and putting them over the book.

This made a pulse go through the book, with exploding stars floating down over it. I looked around my bedroom, feeling like it was a sunny day, with the glow that was being emitted off me.

I turned to look in the mirror on my wardrobe, smiling at myself with a white light swirling around me and my eyes were shining brightly. A loud sigh came out of me as though something had finally been released.

I took deep breaths, feeling alive at last, instead of the numbness I had felt for many years. I put my finger on the knot I had put in the string, *"untie this string and let this Dragĕ in."* It undid by itself, opening to the first page I had seen before, with the family tree.

I took Mum's letter out putting it aside. The symbol that was next to Matilda's was now next to my name.

The page then turned by itself with an introduction appearing in script writing as though it was floating in water, *"Welcome Hannah to the Dragĕ Family Book."*

I smiled at this acknowledgement, when it changed saying, *"A token must be given for you to proceed."*

A picture of an empty inkwell was on the page, with a real white feather appearing on top of the page.

I wasn't quite sure what to do next, thinking about it, when the feather started to quiver near my hand. I picked up the feather looking at it, noticing it had quite a sharp point on it; almost like a pin. The hand that Matilda had touched guided me to prick one of my fingers on the other hand, making it bleed.

I realised what it was doing, letting the blood slowly drip into the inkwell. Once the bottom of the inkwell was covered with my blood the feather disappeared and a bright light flew up from the book and into me, as though it was scanning me, making me groan.

Another wavy message came out, "*You have been confirmed with the blood of a Dragĕ, you are at one with the family book and may continue.*"

I sat there stunned, beginning to wonder if I was dreaming all of this, looking down at my finger with the blood still coming from it. I put it up to my mouth and sucked on it, thinking, '*Well that is real blood, so I must be awake.*'

The book let me turn the pages, as I looked through it with different spells and chants on them in undecipherable writing. I sat there briefly thinking about it, then I thought maybe if I waved my hand over them, they might become clear.

I did this on one of the chants and sure enough the words turned into a chant I could read, putting a donkey chant on someone. I smiled at the words, thinking, '*I'll definitely have to remember that one.*'

I started to feel a little weary with everything I had just experienced, deciding to put the book away. I will have to find a better place to put it as well, even though it appears to be protected by a blood spell, which made me feel better.

I did remember how to put a protecting spell on the house, which I always did anyway, so I cleansed it first with some bay leaf and then put a protecting spell around, feeling safe within the walls of my unit.

I had a shower, standing in there thinking about all the things I had just experienced, along with all the bullshit I had experienced growing up; feeling the anger build up within me.

I got out, getting dressed and drying my hair off, looking at the glow still within me from the magic, feeling sad and pleased all at the same time. I put some music on and got some more wine, sitting with just a couple of candles burning and some incense, turning things over in my mind, as Kimba came and sat on my lap. I probably shouldn't have kept drinking but I did, thinking about all the years I've lost not being true to myself with my own decisions but also the decisions of my family not letting me make up my own mind on whether to accept the family magic.

Katy Perry's 'Roar' came on yelling the words to no one in particular, as I had another glass of wine feeling the anger well up inside, needing to escape, as a loud clap of thunder clapped over the unit.

Getting up, swaying to get another glass of wine with Shania Twain, 'Man I feel like a woman' coming on dancing around the lounge with Kimba in my arms. Poor baby must have wondered what she had done to deserve this.

I ran out of energy and wine, laying down on the sofa with Kimba and America's 'Sister Golden Hair' coming on, reminding me of my teenage years, going through puberty and a magic that I wasn't allowed to try. I was also getting harassed by people that were basically just horrible human beings and who I should have been able to trust and love. I eventually dropped off on the sofa with angry thoughts still in my head and a lot of wine swirling around, making me numb.

The candles eventually went out, when a figure appeared in the lounge, picking me up and putting me in my bed, stroking my hair gently saying, "You need to dream about me Hannah so I can come to you."

I stirred a little, mumbling. I slept heavily at first but once the effects of the wine started to wear off, I began to dream. It started off with my mother constantly telling me off about things I did more out of anger than on purpose, then my teachers constantly growling at me, making me roll in the bed.

I woke finding it still dark, so I got up staggering to go to the toilet and having a drink of water. I put some food out for Kimba so I could sleep in, getting back into bed shivering with the temperature dropping, feeling the coolness in the unit.

I lay there briefly thinking, '*I must have climbed into bed*' then dropped off. I went into a deep sleep with a dream starting of me in our old house in New Zealand looking at all the familiar things.

The 1970s wallpaper that we helped Dad put up with its browns, greens and yellow crazy designs. I walked down the hallway looking to the right to see my parents' bedroom with their familiar double bed and the 70s headboard, along with built-in lights on either side.

I turned running my hand down the wall feeling the wallpaper under my hand as I walked down coming to my brothers' bedroom, that they shared, with posters of cars on either side and two single beds. I could still hear the sounds of them arguing about who was going to have the best car, when they started working. I carried on down hearing the squeaky board that always squeaked when you walked on it, especially when I was trying to sneak back into the house, after being out to the pub.

I moved down, looking at the bathroom that was straight ahead, but on the right side was my bedroom. I walked in looking at the bed and dressing table that my father had built me with a yellow chenille bedspread on the bed. I looked around at the familiar yellow flowers on the wallpaper with posters of David Cassidy and dogs and cats. I smiled, '*I never could make up my mind whether I liked popstars or dogs and cats better.*'

I ran my finger over the dressing table, with my teenage bits and pieces on it. Even then I had crystals sitting in glass bowls along with candles that I had bought from op shops, much to my mother's annoyance.

I looked over to the other wall to see my stereo on a cabinet with all my records and tapes that I used to play all the time to stop some of the visions coming into my head or just to take me away to another world.

I felt sad at the thought of how much I could have learned while I was in this room but instead, I would hide out in it closing myself down so I wouldn't be called names or picked on. I looked at the window that had the familiar yellow curtains with sheer ones in between, which moved gently in a breeze blowing through. I remembered I would constantly look out at the moon, which shone brightly over the roof tops as I dreamt of flying high over them, when I was young.

I got up, feeling I had seen enough, walking towards the door, when all of a sudden, I heard this piercing noise, like finger nails being scratched on a blackboard. I covered my ears with my hands, crouching wondering where it was coming from as it sent shivers down my spine.

A loud thump sounded on the roof above me, then more scratching noises making me groan, "Agghh," and holding my ears still. I walked towards the door feeling my heart starting to race, getting ready to flee. A huge bang sounded, with bits of ceiling coming crashing around my old bed, I had been sitting on.

I stood in the doorway getting ready to bolt, when a huge purple foot with big talons on it came through, crushing my old bed beneath it, hearing the wood splinter.

All my posters on the walls were shredded and the curtains were getting ripped and dusty from the ceiling being pushed in. I was just thinking, '*Time to go;*' when a voice sounded out, "Hannah don't leave, stay where you are," It made me hesitate, as I watched another foot come through the roof.

I could feel my heart racing still, wanting to flee, but the voice sounded familiar for some reason staying where I was, yelling out, "Who are you?"

A big gap opened up in the roof with some front paws and a head of a dragon, with big yellow eyes, that appeared to be smiling, with a wide toothy grin.

I stood there thinking, *'Ok this is a weird dream.'* The dragon made a bigger hole in the roof with its front paws, peeling the iron roof back like a can being opened, moving closer to me smiling, "Come for a ride, Hannah."

I was covered in dust which made me cough, still with my hands on my ears from the screeching noise, slowly taking them off my ears, "What did you say?"

He chuckled with a little flick of flame coming from his mouth, "Come for a ride Hannah, like you used to when you were young."

I started to back up, "No I don't think that's a good idea, I'm too old for this stuff now."

He grabbed me with his front paw, as I struggled to get out of his grip. He chuckled holding tightly so I wouldn't fall, "Come on, it'll be just like when you used to jump off the garage roof, when you were young trying to fly. I won't hurt you."

I started to relax with the sound of the familiar voice, when he put me on his other front paw, helping me to go up onto his back thinking to myself, *'It's only a dream, let's have some fun.'* He lowered himself to let me get on his back, near the top part of his neck.

As I was climbing up his scaly purple neck, I asked him, "What's your name?"

He chuckled again, "Don't you remember? It's Ferdinand."

I got on the back of his neck, when he lifted us up through the roof, while I was trying to find something to hold onto, with him looking back saying, "There's a harness there to hold onto."

He took a giant leap up in the air, like a horse bolting, lifting us out of the house, as I looked back at the giant gash in the roof with debris falling everywhere that had fallen on him, as I squealed in terror holding on tight to the harness.

He looked back chuckling, "Hold on Hannah and relax," he pushed his wings out to full span, flapping them so we flew higher up in the air.

My knuckles were white, holding onto the harness, with my heart nearly jumping out of my chest. I started to look around me taking deep breaths to calm myself, at all the different coloured roof tops and streets winding around the area, where I used to live, that were slowly getting smaller as we flew high up into the air. I relaxed with the cool air rushing past my face, with my hair fly out behind me, as a smile was forming.

Ferdinand looked back, chuckling, "That looks better," as he continued to climb reaching the clouds, as I squealed in delight, feeling the dampness within them.

He flew over my old school where I would constantly look out dreaming of flying and now, I was looking in and flying; it was a wonderful feeling. He flew towards the sea smelling the delights of the salt and water coming to me, even before we got to it.

Below, I could see lush bush, with the earthy damp smell and huge ferns sticking their leaves up into the air to get as much sun as they could.

As we got closer to the sea, I could see a huge Pohutukawa tree with its beautiful red flowers shining out like a beacon, with the sea behind it.

When we flew over the sea, he went down lower getting some of the sea spray flicking up just enough to wet me, making me giggle in delight.

Dolphins started to jump up in front of us as though we were the bough of a ship, relaxing enough to lean forward over his neck, watching them jump and race us.

We got further out to sea with what appeared to be no land mass around, spotting a huge whale swimming along spouting water every now and then creating a huge wake in its path. The rays of the sun were shining off its magnificent body, looking like it had wetsuit on.

It started rolling over and waving its huge flipper at us, as though it was saying hello. It appeared to take only a short while and we were over the coast line of Australia, heading up towards Sydney, with the sun starting to rise over the headlands. It looked divine as little rays of yellow light sneaked through different parts of the rocks and over the land, as we flew over them.

I could hear the waves crashing into the large sandstone rocks and seagulls waking up starting to squawk. He flew over the opera house and Bridge, feeling the warmth of the sun compared to New Zealand's cooler climate.

Sydney was just starting to wake up with cars appearing on the bridge and in the city, along with people walking through the parks for their morning walks, looking like little ants.

He flew back towards Cronulla, landing on my balcony, making himself smaller so he could fit in it.

I jumped off his back looking at him unsure what to say, but eventually I thought of something, "Thanks for the great ride. I've always dreamt of flying like that."

He smiled at me, "I know Hannah, now you can actually do it." He gave me a hug, "See you next time," pointing at me, putting me in my bed and taking off.

I woke not long after in my nightie sitting up in the bed with a bit of hangover, smiling at the thought of the wonderful dream I'd had. I looked at the time with it being 9.00am groaning, as I lay back down not really wanting to get up.

I felt too awake though and knew I wouldn't go back to sleep; so I got up opening the curtains with a sunny day coming through sending sun rays all around my room dazzling my eyes.

My nightie sleeve moved up my arm as I opened the curtains, when I noticed something on my wrist that wasn't there before. It was a small tattoo of a dragon.

I sat there mystified wondering how this got on there, when a distant memory came to me of a dragon that had come onto my wrist, when I was young but it was more like a cartoon one then.

This one was more defined and looked more like an actual dragon. I remember Mum going off at me, accusing me or drawing on my wrist all the time and my brothers kept bullying me about it. It did eventually fade when I started to shut myself down.

With my mood better, than when I went to sleep last night, I just shrugged it off, especially with that dream; so, I got up putting my dressing gown on as it was a bit cool.

I made some breakfast and cleaned up watching a bit of the news on the TV looking at all the trouble going on in the world, feeling a bit miserable as I watched it. I decided to turn it off, putting some music on.

I went and got the book bringing it into the lounge to take another look at it. I undid the string opening it by enveloping it with my hands again, as it turned to the first page with the family tree on it, looking at my girls' names.

I sighed thinking, *'They have missed out on the magic as well, but at least they are younger than me. I can make it my mission to let them decide whether they take this on or not.'*

My anger started to well up again inside me at all the horrible snide remarks I had put up with from different people through the years.

I sat there for a couple of hours just going through the book looking at different chants and spells coming across the Dragĕ coat of arms and a motto *"My family is my bond; My ancestor's blood in my veins; Together we fight any enemy until they are all slain."*

I said it out loud nodding, "Mm not a bad motto. I'll have to remember that one."

I had a thought while I was there about magic movies like Harry Potter and Practical Magic etc., thinking what I would like to learn first.

I thought about all the times I sat in classrooms or work places wishing I could fly, which was something all those movies had in common as well. I put that to the book, summoning a spell so that I could fly or teleport, which would be better.

The book started flipping its pages over, stopping at a page that had a picture on it of wings. I passed my hand over it, with the words turning it into a spell, requiring it to be done with a feather waving over me saying, *"I cast this spell upon thee now to teleport here and there within this realm lanuae lanuae lanuae."*

My phone rang making me jump, as I was deep in thought, looking at it realising it was Amelia ringing; which she usually did on a Sunday to see how I was going.

I answered, telling her, "I've got the family book out to have a look at." She asked what was in it, with me saying, "It's difficult to explain you'll have to come and have a look at it." She was intrigued but said, "I've made plans for today but I will give you a ring through the week and come over."

I was happy with that, ending the call. I got back to the spell deciding to try it, taking my dressing gown off, standing up in the middle of the lounge getting a feather. I always had one around, taking a deep breath waving the feather over me as I recited the spell, *"I cast this spell upon thee now to teleport here and there within this realm lanuae lanuae lanuae."*

After the third time of reciting it, I felt a shiver go through my body, then starry wings appeared around me gently floating down and hitting me, sending a fluttering feeling through me. I felt pleased with how it went, deciding to have a go once I got dressed.

I put the book away again getting dressed thinking about lunch, but not feeling hungry right now, deciding I would go to a local café afterwards.

I decided to go for a walk while it was warm enough, but to teleport down to where I wanted to go. I didn't feel like being around too many people, so I teleported saying, "Lanuae" with Greenhills in my mind, taking my crystals to cleanse them, hoping this would settle my temper down as well.

It freaked me out at first, feeling the whirling of things going around me, like a picture that had been smudged, going out of the unit, as I squealed, but not landing exactly where I wanted to land. I landed with a bit of a thud on the sand falling to my knees then dropping down.

Luckily there weren't too many people around and I hadn't landed on anyone, smiling as I thought of it. I will certainly have to practice that one.

I decided to try again, getting closer to where I wanted to be, saying, "Lanuae" with Greenhills in my mind again.

I still landed a bit roughly, falling over with someone, walking past looking at me, as I smiled saying, "Oops, bloody sand," then getting up.

I walked a little further taking in the sunshine on my face, listening to the waves gently caress the shore, with the odd seagull squawking. I walk on, finding a quieter spot not far from the Wanda surf club. I headed towards the water lifting my pants up to my knees wading in, feeling the cool clear water, bringing goosebumps on my arms and around my legs as it ebbed and flowed, gently lulling me into a bit of a trance.

My body slowly accepted the cold water as I waded out a bit further getting my crystals out, which I always put in my bra, so I didn't drop them.

I got them out to dip them in the water starting to cleanse them saying, "*I ask from the fire, wind, earth and air to cleanse these gems of any negativity and to be clear, for me to use with peace and harmony, coming over me so mote it be.*"

A pulse rang out from them as they were immersed in the water, which then came back to me, through the water within a wave, hitting me, throwing me off my feet.

This sent me under the wave making me gasp as I pushed myself up through the water, feeling the cold water enveloping my body.

It made me feel wonderful, like a caterpillar coming out of its pupa, with the anger I had been holding onto for all those years in the pit of my stomach, escaping, sending it through the water. It looked like a small bomb had been exploded under the water, with the vibrations going out to sea.

I turned to look towards the shore feeling renewed and ready to make my way in, when I heard a voice yelling something at me. I could see someone coming to the water's edge yelling at me, "Don't you do that here, you witch!" As I stood there watching with a steely look in my eyes, at the man who was saying it.

He was a rounded man starting to go bald, wearing all black, shaking his fist at me. I smiled wickedly as I built my anger up hearing a bolt of thunder up in the sky, putting the crystals back into my bra. I backed back into the sea, putting the water around me at hip level.

He took his shoes off rolling his pants up, walking into the water, yelling at me, "Stop that, you witch!" As I lowered myself, feeling something coming from the book, *"Waves of thunder hit thee now, knocking this fool, acting like a floundering fish into the sea with all your power hitting thee, this man I see before me going in and out of the sea."*

I stood up bringing my arms from behind me, with water coming up like a huge wave knocking him off his feet. I watched him fall over and roll on the sand as the waves hit him again and again, along the shore line with him unable to stand up. I growled like a satisfied lion, who had just caught its prey, going under the waves in satisfaction, that I can finally get my own back.

I went under another wave swimming down the beach just in case someone else saw me, heading back towards my unit. I looked back to see a crowd form around the man, who couldn't stand up as the waves kept buffeting him. I knew it wouldn't last that long as my magic wasn't very strong, but it was funny to watch—I still had a sense of humour.

I sighed in relief at finally being somewhere I felt I belonged, walking out of the water, making sure my key was still in my pocket thinking, *'Oh I don't need it, if I can teleport into my unit,'* and smiling at the thought of it. I hadn't quite got out of the water when I felt someone standing near me.

I turned to see the guy from the mediation class standing next to me with a scowl on his face. I decided to ignore him wringing my hair out as I walked, hearing him say, "Hannah, take that chant off that man."

I was still pushing up against the water, with the waves going in and out fast, when I felt his arm going around my waist. I pushed him away, throwing him in the water, yelling at him, "Bugger off!"

He got up quicker than I expected putting me in a bear hug, "Hannah Dragé you need to take that chant off him, now!"

The sand was soft and moving with the waves, when a large wave came in pushing us both over, falling back as he still held onto me in a bear hug. I pushed my head up, coughing after taking some water in, throwing my elbow into his stomach, which made him let go.

I got up to walk out of the water, getting ready to take off, when he appeared in front of me with a wicked grin on his face, "You've been misbehaving, Hannah, take that chant off that man."

I screwed up my face in conceit, "I don't know what you're talking about. Now go away and leave me alone."

A cool breeze was coming off the water sending a shiver through me, as I thought to myself, *'It's time to go, I'm getting cold.'*

He grabbed my wrist before I could take off making me angry. I tried to shake it free but realised I couldn't take off because he was holding me. I glared at him, "Who are you and why are you annoying me?"

He turned my arm, revealing the tattoo on my wrist; pointing to it said, "That is who I am Hannah; I'm Ferdinand."

I laughed sarcastically at him pulling my hand out of his grip getting it free, "I think you've been smoking something you shouldn't have." I teleported away from him, landing not far from my unit on the sand; falling over again.

Ferdinand stood there surprised that I had learned how to do that so quickly, magicaeing after me.

He landed just behind me, picking me up, putting me into bear hug again, holding onto my hands, "Hannah come back and take that chant off that man."

I could feel my anger build now, as a clap of thunder sounded out to sea, with a chant coming into my head, *"I put manacles on this man to stop him with his demand ..."*

Ferdinand realised I was about to put a chant on him, "Don't you use your magic on me Hannah!" Putting his hand over my mouth so I couldn't say the full chant, but I had said enough for handcuffs to appear on his wrists.

He tried to wrestle with me as I slipped out of his grip, turning to smile at him blowing him a kiss and teleporting again, going to my unit.

Ferdinand angrily tried to use his magic to get out of the cuffs, watching me disappear in front of him. He was surprised again, that I had worked out how to teleport, thinking she has probably gone to her unit. He knew it well having, visited at night when I was asleep, so he magicae there onto the balcony.

I had teleported onto the balcony, landing on my knees, skinning them, swearing as I did so, with blood instantly appearing through the hole I had just made in my pants. I got angry, feeling cold, with a shiver going over me again, knowing I couldn't go into the unit through the door as I bolted the door from the inside. I calmed myself, sitting on the chair looking at my knees planning on going into the unit again by teleporting.

Ferdinand arrived not far behind me, still with cuffs on, looking angry as I thought, "Oh crap," and got up, grimacing with the pain from my knees to move away from him.

I looked at him unsure what to make of this guy, getting ready to teleport into the unit, when he grabbed me, turning my back to him putting his cuffed arms around me, "Get these off me, Hannah."

I struggled, "You obviously have magic in you, do it yourself!"

He moved in closer to my cheek, "It's your chant, I can't take them off because of that. Now take them off."

I grinned wickedly, "Wow, I'll have to remember that."

He wasn't amused, growling, "Hannah!"

I touched the cuffs but hesitated, "You know you sound just like my teachers back at school. You're not going to try and punish me or anything are you? This may lead to more magic being used otherwise."

He squeezed me with his arms trying to control his anger, "Ok, but you behave yourself as well."

I took a deep breath, "Alright, but you better have a good story."

I touched the cuffs releasing him then he magicae us into the unit.

I went to push his arms away to move away from him, but he held tight. I tensed up in his grip, "You made a deal, let me go."

He spoke quietly to me, "There is still the matter of the man with the chant on him."

I smiled to myself at the thought of him wallowing in the surf, "He deserved it. I wasn't doing anything to hurt him, so let me go."

He chuckled, which unfortunately sounded familiar, when a whirling sensation happened around me, finding myself flying on the back of a dragon squealing "OMG stop it, Ferdinand!"

He flew high at first going over the sea with the waves crashing into the shoreline, then soaring back down to where the man was, still thrashing around with people trying to help him.

I felt my anger building, "You promised there wouldn't be any punishment, now take me back or else I won't keep my side of the bargain." He reached back holding onto my leg, which meant I couldn't teleport off him, "Take it off him, Hannah"

I could see an ambulance arriving at the surf club with a stretcher being unloaded, "He'll be alright soon, my magic isn't very strong—yet!"

He landed not far from where everyone was, with the dragon turning back into male form holding onto my arm. He put his arm around my waist pulling me up closer to where the man was rolling around, with Ferdinand saying quietly, "Take it off him Hannah, now!"

I growled, "I don't know how."

He chuckled, "I think you do."

My knees were starting to ache and I could feel myself getting cold, as I was still wet.

I decided to do as he asked, moving away from Ferdinand, putting my hand up, "Stay there," and getting closer to the man, as I took a deep breath, saying quietly, "*Stop the floundering now like a fish but leave a smile like a Cheshire cat, like the fool you are, so take that.*"

It stopped the man floundering on the ground, turning to Ferdinand, "There, now goodbye."

I turned away from him about to take off.

Ferdinand grabbed me around the waist, "I think I'll take you home."

Ferdinand glanced one more time at the man as he sat up rubbing his face with his hands, feeling satisfied that I had taken the chant off him.

I took a last look before Ferdinand took me home, grinning as the man put his hands down, smiling like a Cheshire cat, that Ferdinand didn't see.

Ferdinand and I arrived back in my unit in the lounge area, still holding onto my waist turning me, "let me look at your knees."

I looked at him annoyed, "They will be alright, I'll go and have a shower which will stop the bleeding."

He growled, "Come here, Hannah," taking my wrist, pulling me towards him, pointing to my knees as they healed.

I pulled my arm out of his grip, getting angry, not realising at first what he had done, then I felt the sting had gone from my knees I looked down at them in disbelief. "Wow that's cool. I wish you were around when I was younger, especially when I was jumping off the garage roof."

He smiled sadly, "I was, but you blocked me out."

This just made me annoyed, "Yes, well it wasn't by choice. I suppose this is another dream with my purple dragon coming to see me now in the form of a man."

He came up, pinching me on the arm, making me wince in pain.

"Ouch!" I exclaimed as I rubbed it.

He chuckled, "See it isn't a dream this time, Hannah. Go and have your shower, I'll make you some lunch as I know you haven't eaten much."

I laughed nervously, "I don't know you. How do I know you won't attack me while I'm in the shower? You go away and I'll meet you somewhere in a café or something."

He was getting annoyed, moving suddenly, putting me into a fireman's lift, picking me up, "I can put you in the shower if you like or you can go by yourself. It's up to you."

I thumped his back, then put my cold hands on his bare skin making him recoil, "agghh your bloody hands haven't changed much."

I slid them over his back more, "Put me down Ferdinand. Alright, just remember I have these and I know enough magic to get back at you."

He put me down in front of the shower taking my wrists in his hands, "Don't be too long," and went out to the kitchen.

I got the shower running coming back out to find him busy in the kitchen preparing something, shaking my head, "This is just strange again—another strange day."

He looked at me about to ask what I was doing, "I'm just getting some clothes."

I had a shower coming out to see Kimba in his arms while he was stirring something that smelt quite nice on the stove.

I looked at her purring away as I sulked, "She doesn't normally go to other people. Must be the dragon thing, is it?"

He smirked, "She knows me well."

I just shook my head putting some music on, turning it down so it was just in the background, intending to talk to him, to see who he was etc.

I had put a sweatshirt and some track pants on as I could feel a bit of a chill coming over me from being wet so long.

He put Kimba down, washing his hands and serving up some pasta with a pesto sauce in a couple of bowls. It did smell nice as I looked at it, when he brought it over asking if I wanted parmesan cheese on it. I nodded, "Yes thanks. What's this called?"

He smiled, "Pesto alla Genovese pasta. Now I expect you to eat as much as you can."

I sighed, "No pressure then! I'm not a big eater especially of pasta, so don't get annoyed if I don't eat it *all*—mother!"

I got up before I started, "Do you want a drink of water or wine?"

He sighed, "Yes some wine would be nice."

I got two glasses filling them up and bringing them over along with a glass of water for me. He looked at them both starting to eat his pasta as I took a drink of water first. I started to eat the food, which was delicious, sipping on my water and wine as well.

He ate his sipping his wine, "So you've learned how to teleport or what we call magicae?"

I was a little surprised at what he called it, "Yes. It was in my book of tricks, so I thought I would try it. As you saw I'm a not that good on the landing and sometimes my final destination, but I'll keep practicing."

He smiled, "You were always falling over at the best of times, especially in your sports."

I took another sip of wine frowning, "So are you going to tell me who you are?"

He finished off his pasta, sitting back having a drink of wine, "Come on Hannah, you remember me. I used to take you for rides when you were young, at night in New Zealand."

I looked down at my food trying to remember with a frown coming over my face, "I have blocked a lot of that out Ferdinand, plus I don't remember you being a man that much."

He chuckled, "Yes you do. You saw me a few times, giving me cheek usually."

I slowly ate the pasta, managing to eat it all, which pleased him, trying to remember some of the times I might have seen him.

Some of it came to me, "You were in the pub that time when I had had too much to drink."

He chuckled, "Yes that was me. It will come back to you now that you've opened yourself up. I am your spirit animal assigned to you when you were born Hannah. Everyone gets one, but in your world, they generally don't accept them.

The American Indian people are great believers of us, but your people have blocked us off, which is sad."

I thought about it, "I have read about some of their beliefs. It's strange how our "modern" world has blocked a lot of things out of our lives. My mother tried really hard at that, something I hope to put right for my girls. I'm just annoyed that I'm getting too old to enjoy it properly now."

He looked at me seriously, "You need to control that temper of yours and not take it out on people just because you can. I know why you're angry but it won't help you or your daughters. Besides you've still got plenty of time to use your magic for *good* use."

I finished off the meal, "I will try Ferdinand, but I can't promise anything."

He took my bowl going to the kitchen starting to do the dishes with me coming over to help him. Once we had finished, he hugged me, "I'm here to help you Hannah not to try and control you. Please don't keep pushing me away. I'll go now and see you later."

I looked at him with mixed feelings still, "Like I said Ferdinand, it's been a long time, but I will try."

Chapter 3

He took off, leaving me alone with my thoughts. I felt a bit of a chill come over me thinking to myself, '*I think I'm going to get a cold being in that water and wet clothes today. I think I'll ring my boss now to tell him I won't be in for a few days. I have plenty of sick leave, so I may as well take it, which will also let me get my head around some of these changes as well.*'

I rang Tom, my boss, leaving a message for him that I wouldn't be in for three days at least because of a cold.

I rang Suzannah before it got too late with a little old lady's soft voice answering the phone, "Hello, who is this?"

I rolled my eyes thinking, '*I'm not sure if I should be doing this.*' I hesitated with her saying, "Hello who is this?" again, with me replying, "Hello my name is Hannah Drage̋, a lady called Miranda from my meditation group gave me your number to ring about a special meditation group you might recommend."

Suzannah paused, "Oh yes, Miranda, I think she did mention you, Hannah. Can you come and see me sometime this week?"

I thought about it, "I think I'm getting a cold so I will have to leave it a couple of days. When will suit you?"

She paused, "Oh how about Wednesday around 7.00p.m., will that suit you?"

I hesitated, "I can make it earlier as I might take a few days off to recover from this cold. Can you make it around 3.00p.m?"

She didn't hesitate, "Yes that would be wonderful. I'll send you my address in a text. See you then, Hannah"

I received a text not long after with the address of her house in Newtown, which was an older part of Sydney. I started to sneeze with my nose running thinking, '*Oh crap here it comes. That's the good thing about being this age, I know my body well enough to know when I'm going to be sick.*'

I got into my nightie and thick dressing gown and made some vegetable soup with whatever vegetables I had in the fridge.

While I was sipping on my soup, I thought about what Ferdinand had said knowing me for all those years and not really being able to connect with me because I had blocked myself off so much.

It still angered me, all the people who used to pick on me because *they* said I was different or whatever, making me have to block myself off.

After I had finished my soup, I got a pad and wrote down all the people who made my life miserable over the years. There were a few in New Zealand and a few here in Sydney, especially my brother, Christian.

I sighed, thinking I might look them up and then decide what to do; you know karma might have dealt them enough of a blow to not worry about them. I got up and made myself a cup of green tea while I watched the news. I was just taking a sip of tea, when a headline came on about a guy having a fit on the beach in Cronulla choking on my tea.

Someone had taken a video on their phone of him flopping around in the waves not being able to get up. It then showed the paramedics putting him on a stretcher still thrashing, then all of a sudden stopping.

The next shot was the paramedics taking him away grinning like a Cheshire cat yelling, "stop that, witch!" Then smiling again, giggling at this.

Unfortunately, the person who was taking the video panned it over the crowd showing me and Ferdinand in the background.

I lay down on the sofa flicking the TV over to something else, deciding to ring Charlotte to see what she was up to. She was out with friends, saying she would ring me tomorrow. I lay on the sofa putting the throw over me while watching TV not really interested in it, deciding to do a search for some of the people that were nasty to me.

Now these people didn't just play pranks on me or say "you're weird;" they bullied me mercilessly, making me wonder if I should stay alive, kind of bullying.

I found a couple of them on FB and other places looking at their profiles to find they were divorced and one was in prison. I won't bother about those two at least.

As I searched, I kept having to blow my nose dropping the tissues on the floor, meaning to pick them up later.

I started to feel tired with my eyes drooping, deciding I had had enough and going to bed. I looked at the tissues and the kitchen feeling too sleepy thinking, '*I'll clean it up tomorrow, plenty of time.*' I stood up, closing the curtains on another day, looking at the sun setting, smiling to myself, '*I've finally got what I always wanted—the gift of magic.*' I got up, getting a glass of water, another box of tissues, some painkillers and my chest rub, which I always used when I had colds, putting them next to my bed.

After I brushed my teeth, I got into bed, took the painkillers and rubbed my chest with the rub. I managed to sleep for a little while, but then I started coughing and blowing my nose after 4–5 hours' sleep, getting restless in bed. I sat up in the dark taking some more painkillers and went to the toilet; finally managing to drop off only to be woken by Ferdinand around 8.30 am, calling me from the lounge. I groaned with Kimba jumping off the bed to greet him, hearing him open the curtains in the lounge.

He came in with her in his arms, "Where's your mother, Kimba?"

I was on my stomach pulling the sheet over me with him saying cheerfully "oh there she is, still in bed. Aren't you going to work, Hannah?"

I pulled the sheet over my head, "No I'm sick, Ferdinand go away."

I knew he was standing there looking at all the tissues on the floor.

"I'll feed Kimba for you." He went and did this as I thought, '*Oh crap I've left that mess in the kitchen.*' I wasn't getting up. So too bad. I could hear him moving things around out there as my nose started running again. Blowing it.

He went and got the throw from the sofa, noticing my list on the coffee table and all the tissues lying around it, picking them up first and putting them in the bin.

He came back into my room with the throw looking at the rub. He picked it up opening it, "Oh I remember you using this when you were young." He pulled the sheet off me, pulling my nightie up, making me angry, "What are you doing Ferdinand, get out!"

He had me at an advantage, as I was on my stomach still, so he just pushed me down, "I'll put some on your back."

I tried to push myself up, "Ferdinand I don't need your help. I can look after myself now get out!"

He wasn't taking 'no' for an answer pushing me down again, starting to rub on my back, "Just stay still while I do this."

I growled not able to get up, with Ferdinand moving down my back, "Now if I remember correctly, you had a little sensitive spot just near one of these tattoos you have on your back."

My hair was flopping all over my face, as I tried to push myself up, "Ferdinand, don't you dare."

I kicked my legs out to try and hit him. I started to cough again, grabbing a tissue to blow my nose, which was going red, as he stopped going down my back, "I'll leave it for now, but just remember I know about that."

He then got the throw from the lounge, wrapping it around me, so I couldn't get my arms out, picking me, "I want to stay in bed. Ferdinand put me down," bringing on a coughing fit again, pulling me in closer to him, sitting my head up a bit.

He walked out to the lounge, taking a pillow from my bed with him, "I think you need some fresh air and food for a little while, then you can go back to bed." He put me on the sofa propping me up with the pillow, making sure the throw was covering me.

I gave him a deathly stare, "I am capable of looking after myself, Ferdinand."

He ignored me turning on the TV. He went back into the bedroom picking up all the tissues, opening the curtains and window and bringing in the painkillers, tissue box and rub putting them near me on the coffee table. He sat next to me opening the rub again, "I'll put some on your neck and chest."

I glared at him, trying to get my arms out of the throw, "No, I can do that."

He had a determined look on his face putting his hand to hold my hands still, rubbing it on my neck and little down on my chest. He smiled, "Don't you think of using any of that magic on me Hannah, there will be penalties."

I started to cough again, turning my head away sounding croaky, "You sound just like my principal."

He finished putting the rub on touching my forehead, "I don't think you've got a temperature. Did you eat anything last night?"

I tried to wriggle out of his hold, "Yes, you saw the mess I left in the kitchen. I made myself some vegetable soup; like I said I know how to look after myself." I tried to pull one of my hands out, as my nose was running, with him still holding onto them, "Ferdinand, I need to blow my nose, let go of my hands."

He let go of my hands, as I pulled one out, he gave me a tissue to blow it, "What do you feel like for breakfast?"

I leaned back on the pillow coughing a croaky cough, "Sleep."

He smiled, "You will sleep better with something in your stomach, now tell me what you want to eat or I'll just cook something and expect you to eat it."

I glared at him, "You're determined to boss me around, aren't you? I remember you saying yesterday that you weren't here to do that."

He smiled, "Not when you're sick though. Tell me what you feel like."

I yawned, thinking of something I knew I didn't have in the fridge, so he would have to go out, "Mushrooms on toast."

He smiled, "See that wasn't hard, was it? Do you want some coffee?"

I shook my head, "No, just some green tea."

Before he got up, he noticed a recap on the news from yesterday of the guy I had put a chant on, ranting on the TV about witches being around.

I went to grab the control, with him holding my arms in place, "No you don't madam."

This brought on a coughing fit again, moving down the sofa to get comfortable with him looking at me, shaking his head, "See what you have done, you little minx."

I stopped coughing, "I don't care Ferdinand, he started it. I was just minding my own business cleansing my crystals."

He put his hand on my chin pulling me around to look at him seriously saying now, "you don't understand, there are people in this world who know you have magic in you now. It's like a vibration going over a pond. Some people are sensitive enough to know you have it."

I shrugged my shoulders sulking, "I'll deal with it as it comes. If you don't like it you can go."

He looked at the list of names I had on the pad. "I recognise a couple of those names are they some of the people who were really nasty to you?"

I started coughing again turning my back to him, not bothering to answer.

He got up shaking his head going to make my breakfast, as I turned to flick the TV over to something else that I preferred to watch.

I sighed, '*He's brought them in magically, hasn't he?*' He brought two plates over with the mushrooms and toast smelling good. He helped me sit up, putting a stable table on my lap so I could eat my food.

I looked at the food not really that hungry, but I could see he was watching me still, so I made an effort. It was nice food, eating it slowly as my stomach was sore from the coughing. He was waiting for me to finish, which I did, giving me a glass of water with some painkillers.

He then put the tea next to me taking the plates away and tidying up the kitchen. I took the painkillers laying back down, blowing my nose and getting comfortable. I had to admit it was nice being pampered when I was sick, but I wouldn't tell him that.

Once he had finished cleaning the kitchen up, I thought he would go, but he came and sat down by my feet pulling the throw off them checking to see how cold they were.

He gasped, "How do you have cold feet, when you are warm everywhere else?" He started to rub them as I tried to stop him, "I've always had bad circulation. You don't have to do that I'm used to having cold feet."

He just pulled me down a bit more, putting my feet on his lap as he rubbed them watching the TV. I didn't have the energy to fight with him and the painkillers were kicking in, making me feel tired again, along with his massage of my feet.

I eventually fell asleep, waking up when I heard my phone go off, sitting up to search for it, realising it was in the lounge, hearing Ferdinand answer it.

I heard him say, "Oh hi Charlotte, yes I'll just get her for you," as he came into my bedroom smiling giving me the phone.

I shook my head annoyed at him, lying down to talk to Charlotte with her giving me the third degree, plus she had seen me on the news, which had been posted on FB, noticing Ferdinand next to me.

She has always been difficult when I've had a man around, so I made up the excuse that he was an old friend and was gay, who was checking on me while I had a cold.

That satisfied her for now, changing the subject and talking about the family book. She sounded interested as well, telling her that I'll try and get down to her soon, to show her.

I got off the phone, realising I had slept for just over 4 hours feeling a bit better, but I think my cold had moved to my chest and lungs, feeling a bit wheezy.

I got up finding bed socks on my feet, smiling, going to the toilet coming out to find Ferdinand in the kitchen waiting for me. I could smell some baking had been done, looking at Ferdinand, not looking very happy now, "You told her I was gay, didn't you?"

I stood there wheezing a bit, nodding my head, "Yes, it was the only way to calm her down. She saw us on the news report as well."

He came closer to me, taking my hands, "You know I have been waiting a long time to be back with you, so Charlotte is going to have to get used to the idea of me being around because I'm not going away again. I would appreciate you telling her I'm not gay next time you talk with her."

I took a deep breath, a little agitated, "Alright, she has always been grumpy when I have men around me, which is why I haven't bothered in the end. It is something I'll have to work through with her."

He then realised I was wheezing, as well as looking quite pale, "Your breathing has changed."

I coughed, "I'm alright it always does this going to my chest, it'll pass. I made an appointment to go to the doctor on Tuesday just in case."

He picked me up. "Ferdinand, I can walk."

I protested but he carried me over to the sofa and put the throw over me. I've made some chocolate brownies, as I noticed you like chocolate with the amount of it in the fridge.

I smiled, trying to calm things down a little, "Can I have a peppermint tea with one?"

He went and got my pillow, propping me up then got us a brownie and some tea.

While we were sitting there eating them and watching TV he smiled, "Oh I forgot your boss rang as well, not long after you fell asleep, so I didn't want to wake you."

I rolled my eyes, "Oh yes, I bet he was surprised you answered my phone. You know he's going to give me the third degree when I go back as well."

He chuckled, "I'm enjoying this." He made me look at him.

"What are you enjoying Ferdinand? Your brownie or stirring up my life?"

He chuckled again, "Both, actually," as he rubbed my feet.

I relaxed after having the brownie and tea along with some more painkillers watching a bit of TV with Kimba coming up to be with us, preferring to sit on Ferdinand's lap, making me frown. He smiled at me while patting her as she purred.

I was having coughing fits off and on with phlegm rattling around in my chest. He got up to put some more rub on my chest and back to help it settle down.

I was going to argue with him, but the expression on his face stopped me. He was putting a lot of rub on, making me cough with the fumes hitting my nose, "I think you're putting a bit much on, Ferdinand."

He just rubbed it in more, "It'll be alright."

I sat back after he had finished, getting a tissue to blow my nose, "I think I will do some steam soon, it will help clear some of it, before I go to bed."

He looked pleased, "Yes good idea. I'll start some dinner then you can do it after that. I'm staying the night, by the way."

I looked surprised, "Oh, are you? Where do you intend to sleep?"

He pulled me down onto the pillow a bit more getting close to my face looking determined, "Yes, I am. I will bring in a bed, so don't worry I not going to start sleeping with you—yet!"

I chuckled coughing again, "You're a cocky dragon, aren't you?" He grinned, "Yep" and got up and walked to the kitchen.

We had dinner eating as much as I could. I went to get up to have a shower with him coming over to me, "Are you going to do the steam now?"

I shook my head, "No I'm just going to have a quick shower, it'll help my chest as well; plus, my hair is getting knots in it."

He shook his head, "No I don't think you should have a shower. Just do the steam and then I'll brush your hair out," He turned me around to go back to the sofa.

I took his hands off my shoulders, "Stop it! A shower warms me up and will help to loosen the phlegm, otherwise it goes to my lungs."

He relented, sighing, "Alright but don't stay in there too long."

I had a quick shower, drying off my hair then going over to do some steam in a bowl with a towel over it. I stayed under there as long as I could, as he rubbed my back trying to make the phlegm move. He rubbed the rub back into my back, then I took it this time to do my own chest.

He picked me up, "Come on time for you to go back to bed and I'll brush your hair out there."

I coughed a rattly cough, "I'm not ready to go to bed yet, put me down."

He just ignored me, getting my brush and putting me into bed, sitting next to me brushing my hair gently, getting the knots out of it. He encouraged me to lay down to let him brush it with the action sending me off to sleep.

I woke early in the morning wanting to throw up, rushing to the toilet bringing up some of the rubbish off my chest. I thought to myself, well at least it is moving, it should clear a bit quicker now.

Ferdinand came up behind me, "Are you alright?"

I got up, wiping my mouth, "Yes this is a good sign it is moving from my chest." I washed my face, taking a towel with me back to bed.

He looked at me, "Why are you taking a towel with you?"

I got back into bed, "I think there is a bit more in there. Just in case I don't get to the toilet in time."

He climbed into bed next to me, making me look at him, "What are you doing?" He made himself comfortable putting some pillows behind his head and back, pulling me down onto his shoulder.

"I'm helping you," as I tried to get back up.

"I don't know …" he just pulled me back down, pulling the blankets over us. He flicked his fingers, which turned off the light. My chest started to rattle again along with coughing, as he rubbed my back.

I felt like talking, "Ferdinand did you stop seeing me when I was around 7 or 8?" He sighed, "Yes it would have been around then, why?"

I shrugged my shoulders, "I thought it was around then. That's when Mum and Dad threatened to take me to a 'special' doctor to see what was wrong with me. I remember trying to hide the dragon picture on my wrist as well, with it eventually disappearing."

He rubbed my back a bit more, listening to the rattle, "Try not to worry about it now. Let's just get to know each other and try not to get angry." This made me laugh, bringing on a coughing fit, having to sit up and grab a tissue to blow my nose.

I lay back down on his chest listening to his heart beat, which was a bit fast then slowing down to a calm rhythm, sending me off to sleep. I woke feeling drowsy with my stomach starting to heave, as he pushed me up flicking the light on and putting the towel underneath my mouth, watching me bring up some more stuff. I managed to get up with his help, going to the toilet and bringing up a little more.

He had a glass of water and some painkillers waiting for me, when I came out, having it then going back to bed.

It was around 5.00am and I was feeling worn out, laying down with him putting some more rub on me, feeling a bit better. I set the alarm because I had the doctor's appointment at 11.30 and didn't want to miss it. He stroked my hair as I dropped back off to sleep.

I woke around 10.00am just before the alarm looking at him, still feeling strange that he was here helping me. My ex-husband wouldn't have done this, so I still found it odd that he was here helping me and we hardly knew each other.

I smiled to myself, '*At least he's not bad looking, even though he is a bit bossy.*'

He smiled, "I'm afraid I can read your thoughts, Hannah"

I sat up, "Oh that's not fair. Besides I thought you were asleep still."

We got up just having some toast for breakfast and a cup of tea. I told him about the appointment I had with Suzannah tomorrow.

He smiled, "Ah so you planned on having most of the week off, didn't you?"

I smirked, "I know when I'm going to be sick, so yes. Besides I don't take a lot of sick leave so I'm entitled to this. That reminds me, I didn't ring my boss back; I'll ring him after I've been to the doctor."

I got dressed ready to go to the doctors, which was just in the Cronulla Mall, so I could walk there. He came out of the bathroom ready to go, I thought to wherever he goes, but he took my hand smiling, "I'll come with you. We can then have some lunch afterwards."

I looked at him, "You're not going to change your mind, are you?"

He shook his head, "No. Besides I can show you how to teleport a bit better."

I put my hand up, "I'll just get my bag as I need my card for the doctor."

I came back out to find him shutting the balcony door, then he took my hand, "Are you ready? Now just think of the place where you are going and keep your eyes open."

I smiled nodding, "Ok, I wasn't keeping my eyes open which was part of the problem. We'll just go down to the car if you like and walk out of the driveway. There shouldn't be anyone down there."

He nodded, "Yep sounds good." We teleported down there with me stumbling a little, luckily, he was still holding onto my hand, laughing, "You'll get it eventually."

We walked the rest of the way with just a light breeze blowing off the sea and a little bit of warmth in the sun. I went in and saw the doctor, as he waited outside for me. The doctor gave me the rest of the week off and some antibiotics to make sure my chest didn't get worse or it went to my lungs. I came out telling him this with him smiling, "That's good I can annoy you a bit more."

I smacked him on the arm, "Stop it."

He looked around, "So where would you like to go to lunch?"

I pointed over to Nulla. I generally go there, but there is another place near the water called Barefoot Café if you want a water view. He took my hand, "We'll check out the Nulla Nulla first, see how busy it is."

I felt a little unsure now, as I don't normally get that much from there and sure enough, as I walked up to it Cecilia was there smiling, who, with her Filipino accent, "Ah Hashbrown Hannah, how many do you want today? Oh, you've got a friend with you this time, does he want hashbrowns too?"

Ferdinand looked at me shaking his head, "No it's ok thanks. Hannah is off the hashbrowns for now."

Cecilia laughed, "I keep telling Hannah we have other food."

Ferdinand squeezed my hand, "We'll come back another day, you look quite busy. I think I'll try something else."

Cecilia looked disappointed, "Aww, make sure you come back next time though."

Ferdinand nodded, "Sure, Cecilia."

We went to Barefoot Café sitting down feeling a bit nervous, as I hadn't been out with anyone for a long time. He smiled, "You're nervous, aren't you?"

I put my eyes down looking at the menu, "A little. It's been a while."

He poured some water from the jug, "Just relax. I won't bite you."

This made me laugh and wheeze, "You are a dragon, you might."

We made a selection with him going up to order the food, coming back with a number. I was sipping on the water looking out at the view when he came back, "Don't forget to take your tablet that the doctor gave you."

I rolled my eyes, "Bossy dragon."

I thought of something I wanted to ask him, "So where do you go when you aren't here?"

He looked at the view almost as though he was visualising something, "To a beautiful place that is peaceful. You have actually been there when you were young but you probably can't remember it."

I felt a bit sad at that. "I do remember having some sort of dream of a beautiful lush place with lots of women around and animals walking freely. Is that it?"

He nodded, "Yes that sounds like it. I will take you there again soon."

I looked surprised at that, "Really! That will be something to look forward to."

A cheeky grin came over his face, "You have to learn to behave first and get that temper under control."

I groaned, "There's always rules or conditions isn't there." Our food came with him, looking bossy at me, saying, "Yes, Hannah."

We walked back to my unit taking in the smell of the sea and fresh air with just an odd cough coming from me. I was feeling a lot better having got rid of that stuff off my chest, plus some fresh air and nice food helped.

We were getting near the unit when I spotted the man, I had put a chant on, sitting on a seat talking on the phone. I smiled, with Ferdinand looking at me, then looking at the guy realising who he was.

Ferdinand took my hand saying quietly, "Don't you dare, Hannah. You've already been sick because of him."

I leaned into him, "It was worth it, Ferdinand. I'm not going to do anything, but it was funny."

He shook his head, "Remind me not to get on your bad side." Ferdinand steered me away from the man, but it was too late the guy looked up from his phone call, staring at me with that look of 'I've seen you somewhere before.'

Ferdinand squeezed my hand, "Don't look at him, Hannah." The guy stood up watching me walk away with Ferdinand, starting to follow us as I said, *"The laces that tie your shoes shall join together like a snake and make you fall like the fool you are."*

Ferdinand pulled me closer to him, "Hannah Dragĕ you said you wouldn't do anything."

We heard a yell of "agghh" turning to see the guy fall down tripping over his laces.

Ferdinand carried on walking saying quietly to me, "Why did you do that?"

I looked up to him annoyed, "He was going to follow us. I didn't want him to know where I lived."

Ferdinand sighed in frustration, walking on a bit further then teleporting back home. Ferdinand held my hand, not letting it go. I tried to take my hand out of his. "Don't get annoyed with me Ferdinand. I'm not having a creep like that hanging around my place just because he thinks I'm a witch. Now I've had a nice day with you, but I'm going to ring my boss and then have a nap. You can get as annoyed with me as you like, but I'm going to defend myself if I feel I have to. That chant won't last long either."

Ferdinand looked at me, admitting defeat, "You're probably right with him wanting to know where you live. I just get nervous when you use magic out in the open like that. Like I said, there are a lot of people who would try to get you in their dark corner or worse try to get your magic."

I sighed, "How do I know you're not the dark corner?"

He looked seriously at me, "You will know the difference, Hannah. Like other things in your world, there are good people and bad people, who will do anything to get what they want, no matter what."

I chuckled, "That sounds like most of my life."

He let me go but pointed at me changing my clothes to my nightie and putting me in my bed growling at him as he came in behind me smiling, "But it doesn't mean I can't punish you."

I tried to get up before he got there but he came in behind me holding tight, "No you don't, you little minx." I started to laugh which also made me cough, trying to make it sound worse than what it was.

He chuckled, "It's not working, Hannah, putting on the cough."

I was running out of energy, "I've just got to ring my boss, then I'll have a nap, ok."

He brought my phone out magically still holding me dialling the number "no Ferdinand let me talk to him." He was chuckling as Tom my boss answered.

I went quiet, mouthing to Ferdinand, "Give it to me." Ferdinand spoke into the phone, "Hi Tom, this is Ferdinand Hannah's boyfriend, she just wants to talk to you," giving me the phone as I slapped him angrily. Ferdinand grinned, blowing me a kiss going out of the bedroom.

I told Tom I wouldn't be back until next week, with him sounding surprised that I had a boyfriend, more than worried I wasn't coming in for the rest of the week. I tried to explain that he was more a friend, with Tom saying, "Oh yeah ok, Hannah."

I hung up with Ferdinand coming back to sit on the side of the bed now, "You're a bad dragon, Ferdinand."

He chuckled, "I told you there will be repercussions when you misbehave."

I pointed a chant at him then quickly got off the bed, giggling as he yelled, "Hannah you little minx get these off me now," he was standing up with cuffs on, looking menacing at me, as he cornered me in the bedroom.

I ran out of room speaking quickly, as he was getting closer, "You have to trust me Ferdinand, when I use my magic alright? I'm not an 8-year-old girl now. I might make the wrong decisions sometimes but I'm not putting up with creeps like that."

He took a big step putting his cuffed arms around me, "Take these off me, Hannah."

I shook my head smiling, "No Ferdinand, not until we get it clear that I'm going to use my magic if I have to."

He turned me around so my back was to him, picking me up and putting me back on the bed, "You're a stubborn woman Hannah, but alright. I won't try to interfere too much. Now let me out of these."

I felt satisfied we had come to a truce, so I took them off him. I got up to go to the toilet and have a drink of water, taking my time. Ferdinand ended up picking me up over his shoulder, "I think you're taking too long Hannah Dragĕ, time for your nap." I squealed as he walked back into my room lying me down changing his clothes and lying down behind me, holding onto my waist, "Now go to sleep, Hannah." I had no energy left now, so I held onto his hands that were around my waist, "Tell me about the place you go. What's it called?"

He got comfortable, "It's called Jardine. You will be told the full story later about it, but it is probably what your world would call the Garden of Eden. We don't have money; everyone has a roof over their head and food. We work as a community and animals are not eaten with some being assigned as guardian or spirit animals like you and me."

As my eyes started to close, I started to dream of a place that was lush and green with animals roaming free. Ferdinand could hear my breathing deepen as I dropped off to sleep.

Chapter 4

Ferdinand stayed the night again, then left after breakfast, giving me a hug saying I'll be back for dinner. I started to smile, "Thanks for looking after me while I was sick. My ex-husband would never have done that." He leaned in kissing me on the cheek, "It's been nice and *challenging* with your temper."

I laughed, "With your temper as well, Ferdi." We gave each other a hug again with him disappearing.

I did a bit of cleaning, then went for a walk as the sun was coming out, to get some fresh air, keeping an eye out for that guy, but not seeing him thank goodness. My cold was a lot better feeling a lot stronger, thinking to myself, '*I got those antibiotics in time, thank goodness.*'

I decided to go to the supermarket to get some cat food and fruit, going over to the apples. A plump woman came up beside me looking at them, when I noticed she was breathing quite heavily with little beads of sweat appearing on her forehead, even though it was a cool day. As she sweated, her curly blonde hair looked a bit like medusas' snakes on her head—all messy and intertwining.

I moved away to look at the different apples, with her taking a step over towards me. I picked a couple of apples up and put them in the bag hearing her laugh, "Well it's good to see you're picking a good fruit love!"

I thought to myself, '*Oh no, a nutter.*' I just smiled at her, noticing a necklace around her neck that looked almost like a black diamond, which gave off a bit of sparkle as she moved.

I tried to change the subject, "Gee I like your necklace, did your partner give you that?"

She breathed heavily, "Oh this was given to me by a friend. It's lovely, isn't it? You know apples were in the Bible, you should eat plenty of them, as they are good for you."

I smiled, "They were in a lot of fairy tales as well, maybe I should put them back in case they are poisoned."

This made the woman start to get agitated, "Only witches used them in fairy tales, are you a witch?"

I rolled my eyes, 'Here we go again' moving away from her, but she put her chubby hand on my wrist, "Well, are you a witch?"

I tried to stay calm feeling as though she was being controlled by that stone, "Not that I know of. Are you?"

This made her gasp, "No I would never call myself a witch, how dare you."

I shook off her hand, "It's only a label that horrible people, especially men, used to justify killing women for no reason at all. You should feel sorry for those women."

She followed me around the supermarket, which isn't very big, finally getting annoyed and saying a chant: *"leave me be this woman who is enchanted go back to where you were planted by whom I'd like to see."*

This stopped her annoying me, allowing me to pay for my things, then I went out over to Nulla Nulla getting a hashbrown from Cecelia. Who joked with me not having Ferdinand with me this time. I then sat on a seat under a tree nearby, watching to see where she went.

She came out of the supermarket looking a bit dazed with two men coming up to her; one of them was the one I had put a chant on before. I watched them as they spoke to her, not being able to hear what they said, as they were too far away. The chubby one took the necklace off the woman letting her sit down as she held her head.

I ate my hashbrown watching with intrigue; with the two men grouping together away from the woman so I said, *"A dust devil shall appear swirling whirling to form around this pair I see blinding them with dirt temporarily while they plot their evil."*

A little whirlwind formed around the men, twisting in a gust of wind, sending dirt into the air surrounding them, as I giggled to myself. I watched them stagger around putting their arms out to try and stable themselves because they couldn't see.

Tears of laughter started coming down my cheeks, watching the two men staggering and falling on the ground like a comedy act.

I calmed down continuing to eat my hashbrown and watching them, when I felt someone sit next to me, putting an arm around me. He leaned over to give me a kiss on the cheek, "You're being naughty again, aren't you?"

I passed my hashbrown over to Ferdinand, "Do you want a bite, they're quite nice." He looked over to the two guys walking as though they were in a wind tunnel now with dust swirling around them shaking his head, "Yes I think I will try some," and took it out of my hand and bit into it, "Mm not bad. I think I could make better ones than that. Now are you going to stop the whirlwind?"

I looked horrified, "Oh, you think that was me?" He moved in closer giving me the hashbrown back looking at me sternly.

I took my hashbrown back, sighing, mumbling the chant to stop, then carried on eating my hashbrown. The two men stumbled onto a seat brushing themselves off.

Once I had finished the hashbrown, Ferdinand stood up, picking up my groceries, putting his hand out for mine, to walk me back to the unit.

I took it, sighing, turning once more to see what they were doing, smirking with the men clearing their eyes, looking around to see where it came from. Ferdinand growled, "Hannah that's enough" holding tight onto my hand pulling me a little, walking away as quickly as possible.

As we walked, "Now I didn't start that—again! They did by sending that enchanted woman next to me. I'm just defending myself Ferdinand." We got to a quieter part of the path, with Ferdinand putting his arm around my waist taking me home.

He put the groceries on the bench shaking his head, "Alright you were defending yourself. I'm telling you, just be careful, besides I don't want to end up in cuffs again."

I smiled, kissing him on the cheek, "See that didn't hurt did it." He helped me put the groceries away noticing more chocolate in the bag, "Haven't you got enough chocolate in the fridge already?" I took it off him, "You can never have enough chocolate or wine Ferdinand, it's a number one rule of this world."

He gave me a hug, "I know you have that appointment with that woman today, try and behave yourself. I'll see you afterwards for dinner."

I looked into his eyes, seeing a flicker of love in there, feeling a little nervous, but decided not to think about it, "Sure. What delight are you going to cook for me tonight?"

He continued to hug me, tapping my bum, "Depends on how good you've been, you'll have to wait and see." He gave me a kiss on the cheek then moved away from me and disappeared.

I felt a little stir inside of me, knowing I hadn't felt that for a long time as I touched my cheek feeling nervous. I took a deep sigh, scolding myself, *'Stop over thinking it. Just see what happens. Besides he's a dragon, am I allowed to think that way about a dragon?'*

I decided to get the family book out to see if I could get a better security system on it before I went to Suzannah's house to take my mind off things.

I put the thought into my head with the pages turning over to the back of the book, almost where the Dragĕ coat of arms was. I looked at the dragon in it, which was facing straight ahead, with its wings spanned out and it was holding a sword with a unique handle design. It looked like flames in metal, forming part of the handle, that the dragon was holding onto with its front paws.

I sighed, *'Mmm I wonder why it's showing me this? I wonder if I need the sword to change the security on the book.'* I looked through some of the other pages not finding anything else, so I put it away and got ready to go to Suzannah's.

I got changed, thinking I had better drive there rather than use magic, just in case she comes out not finding the car. I took off, getting to Newtown after having to go through a bit traffic, wishing I had used magic to get there now. I finally found the place, using my map app, pulling up in front of a small house. It was one of those narrow red brick places built in the federation style, which was popular in Sydney around the 1900s. It had the traditional red, green and white paintwork and lattice iron work around the bullnose veranda on the front. I walked up the path on the original Victorian era pattern work of green, red and white tiles surrounded by old fashion rose bushes with their scent hitting me as I walked down. This reminded me of my mother who always loved roses.

As I got closer to the door, I could see fruit trees that were covering the corner of the house. A light breeze blew gently as I approached the door with the sound of a wooden windchime sing its song in a low-pitched sound, as they hit each other.

I took a deep breath and knocked on the door waiting for a few minutes. I was about to knock again, when I heard shuffling behind the door and a lock being turned. The door finally opened with a small woman with a round moon face and fine wrinkles showing her age but making her look wise. She had long hair that was tied in a knot on her crown, that looked like it had been blonde once, but the white streaks were now taking over, merging through it. Her hair appeared to encase her face making her icy blue eyes stand out more.

She brought a gentle smile to her lips, but her eyes were checking me out as though they were trying to search my soul. I could smell the faint aroma of white sage incense burning somewhere in the house, as she opened the door wider, allowing her shiny marmalade cat to sneak out of the crack, coming to rub itself around my legs. I smiled, "Hi I'm Hannah Dragĕ, I rang you about the meditation meeting."

She smiled at me, opening the door inviting me in. "ah yes. It is a good sign when one of my cats likes you, Hannah. Please come this way." There was a big arch over the hallway with a keystone in the middle, blue runner rugs covering the wooden floors and an old-fashioned coat stand against the wall on the right.

She showed me to the lounge which was full of two sofas and heavy bureaus made out of dark stained oak. Big leafy pot plants were intermingled with the furniture, giving it a Victorian feel, but homely as well.

She asked me to sit on a sofa, that was covered with a patchwork fabric of pinks, purples and blues. As I sat down her other cat, a black one this time, jumped on my lap wanting some attention.

Suzannah made a fuss, "Oh Sooty don't be naughty you don't normally do that to my visitors."

I smiled at Suzannah, "Don't worry I have a cat myself and love them. They usually are a good judge of character, aren't they?"

I started to feel a little more relaxed with the cat on my lap making a fuss of her, which she thoroughly enjoyed.

Suzannah smiled in a worldly way, "Would you like a cup of herbal tea Hannah?"

As I rubbed Sooty's ears, "Yes thank you, that would be lovely. I hope I am not putting you to any trouble though."

"No, I was going to have one anyway." She then got up to go to the kitchen to make it.

I had noticed when I walked in the lounge a large ornate dresser with a lot of crystals on it. With my magpie instincts kicking in, I got up with Sooty still in my arms, scratching her ears walking around looking at them all; listening to Sooty's purring getting louder with all the attention.

There were all sorts of crystals on there, along with little statues of women and photos of, what I presumed were here family in old-fashioned frames. I have always loved collecting crystals and have a few of my own, so I was enjoying myself looking at her collection.

One crystal stuck out in particular which had rose quartz for the stem and clear quartz crystal for the crossbar in the shape of a dagger being joined together with delicate silver lacing going around it—I just had to touch it.

I noticed, as I picked the dagger up, feeling the weight of it in my hand, that it had a handle on it very similar to the one in my book I had just seen. As I turned it around in my hand, I thought I could feel a little pulse come off it. I had felt pulses off my crystals before but not normally other people's. I put it down going back to sit on the sofa, as I could hear Suzannah shuffling back to the lounge with a tray.

I put Sooty down offering to help her but she said, "I'm fine go and sit down and make yourself comfortable." She put the tray on the coffee table that was a chest as well as a coffee table carved with intricate designs, some of which I hadn't seen before.

As she gave me my tea looking at me intently with those icy blue eyes, "Did you find anything you liked, Hannah?"

I looked a little embarrassed at her, realising she must have seen me get up to have a look around. She smiled, "Don't be embarrassed, Hannah, have another look and show me which one you felt drawn to?"

I got up going back to the bureau I had looked at the crystals on, going straight to the dagger picking it up feeling that hum again. I turned to smile at her, "This is beautiful and one that I feel drawn to."

Suzannah's expression changed briefly, putting her smile back on. "Well, it appears to be yours. Please take it home with you as a gift from me."

I gushed, "I can't take this home I am sure it is worth a bit of money, having crystals myself."

Suzannah patted the sofa saying, "Come and sit down here and bring the dagger."

I did as she asked bringing it over to her going to give it to her. She put her hands up, "No I insist. It is yours now. Use it as much as you can in your meditations."

I felt a little awkward but relented at her insistence saying, "Thank you very much, I appreciate it."

As we sipped our tea Suzannah asked about my family and its history. Ferdinand's warning to be careful around people came into my head and I really didn't know this woman, so I just shrugged, "I really don't know a lot, Suzannah. My mother wasn't the type of person to go into the history of our family very much. All I know is that my grandmother came from Norway and my grandfather came from Germany."

Suzannah had a little glint in her eye making me look more intensely, at her as she put her eyes down so I couldn't read them.

As we drank our tea, she asked me, "Why do you think your meditation teacher has sent you here, Hannah?"

I took a sip then put my cup down thinking about it, "I think mainly because I was getting a few visions in my meditation. I had actually spoken to her about this before, but she wasn't really interested; so, I am not sure why she has taken an interest in me now."

Suzannah looked at me, still guarded, "I think you are opening yourself up a lot more now that you have reached a certain age. Your subconscious is making you see that you have a special talent that has lain dormant for some time. It is time to wake it up Hannah. I will give you some information to read, to teach you how to get yourself into a deeper meditation to show you what that talent is. It may come to you directly or indirectly depending on how, strong you are. You need to follow these instructions to enable you to get stronger as well as reach your full potential. I do feel in the past that your shyness along with your temper has restricted you, stopping you from reaching your full potential."

I sat there perplexed, listening to Suzannah, "Wow, you can tell that just from being with me in this short amount of time?"

I thought of something silly to say to make it look like I didn't know anything, "So do you think I could read hands or something like that?"

Suzannah chuckled quietly, "I think you have something a bit stronger and deeper than that buried deep within you. Anyone can read hands or tell peoples fortunes."

I smiled, "Well I guess I really don't want to read fortunes."

Suzannah put her cold hand on mine, "Now you are being truthful with yourself. Read the information I gave you as well as do your meditation with the dagger. Make sure you cleanse it well first, in the sea, as that would be the best way to cleanse it. There is a meditation group that will meet tomorrow in Newtown. I think you should go to it as it will also help you to become stronger in your meditation. I don't think you need to come and see me again, but if you would like to talk to me about anything, you have my number, just ring me."

I got up, helping her up, taking the information she had given me, walking towards the door, "Thanks Suzannah, you have been a great help. I will let you know if I need anything else and thanks again for the dagger."

I got into my car looking back at the house before I started it up, noticing a twitch of the curtains with a little pale face disappear, when she realised, I had seen her.

I shook my head, 'She was certainly different to what I expected.' I blew my nose as it was still running from my cold getting a cough lolly to suck on thinking, '*Thank goodness I didn't start coughing around her.*'

I drove back home with the traffic just as horrible, feeling a bit weary, by the time I came back. I decided to go and cleanse the dagger quickly, just ducking down to the beach near the unit, hoping I won't have any trouble this time.

I put a beanie on as it was a little cool outside and I thought it might disguise me a little if that guy was hanging around. I put the dagger into a little towel I had, hiding it.

I got down to the water taking my shoes off to put my feet into the water, feeling a shiver and goosebumps going over me, but it also helped to ground myself. As I walked in a little further, I was about to do my usual chant that I did for cleansing, when another one came into my head, "*With this dagger I ask that all the elements earth, air, wind and fire cleanse it well and relieve it of its past. Make it fresh, make it new without any doubt or negativity to be passed from you to me while in this cleansing sea. So, mote it be.*"

I was dipping it in the water saying this when a pulse went out from it, then a white light came back into it, sending it through me, making me take a deep breath, nearly knocking me over. I stabled myself, putting it back into the towel I had brought it down in, walking out of the water, feeling the buzz from the pulse I had received.

I walked towards my shoes looking up to see that guy coming towards me again thinking, '*Oh for crying out loud*' bending down to pick up my shoes walking down the beach, so I didn't have to confront him.

He caught up with me putting his hand on my arm, when it recoiled off me quickly, as though he had been burned at the touch of me. He was puffing at the exertion of walking quickly, with a look of shock with the jolt he had received. I turned to face him, "What do you want? Just leave me alone. I'm not hurting you or anyone else."

He had a scowl on his face, "You are a witch; you shouldn't be doing this stuff. I think you need to go and get your soul saved."

I laughed sarcastically at him, "You've got to be kidding. Why don't you go and save all the souls of the paedophiles you have in your *church* and leave me alone? Besides what are you going to do about it if I am a witch, which I am not! Are you going to burn me at the stake like all the other innocent women your kind have killed over the years?"

This made him angry, "You think you are so clever with you spells; your day will come."

I could feel my anger building now with a clap of thunder heard out to sea looking at him with a death stare, which made him gasp, not sure what to do.

A chant came into my head but I decided just to say, "Your day will come little man! If you keep hassling me, I'm going to report you to the police, then we will see how you go. I imagine you're some sort of priest and the *church* won't like that."

I then teleported out of there going home. I got home growling having a drink of water to calm myself down while I went and sat on the balcony, taking some deep breaths.

After about 15 minutes, I felt calm enough to bring the book out to have a look to where the sword was on the dragon. It certainly looked very similar in the handle putting it down on the page to compare it, when the dagger moved over the sword, with a bright white light forming in a circle around it for a few seconds then it stopped. I shook my head, '*Wow I wasn't expecting that.*'

I closed the book leaving it on the coffee table deciding to do some meditation with the dagger, as Suzannah had suggested. I lit some incense sitting in front of the balcony doors so I could get the sea air on me, deciding to leave the beanie on so it wouldn't freshen up my cold.

I put the CD on, starting my meditation, going into my breathing, feeling myself go deep quite quickly. I could feel myself being enveloped with a radiated light going deeper; feeling myself have an out of body experience.

I've had those before in my meditation, so it didn't frighten me, I just floated around myself watching the dagger lift off the ground slowly twirling around then it pointed towards me, sending a beam of white light through me. I felt a shudder hit me as I gasped for a few seconds then the light went back to the book as it to lit up.

This whole process only took a couple of minutes then the dagger righted itself still in the air in front of me twirling. The white light, that was around me, swirled like a mist sending a calm feeling through me and connected to both the crystal and the book.

I heard a noise, realising Ferdinand had arrived back, looking at me then noticing the book on the coffee table. I was curious to see what he did, so I stayed out of my body; I knew he couldn't see me.

He sat down on the sofa moving over to the book, looking at the name on the top of it. He put his hand on it to ensure it didn't have a spell on it or anything, then turned the front cover over. He saw the family tree there with me and my girls in it along with my mother and the other two grandmothers. I could see he was curious as to why the others weren't there putting his hand above my grandmother's names to see if there was anything else there.

He tried to turn the next page but it wouldn't let him because he wasn't of my blood, showing me the security on the book worked.

It was time to come back, starting to change my breathing, which Ferdinand could hear, so he quickly closed the book and moved over to the kitchen sitting on the barstool. I slowly came out of my meditation with the dagger going back down onto the floor opening my eyes.

I looked at myself with the white mist still faintly around me, stretching out my legs slowly. Ferdinand got up making me look around smiling, "Oh hello, I didn't think you would be back yet, or did I take too long in my meditation?"

I rolled over onto my knees and hands as he came over to help me up laughing, "Why did you sit like that when you have trouble getting up?"

I groaned, "I don't know it seemed like a good idea at the time."

He helped me up pulling me close to him looking at the beanie smiling, "Well at least you're not trying to get sick again."

I smiled, pulling it off, with my hair falling out with a bit of static in it, "Oh heck now it's going to be a pain in the bum." I went to move away but he held onto me, "I want to ask you something." I looked at him curious, "Oh what's that?"

He pushed some of my hair off my face, "I'd like to get to know you better and would like to start sleeping here more. I enjoyed it when you were sick, well not you being sick, if you know what I mean; but I enjoyed us being together."

I smiled looking a little coy at him making him chuckle, "No there will be no sex, not as you know it anyway."

I looked bemused, "What do you mean not as I know it?"

He hugged me, "When we are *both* ready, we do it Jardine style."

I moved out from him, "Jardine style." That sounds interesting.

I sighed thinking about it, 'I'll have to warn you, and you probably already know this, it's been a long time since I've lived with anyone, especially a man or dragon for that matter. You already know I have a temper, so if you're willing to tolerate that, I guess we can give it a go. There is one other thing though, we have to keep it quiet from the girls, especially Charlotte, until I think they are ready to know.'

He gave me a hug, "Yes alright dear."

I laughed, "Oh we're getting to that already as well. You don't muck around, do you?"

I thought of something else, "Are we breaking any rules doing this?"

He grinned cheekily at me, "I broke some going to see you from time to time when you blocked me off, but no we're allowed to do this."

I teased him, "Oh you naughty boy."

He kissed me on the cheek changing the subject, "You did well with that guy again today, I'm proud of you."

I sighed, "It's like he has a homing device or something as soon as I go in that water. It's starting to annoy me. I really had to try hard not to put something on him."

Ferdinand's expression changed, "I wonder if they do have something that tells them where you are."

I shook my head, "I don't know, but like I said it is getting annoying."

He kissed the top of my head, "I'll cook something nice up for dinner. Did you take your antibiotic today?"

I put my hand up to my mouth, "Oh no I keep forgetting. Luckily you remembered and there aren't too many to take. I might go and have my shower now to fix up this hair before it drives me nuts."

I remembered about the family book, looking at him smirking, as he watched me pick it up, "Do you want to have a look at it?" He shook his head, "No that's alright." I put it away getting my things ready for a shower. I came out of the shower getting a glass of water for us both, going to sit on the sofa to check my phone, to see if I had missed anything.

Just as I was sitting there sipping on my water, checking FB; a message came in, *"Hi Hannah it's great you're coming to my wedding with your new boyfriend. Do you want to use my hair and makeup lady? Tania."*

I turned to look at Ferdinand, who was just putting the plates of food on the bench he had cooked, smiling at me, "Dinner is ready." My face changed, making him look nervous, "What's the matter dear?"

I scowled at him, "Don't you dear me. Why is Tania saying I'm going to her wedding?"

He smiled cheekily, "Oh yes, she rang while you were sick. I thought you might like to go so I said 'yes plus one' as it said on the invitation."

I got up taking a big gulp of water, "I'm going to have to make sure I don't leave my phone around you anymore, aren't I? I wasn't going to go to the wedding because I don't believe in weddings any more, plus I don't have anything to wear."

He walked around the counter putting his arm around my waist, "That's alright we can go shopping tomorrow for a dress."

I growled, "Ferdinand, I didn't want to go."

He looked down at me, "You need to socialise with your friends more. You've built yourself a little cocoon here; it will do you good to get out."

I growled again, "You better behave yourself!"

He smiled wrapping his arms around my waist with a glint in his eyes, "I always do, it is you that misbehaves, remember," giving me a kiss on my forehead again, "Now come and eat your dinner while it's hot. Your tablet is on the bench as well."

I sat down taking my tablet, sulking while eating the food, which was delicious, not talking very much. He was trying not to smirk too much, taking a sip of his wine, looking at me every now and then.

We cleaned up with him going to have a shower while I lay down on the sofa looking at different dresses, I could possibly look at to buy.

I decided to have a bit of a stir, putting a chant on Ferdinand, chuckling to myself saying, *"Bubble, bubble make the soap keep on bubbling giving Ferdinand trouble."*

All of a sudden, I heard a yell, "Hannah you little ..."

I giggled to myself, when all of a sudden, he appeared behind the sofa naked and soapy. I realised I was in trouble, quickly putting down my phone, getting up to move, when he grabbed me picking me up and magicaeing into the shower, as I struggled laughing.

He put me down holding on making sure I got wet and soapy, "Take it off Hannah."

I struggled against him laughing. I was laughing so much it started a coughing fit, deciding it was time to do a reverse chant, with the soap stopping.

He shook his head getting all the soap off himself looking at me determined, "I think you need to go to bed."

I stood there looking at him naked admiring the view, "No dear, not yet."

He had a big smile on his face, "Do you like what you see?"

I chuckled, "Yes I do, actually."

I walked out of the shower, stripping off my wet nightie and knickers; grabbing a towel wrapping it around myself to go to the bedroom, noticing he was getting a good look as well.

He came out putting a towel around his waist grabbing me and lifting me up in a fireman's lift as I yelled, "Ferdinand I'm not ready to go to bed yet, put me down."

I was laughing and coughing still, with him holding on tight. As I tried to get out of his grip, he turned off the lights, shut the balcony door and grabbed my phone.

He put the phone on his side magically putting some clothes on me and drying my hair, while still holding me down, with a big grin on his face.

He got the rub, starting to rub it on my chest, while I tried to stop him, but he was a bit stronger than me. He then turned me over to rub it on my back, going down to my sensitive spot, "Ah that's right there's that spot you have."

I squirmed under him pushing myself up to try and turn, "No don't touch that Ferdinand," but it was too much of a temptation for him as I wriggled around squealing.

He lay down beside me holding on, "Have you had enough?"

I took a deep breath nodding when the phone went.

He looked at me with a wicked smile, because it was on his side, with both of us going to grab it. He got to it first seeing who the caller was; it was Amelia as he held it out of my reach, "Are you going to behave?"

I sat down out of breath, "Yes, just let me answer it." He gave me the phone answering it to speak to Amelia. He put some clothes on, turned off the main light putting the lamp on and got comfortable beside me cuddling in.

I was trying to talk to Amelia about going out to lunch on the weekend but he kept distracting me, kissing me on the cheek every now and then.

Amelia could hear I was distracted, eventually asked, "What are you doing?"

I had to think fast, "Oh Kimba is being silly for some reason," as I slapped Ferdinand's hand that was around my waist.

I eventually hung up, putting the phone over my side this time, turning to look at him with his eyes closed as I smiled thinking, '*I still can't believe this is happening. Why have I let him in so quickly. Am I making a big mistake again?*' I scolded myself, '*Just go with the flow and make it an adventure.*'

He flicked his fingers, turning the light off saying, "Good night, dear."

Chapter 5

I woke to find Ferdinand awake lying there looking at me smiling, realising I was waking up.

I stretched like a cat smiling at him putting my arms around his neck, "What are you looking at, Mr Dragon?" He chuckled, "Just glad we are finally together."

I kissed him on the cheek, "Aww that's nice. Let's just cuddle and go back to sleep."

He chuckled again making me get suspicious, as he reached up moving some hair off my face, "No dear, I'm going to take you shopping remember. We can get up now and go somewhere to have a nice breakfast then beat the crowds in the shops."

I groaned, "No that doesn't sound that good, I liked my idea better," stroking his hair trying to soothe him. Unfortunately, it was doing the opposite, stirring him up a little and getting up, "Come on, we'll go somewhere nice for breakfast."

I rolled over, "No you just cook something nice for us. I like your cooking better."

He got up going to the toilet, "It's not going to work Hannah get up."

I stayed where I was hoping he would change his mind, when he came back and opened the curtains making me groan again, pulling the sheets over me.

I don't know why I bothered, he just pulled them off, picking me up in his arms, "Oh come on Ferdinand, it's too early, look there are grey skies as well so it might rain. Cough-cough."

He shook his head, "Go and get dressed. You have that meditation meeting tonight don't you as well."

I screwed my face up, "Yes. I don't know if I'll go yet."

He put me down, giving me a kiss on the top of my head, "Come on let's go and have a nice breakfast and go shopping."

I sighed going to get dressed, "I'll have to get you to show me how to get dressed magically like you do."

He smiled, "You've worked out how to teleport, I thought you would have worked it out by now."

I stood there thinking about it. It must be all in the mind, so I thought about what I wanted to put on, taking a deep breath, waving my hand over myself.

The clothes I had wanted to put on appeared on me, as I jumped up in excitement. The only thing missing were some knickers and a bra. He came in smiling, "Not bad for your first attempt."

We took off going to have some breakfast at a café called Settlement on Quay, watching all the people go past as we ate.

I felt a little nervous going there, which Ferdinand picked up, "What's the matter, Hannah?"

I smiled, "It's not far from where I work Ferdinand, they might ask why I'm here when I'm off sick."

Ferdinand smirked, "Oh I forgot about that. It's a bit early for most of them anyway, isn't it?"

I nodded, "Yes thank goodness."

We took our time, then walked slowly up to the shops just in time for them to open. We went into Myers with Ferdinand finding a soft teal blue wrap dress, getting me to try it on.

The sales lady, whose name was Jasmine, was gushing around Ferdinand, "Oh a lovely choice."

Ferdinand says, "Come out so I can have a look at it."

I felt a little embarrassed not used to having to do this, but I did like it anyway so no matter what he said I would probably buy it. I went out to show him, as he smiled lovingly at me, "That is nice, Hannah."

I went back into the cubicle to get changed feeling a bit strange still at his look and how fast this was going. I went and got changed, with us both arguing, who was going to pay for it. He insisted that he pay for it as it was his idea to go to the wedding. I gave in, "I'm going to need some shoes so I will pay for them, do you understand!"

He just leaned in giving me a kiss on the cheek, "Yes dear." Jasmine was looking on dreamily at him.

We went to the shoe department finding some nice shoes that I wouldn't fall over in but high enough to look nice. I tried them on then paid for them.

I took Ferdinand's hand, "Wow that's the fastest I've done clothes shopping in a long time."

He smiled, "I'm good at this and see we have beaten the crowds. It's well worth getting up early."

I rolled my eyes, "Yes dear." We walked to a quieter area of the city then magicae home, landing in the unit with his arm around my waist. I put the dress and shoes away, sitting on the sofa while Ferdinand opened the balcony door, coming to sit next to me.

He put his hand over mine making me curious, "The meditation meeting you are going to tonight; there is a woman that goes there from Jardine and her name is Lilith. She has helped me through the years when you were not around, but we have not been intimate or anything, which is what we call it in Jardine."

I raised my eyebrow, "Oh yes."

He smiled, "She has a guardian animal as well, so don't be silly."

I laughed, "It's ok Ferdinand. I actually have something to tell you as well. I've found out an old boyfriend is going to be at the wedding, so do you still want to go?"

He chuckled, "Yes dear I do. I'll tell you what if it gets too uncomfortable for you, we will go once the ceremony is over ok? I just think it will be good for us both to have a bit of fun."

I squeezed his hand, "Ok, that makes me feel better. They aren't that bad I just get a bit sick of them going on about me not being with anyone or if I do bring someone they go on and on about when am I going to get married again blah blah blah. I mean they try to look after me in a friendly way, but I think I'm old enough to know what I want."

He sighed, "Yes, I guess you're right. Do you want to go for a walk on the beach before I go?"

I nodded, "Yes that will be nice."

We went for a walk along the water line, getting a bit of chill at first, when the water hit our feet with it being cold. We chatted about different things as we walked, mainly me asking about Jardine. We didn't run into anyone annoying which was nice for a change.

We went back home with him taking off, letting me catch up with the girls, as well as getting the book out again. As I was studying it, I thought about how to secure the book better, thinking like a computer file, when something came into my head; I felt from my ancestors. It was almost like a vision showing me what to do, so I set about getting it ready to start the process.

I needed some herbs of angelica root, bay leaf and some crystals which were labradorite and clear quartz crystal, which I managed to pull in magically, feeling pleased with my ability. I cleansed myself with some sage and made a circle putting the elements around me of earth, air, wind and fire putting the book, a white candle, the herbs and the crystals in the middle with me.

I went around the circle asking for protection from the elements as well as security for my book. It then showed me how to lock the room taking a deep breath saying, *"Lukk taigh"* with the sound of locks clicking around the unit being heard. I put the crystals around the book and lit the candle saying, *"With this candle I do ask for security and protection for this book once the chant my lips has passed."*

I then put the herbs into my hands resting them on my palms closing my eyes with a spell coming into my head, *"Blood is thicker than water, blood is true, I ask for protection of this book through and through. No one is to touch or see it unless their blood flows as thee. A penalty exists should they try times three. The protection is the breath of a blood with apen leabhar to open lukk leabhar to close. So, mote it be."*

I said this three times opening my eyes then brought my hands together with the herbs hitting each other above the book with a white light going from my hands over the book, making it disappear.

I smiled, *'Now let's see if I can get it back.'* I put the herbs down on the floor then brought my hands together and blew on them saying *apen leabhar* with the book reappearing on my hands.

I put the book down on my lap grinning like a little kid in a lolly shop, punching in the air, *'Yes!'*

While I had it there, I thought again what else I would like to learn to do having teleporting just about under control. I smiled, thinking, Ferdinand helped a bit with that one as well making sure I don't fall over. I will have to keep trying it without him to get stronger in it.

I looked at the elements around me with a thought coming to me, 'I know I would like to be able to use the elements if I'm in trouble or just as added strength.' I started with fire putting the thought into the book with the pages flicking over and stopping with a spell to bring in fire.

I put my hand over it watching the words change to a spell. I took a deep breath rubbing my hands together at first then opening them a couple of inches apart, visualising fire saying, *"Fotia."* A small flicker of flame started to emerge from the small gap between my hands. The more I concentrated the bigger the flame got. I opened up my hands with the flame sitting just above my palm, not like you see in the movies in a ball, but actually like a flame of a candle.

I waved my hand over the flame making it flare, sending out little sparks hitting the mat, thinking, '*Oh shit*' as I tapped them with my free hand to put them out. The smell of burned carpet came up to my nose, '*Luckily it wasn't on the main carpet and only on the rug.*' I put my hands together extinguishing the flame.

I then looked at the smoke coming from the incense representing the air, putting my hand out again with palm up, swirling my finger around my palm saying, *"Aeras"* bringing in a little whirlwind, smiling as I thought about those two guys' I had used something like this on.

I put my hand above it, stretching it out, with my hair start to waiver and blow and things around me starting to flutter around. I moved my hand back down making it smaller with everything settling down, then I sent it away.

I looked at the water next to me, putting my palm out not sure what is going to happen with this one, putting both my palms together pulling them apart, but cupping one saying, *"Nero"* as a small pool of water appeared in the cup of my hand.

I nodded, feeling happy with that. I put my hand back over it to see if I could make it bigger, watching it grow, starting to overflow from my hand with water dripping onto my pants. I closed my hand again before it got too messy.

I sighed, well the last one is earth looking at the dirt that was in the circle on a plate. Again, I put my hand out cupping it and putting the other one over it saying, *"Terra"* with some dirt appearing in the cup of my hand. I expanded my hand as the dirt filled the cup of it, spilling over hitting the rug.

I let out a satisfied sigh, '*Well I am happy with that effort. I will certainly have to practice those things, should I need them. I knew that I was joined with the book bringing in chants, so I was feeling really good about my magic.*'

I chuckled to myself, '*I wonder what my mother would say now?*' I cleaned my hands picking up the book, closing it and sending it away by blowing on it saying, *"Lukk leabhar,"* watching it disappear. I rubbed my hands together in satisfaction at my achievements.

I closed the circle taking the elements, herbs, crystals and candle away checking the singe marks on the mat. They weren't too bad, still smiling at the thought of what I was able to do.

I sat there thinking, *'There's something else I need to do? Oh yes open the unit back up saying, "Apne taigh" hearing the sound of locks opening up.'* I got up, stretching my legs, doing some yoga moves to stretch my back out as well. I sat out on the balcony breathing in the cool fresh sea air, feeling quite satisfied; something I hadn't felt for a long time. The only regret is, I wish I was younger, but I can't do anything about that unfortunately. I chuckled again to myself, *'Well I don't think I can.'*

It was lunchtime, but I didn't feel that hungry just yet, so I decided to do some meditation, cleansing myself first. I lit another incense, put my CD on and lay down this time for the meditation, so I didn't get too stiff.

I was thinking of everything I had just achieved, so it took a little longer to clear my mind. I concentrated hard on my breathing going in and out when the usual vision came into my head of floating down a stream with the boat stopping, making me sit up.

For some reason, I could feel my anger building, which wasn't normal for my meditation. I got out of the boat standing on the fresh green grass with the smell of it hitting my senses. I turned my head to see what was around me, noticing a little cottage to the right of me with smoke coming out of its chimney.

I was curious, so I started to walk towards it with my bare feet crunching on the grass, feeling the anger building, along with hearing a thunder clap around me, as I got closer to the cottage. I stopped to look up at the sky noticing it getting darker with the clouds converging, as I continued to walk towards the cottage.

I was quite close to the cottage when I saw the door open with a familiar face appearing at the door, looking a bit uncertain. The anger that was buried deep within started to rise, as I stopped short of the cottage.

Ferdinand appeared near me in male form, moving over to take my hand. I took a deep breath going closer to my mother, who had moved away from the cottage to greet me.

She smiled nervously at me, "I know you're still angry Hannah, and I don't blame you, but I am hoping one day we will be able to close the gap because I do love you. I'm coming to you now because I know you are picking up things very quickly; which is what I expected of you. Just be careful that's all I ask.

There are a lot of people out there who are willing to harm you and the girls to get what you have."

I looked down at my feet finding it hard to control my anger, looking at my mother, "It's going to take time, Mum. I don't hate you; I'm just holding onto a lot of anger not just at you but other people as well. I will be careful and I will show the girls as much as possible if they're interested."

Mum looked at Ferdinand, "Make sure you look after her as well."

Ferdinand smiled, "I will," and squeezed my hand.

I looked back at the boat, "I have to go, Mum."

Ferdinand changed into a dragon putting me on his back, making Mum smile and shake her head, "She always told me stories about a flying dragon." She went back to the cottage. Ferdinand flew over to the boat, helping me to get back in, giving me a little kiss on the cheek, "I'll see you at home."

I lay down as tears started to well up, "Ok." I could hear my breathing coming into my thoughts, taking over the vision of being in the boat, feeling myself come back to the room. As I breathed deeply, tears were flowing down the side of my face, putting up my hand up to wipe them, then opening my eyes.

I rolled onto my side, then went into a crouch position to start to get up, wiping my eyes. I finally got up going over to get a drink of water, aware that Ferdinand was near me.

Once I had finished having a drink he came and gave me a hug wiping the tears away.

I leaned in hugging him taking a deep breath, with Ferdinand saying, "Did you hear your mother say about the story you had told her of flying on a dragon?" This made me smile, "No I didn't. I told her a few times that story. At least, she now knows I was telling the truth. Thanks for being there for me."

He brushed the hair off my face, "That's ok."

I looked up, "I'm just going to wash my face." He let go of me as I went into the bathroom and washed my face.

Ferdinand went over to the balcony opening the door, smelling something different around there, looking at the mat with little burn marks along with a bit of dirt and water on the mat. He shook his head wondering what I had been doing now.

He sat on the balcony waiting for me to come back out. I finally came out sitting on the chair next to him, taking another deep breath, "Well I didn't expect that in my meditation."

He took my hand, "Sometimes we just have to deal with these things when we least expect them. So, what have you been doing to get her worried?"

I shook my head, "Nothing different just looking at the book, why do you ask?"

He smiled, "There are burn marks, water and dirt on the mat near the door, that is why."

I had to think quick. "I was just strengthening the protection on the book and I needed the elements in the circle to do it. I spilt some of the things when I was moving them as usual."

He looked at me hesitating whether to say something else, but decided not to, getting up, "I haven't had any lunch yet, do you want something?"

I knew what he was doing, "Yes just a cheese toasty would be nice." As he was making them, I went and got us both a drink taking them out on the balcony to wait for him to finish.

I looked out to the sea thinking about my mother and what she said about people wanting to get at me and the girls because of the magic. I guess we will have to sort it out as we go and make sure we are strong enough to combat anything that comes our way.

We ate our lunch not talking much, just watching the sea and people walk past us. I finished up having a drink of water feeling a bit weary, "I think I might have a bit of a rest it's been a bit of an emotional day." He nodded, "Yes, I think that's a good idea. Then you'll be fresher for tonight."

I groaned a little, "Oh yes tonight," and walked out with my plate and glass putting it in the kitchen. I went into the bedroom and lay down with things whirling around my head trying not to over think things, when he came in and lay down next to me.

He rolled me over putting his arm around my waist, "You've got too much going on in that head of yours, try and calm it down."

I took a deep breath trying to relax myself, "Can you tell me a story?"

He chuckled, "Ok, well there was once a little girl who was born in New Zealand who had this handsome dragon."

I chuckled with him squeezing me, "I'll continue, who had a handsome dragon to look after her. He used to take her for rides on his back late at night which made her laugh and giggle in delight. He showed her little tricks to do with magic which made her look at him with wonder in her eyes. As she got older, he took her to Jardine making her squeal and not wanting to go home …"

I was dropping off with my breathing changing as he smiled giving me a little kiss on the head. He lay there wondering what I had been doing with the family book, he could usually pick up my thoughts but he was blocked out for part of the time.

He realised he would have to keep an eye on me, as I was getting strong in my magic quickly, especially after what my mother had said about being careful. He knew there were some bad people out there, who would be quite happy to get me to turn to them. He drifted off to sleep with little visions of his own, that he couldn't understand as well.

I woke after about an hour turning to see him still there, which surprised me, making me smile moving onto his chest laying my head on it, "I thought you would have gone."

He put his arm around me, "No I like to be with you. I did drop off a little myself but then your snoring woke me up."

I giggled, "I don't snore, well not very loud anyway. What's the time?"

He looked at the clock beside the bed, "4.30pm by the look of it. What do you feel like for dinner?"

I yawned, "Something light. I'm not that hungry. I'm still unsure about this meditation meeting, I have a feeling about it." He put his hand on mine, "I can come with you if you like, or at least take you there and just hang around. I'm not very good at meditation to be honest. I only did it to be near you."

This made me smile, "That's nice. It would be nice if you can at least take me, you can introduce me to Lilith as well."

While he was preparing the meal, I thought about the book Suzannah had given me, realising I hadn't really looked at it properly. I got it out skimming through some of the pages basically saying to get in tune with nature and meditate as much as possible with either the elements or the chakras. I sighed thinking, *'Well I have been doing most of that. I might try my chakras next time, as that sounds interesting.'*

We had our dinner, then Ferdinand took me to the meeting which was in an old church in Newtown. It reminded me a little of when I first started to do meditation in New Zealand, with that group meeting in an old church.

We landed just near the doorway, watching people go inside. The street was dark with the light from the church spilling out of the doorway, like an inviting ray of light, and the distinct smell of incense burning, which smelt like dragon's blood—one of my favourites.

There was an old wrought iron fence in front of the church with a gate that was open for people to go in. Ferdinand looked at me, "Are you ready to go in?"

I nodded, "Yes it looks alright. I still have a bit of a funny feeling, but I suppose I can always leave if I don't like it."

We walked in looking at the people milling around in little groups chatting. It was an old building with big oak beams going across the room holding up the ceiling, the walls were brick that had been painted white and the floor was a lovely polished oak. The door was an old wooden style with big hinges and an old-fashioned lock which used a big old key.

Ferdinand pointed over to a lady with raven black hair pulled up into a messy bun, who was quite slim with pale skin. She wore a long black dress with a cardigan over top and boots on her feet, looking up as we came in smiling.

She was talking to someone but excused herself moving over to us. She smiled at Ferdinand with stunning green eyes giving him a hug, "I haven't seen you around for a while, where have you been hiding?"

He returned the hug, turning to look at me, "This is Hannah. I've been getting to know her again, as well as to get her to behave herself."

I sighed, shaking my head, "Hi Lilith. He makes me sound like a trouble maker, but I'm really quite sweet."

Ferdinand coughed, "You do have your moment's, I guess. Anyway, I'll leave Hannah in your capable hands, Lilith."

He turned to look at me squeezing my hand leaning in talking quietly, "Try to be good."

I could see Lilith looking at us not quite sure of her reaction, but I just nodded, "Ok, just for you."

Ferdinand left leaving Lilith and I standing there, feeling a little awkward, so I spoke first, "I haven't been to this meeting before. Suzannah recommended I come here to help strengthen my meditation or something."

Lilith's forehead creased, "Oh Suzannah, I'm not sure who that is?"

I looked around wondering if I had come to the right group, "Suzannah Keller; I think her surname is."

Just as I said that, Suzannah came towards me, smiling from a group of women. She looked at Lilith suspiciously, then back to me, moving forward to give me a hug, "Good to see you made it Hannah. I wasn't sure if you would come or not. Did you bring the dagger with you?"

I felt something as we hugged, but couldn't quite put my finger on what it was, so I just smiled, "I must admit I wasn't sure if I would come. I have in a way. Suzannah this is Lilith a friend of a friend."

Suzannah smiling insincerely at Lilith, "Oh hello Lilith, I haven't been to this meeting that much, so I probably haven't met you before."

Lilith looked at her a little unsure, "Nice to meet you to Suzannah."

Suzannah turned to look at me, ignoring Lilith, "I'll introduce you to some of the others, Hannah," and put her hand out to guide me over to a group of women. I looked at Lilith unsure, "I'll catch up later, Hannah."

I nodded, "Ok, thanks Lilith."

I followed Suzannah over to a couple of women who she introduced as Hildegard who had long blonde messy hair down her back, a bit taller than me, but stockily built with black pants and a blue top that set off her blue eyes.

Suzannah leaned over to Hildegard, "This is Hannah, the one I told you about." Hildegard smiled putting out her hand to shake mine noticing a ring on her finger with a big black diamond set in a gold setting, shaking mine feeling something odd as we did.

I quickly released my hand, not liking the feeling I got from it. Hildegard breathed in sharply as we let go of hands, changing her expression quickly, with what sounded like a German accent, "Oh yes, Suzannah, you did tell me about Hannah. Nice to finally meet you."

Suzannah smiled then introduced me to Allegra, who had a moon face, surrounded by wild brown curls and deep brown eyes. She was around the same height as me, quite slim, wearing jeans and a black top with boots on her feet. She too leaned in to shake my hand wearing a similar ring on her finger as Hildegard's, as that odd feeling came over me again, when we connected hands.

Allegra hesitated then smiled, "Nice to meet you, Hannah. I hope you enjoy our meeting."

I was beginning to wish I had worn one of my clear quartz crystals now as I was picking up some strange vibes from these people.

I played along, "Thank you. I'm looking forward to meditating with different people in this great old church. It reminds me of my younger days actually."

Hildegard looked curious, "Oh you have done meditation for a while have you?"

I nodded, "Yes since I was in my teens at least."

Allegra looked around, "Well we had better start, so just join in and see how you feel."

I felt a little trapped for some reason by these women so I asked, "Is there a toilet I can use before we start?" Allegra pointed to a little serving area then there was a door leading outside to where the toilets were.

I thanked her, "I won't be long."

I could feel their eyes on me as I walked out going through the door, which led to a little courtyard, with only one small light on, looking quite dark.

It was paved unevenly, encased with a painted brick wall with artwork on it and a big jacaranda tree in the corner, just starting to bloom a carpet of purple flowers with sprigs of green leaves in between them.

I looked around finding a door open with light coming out of it, of what looked like a little office; so, I headed towards that carefully, finding the toilet next to it. I did what I had to, coming back out noticing a pathway leading around the side of the church with me thinking, *'It probably leads to the street, I might just go.'* I decided to bring in one of my necklaces magically first, to get rid of that feeling, bringing in my clear quartz one into my hand putting it around my neck.

Just as I was doing this, Lilith came out looking for me, "Hi Hannah. I was looking for you. We are about to start, are you alright?"

I wasn't sure whether to say too much to Lilith so I smiled, "Oh I just needed to go to the toilet."

She smiled, "You were going to leave, weren't you? Did you get a funny vibe off those women?"

I nodded, "Yes I did," still not sure how much to say.

Lilith noticed the crystal around my neck, smiling, "You need as much protection as you can get here Hannah."

I wasn't sure what she meant by this as Lilith continued, "You will see what I mean soon. When we go in the circle there are two young ones you should go with. I don't want to be too near you, as they will get suspicious."

I stopped her, "What do you mean by all this?" We could hear Hildegard calling everyone to form a circle with Lilith putting her hand on mine, feeling a different vibe from her, making her turn to look at me with a surprised look on her face, "Just go to the two I show you and I will explain later."

We walked back into the room with Lilith lagging behind me, so it didn't look as though we had been out there together. I watched Lilith go up to a young girl and guy looking at me with them coming over to the circle that was forming.

Lilith joined in a couple of people down watching Hildegard and Allegra smiling wanly but following me.

Hildegard clapped her hands, getting our attention, "Ok everyone form a circle, so we can get started."

Allegra went to the middle of the circle to check on the sage that was burning in a metal pot, blowing on it, to get it smoking a bit better.

She put it back joining the circle on the other side of the young girl who was standing next to me. Hildegard was watching this, glaring at Allegra, who shrugged her shoulders because the young girl wasn't going to relinquish her spot.

Hildegard sighed, "Now can everyone introduce themselves to the person next to them and then join hands."

I turned to look at the young girl who was smiling at me about the same height as me with blonde curls wearing Indian baggy pants, a loose multicoloured top and wearing heavy makeup, "Hi I'm Hannah," with her turning smiling at me in a bubbly way, "Hi I'm Harriet, nice to meet you, Hannah"

I turned the other way, with a young guy with a lopsided relaxed smiling at me, with brown hair with blonde streaks and shaved on the side, wearing track pants and a loose tied died top, "Hi I'm Jonas."

I smiled back, "Hi I'm, Hannah."

Both he and Harriet took my hand so no one else could get in between us, feeling a bit of a buzz between us, making us look at each other.

Harriet smiled, "I think it's going to be an interesting night."

I just smiled, thinking, *'I think I'll have to try and control myself.'*

Hildegard instructed us to walk slowly in a clockwise direction, "Now I am going to sing a chant that I want you all to sing with me." She started off singing:

I call to thee from earth, air, fire and water to join these souls to you now;
My sacred soul connected to thee
To Earth this truth I show,
To sing with birds to love each cloud,

Brings goodness all around
As it is so.

We all started to sing the chant with Hildegard singing louder now, saying, "Come on louder," as we moved around in the circle. The pace started to pick up, with our voices getting louder. The vibrations from our voices felt as though they were bouncing off the walls.

The smoke coming from the sage was starting to twist like a mini tornado in the centre of our circle along with embers flaring in the metal bowl it was in, as the air in the room was being pushed around in the circle. We were all smiling now, as an electric buzz was coming through our hands connecting us all as one.

Hildegard then asked us to slow down eventually stopping. As we stood there holding hands, you could see our faces were bright and smiling. Hildegard then instructed us to close our eyes while still holding hands, "I want you to breath like a meditation breath, bring the air deep into your lungs, taking the sage within you to cleanse you deep within. Now close your eyes and say after me:

'Negativity that invades my sacred space, I banish you away with the light of my grace, you have no hold or power here, for I stand and face you with no fear, be gone forever from this day, for this I will say this is my sacred space and you will obey.'

As we stood there chanting it over and over, I could again feel a build-up of energy, almost like an electrical charge coursing through my body, spreading it to the hands of Harriet and Jonas; who I could hear breathing deeply taking it in.

My heart was beating fast within my chest making me ecstatic. I could feel the strength from the others in our circle, as though I was taking their energy from them, then shooting it around my body, boosting the vibrations coursing through my body.

The smoke from the sage which had formed a mushroom high up on the ceiling, was falling to cover us now like a blanket, protecting us, as it swirled around while we chanted. The small embers that were around the sage as it smouldered, were lighting up, rising from the sage into the air, above the metal pot, like a funnel. The chant was getting to a high-pitched static, as it encircled the group.

I stood there with my eyes closed listening to Hildegard behind us, calling to the circle, "I need you all to bring the chant down to a stop and come back to the circle, now as one."

People were slowly stopping the chant at different times, releasing the power that was surging within us. I started to take deep breaths, while releasing my hands from Harriet and Jonas, calming my heart rate, which was beating fast. I bent down, putting my hands on my knees to breath and relax my heart rate.

Harriet was giggling saying, "Oh yes!" Punching the air, "That was fantastic! Let's do it again!" Jonas was standing looking stunned with his spikes, standing tall.

Some of the others fell to their knees with the exhaustion of it. The embers and smoke from the sage returned to normal, once the power had released.

Allegra was panting, turning to look at Hildegard and Suzannah, who were on the side watching us and then to me with a "I told you so" look on Suzannah's face.

I stood up, shaking myself out, with my heart rate returning to normal, feeling better. I looked at Harriet who was giggling with the energy within her, moving closer to me, giving me a high five, "That was amazing!" I was laughing with her, acting innocent, "Wow this is an electric group, does that happen all the time?"

Harriet giggled, "Heck no. This is the first time that has happened."

I looked at Lilith, while shaking myself out, noticing a worried look on her face. I sighed thinking, '*Oh no, I think I've let too much go,*' turning to look around noticing Suzannah standing near the door that led to the toilet area smirking.

Hildegard clapped her hands again, getting our attention, "Ok we will have a break now before we start the meditation." Hildegard and Allegra went over to Suzannah, talking excitedly.

A few of the people were excited with what had happened, others said it felt like they were being drained of energy. Harriet came up to me with a glass of water in her hand smiling a wide brimmed smile, "Gee I hope you are coming again. That was fantastic."

I smiled nervously, "Do you think it was me?"

She leaned in, "It certainly wasn't this lot; I have been coming here for a few months and you're lucky to get a spark out of them."

I giggled, "They may not want me back."

I got a drink of water, thinking about what had happened, sipping on it, watching Suzannah, Hildegard and Allegra, with downcast eyes so I didn't look so obvious.

Lilith came over talking quietly, "Hannah you need to tone it down a bit, they have picked up your magic. That's probably why they invited you here. I will tell you more later."

I turned my back to Suzannah speaking quietly to Lilith nodding, "Ok."

Allegra called us all in to get ready for the meditation. There were mats and pillows to the side of the hall, which everyone grabbed to get ready for the meditation.

I found a spot with Harriet and Jonas going either side of me smiling as we got down on the floor. I laughed saying to Harriet and Jonas, "I'm ok going down but I'm not very good getting up."

Jonas smiled, "Don't worry we will help you to get up if you need it."

As we were getting comfortable Harriet asked me, "Do you mind if I get close to you. I know some people don't like their space taken up?"

I shook my head, "No I am fine with that." She shuffled over so there wasn't much of a gap between our mats, laying down and getting comfortable.

Another incense had been lit, this time smelling like frankincense which slowly creeped around the hall.

Allegra asked us to close our eyes and to get comfortable. I adjusted my position a little to make myself comfortable then closed my eyes laying down with my palms up starting to breath, relaxing quite quickly, even though I was in a different place.

Allegra with a louder voice, almost as though she were singing now, to lull us into our meditation, saying, "Breath in pause and then out. Clear your minds as much as you can from your busy day. Relax your bodies, starting from your head relaxing all the muscles in your face and jaw. Go down to your neck, release all the tension from there. Carry on down to your shoulders and arms squeeze your muscles then let all the tension out as you do this. Your chest, stomach and solar plexus, squeeze them now and let all the tension of the day out. Finally, going down to your legs and feet, squeeze the muscles releasing all the tension. Now put the vision of your lungs being filled deep with fresh clean air then see it being released. Continue to do this now until you cannot think of anything else, breathing in, pause, then out."

I could hear her moving around us, looking to see if we needed any help. As I went deeper, I could hear her voice saying, "I want you to imagine that you are in a beautiful land filled with green fields and shrubs along with scented flowers. Now I want you to go to one of the flowers that you like and pick it and put it up to your nose and smell it. This flower can smell of any scent you want, as long as it brings you happy memories. Now I want you to inhale the scent of your flower, letting it fill you with the delightful smell it sends off to you, filling you with happiness."

"Now I want you to look over to your left where you will see a small hill which will have an animal on it. Now this animal can be anything you want it to be either sitting or standing there waiting for you to come over to it. I want you walk over to it and stroke it as though it was your long-lost friend."

"As I followed her voice in the meditation, I turned to look to my left to see what animal was waiting there for me. It was a huge purple dragon sitting there looking at me with its big yellow eyes."

"I moved closer to him, smiling at him with familiarity, as he smiled back with a flick of flame coming out of his mouth. He put his head down as I stroked his scaly face, which he reciprocated, moving closer to me pulling me into him, as I could hear his heart beating. It was Ferdinand. I gave him a long hug, then walked back towards the flowers as he watched me go."

Allegra was talking again, "Now say goodbye to the animal you have seen and made contact with giving it a hug. I want you to walk back through the grass towards the flowers now. I want you to go to a flower you don't like. I want you to pick it but not smell it this time. I want you to set it free in the breeze that is now blowing. I want you to turn to your right to see who that flower represents as someone you don't like or have had problems with. I then want you to feel peaceful that you do not have to deal with that person anymore."

I turned to my right seeing the guy who called me a witch with his smug face, smiling at me. I could hear a clap of thunder growl in the distance, with the wind picking up. I was angry now, with another clap of thunder peeling in the distance, when my body vibrated sending a sonic wave through me. The sonic wave pulsed through me, towards the man sending him off into the air screaming.

As this was happening in my meditation, a sonic vibration coursed through my body. Harriet had moved her hand closer to mine as I went under in my meditation, so she received some of that jolt along with Jonas, who was quite close as well.

Allegra started to bring us out of the meditation; I thought a little quickly, as she said to find a happy space and start listening to our breathing. I opened my eyes lying there feeling really good.

Harriet and Jonas opened their eyes, lying there stunned. Harriet turned to her side, "Oh wow I'm only guessing, but you really don't like someone with that boom."

Jonas lay there on his back dazed, saying, "Oh wow what a trip."

I was a little embarrassed, trying to shrug it off. I sat up turning to go onto my knees to try and get up. Harriet came over, helping me up, making me feel like an old lady; but I appreciated it. I thanked her as I shook myself out, relaxing my muscles, bending down to get my mat and pillow to take it back to the storage area.

Hildegard and Suzannah followed me over, waiting for me to put the mat and pillow back where they belonged, smiling as I came out, "Hannah did you enjoy the meeting tonight?"

I calmed myself, "Oh yes it was good. Not much different from the other one I go to though."

Suzannah looked disappointed, "Surely Hannah you have felt a little different to the other group you went to?"

I shook my head, "No not really. Some of the people are nice here compared to the other place, but meditation wise, I feel the same. I think I might get a drink of water if you don't mind and then I'll have to get going."

Suzannah went to put her hand out to stop me from going, but I sneezed moving my hand out of the way, "Oh sorry about that I'm just getting over a cold and it's still hanging around a bit."

Suzannah tried one more time, "Can you show Hildegard the dagger you found at my place Hannah; she is interested to see it."

I shook my head, "No I didn't bring it. I thought I had put it in my bag but I must have forgot to bring it."

Hildegard looked impressed, "So you had all that energy going through you without it?"

I chuckled weakly, hoping it sounded real. "I think I was just getting some of that from the young ones I was holding hands with. They were buzzing; I'm surprised my heart is still ticking. Maybe it is them you should be talking to."

I tickled the tattoo on my arm letting Ferdinand know I wanted to go. It wasn't long before he came to the door looking for me, coming over to where I was, talking to Suzannah and Hildegard. He didn't smile putting his hand in mine, "Have you finished Hannah, as I don't have a very good car park?"

I feigned surprise, "Oh sorry Suzannah I have to go, my ride is here. My car was playing up so Ferdinand gave me a lift. Ferdinand this is Suzannah, Hildegard and Allegra who were running the group tonight."

He nodded, "Nice to meet you all, but I do have to go, Hannah."

I waved goodbye to them walking out with Ferdinand going down the street a little with Ferdinand stopping, "What's going on?"

Just as he said that Lilith appeared next to us surprising me, "Oh shit I didn't expect that."

Lilith looked back to the church, "Come on we better get out of here" and took my hand and Ferdinand taking the other, to go back to my unit.

We landed in the lounge with Ferdinand looking worried, "What's happening Hannah or Lilith?"

Lilith looked around, then went and sat on the sofa, "Hannah was purposely invited there because of her magic by that Suzannah. She must have picked it up."

I sat down near her, "I went to her house to see about the meeting, as recommended by my other meditation teacher. While I was at her house, I found a crystal dagger there that appeared to call me and she let me have it. I was a bit suspicious of her and wasn't going to go, but Ferdinand said that you will be there, so I should go."

I didn't want to tell her the rest that it looked like the one on the family crest and that it joined with me, as I didn't know if I could trust her.

Ferdinand looked at me and then Lilith, "I knew you would be there Lilith that was my main reason for wanting Hannah to go."

Lilith got up, looking from me to Ferdinand, "What magic have you been doing, Hannah? It must be something strong for them to pick up?"

I was getting a bit agitated now, being asked all these questions, "Why do you need to know, Lilith?"

Ferdinand could tell I was getting annoyed, coming over to me to hold my hand, "Just summons an elder, Lilith and see what she says."

Lilith noticed Ferdinand taking my hand, "Do you think it's necessary to get Jardine involved, Ferdinand. I could just keep an eye on Hannah and make sure she doesn't get into any trouble."

Lilith started to fiddle with her hair as though she was nervous, "I hope you're not showing Hannah anything technical, Ferdinand, or hanging around her too much."

Ferdinand was getting agitated now, "No I think Hannah needs to talk to an elder at least to see what is best for her."

He was about to say that he had been staying here, but I knew a jealous woman when I saw one, butting in, "He has helped while I had a cold, that is all and with regard to magic all he has helped me with is to magicae and heal my knees."

Lilith reluctantly summonsed an elder, when a woman appeared in the lounge, who had long brown hair with streaks of grey, like ribbons going through it and flowing dark green and black robes. She had a kindly face that was just starting to crease with age and soft blue eyes.

She turned to look at everyone, then came over to me with a fond smile, "Hannah it is so nice to see you again," as I stood up, with her taking my hands in hers.

She closed her eyes taking a deep breath, "Ah you have finally started working with your family book, haven't you?" She chuckled, "You are quite strong already in your magic, Hannah"

I looked at her, trying to remember her face, then looked at Ferdinand puzzled as to who this woman is. Ferdinand smiled, "This is Morag, one of the elders at Jardine, Hannah. You met her when you were very young and obviously do not remember her now."

Morag sighed, "Oh that is a shame. You always enjoyed it when Ferdinand brought you to Jardine to see us."

Lilith moved closer to Morag acting as though she was in charge, "I am worried that Hannah has been exposed to a group that is after her magic Morag. It is the one that you asked me to watch in case anyone came along with magic in them."

Morag nodded, "Ah yes, they are not very nice. We have heard that some women are going missing but we cannot tell if it is them or not."

I was looking confused again, "Do you want to sit down Morag or have a drink of water or something else?"

Morag put her hand up to my cheek, "You were always a lovely girl so calm and polite," making Ferdinand cough a little.

I frowned at him, squeezing his hand, making Morag laugh, "I have heard about your temper, Hannah. Ferdinand has kept me up to date with what has been happening in your life. You are a bit of prankster now, aren't you?"

I sighed, "Only when provoked, Morag," and looked at Ferdinand scowling at him.

Morag sat down on the sofa, "Oh this is comfortable and no I won't have a drink of anything Hannah; your water isn't very nice here. Well sit next to me Hannah so we can discuss what to do next."

I sat down next to her, looking determined, "I'm not giving up the book now Morag just because of these people; it's taken me too long to get it."

Morag put a gentle hand on mine, "We don't expect you to Hannah and we don't want to control you in any way either. You did a ceremony many years ago when you were young to come to Jardine as one of us, but because it has been so long and you obviously don't remember a lot of things, I would like you to do it again; that way we can protect you. This, of course, is entirely up to you; we cannot force you. Ferdinand will always be there for you but you are getting very strong quite quickly in your magic Hannah. If your daughters join you as well the power of three with your old family magic is very strong and groups like the one you have just been to, will seek you out, one way or another. You have obviously already sent vibrations out to those type of people. Did Ferdinand explain that part to you?"

I nodded a little guilty, "Yes he did, but I really didn't believe him," looking to him standing there with his arms crossed looking clever. I took a deep breath, "I wish I could remember some of these things, I've closed so much off in my mind. I just want to get some fresh air if you don't mind to think about it."

Morag patted my hand again, "That is fine Hannah, take all the time you need."

I opened the balcony door walking out, getting a hit of cool air in my face, looking out to sea, breathing in a big lung full of air. I felt in a bit of a daze with everything happening quite fast as well as feeling frustrated, that I couldn't remember a lot of things when I was young. I looked up to the sky, noticing the moon for the first time, nearly formed looking bright and shiny in the inky black sky with little twinkling stars shining around it. The gentle caress of the waves hitting the shore calmed me, letting me think more clearly, especially what Morag said if my girls join me in the magic.

I hoped that they would join me but it is up to them in the end. I knew I was getting stronger in magic and I was sure either one or both of my girls would pick it up really fast as well, which worried me. I groaned a little, leaning on the balcony wall looking out to the water, if only I had had more time to learn this when I was younger.

Ferdinand came out to see how I was going, "Do you want me around, Hannah?"

I nodded, "Yes that would be nice."

He stood next to me, putting his arm around my waist, as we both looked out to sea, "It's happening a bit quick for you, isn't it?"

I frowned, "Yes, just a bit. You do know me, don't you? I just wish I could remember some of these things as well."

We stood quietly for a few minutes, when a dark figure walked past, looking up at the units. We didn't have the balcony light on, so he couldn't see who was on it, but we could see him searching in the darkened street with just the street light, making him visible to us.

I sighed, "Well there's another reason I guess to protect not only me but my girls as well. Let's go and do it."

Ferdinand gave me a hug, kissing me on the forehead, moving into the lounge; I hesitated long enough to see Ferdinand go in the lounge, putting up my hand twirling a little whirlwind in the palm of my hand with the finger on my other hand saying, "*Anemos*" and blowing it down to the man in black.

I stood back and watched hearing a scream rise from him as a mini whirlwind buffeted him around, blowing him off his feet smiling to myself.

Ferdinand came back to the door to see if I was alright but then heard a scream rise from the footpath. He looked out to see the man being harassed by the whirlwind, making him shake his head with a smirk appearing on his face, grabbing my hand, "Get in here, Hannah, before you do anything else."

I came back into the lounge with Ferdinand holding my hand, feeling like I was back in school again in trouble with a big smile on my face.

Morag chuckled, "What have you been doing now Hannah?" She walked out to the balcony noticing the man in black being knocked about by a mini whirlwind falling down then trying to stand up and screaming in frustration. Morag came back in laughing, "Oh Hannah, you are terrible. You've learned how to use the elements, haven't you?"

Ferdinand growled, "I think she should stop it, don't you Morag?"

I dropped Ferdinand's hand, crossing my arms in defiance, "He shouldn't be hanging around here at this time of the night."

Morag shrugged her shoulders in a relaxed way, "It'll wear off Ferdinand, let her have some fun, she's waited long enough for it."

This made me smile again, "Thanks Morag. So, what do I have to do for this ceremony?"

Morag put her hands up and summoned the ceremony team consisting of three women whose names were Cara, who had stunning red hair, was small and petite with creamy white skin and stunning green eyes.

Adesa, who had dark skin with curly black hair, big round dark eyes encased in white pools with an athletic face and chiselled cheek bones. She was tall and athletically built everywhere else as well.

There was also Louella an older looking woman with long brown wispy hair tied up in a bun. She had a rounded face that looked wise and gentle with hazel eyes and was just a bit taller than me with a fuller figure. They all wore white robes with bare feet.

Morag greeted them asking them to come over to me, "This is Hannah. I don't know if any of you remember her but she did the ceremony when she was very young. Unfortunately, due to different circumstances, she needs to do it again and hopefully her daughters will want to have it done as well."

Louella smiled at me, "I do remember the name vaguely and those dark blue eyes. I think you set fire to my robe one time, didn't you Hannah?"

I didn't know where to look, "I can't remember doing something like that Louella," and hearing Ferdinand laughing behind us, "Sounds like Hannah. She's just blown a man off his feet a few times."

Morag chuckled, "Well let's get this started. Hannah, can you take your shoes off and ladies can you please get ready to do the ceremony. Now I need to ask one more time that this is your decision Hannah, you can still back out if you want?"

I nodded, "Yes I want to do this Morag and it is my own free choice."

I took off my shoes putting them aside with some dirt appearing just in front of me.

Morag came closer to me, "Lilith will get you ready for the ceremony and once the ceremony starts you will feel roots forming over your feet; these connect you to mother earth."

"The women will surround you saying a chant that you probably won't understand, but just close your eyes and relax; that is all you need to do. While Lilith is getting you ready, I will lock the house so we don't get any interference from outside forces." She then went to all corners of the unit, saying a chant to lock it.

Lilith came over giving me a hug, "Welcome again to Jardine, Hannah. I will change your clothes and cleanse you so you are ready for the ceremony."

I looked a little unsure at first at Lilith, thinking she would give me something to change into, but she pointed at me changing my clothes to a white robe similar to what the others had on. I ran my hand over the material as I had not seen anything like it here in our world.

Lilith then got a sage stick, lighting it with the click of her fingers, waving it over me saying, *"Cleanse this woman now ready for her rebirth with mother earth once and for all."* A wave went through me as my body cleansed under the smoke of the sage. Lilith then smiled at me, "You are now ready for the ceremony, Hannah; can you place your feet on the soil please?"

I nodded nervously at Lilith, then looked over to Ferdinand who was grinning at me, turning to then look at the dirt on the floor. I stepped onto it feeling a connection straight away making me look down to see a glow appear around my feet.

The three women surrounded me looking at this happening with puzzled looks on their faces, briefly glancing at Morag, then coming back to look at me.

They put their arms around each other's waist enveloping me in their circle starting the chant, signalling me to take a deep breath and close my eyes. I stood there with my palms facing up feeling like the vibrations from the chant were forming around my body, then I could feel something going over my feet. I opened my eyes briefly to look at the roots that were forming over my feet, sending energy through my body making me hum.

As the women got deeper into their chant, the energy turned into a white light forming around my body, with a vision of the dagger spinning in my head, joining with the Jardine magic. This made a pink and white misty light form around me, growing stronger as it all connected with the earth, hitting the women that were surrounding me, making their voices go higher pitched.

This intense energy felt like an intoxicating power surge, coursing through my blood making the three women's chanting get faster, while feeling my heart race in my chest.

The white light now formed around us all, encasing us like a huge orb, when I heard some of my ancestors' voices within me, rejoicing to finally feel the magic release in me.

I could hear a voice within me, telling me to breath deep now, to bring the energy down to release the women around me. I did as it asked, taking deep breaths, calming my heart as the white and pink mist retreated back inside me, through my crown chakra.

After a short period of calming everything down, I opened my eyes to find the poor women around me, looking exhausted hanging onto each other, with their hair sticking up in all directions.

I stood there taking deep breaths trying to see Ferdinand, Morag and Lilith who had moved away from us, so they didn't get hit with the power surge, going on in the circle.

I looked closer at the three women feeling a bit wobbly and a little guilty, "Are you three alright? Does that normally happen?"

Cara, looking a lot paler than what she was before, shaking her head taking deep breaths, "No Hannah, it doesn't."

They released their arms, wobbling over to the sofa to sit down, to regain some energy. The roots from my feet released me with the dirt disappearing making me feel a little giddy, with Ferdinand coming over putting his arm around my waist and walking me over to a chair.

Morag came over smiling, "Well that was a bit different than what we usually experience, Hannah."

I felt a little worried, "My family magic joined with Jardine, is that why it was so intense?"

Morag sighed, "Yes I am sure that is why."

She went over to talk to the other women sending them back to Jardine with them waving tiredly at me. She also went over to Lilith asking her to change my clothes and to give me the book from Jardine then to go as she wished to speak with me privately.

I could see Lilith was wanting to stay, but had to do as she was told, pointing to me changing my clothes.

She came over giving me another hug, feeling a small power surge still within me, "Wow you're still buzzing, Hannah. I have a book for you to read giving you the history of Jardine. Please keep it safe as no one else is allowed to see it."

I lifted my hands to take the book, noticing a dim white misty light, still floating around them. I smiled nervously, "yes, I am, aren't I? I'll see you later Lilith, thanks for the book and your help tonight."

Lilith patted my hand, "That's ok Hannah," and turning to Ferdinand, "See you later Ferdinand," with Ferdinand smiling, "See you Lilith," as she disappeared.

Ferdinand went and got me a drink of water coming back looking a little worried, "Are you alright?"

I nodded, "Yes it's just given me a big buzz."

Morag sat on the sofa, "Hannah come and sit next to me I wish to talk to you."

Ferdinand helped me over to the sofa feeling a bit wobbly still, sitting down next to Morag.

I smiled, "I feel like I'm back in school in trouble."

Morag chuckled, "Yes, I have heard about some of your school activities. No, Hannah you are not in trouble, I just wish to talk to you about your family magic, especially now you have joined with Jardine."

Ferdinand sat down quietly on the single chair near us. Morag surprised me, "Can I have a look at your family book, Hannah?"

I felt a little uncomfortable turning to look at her, "Can I ask why, Morag?"

I could hear Ferdinand sigh quietly moving in his seat wanting to say something, but couldn't in front of Morag.

Morag looked at me unsure, "You are quite protective of your family magic, aren't you? I can't blame you with the long period you have been denied access to it. I just want to have a little look to see what we are dealing with. We know you have a bit of a temper Hannah. You will have not only your family magic but Jardine magic at your disposal. We just want to teach you to control that temper, with all that magic, if you get attacked. We don't approve of anyone getting killed."

I relented, "Yes you do have a point there, although I have never really wanted to kill anyone. I will tell you though I have protected it very well and I don't know if you will be able to touch it."

Morag looked impressed, "Well Hannah that sounds impressive! Let's see what happens."

I cleared my throat, "I know you have put a lock on the unit but I want to put mine on as well."

Morag waved her hand, "Feel free, Hannah."

I got up shaking myself out a bit then pointed to the four corners of the unit saying quietly, *"Lukk Taigh."*

I could see Morag and Ferdinand watching me as I did this feeling like I was on a test with the sound of locks clicking being heard, with Morag smiling, "Ahh very good Hannah."

I then sat down with them both looking at me, curious, "I have locked it away in a special place."

I then put my hands out palms up in front of me, like I had a book sitting on them, saying quietly so they couldn't hear what I said, *"Apen leabhar"* blowing on my hands with the book appearing on top of them.

Morag giggled clapping her hands, "Oh, you clever woman."

Ferdinand just sat there stunned, eventually saying, "You saw me looking at the book when you were meditating didn't you, Hannah?"

I nodded, "Yes Ferdinand, I don't blame you I would have done the same thing. I knew I had to put it away a bit better that is all." I put the book on the coffee table, with Morag leaning forward, to open it. I stopped her taking hold of her arm, "I will warn you, Morag, it is also protected by a blood spell."

Morag smiled again, shaking her head, "You are full of surprises, Hannah." She gingerly leaned forward touching it, when her hand flew back saying, "Ahhh" then laughing. She looked at the both of us laughing again, "Sorry I couldn't help it. I might be old, but I still have a sense of humour."

I giggled, "It's nice to have someone with a similar sense of humour," looking over to Ferdinand, who was smiling, then shook his head, "I have a sense of humour too, Hannah." I just smiled, "Yes Ferdinand."

Morag touched the book again turning the first page over with the family tree appearing, starting at grandma Matilda then showing my mother, myself and my girls. She looked at me, "I wonder why it doesn't show the rest of your family tree?"

I shrugged my shoulders, "I don't know Morag; I was hoping to work it out eventually."

She looked at the symbols next to the names, "The symbol next to Matilda's name means she has been initiated into Jardine. As you can see your mother's name has a different symbol, meaning she has no magic."

I looked at my name "oh the symbol has changed from when I first saw it" looking at my daughters' names, "It was the same as Amelia and Charlotte's."

Morag nodded, "Yes you have been initiated into Jardine. If your daughters follow you, theirs will change as well."

Ferdinand came over kneeling on the ground to have a look at the book.

Morag went to try and turn the next page with a message coming up on the page opposite the family tree in blood, *"hello Morag from Jardine. Do you have permission from Hannah Dragĕ to enter this book?"* with a light flashing like a computer arrow.

We looked at each other surprised as I smiled, "Well I give you permission but how do I do that?"

Something came into my head, so I put my hand up and blew on the page, as it scanned my breath, going up the page like a computer screen analysing it. It then asked for Morag to put her thumb on a dot on the page, which she did scanning her, then allowing her to proceed with another message coming onto the page, *"You now have Hannah Dragĕ's permission to proceed."*

Morag turned the page over, looking at me, "You are connected to the book aren't you, Hannah? You get messages from it when you need something?"

I nodded, "Yes Morag. Is that normal?"

Morag smiled, "I haven't heard of it before, but then you have learned a lot as well as tried a lot of different things in a short time. I'm not agreeing with what your mother did, but maybe that is partly why you were stopped from learning some of this. You were too far ahead of your time."

I looked sadly at both of them, "Yes maybe. I am sure she had her reasons but I still feel cheated. If Matilda had been to Jardine and had survived after I was born it would have been a lot better with her support as well as Jardine's."

I sighed, "I guess we just have to carry on. I wonder what my girls will bring to it, as they are a lot smarter than me."

Morag turned some more of the pages, "I see the spells and chants are still encrypted. I assume you can read them."

I nodded finding an easy chant putting my hand over it with the gibberish words turning into English, with Morag putting her hands up to her mouth in surprise, "It certainly has a lot of security on it, Hannah."

I smiled, "This was already in place when I opened it. I just added the other security."

Morag went to the end of the book where the family crest was with the dragon holding the sword and shield.

Ferdinand looked at it with a puzzled expression coming over him, "I just need a drink of water." Morag and I looked puzzled at each other.

I called out to him, "Are you alright Ferdinand?"

He nodded, "yes, I just wanted a drink of water. Do you two want anything?"

Morag shook her head, "No I am ok, thank you Ferdinand. I think I will go soon and let Hannah get some sleep, it has been a big day for you."

I nodded, "Yes I will have a drink of water." He brought one over for me then sat back in the chair away from the book.

Morag looked closely at the dragon, noticing the sword was complete whereas the shield was like it was pencilled in, "Hannah have you noticed the sword is filled?"

I nodded, having a sip of water, "Yes, I have Morag. That happened when I got the crystal dagger from that woman Suzannah. I wonder if she knew its history and had been waiting for someone to come along and claim it from the Dragĕ family."

Morag sighed, "Yes that is probably correct. You have to find the shield now I guess?"

I nodded, "I guess it will come to me or my girls, eventually."

Morag closed the book with a bright light sealing it. I put it on my hands blowing on it saying quietly, *"Apne leabher"* sending the book away. I then got up pointing to the four corners *"apne taigh."*

Morag was smiling at me as I sat down, "You have done very well, Hannah. All I ask is that you be careful and try not to use this when you are really angry."

I nodded, "I will be careful. It's so nice to be able to talk to someone about my magic and not be told it's bad. Mr bossy dragon over there is keeping an eye on me as well," looking over to Ferdinand smiling. He looked a bit better leaning forward, "That's right, Hannah, and I'm not going anywhere, so get used to it."

Morag turned to look at me a bit better, "how are you feeling; are you still buzzing?"

I nodded smiling, "I'm alright but I feel as though I've had 10 cups of coffee."

Ferdinand groaned, "Oh no, she is bad enough on one cup of coffee."

Morag looked at me then Ferdinand, "You two appear to be getting on a lot better now, which is nice to see. He has been waiting a long time to come to you, Hannah."

I felt a little guilty at the way I treated him at first, "Well it's another thing we will just have to make up time for won't we. Although he gets a little bossy at times, but we have come to an agreement."

Morag looked at Ferdinand raising an eyebrow questioning, "You're supposed to be here to help and protect her Ferdinand not boss her around." He fidgeted, "I'm just trying to slow her magic down and stop the wrong ones from being aware she has magic in her."

Morag took my hands in hers, "Well I will go now," rubbing her thumbs in my palms sending me to sleep, dropping onto the sofa backwards like a rag doll.

Ferdinand got up in surprise, "Wow that was good. Can I learn to do that?"

Morag chuckled, "No Ferdinand, you can use sleep dust only. I could feel her resisting it, so if she gets angry at you, tell her it was my idea and that you'll take her to me in Jardine, if she doesn't calm down."

He sighed, "You know she will get angry, don't you?"

Morag shrugged her shoulders, "I've told you what to do. Unfortunately, the Dragĕ women have a good temper as well as a weak chest and lungs, which you have seen already with the cold she has just gotten over. Her mother and grandmother were the same."

Ferdinand looked curious, "So you met her mother?"

Morag nodded, "Yes only once. Something had frightened her so much, swearing not to deal with magic ever again. I never found out what it was. Her grandmother Matilda had joined us, but wasn't interested in being a real part of Jardine, preferring to go on her own. Don't you say anything to Hannah, if the time comes, I will tell her that, but like I said, I don't know what frightened her mother."

Ferdinand nodded, "Ok I'll leave that up to you. She has spoken with her mother in her meditation recently. Her mother just asked her to be careful."

Morag sighed, "Well maybe she will tell her one day. Anyway, I am going. Please keep me informed of anything you might be concerned about or anything new really. I believe Hannah is meeting with Amelia over the weekend to discuss the book, so we will see what happens with that. I think you are going to have some trouble with Charlotte as she is just as stubborn as her mother, especially when new men are concerned."

Ferdinand groaned, "I have heard that. I'm hoping I will win her around."

Ferdinand picked me up ready to take me into the bedroom, pulling me into him.

Morag laughed, "Good luck with that Ferdinand." She stroked my hair, "Sweet dreams, Hannah. Good night, Ferdinand you're doing well," and disappearing.

I mumbled something with Ferdinand smiling, "Bedtime for you, so don't fight it you little minx."

Later on, that night a dark hooded figure appeared in the lounge of my unit. It floated stealthily around the unit looking for something, quietly opening cupboards and draws magically. It came into the bedroom looking in the wardrobe gently gliding it open magically. Getting frustrated, going over to the bed to look under there, the figure noticed Ferdinand and I sleeping together.

Ferdinand started to stir, making the figure raise a cloaked arm, when a voice sounded from a dark corner of the bedroom, "Not this time!" The cloaked figure turned suddenly to find a ghostly figure coming forward with an angry look on her face, "Get away from my daughter, you beast."

The figure growled, raising its arm towards the ghost, throwing a spell without any affect. The ghost chuckled moving closer to Ferdinand and I sending a spell towards Ferdinand and I as a protection.

Ferdinand stirred again making the cloaked figure angry and disappear. He woke looking around the room, then over to me smiling briefly, that I was still asleep, falling back into a contented sleep.

The ghost went beside the bed on my side, whispering in my ear, "Put more protection on your unit Hannah. I love you dear."

Chapter 6

I woke feeling quite refreshed with a strange dream coming to my mind looking around the room with just a small crack of light coming in through the curtains. I lay there thinking about it, deciding to put some more security on my unit, now that I have this magic within me.

I turned to see Ferdinand still sleeping, pleased at first to see him there, but then feeling annoyed that I had a chant put on me to sleep. I growled inwardly thinking I will have it out with him when he wakes up. Kimba jumped up next to me to give me a cuddle as I gently patted her.

Ferdinand rolled over putting his arm around my waist reaching over to pat Kimba as well, "Oh you're going to have it out with me, are you?"

I tapped his arm, "I'm not happy with you letting Morag put me to sleep like that. I was going to have a shower and an herbal tea to relax, I do know how to relax myself you know."

He moved in closer, with Kimba getting annoyed and jumping off the bed, "If you're going to get angry about it, Morag said I was to take you to Jardine and let her deal with you. Besides it wasn't my decision to do that, so don't get angry at me."

He made to get up, "Come on you can go and have your shower while I get some breakfast then I'll take you to Jardine with me."

I knew he would do it to, having to back down, "Alright I know you didn't know Morag would do that. I don't want to go to Jardine for an argument; I want to go there for a good reason."

He grinned knowing he had won that argument, laying back down hugging me, moving his hand towards the small of my back, "Ferdinand what are you doing?"

I moved quickly to get away from his hand, "Don't be naughty, my back is a bit sore this morning,"

I giggled, "Stop it you rat bag."

He pushed me over onto my stomach, as I tried to push back, with him lifting my nightie up tickling my back, then all of a sudden, he stopped. I looked to see what he was doing, "What is it?"

He rubbed his hand over my hip, "There is a tattoo forming on your hip similar to the family crest you had in your book last night," with the sight of it making him turn pale again.

I sat up suddenly hitting his chin, as he fell back on the bed, "Geez Hannah are you trying to knock me out now." I tried to supress a giggle, putting my hands up to his chin, "Sorry I didn't mean to do that," and got out of bed to look in the mirror at my hip. Sure, enough there was a tattoo outlined on my hip similar to the family crest, "Oh shit I wonder what that means."

He got up sitting on the edge of the bed rubbing his chin, "Maybe it's you joining the family magic or something? I'll ask Morag when I go to Jardine."

I sighed, "Yes there is certainly a few things going on with this family magic that I am going to need help with, I think. My family crest appears to affect you? Do you know why?"

He looked confused, "No not really, it just sends a funny feeling running through me."

I sat next to him looking at his chin as he rubbed it, "Lilith seems nice. She could almost be related to you with her colouring." He stopped rubbing his chin as he thought about something but it appeared to go, "She is just a close friend. I can't have children and don't have any family. That is why I can only be intimate with you—should we get to that stage."

I was just about to say something else when a text came onto my phone making it ping, with Ferdinand grinning going to grab it.

I jumped on his back, "Leave it Ferdinand," as he laughed grabbing the phone, playing with me, keeping it out of my reach, as I tried to get it off him. He rolled me onto my back sitting on my hips with the phone in his hand just out of my reach, "Now I think you need to tell your girls that I am not gay and are becoming more than just a friend?"

I was trying not to laugh, wriggling under his weight on me, "I will have to see how they are; you know they can be difficult, especially Charlotte. Now give me the phone otherwise I might be forced to use magic on you."

He smiled, shaking his head, "No magic when we are mucking around Hannah you are a lot stronger than me, so it's not fair."

I laughed, "You are a lot stronger than me strength wise, but ok as long as you don't do anything silly to hurt me, because then I will use my magic."

He looked at me passionately leaning down to kiss me on my neck, "You know I love you and won't hurt you, Hannah."

I stopped struggling under him taking a deep breath feeling a little scared at this declaration of love.

I started to stroked his hair deep in thought, "I know and my feelings are getting stronger for you Ferdinand, but it will take a little more time for me."

He came back up looking at me with love in his eyes, "That is all I ask. There is one thing I remember though, that you have another ticklish spot around your ears for some reason," looking deviously at me.

I feigned ignorance, "I don't know what you are talking about, now get off me and give me my phone."

He chuckled, "Mmm maybe I should tell Amelia Mummy isn't available today as she is going to Jardine with me."

I pushed myself up trying to get to my phone, "Ferdinand stop being naughty," with him leaning down gently touching my ear as I giggled, "No Ferdinand," kicking my legs and my arms to try and get free while laughing. I pleaded with him, "Ferdinand I need to pee and you're sitting on my bladder, let me up."

He rose up looking triumphant "so you are promising to be nice today and talking to Amelia, at least?"

I flopped back defeated and out of energy, "Yes Ferdinand. Now let me up."

He finally let me up, pulling me into him, giving me a hug, "I meant what I said before," with me hugging him back, "So did I." We stood there just relaxed in each other's arms with him kissing me on the cheek, "Send your text to Amelia then go and have your shower and I will make breakfast. Any special requests?"

I smiled at him, "No you can surprise me."

I read Amelia's text saying she was free for lunch today as well as the rest of the afternoon, do I want to meet? I sent one back saying, 'That would be great see you at our usual place.'

I had my shower coming out, with him saying, "Breakfast is ready."

I grabbed the remote control turning on the TV to see what was happening in the world, moving over to the breakfast bar to sit and eat my breakfast. The news came on with an article about a priest in Cronulla being buffeted by a "dust devil" or mini whirlwind last night as he walked along the footpath.

I went to grab the remote with Ferdinand putting his hand over mine, "Leave it Hannah," as I grimaced, "Fine, he deserved it as Morag said." It at least gave us his name being John Adams, who was a priest at St Andrews Church in the city.

I screwed up my mouth, "I wonder why he is hanging around here? Maybe he lives around here or something?"

Ferdinand continued to listen to the article, "he has probably picked up on your vibrations like I said; either that or he has someone else who has picked up your magic and he is monitoring it. That is why I get nervous when you do pranks like that, it tells them where you are."

I shook my head, "It's like being in the dark ages with churchmen picking on women because of their abilities just for the power hit. Just remember I didn't start it; I was just minding my own business like he should have been."

We finished breakfast with Ferdinand saying, "Go and read your Jardine information I will clean up."

I grinned, "You're handy to have around," and went to get the shabby book sitting on the sofa to relax and start reading.

Ferdinand brought over a cup of coffee for me waiting to see what happened next. I let out a surprise, "Wow I didn't expect that," with the book turning into an iPad. Ferdinand smiled, "Jardine are full of surprises as well."

I got comfortable while Ferdinand tidied up in the kitchen as the screen came to life with Cara coming on smiling at me, "Hi Hannah and Ferdinand how are you both?"

I smiled at her relieved she looked a bit better than yesterday, turning the screen at Ferdinand with him waving "we are good Cara. I hope I didn't blitz you too much yesterday?"

She laughed, "Well, it was a different experience but it wasn't too dramatic. Before we begin with the history of Jardine, I need to tell you a couple of things. You will be assigned a sister from Jardine who works at your place of work; her name is Alira Kingy. I don't know if you know her, but she is an Aboriginal woman who has been with us for little while. Everyone who joins Jardine gets a sister to help them through their journey in life."

I nodded, "Well, that will be nice to have a sister for a change, as well as having someone to talk to about things, without having to be too careful."

Cara nodded, "We have found that it works really well. We also know that you have already started practicing magic from your family book and have learned to magicae, as we call it, or teleport."

I smiled, "Yes that's correct. Ferdinand found that out the hard way," and chuckled as I heard him sigh behind me. Cara smiled back, "I believe you would normally say a magical word like *'lanuae'* when you used your old magic but with Jardine magic all you need to do is visualise it and it will happen. It doesn't really matter which method you prefer; it is up to you in the end Hannah. Now get comfortable while I tell you the history of Jardine."

I took a sip of my coffee, "Is it alright for Ferdinand to be here while I do this, Cara?"

Cara smiled, "That is good that you are thinking of the security of the information; yes, Hannah it is alright. Ferdinand has been with Jardine for a long time, we can trust him. Adesa will also narrate some of the story after a while as well. If you need a break, just let either me or her know and we can stop to let you have one."

I could hear Ferdinand making something in the kitchen smiling, "yes, I will let you know Cara thanks. By the sounds of it, Ferdinand is going to make sure I don't die of starvation"

Cara laughed, "Well if it's anything nice, let me know and I will pop in and sample it."

I chuckled saying quietly, "I think he is making something chocolate."

He spoke up, "Yes Cara, I am making chocolate brownies. You're welcome to come and sample them when you are ready."

I turned to look at him, "You've got good hearing when you want, Ferdinand."

Cara smiled, "Well, we will begin. Now I know you have been to church before so you know about the story, they have told you about Adam and Eve and how they were expelled from the Garden of Eden?"

I nodded saying, "Yes, I do. I mean, I feel as though there were bits missing as I know books were taken out of the Bible to suit different religions so who knows what they have told us."

Cara smiled, "Well that is right, Hannah. This is how it happened but keep in mind this is a shortened version, the rest of the information is on the iPad should you wish to know more."

I got comfortable as Cara continued, "There was a Garden of Eden but it was called Jardine. Now this garden was beautiful with lush plants open plains and dense bush. There were clean oceans with all kinds of animals swimming in them. At first, we were learning to live with what we had. As we grew and developed so did our minds, letting us discover all kinds of things. Magic, as you call it, was always there. It was our birth right, given to us by mother nature. The problems started when men wanted more magic or power. Women always had the majority of power, because they were at one with mother nature."

Cara hesitated, "You did the ceremony with the roots of mother nature, making you one with her. Well men cannot do that. They had some powers, but not as much as women."

"Mother nature controlled our population along with how long we lasted, this balanced life in Jardine. Animals were a part of us being spirit animals as Ferdinand is with you. Animals were not eaten as they were one with us, with mother nature giving us a food that sustained us. It was mentioned in your Bible called mana. We were happy living in harmony until things started to change especially with one man known as Adam, who had always been a difficult boy and who eventually grew to be an angry young man."

"As we grew in knowledge alongside men, who excelled in things like maths and science, accepting this, with them developing some great things to help us grow our abilities, along with anything else we needed in our world. Our society was developing into a more technical world, but we were still living in harmony. Women and men lived together in harmony. We had our problems from time to time but it eventually got sorted out without any harm. We don't claim to be a perfect society, but we do strive for harmony in our lives."

I thought about what she said nodding to let her know I understood so far. Cara continued, "With this knowledge growing amongst men, Adam and a group of men found that if they ate a lot of pomegranates or apples, it boosted their testosterone levels, which made their muscles grow This also changed their hormones in their bodies, bringing out a lot of anger. They eventually worked out how to make them in concentrate forms, so that they could ingest high amounts of the fruit in another form, causing them to become even more angry and rebellious to the authority. They grew very muscular and strong along with their hormones changing their bodies, allowing them to grow scrotums; which they didn't have before."

"In our society, everything living was sacred; this included trees, land, water and animals. Men had to ask the elders to use a tree for something they were working on which they hated."

"Adam wanted a mate to be intimate with. Now we did not have sex as you have it in your world. It was a private time when our souls were shared, perhaps similar to how you fall in love, with that feeling as your souls joined. Adam wanted Lilith, but she refused, as she felt he was too demanding. The women had the right to do this as the men were not in charge in our society. This made Adam angry, but he managed to convince another woman called Eve to become his mate, although he was not really happy with her, as he still wanted Lilith."

"It slowly got to a point of no return, with the men growing strong and rebellious in large numbers, like a disease spreading through the garden. The elders had noticed this bringing everyone together warning the different groups to comply or they would be dealt with."

"Upon hearing this, the men became cunning and convinced some of the weaker women to use their powers to shield their activities from the elders—Eve was one of them wanting to please Adam as she knew Adam still loved Lilith; making her jealous. Some men started making fine jewellery out of gold and gems for these weaker women who became jealous and envious, emotions we hadn't had to deal with before. These women were like magpies after shiny objects."

"It came to a head when Adam and a group of men schemed to kill Lilith for not wanting to be his mate. He took the apple seeds which contained arsenic, crushing them and putting it in her food, killing her. They then went out into the forest and killed some animals to eat them, spilling the blood on the earth, sending turmoil throughout the land. This sent huge ripples throughout Jardine making the elders angry."

Adesa took over now from Cara. "Hi Hannah, do you need a drink or anything?"

I nodded, "I will go to the bathroom I won't be long." When I got back Ferdinand had a drink of water sitting there for me. I smiled at him, sitting down ready to listen to the rest of the story.

Adesa carried on, "While we did not have an authoritarian rule like your world with kings, queens and politicians, we did have three goddesses the mature, mother and maiden. They held the ultimate power in our world. They met with the elders as they had felt the vibrations going through the garden."

"The elders had asked for more time, but the goddesses refused, deciding to do something straightaway, as it was infecting the whole garden. They called everyone together with a thunderous roar around the country. Now at this stage the world was a lot different, with just one land mass, so we all lived in the same part of the world. We all spoke one language as well."

"Everyone came together at the goddesses' request except for the ones that were causing all the trouble, who were trying to hide. The goddesses put a binding force over both the men and women who were causing the trouble, bringing them to the meeting, whether they liked it or not."

"The goddesses made a decree that day from now on you will no longer be a part of this world. We are going to separate you from us, as you are no more than a disease on the side of our face. We turn our backs on you from now on. As punishment we will give Adam and your male followers the sign of the apple forever, as an Adam's apple, in your throat because of the vile things you speak. You will have to hunt for your food and will die early. You will be like the snakes that slither along the ground having penises, which will be used to defile the women that have followed you. You will never be happy with what you have, killing each other for trinkets and power."

"As for the women who have followed you. You were the highest in society, so now you will be the lowest in society, needing men to look after you. You will be forced to produce children out of a womb, shedding blood as you do, forever, for the blood of your sister Lilith, that Adam has taken and whom you did not protect. You will have your powers but they will only be passed on to your offspring, who show goodness in the world. For those who try to hide their powers from the world, you will turn into fairies and other mythical creatures, to escape any torture that men will later inflict, on many women because they show magic or independence."

"Jointly now, you will be ruled by men who are evil and controlling, killing you whenever they please. Women will be hunted as witches for those who do retain their powers. The animals who were once joined with you in your soul will kill you and you will kill them in return, making the blood lust continue, falling to the earth returning to mother nature. Men will continually rule through the ages making themselves 'god like' becoming kings, messiahs and dictators, killing thousands in their wake. This will continue for many years until Adam and Eve's bloodline has gone forever and the blood spilling into the earth finally stops."

"We are now going to separate from you so you will no longer see us as the sight of you all disgusts us! We will become myths in your stories to your children out of shame. You will no longer understand each other, having different languages and customs, which will also bring wars because you cannot get on together, causing hate and mistrust."

"Some women screamed at the thought of being separated from their sisters, but it was too late; the decision had been made. Unfortunately, some innocent women were caught up in the separation, but it was too late the goddesses were angry now and had begun the process."

"The elders along with the goddesses, went to all corners of the land forcing those who had rebelled out into the open, gathering them together as they began the separation."

"The goddesses and elders joined together using their powers starting to chant, forcing the land mass apart, making all those on the other side run. Some of them fell down the great canyons that were forming from the chant that the goddesses and elders were saying. As they chanted the land separated into different parts, but only Jardine remained as one piece."

"As they raised their hands a dome formed covering the land of Jardine to protect it forever. The people in Jardine wept continuously for five days for their sisters and brothers, forming large areas of water that became oceans and lakes. Once the dome had formed the goddesses said there will always be a sign to show that you were once a part of Jardine; with a rainbow forming over the dome in different colours of the spectrum."

As I sat there listening to the story, I couldn't help it as my eyes filled with tears, falling down my cheeks of the sad story that was unfolding.

Both Cara and Adesa saw the pain in my eyes, moving forward sitting next to me giving me a hug. Cara gave me a tissue to wipe my eyes, saying in a comforting voice, "Are you alright, Hannah?"

I leaned back to wipe my eyes nodding, "Yes, sorry it was just so sad. To think that all the heart ache and killing that this world has experienced could have been stopped. I don't think it is going to stop for a long time either."

Cara rubbed my arm, "Things are slowly improving Hannah, but yes there is still a lot of unnecessary sadness in your world. I know you enjoy history and have seen the different stages of the people of the world like the Mayan or Romans coming through but they all crumble in the end, with power setting in to control everyone, but people just don't learn. We have tried to help at different times sending people to teach them like Jesus, Mohammad, Buddha but the greedy people just use it to collect riches or control people."

"Even people like Leonardo di Vinci and Florence Nightingale were sent to bring beauty and better health in the world. It has helped a little, but not enough to stem the greed and the hate."

Ferdinand came over with a plate of chocolate brownies looking concerned, "I have baked some brownies if that will help," bringing a smile to me through my tears, "Thanks Ferdinand."

Cara and Adesa looked at them longingly then back at me, "Please help yourself otherwise he'll expect me to eat them all." As we ate our brownie, we sat there reflecting on the story that had just been told.

After Cara had finished her brownie, she looked at me, "Now that is enough of the negative stuff; we will get on to something else. If you want to read some more about that happening there will be a folder on your iPad you can read, to get a better idea of it. Do you have any questions, Hannah?"

I wiped my mouth with a tissue nodding, "Yes actually I do have one. I know this is all fantasy on TV etc. but it has been around for a long time on how women used to use brooms to fly and wands to cast their magic. Is there any truth in this and why did they have to use these things?"

Adesa patted my hand, "That is a great question, Hannah. They had to do this because they were separated from mother earth. Using a stick or a piece of wood from a tree for a broom was their connection to mother earth. You will notice this when you cast spells or chants now, that you have joined with Jardine, that you don't have to use so many magical words or items that you would normally, with your old family magic. Jardine magic is mainly all thought based, but every now and then we might use something in the way of herbs or crystals."

I nodded smiling, "Well that makes sense, thank you." I watched Ferdinand finishing off his brownie, "Just one more question."

Cara was wiping her mouth, "Yes, what is it, Hannah?"

I hesitated, "Were the spirit animals put there to balance with the women, sort of like in the Chinese culture of Ying and Yang?"

Ferdinand grinned, but let Cara answer, "Yes Hannah. There is always two parts to nature and it is so with women and men."

I smiled, "I thought it was something like that, thanks."

Cara and Adesa got up after enjoying another brownie and a drink that Ferdinand had prepared for us. Cara gave me a hug, "If you want to ask any more questions, just open your iPad and one of us will be there for you Hannah. We are here to support you in any way we can."

Adesa gave me a hug as well, "We know you have Ferdinand and will have Alira soon as well, but like Cara said we are here to support you."

I sighed smiling, "It's nice to know, thank you both," as I watched them disappear waving.

I took the cups and plates over to the kitchen checking the time. I still had just over an hour until I was due to meet Amelia, with Ferdinand coming over giving me a hug, "Are you alright?"

I leaned into him nodding, "Yes just a bit to take in, I guess."

Ferdinand pulled away, "Do you want me to hang around a bit longer or take you to your lunch?"

I smiled, "You just want to meet Amelia, don't you? No, dear I will be alright and I will have to break things to Amelia slowly. I might do some meditation before I go, just to calm myself."

He chuckled, "You're starting to work me out. I'm going to have to be more cunning I see. Well, I will get going to Jardine, just be careful and if you need me, you know how to call me."

He gave me a kiss on the cheek, "No pranks just get out of there."

I tried to act serious, "I'm not expecting any trouble dear, but I will call you if I need help."

He groaned, "Mmm that's what you keep saying, but it appears to follow you around. I'll see you later otherwise."

Chapter 7

He disappeared, leaving me thinking about what I he had just said about it following me around. That priest appears to know where I am for some reason, surely it can't just be the vibrations from my magic. I mean I don't use it until he or someone else has threatened me.

I sat down pondering over it for a bit not really coming to any conclusion. I got up and cleansed myself with some bay leaf getting rid of any negative thoughts and lit an incense.

I remembered the thought I had this morning about putting some more protection around the unit with a spell coming to me, *"In this unit we will be protected and safe from any foe or enemy. Protect us now and protect us well so mote it be."*

I put my hands above my head turning slowly around in the lounge, saying the spell, seeing a white light of protection go around the unit, then a small pulse sound at the end.

I felt happy with this, deciding to ask another question about how people manage to find me. I went and got some of my crystals placing the white quartz for my crown, purple for my third eye, blue for my throat, pink for my heart, yellow for solar plexus, orange for sacral and brown for the root chakra laying down and positioning them in their correct places.

I started my CD off clearing my head, starting to relax my muscles listening to my breathing. I found it a little difficult to clear my thoughts at first, but I finally relaxed with the vision of the boat coming into my thoughts, floating down the river with soft clouds above me, the sound of birds and insects around me, when all of a sudden, the vision stopped.

I appeared to be just floating in the boat with nothing happening around me, making me sit up in the boat to see what was happening. I looked around with just a white space around me, feeling confused, then I turned to see a figure sitting at the other end of the boat. The figure wasn't very clear but I did realise it was a ghost, having seen a few in my time.

I sat up properly looking at the figure before me, "Who are you?" The ghost lifted its head, making me realise it was a woman looking at me intensely "Jeg er din stamfar Hannah (I am one of your ancestors Hannah.)"

I sat there confused at first, realising she was speaking Norwegian, but what made me confused was, I could understand her. I had looked at the language before, but never really studied it. I spoke back, "Hvilken (which one)?"

She chuckled, "Det er ikke vikitg (that is not important)." She moved closer to me floating in a ghostly way, looking me up and down, "Du er en Dragĕ kvinne (you are a Dragĕ woman alright)."

I started to get agitated with her laughing, "Sporsmålet du stilte er I juvelene dine (the question you asked is in your jewels)" floating closer now stroking her ghostly hand on mine, "Du har din bestefars temperament (you have your grandpa's temper)." She then disappeared with the vision of the river and green fields coming back, feeling unsure of what to make of this lying, down hearing my breathing come back into my mind.

I lay there for a few minutes taking it all in, wondering who she was and what she meant about it being in my jewels. I shrugged, '*I don't even know how I understood her,*' and sighed, '*Things are certainly getting a lot more different than what I am used to.*'

I took the crystals off my chakras getting up to shake myself out. As I did this, I looked at the jewellery I had on, thinking about what she said. I wore a couple of rings on my right hand, one of them was a signet ring of a shield with my initials in it that my mother had given me when I was young and a ring that my girls had given me a couple of years ago. I haven't worn an engagement or wedding ring for years.

I checked the time, realising I had taken longer than I thought, so I quickly put some jeans and a light top on, taking a jacket in case the weather changed. I landed near the nurses walk, hoping it wouldn't be too busy, slipping a bit on the old cobbles that were around there.

A couple walking past looked as I stumbled, feeling a little embarrassed, regaining my composure. I headed towards the end of the main street going down to the pub called Fortunes of War. It had a café attached to it as well as a beer garden, which I thought would be nice to sit in today as the weather had turned a bit warmer.

I went into the beer garden getting a seat, looking at the magnificent jacaranda tree with its light covering of purple flowers that would occasionally drop to the ground, forming a purple carpet. As people walked on, the flowers a gentle smell of their scent, would rise up to hit you. The old architecture of the pub made you feel you were in the 1800s with Tasmania oak and tiles on the walls and floors.

Amelia arrived not long after, wearing some dark blue denim jeans and a light blue top, which set off her eyes that were similar to mine. She wore her long blonde hair out with just a light covering of makeup.

I could see the waiter looking at her, then looking at the both of us smiling, as you could see we were mother and daughter. He had brought the menus over asking if we wanted anything to drink. My daughter hadn't had a lot of success with men either; I was beginning to think we had a curse on us or something when it came to them.

I felt like a nice glass of wine ordering one with Amelia deciding to join me. As I picked up the glass my sleeve rose up, revealing the tattoo of the dragon.

Amelia noticed it laughing, "OMG Mum, really a dragon tattoo. Aren't you getting a bit old for those?"

I pulled the sleeve down, "No I thought it was cute so I decided to get it," feeling it move a little as I said this.

We chatted about general things, having our lunch and by the third glass of wine we were feeling quite relaxed. I got up, "I'm just going to the toilet and I'll pay the bill."

Amelia nodded, "Yeah ok, I'll wait for you here."

The toilets were in an older part of the building with creaky old floor boards and squeaky doors that were quite narrow.

I felt a little tipsy smiling in the mirror afterwards thinking, *'Well, here we go for the talk.'* I went out and paid when I noticed Amelia was talking to that pesky priest. My temper stirred going towards him, but tripped on one of the chairs, drawing attention to myself.

This alerted him, giving him enough time to take off, before I got there. I thought about saying a chant but I tried to calm myself down to see what he said to Amelia. Amelia looked at me confused, "What's the matter, Mum?"

I sat back down, taking another swig of the remainder of my wine, "That man is a bit of a nutter and has been hanging around for a while and is really starting to annoy me. What did he say to you?"

Amelia chuckled, "We're in Sydney Mum, there are a lot of nutters here. He was asking about you and your beliefs or something, I really wasn't listening to be honest. I was just about to tell him to go away, when you came out falling over the chair."

I finished off my wine, "You know I'm a bit of a klutz with my feet," with her looking at the wine. I finished it off, "Yes, the wine probably isn't helping. I'm not having any more. Come on we'll go for a walk, as I want to talk about a couple of things with you."

We walked towards the bridge going to a park bench not far from the water, looking over to the harbour. As we walked, we watched the water being churned up by the ferries going past, sending sea spray up towards us, in the light breeze.

It was Friday afternoon, so a few business people dressed in suits and dresses were going for a long lunch, with me hoping I wouldn't see anyone from work.

The park bench we found was surrounded by small bushes, so we could see the footpath, but people couldn't really see us, which made it perfect for our private chat. I didn't really know how to start so I just said, "Do you know anything about the family book?"

Amelia got her phone out to take a photo of the bridge, which she always enjoyed doing, then took a photo of me and her. I sighed, "So do you know anything about it, Amelia?"

She looked at me, "It depends on your mood, Mum?"

I frowned, "What do you mean by that?"

She smiled wanly, "Well, you do have a bit of a temper. Ok, I do know about the family book. I have seen it, but haven't looked in it."

I sat back on the seat trying to stay calm, "Did Nanna show you the book?"

She nodded, "Yes, when we were young. When she used to babysit us for you, she would let us do little magic shows for her and then one day she brought out the (saying dramatically) 'family book'. She said she couldn't give it to us as it was your birth right first."

I got up feeling the anger in the pit of my stomach churn up again, trying not to show it to Amelia, but she knew me too well, "Look Mum, if you're going to get angry, I may as well go home. This is why we never said too much to you about it, because you kept closing yourself off to us or would just get angry."

I took a deep breath, putting my hands up, "I'm sorry, your Nanna kept it from me, for a long time and I am just finding some things out, that is all."

I sat back down trying to keep myself calm, putting on a smile, "So what tricks would you do for her?"

She smiled, "Well I don't know if I can do them now. Charlotte was better at them than me, that's probably why she is a science teacher. There was one I think I can remember" as she put her hand out thinking of the word, then recognition coming over her face, "Oh I think I remember it now," '*Fotia*' as a small flick of flame appeared on her hand.

Again, I took a deep breath smiling, "Wow that was good Amelia. Do you ever find if you get angry or annoyed at someone that things happen?"

She laughed, "Well I don't get as angry as you or Charlotte, but yes when someone pisses me off, I do think of something to get them back."

She looked a little puzzled, "Just lately if that happens, something comes into my head, almost like a poem. One time I said it and the person slipped all over the place as though they were on an ice-skating rink. I must admit it was funny."

I laughed with her, "Well you have that part of me with a strange sense of humour." I could hear the bush rustling beside us, turning to look at Amelia, getting up to see who was there. I growled as John Adams came out with a smirk on his face, "Mother and daughter are alike, I see," grabbing Amelia by the arm trying to pull her away, "Bugger off, you creep."

I didn't want to send anything to him in case I hit Amelia, so I touched my tattoo, with Ferdinand appearing next to me, instantly reacting to what was going on. He lunged towards John Adams punching him in the jaw.

John Adams stumbled on a tree root that was sticking up from the ground releasing Amelia's arm, hearing him groan when he landed on the ground, then hearing a crack.

Amelia came over to me, rubbing her arm and looking puzzled at Ferdinand as I said, "Are you alright, Amelia?"

"Where did he come from Mum?"

Ferdinand came over to us, noticing my anger flaring, about to put a chant on John with Ferdinand looking determined, "Don't Hannah he has hurt his arm and he will have a sore jaw as well; so that's enough."

Amelia looked at me then him, looking at Ferdinand as though she had seen him somewhere before. Ferdinand grinned taking our hands. I realised what he was going to do trying to stop him, but it was too late, we magicae out of the park to my place.

I could hear Amelia squealing, as we travelled landing in my lounge, with Ferdinand holding us both up as we landed, stumbling. Amelia's hair shot forward landing over her face then shook her head in annoyance.

He laughed, "You can see you two are related."

Amelia shook his hand off, looking dazed then, realised where we were, "How did we get here?"

I groaned, "Well I was going to get around to this part, but Ferdinand has beaten me to it."

I sighed, "This is part of the magic in the book, Amelia," and walked over to the kitchen to get us a drink of water.

Amelia went over to the sofa, still a bit dazed, as I brought the water over. I looked over to Ferdinand, "Did you want one?"

He shook his head, "No I'm fine, thanks."

She looked at him then me, "So is this the gay guy that's been hanging around you?"

I turned my head away from Ferdinand, smirking as I knew he would be annoyed, getting my composure back, "This is Ferdinand. He isn't gay and he is part of the magic."

Amelia took a sip of the water, "What do you mean part of the magic?"

I was about to explain when a dawning look came over her face, "Is he your guardian animal?"

I looked at Ferdinand and then back at Amelia, "How did you know about that Amelia?"

She sighed, "Nanna told us these stories about it. We didn't believe her though. So, what do you change into—I know let me guess the dragon that Mum has on her arm?"

Ferdinand got up, "Nice to finally meet you Amelia," then changed into his dragon form. Amelia gaped at him in amazement dropping the glass of water onto the carpet, realising picking it up. I pointed at the wet patch with my finger drying it instantly.

She grinned looking at my handiwork, then put the glass down on the coffee table walking over to Ferdinand, "Wow so Nanna wasn't completely nuts then."

Ferdinand shook his head, "Your family have a way with words, don't you?"

I sat down watching Amelia touch Ferdinand's scales and the talons on his feet.

I could see a mischievous look in his eyes, grabbing Amelia's arm, "Come on let's go for a ride, Amelia," and heard her squeal as he magicae out of the room putting her on his back flying over the sea. I smiled watching from the sofa as they flew out to sea, with Amelia still squealing trying to find the harness around his neck to hold onto.

By the time they came back, she was giggling like a kid, "Wow do I get a dragon?" She slipped off his back fixing up her hair that had been blown everywhere and Ferdinand changing back to his male form. I shrugged my shoulders, "I don't know Amelia that is up to Jardine I think?"

Ferdinand sat down on the chair by the door, surprised, "So you know about some of this stuff, Amelia?"

She nodded, "Yes I was just telling Mum that Nanna used to let us do magic shows for her when she looked after us when Mum worked or went out on the odd date; that never lasted very long."

I sighed, "Thanks for that Amelia."

Amelia smiled, "I think I'll have a glass of wine Mum; do you and Ferdinand want one?"

I nodded, "Yes I think I will have one."

Ferdinand smiled, "Yes thanks."

She brought them over shaking her head, "Wow I really thought Nanna was going gaga, but she's proved us wrong."

I took the glass from her looking at Ferdinand, "Amelia did a little magic trick for me, I think that John Adams saw it, that's why he came out. I'm trying to work out how he is finding me all the time, it is really starting to get annoying."

Ferdinand took a sip of wine thinking about it, "Yes, it is too much of a coincidence now."

Amelia sat down with a plate of Ferdinand's brownies, "Did you make these Mum they look nice?"

Ferdinand laughed, "No I made them, Amelia." She took one passing them to me and Ferdinand, as we took one each.

Ferdinand produced some paper napkins making Amelia look, "So you can do magic as well?"

Ferdinand nodded, "Only basic things though, nothing like your mother."

Amelia turned to look at me, "What sort of things can you do Mum?"

I put my glass of wine down, "I've just been dabbling a bit," putting my hand out swirling my finger in my palm bringing in a really small whirlwind, then changing it to a small pool of water, changing to a small fire like she had produced and then some dirt.

Amelia sat there quietly, "Wow that looks good."

Ferdinand sat quietly eating his brownie looking at me making me feel a little uncomfortable.

I picked up my glass of wine, "I can do other things but I'll show you later. We need to discuss something else."

Amelia sat back on the sofa getting comfortable, "Is that Jardine?"

I looked at her again disappointed, "So Nanna told you about that as well?"

Amelia could tell my mood had changed, "It's no use getting annoyed about it, Mum, she must have had her reasons for not letting you do the magic. You look as though you've picked it up quite quickly, maybe it was because of that?"

I pursed my lips, calming myself, "People keep telling me that, but anyway what do you know about Jardine?"

She finished off her brownie thinking, "Well Nanna said it was a beautiful place where women ruled, that you had guardian animals," and looked at Ferdinand, "And that magic was normal there."

I put my glass down getting up shaking my head, mumbling under my breath in annoyance, going to the balcony to get some fresh air. I got outside growling, taking deep breaths with a clap of thunder being heard in the distance.

Amelia pulled a face, sighing at Ferdinand as he said, "Just let her calm down a bit. She is just only finding out a lot of this stuff."

Amelia shook her head, "I can see where Charlotte gets her temper from. You know Charlotte is going to give you the third degree, especially since you're sleeping with Mum."

He looked surprised at her, "How do you know I'm sleeping with your mother? Besides it's not sex like in your world."

Amelia snickered, "Oh boy I would be very careful when you meet Charlotte then. Just make sure I'm there when you do meet her."

Ferdinand groaned, "Something to look forward to I guess."

Just as they were talking, a woman appeared on the balcony, making Amelia turn to look, "A woman has just appeared on the balcony with Mum. Is she from Jardine?"

Ferdinand got up to have a look, "Yes that is Morag, an elder. She is good at calming your mother down, so let them talk."

As I stood out on the balcony taking deep breaths with tears of anger welling up, Morag appeared after a short time. Morag put her arm around my waist, "What is it, Hannah?"

I quickly wiped my eyes in frustration, "Mum has been to Jardine and never told me but she told Amelia and Charlotte. Did you know?"

Morag sighed, "Yes, I knew, but it was only a quick visit with Matilda and you when you were young. That is when something happened and she swore she would never be back or use magic again. That is all I know."

I turned to Morag frustrated, "She even let my girls do little magic shows when she used to look after them. She better have had a good reason to put me through the rubbish she put me through that's all I'm saying."

Morag gave me a hug, "Come on Hannah it is no use staying angry at your mother, we all make mistakes, as you know with your children; I am sure it will come to light eventually."

I took a deep breath as I hugged Morag crying, "You're more like the mother I should have had. I wish I had known you earlier."

Morag patted my back, "Come on wipe your eyes and introduce me to your daughter and we will see if we can convince her to join you. At least that way you can support each other."

I took a deep breath, "Ok, I'll just go and wash my face."

Morag smiled, "Here, I'll fix you up," as she waved her hand, "There that looks better. That is a refresh which you can use for your face or if you get wet. Try it next time, it comes in handy."

We walked into the lounge, with Ferdinand coming over to me, "Are you alright now?"

I nodded, "I'm getting there," looking at Amelia, "Morag, this is Amelia my eldest daughter."

Amelia got up smiling nervously, "Hi Morag, it's nice to meet you. Ferdinand was saying that you are an elder in Jardine."

Morag came up to Amelia giving her a hug, "Well you are like your mother in looks, aren't you?"

Amelia laughed, "Yes but not in temper. Charlotte was lucky enough to get that part of Mum, as well as similar looks."

Morag sat down, "Come and sit with me Amelia so we can talk."

I went over to the kitchen to get some more wine, "Morag would you like a glass of wine?"

Morag turned to look at me hesitating, "Yes that would be nice, thanks Hannah."

Ferdinand came over to help me, getting some more brownies out, with me shaking my head smiling, "They are nice Ferdinand. I am sure Amelia will have another one."

He gave me a hug, "I'm hoping you will as well. Actually, I might order some pizzas soon, what do you think?"

I shrugged my shoulders, "Yes if you like. Just use my phone if you like as you already know how to use it."

Amelia and Morag sat down together with Ferdinand bringing over the glasses of wine and brownies.

Morag smiled at him, "Mmm they look nice Ferdinand, did Hannah make them?"

He shook his head, "No, I'm the cook here."

Morag shrugged her shoulders, "Well I will have one thank you." She took a bite, "Mm nice."

After Morag had a bit of brownie and a sip of her wine expressing it was nice, she put it down, "Well Amelia you appear to know a little bit about Jardine and magic. How would you like to join with your mother to help her? She has joined Jardine, so she can get help from us when she needs it, as well as be part of a community. It is entirely up to you though Amelia, you can just stay as you are without the magic or even just to be a part of your family magic."

Amelia took a big sip of wine, "I was thinking about it while you and Mum were talking actually. I know Mum is angry with the way things have turned out, but I think if I learn the magic and join, we can at least get a bit closer. She has pushed us away a bit over the last few years as well. I also like the idea of having a guardian animal who turns into a man. As you know Dragĕ women don't have much luck with men and that appears to be the case with me and Charlotte as well. At least with a guardian animal/man he *has* to hang around," laughing as she said it.

Ferdinand had just finished ordering the pizzas hearing that part shaking his head, "You Dragĕ women have a strange sense of humour."

I started to splutter on my drink trying not to laugh, "I never thought of it like that Amelia," and turning to look at Ferdinand, "Looks like you're stuck with me Ferdinand."

He smiled coming over to sit next to me putting his arm around me, "I don't mind that at all. It's been well worth the wait."

I smiled leaning into him, while Amelia watched turning to Morag, "Wow are the guardian animals allowed to get that close?"

Morag looked at Ferdinand and I, "Yes, they can; they can also become intimate, which I won't go into right now. There are a few rules that they have to follow, but again I won't go into that now, at least not until you get your own guardian animal."

This brightened Amelia's eyes, "Oh wow, I can't wait. Is the dragon a family thing or do I get something else?"

Morag smiled, "No an animal gets assigned to you through mother nature. Just because your surname means dragon doesn't always mean you get a dragon."

Ferdinand chirped in then, "There's only one of me, Amelia" making her cough, "Good grief, just be careful with that attitude around Charlotte Ferdinand."

Morag put her hand on Amelia's, "So what is your decision, Amelia? Do you want time to think about it, doing it another day or we can do the ceremony now?"

I sat forward, "Only do this if you really want to Amelia, there is no pressure."

Amelia (taking after me) took a big gulp of wine, "No I want to do it now. Time is ticking away for me as well and I want to have some excitement in my life before I get old and miserable like Mum."

I sat back with Ferdinand giving me a hug, "Thanks Amelia."

Amelia laughed, "Come on Mum, I'm just trying to stir you up."

Morag clapped her hands, "Oh this is wonderful. We can arrange it after I've finished this lovely brownie and glass of wine. Do you think Charlotte will be as willing as you?"

Amelia chuckled looking at me, making me grin, "No, but I am sure we will get her to change her mind."

We finished our wine as I got up to go to the bathroom, taking the glasses on the way. I looked at Amelia, "Can I talk to you Amelia before you do the ceremony?"

She got up, "We won't be long I just want to check something with Amelia," with Morag and Ferdinand nodding finishing their drinks.

I took Amelia into the bedroom, shutting the door, "Before you do the ceremony, I would like to join you with the family book first."

Amelia smiled, "Should we tell Morag that we are going to do this?"

I shook my head, "no I would rather not, as this is our side of it. This won't take long."

I locked the room and brought out the book on my hands as I had done before, with Amelia standing there with her mouth open, "Wow Mum, you have been working hard."

I nodded, "Just touch the book and see what it says." She did as I asked, as the book turned over to the page with the family tree on it and then words coming up *'welcome Amelia Dragĕ please put your contribution in the ink well.'*

A feather came out again with a sharp point and Amelia looking at me, "Just prick your finger with the feather point and then put your blood in the ink well on the page."

Amelia nodded, "Ok" doing what I asked her to do. Her blood went into the ink well watching the book scan her and then accepting her as a family member. Her eyes lit up with surprise, "Wow that is almost like a scanner doing my DNA," and gave me a hug, "You are quite clever, Mum."

I sent the book away unlocking the room, "You can have a look at later in your own time. We better get back out there." Before we went out, I stopped Amelia, "Don't say anything to them for now, ok, and suck your finger to stop it bleeding. Just say I wanted to check that you were sure that you wanted to do the ceremony."

Amelia nodded, "Yes sure Mum, don't worry."

Morag stood up smiling at us both, "So you've had your mother daughter talk and are sure you still wish to join us, Amelia?"

Amelia looked bright eyed at Morag, "Yes Morag I am more than sure that I want to join now and it is my free choice."

I put my arm around Amelia giving her a hug, "I'm proud of you, Amelia."

Morag called Lilith, Cara, Adesa and Louella in for the ceremony. Lilith looked around smiling at Ferdinand then noticed Amelia with me.

I noticed her smile drop briefly, but then it looked as though she was forcing it, coming over to me, "Hi Hannah is this your daughter Amelia?"

I nodded, "Yes Lilith and she is quite ready to join Jardine."

Lilith had a job to do, so told Amelia that she was going to cleanse her and get her ready for the ceremony. She then told her about the roots going over her feet but not to worry about it as it is the joining of her to mother earth.

She introduced Amelia to Cara, Adesa and Louella saying this is Hannah's daughter.

Louella's smile drained from her face, "Does she have the same strength as her mother?"

I tried not to smile at the thought of those three with their hair crazy and looking drained after my ceremony. I turned away from them so they wouldn't see me smile making myself busy putting the glasses in the kitchen.

Lilith looked at Louella, "I am sure Amelia is not as strong as Hannah yet." She then changed Amelia's clothes for the robe like I had had, with Amelia looking down in amazement. Lilith now cleansed Amelia for the ceremony saying: *"cleanse this woman now ready for her rebirth with mother earth once and for all."*

Ferdinand came over to me putting his arm around my shoulder guiding me away, "I don't think you need to be that close, as you are just likely to put your bit of energy into the ceremony, nearly cooking them again."

I was trying not to giggle, as he walked me over to the barstools standing behind me with his arms around my waist, letting me lean into him. It felt nice seeing my daughter do this for me as well as having Ferdinand's support.

They asked Amelia to take her shoes off now, putting the dirt on the floor with her stepping onto it. She looked over to me for reassurance as well as looking at Ferdinand behind me with his arms around my waist. I smiled at her nodding, "It'll be ok. Don't worry."

Morag went over to Amelia giving her a hug, "Just relax, close your eyes and enjoy the ceremony."

Amelia stepped onto the dirt as Adesa, Cara and Louella formed a circle around Amelia starting to sway as one saying the chant. Amelia took one last look at me for reassurance with me blowing her a kiss from my hand. A fine misted heart went to Amelia landing on the top of her head as she stood there closing her eyes.

I cringed, stiffening up, hoping Ferdinand didn't see that, when he wrapped his arms around me, "What did you just do?"

I shrugged my shoulders, "I don't know what you're talking about."

He growled, "Hannah, I hope you haven't sent anything too strong to Amelia?"

I looked up to him as he held me, making sure I didn't do anything else, "I just blew her a kiss."

Morag came over noticing Ferdinand holding me, "What's happening Ferdinand?"

Ferdinand kept his hands where they were, "Hannah sent something to Amelia. It will probably send a serge to the three women doing the ceremony."

Morag smiled looking knowingly at me, "I think that little kiss won't do much but the joining of the family book will be the energy builder. We will have to wait and see what happens I guess."

Ferdinand looked down at me, "Is that what you did in the bedroom Hannah?"

I tried to escape Ferdinand's arms, "They will be alright she hasn't been practicing magic to make her strong. I just wanted the family magic in there that is all."

Ferdinand sighed, "We will have to wait and see won't we."

As the chant grew stronger, I could see the roots forming over Amelia's feet making her one with mother earth. As the swaying and the chanting came to a pitch, a white light sprung from Amelia hitting the ceiling and forming around the circle as a protection.

Amelia's body lit up with the light as she was being accepted by mother earth to become one with her. The heart that I sent to Amelia mixed with the energy from mother earth sending gentle heart shaped lights around the women doing the ceremony, like a mother's love being passed around.

It was still full of power making the three women's hair stand-up but not as strong as when I did the ceremony. Right near the end I noticed a small pink misty light swirl briefly around Amelia, which I recognised was the family book.

Lilith came over smiling, "It appears to be going well so far, a bit more of a buzz than what we would normally see, but not as strong as yours Hannah."

I went to move feeling Ferdinand's arms hold firm, "Yes it has gone well."

Lilith noticed Ferdinand with his arms around me, "I don't think you need to hold Hannah so tight Ferdinand; she isn't going to do anything." He grimaced, "She already has, but luckily it didn't affect the ceremony."

The three women slowed their chant and swaying down taking deep breaths. Amelia's light energy started to dim with an added burst of stars coming down on everyone in the circle making her look angelic with her blonde hair sparkling as we looked on in wonder.

Morag's eyes lit up, "Aww that was a nice little flutter at the end."

I tried to move again, "Come on Ferdinand it's finished and everyone is safe. I want to see how Amelia is." He sighed kissing the top of my head leaning down saying quietly, "You're lucky madam," and letting me go.

I stepped closer to Amelia watching the light dim with an ethereal look come over her. A big smile came over her face turning to look at me, "Wow that was amazing Mum. I thought I could hear voices in there as well; was that the ancestors?"

I nodded, "Yes probably."

Morag moved closer, "Welcome to Jardine, Amelia."

I let her settle, checking on the others as Ferdinand came with glasses of water for them all. Louella sat down to rest having a drink of water, "Are there any more family members?"

I smiled at her, "Yes, I have one more daughter why?" She looked at me sighing, "This is making me older, but at least this one wasn't as strong as you, Hannah."

I patted her on the shoulder, "Sorry about that Louella. I am sure if Charlotte goes ahead with the ceremony, she won't be very strong either."

I could see Lilith hovering, listening to us wondering what she was up to.

Morag called for everyone's attention, "Now that we have the ceremony over with it is time to introduce Amelia to her guardian animal. Ferdinand, can you get some extra chairs in so everyone can have a seat. Amelia come and stand next to Cara as she will bring him forward for you."

Amelia grinned, turning to look at me, with bright eyes, reminding me of when she was little, then moving over to Cara sitting next to her.

Ferdinand brought in some chairs with an excited feeling going around the room, while everyone got settled into a chair. I could hear Louella chatting excitedly with Adesa, "I love this bit."

Ferdinand came up to me, "Do you want to sit down?"

I shook my head, "No I'll watch from here; I can see everything."

Ferdinand helped Morag and Lilith get settled, noticing Lilith looking sulkily at Ferdinand watching him come back over to me, standing behind me putting his arms around my waist. I leaned into him feeling happy at last that Amelia is a part of something that I belong to.

Cara then looked at Amelia, smiling warmly, "It is time to introduce you to your spirit animal, who has been waiting for a while to see you, Amelia." She looked over to me, excited.

Cara then went to a part of the lounge that had no furniture in it, rubbing her hands together causing a white light to form between them. She pulled the white light apart, like you would a bread dough, forming a big circle. It was pulsating gently with little wisps of mist coming off it. You could feel the anticipation in the room, waiting for something to come out.

Cara now said, "I summon Amelia Dragĕ's spirit animal please come forth." A beautiful grey and white wolf with its fur encasing dark mysterious eyes poked his head out of the circle. The wolf stopped briefly taking in the surroundings around him before he fully emerged from the circle panting, looking as big as a great Dane.

I heard a gasp from some of the Jardine women, then, "Aww it's a wolf, how beautiful."

Amelia put her hands up to her face in surprise, with the wolf looking around at all of us, then going straight to Amelia rubbing himself on her legs, as she sat there not quite sure what to do. The wolf sat down near her legs as she leaned forward giving him a big hug welling up at the sight of this beautiful animal. This made me have to wipe my eyes as Ferdinand squeezed me.

Cara then said, "Reveal your male form."

The wolf changed growing into a tall man with broad shoulders and strong arms. He had long dark hair with flecks of white through it. His skin was olive, making his dark brown eyes look striking, with him reminding me a little of Jason Momoa.

He had tightly fitted black jeans on with a shirt that looked native American. Over that he wore a waist coat made of cloth in dark colours with symbols imbedded in the material. He wore a black band on his wrist with an amber stone threaded through it.

He turned to look at Amelia embracing her around her waist, picking her up off her feet, making her squeal. He smiled showing pointy teeth, something she had always had in the front as well, with him saying, "I finally get to meet you."

He let her slide down while looking at her with love in his eyes. She blushed not taking her eyes off him saying, "What's your name?"

He had dimples at the end of his mouth making his smile look contagious, saying, "My name is Shiro Amelia," as he got her hand and kissed it lightly.

I could hear Louella, Adesa and Morag sigh, "Aww that is beautiful."

I was trying to hold in my pleasure, wiping my eyes with Ferdinand producing a tissue in his hand. I took it wiping my eyes watching them.

I went to move forward thinking he is getting a little cosy quickly, when Ferdinand stopped me. He looked at me, "She is alright. That is probably what it would have been like for us, but you were too stubborn."

I turned to look at him, "I was stubborn; who kept telling me off for using my magic and nearly drowned me." He turned me around putting his hand over my mouth saying, "Shh."

I put my hand up to his trying to take it away, with him bending down, "Are you going to be quiet?" I rolled my eyes nodding, as he dropped his hand.

Shiro then took Amelia's left hand as she stood there transfixed at this man standing in front of her saying, "This is your calling card for me if you ever need me," touching her wrist gently leaving a little tattoo there of a wolf.

Amelia winced a little, taking her eyes off him briefly looking down at the little tattoo he had put there for her. She kissed it saying, "Thank you," going back to stare into his eyes mesmerised.

The buzzer went for the door security breaking the spell between them, with Shiro looking around at us all smiling, "Hello everyone. It is nice to finally be here."

Ferdinand went over to let the pizza guy in waiting for him to come to the door. I went up behind him, "I didn't give you any money, how did you pay for it?" He bent down kissing me on the cheek, "Don't worry about it, I have money. Go and see how everyone is and if they want any pizza before they go."

I went back over to everyone asking if they wanted to stay for pizza and some wine. Cara, Adesa, Louella and Lilith all looked pleased with Louella's mood picking up, "I haven't tried your world food very much, it will be interesting to try it, thanks."

I went and checked on Amelia who was still staring starring eyed at Shiro holding his hand, "Hi Shiro I'm Hannah Amelia's Mum, welcome to the family."

I gave him a hug, with him not wanting to let Amelia's hand go, "Nice to finally meet you, Hannah. Ferdinand has told me a lot about you all; so, it is nice to finally get together." I looked at Amelia waving my hand in front of her, "Earth to Amelia."

She came out of her daze, "Oh hi Mum, this is Shiro."

I gave her a hug, "I know Amelia, we have already introduced ourselves. Do you want some pizza and wine, we have just had it delivered?"

Shiro's eyes lit up, "Oh yes, I'm starving. I haven't tried your world food either, so it will be a new experience," and turning to Amelia, "Maybe you will help me by explaining everything to me Amelia."

Amelia leaned into him putting her arm around his waist looking like a kid in a candy store, "I certainly will Shiro."

After we had all eaten, Cara went over to Amelia, who was sitting closely to Shiro still, giving her the book ensuring that Amelia make sure that no one else sees the book keeping it secure somewhere.

She also told her she will be assigned a sister who is of Māori origin called Hinemoa Tanĕ. She will make herself known to you next week sometime. Amelia looked at the tatty old book screwing her nose up, "I'm not a very good reader but I will try my best," putting it in her bag.

Morag went and sat down next to Amelia after Cara had moved, talking to her taking her hand, "Are you alright, Amelia?"

Amelia was still grinning, "Yes I am great, thanks Morag."

Morag smiled, "It is nice to finally see you with your spirit animal. Shiro knows the rules so just get to know each other before you get too close Amelia. Your mother also mentioned you joined the family book. If you need any help or feel something isn't right, please call on me, Cara or Adesa, won't you?"

Amelia chuckled, "We can't pull the wool over your eyes, can we?"

Morag looked a little confused, "I am not familiar with that expression, does that mean that you cannot fool me?"

Amelia nodded, "Yes, sorry I forget you don't know these sayings. Mum always said them to us, so we tend to repeat them."

I got another bottle of wine out of the fridge with Ferdinand coming up behind me wrapping his arms around me, "Are you happy, Hannah?"

I turned around in his arms, smiling looking up at him, "Yes I am, thank you," leaning into him giving him a hug. I could feel some eyes on us, noticing Lilith looking our way, but then turning away as I looked over to her.

After a couple of hours of eating, drinking and chatting everyone left except Shiro and Amelia. I started taking glasses and plates to the kitchen with Amelia coming to help me.

Ferdinand was already getting the sink ready to wash them and Shiro was in the lounge getting rid of the extra chairs.

Amelia smiled at me giving me a hug, "Thanks Mum, it turned out to be a great day after all, didn't it?" It felt nice to hug my daughter again; I had cut them off and they had in return, cutting me off.

I kissed the top of her head, "You go with Shiro now, I am sure you would like to get to know him. Let him show you how to magicae as well, it is a handy thing to know. Oh, and don't say anything to your sister. You know we have to approach her a bit differently."

She turned to look at him feeling a little shy, "Wow I still can't believe he is in my life now. We feel very similar almost like brother and sister but there is just this inner love there. I'll call you tomorrow to talk about Charlotte."

I nodded hugging her again, "Just take it easy with Shiro as well, he is new to this world." She rolled her eyes, "Ok Mum. See you, Ferdinand."

She walked over to Shiro taking his hand, "Are you ready to take me home Shiro?" He looked down at her lovingly, "Yes, I am. See you Hannah and Ferdinand."

I sighed feeling quite happy with the way things had turned out with Amelia, smiling to myself as I dried the dishes.

Ferdinand was watching me, turning to give me a hug, "One down and one to go."

I chuckled, "Mmm yes, the difficult one to go. Can we go for a ride after this?"

He gave me a kiss on the cheek, "I thought you'd never ask." We finished the dishes with him flicking water at me just as he was about to pull the plug. I giggled then quickly got the towel to flick him in the bum, getting him just in the right spot.

He grabbed the towel then me, "Agghh you little minx," magicaeing out of the lounge landing on his back soaring across the water.

I couldn't stop giggling feeling like a kid again, with the delight of the sea air rushing up to me, the inky black sky above with twinkling stars making me feel free.

I leaned on his neck putting my arms around him, looking at the sea hearing a splashing noise with Ferdinand pointing "look, a whale." There was only a quarter moon but there was enough light hitting the whale's skin, as it rose out of the water making its skin look shiny and clean.

As it went under it flicked its tale at us as though it was saying hello, making me grin with delight.

Chapter 8

I woke to the phone ringing, groaning to pick it up, noticing it was Amelia. Ferdinand had Kimba next to him, stirring to look to see if it was anything urgent.

I rolled onto my back, "Hi Amelia, is everything alright?"

She sounded all excited, "I've spoken with Charlotte already and told her we will come down to see her."

I groaned, "Amelia what did I say last night about not saying anything to her?"

Amelia started talking fast now, "We have to get this done Mum, Lilith was saying that there are people out there who would love our magic, especially our old family magic."

I yawned, "When did you say we would come to see her?" She was giggling, "Today. Shiro and I will come around soon and pick you two up."

I yawned again, "No Amelia we are still in bed and it's too early to go. Give us a couple of hours at least and message me when you're coming."

Amelia giggled again, "Oohh what are you two doing?"

I sighed, "Amelia we aren't doing anything but sleeping, well trying to, at least. Do your Jardine reading then message me in a couple of hours to see if we are up."

Amelia sounded disappointed, "Ok. See you later."

I looked at the time, "Good grief it's only 6.00am. That's early for her to be up on a Sunday." Kimba jumped off the bed, with Ferdinand rolling over to me, putting his arm around my waist, "Sounds like we're going to see Charlotte?"

I sighed, "Yes, and Amelia has already been talking to her, so just be ready."

Ferdinand groaned, "I won't hang around too long at first, so you can get her used to the idea; but I will be back in the evening."

I rolled my eyes, "Ok sounds like a good plan." We went back to a light sleep hearing a beep exactly after 2 hours from Amelia saying she would be there in half an hour. Ferdinand leaned over me picking up the phone reading it, "Hannah, Amelia and Shiro will be here in half an hour."

I groaned rolling into his neck, kissing it, "I might tell her we'll go tomorrow."

He chuckled, "I think she has already made up her mind, like another stubborn person I know. Come on, we may as well get it over and done with."

We eventually got up getting dressed with Amelia and Shiro arriving just as Ferdinand was starting to cook some scrambled eggs on toast, while I was still in the bathroom. Shiro looked at Ferdinand, "Mm what are you cooking Ferdinand?"

Amelia came into me, "Hi Mum are you just about ready?"

I was putting some mascara on, "Yes, we just have to have some breakfast then we can go. Are you having some?"

Amelia looked ready to go, "Oh I suppose Shiro will want something more. We had toast at home, but then we have to go. We thought it would be best to stay the night; you know how stubborn Charlotte is with new things."

I nodded, "Yes, I'll put a couple of things in a backpack. Have you got anything?"

She smiled, "You'll be proud of me I have only brought a backpack as well; Charlotte is going to die of shock."

We had some breakfast and put some extra food out for Kimba to save coming back. I put some magical locks on the unit just in case, putting a jacket on, then took off to Devonport in Tasmania. We landed down by the water near the cenotaph in the park, looking around to see if any people noticed us just appearing, but there weren't too many people around.

The sea looked beautiful, clean but menacingly cold with just a slight wave action hitting the pebbles on the beach, moving them up and down with a clattering noise.

A ferry had not long docked in the harbour, so you could hear cars and people coming off it, from the mainland.

A sharp cool breeze came off the water hitting us as we all shivered. Ferdinand rubbed my hands, "I think you should put gloves on those hands of yours and do your jacket up, you've just gotten over a cold?"

I smiled, "Yes dear. I don't think I need the gloves; Charlotte's place is not far from here" looking down to do my jacket up.

We headed towards Charlotte's place which was a short walk from the water. I stopped before we turned into the Charlotte's Street, "Maybe you and Shiro should go, that way we can get her used to the idea of you two being around."

Amelia grumbled, "Oh stop fussing Mum, I have spoken to her about Ferdinand and Shiro. She is going to have to get used to it."

I didn't feel very optimistic, with Ferdinand shrugging his shoulders, "We'll see what happens. If she gets too annoyed Shiro and I will go and let you two sort it out. We won't stay that long anyway, but we will be back in the evening."

We got to Charlotte's place, which was a simple wooden bungalow with a veranda in front to protect the door from the weather, which was just off the main street. It had a lawn out the front with a small garden near the lounge window in the front.

Amelia smiled, "We should just magicae into the lounge and give her a fright."

I shook my head smiling, "You're terrible Amelia, no we will knock on the door."

Ferdinand chuckled, "Gee I wonder who she got that sense of humour off?"

I glared at him turning to knock on the door.

I couldn't hear anything, so I got my phone out to ring her, when she opened the door, looking at us all standing there. She looked a little sleepy, "Hi, you are early."

She was wearing sweat pants and top with big thick socks and fluffy slippers on. Her hair was just bundled up into an untidy bun, but she still managed to look good.

Charlotte yawned, "Come in it's a bit cold out there," looking past me and Amelia not saying anything to Ferdinand and Shiro.

We went into the lounge with the fire smouldering, with two big sofas and some bean bags and a big rug down in front of the hearth.

She looked sarcastically at Amelia, "So where's your big bag, Amelia?"

Amelia laughed, "Just travelling light, Charlotte. This is Shiro and that is Ferdinand who I told you about."

Ferdinand was holding my hand looking unsure how to approach Charlotte.

I could see Charlotte's mood change as she made a motion towards Ferdinand, feeling his hand whip out of mine. I heard a thud as he was sent to a chair with his hands cuffed behind his back.

Ferdinand yelled, "Agghh Hannah tell her to let me go!"

I looked bemused at her trying not to smirk, "Charlotte why did you do that?"

Ferdinand was struggling looking annoyed at Charlotte, "Let me go Charlotte, now!"

Charlotte growled, "Nanna told me to keep a dark-haired man away from you Mum and that is what I am doing. Why was he holding your hand?"

I shook my head, "Well Nanna isn't around and I am sure this isn't the dark-haired man she was talking about because he is my guardian animal and friend. Now let him go!"

She was being stubborn crossing her arms, "He doesn't look gay; how do I know he isn't the guy Nanna was talking about?"

Amelia was losing her patience as well, "For goodness' sake Charlotte, I told you about him last night when we were talking, now let him go."

I took my jacket off putting it on the sofa, "Let him go, then he and Shiro can go away for a while to give us a chance to talk."

Shiro looked nervous moving closer to Amelia, whispering, "She's not going to do that to me is she?"

Amelia looked annoyed taking her jacket off, "She better not."

Charlotte heard Amelia deciding to relent in the end, waving over to Ferdinand releasing him as she watched him get up and rubbing his wrists, "You Dragĕ women and your tempers."

I went over to him, "Are you alright?" He put his arm around me looking wide eyed and daring at Charlotte, then gave me a kiss on the cheek, "Yes, I'm alright. I think we'll get going though. We'll see you later this evening. I'm not going anywhere Charlotte so you had better get used to me being around," and taking off with Shiro.

Charlotte glared at him, flopping on the sofa, not saying anything until they left. I moved over to the fire giving it a stir to get the embers flaring and putting some wood on it. I put my hand out visualising fire in the palm of my hand and blowing it towards the fire. It burst into life as I put my hands out to warm them against the flames.

Charlotte was watching me, "So it is true that you've got your magic?"

I got up nodding, "Yes finally, and I'm learning a lot."

I moved over to sit on the sofa, "So why did Nanna say to keep the dark-haired man away from me?"

Charlotte shrugged her shoulders looking sulky, "I can't remember what the reason was."

Amelia sat down on the sofa as well challenging Charlotte, "It didn't matter what coloured hair the bloke had, you frightened him away."

Charlotte turned looking annoyed at her sister with me, feeling the tension between them rising said, "That's enough you two. Amelia said that Nanna used to let you two perform magic shows. You have obviously retained some of your magic. What else do you know?"

Charlotte was still annoyed shrugging her shoulders, "Just little things come out, especially when I'm angry at someone. Just lately though, things have been coming into my head and I've been having dreams about relatives. I'm not sure who they are though."

Amelia sighed, "Well are you going to join with us Charlotte?"

I looked over to her annoyed giving her a look, with Amelia putting her hands up questioning, "What Mum? I had a good talk with her last night and she was alright; so, I don't see why she is being so stubborn."

Charlotte got up frustrated, "Oh be quiet Amelia, I can make up my own mind."

I turned to look at Amelia shushing her quietly. I got up, "Tell you what I will bring the family book out so you can have a look at that part at least. You don't have to make up your mind about Jardine or anything else until you are ready."

Amelia jumped up excited, "Yes that's a great idea, Mum."

Charlotte half-heartedly agreed, "Do you want a drink of water or something before we do that?"

I nodded, "Yes a drink of water would be good."

Amelia followed her out, "Do you have some juice or something?"

Charlotte groaned, "It's not a coffee shop you know."

I pointed to the fridge putting some juice in there, hearing Charlotte in exclamation, "How did that get in there?"

Amelia giggled, "Mum did you do that?"

I smiled nodding, "Yes, I did. It's fun sometimes, isn't it?"

They came back with their drinks and one for me, as I sat on a beanbag leaning up against the sofa for support and my legs out in front of me.

Amelia laughed, "Are you sure you should sit like that, Mum?"

I sighed, "I probably shouldn't, but it is the best way for you two to see what I'm about to do."

Amelia and Charlotte came and sat next to me ready to watch what I did, feeling nice having just us three again, in front of a roaring fire, doing something together.

I pointed to the four corners of the room we were in saying, *"Lukk Taigh"* with the sound of locks being heard going around us, "You have to do this every time you bring the book out girls, because there are a few people who would love to get their hands on it."

Amelia looked at Charlotte excitedly, with Charlotte trying to hide her expression.

I put my hands out together with my palms up, blowing a white mist onto them saying, *"Apen leabhar"* bringing the book onto the palms of my hands with the Dragĕ name standing out on the leather binding; as the girls move in closer to have a look at it. I opened the front cover revealing the family tree, pointing out to the girls their names along with the different symbols next to them, as shown to me by Morag. They quietly looked at their names emblazoned in the book with their other relatives along with mine.

On the opposite page as before a notification came up in blood, "Welcome Hannah and Amelia is Charlotte ready to join the family book?"

Charlotte gasped, "Wow I didn't expect that. It looks a lot different from when Nanna showed it to us."

I took a deep breath, trying not to bring those feelings out again, clearing my throat, "I have made some modern improvements to bring it up to the 21st century."

The ink well appeared along with the feather, which sat on top of the page. Charlotte looked at me then back at the page, "What does it want me to do?"

Amelia butted in, "It wants you to prick your finger and give your blood for a DNA match, just like in one of your labs."

I smiled at her, "It's up to you whether you want to do it Charlotte. It gives you access to the book whenever you want to have a look at it."

Charlotte took a few short sharp breaths, "This feels so strange, even though I know Nanna has talked about it for years. To be honest I thought she was just going a bit senile or something, especially since you two didn't have a very good relationship."

Amelia sighed, "Well if you're not going to do it, you can't look at the book. I would like to have a look at it while Mum has it out at least, so you'll have to move away from it."

Irritated now Charlotte grabbed the feather, pricking her finger, "Ouch" making it bleed and putting the blood in the inkwell. Her blood slowly dripped into the inkwell filling it enough to cover the bottom, with a cursor appearing as though it was thinking, then a light scanned Charlotte.

Charlotte smiled, "Wow you have made it really secure, haven't you Mum? Maybe that is why you were denied access to it for all those years; you're quite clever."

I grumbled, "Yes, a few people have said that to me. I still feel cheated that I haven't had the choice, but I am not going to dwell on that," and taking a deep breath, "I'm going to enjoy the experience with you two girls."

The book finished scanning Charlotte with a wavering sentence coming up, *"Welcome Charlotte Dragĕ to the family book. This completes the Dragĕ family who are currently living and you now have the power of three. We hope you enjoy your experience with the family magic."* The fire in front of us, roared with bursts of stars popping out of the fireplace, as the book confirmed that all three were initiated into it.

We all looked at each other grinning like we had just won the lottery, with me grabbing their hands, "Wow I didn't think that was going to happen, but I'm glad we are all in it now."

Amelia and Charlotte gripped my hands in delight with Amelia saying, "This is going to be fun."

Charlotte, the realist, was sucking her finger, "Technically I'm not a Dragĕ by name but I suppose I am by blood."

Amelia sighed, "You are the only one who has chosen to keep Dad's surname but, yes you do have the Dragĕ blood in you."

I looked at the two of them, "Is there anything in particular you would like to look at?"

They sat there thinking for a few minutes sighing, "Even if you think of something from Harry Potter or some other witchy film, which is what I did in the end."

Amelia put her hand up, "Ah change our looks. Do we need a special potion for that?"

I shrugged my shoulders, "I don't know ask it for a spell to change your looks?"

Amelia put her hand over the book, "Show me a spell how to change my looks."

The book started to flip pages as the girls watched amazed. I leaned back on the sofa a bit more watching the delight in their faces, with the shine of the fire hitting their eyes light them up brightly.

The pages stopped flipping over with Amelia, Charlotte and I moving forward to have a look at where it stopped. Charlotte looked at the words on the page, then back to me, "It doesn't make sense."

I smiled knowingly at them, "Because that is the original security system and I left it on. You have to put your hand over it to make it turn into something that you can understand."

Amelia leaned forward putting her hand over the page as a white light appeared from her palm, watching as the words turned into something legible. She opened her mouth taking a deep breath, clapping her hands, "Oh wow that is fantastic."

She moved forward a bit more reading it, "*A sprig of lavender a white ribbon with a gem of smoky quartz on the wrist will see the change you envision and wish. Say this rhyme to say what age, gender you wish to be at this time. This will last only half past the hour unless you repeat thrice for the full hour.*"

Amelia sat back, "Oh we don't have those things."

I put my hand out putting the other one over top, envisioning lavender, white ribbon and smoky quartz times two, with it appearing and handing it to them.

Their faces brightened up, with Charlotte finally getting into the mood, "I'm going to have to practice that one. I'm always forgetting things."

They threaded ribbon through the smoky quartz putting it on their wrist not sure where to put the lavender. I suggested, "Put it in your bra for now, that way you won't lose it. Now remember you don't want to stay like it too long this time." They smiled putting the lavender in their bras.

I could see them thinking of who they would want to look like, giggling as Amelia said the rhyme changing into Kim Kardashian while Charlotte said the rhyme changing into Jennifer Aniston from *Friends*.

They looked at each other laughing hysterically, as I chuckled with them, looking at them, "Wow that works well. It might come in handy later on."

They both got up dancing around the lounge then looking in the mirror. Amelia flicked her black hair as she looked in the mirror, "Wow this is fabulous. I wonder if you don't want to do it for so long how to break the spell. Maybe just take the charms off. I'll try it."

She took the lavender out of her bra and the white ribbon and crystal off her wrist, which changed her back to herself instantly, "Oh that's good to know as well."

Charlotte was stroking her hair like Rachel would in *Friends*. "Imagine the looks you'd get as you walked down the street." She too took the charms off, changing back to herself.

They were still both giggling like they used to when they were young, making me feel quite content. Amelia took the book off my lap, "Here I'll take it and help you up Mum. I'd like to just have a bit a look through. I'm sure Charlotte wants to, as well."

I put my knees up rolling over as they both took an arm each helping me up, "Gee that makes me feel old. My hips just don't want to work like they used to."

I got up shaking my legs out poking the fire and putting some more wood on, while they took the book over to the table to have a look at it.

I sat back on the sofa drinking my water listening to them chatter over different things they had found in the book. They must have gone over to the back page and found the family crest with Amelia calling out to me, "Is this the family crest, Mum?"

I went over to have a look, "Yes. It needs to be completed, doesn't it? I got a crystal dagger from this strange woman and once I joined it to the book it filled in the sword part. Now we have to find the shield. I'm not sure why the dragon isn't filled in, as I have Ferdinand who is a dragon. Maybe it is another dragon' I'm not sure."

Just as we were standing there pondering over the family crest, I felt a presence in the room, feeling goose bumps come over me as the temperature dropped, "I think we have a visitor, girls," as they looked up from the book.

I looked around the room finally seeing a ghostly figure start to appear near the fireplace, with Amelia coming over to me. Charlotte stayed with the book closing it and bringing it over to me.

I looked at them both, then turned to the ghost realising it was the one that had come in my meditation, "Hello bestemor (hello grandma)." As the face formed a smile appeared, "Hei Drage familie (hello Drage family)." She floated over towards us with Amelia moving closer to me, "Who is it, Mum?"

I shrugged my shoulders, "She won't tell me her name, but she is a part of the family." She smiled, "Du har gjort det bra Hannah (you have done well Hannah)."

Charlotte hung onto the book, "What language is she speaking, Mum?"

The ghost moved closer to Charlotte who was hanging onto the book, "Familieboka. Beskytte den godt Charlotte (the Family book. Protect it well Charlotte)."

Charlotte smiled nervously, "Can you speak English?"

I looked over to Charlotte, "She is speaking Norwegian Charlotte the old family language."

The ghost laughed softly, "Auf Wiedersehen meine familie (good bye my family)" fading out.

I sighed, "She spoke German then; I didn't know there was German in the family."

Amelia looked at me, "Did you understand her mum?"

Charlotte moved closer still holding the book, looking at me, as I nodded at them, "Yes, I did for some reason. Since I got this tattoo on my back, I have been able to. I meant to show you before, but got side tracked with showing you the book."

I turned lifting my top showing them the tattoo on my back, which was just about completed. Both my girls bent down to look with Amelia touching it, "It is the same as the family crest and it is just about complete."

I turned to look, "Oh is it. I wonder if that is because you girls are joined to the book? Where's your mirror, Charlotte?"

She pointed to her bedroom, "In my bedroom over there."

I went and had a look wondering what it meant. I came back in sitting on the sofa with the girls coming to join me on the sofa.

Charlotte put the book on her lap opening it up to look at something else "maybe there is something in here about the tattoo Mum?" The girls continued to look at the book a bit more with the fire burning well, feeling relaxed again.

I started to yawn, "I'm feeling a bit sleepy, do you want to get some fresh air and go and get some lunch. Is there a nice café near here Charlotte?"

She thought about it, "Yes Café XoXo is quite nice and it's not far from here."

I yawned again, "We'll put the book away and open up the house. Do one of you want to do that for practice?"

Amelia spoke up before Charlotte, "I'll send the book back. Charlotte can have go at unlocking the house."

I told Amelia what to do as I watched her do it. She put the book on her hands blowing on it sending it back saying, *"Lukk leabhar."* We all watched as it disappeared from her hands, with a big smile coming over her face.

I told Charlotte what to say, watching her point to the four corners of the room, *"Apen taigh"* hearing the lock sounds open around the room. Charlotte and Amelia hugged each other then, hugged me in excitement like little girls.

I moved away smiling putting my jacket on, "Oh where do we put our bags, Charlotte?"

Charlotte was just putting her jacket on, "Just in that room off the lounge. Amelia can sleep with you as your snoring will drive me nuts."

I looked rebuffed "I don't snore, it's just when I've got sinus."

Amelia chuckled as she was putting her jacket on, "Yeah sure Mum," turning to look at Amelia, "Thanks Amelia."

Amelia had a cheeky look on her face, "Ferdinand can take Mum to a hotel, that way I can have Shiro with me."

Charlotte went quiet, "You're sleeping together? I thought he was your guardian animal?"

I looked disappointed at her, "He is also a man and I like the company, as I've been on my own for a long time. We aren't having sex either. Amelia is sleeping with Shiro already. You're not going to carry on making a fuss are you, Charlotte?"

She sighed, "No I won't make a fuss, but it doesn't mean I'm happy with it."

Amelia smiled at me, "We should show Charlotte what else we can do," and looked at Charlotte with a cunning grin.

I put my hand up, "Hang on put the fire guard up and lock the door, Charlotte."

Charlotte looked confused going to lock the door, putting the key in her pocket.

Amelia waved her over, "Come here, Charlotte," and taking her hand, "Come on Mum, take Charlotte's other hand" and doing as she asked, smiling, "Get ready Charlotte," as we magicae out of the room.

We could hear Charlotte squeal, "OMG" landing a short distance from the coffee shop. Charlotte stumbled, nearly making me fall, as she pulled me up, "Wow that was amazing." We all giggled, "It's fun, isn't it?"

We walked up to the café finding a seat and ordering some food. Charlotte had one more question with regard to Ferdinand, "So are you going to tell Dad you have a new boyfriend?"

Amelia shook her head in disbelief, "Good grief Charlotte, Dad hasn't been to see Mum for years, why would she bother to tell him that."

I put my head on the side with a faint smile, "That's right Charlotte, you know your father and I don't talk and haven't for a long time. I'm not stopping you from spending time with him, but don't think I'm ever going back to him." She put her head down looking at her hands, "Ok, I just thought I would ask."

Chapter 9

We had a nice meal and a coffee deciding to walk along the waterfront to get some fresh air, as it was quite warm in the café, filling up with a lot of people.

We were all relaxed and joking with each other as we walked along throwing stones in the water to see who could skip them the most. Amelia starting joking with Charlotte, "So are you going to get your guardian animal now Charlotte, I wonder what it will be?"

Charlotte smiled nervously, "I don't know yet Amelia, stop being pushy."

I gave Amelia a look making her settle down. Charlotte moved away from us to get some stones to throw in the water, when a woman approached her almost as though she came out of nowhere.

I stopped to watch her talking to Charlotte, with an uneasy feeling coming over me. I moved closer, indicating to Amelia to come over. As Amelia and I approached Charlotte, the woman looked nervously at us.

I reached Charlotte first, trying to sound calm, "Charlotte we are going home now, as I'm getting a bit cold?"

Charlotte looked at me not sure of my expression, then looked at the woman she was talking to, "Mum this is Sarina who I met in the pub the other night." Sarina was moving closer to Charlotte as though she was going to grab her.

A chant came into my head while I smiled, trying to look friendly, putting my hand out to shake her hand, "Hi Sarina I am Charlotte's mother."

She smiled nervously, feeling obligated to shake my hand; once I connected, I said the chant, *"Liar, liar, Sarina your plans will misfire; until you tell the truth your hand will feel on fire so mote it be."*

Sarina's face screwed up in pain as I held onto her hand, "What's your plans Sarina?" She was trying to shake her hand free, "I don't know what you mean, let me go, Hannah."

Charlotte was looking confused, "Mum what are you doing?"

I smirked at Charlotte, "I didn't tell her my name, did you?"

She thought about it, "No I didn't."

Sarina buckled under my grip that was burning her hand, "Tell me what your plans are, Sarina."

Amelia and Charlotte shielded me and Sarina from passers-by. Amelia looked angrily at Sarina, "Come on, Mum will hurt you more, if you don't tell us."

Sarina's face screwed up in pain, "I was trying to get Charlotte to join us. We know about your family magic and that Charlotte hasn't joined Jardine yet, agghh let me go, Hannah."

I let go of her hand, noticing welt marks on her hand, from my hand, "Who are you with Sarina?" Another two women appeared behind us, with Sarina giving them away by smiling cunningly at them. Amelia and Charlotte turned to confront them with Amelia growling, sending a bolt of light to one of them, knocking her over. The woman emitted a loud cry of pain as she rolled on the ground. Charlotte blew a whirlwind towards the other one knocking her off her feet, as she screamed while being buffeted by the wind.

Sarina tried to run for it, so I sent a mini whirlwind towards her knocking her over. I then moved my hands up levitating her in the air as she flayed her arms and legs getting angry, "Let me go Hannah!"

Ferdinand and Shiro appeared taking in the scene, with Ferdinand calling to me, "Let her go Hannah, we have to go."

I smirked holding Sarina in mid-air while she yelled at me, "I didn't call you?"

Ferdinand came over to me with a determined look on his face, "There are others coming" and took my hand, walking over to Charlotte who had sent a bolt of light to the other woman.

Ferdinand grabbed her hand as she tried to pull away, "Let me go Ferdinand, we are alright," magicaeing out of there putting us on his back, flying over the water.

Shiro in the meantime had run up to Amelia taking her hand, "Come on Amelia, it's time to go," with Amelia stopping smiling sweetly at him, magicaeing out of there.

Charlotte was yelling trying to find somewhere to hold on, so I leaned forward guiding her towards the harness, "Here hold onto this, Charlotte."

She took it nervously holding on, "Why did they come and get us; we were doing alright?"

Ferdinand flew back over where we were, "Look down there, a group of women were coming to fight with you," as he dipped his body showing us a group of women forming.

Charlotte was still holding on tightly, "We can fire at them from here," with Ferdinand looking back shaking his head going out to sea.

I held on to Charlotte, "Mum we could have fought them." I shook my head, "No I think we would have been out numbered, you will probably find that Ferdinand and Shiro were sent by one of the elders. Just relax and enjoy the ride for now."

Charlotte leaned back onto me holding onto the harness, "Wow this is beautiful isn't it, Mum. No wonder you don't want to let him go."

I smiled lovingly, "Yes that is one of the reasons I don't want to let him go. Look down there a whale is breaching for us," and watched it jump up into the air with Charlotte smiling, "Oh its wonderful seeing it up close isn't it, Mum?"

Ferdinand looked back, "Are you ready to go back there are people waiting for us?"

Charlotte looked back at me, "Yes Ferdinand, we better get back."

He magicae the rest of the way back, landing in the lounge, with Ferdinand holding both of our hands, landing unsteadily, having to hold us up, shaking his head. He then dropped our hands quickly, "Is it a family trait of falling over on landing and having no blood circulate through your hands."

He pointed to my hands putting gloves of them with a look of agitation, "I don't need these on Ferdinand," and went to take them off.

He came over, "Leave them on until your hands warm up—please." He put his hands on my shoulders turning me around to show me who else was in the room, "We are not alone, Hannah."

I looked around to see Morag and Lilith standing there with solemn faces.

I looked up at Ferdinand, "We aren't in trouble, are we?"

He helped me take off my jacket, shaking his head, "No I don't think so."

Charlotte took off her jacket looking around coming over to me, "Who are they, Mum?"

I put my arm around her shoulder steering her towards the women, "One of them is an elder of Jardine, so be nice."

Amelia was already on the sofa with Shiro waiting for us to come in.

Morag came over to me giving me a hug, "Are you and your girls alright Hannah?"

I hugged her back, "Yes Morag, we are fine. I guess we didn't expect that attack though; thank you for sending Ferdinand and Shiro to help."

Morag pulled back from me looking at the gloves on my hands, as I looked over to Ferdinand, "He doesn't like my cold hands for some reason," making her chuckle.

I brought Charlotte forward, "This is my youngest daughter, Charlotte. This is Morag Charlotte, an elder of Jardine."

Charlotte looked a little unsure, with Morag coming in and giving her a hug, "It is nice to finally meet you, Charlotte. It is unfortunate we had to barge into your home like this, but we could see trouble brewing, which is why we sent Ferdinand and Shiro in to help you all. I see you have some magic within you, but I don't think you would have been strong enough to combat all of those women."

Charlotte looked at me for reassurance, with me smiling at her, "I assume you are from Jardine. Nanna told me a little bit about it, which in some ways is why I have always tried to fight for nature."

I took the gloves off feeling my hands warm up putting them in my pocket.

Morag looked kindly at Charlotte putting a hand up to her face, "You are like your mother, but remind me of someone else, I just can't remember who though. As long as you are all safe that is why we came."

Amelia came up to join the group, "So Charlotte are you going to join Jardine now?"

Charlotte groaned, "Just stop it Amelia I want to get over being attacked first!"

I watched Lilith talking to Ferdinand who was poking the fire to get it burning again. Ferdinand appeared not to be concentrating on what Lilith was saying, but watching the fire as it started to build up. Lilith tapped him on the shoulder, making him look up with a look reminding me of myself when I'm in a bit of a daze. He smiled briefly at her, "Sorry I was thinking about the attack." Lilith looked annoyed and walked off.

I turned back to Morag, "I am worried about how those women found out so quickly that Charlotte had joined with the family book Morag. Do you have any thoughts on it?"

Morag looked concerned as well as she watched Charlotte walk over to the kitchen, "Yes, I am worried as well, Hannah. What did that woman say to you when you put the liar chant on her?"

I smiled amazed, "You don't miss much do you Morag. She said that she knew Charlotte had joined with the family book but wanted to get to her before she joined Jardine."

Morag put her hand up to her chin thinking, '*Mmm this group must be quite strong here if they can pick that up. Did you lock the house before you brought it out?*'

I nodded, "Yes I did, and I showed the girls how to do it if they wanted to bring the book out."

I sighed, "Someone has suggested to me that a piece of jewellery I am wearing has had a spell put on it. I was going to sit down once we got back from lunch to check some of my jewellery."

Morag thought for a few minutes, "Yes that is quite possible, Hannah, especially when you went to that meditation meeting. It doesn't take much to do that, if they are good at it. Can I ask who the person was that suggested it?"

I smiled at her knowingly, "You know I have a connection with ghosts; let's just say it was one of my ancestors."

Morag smiled then looked at the jewellery I had on, "Do you want to take off your jewellery and we can put it under a cleansing spell?"

I walked over to the table in Charlotte's dining area, taking all my jewellery off putting it on the table. Ferdinand came up behind me, putting his arm around my waist, "What's happening Hannah?"

I looked up to him smiling, "Morag is going to check my jewellery to see if I have a tracer on them. They appear to be finding us a bit too quickly for my liking."

I put my clear quartz necklace that I quite often wear and had worn to the meditation meeting I went to, on the table as well, looking over to Morag. Lilith, Amelia and Charlotte came over to see what we were doing, as Morag waved her hands saying a cleansing chant over my jewellery.

The clear quartz necklace started to rattle on the table with a loud pop and a black wisp rise from it. I shook my head, "Wow there it is. I wonder how that got on there?"

Amelia and Charlotte stood there staring with Amelia saying, "Did that have a tracker on it or something Mum?"

I nodded, "Yes Amelia, that is how they knew where I was all the time."

Charlotte moved off, "I think I need some wine, anyone else want one?"

Shiro followed her into the kitchen, "I'll help you Charlotte, just in case you need some extra things."

They came out with some glasses of wine on a tray with everyone helping themselves as they walked around.

Ferdinand brought out some snacks handing them around coming back to me, "Well that was interesting about the jewellery, who do you think put it on."

I shook my head, "I don't know, but if I find out, I'll be dealing with them."

I leaned into him as he put his arm around my waist, "Thanks for coming to get us. It has helped with Charlotte towards you a little, as well."

He smiled, "I knew my charm would get there eventually."

I laughed, "You are funny. I think I will text my boss and take a couple more days off on sick leave. Charlotte is still hesitating about joining Jardine and I don't want to pressure her because I have to get back to work."

He squeezed my waist, "Anything to get out of going back to work, I know you Hannah Dragĕ."

I looked shocked, "Ferdinand I have lots of sick leave thank you very much, but there is someone who I am enjoying being around."

He bent down giving me a kiss on the cheek, "I'm enjoying it to."

There were a couple of sets of eyes on us while we did this. Charlotte took another sip of wine sighing not sure how she felt about me being with this man. Lilith came and sat next to her, "Hi Charlotte I'm Lilith, we haven't really been properly introduced."

Charlotte smiled, "Hi Lilith, so where do you fit in to all of this?"

Lilith glanced over to Ferdinand and I and then back, "I'm not an elder but I am a senior woman in Jardine, I guess you would call it that. At the moment, I am helping Morag with your mother and you two with your new found magic. How are you finding all of this?"

Charlotte shrugged her shoulders, "I've known about it since I was young, Nanna would talk about it to us constantly. I'm not sure if Nanna was quite right in the head near the end though talking about Mum keeping away from some man."

Lilith looked curious, "Oh why do you think she would say that, Charlotte?"

Charlotte started to feel uncomfortable talking to this woman she didn't know that well, "I don't know Lilith maybe she just didn't want Mum getting hurt again. I know she looks a lot happier than she has been for a long time." This made Lilith flop back in the sofa taking a sip of wine which Charlotte noticed, deciding to change the subject, "So where is your spirit/guardian animal, Lilith?"

Lilith not really interested in the conversation, vaguely said, "Oh he is in Jardine."

Charlotte was getting suspicious now (she was a bit like me in that regard), "So what animal is it?"

Lilith was thinking not really listening, "Oh he is a leopard and his name is Pardus."

Charlotte kept on, "So what animal do you think I will get? Would it be a dragon like Mum?"

Lilith shook her head, "Generally you don't get the same animal as another member of the family, it is up to mother nature in the end. As you see your sister got Shiro. Are you thinking of joining?"

Charlotte realised while she was talking to Lilith that I was happier than I had been in a long time. She knew part of that was being back with herself and Amelia, but she could see the love growing between Ferdinand and I, as well as the motherly relationship she had developed with Morag; something she didn't have with her own mother. This was enough to help her make up her mind, "Yes I think I will join."

Lilith looked surprised, "Oh I got the impression you were a bit reluctant."

Charlotte sighed, "I admit at first, I thought it was one of Mum's 'spiritual' things she was trying to get us into again. She used to take us to church, which, I admit I enjoyed in the children's groups, but I knew they used to treat her terribly, because she was a single parent. You just made me realise it is more than that, thanks Lilith."

Charlotte got up smiling at her, walking over to me looking at Ferdinand, then back to me, "Mum I'm ready to join Jardine."

I grinned hugging her, "Oh Charlotte that is wonderful. Go and let Morag know and she can organise it."

Ferdinand smiled, joking with Charlotte, "Was it my charm Charlotte?"

Charlotte groaned, "I'm still deciding on you Ferdinand, don't push it; you now have three magical women to deal with."

I chuckled walking away to compose myself but Ferdinand caught my hand looking nervous, "You know she is right, what have I got myself into."

I turned to hug him, "You'll be alright."

He hugged me back, "You don't need to take the time off work now."

I giggled again, "It's too late I've already sent the text and he has said it was fine." He gave me a squeeze, "Oh well more time for us to spend together."

Morag clapped her hands in delight giving Charlotte a hug, "Oh that is wonderful Charlotte, I will send for the ceremony team straight away."

Amelia came over to Charlotte giving her a big hug, "You won't regret it, sis."

Cara, Louella and Adesa arrived surprising Charlotte still, smiling at me, "I still can't get used to people popping in and out like this."

Lilith came over putting her arm around her shoulders, "I'll just tell you what is going to happen Charlotte. I will change your clothes," waving her hands in front of Charlotte changing her clothes to the white robes the others had on.

Lilith continued, "Dirt will be placed on the ground that you will stand on. The three women will surround you doing a chant that you probably will not understand. Once this chant starts, roots will cover your feet to join you with mother nature. From the experience of your mother and sister you may feel a power surge, how strong your magic is, depends on how strong the surge will be. Are you sure you wish to proceed, Charlotte?"

Charlotte looked at the robe that she had on with its different kind of material she had never seen. She smiled nodding, "Yes I am happy to proceed Lilith."

I went up and gave her a hug and a kiss, "Just relax, close your eyes and enjoy it, Charlotte. We all did it and we are alright."

Ferdinand came over putting his arm around my waist, "Enjoy it, Charlotte you will belong to a great family once it is over."

Charlotte looked at both me and Ferdinand and said, "Thanks."

Ferdinand steered me away from the ceremony "no sending kisses or anything Hannah. We want the women to survive this last one."

I chuckled, "You're just exaggerating, Ferdinand. Amelia's ceremony was alright."

Ferdinand moved us away from the ceremony, enough so any powers off me, wouldn't connect. Ferdinand stood behind me with his arms around my waist as we watched Lilith get Charlotte ready for the ceremony asking her to take her shoes and socks off and step onto the dirt. Charlotte looked over to me with her eyes bright and a nervous smile on her lips.

I nodded going to send her a kiss with Ferdinand putting his hand on my arm leaning down, "Hannah don't be naughty."

I sighed, "It's alright I have already given her a kiss on the cheek anyway."

Ferdinand groaned, "I hope there wasn't any magic in that?"

I shook my head, "No just a mother's love."

The ceremony began as Charlotte stepped onto the dirt, along with the three women doing their chant. The roots formed over Charlottes feet, joining her with mother earth. I could feel my emotions well up again, but because this was Charlotte, who was the stubborn one, tears fell. I wiped my eyes, with Ferdinand leaning down giving me a kiss on the cheek, then producing a tissue to wipe my eyes.

As the three women got deeper into the chant, a white light formed around Charlotte then a pink sparkly light followed, entwining around her body, hitting the three women doing the chant. Ferdinand leaned down, "Hannah did you do anything?"

I wiped my eyes shaking my head, "No you know I haven't done anything dear."

Just as the three women got to the pitch of their chant, small orbs came from the pink and white light with the sound of voices coming from them, bouncing around the circle. Two of the orbs came out of the circle hitting me and Amelia in the chest, making us throw our arms out, pushing Ferdinand and Shiro away from us.

I threw my head back groaning. Taking it in, while I heard the ancestors chuckle with glee, *"At last the power of three."* It was only brief, but I knew it was a powerful surge, feeling the strength within. I looked over to Amelia who was grinning with the power surge hitting her, "Wow Mum that was fantastic."

We both then looked at Ferdinand and Shiro, getting up off the floor, as I flinched, "Oops."

I went over to help Ferdinand up, as he glared at me, "Are you sure you didn't do anything Hannah?"

I shook my head, "No I didn't. You already know she has been accepted by the family book ... oh did I tell you that?"

He shook his head, "Your incorrigible, aren't you?"

I grinned, "I guess not dear. Looks like the family are happy at least. Look it didn't hurt the Jardine women either, so stop fussing."

The three Jardine women didn't get any benefit from the power surge, other than making their hair stand up a bit again. Once they had stopped chanting, they looked at each other smiling feeling peaceful, separating and patting each other on the back as Louella said, "Thank goodness that was the last Dragĕ woman. If they have any children, I'm going to retire."

I went over to Charlotte to see if she was alright, with Amelia following to, giving her a hug smiling, "Wow that was a great power hit, sis."

I hugged her, "Looks like the family are happy with us joining together."

After a few minutes, we separated and Morag came over to us with a nervous smile on her face, "Well you Dragĕ women certainly know how to surprise us. We didn't expect that."

I looked a little sheepishly, "Sorry Morag, I didn't know that would happen either."

Morag chuckled, "It's ok, there was no harm done. The three Jardine women weren't blitzed, which is what we like to see."

Ferdinand came over taking my hand, "Are you alright, Charlotte?"

Charlotte still with bright eyes, smiled at Ferdinand nodding, "I feel great. Mum and Amelia look like they are still buzzing as well."

Ferdinand looked at me, "Yes, they are. Come on do you want a drink of water of something you three."

Shiro came and got Amelia putting his arm around her shoulders giving her a kiss.

We went and got a drink of water offering the others a drink. We went back out to the lounge sitting and drinking the water chatting to the Jardine women.

Cara was stunned shaking her head, "Wow there was a bit of power there. Are you alright Charlotte?"

Charlotte took a satisfying breath, "Yes I feel wonderful thanks Cara."

Cara smiled, relieved, "Well it is time to introduce you to your spirit animal now, are you up to it?"

Charlotte grinned, "Oh yes I've been looking forward to this."

Cara gave Charlotte an old worn out book, "Charlotte this is to be read by you with the history of Jardine and some of the rules we live by. Make sure you don't show it to anyone else or leave it lying around. You will also be assigned a sister whose name is Sophie Dumont. She will help guide you and answer any questions you might have. If anyone else approaches you saying they're your sister, please get away from them, especially after the incident earlier today."

I looked at Ferdinand upon hearing Cara, "Do you know what her spirit animal is?"

He put his arm around my shoulder, "Yes I do, and no I'm not telling you."

I put my arm around his waist, "Oh come on don't be mean."

He turned me around putting his arms around my waist, "Just watch and don't interrupt when they are looking at each other this time."

I had a thought, "Do you think we should order some food or something for afterwards?"

Ferdinand patted my hand, "I've already done that; it should be here soon."

Everyone got comfortable ready for the reveal of Charlotte's spirit animal, feeling the mood change in the room to one of excitement. Charlotte sat down on the sofa not far from where Cara was going to let the spirit animal enter the room. She looked over at me in Ferdinand's arms biting her lip in apprehension, as I smiled at her. Shiro had brought in extra seating for the others and once everyone was settled the room went quiet, with just the crackle of the fire to be heard.

Cara put her hands together forming a white light in her hands, then separating them to form a circle with wispy mists forming around it saying, "I summon Charlotte Dragĕ's spirit animal, please come forth."

You could feel the anticipation in the room as a beak appeared from the circle, then some magnificent strong brown eyes which were scanning the room. An eagle looked down then jumped out of the circle into the room, doing a little squawk.

He stretched up and flapped his wings showing a beautiful plumage of dark brown feathers with strong wings and big talons on his feet. He stood just outside of the circle, looking around the room at all of us. He then stopped and focused on Charlotte moving over to her, as she lowered herself, embracing the bird in her arms.

Cara then asked the eagle to reveal itself in male form, asking Charlotte to stand up to allow the bird to change. The bird flew up into the air, then came back down beak first, letting out a high pitch squawk, forming into a man, landing right in front of Charlotte as we watched him form.

We all let out a gasp in delight, as we watched this happen. Charlotte stood there wide eyed, as the eagle developed into a man, slightly taller than her with brown wavy hair, deep set dark eyes, a square jaw, looking stunning with olive skin. He had a slim body, but strong shoulders and arms. He was wearing a white shirt with black jeans along with black boots on his feet. He stood there looking at Charlotte with a gentle smile on his face, then moved closing the gap to give her a big hug.

I could hear Amelia squeal in delight, as she watched her sister hug him in return, looking relaxed with tears welling up in her eyes, dripping down on his shirt, for the love of this man, she has just met.

She put her head up with pools of moisture in her eyes, "What is your name?"

He looked at her now not far from her face saying, "Aetius." He wiped her eyes gently with his thumbs, then picked up her hand kissing it gently, putting his tattoo on her wrist.

She looked away briefly from his face, looking at her arm, as he put it in his hand again kissing it, "This is so you can call me whenever you need me."

She nodded still, smitten with this man in front of her, looking in her eyes with intense love. She put her arms around his neck, giving him a hug.

I could feel the pride build up inside of me at this moment seeing the love Charlotte had for Aetius so quickly. Tears started running down my cheeks, hitting Ferdinand's hands with him lean down giving me a kiss on my cheek, "You softy." He gave me a tissue to wipe my eyes calming myself, watching them for a little longer, leaning into Ferdinand, as he cuddled me.

All of the Jardine women clapped softly with sounds of "aww isn't that lovely," hearing sniffles and blowing noses, come from that direction. Ferdinand heard a knock at the front door leaning down, "That should be the food, come and help me bring it in."

I nodded, "Ok" still watching Charlotte and Aetius staring at each other. Ferdinand had ordered vegetarian Chinese meals, smelling delicious as the man passed over four bags of food, "Gee Ferdinand, how much did you order?"

He smiled, "Don't you worry about that, it's a good celebration with the Dragĕ women finally initiated into Jardine."

We took the food over to the table opening it all up with Amelia and Shiro coming over to help, getting plates along with wine, water and glasses for everyone.

I shook my head amazed, thinking a few weeks ago I was at a loss what to do with myself, now I am joined with not only my family again but also the Jardine family. Ferdinand came up to me smiling, "Stop daydreaming again, Hannah," and gave me a kiss on the cheek.

I went up to Aetius while I had a chance, to welcome him into the family, giving him a hug. He smiled a relaxed smile, "Thanks Hannah, it is so nice to finally be here."

We all had a nice time eating and chatting about the ceremony as well as the other two ceremonies having a good laugh about it, especially after a couple of wines.

I called Morag over into the kitchen while everyone was chatting still, showing her the tattoo on my back, which she commented was fully formed. I tried to look behind me, "Oh I wonder if that happened when we got hit by those orbs?"

Morag nodded, "Probably Hannah. This is a strange one, as we have had other families with old magic, but nothing like this has happened. Can you keep in touch with me if anything else happens? I will give you the power to communicate with me without having to go through anyone else."

This made me look over to Lilith, who was glancing over to us every now and then, wondering what we were talking about, deciding not to say anything about her at this stage but nodding, "Thanks Morag, I appreciate that."

We came out of the kitchen with more wine, filling up glasses. Everyone was getting quite tipsy, evidenced by Louella getting up to give me a hug, when I came around with the wine, "You're a good woman Hannah, but gee you were a cheeky girl when you were younger."

I hugged her back, "I wish I could remember it Louella, but thank you."

Everyone eventually left, leaving just the six of us, to clean up. I felt a bit anxious with Charlotte and her dislike of Ferdinand being with me, so I decided to confront her, "Charlotte, I'm just letting you know that Ferdinand and I sleep together, there's no sex but we are very close."

She looked at me relaxed and starry eyed, "That's ok Mum. You look happy that is what is important."

I sighed, "Wow I wasn't expecting that."

I watched Charlotte and Aetius go into the bedroom, feeling a little unsure whether they should do that straight away, with Ferdinand coming up behind me, "Leave them alone, they will sort themselves out, just like we did."

I chuckled, "That's what I'm worried about. I'm still her mother and that's what we do."

He took my hand, "Come on we need to sort out where we are going to sleep;" watching Amelia and Shiro go towards the bed, where we were supposed to be sleeping in.

I sat down on the sofa watching the fire, "We can sleep out here, I suppose."

Ferdinand grinned a cheesy grin, "Great idea, Hannah." He moved the sofa bringing in a bed testing it with his hands, "Looks soft enough, what do you think Hannah?"

I chuckled going over to it lying on it, "Feels good Ferdinand. I don't think it will take long to fall asleep tonight. I'm just going to have a quick shower; I won't be long."

I came back to find him building the fire up nicely, going to lie on the bed relaxing at last. As I lay there, he was crouching in front of the fire watching it burn, with a vision coming to me of another time that I had never seen before. It looked medieval feeling the walls change around me like I was in a castle in a big four poster wooden bed and woollen blankets around me, watching a man by the fire, just as Ferdinand was doing now.

The man turned to look at me smiling with love in his eyes who looked similar to Ferdinand coming towards me, but then it changed to Ferdinand, "Hannah are you ready to go to bed?"

I shook my head, taking a deep breath realising where I was again, "Yes Ferdinand."

He leaned over me, "Were you daydreaming again?"

I smiled, "Yes, I think I was. There is something about open fires that make me daydream. I do miss a fire sometimes."

He gave me a kiss, "I'll just have a quick shower."

I nodded, "Ok, thanks for being there for me today, Ferdinand." He stroked my face gently, "I told you I would from now on. No getting rid of me now Hannah Dragĕ."

I put my hand up to his, "I don't want you to go anywhere Ferdinand." We hugged, "I'll be back soon."

While he went to have his shower, I didn't want to fall asleep until he came back so I got off the bed, sitting in front of the fire poking it gently to make it burn, while feeling the warmth hit me, as the temperature was dropping outside.

As I sat there, I could feel the temperature drop inside, making me look around me, "Hallo bestemor (hello grandma)."

She chuckled, "Du blir flink (you are getting clever)."

I sighed with satisfaction, "Vi tre er sammen nå er du lykkelig (the three of us are together now are you happy?)." She moved in closer, "Ja Hannah. Men du må holde fokus. (Yes Hannah. You need to stay focused though)."

I sighed, "Jeg prøver. Hva heter du? (I am trying. What is your name?)"

She turned away from me at the sound of someone coming, disappearing as Ferdinand came back into the lounge looking at me, "Were you talking to someone?"

I smiled, "no just talking to myself. I'm ready for bed though, are you?"

He helped me up, pulling me into him, "Yep, it's been a long day."

Chapter 10

I went to sleep alright, but started to dream all sorts of dreams about ancestors and being attacked. I woke up suddenly with the sound of a bell going off making me sit up. I took a deep breath, hearing the bell go off again.

Ferdinand said sleepily, "What's the matter Hannah?"

I turned to look at him, "Someone is trying to get into my unit." He woke up a bit more now, "How do you know?"

I got up getting dressed, "I put a magical alarm system on it."

He sat up rubbing his eyes, "You've locked it both ways though, haven't you?"

I nodded, "I just want to go and check I won't be long."

He moved over quickly getting dressed, "No you don't, you wait for me."

I sighed, "I won't be long."

He growled, "Hannah, just wait for me," taking my hand, magicaeing out of the room to inside the front door of the unit. Kimba came up meowing making Ferdinand have to pick her up to quieten her down. I could hear someone trying the lock on the door and turning the handle.

Ferdinand put Kimba down whispering, "I'll go down the hall to see if I can see anyone."

I shook my head, "No I'll come with you just in case they are magical."

He pursed his lips, "You're stubborn," taking my hand magicaeing near the stairs that took us down to the carpark. We crept forward in the dark noticing two dark figures, with one trying the door with something in his hand, emitting a small spark, while the other one kept watch.

Ferdinand ran towards them, yelling, "Who are you?" The one that was keeping watch moved towards him menacingly with a wand, which I could just see in the dim light, so I sent a deflecting bolt towards him. The person who was holding the wand yelled in pain as it flew out of his hand. Ferdinand punched him in the face, but it wasn't strong enough to knock him out.

The one that was by the door used his wand to disappear. The one that Ferdinand had punched, got up suddenly, knocking into Ferdinand, then running past me, knocking me over falling down a couple of stairs. I yelled, "You mongrel," sending a bolt but missing him.

Ferdinand came over to me, "Are you alright Hannah?" He helped me up as I winced, "I think I've sprained my wrist." We magicae back into the unit turning the lights on.

Ferdinand looked at my wrist, "I think we should go to the hospital to get it checked out?"

I tensed up, "No it is alright; I am sure it is just sprained. I have some strapping in the bathroom I can put around to support it."

He didn't look happy about it, but went and got it, strapping it up for me, "I wonder who they were, that were trying to get in?"

I shook my head, "I don't know, but they were definitely magical. I wonder if they think I have the book lying around or something?"

Ferdinand nodded, "Probably. Come on we'll give Kimba a bit more food and get back to Tassie."

We got back to Charlotte's place in the lounge that had cooled down because the fire had died. Ferdinand bent down and poked it putting some more wood on to get it burning well again. I changed and got back into bed watching him as he did it.

That vision I had, came back into my mind, wondering where it had come from. Ferdinand changed and got back into bed cuddling in, as I smiled, "Mm it's nice cuddling in with a fire burning, isn't it?"

He chuckled, "Yes, it is, plus I'm trying to stop your hands getting too cold again."

I smacked him playfully on his arm, "Don't be naughty, they're not that bad."

He looked at my hand again in the fire light, "Are you sure it is alright?"

I nodded, "Yes dear. Let's try and get some sleep. I think we will stay for a little while then go home." He kissed me on the cheek, "Yes sounds like a good idea."

I woke to the sound of the girls giggling and talking to Aetius and Shiro, looking over to Ferdinand who was still sleeping. I slipped out of bed leaving him there to go to the toilet and then started making some French toast for the girls, as a surprise.

This was enough to wake Ferdinand, he grinned, "What are you making Hannah?"

He came behind me putting his arms around my waist as I mixed the egg mixture, "Some French toast. The girls always liked it, so I thought I would do it for a surprise."

He looked at my hand, lifting it, checking the bandage, "I think I will take over and give your hand a rest."

I turned around to face him, "You just don't trust my cooking, do you Ferdinand?"

He leaned in so I couldn't see his expression, "No it's nothing like that dear, I'm just concerned about your hand."

I giggled, "You're a big fibber. Can you send the bed away first so we can have some more room?" He did that, then took over making the French toast.

After breakfast Ferdinand, Shiro and Aetius took off to Jardine for a couple of hours to give us some time to chat. I told the girls about what happened last night, getting annoyed that they were hassling me so much.

Amelia looked cross, "We'll have to find out who they are and deal with them Mum. This has to stop."

I nodded, "Yes, but we do it together, don't try and do anything yourself."

Charlotte brought out the book from Jardine looking at it then gasping as it changed into an iPad, "Wow that's clever."

Amelia and I looked at each knowingly, "Yep Jardine are full of surprises."

Cara came on the screen smiling at Charlotte, "How are you feeling today Charlotte after your ceremony last night?"

Charlotte sighed, "Oh I feel great Cara, thanks."

Cara noticed Amelia and myself there, "Hi you two. Instead of doing the history today Charlotte we'll get your sisters to introduce themselves, then you can come back to me for the history lesson and rules."

Charlotte smiled, "Ok sounds good. See you later, Cara."

Not long after she put the book away, there was a knock at the door. Charlotte went to see who it was with me following behind her, just in case it was trouble.

Once she opened the door a cool gust of wind greeted her, revealing three women standing there smiling. A lovely looking lady with shoulder length hair, whose face looked flawlessly pale with red lipstick and hazel eyes, a slim body with jeans and jumper and a sleeveless jacket on, spoke first, "Hi Charlotte my name is Sophie Dumont," shaking Charlotte's hand. She stepped aside to let the next lady introduce herself.

Another woman moved forward, "Hi I'm Hinemoa Tanĕ. I'm here to meet Amelia."

Amelia come over to see who was there. Hinemoa who was a Māori woman with long thick black hair in a plait, quite a stocky build, but not fat with big brown smiling eyes with jeans, boots and a dark green jumper on came in smiling looking at Amelia, "Hi Amelia, I'm Hinemoa or Hine or just Sis, which every you prefer."

Amelia grinned, "Come inside it's a bit cold out there."

The next woman that came in was Alira, an Aboriginal woman, who was short with jeans and a black jumper on. She had black wavy hair, that she had pushed up into a bun, making her big brown eyes stand out, even more. She came into the house rubbing her hands, "Gee its freezing out there. I'm Alira Kingy and I'm here to see your mum, Hannah."

Charlotte shut the door, "Come in ladies and take a seat near the fire."

I went over to give the fire a bit of a stir up with Alira coming over with me, "Hi Sis I'm Alira. Aww move over so I can warm my hands up."

I giggled, "Oh good, another one that has bad circulation in the hands. I'll have to tell Ferdinand; he will be pleased."

Alira put her hands out to the flames to warm them then turned around to look at the other women, "Well here we all are finally with the Dragĕ women. Should we have a chat then go somewhere for lunch?"

Hine sat down getting comfortable, "Yep sounds good to me."

We sat around for a while chatting getting to know each other having some laughs as well. Sophie got up, "So ladies did you have anywhere in mind to go and have some lunch?"

I hesitated, "Can I ask for something before we go?" Everyone looked towards me wondering what I was going to ask. "I want a memory spell on me so I can remember from when I was young to when my mother was threatened by someone—is that possible?"

Alira came up to me putting her arm through mine, "Of course we can do that. Are you sure you want too though?"

I thought about it again sighing, "yes, I do. It might stem my anger for my mother and also see who the hell frightened her enough to stop the magic in our family."

Alira looked at the others, "Do you mind if I do this?" She didn't get any objection as she turned me to look at her, "Close your eyes, Hannah and I will put a spell over you. It will appear in your head like a movie. You can choose to tell us or not, that is up to you."

I took a deep breath, "Ok, that sounds good to me." I closed my eyes letting Alira put the spell over me. I stood there with a vision coming over me of when I was very young and Ferdinand, who was also very young, hovering around me, making me giggle in delight.

I could feel myself grinning at the sight of this. The vision then flicked to when I was around 3 years of age going to Jardine with my mother and doing the ceremony. I could feel the jubilation of doing the ceremony and the pride in my mother. I could see the sights of Jardine along with the huge prides of cats, which always drew me in, going to talk with them and sleep with them.

The vision changed again with a vision of dark feelings coming over me with my mother's attitude changing towards me as though I was someone that shouldn't be in the family. My brothers were getting all the attention now and my mother expecting me to be like a 1950s housewife, almost, cleaning up after them and making their food. I refused in the end building up my temper and not knowing why I was being ostracised like this. My brothers were constantly picking on me. My father, while I felt he loved me, felt distant as well.

I felt abandoned and unloved for who I was. I looked different from the rest of the family and also acted differently, bringing my temper out even more, through school and my life generally. I could not see the person who spoke to my mother deciding to end the spell and coming out of it.

I stood there waking up feeling tears falling down my face with Alira looking concerned, "Hannah are you alright?"

I brought in a tissue with my girls coming over to me giving me a hug, "Do you want to talk about its Mum?" I thought about it saying in the end, "No, it's what I expected. It didn't show the person who threatened my mother, so it's no use."

I wiped my eyes, giving my girls a hug again, "Have you decided where to go for lunch; I need some fresh air."

Hine sat forward, "Well there is a great little pub in Hobart that has great beer and a good band. It will give Amelia and Charlotte some practice to magicae bigger distances as well."

Alira got up, "Well that sounds great to me, shall we go there?"

I put a warmer jumper on and Amelia and Charlotte changed into something warmer getting excited to do some magic. This also made me feel better about what I had seen in my vision, taking my mind off it.

Charlotte went and locked the doors and put the fire guard up to the fire, "Well, are we ready to go?" We held hands with our Jardine sisters with a look of excitement coming over me and my girls faces and Alira saying, "Let's go ladies." We took off with the sound of Amelia and Charlotte yelling, "Yahoo" as we took off.

We landed in a park not far from the pub with Amelia and Charlotte, stumbling a little on landing, as I giggled, "Usually that's me. You did well girls." We walked over to the pub which was a big stone building with umbrellas on the outside that didn't have anyone sitting under them because it was too cold.

We went inside with the warmth of the pub hitting us, which wasn't very busy. It was one of those old pubs with wooden floors, a big wooden bar with glasses hanging from a wooden false ceiling that had downlights making it look cosy. It had an old sign done in gothic writing saying Milliner Drapery imbedded in the wood. You could still smell the faint smell of the wood and polish, which I think was Tasmanian oak. The girls went straight up to the bar ordering their drinks with us older ones following them looking around to see who was around.

Alira smiled, "You're as bad as me Sis, checking out who is around."

I smiled back at her, "Well I've been a bit bombarded lately, so I'm finding I have to be careful."

Alira got her drink, "Yes, I've heard about that. Don't worry we'll keep an eye out for you as well."

We all sat down having a look at the menu, with a waitress coming over to take our orders. Once she had gone the band started playing a typical Irish jig.

Hine and Amelia had tall glasses of Guinness looking pleased with themselves clinking their glasses, as they took a big mouthful of beer, giggling at each other with their bear moustaches.

We were enjoying listening to the music eating our lunches with a great atmosphere in the pub.

After another drink, one of the band members came over to us, "Come on ladies we want a volunteer for a dance off."

Amelia who was nice and relaxed after the beer got up, "I'll do it."

She went onto the floor where five other women were standing, as well as an Irish woman, in traditional dress, "Well, ladies come together and once the music starts just follow me."

Amelia looked over to us smiling. A small Irish guy dressed in black pants white shirt and a green vest with a rounded face and big ears, who appeared to be their spokesman, got up with an Irish brogue, "Now everyone we want you to clap with these brave ladies and then at the end you can vote who did the best jig."

The music started with the Irish lady tapping her feet, encouraging the six women to start tapping their feet.

I could see Amelia giggling away, as she was watching the Irish woman. I noticed the lights were slowly being dimmed, making it harder to see the women dance, thinking, *'Aren't we supposed to be judging them?'*

I looked at Alira who was also looking at the lights being dimmed, noticing small sparks coming off the Irish woman's shoes. Charlotte and the others in our group were clapping and laughing at the women dancing, but Alira and I noticed the music felt like it had a strong vibration to it.

I looked around the pub noticing the peoples clapping adding to the vibration the music was sending out, which was cascading around the women on the floor, as well as people in the pub.

The little guy, who was the spokesman for the band, appeared in front of Alira and I with his Irish brogue, "So you're not getting into the spirit of the music ladies."

I looked at Charlotte, Hine and Sophie who were clapping and appeared transfixed on the music watching the women dance.

Alira put her hand on mine, "No, we think it is time for it to stop now, so we can judge the women before they get worn out." He had a broad smile that turned menacing "it'll stop when we're good and ready Hannah and Alira. Your daughter is doing fine up there Hannah, so don't be going to interfere. It's time to have a talk to some people who want to ask you a few questions."

I was angry now, "You're a leprechaun, aren't you? Who has put you up to this?"

He waved his hand towards a small group of women near the bar, which must have been the signal for them to come over.

Alira and I touched our tattoos to get Ferdinand and her spirit animal here. Four women made their way over to us with a tall woman with long blonde hair came over smiling, "We finally meet Hannah and Alira," and looking at the Irish guy, "Thank you Toby go and keep an eye on Amelia for us, will you?"

He nodded, "Sure thing Harriet."

I thought to myself, '*I've heard that name before*' making Harriet smile, "Oh Hannah, you must come back to the meeting it's given us such a buzz."

That jogged my memory with the recognition coming over my face, smiling, "Did you like my disguise, Hannah. I believe you have tried that spell yourself."

Alira looked at me confused, so I explained to her, "Harriet was in a mediation meeting I went to, looking a bit younger and too eager to be near me."

Alira nodded, "Oh I see. Well Harriet what do you want we've had enough of this Irish stuff."

Harriet chuckled, "Now there isn't any rush ladies we just want to talk to you about joining our group or giving us some of your powers."

I could see the door to the toilet area opening with some men walking in recognising one of them being Ferdinand.

Harriet noticed me glance over, "Oh Hannah, you called your dragon how sweet." She pulled out her wand, making me send a bolt towards her hand, then saying a chant that had come into my head, "*Release them now or I'll deal with you so. Your strings on your fiddles with break along with your bow.*"

Alira sent another bolt over to someone else who was getting their wand out.

I could hear the musicians' strings go twang with the music stopping. Ferdinand, Fia, Shiro and Aetius were coming towards us, when bolts were being fired towards them, making them duck for cover.

The music had stopped which also made the spell around the room lose its strength. Harriet signalled to Toby to get Amelia but Shiro magicae to her before he could get there, taking her in his arms and magicaeing out of his reach.

Amelia looked dazed but came around quickly, "What's happening Shiro?"

Shiro pointed, "That guy is a leprechaun and there are women over there trying to get to your mother and Alira."

Amelia could see some bolts being thrown, so threw one from her direction confusing the women where it was coming from.

Ferdinand magicae to me knocking two of the women out of the way. Harriet found her wand pointing it at him saying, "*Levita*" watching him levitate in the air struggling yelling, "Let me down!"

Harriet grinned wickedly, "Now come on Hannah we don't want anyone else getting hurt."

Hine, Sophie and Charlotte were coming out of their dazed state with Aetius diving under the table to get near Charlotte to help her.

Alira and I stood up holding hands, "Let him down Harriet."

Harriet flinched a little with the look on our faces and the tone of our voices, but put on a brave act, "I can really hurt him if you don't do as I ask, Hannah."

A clap of thunder could be heard outside with Harriet and a couple of her accomplices look anxious, but Harriet still felt brave, "Ah there's that famous temper from you two. Just imagine what we could do with that temper in this pathetic world that is run by weak minded men."

I could hear Ferdinand struggling, "Don't listen to her Hannah."

Amelia and Shiro got closer finding Fia in the darkened room, who was edging closer to Alira.

I smiled cunningly at Harriet, who was still pointing her wand at Ferdinand, throwing a small bolt at him every now and then to make him groan; with an uneasy look coming over her again, "Come on Hannah and Alira, you know you want to join a real group, show us some of your tricks?"

I looked at Alira, putting my hands up in the air in surrender, as though I was giving up, but I had actually sent out a spell to freeze everyone in the room.

Alira grinned at me, "Not bad Hannah, but I think Ferdinand is going to be pissed off because you've frozen him."

I looked up at him, "Oh shit."

Harriet smiled, "Very nice and you did it so easily."

I could see Ferdinand struggling against the spell, but there wasn't anything I could do. I looked back to Harriet looking serious, "So where is your friend Jonas? If I'm going to join a different group, I want to see who I'm joining with."

Harriet grinned, "I'll call him, he was my back up plan."

Just as we said that Jonas appeared, "Hi Hannah and Alira. So, you're thinking of joining us?"

I looked at him, "Wow you look a lot different from the meditation meeting."

Jonas smiled, "Yes not the young thing I was at the meeting, looking cool and calm. So, why don't you come with us Hannah and Alira and we can take you to a better place to talk about what we want to do with this organisation."

I could hear whispers in the background from my girls and the others. I squeezed Alira's hand indicating I was about to do something, with her squeezing back in recognition. I smiled back at Jonas delaying for time, "I just need to talk to my girls, so they don't try to attack you or get upset."

Jonas and Harriet grinned slyly with Harriet saying confidently "don't take too long or try anything, Hannah."

I grinned at her, "No I won't try anything."

I turned to look at my girls grinning putting my hand up, as we joined together with the book, saying a spell quietly together, *"A clap of thunder a bolt of lightning, a water spout turning again and again around these two in front of me and you,"* and turning quickly to point at both Harriet and Jonas before they realised what we were doing.

This caused a water spout to appear instantly around Harriet and Jonas sucking them up into it swirling around and around with claps of thunder reverberating around the room.

Every time a clap of thunder sounded it struck Harriet and Jonas hearing them scream as it hit them. This also sent their wands flying off with Hine pointing to them smashing them to pieces.

Hine, Sophie, Amelia and Charlotte sent bolts or binding spells to the others that were trying to escape.

Alira giggled calmly, "Can I do something now, Hannah?"

I smiled, giving her a high five, "Sure can, Sister."

Alira then moved forward a little, *"I box them in to keep the water within like a washing machine around both of them,"* putting her hands up to form a square around Harriet and Jonas as an invisible box formed around them.

We smiled at each other watching Jonas and Harriet struggling like mimes against the walls of the invisible box with the water spout thrashing them like a washing machine, along with strikes of lightening, hitting them every now and then.

The water was collecting in the box from the water spout slowly filling it up. Harriet and Jonas were banging their hands on the box yelling at us to let them go.

I looked at them putting my head on the side, "Do you think I should lower the water level just in case they drown or something like that?"

Alira put her head on the side as well, "Yes, I think so."

The water level drained a little, while the water spout agitated them around like a washing machine. Both Alira and I, felt intoxicated being able to do some real magic, starting to sing a song together, "This girl is on fire …"

Amelia and Charlotte came up behind us giggling at us, "Mum and Alira you are silly," joining in with us swaying and singing.

Hine and Sophie, who still had Toby in their grip looked worried, with Hine giving a nervous chuckle, "Hee hee you two know how to have fun, but do you think you had better stop now?"

Toby who was struggling to get out of their grip in his Irish brogue, "Now come on ladies it was all just a bit of fun. Let Toby go, as I was under a lot of pressure by those witches to do this."

Charlotte stopped dancing with us taking Aetius' hand, "You know they deserve everything they get. We just came here for a quiet drink and we get attacked. I say the leprechaun is next. Can I have a go, Mum?"

I giggled, turning back to the two in the cube, going around like clothes in a washing machine, "I'll just put a finishing touch on this one," pointing to the cube and putting a big red bow on the top, "There, what do you think of that Alira?"

Alira clapped her hands giggling again, "Oh perfect, Hannah."

Charlotte grinned now moving forward to try something on Toby as he struggled against Hine and Sophie, when Morag and Cara appeared in front of me and Alira.

Alira whispered to me, "Oh crap!"

Morag moved forward looking at the situation, "Mm looks like you two have been having some fun."

She looked at Ferdinand up in the air, "Come on Hannah let the room go. You are not supposed to freeze your guardian animal, unless they have done something really bad to you."

I swayed a little with the alcohol along with the fun of using our magic together feeling like I was back in school whispering to Alira, "Is there a rule that you're not supposed to freeze your guardian animal?"

Alira turned her head away from Morag talking quietly, "I'm not sure, we must look that one up in the rule book."

Morag didn't look impressed, hearing those comments, then turning to Charlotte, "I'm afraid you can't have a go at the leprechaun Charlotte, I'm going to send him back to his realm so they can deal with him."

Toby sighed in relief, "Thank you Morag it was all just a bit of fun to be sure, but these two are a bit tipsy and took it seriously."

Morag chuckled, "Don't play me for the fool Toby McGuire, or I will let Charlotte do her bit on you."

I looked petulantly at Morag, "Oh come on he has his own realm to go to? That's not fair, he is just as guilty as those two. I should have put him in the box with them," and looking at Harriet and Jonas being agitated, going around and around in the box.

Morag didn't bother to argue looking at Cara, "Can you do that for me Cara, while I sort this out."

I could see Cara looking at Harriet and Jonas trying to stifle a smirk, "Sure Morag." She pointed at Toby but before she could send him away, I pointed a finger at him sending a little bolt towards him hearing a yelp, "You damn witches," then Cara sent him away. Hine and Sophie put their heads down trying not to laugh.

Morag looked at me annoyed, with a hint of mirth in her look, biting her lip, "Hannah there was no need to do that, he will be dealt with by the other leprechauns."

She went over to the box with Harriet and Jonas in touching it; I think to see if she could break the spell. She didn't let on but she couldn't, turning back towards me and Alira, "Ok stop this now, we will let Jardine deal with these three and the other two that are over there."

I sighed, "Alright Morag, but I have to remember where the stop button is," and turned to Alira, "Do you know where it is Alira?" and giggling to each other.

We turned back to Morag who wasn't smiling, but Cara had put her hand up to her mouth to hide her giggle as Alira said, "Oh alright. They should be nice and clean now I guess."

I stopped the water spout from spinning them in the box, watching them flop onto the bottom of the box like drowned rats, gasping.

Alira put her hand on the box making it disappear, watching the bow fall, as I leaned forward to catch it, "Can't let that go to waste."

Harriet and Jonas coughed and spluttered on the floor, taking deep breaths, growling in between breaths, "You should put a leash on those two Morag."

Alira and I held hands giggling, pointing at them both putting a collar and leash on them binding their hands with the leash.

Meanwhile, we could hear Ferdinand growling behind us wanting to be freed.

I looked at Alira ignoring him saying calmly, "Oh I do love the colour of your collar Alira. Is that an Aboriginal design?"

Alira looked pleased, "Yes, it's a new range out."

Morag was trying to stay patient "Hannah and Alira that is enough! Now Hannah release the room," as two guards from Jardine came into the room taking Harriet, Jonas and the other three away with them.

I knew it was time to release the room, so I put my hand up quietly saying, *"Liberate."*

Ferdinand fell to the floor. I went over to help him up, "Sorry about that dear, I'll have to learn to aim better."

He took my hand getting up glaring at me, not saying anything, but making me feel a little nervous.

He kept a firm hold of my hand taking me back over to Morag. Fia was standing behind Alira with his arms around her waist. I put my head down, "Mm this doesn't feel good Alira," as we both giggled.

Morag was talking to Cara, "Can you go and send a calm wave around the room so they don't remember anything Cara, and can you also see what you can do with the band's instruments. They are not looking very good."

Alira and I still had our heads down to hide our chuckles. Ferdinand quietly said in my ear, "Stop it, Hannah. You're in trouble."

A drunk guy came swaggering up to us holding a beer in his hand, "Wow that was some dance ladies. Can we do it again?" This was enough to make Alira, Charlotte, Amelia, Hine, Sophie and I all burst out laughing.

Ferdinand squeezed my hand growling, while Morag smiled back nicely, "No I think you've had enough for tonight. Maybe another night." He swaggered off again, "Ahh come on, this has been a fun night."

Morag turned back to us, "Ferdinand and Fia can you take Hannah and Alira back to Charlotte's house."

Charlotte came forward looking annoyed, "You know we didn't start this, they did! I don't see why we should be in trouble because of them."

Morag nodded, "No Charlotte you shouldn't be in trouble but your mother and Alira are strong in their magic and need to learn to control it. I want you four to go and help Cara to put a calming feeling around the room then go back to your house."

Ferdinand put his arm around my waist magicaeing back to Charlotte's house. I moved away quickly, once we landed, giggling, "Don't you get angry at me Ferdinand, I was protecting all of us."

Alira got out of Fia's grip as well coming over to me holding my hand, "We were only doing what we could. You two were unable to help us."

Ferdinand looked at Fia both grimacing, when all of a sudden, I started to hiccup, which started Alira giggling. Ferdinand made a move towards me, as I let out another hiccup again, giggling, "Ferdinand don't be a naughty dragon."

This started Alira off giggling again, when Fia caught up with her, putting her over his shoulder in a fireman's lift making her squeal with laughter, "Fia put me down you silly bugger."

Ferdinand had a determined look on his face catching up with me, "Hannah!" He wrapped his arms around me lifting me up, pushing my legs around his hips, "Stay there, Hannah"

Lilith arrived in the lounge looking at the scene smiling briefly, "Good grief, are you two arguing again?"

I struggled hiccupping and giggling turning to look at Lilith, "Here comes the Lilith calvary."

Alira was hitting Fia's back letting out a burst of laughter, "You crack me up, Hannah."

Ferdinand sat on the sofa holding onto me, putting his hand up to my head pushing me into him, "Shush Hannah, behave yourself." He wrapped his arm around my back pushing me into him more as I struggled against him, "Let me go, Ferdinand."

Ferdinand was trying to hold onto me, when Lilith moved closer, "Are you alright? I heard you were attacked?"

Ferdinand frowned, "I'm alright, just a few scratches and bruises. I'm trying to settle Hannah down at the moment so Morag can talk to her."

I hiccupped again unable to turn my head to look at Lilith, because Ferdinand was holding me, "Stakkars lille Lilith (poor little Lilith)."

Ferdinand put his head down looking puzzled, "What did you say Hannah?"

I turned my head on his chest hiccupping trying to push away from him, "Nothing."

Fia sat next to us with Alira on his lap in a similar way holding onto her. We looked at each other giggling. I poked my tongue out at her, "You're in trouble now Alira Kingy."

Alira struggled against Fia managing to get her hand out putting her thumb up to her forehead, "So are you Hannah Dragé."

I could hear Ferdinand growling, "Hannah, behave yourself." He noticed some tablets on the coffee table calling to Lilith, "Lilith can you give me those tablets? I want to look at them."

Lilith picked them up looking at them, "They're painkillers."

Ferdinand was struggling to hold onto me, "Can you read if there is anything about drinking alcohol with them?"

Lilith looked pleased that she was able to help Ferdinand, reading the side of the box, "No you're not supposed to drink with them."

I was still looking at Alira trying to reach her hand but Ferdinand kept stopping me, "Hannah did you take those painkillers before you went out tonight for your wrist?"

I stopped and thought about it hiccupping again then saying like a sulky teenager, "Yes dear."

Alira managed to get an arm out without anyone noticing pointing to Lilith, *"Twinkle, twinkle little Lilith make her a pirouetting ballerina star."*

Lilith squealed as she put her hands up in the air pointing her toes pirouetting around the lounge.

I could just see what was happening, as I burst out laughing. Ferdinand moved me out a little trying to hide a smile, but sounding annoyed, "Hannah did you do that?"

I put my hand up to his chin looking at him with puppy eyes, "Ingen Ferdinand. Gi meg et kyss (no Ferdinand. Give me a kiss.)."

I moved in trying to kiss his lips as he tried not to grin, pulling me into his chest and wrapping his arms around me, "Stop being naughty, Hannah."

He looked up at Lilith pirouetting around the lounge trying not to laugh turning to Fia who was grinning, but putting his head down talking to Alira.

Lilith was growling, "Tell Hannah to take this off me Ferdinand, now!"

Ferdinand was just about to say that I didn't put it on her when Morag appeared in the lounge, followed by all the others having, finished at the pub noticing, Lilith pirouetting around the lounge.

Morag looked away at Cara, trying to compose herself, taking a deep breath turning back to Lilith, "What are you doing Lilith?"

Lilith tried to stop herself doing the ballet move, "Bloody Hannah has put a chant on me, make her take it off."

Morag coughed still struggling to compose herself, turning to Ferdinand and Fia who had their heads down trying not to watch Lilith. She moved closer, "Ferdinand tell Hannah to take that off her."

Ferdinand was chuckling quietly shaking his head saying quietly, "It wasn't her."

Cara came up behind Morag, talking to Alira quietly, "Take the chant off Lilith, Alira."

Alira looked sulkily at her but noticed all the others trying to hide their laughter, "Oh alright." She pointed towards Lilith saying a reverse chant to stop Lilith pirouetting.

Morag composed herself flicking her hair back off her face, "Oh hello Lilith what are you doing here?"

Lilith stopped being a ballerina looking angry, "I had heard there was some trouble here so I thought I would see if I could help in any way."

Morag looked at Ferdinand and Fia holding onto Alira and myself, "Well you can see it is not going very well at the moment."

Charlotte and Amelia butted in looking at Ferdinand holding onto me, "What are you doing Ferdinand, let Mum go."

Ferdinand growled, "Your mother took these tablets for her wrist and went out drinking when she shouldn't have."

I let out a big hiccup, making Alira giggle again.

Morag pointed to the fire making it roar into life, warming up the lounge. She looked annoyed, "Hine and Sophie can go now. I will get in touch with you two later. I need to talk with the others."

They nodded, "Sure Morag, see you later Amelia and Charlotte."

Alira giggled, "See you later girls," hearing another hiccup from me along with a giggle.

Amelia looked at the packet reading it, "Oh dear, you're not supposed to drink with these tablets," and trying not to laugh.

Ferdinand just glared at her, "Where did she get those tablets from?"

Charlotte looked a little guilty, "I had them in my cupboard for a sore hand, I thought they would be alright."

Morag took a deep breath looking at Cara, "What do you think we should do with these two?"

Ferdinand spoke up then, not waiting for Cara to answer, "I think they should all go to Jardine and be taught the rules." A loud hiccup sounded out from me with laughter coming from both Alira and myself.

I tried to reach out to Alira again to get her hand, but Morag saw what we were doing, "Stop them from holding hands you two. Their intoxication appears to be within them both and when they connect it gets worse."

Charlotte was getting annoyed, "You know it's not our fault that this happened. We were about to go home when they attacked. They probably spiked the beer as well, making them two drunker than they should be. I mean, Alira didn't take the tablets and she is just as tipsy as Mum."

Alira giggled again getting frustrated she couldn't hold my hand so she started making the noise of a digeridoo, "Wow wow wow brr brr."

This set me off again hiccupping and then slapping my hand, that I had managed to get free, against Ferdinand's back in tune with her. Ferdinand grabbed my hands wrapping his arms around me, to hold on more, looking at Morag, "Well what are you going to do Morag?"

Morag moved forward stroking her hand over my head, "Relax Hannah," with realisation coming onto my face. I struggled against Ferdinand's grip but he was holding me tightly against his body, "Ingen Ferdinand (no Ferdinand)."

Ferdinand leaned in closer, hearing it this time saying quietly, so no one else would hear him, "Gå i dvale Hannah (go to sleep Hannah)." I collapsed in the end, against Ferdinand.

Alira turned to see this happening, looking scared trying to pry Fia's arms off her, "You're not going to do that stuff on me."

Cara was there stroking Alira's head, "Go to sleep Alira." After a few minutes, Alira collapsed against Fia's chest as he sighed in relief, "She was getting strong, I don't think I could have held her much longer."

Charlotte and Amelia looked at each other worried, with Amelia saying sternly now, "What have you done to them?"

Morag came over to her putting her arm around her shoulders, "It is ok they are just asleep. We need to sort out what is going on, as you said Alira didn't take the tablets, so why are they both out of control?"

Ferdinand sighed in relief, "I don't think I could hold on much longer either, she was getting stronger," with a hiccup being omitted from me.

Morag chuckled pointing at me stopping the hiccups. She then looked at my wrist, "What did she do to it Ferdinand?" He relaxed back onto the sofa, "She sprained it when her unit was being broken into last night."

Morag took my hand in hers feeling it, "I think it is broken, I cannot mend it."

Ferdinand shook his head, "Little minx, I wanted to go to the hospital but she insisted it was just sprained."

Morag walked back over to the fire to warm herself, "I think you are right Ferdinand; we will take them to Jardine to get them checked over and tell them the requirements we expect of them."

She turned to Amelia and Charlotte, "I would really like you two to come as well to see Jardine and support them."

Lilith spluttered, "Surely, they don't need to go to Jardine, can't they just be restrained with their powers for a short period of time until you sort them out. It's obvious they are still doing pranks, like they did when they were younger."

Morag looked over to Lilith annoyed, "No Lilith I want them to come anyway so this is a good chance for them to do this. You can go now."

A look of annoyance crossed Lilith's face briefly then nodded, "Alright, but I think you are wrong. Hannah has become too strong too quick for my liking," with her disappearing.

Cara and Morag looked at each other frowning, but put on a happier face for Amelia and Charlotte, "Can you two take a couple of days off work to come to Jardine; you won't regret it."

Amelia looked at both Alira and myself sleeping on Ferdinand and Fia's laps "this isn't about controlling Mum or anything, is it? You know she called us in to the water spout spell, so it was the power of three, just remember that when you try to work it out."

Cara came to her putting her arm around her shoulders, "No Amelia, we just need to see why these two were affected so much. We don't always have all the answers, Jardine will sort it out a lot better than we can."

Morag looked over to Charlotte, "Well what do you think Charlotte?"

Charlotte nodded, "I can take a couple of days off; I know Mum wasn't going back to work until Wednesday so we may as well get this sorted out. I must admit I am curious about Jardine."

Morag smiled properly for the first time tonight, "That is wonderful. Ferdinand and Fia can take them back to Sydney and I want you two to join us early tomorrow morning at your mother's place. We will go through the Blue Mountains gate to Jardine."

Charlotte and Amelia looked at each other nervously smiling, with Charlotte saying, "Wow this sounds interesting."

Cara gave Charlotte a hug, "I will run through with you the history of Jardine tonight as we had originally planned; that way you will be better prepared."

Morag looked over to Amelia, "Are you going home to Sydney Amelia?"

Amelia shook her head, "No I think I will come with Charlotte in the morning."

Ferdinand stood up changing my position so he could cradle me in his arms, disturbing me as I mumbled something, making Ferdinand put his head down to listen, "Jeg vil ikke legge meg (I don't want to go to sleep)." He kept his head down so no one else could see his expression on his face.

Morag put her hand on his arm, "What did she say Ferdinand?"

He shook his head putting it up, "I think she said 'I don't want to sleep' Morag, which means she is trying to fight it, so I will get her home."

She looked into his eyes then noticed a few rips in his shirt, "Oh dear did you get hurt?"

He shook his head, "I'm alright Morag, it's only a bit of bruising and the odd cut. Jardine will fix that tomorrow."

He asked Amelia to get my things and put them into the backpack putting it on Ferdinand's back. Amelia gave me a little kiss making me stir again, "See you tomorrow, Mum."

Ferdinand grimaced, "I think it's time to go. I'll see everyone tomorrow around what time, Morag?"

She looked at Amelia and Charlotte, "Make it around 8.00am, is that alright girls?"

They both shook their heads saying, "Yes."

Fia picked Alira up, "See you all at Hannah's place."

--ooOoo--

Ferdinand and I got back home turning the lights on and putting me on the bed. He turned away to take the backpack off himself, when he heard me say, "Ferdinand." He turned around with a taut smile, finding me with my eyes wide open, looking at him confused.

I felt dazed as I went to get up, but he came over to me, putting a bag of sleep dust next to the bed just in case. He took my hands and leaned on me so I couldn't get up, "You're supposed to be asleep Hannah, what are you doing awake?"

My head felt fuzzy, "Why did Morag send me to sleep again?"

He sighed, "Because you had taken some tablets and then drank alcohol with them which was making you and Alira misbehave."

I creased up my face thinking, '*Oh did I. Was it those tablets for my sprained wrist?*'

He smirked, "Yes it was those tablets for a broken wrist you little minx. Morag was going to fix it for you but found it was broken. Now why don't you go back to sleep because we are going to Jardine in the morning."

A look of surprise came over me as I tried to sit up but he wouldn't let me, "What, why are we going to Jardine?"

Ferdinand had to think quickly, "Morag thought it would be better for you to have a break from all the attacks that have been happening and they can fix your wrist as well. It's just for a couple of days; you were taking them off anyway with your sick leave."

I relaxed nodding, "Oh that sounds like a good idea. Are my girls coming as well?"

Ferdinand nodded, "Yes as well as Alira. So, I'll be able to show you around Jardine for the first time. I know you'll like it and want to stay."

I smiled, "It does sound lovely."

I looked at his shirt which was torn in different places, "Are you hurt from that attack Ferdinand?"

He looked a little unsure, "Don't you remember what happened Hannah?"

I lay there thinking frowning, "It all seems a bit of blur, some things come to me then it fades out. I know you don't want me to get up, but I'm hungry, can you cook me something?"

He sighed smiling, "Ok, but just behave yourself." He sent the bag of sleep dust away helping me to sit up. I had a bit of a head spin taking a deep breath, "Wow that was a bit of a spin, they must have been some tablets."

He looked at me, "Do you feel alright now?"

I nodded, "Yes I might go and have a shower while you are cooking."

He gave me a kiss on the cheek, "Alright, but be careful in there. What do you feel like?"

He helped me go to the bathroom making sure I was alright and let me have my shower, while he went into the kitchen to cook something.

I didn't really talk much as I felt quite confused. I could see Ferdinand was watching me getting the feeling he was wanting to ask me something, but didn't know how.

He replaced the bandage on my wrist making sure it was firm to hold it in place, "Is it aching Hannah?"

I nodded, "A little, but it doesn't feel broken Ferdinand."

We went to bed rolling over with his arm over my waist, "Ferdinand can you tell me what Jardine is like?" He pulled my hair away from my face cuddling in, "When you get there you will have to go through a special process to be cleansed from this world, but once you are in there it has beautiful lush plants, the rivers are clear and the skies look as blue as blue." His stories always relaxed me and it didn't take long for me to drop off.

Chapter 11

I woke early, sneaking out to the lounge, opening the curtains sitting on a chair to watch the sunrise; with Kimba coming to join me, sitting on my lap. I put a throw around my shoulders to keep me warm from the morning chill. It was going to be a warm day but the mornings were still fresh.

Sitting like this made me think of when I was younger waking up to the sunrises just in awe of the magnificence of the way the sun would rise spreading light everywhere. There was a small scattering of clouds still around that would probably move off when the sun started to warm up the place.

Ferdinand woke to find me gone, feeling worried at first, getting up to find me. He went to the doorway to see me sitting in the chair with Kimba cuddling in, watching the sunrise. Kimba noticed him there, making her do chirpy little meows, as I turned to see what she was meowing at.

He came over giving me a kiss on the top of my head, "Are you watching the sunrise?"

I nodded smiling, "Yes, they are wonderful, aren't they? I suppose they are even better in Jardine?"

He sighed, "Yes, they are. Having no pollution around or high-rise buildings helps it as well. I'll get some breakfast then we can go for a walk along the beach before everyone arrives if you like?"

I nodded, "Yes that will be nice thanks."

We had our breakfast, got dressed and went for a walk along the beach with hardly anyone on the beach "I think it's going to be a warm day here today."

He took my hand, "Yes, but it will be nice in Jardine as well."

I smiled, "Of course it will be dear." As we walked, I could see he was still toying with something when he eventually said, "Have you remembered anything else that happened yesterday?" I sighed, "I remember meeting everyone at Charlotte's place, going to the pub in Hobart, having a couple of beers. We decided to get one more beer before we went home, not feeling drunk, but just relaxed, going back to the table with some guy coming up asking for a volunteer for the dance competition. We hadn't sat down at that stage but Amelia volunteered in the end to do it. I remember sitting down with Alira getting ready to watch the competition and then the music starting. Alira and I realised something was wrong with the dazed looks on people's faces, but it wasn't really affecting her and I."

I continued to run things through my mind thinking, '*I remember taking Alira's hand and holding it tight because I could feel danger around us. I recall meeting Harriet and Jonas but that's when things start to get hazy. It was almost like something took over but it was me doing things. I remember Morag being there and you holding me on your lap as she rubbed my head to help me to sleep. It is a really strange feeling; it was almost like I wasn't in control but I was. I guess it's a bit like being hypnotised.*'

He shook his head, "Well I'm not sure what was going on, I guess we will have to see what Morag makes of it. Husker du at du snakket norsk? (Do you remember speaking Norwegian.)"

I stopped walking hesitating trying to look innocent shuffling my feet in the sand "oh did I? When did I do that?"

He stopped walking taking both my hands, "Look at me," making me look up sheepishly. He was smiling, "You just gave yourself away Hannah because you understood what I said."

I moved in to hug him, so he couldn't see my eyes, "I only know little bits I have picked up from my travels that is all."

He chuckled again, "Jeg tror du vet mer enn di sier Hannah (I think you know more than you say Hannah?)"

I cuddled into him not wanting to say anymore but it just kept coming like verbal diarrhoea "Nei, Ferdinand slutter ikke å prøve å lure meg (no I don't Ferdinand, stop trying to trick me.)"

I moved away from him cursing, "oh shit! This is not fair, Ferdinand. I'm still getting my head around yesterday and now you are quizzing me about this."

I stormed off with him running after me, grabbing my hand stopping me grinning, "I'm sorry Hannah I don't mean to upset you. You just surprised me when you said it last night. Can you tell me how you picked it up, then I won't ask any more questions?"

I groaned starting to get angry, "Bestemoren min. Jeg vet ikke navnet hennes. (My grandma. I don't know her name)."

He cuddled me trying to calm me down, rubbing my back, "Ok, no more questions. Come on we will go back as they are due to arrive soon. I am getting excited to show you around Jardine and hoping you will like it enough to come and live with me there."

I moved out from him looking at him, "Do you really want to do that?"

He smiled, "yes, I do because I am getting worried with all these attacks on you. I want you safe with me and having some fun."

I put my arms around his waist, "I'm looking forward to it Ferdinand but can we just take one day at a time. Come on let's get back and sort poor Kimba out before they arrive. She must be feeling a bit deserted."

We magicae back to the unit sorting Kimba out and shutting the unit up just in time for people to start arriving. Amelia, Shiro, Charlotte, Aetius, Alira and Fia arrived first giving hugs all a little excited and anxious at the same time about going to Jardine.

Alira pulled me aside, "Do you remember much about what happened yesterday, Sister?"

I frowned, "No not really, it keeps fading in and out. How about you?" She shook her head, "No. My mum is a bit worried about it as it just sounded so strange." I sighed, "I'm looking forward to talking to Morag about it, hoping she might have some insight on it."

Alira smiled, "Maybe we are just a bit naughty when we drink?"

I chuckled, "I've always been a drinker, although I didn't have strong magic in me, I don't think it would have affected me that much. I feel it was something stronger than that."

Morag and Cara arrived smiling with Morag walking towards us giving us a hug, "Well hello everyone, are you ready to come and stay in Jardine?"

She went around everyone giving them a hug finally coming up to me giving me a hug, "How are you, Hannah?"

I smiled giving her a hug, "I'm ok Morag; a little confused but I am hoping you will be able to help me sort that out."

Morag patted me on the back, "Let's just give you a good rest and see what happens."

She gave Alira a hug, "Are you looking forward to going to Jardine, Alira?" She smiled looking at me, "Yes Morag. It will be nice to be out of this realm, even for a few days."

Morag moved out, "Well it is time to go. Please take your spirit animals hand and they will take you to the spot where we need to go."

I took Ferdinand's hand watching everyone else take their spirit animal's hands disappearing. We met in the carpark of the Hydro Majestic Hotel in the Blue Mountains, looking around me to see where I was.

Ferdinand smiled at me while holding my hand, "Do you know where you are?"

I nodded, "Yes I do, is there something here leading to Jardine?"

He smiled knowingly, "Yes but you will never guess where."

Hine and Sophie appeared near us giving me and Alira a quick hug, "Hi you two. Are you feeling better?"

I hugged them back, "A little dazed but a lot better, thanks you two."

Alira chuckled giving them a hug, "You might have to fill us in on a few things."

Morag and Cara arrived, "Alright everyone quickly follow me before we attract too much attention," as she walked towards a bush area on the side of the road near the Hydro.

I looked puzzled making Ferdinand smile, "Just follow us."

Morag waved her hand with a track appearing, then waved us on, "Come on everyone please move quickly down this track. Cara can you be the last one and close off the area."

Cara nodded, "Yes certainly, Morag."

Ferdinand was still grinning, "Come on, make sure you hold my hand as I know you slip on these types of tracks."

Amelia came up behind me, "Yes Mum, make sure you hold Ferdinand's hand we don't want you hurting yourself again."

We went down a narrow track with Cara closing it off as we went. Small lights came on like on an airport landing strip, as we moved down the track, flicking off once we had passed them.

As we went down the track the light grew dimmer with the canopy closing in around us and the smells and sounds of the Australian bush becoming louder as we got away from the road.

Amelia was behind me looking nervous, "I hope there aren't any snakes around here?"

Shiro held her hand, "Don't worry they won't bother you with us around."

We got to a clearing at the end of the track with a sandstone boulder sitting in the middle of the clearing. Morag asked everyone to form a circle around the boulder holding hands. We all stood there in anticipation waiting to see what Morag and Cara were going to do next.

Morag got some water from a special bottle pouring it over the rock saying a chant when all of a sudden, some iridescent blue symbols appeared on the rock, making me look at Ferdinand smiling. He smiled back, "Are you impressed so far?"

I nodded, "Yes."

Morag turned to look at everyone, "Now hold on tight to each other's hands and don't let go." She turned with Cara and herself putting their arms out from their sides starting to chant and sway for a few minutes when all of a sudden, we could feel ourselves being pulled from where we were to another dimension.

I could hear my girls squeal in delight, looking at them as though they were being sucked through a funnel and like they were in a cartoon in one dimension. We landed in another bush clearing still holding each other's hands feeling excited, "Wahoo!"

I looked around me seeing typical Australian bush with eucalyptus trees, ferns and the sound of a waterfall in the distance. I could smell all the distinct smells of the Australian bush while still holding Ferdinand's hand. He pulled me in a bit closer, "Not far now."

Morag led the way, "Come this way please." We went down a small track again being lit as we walked towards a waterfall. Morag said a chant, making the waterfall halve its flow, letting us walk underneath it into a cave, that was also being lit up as we walked in.

Charlotte came up beside me, "Wow this is like something you see on TV isn't it, Mum?"

I smiled, "Yes we are certainly having our own adventure now, aren't we?"

Morag waved us on, "Come on we are nearly there." We walked out of the cave into another bush area then went into another cave when I noticed a lot of drawings on the walls.

Cara came up behind me waving her hand over the drawings, "Here you go Hannah, they move when you have the right magic."

I turned to smile at her, then back to the drawings that were moving after she had waved over them, "What are they about Cara?"

Cara took my hand, pointing to different pictures, "This is the history of Jardine done in picture form."

I watched briefly as the figures moved along the wall showing the relationship between the animals and the people living in amongst the bush.

Ferdinand squeezed my hand, "Come on we better catch up."

Morag waited for everyone to regroup, "Now this is where you meet a gatekeeper called Seneca. A word will be put into your head and you must repeat it back to her to be able to go any further."

I looked nervously at Ferdinand, "Oh dear, I hope I don't muck it up."

Alira came up to me smiling, "I was going to learn mind thought, I wish I had done it now."

"I just hope I don't muck it up."

Morag called to the spirit animals, "all of the spirit animals can go now and we will meet you on the other side."

Ferdinand gave me a quick kiss on the cheek and disappeared.

One by one we said the word to Seneca who was a tall muscular woman wearing just a plain outfit with a silver headband that had a crystal in the middle. She also had a staff with a large white crystal at the top of it.

I nervously listened for the word to come into my head, which were all different from the others, hesitating with Seneca looking at me sternly, "did you not get the word?"

I nodded, "Yes, sorry I was just sorting it out in my head." I told her the word and she let me pass, meeting Ferdinand on the other side who looked a little worried, "Everything alright?"

I smiled, "Yes, just nervous."

We moved forward into a meeting area with all of us looking around curious. There was a long table and chairs with food and drink on it. A couple of other women came forward to greet us, "Please help yourselves to the food and drink and then we will take you to another area where we have to cleanse you from your world, so you can enter ours."

After milling around having a drink and a light snack Morag got us to follow her to another area that had a big building built in a classical style with animals and bush imbedded in the building's architecture, "There are cubicles where I want you to disrobe and put the clothes on that are in the cubicle then follow the assistant to walk through a machine. This machine is just crystals that will cleanse you, so please don't be afraid."

I went into the cubical putting the clothes on feeling the material, 'Wow that is different' coming out on the other side, watching everyone else go towards a tunnel with lights flashing along it and everyone walking through it.

As I walked through the tunnel, I felt this overwhelming feeling of peace and happiness coming over me as I walked through. I looked at my hands watching my skin firm, feeling my joints free up and my wrist felt as though it was being healed. I pulled the pants out that I had on, looking at my varicose veins that had started to appear, were now fading.

By the time I got to the end of the tunnel I felt wonderful, emotionally and physically.

I walked out meeting everyone at the other end, looking at them, who were grinning like me. Amelia and Charlotte came up to me with Charlotte jumping around like a little kid, "Wow do you feel wonderful, Mum?"

I nodded, "Yes, I actually feel like going for a big walk or something now. I'm just full of energy."

I looked at the bandage on my wrist, "I suppose I can take this off now," flexing my hand and wrist not feeling any pain.

Two women approached our group, one being a tall but athletic dark woman who introduced herself as Zoya, with a big smile appearing, showing beautiful white teeth and sparkling dark eyes. The other woman who was tall with long blonde hair called Tama had striking blue eyes and clear pale skin smiling, "Please follow us and we will take you to your accommodation."

Zoya came up to me and Alira, "Morag would like to speak with you two before you go to your accommodation; can you please follow me?"

Amelia and Charlotte came over to us with Charlotte looking anxiously at me, "Are you alright, Mum?"

I nodded, "It's alright. You two go and get settled with Aetius and Shiro, we will be along soon."

Alira and I looked at each other feeling a little disappointed, but followed Zoya to a room not far from the cleansing area. We went into a small room finding Morag, Cara and another woman called Demi there. I looked at Alira who I could see was nervous as well, as we went into the room with Morag ushering us in, "Come in and sit down. Please don't be nervous we are just trying to work out what happened yesterday."

I sat down showing my disappointment, "I know we need to get this sorted Morag I just thought we would have some time to relax first after all the attacks we have had."

Demi sat down, "You will be joining the rest of your family soon Hannah. We are just trying to help, so you will be able to stop whatever happened yesterday, happening again."

Alira sighed sitting down, "We don't know what happened. All we know is that we were attacked by some witches and a leprechaun and we defended ourselves, but now feel we have done something wrong."

Morag could see it wasn't going well, "Please Hannah and Alira we are not trying to stop you, but just want to know what we are dealing with. This could turn nasty if you don't learn to control it."

I sighed, "You're probably right, what do you want to know?"

Cara flicked her fingers, "Can you just tell us what you remember, which we would like to record. That way we may be able to see where something happened when you two joined together to fight them. We may need to talk to the other people who were there as well."

I started off first, "As far as I know, that leprechaun put something in our last drink, which reacted with our magic, turning it against them; which we all didn't expect. I will tell you what I remember then I am going to my accommodation."

Alira nodded in agreement putting her hand on top of mine, "I am the same."

Morag, Cara and Demi looked at each other with Morag smiling weakly, nodding her head, "That's fair enough Hannah and Alira. Please tell us what you remember then you can go and join the others."

Both Alira and I told our version of what happened yesterday with the three women listening intently, nodding every now and then saying, "Oh yes, oh dear."

We finished telling them our version. Morag then asked if we could put our hands together to see what happened. I looked at Alira and smiled as we held hands noticing a spark being emitted when we touched hands. I grinned at Alira with her grinning back, "Looks like we were meant to be sisters Alira."

Alira giggled, "I knew that before that happened, Hannah."

Morag smiled, "You two are certainly close. It looks like you are exchanging magic between each other. We have some thoughts on that, but would like to talk about it between ourselves before we come to any conclusion. All we ask is that you both be careful when you are together to control your magic," and looking mischievously at us, "Especially when you are drinking."

I looked curiously at Morag, "I remember bringing my girls into the spell I did for the water, would that have passed onto Alira as well?"

Morag hesitated, "That is quite possible. Hannah. I also know you two woke up once you were taken home, which shows you had a bit of power there."

I grinned at Alira joking with her, "We are the ebony and ivory power sisters."

Alira put her hand up to high five me, "Sure are, Sis."

Morag got up, "Well that is all we need to know for now. Go and enjoy yourself in Jardine. We will see you at the evening meal and try not to get into any mischief you two."

Alira and I got up as Zoya came in to take us to our accommodation. We walked along a narrow path opening up to a big market place with lots of tables, open areas and covered areas. We carried on through lush bush with animals walking around helping Alira and I start to relax a bit now.

A big leopard came up to us brushing itself up against our legs making Alira and I look at each other nervously. When it carried on, we sighed in relief, "Wow something we will have to get used to I guess, while we are here."

Alira who was a little pale, "Yes, but I hope it doesn't happen too often otherwise I'll be as white as you."

I chuckled, "You silly bugger."

I could see Ferdinand and Fia waiting near some bungalows with an anxious smile on their faces. Ferdinand came up to meet me and Fia with Alira putting their arms around our us, "Everything alright?"

Alira and I looked at each other then back to them with me saying, "It's alright. They just wanted to know what happened yesterday. Come on let's see these bungalows."

Ferdinand led me down a little path through bush and thick green grass as I waved goodbye to Alira. He picked me up as we approached a small house with a balcony on the front of it, "This is our pad, Hannah."

I chuckled, "You silly dragon," taking me into the bungalow, still holding me in his arms, "What do you think?"

I smiled, "Can you let me down now so I can have a look around?" He kissed me on the cheek putting me down in front of him as he put his arms around my waist, "This is the lounge area," then taking my hand, "The kitchen and bathroom," walking a little further, "And this is our love making area."

I giggled feeling a little shy, "Ferdinand we've been sleeping together for a few weeks but haven't made love." He wrapped his arms around me, "Mmm but Jardine is the best place to start."

He picked me up as I laughed again, laying me on the bed, "Mm just having you here makes me excited Hannah. I know you're not ready yet, but I want to help you relax." He lay down beside me, grinning lovingly, moving over to kiss me gently on the neck.

I could feel myself relax playing with his hair, "You're supposed to be showing me Jardine, Ferdinand," when we heard a knock on the door, "Mum are you here yet?"

Ferdinand rolled onto his back groaning, "Well it looks like you will get your wish."

Ferdinand got up, helping me up off the bed, going out to find Amelia, Shiro, Charlotte and Aetius standing on the balcony waiting for us to come out.

I smiled looking at them in the Jardine clothes, thinking that they suited them, "So what have you all done so far?"

Amelia looked at me, "A bit more than you two by the look of it. What did Morag want to see you two about?"

I moved out to sit on the deck, "Oh just asking what happened yesterday. She might want to talk to you two as well. Don't worry about it for now, I want to enjoy being here."

Charlotte shook her head, "I'm a bit annoyed about this, but like you said we may as well enjoy being here. Have you been shown what the houses do?"

I looked at Ferdinand smiling, then back at them, "I was just being given the tour of the general things, but no, I haven't been shown what the houses do."

Charlotte walked into the lounge area, "What colour would you like the walls?"

I wasn't sure where this was going so, I just said, "A deep blue."

Charlotte got my hand and put it on the wall, "Now say that."

I looked unsure, "Deep blue, when the walls in the lounge changed to that colour," with a surprised look on my face, "Wow that's clever."

Amelia also came in, "You can also change the furnishings to your taste as well, by saying what you want."

Charlotte looked at Ferdinand grimacing, "You obviously got distracted."

Ferdinand sighed, "Does anyone want a drink or something to eat?"

Shiro and Aetius came in, "Yes thanks."

After having a drink and a snack, Ferdinand came up to me, "Are you ready for a ride around Jardine?"

I nodded, "Yes, that sounds exciting." I looked at the girls, "So what have you seen so far; do you want to come with us?"

Charlotte shook her head, "No, we have been shown quite a bit with Aetius and Shiro. You two go and enjoy yourselves and we'll meet up for the evening meal, if you like?"

This made Ferdinand perk up, "Ok girls, that sounds good. We'll see you all then."

They took off, with Ferdinand grinning, giving me a hug, "Now where were we?"

I smacked him playfully on the arm, "You were about to take me for a ride to see Jardine."

He took a deep breath, "Ok, let's go." We took off, with him putting me on his back, flying high over bush land with fresh air rushing past, feeling alive.

I couldn't stop smiling looking at the huge trees rising up before us and beautiful blue skies with gently moving clouds above us. Ferdinand pointed out beautiful cascading waterfalls flowing into clear rivers where animals were drinking side by side with each other.

People were also sitting alongside some of the animals or just wading in the water naked, without any fear of being seen, looking so free and natural. There were houses scattered here and there but weren't densely put together, like in my world.

Ferdinand then flew over to a mountain area with snow-capped peaks revealing a tree line further down. I could see something going around the mountain in the distance but couldn't quite make it out.

As we flew closer, I could feel the coolness in the air coming from the snow. Ferdinand turned and pointed to my hands putting gloves on them as I slapped him, "There is no need for these Ferdinand."

He wobbled a little, as I squealed, holding onto his harness, "Leave them on Hannah I don't want to die of fright with those things."

I groaned, "Talk about over dramatic."

As we moved closer to the shapes I could see before, they became clearer, realising they were dragons, frolicking around the mountain with one of them coming up to us, "Hi Ferdinand, who do we have here?"

He hovered as he flapped his huge wings, looking at me smiling, "This is Hannah. Hannah this is Omar. He can be a bit annoying but he's not too bad."

Omar flew up to me, "Nice to finally meet you, Hannah. You should come back to Jardine more often it's better than looking at Ferdinand all the time."

Ferdinand threw a bit of fire towards Omar's tail as Omar yelled back, "You dirty rat."

Ferdinand laughed, yelling to me, "Hold on Hannah, he thinks he's faster than me."

I held on tight to the harness, squealing in delight, as they ducked and dived through trees.

Ferdinand flew low over a river dipping his feet, then flicking his tail up at Omar wetting him, just as Omar was about to send some fire his way, reducing it to hot steam coming out of his mouth.

I laughed out loud, with Ferdinand turning to look at me, "Wouldn't you rather stay here and have fun, Hannah?" I leaned onto his neck, "Soon, Ferdinand."

Ferdinand yelled back to Omar, "See you later old man," and flew back towards the main area of Jardine going via the ocean landing down on the beach, changing to his male form.

I took the gloves off, putting my hand out to take Ferdinand's hand. He looked at me touching my hand gingerly, "Is the blood flowing in that hand Hannah?"

I chuckled, "Don't be silly," grabbing his hand, "I thought you are a dragon."

He wrapped his arms around me giving me a kiss on the neck, "You know I am and if you let me, I'll show you more of me."

I looked down feeling shy again, "Mm Jardine does make you frisky, doesn't it?"

We walked down the beach holding hands smelling the fresh sea air that was clean and clear, sighing as I leaned into Ferdinand, "It is beautiful here, isn't it?"

Ferdinand nodded, "Yes and it could be your home as well, with me. No attacks from people wanting your powers to put up with."

He stopped to look at me, "Are you at least thinking about it, Hannah?"

I looked at him with love in his eyes, "yes, I am Ferdinand; I just need to make sure my girls are alright and I need to sort a few things out in my head. You also have to remember I am still learning a lot about my magic and my family. Please be patient."

He did a little sigh, "I understand. Come on let's get back and have a rest before the main meal event. You'll like that, everyone gathers around to talk and drink just like a big family."

I felt a bit mischievous as a big wave came in, flicking water up at him magically, soaking him, then running off laughing. I could hear him growling, "Oh you little minx," and running after me catching up and throwing me over his shoulder in a fireman's lift, walking into the water. I was laughing and trying to wriggle free from him, "Ferdinand don't be naughty I only wet you a little bit," but it was too late he dropped me into a wave, as it crashed over his legs. I went under still laughing but rebounded quickly, grabbing his legs and pulling him down. All I heard was him yell, "Agghh" not expecting me to get him so fast, as I walked out of water laughing getting my breath back.

He got up looking for me, spluttering from the water wiping his eyes with a determined look on his face, coming towards me.

I giggled at him then saw his look, "No Ferdinand, we are even now," raking his hand through his hair that had fallen over his eyes, "Come here, Hannah."

I went to magicae away from him, but he was quicker than me, putting me in a bear hug, "No you don't, I can still read your thoughts remember," as I squirmed in his grip.

He was just about to pick me up again, when we heard a voice coming not far away, making him look up.

I couldn't see who it was as I was facing the opposite way and he was still holding onto me, "Who is it, Ferdinand?" and trying to look.

He leaned down talking quietly, "It's Lilith." He loosened his grip letting me turn to see Lilith, standing there watching us with a sombre look on her face, "Oh hi Lilith, how are you?"

Ferdinand dropped his arms taking my hand, "Hi Lilith how long have you been back?"

Lilith moved closer, "Only for a couple of hours. They told me you were all here so I thought I'd come and say hello. I couldn't find you in your bungalow so guessed you two would be down by the water somewhere."

I let go of Ferdinand's hand to wring my hair out and get it off my face, "Yes, we always seem to end up in or near the water, don't we? Are you coming to the main meal?"

Lilith nodded, "Yes, I always enjoy those and I am sure you will to Hannah. I see Jardine has healed your wrist, which must feel better."

I looked down at it, "Yes it feels wonderful now. I don't have to wrap it either thank goodness."

Lilith smiled, "Or have to take any more painkillers."

Ferdinand looked at me, piqued, "Especially when you are going to drink, Hannah."

Lilith looked at Ferdinand then back at me curious, but didn't say any more about it, "Well I will let you two get changed. I'll see you at the main meal."

Ferdinand nodded, taking my hand with Lilith glancing to look, then taking off. I didn't say anything but he could hear it in my thoughts, "We are only friends and have been for a long time."

I smiled, "I don't think she quite sees it that way, but I'll leave it with you."

He put his arms around me and magicae back to the bungalow looking up to him, "I'm just going to have a shower." He pushed some wet hair back, "Ok, giving me a kiss," smacking his lips together licking them, "Mm salty," as I smiled.

I came out in my towel, "The shower is free. I'm just going to do a quick meditation before we go out."

He came over to me giving me another kiss, "Mm that's nice too. Are you sure you don't want any help drying yourself?"

I shook my head, "You really are naughty here in Jardine, aren't you? Go and have your shower to cool yourself down."

He pouted his lip, "I'm wearing you down, aren't I?"

I did a little growl looking at him walking off into the bedroom to do some meditation. I took a couple of deep breaths thinking, *'He is working me up, I have to admit.'*

I dried myself off, realising I wasn't sure how to get some more Jardine clothes in trying to imagine it, but nothing came in. I resigned myself to sitting in my towel for now until Ferdinand came out of the shower. I got comfortable in front of a big window that looked out onto the bush in the bedroom, relaxing me quite quickly.

I brought some incense in lighting it and playing my usual meditation on my phone. With the Jardine cleansing, I felt good enough to sit up without getting too stiff or sore, so I closed my eyes listening to the meditation, starting to breathe.

The vision of me on the boat came into my head as I went deeper, then the vision disappeared, realising I had a visitor again, "Hallo bestemor (hello grandma)."

I heard a little chuckle, "Du blir flink (you are getting clever)."

I saw her in a white ghostly form in my vision moving closer to me, "Jardine er enig med deg (Jardine agrees with you)." I laughed, "Jeg liker det her (I do like it here)."

I didn't know it, but Ferdinand had finished his shower coming into the doorway to see if I had finished, just wrapped in his towel. He stood there noticing my towel, that had fallen off me, sitting around to my hips, facing the window, as I spoke Norwegian.

He was thinking about whether to try and get into my vision, which he can do and has done before in my meditation, when he heard a voice coming from the door.

He turned to see Lilith smiling coming in, "Hi Ferdinand, I thought I would come and have a drink with you two before the meal."

He sighed looking back at me, then closing the door on the bedroom, "Hannah is just doing some meditation; I am sure she will like that once she is finished."

Lilith looked at Ferdinand, smiling at him with just his towel around his waist, moving to go nearer to him. He saw her look remembering he was just in a towel, waving his hand over himself, getting dressed. Lilith, a little disappointed, kept a smile on her face, "We don't seem to have much time to talk any more like we used to."

Ferdinand moved over to the kitchen, "You know I am trying to get to know Hannah better Lilith. I do still come to Jardine for a few hours each day, but you are never here then. How is Pardus?"

Lilith sighed sitting on the barstool, "No Morag is keeping me busy with other things at the moment, that is why I am not able to come as much as I would like to, especially to talk to you. Pardus is fine, we haven't seen that much of each other lately."

Meanwhile in the bedroom grandma knew Ferdinand was watching "Ferdinand skulle bli med oss, men noen kom inn (Ferdinand was going to join us but someone came in)." This made my breathing change losing my concentration, "Å var han (oh, was he?)"

Grandma chuckled, "Hvis de er intim med ham vil det gjøre deg sterkere (if you are intimate with him, it will make you stronger)." It was too late I was starting to lose my concentration with Grandma sighing, "Hei Hannah husk hva jeg sa (bye Hannah remember what I said)."

My breathing came back into my head feeling myself back in the room, smelling the white sage incense I had lit, hit my nostrils. I slowly opened my eyes looking at the scene of the bush in front of me, taking a deep breath.

I thought to myself, '*Now here is the test whether I can get up*' stretching my legs out in front of me, letting the towel drop, so I could put my hands on the floor to push myself up.

I did a little wiggle, '*Yahoo I got up without too much trouble, great one Jardine!*'

I wrapped the towel in front of me but not wrapping it fully around, walking out to the kitchen to ask Ferdinand how to get the Jardine clothes in. He was already coming towards me, probably having read my thoughts, when I realised Lilith was there, "Oh sorry I didn't realise anyone was here. I don't know how to get the Jardine clothes in Ferdinand," and feeling a little embarrassed.

I turned quickly to go back into the bedroom with my back and bum showing, along with the family tattoo. Ferdinand rushed up behind me, "Hannah, you're revealing yourself more, come here I will dress you."

Lilith noticed the tattoo, squinting her eyes to zoom into it. I turned to look at Ferdinand noticing Lilith do this, when some clothes came on me replacing the towel.

Lilith quickly turned back to her drink, "Sorry Hannah I thought I would come and have a drink with you two, before the meal."

Ferdinand took my hand, "Come and join us now that you are dressed."

I smiled briefly, "I'll just give my hair a brush and then I'll join you both. Why don't you go and sit on the deck, it's nice out there? I am sure Amelia and Charlotte will be along soon as well."

Ferdinand looked at Lilith, "I'll be right back."

Lilith waved her hand getting up to go out to the deck area, "That's ok. I'll wait out here."

Ferdinand came in as I was brushing my hair, "Bestemor fortalte meg at du lyttet (grandma told me you were listening)." He took the brush out of my hand brushing my hair for me, "Ja jeg var (yes I was)."

I gave him my hairband to put my hair up, looking at me in the mirror, "You're not used to people popping in and out all the time, are you?" I leaned into him once he had finished putting my hair up, "No I'm not, especially one that has an eye for you."

He smirked, "Mm that's a good sign, you're getting jealous."

I turned around trying not to smile, "Oh you're just full of yourself now," trying to push him away. He wrapped his arms around me, giving me a hug, kissing me on the neck, "I'll show you how I feel later."

We heard other voices on the deck area as I giggled, "It's a busy spot lately, isn't it?"

He groaned, "Yes especially when we get a bit cuddly. Come on we'll have a drink and then go to the meal. Not too much alcohol for you though, I need you to behave yourself while you're here."

I sighed, "I'll try, but it doesn't always work out that way. I'll be out in a minute."

He kissed me on the cheek, "Ok, don't be long."

I tidied myself up, feeling a little nervous to meet so many people, like Ferdinand said I'm not used to being around a lot of people all the time. It just slowly creeps up on you that you become more and comfortable with your own company.

I took a deep breath and went out to greet everyone. We had a drink on the deck chatting with other people walking past and joining us. We then went to the area where all the chairs and tables were, as a large number of people were gathering.

I stayed close to Ferdinand my girls and Alira at first but started to relax once we had eaten then started mingling afterwards.

Everyone was very nice, asking about different things from my world. Amelia and Charlotte were in their element chatting away to different people about things going on in our world. They found people who had similar interests to them comparing our world with Jardine's, which made it interesting for them.

Morag came up to me, "Hi Hannah, you are looking very much a Jardine woman already."

I smiled, "I must admit I am not used to having people pop in and out all the time or eating with so many people."

Morag looked dismayed "oh, who is popping in and out all the time Hannah?"

I felt a bit silly saying it now, "Oh it doesn't matter Morag; I am sure she is just being friendly."

Morag pursued "no, I would like to know, Hannah, is it Lilith?"

I nodded, "Yes, but Ferdinand said that she has been friends with him for a long time and not to worry." I could see Morag thinking about it, "She must respect your privacy though, Hannah. If she keeps doing it, please let me know. It is different out in these open areas but if she is popping into your accommodation unannounced, that is not acceptable."

I sighed, "Alright Morag. I am sure she will settle down, although she managed to get a look at my family tattoo, which I didn't want to happen."

Morag shook her head, "Well that is not on. I will have to speak to her."

I tried to calm it down, "It's alright Morag. If she does do it again, I will say something and if she gets offended, I will let you know. How about that?"

Morag nodded, not really happy about it, "Alright Hannah. I'll do it your way. She does have to understand that you and Ferdinand have a lot of catching up to do plus, he needs to make sure you are safe and not be worrying about her."

I nodded, "Ok. Like I said if she keeps doing it, I will say something."

Morag looked a bit happier, "I will also want to have another meeting with you and Alira before you go. I know you and Alira have told us everything you know, but we just want to let you know the conclusion of our findings."

I sighed with acceptance, "Ok Morag. Have you told Alira or do you want me to?"

Just as I said that Alira came up, "Did I hear my name being spoken?"

I laughed, "Yes you did. Morag wants to meet with us before we go home about their thoughts of what happened the other night." She let out a big sigh, "Oh alright," teasing Morag, "I suppose we can make it."

Morag chuckled, "You two are just naughty. I'll see you later."

Alira and I moved over to get another drink, looking over to see where Ferdinand was. He was talking to Shiro, Aetius, Fia and I wasn't sure who the other guy was.

I looked at Alira taking a sip of my drink, "Who is the other guy talking to Ferdinand and Fia over there?"

She glanced over, "Oh that is Lilith's spirit animal Pardus. He's a nice guy, I don't know why she isn't that interested in him."

I groaned a little, "I think I know why, but I've made Morag aware of that. I'm sure she will settle down. This wine is nice, isn't it? It's a shame we can't take it back to our world and sell it."

I laughed, "We could call it Jardine grapes or something."

Alira giggled, "Jardine grapes, good grief. No, I know, how about Jardine magic?"

I chuckled starting to feel the effects of it, "Hey, yes that sounds better."

As we stood there, Alira got called over to a group of women to talk to, so I moved off bumping into Lilith, "Oh hi Hannah. How are you liking the food and wine here?"

I decided to try and be nice, "It is lovely. I was just saying to Alira it would be good to take it back to our world and put it on the market, trying to think up a name to call it."

Lilith shook her head, "Trust you two. Are you feeling a bit more relaxed now?"

I nodded, "Yes, a bit more. I'm just not used to having so many people around me all the time, I guess. I've only just got used to having Ferdinand around all the time except for when he goes to Jardine."

This appeared to surprise her a little, "Oh he is staying at your place a lot, is he?"

I hesitated thinking, '*Oh my be quiet*' "well it appears that he is there all the time. Like I said I'm used to being on my own a lot."

Lilith fell quiet, obviously thinking about it, "We have a lovely dessert; I don't know if you've tried it?"

I looked interested (having a bit of sweet tooth) "oh what is it called? I have tried one of them, that was on the table."

She put up her finger, "I'll get you one, putting out her hand producing a plate with a small purple dessert with a meringue kind of texture on it." She handed it to me, "We call it a fuzzy wuzzy, it's great for people with a sweet tooth but it's not too big."

I put down my glass tasting a small piece of the dessert, "mm it takes nice."

Lilith was smiling, "It is a nice dessert, isn't it?"

I tried to change the subject while eating it, "You must introduce Pardus to me. He looks nice from what I have seen."

She nodded, "I will. I think he has gone now though."

I finished the dessert with a feeling of total relaxation going through my body, picking up my drink to wash the last bits down, staggering slightly.

Lilith looked mildly concerned, "Are you alright, Hannah?"

I started to yawn, "Oh I feel quite tired now. I might go back to the bungalow and have a sleep."

Lilith looked at me, "Yes, you are looking a bit tired. Here I'll point you in the right direction, just follow that path and you'll get there alright."

I put my glass back down with an overwhelming feeling of just wanting to go to bed, not bothering to tell anyone I was going.

Lilith must have thought I might want to do this, "I'll let Ferdinand and your girls know you are going to have a nap."

I nodded waving, as I swayed a little, moving down a path through the bush, out of the meeting area.

Lilith smiled watching me swagger down the path and eventually out of sight. She turned to look around to see where Ferdinand was, going to the bathroom to tidy herself up first then moved over to talk to him properly, without any interruptions.

Lilith stood by Ferdinand who was talking to some other people, when Lilith finally got his attention as he turned smiling at her, "Hi Lilith, are you enjoying yourself?"

His smile made her feel like how he used to be before Hannah came on the scene, making her relax with her decision to give me the dessert. Ferdinand looked at Lilith, "I was talking to Pardus before and he was saying he'd like to do something together with the four of us tomorrow."

She tried not to show her disappointment, "Oh, what sort of things? Isn't Hannah going home tomorrow?"

He shook his head, "No Morag wants to have another meeting with her so we aren't going until the morning after. She can just go to work from here."

He started to look around the crowd that was thinning out now, "Have you seen Hannah? I am sure I saw her talking to you not long ago."

She knew she couldn't brush it off so she lied, "oh she was feeling a bit tired, so decided to go and have a lie down. I thought she said she was going to tell you before she went?"

He put his drink down feeling concerned, "She doesn't know her way around here Lilith, she might have gotten lost."

She looked a little irritated, "She will be alright Ferdinand; she won't come to any harm in Jardine."

Ferdinand got suspicious now, looking at Lilith in the eyes, "Did you give her something?"

Lilith acted offended, but couldn't look in his eyes because she could see anger in there now, as he took her arms, "Lilith answer me," shaking her a little.

She could feel her anger well up, getting upset, deciding to lie again, "She said she would have trouble sleeping, so I gave her a fuzzy wuzzy dessert. It was only a small one and I pointed her in the right direction to go back to your bungalow. I am sure she is there now, sleeping like a baby."

Ferdinand got angry, "She better be, Lilith. I brought her to Jardine because she has been attacked a lot lately, made to sleep and now you do something stupid like this. She got into trouble because they put something in her and it made her magic stronger turning on the people who did it. You better hope this doesn't happen with you!"

Lilith looked defiant at him, "She's not allowed to do that to Jardine people, she needs to learn the rules."

Ferdinand growled, "You're not always in Jardine, are you?"

He stormed away getting Amelia, Charlotte, Shiro, Aetius, Fia and Alira gathering them together in a small circle. Ferdinand told them only part of the story saying that I had wondered off a little drunk and was worried about me being lost.

He went back to the bungalow not finding me there, coming back straight away, "Ok, we need to separate to see where she is. She won't get hurt, but I'm just worried about her. We will come back here in 10 minutes to see what we had found."

Amelia and Charlotte, who were suspicious like me, with Amelia looking at Ferdinand, "I know there is something you're not telling us but we will go and look. She better be ok!"

Morag saw them grouping together but could not to see me around. She then looked over to Lilith who had her head down, stubbornly wiping her eyes, moving off in a huff. They all went off in different directions, going through the bush calling my name looking under bushes in case I had fallen asleep there.

Alira found a path, deciding to follow it feeling nervous, as she still wasn't used to different animals walking freely around her. She was just about to turn back after hearing the sound of lions near her, making her anxious, when she noticed something on the ground ahead of her. She gingerly moved forward finding a pair of shoes on the ground, with big paw prints around them as she screwed up her face, "Oh no, this doesn't look good."

She looked up, noticing another piece of clothing that looked like something I had on. She could hear the lions roar getting closer, putting her hands up to her mouth so she didn't scream; quietly moving closer to find a top on the ground. She looked at the top crouching down to look at it, hearing a lion roar very close now, feeling like she was going to be sick. She crawled up behind a bush to see what was going on, opening the bush carefully to see a pride of lions asleep under a tree, letting out a roar every now and then.

Alira could feel her heart beat quicken and her palms get sweaty, so she magicae back to where they were supposed to meet. Morag was there waiting along with Ferdinand.

All the others slowly came in, looking at Alira, who was now very pale saying, "I think she's been eaten by some lions."

Ferdinand looked in disbelief, "Don't be silly, Alira they don't do that here. Where did you go?"

She pointed a shaking hand with everyone taking off. They landed near the bush where Alira had been, finding the discarded clothing on the ground. Morag took the lead, putting her finger up to her mouth, "Shh" and creeping up to the pride of lions.

Amelia and Charlotte looked fearful at each other because they recognised the clothing as mine, following Morag and Ferdinand.

Alira caught up to Ferdinand and Morag pointing, then jumping onto Ferdinand's back in fear. Ferdinand yelled, "Get off me Alira, what are you doing?"

Alira pointed, only being able to see a leg on one of the lions, "I can see just a leg, she's been eaten, I'm sure of it."

Morag looked angrily at Alira, "Get off his back Alira, Hannah is asleep in the pride. We just don't want to frighten them."

Alira slowly slid down Ferdinand's back with him turning shaking his head, "You crazy woman, go back to Fia and be quiet."

One of the lions on the outside of the pride woke to see Morag standing there, getting up stretching "hi Morag what brings you here?"

Ferdinand walked up slowly towards Morag, looking over to the group of lionesses, to see me asleep in the middle of them all, naked. Ferdinand pointed to where I was, showing Morag, who was trying not to chuckle, "Libua we were looking for the one that is asleep in the middle there."

Amelia, Charlotte and Alira gasped, putting their hands over the eyes of Shiro, Aetius and Fia telling them to turn around. Ferdinand shook his head cringing trying to think how to get me out, without disturbing everyone.

Libua looked over to me in a purring voice, "Oh she came in a little while ago, quite happily going to sleep with us."

Morag put her hands up to calm Ferdinand down, "I'll get her out just be ready to catch her and put something on her."

She checked to see that the others weren't watching then pointed at me levitating me over to Ferdinand's waiting arms, who had a blanket ready to wrap around me. With a sigh of relief, he wrapped me in the blanket giving me a kiss on the cheek, disturbing me, making me grumble and wriggle in his grip, "Hva gjør du (what are you doing?)"

Ferdinand brought me in closer trying not to let anyone else hear me, "Shh go back to sleep, Hannah."

He walked away from the pride of lionesses, letting Morag talk to Libua a bit more, then she came over to the others, "Well thank goodness for that."

She smiled in recognition, "She used to do that when she was young, don't you remember Ferdinand?"

He thought for a moment with recognition coming over him, "Oh yes, she was a little bugger for disappearing, finding her sleeping amongst some animals, especially the lions."

Amelia and Charlotte came over, looking at me asleep, looking annoyed at Ferdinand, "I know Mum didn't drink that much today, so what has made her like this? There aren't any leprechauns around here either?"

Morag picked up my clothes finding bits of dessert on the top, "Who gave her fuzzy wuzzy dessert Ferdinand?"

Amelia looked puzzled, "What's fuzzy wuzzy dessert?"

Morag looking annoyed now, "It's a dessert that was designed to help people sleep, but they are supposed to know this when they eat it, not as a trick."

Ferdinand didn't really want to betray Lilith getting agitated, "I'll take Hannah back to the bungalow and let her sleep it off."

Charlotte was getting angry, "No you tell us now, who gave it to her? We came here to have a break from this rubbish. Whoever you're protecting better be worried Mum doesn't deal with her."

Ferdinand rolled his eyes, "Morag you know who it was, just let me go and take Hannah back to the bungalow."

Morag nodded in recognition, "Yes, I know who it was. I will talk to Amelia and Charlotte, you go."

Morag calmed my girls and Alira down telling them that she will deal with Lilith the Jardine way.

Ferdinand took me back to the bungalow putting a nightie on me and settling me down after being moved. He shut the bungalow up getting changed and climbing into bed with me, feeling relief and disappointment of finding me, but knowing this incident has now spoilt my experience of feeling safe in Jardine, with the possibility of delaying wanting to live here with him. He rolled over, cuddling into me, putting his arm over my waist, eventually going into a fitful sleep.

Chapter 12

I woke early in the morning getting up to go to the toilet and having a drink of water. Ferdinand had been quite restless, waking me a couple of times but this time I just had to get up.

I looked at the time thinking, *'Too early to get up yet'* going back to bed climbing in to have Ferdinand roll over mumbling. I lay there dropping off to a light sleep listening to Ferdinand still mumbling something.

After half an hour of listening to Ferdinand as well as my own thoughts going through my head at 100 miles an hour, especially of what had been happening lately, I decided to do a meditation to the sunrise, getting up quietly so I didn't disturb Ferdinand.

I opened the curtain just enough to let some light in then went out to the deck area quietly shutting the door with just a slight coolness hitting me as I went outside feeling a shiver go over me.

I looked around me smiling to myself smelling the clean air with the scents of all the different plants hitting my senses. The sun was just starting to poke through a low cloud cover that was sitting over the bush area. I worked out the best angle to get the full sunrise on me would be on the lower step, once it had risen. That way I should feel the heat of it on my body.

There weren't many trees and definitely no buildings in front of me to block its progress; so I got comfortable putting my earbuds in my ears stretching my arms and legs to get ready for it.

Just as I was about to start, a big black panther sauntered past me, stopping, "Good morning. You must be Hannah?"

I smiled thinking wow this is strange, "Yes that is right. What's your name?"

He smiled showing a mouth full of really big teeth 'Pantera' with a purring sound coming from him, as he spoke. I smiled, "Nice to meet you, Pantera. Would you like to do some meditation with me?"

He chuckled, "No, that's not my thing. I'll let you get on with it though, happy travels," walking past me with his sleek fur, shimmering in the morning light as he walked.

I decided, rather than doing a visual meditation I would just do a relaxing music one allowing me to turn off, like I'd hoped, from everything that had been happening.

Once the music started and my breathing got into a good rhythm, I could feel my thoughts and body shutting down, like I had done for years, with only the scents and smells of what was around me being present in my mind. The sun was starting to rise hitting my body, warming it through and giving me a sense of re-energising within it.

I had gone quite deep cutting all sounds and thoughts off which felt wonderful for a change, as the sun hadn't risen fully.

Meanwhile Ferdinand had become restless again waking him, with a bit of a start, looking over to find me gone, along with my phone.

Still half asleep and agitated, not finding me there, he started to panic, trying to tap into my thoughts and calling my name but couldn't hear any movement or response from me.

He brushed his hand through his hair in frustration, getting up in the darkened room trying to get his bearings, turning to see some light come from the lounge area from the sun rising. He got up staggering towards it, calling my name again, "Hannah, where are you?"

Again, I didn't answer, feeling his heart rate go up, along with his temper, growling looking around the lounge, kitchen and bathroom areas, not finding me.

In frustration, he pulled open the curtains leading out to the deck area, not seeing me at first because the sun light, that had fully ensconced itself on the deck covering it in bright yellow light, blinded him briefly. I was also sitting on the lower step, so I wasn't fully visible. He pursed his lips into a fine line of anger, finally seeing me sitting on the step, opening the door calling my name again, but I didn't respond.

He stormed towards me frustrated now, "Hannah Dragĕ I've been calling you," picking me up, giving me a fright, not hearing him come up behind me. As he picked me up, he held on tight with his arms encasing me, so I couldn't move. I looked at his face that was contorted with anger getting angry as I struggled against him hitting his chest, "Ferdinand what are you doing?"

Without saying anything, he held my hands, stopping me from hitting him, taking me into the bedroom and laying me roughly down on the bed, straddling my hips as I struggled with him.

I was getting really angry now as I tried to hit him, making him grab my hands and pinning them down growling at me, "I couldn't feel your thoughts and you didn't answer me, don't you do that to me again!" I knew I could use magic to stop him, but I took a deep breath looking at his eyes realising he was panicking, so I tried to calm the situation down, "Let my hands go and I'll show you why I didn't answer you."

When he heard me say this, he too knew he had to calm himself, stopping to take a deep breath, eventually releasing my hands. I carefully put my hands up to my ears as he watched me take my ear buds slowly out of my ears, "I was meditating to the sunrise, Ferdinand trying to shut down for a few minutes."

His face changed to regret bringing his head down beside me, taking a couple of deep breaths, resting his arms next to my head. He kissed me gently on my cheek sounding mournful, "Oh Hannah, when I couldn't find you and couldn't feel any thoughts I panicked. I thought I had lost you again. I'm sorry."

I calmed myself down and stroked my hand through his hair trying to calm him down speaking softly, "I'm sorry, but I needed to shut down. I know you don't like it but I thought you were still asleep."

He lowered himself down on me, calming himself, "Oh shit Hannah, my heart isn't as young as it used to be, feeling it thumping through my chest. I really thought you had gone, especially after what had happened yesterday with Lilith."

I had a gentle smile on my face, "I told you so," as he laughed lightly kissing me on the neck.

We both lay there getting our breath back, as I continued to stroke his hair, feeling my emotions stir with him lying on me, which he hadn't done before.

I tried to slow these emotions down, but they were building as we gently kissed each other on the neck, feeling my breathing start to rise. He put his hand under my head pulling my neck towards him, as I responded moving to allow him to kiss it fully, as his breathing intensified, letting out a gentle groan.

The hand I had going through his hair held his head, guiding it to move down my neck towards my breasts, as he took my nightie off magically, revealing my breasts that were now free for him to cover with his mouth, making me groan.

I wasn't sure what to do as I knew it was different from what we would do in our world, so I put my hand up to his cheek looking at him, feeling our emotions build as he smiled hungrily at me, "Are you ready, Hannah?"

He turned his mouth, kissing the palm of my hand gently going down my arm as I let out a groan, getting my breath back, "Yes Ferdinand."

He raised himself off me enough to point to the door locking it, coming back to me smiling, "No interruptions this time," pulling his t-shirt off then continued to kiss my neck as our breathing intensified. I continued to hold his head with my hand in his hair, hearing him groan.

I could feel my body responding to him wriggling under his hips as he moved taking his shorts off; with our skin touching properly for the first time, feeling my senses tingle.

He continued moving down to my breasts kissing me with butterfly kisses, making my nipples raise in excitement, as I watched him go down. He looked up to me as he kissed between my breasts with lust in his eyes, "Are you sure you're ready, Hannah?"

I put my hands in his hair breathing heavily groaning, "Yes Ferdinand."

He raised himself up looking to the side of the bed clicking his fingers with shards of white crystals and lit white candles appear next to the bed in a staggered formation.

I turned to look at this appear a little confused, but he came back up to my neck turning my head to look into his sultry eyes, "Just relax Hannah, I will guide you." He put his arms around me, lifting us off the bed (magically) levitating above the crystals and with the candles surrounding us like a white halo of protection from their glow.

My breathing was excited with my heart racing, as I looked around me to see the reflection of the crystals in the candle light hitting the walls in the room with it looking like the reflection from a chandelier, gently swaying in a breeze.

He smiled lovingly at me with the light from the candles hitting our eyes which looked like pools of water. He was holding onto me with one arm around my waist and the other moving up to hold my head with his hand running through my hair. He moved my head so he could kiss my neck again, moving up to my mouth, kissing me fully on my lips feeling his passion vibrate through me, as I groaned.

I put my arm around his waist feeling the touch of his skin on mine as his kissing intensified making it hard to breath, but I wanted more, putting my hand up to his head as I hungrily pushed his mouth onto mine hearing him groan.

I could feel an intense vibration going through us when the crystals emitted a binding light forming a crisscross pattern around our bodies joining us together. As our passion rose, I could feel the binding light from the crystals become tighter over us, joining us as one with the vibrations building within me, feeling my sacral chakra pulse.

As the intensity of our passion grew to a point where I couldn't stand it anymore a misty orange light exploded from within me, surrounding us, emitting a groan and shudder.

I tried to move my mouth away; but his mouth was still on mine, not letting me go. I could feel the vibration from him building up, exploding with an orange misty light come from within him. This made me want to hold his head still on my lips as the passion exploded so he couldn't get free from my mouth hearing him groan.

We were both breathing heavily as he released my mouth moving down my neck again with his arms still wrapped possessively around my waist. He moved one hand to hold my head with his hand entangled in my hair.

I groaned again feeling myself orgasm with a dampness between my legs quietly saying, "Meine liebe (my love)."

I felt him flinch a little after I said that, but he didn't say anything. I leaned into his neck feeling spent, holding onto him watching the beautiful lights from the crystals floating around the room, with it looking magical.

We stood there in each other's embrace just enjoying the calming of our bodies and the shared love we had just experienced. He leaned his head down speaking softly, "How do you feel Hannah?"

I looked up to him with the lights reflecting off our eyes showing the love for each other that we had just shared sighing, "Wonderful honey." He smiled then kissed me on the lips gently.

The crisscross lights slowly evaporated into our bodies to be there forever from our shared love.

He then magically took us back to the bed putting me under him protectively covering us with the sheet. He flicked his fingers as I watched to see the crystals and candles disappear. He then brought his hand up to my jaw bringing it back to face him kissing me again on the lips as he groaned. I let out a sigh in satisfaction, putting my hand on his neck holding him there again.

He released my lips then lay down next to me looking at me smiling, "Did you enjoy that, Hannah?"

I felt a bit shy while I held onto him, "Yes, it was beautiful Ferdinand, did you enjoy it?"

He let out a gentle chuckle, "Yes I did Hannah, it was what I have been waiting for a long time."

I sighed in satisfaction, "Well you've exhausted me." We lay there looking into each other's eyes eventually falling asleep in his arms feeling content. I woke with a start, with the sound of my phone beeping, as a message came in.

Ferdinand groaned, leaning over me getting it for me flicking it on, "It's Amelia."

I took it, reading the message, "How are you feeling, Mum? Can we come over soon?" I looked at the time realising it was nearly 10.00am, "Ferdinand it's nearly 10.00am and they're wanting to come over."

He put his hand on my jaw bringing it around to him kissing me on the lips again with me responding but groaning, "Don't be naughty, Ferdinand." He chuckled, "Mm I suppose we better get up."

I got up reluctantly sitting on the side of the bed texting back, *"Give us 10–15 minutes then come. I'm feeling good now thanks. Luv Mum."*

He came up behind me kissing me on my back, "What do you want for breakfast?"

I smiled, "I think you've given me breakfast already." He grinned with a naughty look in his eyes, "I'll just surprise you, shall I?"

Before he left, "Can you bring the Jardine clothes in I still can't seem to get them in?" He smiled again, "Sure honey," waving his hand making some clothes appear.

I got up going into the bathroom to have a wash, looking at myself in the mirror, noticing a fine pink mist float around me. I brushed my hair and put a little bit of makeup on then waved my hands around trying to move the pink mist off me. I mean it was pretty but I couldn't think what I was going to say to my girls.

Ferdinand came in laughing looking at me in the mirror, "You can't get rid of that; it goes on its own accord; that's Jardine style."

I bit my lip gasping, "Oh dear what am I going to say to my girls? Why didn't you say this happened when you were describing it to me before?"

He tapped me on the bum, "Like you told us you had initiated the girls into your family book before the ceremony."

I turned around groaning, "Ferdinand that's not the same!"

He walked out chuckling, "Just tell them the truth," making me annoyed trying to wave the mist that was floating around me.

Ferdinand called out, "Hannah, your girls are here."

I sighed resigning myself to a tirade of questions blah blah from my girls, especially Charlotte. I walked out holding my breath looking at Ferdinand who was in the kitchen grinning like a Cheshire cat as I shook my head walking towards the deck area.

The sun was shining on the deck making the girls hair look as though it had a halo around their heads but as I got closer, I started to grin. Amelia and Charlotte came in to greet me with their eyes downcast looking up at me when we were quite close to each other hesitating then burst out laughing.

I shook my head, "Looks like Dragĕ women get randy together as well." My girls looked at each other with their pink mist floating around them, then over to me smiling, giving each other a hug, walking out to sit down under the shade on the deck.

Shiro and Aetius were there looking a bit nervous at me waiting for my reaction. I sat down, "It's alright Shiro and Aetius. I think the Dragĕ women had the same thoughts at the same time." Relieved, they started to laugh with Shiro sighing in relief, "Yes it certainly does, Hannah. I think I will go and help Ferdinand with the food now, I'm getting hungry. Aetius, are you coming?"

Aetius who was looking nervous but relieved now nodded, "Sure thing."

Alira and Fia came past looking at us with our swirling mist grinning, I looked at Alira chuckling, "Well Alira, it looks as though there were a few randy women in Jardine."

Alira put her arms out looking at the pink mist swirling around her, "Yes it was a great experience but I'm not sure about this, it's a dead giveaway isn't it, Sis?"

I patted a chair, "Come and sit with us and have something to eat and a chat."

She looked excited, "Sure will. Fia you can go and help the guys if you like."

Fia smiled nodding his head, "Yeah sure thing."

We were all chatting comparing notes when Morag arrived, "Well hello the Dragĕ family and Alira. It looks like you have all been having a bit of Jardine intimacy. Do you mind if I join you?"

I smiled, "Of course not Morag come and sit with us, we are about to have some brunch. I'm sure Ferdinand has made enough food to feed an army."

Morag sat down looking at the four of us, "You all look beautiful with your pink mist. I hope you enjoyed it as much as your world loving." A little hesitant at first, I nodded, "Yes it was wonderful, but different to what we are used to I guess."

Morag sighed looking fondly, "Ah I remember my first time, such a wonderful time."

She leaned in closer so the others couldn't hear her, "Just watch them now though, they can become a bit possessive. They might be from Jardine but they still have some annoying male ways." We all leaned back knowingly nodding, "Yes we know what you mean."

Morag looked to see where the men were moving in again, "How are you after your experience yesterday, Hannah? You can't even come to Jardine for a bit of peace and quiet by the look of it."

Alira laughed, "Yeah and you nearly made me as white as you after all with your lions Hannah. Good grief why did you have to pick blasted lions?"

I smiled, "They just looked so cuddly and for some reason familiar."

Morag put her hand on mine, "You used to do that when you were little Hannah. We were forever looking for you with Ferdinand pulling his hair out then. We'd find you in the end cuddled up, usually with the lions, fast asleep."

Ferdinand came over with the food with a cheesy grin on his face, "Yes, I remember that, I'm surprised I'm not bald by now. Looks like you haven't really changed that much, Hannah."

Charlotte laughed, "Yes you are lucky, that happened to a couple of Mum's boyfriends. They had hair to begin with, but went bald."

I looked at Charlotte disapprovingly, "Charlotte don't be naughty."

Ferdinand just shook his head going back to get the rest of the food.

Morag quickly said before Ferdinand came back, "We have dealt with Lilith; she is not allowed near you two without someone else with her for now. We have also taken some of her duties in your world off her, as she appears to be behaving too much like some of your women."

Amelia looked at Morag annoyed, "Well she better not try anything on Mum in our world because she won't have your protection there."

I sighed trying to calm it down, "I am sure she will leave us alone now, especially if she finds out that Ferdinand and I have been intimate."

Morag nodded, "Yes more than likely, Hannah."

Ferdinand came over with pancakes and fruit along with water and coffee for drinks. We tried to forget about all the other stuff laughing and joking about our pink mist and how we had all done it at the same time.

Amelia looked at me, "What did you think of the orbs, Mum?"

I looked a little confused, "What orbs?"

She sighed, "Didn't Ferdinand take you over to that area? That is also where the community make things etc."

Ferdinand looked over, "I wanted to show her my favourite places first, that is all. I'm going to take her there today."

Charlotte nodded, "Yeah sure Ferdinand. We can take her there today if you want to go and hang out with the other spirit animals. Aetius and Shiro are doing that."

I could see Ferdinand wasn't liking being told what to do, "No it is alright. I will do that when Hannah has her meeting with Morag. I prefer to keep an eye on your mum just in case trouble finds her again." I looked at Morag smirking with her acknowledging me with a little grin. I made a move to get up, encouraging the others to do the same, helping with the dishes and tidying up. Morag caught Ferdinand alone as everyone was cleaning up wanting to talk to him, "Ferdinand I need to ask you something?"

Ferdinand turned his back to us looking at Morag, "What is it Morag?"

Morag was trying to find the right words "I know Hannah has been speaking a different language, especially when she is sleeping. Can you confirm this?"

Ferdinand didn't look happy about it, "Yes Morag that is correct, she is speaking Norwegian. I told Hannah I wouldn't tell anyone though. Can I ask how you found out?"

She patted his arm, "Amelia let it slip when I was talking to her about the other night. Has she told you anything about why she is speaking it and who taught her?"

He took a deep breath, "She said her grandma taught her who she sees in her visions, but mainly in her meditation. She was speaking to her yesterday in her meditation and I was going to join her, as I have sometimes, but Lilith came into the house unannounced, which was a bit frustrating. Hannah says she has asked her name but she will not tell her."

Morag frowned, "Yes Lilith has been told to stay away unless she is with one of us from now on. If she starts to bother you again, I want to know about it. Thank you Ferdinand I only need to know what we are dealing with, that is all."

Morag looked over to me then back to Ferdinand, "We are wanting to see how Alira and Hannah act when they have been drinking again. Can you encourage her to have a couple before she comes to the next meeting? I'm asking Fia the same thing."

Ferdinand looked puzzled, "Is that wise, Morag?"

Morag smiled, "If they play up like they did the other night at least we can control it and see for ourselves what is happening between them, rather than it happen in their world."

Ferdinand thought about it, "I suppose it would be interesting to see how they react again."

Once finished Morag gave us all a hug, "I'll see you and Alira before the evening meal for our meeting. Enjoy yourselves."

As we gathered together, I checked with the others if they wanted to come with us, with Charlotte looking defiant, "Yes I'll come with you, I'm sure Amelia will want to have a look again, won't you, Amelia?"

Alira smirked at me, looking down, "I may as well come with you as well Hannah. I didn't get a really good look last time."

Ferdinand didn't say anything shutting the door and grabbing my hand, "Well come on we can walk to some of the things from here."

We walked along with Ferdinand pointing some things out as we went to an area that had what we would call a transport area, with huge pink orbs in an area with platforms going up to each orb. The orbs were surrounded by bush but had winding paths going up to the platform for each orb. Amelia came up smiling, "These are fantastic Mum, you travel in them."

I looked at Ferdinand, "Do you know how to operate them, Ferdinand?"

He smiled, "Yes dear." He walked over to an orb still holding onto my hand, "Here I'll take you for a spin."

Charlotte came up behind us, "Can I open it?"

He stepped aside refusing to let my hand go, "Help yourself Charlotte."

Charlotte put her hand on a panel that had a picture of a hand on it closing her eyes. A door opened from the side of the orb splitting in two with stairs going down and the other half opening up so you didn't bang your head, similar to a small plane's entrance.

I looked at Ferdinand and Charlotte, "Impressive. Is that all thought control Charlotte?"

She nodded, "Yes, it's brilliant, isn't it?"

She went into the orb with us following and sitting down. The others followed us as I tried to get out of Ferdinand's grip. I leaned in, "You don't need to hold my hand all the time Ferdinand everyone is around us; I am sure there isn't any trouble around here."

He brought my hand up to his mouth kissing it looking determined, "I'm not taking any chances Hannah; the others can fly this."

Alira came in, sitting next to me grinning, "He's determined, isn't he?"

I sighed, "I'm sure it will wear off. I have to go to work tomorrow, that will be interesting."

Alira just put her head down shaking it, giving a little chuckle, "I can come and pick you up if you like?"

Ferdinand heard her, "No it is alright, I will take her."

I turned to look at Ferdinand smiling, "You're stubborn."

Amelia and Charlotte did paper rock scissors to see who would drive the orb. Amelia won making me laugh, "They're still competitive." Amelia went over to a panel, placing her hands on it.

Charlotte shut the door sitting down in front of us watching her sister making sure she did it right, pointing to the control panel putting some music on, "Sweet but Psycho" as I listened to the words grinning.

Ferdinand groaned pointing at it, putting on some Chopin music, sounding like we were in an elevator, glaring at Charlotte not to touch it. I looked at Alira trying not to laugh at these determined people.

We moved off quietly floating up into the air as I looked out of the orb at the scenery floating past. We could see through the floor as well with Charlotte pointing out different animals walking past without a care in the world.

She looked like a little girl again with excited eyes, as she was chatting along, "Look Mum there's a dodo bird. It's extinct in our world."

Alira pointed at something moving stealthy through the bush, "Wow that looks like the Tasmanian tiger Hannah. OMG it is," as it came out of the bush area looking up at us. She looked at me smiling, "I wonder if they'll let me take home a breeding pair so they can be put back into Australia?"

Charlotte looked scornful now, "Why, so they can kill them again?"

Alira shook her head disappointingly "yes I suppose you're right, Charlotte."

Charlotte pointed out some buildings with plants growing on their rooves but were quite big compared to other buildings in Jardine, "That's the science areas Mum. They invent things and study things there. I've had a look inside already; they have some fabulous things going on in there."

Ferdinand looked pleased with this kind of talk, "So do you think you would come and live here Charlotte?"

Charlotte thought about it, "I suppose I would be interested, why are you asking, Ferdinand?"

He looked at me then back at her, "I'm just trying to get your mum to come and live here but she is worried about you two."

I looked a little annoyed, "Ferdinand, we'll talk about this later. It's only our second day here."

He squeezed my hand, "I'm going to keep trying, Hannah."

We floated gently over a huge garden area surrounding some buildings, with Charlotte commentating to us what everything was or what they did there. We floated past a market area landing near it, with Charlotte getting up, "This is where they give the things away that people have made. You don't need money or anything. Come on let's go and have a quick look."

She got up and opened the door with everyone filing out moving towards the little stalls. Ferdinand called out to them, "Don't get too excited you may not be able to take some of these things back to your world."

I could hear the girls groan, "Ahh that's annoying."

We came across a jewellery stand with a lady standing behind the counter looking affectionately at us, "Oh you two look lovely together. Are you looking for something nice Ferdinand to celebrate your joining?"

He grinned looking at me lovingly, "Yes, what do you recommend Kósmima."

She moved over to a simple silver bracelet with a rose quartz stone beautifully embedded on the top of it in the shape of a heart, bringing it over smiling, "This one has drawn me to it. What do you think, Hannah and Ferdinand?"

I smiled thinking, '*Oh she knows my name,*' as she gave it to Ferdinand to put on my wrist. He took it looking at me, as I put my wrist up and he put it on giving me a kiss on the cheek, "What do you think, Hannah?"

I looked at it grinning, feeling strange receiving gifts from Ferdinand, "It looks lovely, but can I take it home with me?"

He nodded, looking towards Kosmima, "I'm sure we can ask Morag to take it back with you. Besides you'll be back before you know it to live in Jardine."

Kosmima clapped her hands with a big grin on her face, "Oh that will be lovely Hannah."

I grinned nervously, "We are still talking about it Kosmima, but it will happen eventually. Thank you."

She waved, "Hope to see you again soon, Hannah," as we walked on.

Ferdinand took my hand looking at the bracelet which looked really nice on making me stop, "You're being naughty Ferdinand, telling people I'm coming back to live soon." He looked at me seriously, "I want you to be safe Hannah and I want you with me. I'll keep pushing until you move here."

He put his hand up to my chin making me look at him, "I want to give you gifts whenever I want, so get used to it Hannah."

I moved into him, "I'm just not used to it Ferdinand. Just remember I have had trouble here already as well. You'll just have to be patient."

Alira came up to us, "Ok you two, enough of that. Let's get going before they fill up the orb with stuff."

Amelia and Charlotte had a couple of things in their hands with Ferdinand frowning shaking his head, "I don't know if you can take those back, girls."

Charlotte as determined as ever, "Well we will try Ferdinand. Oh, Mum that bracelet is nice where did you get that from?"

Ferdinand groaned, "We are going now. Save it for another time."

Amelia and Charlotte rolled their eyes with Amelia saying to Charlotte, "He thinks he can boss us around now that he's had his way with Mum."

I heard that giving them a look that only a mother can, that made them be quiet.

We got back into the orb with Amelia taking the controls again, floating up gently going over a housing area that was scattered through the bush looking so peaceful and idyllic.

Ferdinand looked at us all, "Do you want to go for a swim in the sea or lake?"

I smiled, "I would, how about all of you?"

Amelia and Charlotte were interested. Alira wasn't sure, "I'm not a big swimmer but I am happy to walk along the edge."

Ferdinand got up finally letting my hand go, "So what do you want sea or lake?"

I looked at them, "I'm happy with either. What do you girls want to do?"

Amelia moved aside, "I'd like the beach myself," with Charlotte eventually nodding, "Yeah, I think the beach would be nice."

Ferdinand put his hands on the panels changing the direction of the orb to go towards the coast with it finally coming into view like a picturesque scene on a TV as it stretched out before us on the edge of stunning bushland.

I smiled at the sight of it coming in through the orb looking a magnificent blue with white crest waves crashing onto a white sandy beach. There were some people there already swimming or just sitting under shelters.

Ferdinand landed the orb as Charlotte got up to open the door for us to get out. We were all able to change our clothes to swimmers. Alira happy to sit on the beach under a shelter watching us. Aetius, Shiro and Fia came in the water having a great time splashing around.

I came out sitting on the beach next to Alira with Ferdinand and Fia coming to join us panting and wet, drying themselves off. I looked at the water with a big smile lying down on the towel to dry off, "Ahh that was beautiful."

Ferdinand lay down beside me smiling leaning over to give me a kiss, "It's not bad here is it, Hannah?"

I rolled my eyes chuckling, "It is lovely Ferdinand, thank you for reminding me again," hearing a little chuckle come from Alira.

Fia looked at Ferdinand slyly bringing out some wine, "Come you two let's have a glass of wine while we are relaxed and having some fun."

I sat up taking the glass off Fia, "This is nice, thank you."

Alira took one as well, "I don't normally drink on the beach, but this is a special occasion I guess."

Fia and Ferdinand both had a glass sipping on it slowly as we chatted away. Ferdinand decided to make a picnic of it bringing out a blanket and some food.

Amelia, Charlotte, Aetius and Shiro came out of the water to join us looking excited at the picnic. They all got dried and sat down to join us.

We were all chatting away or just relaxing having the wine along with snacking on the food enjoying ourselves without any fear of being hassled.

Both Fia and Ferdinand were passing the wine around quite generously which was not only relaxing us but getting us giggly. Alira and I joked with them, "Are you trying to get us drunk or something?"

Ferdinand grinned, "No, we're just celebrating being in Jardine and being intimate."

Alira nudged me, "I must confess I enjoyed myself, how about you, Hannah?"

I looked shyly, "Yes it was a nice experience," looking at Ferdinand.

We had just finished our third glass of wine when Cara appeared on the beach walking up to where we were, "Hi everyone, are you having a lovely time."

Ferdinand was just giving me another glass of wine asking Cara if she wanted one. Cara raised her eyebrow with a cheeky grin, "Yes I think I will, thanks Ferdinand."

Everyone else had another glass while we chatted to Cara about what we had been doing today.

Once Cara had finished her drink her demeanour changed, "I'm afraid I'll have to spoil your fun. Morag would like to see Hannah and Alira for the meeting she had planned for later, now."

Alira and I giggled looking at each other with me saying, "Well it looks like we're the test bunnies again," giving each other a high five. A spark shot off our hands with us both giggling.

Ferdinand looked surprised at Cara, "I don't think they should go now Cara. Hannah should have a rest."

Cara looked determined, "No Ferdinand, Morag wants to see them especially now."

She got up helping me up and then Alira grinning at us both, "Come you two giggling women."

Ferdinand got up and took my hand, "I want to come with Hannah in case she gets a bit excited."

I giggled, "Relax Ferdinand, we haven't got anyone to put in the washing machine today."

Alira bent over giggling, "That's a shame, are you sure there isn't anyone we can wash today," looking around her. She noticed Lilith walking along the water's edge with another woman pointing to her, *"Abracadabra a snake shall appear to wrap around the snake over there."*

Fia came up behind her taking her hand, "Alira what did you just do?" We all heard a scream, turning to see Lilith wrapped in a snake similar to the ones you would see on the drawings of the Aboriginal people. This started me off giggling as we watched Lilith rolling around on the sand yelling with a white painted snake wrapped around her.

Cara growled, "Alira take that off her so we can get going."

Fia put his arm around Alira's shoulders who was laughing hysterically trying to calm her down. He tried to look seriously at her but had to keep looking away to stop laughing, "Come on dear take it off, Lilith."

I went to take Alira's hand but Ferdinand stopped me, "Hannah, I think you need to have a rest," and went to pick me up.

Cara called out, "No Ferdinand. I am taking them to the meeting. If you are going to be difficult, I will get some help. Come on Alira take that off Lilith so we can get going."

Alira groaned, "There's always a party pooper." She turned towards Lilith reversing the chant then took Cara's hand.

I blew Ferdinand a kiss, "Be a good dragon dear and take the girls back in the orb."

I looked cheekily at them all, quickly turning to take Alira's hand while still holding onto Cara's hand, *"Ring a ring a rosie up in the air we shall be, the sand will blow around thee, a tissue a tissue blowing Lilith into the sea."*

All they heard was a scream come from Cara, as we went up into the air spinning around as though we were on one an amusement ride, moving slowly over the sand towards Lilith. The sand was stirring up slowly at first but when it hit Lilith, who was just getting up from Alira's chant, hitting her again knocking her down. The sand was blowing her around eventually throwing her into the sea.

Cara yelled out, "Cut it out whoever is doing this you two."

I giggled, "Oh alright," watching the sand drop as I did a reverse chant. Lilith was in the water by now looking very angry, getting up and throwing her fist up in the air, "I'll get you two for this."

Cara finally managed to get us to the meeting room landing in front of the door, looking very bedraggled, dropping our hands, "You two let go of each other now!"

--ooOoo--

Amelia and Charlotte were buckling over in laughter with the men looking on trying to be serious. Ferdinand watched as Lilith was thrown into the sea, "Oh shit, she's going to get angry with them now."

As they packed up the picnic, Ferdinand was thinking, then talking quietly to Fia, "I wish we hadn't given them the wine now."

Fia nodded, "I didn't think they would play up that much again."

Ferdinand nodded looking worried, "I agree. They are definitely stronger when they join together."

Amelia noticed Ferdinand and Fia talking, "Well it wasn't those tablets Mum took, by the look of it."

Charlotte joined in laughing, "Lilith got what she deserved though."

Aetius and Shiro put their heads down trying not to laugh then put their arms around Charlotte and Amelia trying to tell them off.

Ferdinand had sent everything away and was going towards the orb, "Does anyone know if anything else has happened?"

Everyone shook their heads with Amelia saying, "No not that we know. It's put a bit of a dampener on coming here with these meetings, hasn't it Ferdinand?"

Ferdinand looked disappointed, "Yes it has, I'm trying to get your mother to come here to live."

--ooOoo--

I looked sulkily at Cara then dropped my hand, "I think we're in trouble again Alira."

Alira pouted, "yep certainly looks like it, Sis."

Cara opened the door, "They are waiting for you in there, please go in."

We went into a plainly painted room with chairs and tables in it. There were two women sitting with Morag, who looked up when we walked in. She took one look at Cara's face and hair getting up greeting us, "Hello Alira and Hannah. Have you two been up to mischief again?"

Cara sighed, "Let's just say Lilith has been paid back for the fuzzy wuzzy desert. I will leave these two with you," as she took off.

Morag looked at us both with downcast eyes trying to hide a smile, "Take a seat Alira and Hannah. I want to introduce you to a couple of experts we have here in Jardine. They are also very interested in your ancestry along with your ghosts—Hannah. Something we don't have a lot of experience with."

I flopped down on the chair with Alira following me. We went to hold hands but Morag came over to us, "Can you not hold hands for now. I'll introduce you to Fantomo and Gua." Fantomo who had long brown hair hazel eyes, olive skin and was wearing white robes. The other lady Gua was of Asian appearance who was slim built with fine features, jet black hair with large brown eyes, making her face look doll like and was wearing white robes as well.

I smiled at the two women trying to behave myself, "So what can we do for you two?"

Fantomo had an iPad in front of her, "I would like to ask you both about your family lines. Morag has said that you don't know anything about your family after a certain period of time. Alira, I know in your culture a lot of the ancestry wasn't written down and was done through song and dance. Do you have any other information on your family?"

I shrugged my shoulders, "My mother wasn't interested in our family line or the magic for that matter, so I am not sure how far we go back. I have been meaning to go to Norway and Germany to check out the family, but haven't managed to get there yet."

Alira was thinking about things while I was talking, "I don't know a lot as well. I will have to ask my mother and her sister to find out more. I know our family has a very long line of magic; how far I'm not sure."

Fantomo was putting this information into her iPad as we spoke. "We may have to assist you both with your research as you appear to have a strong link between you two."

Gua came forward now with a device in her hand that looked like Dr Who's sonic screwdriver, "Can I get you two to hold hands now so I can measure your magical strength with this?"

Alira and I grinned at each other holding hands, with a spark appearing, as Gua put the instrument over them showing a surprise on her face as she watched the readings, "Oh this is very interesting. Can you do a simple chant together while I still take a reading?"

I looked at Alira trying to think of something when Morag moved forward, "Make sure it is something where we will not be harmed Hannah and Alira."

Alira rolled her eyes, "Oh, alright Morag."

I looked around the plain room pointing to the walls putting a moving bush scene around it with butterflies and dragonflies flying in and out of the bush, going around the wall. Alira smiled, "Aww that nice. I think you need a bit of Aussie in there though, Sister," pointing to the walls putting kangaroos and emus bouncing around and going in and out of the bush.

I could hear Morag sigh in relief as she watched Gua take their measurements. Gua again looked surprised raising an eyebrow, "That is excellent Hannah and Alira. That will do for now."

Fantomo now came forward not sure how to word what she wanted to say, "I am interested in your ghosts, Hannah."

She turned to Alira, "Do you have any visions of ghosts Alira?"

Alira frowned, "No, it is frowned upon in our culture. We only visit them in our dreamtime which is a very personal time. We don't like to share with anyone else."

Fantomo nodded, making a note of this, "Thank you, Alira. I will respect your customs and not ask again."

She then turned back to me, "Hannah, I believe you have spoken with family ghosts for a number of years?"

I was starting to sober up, as well get a little tired of these questions, "Yes, that is correct. I found them better to talk to when I was younger than people who were alive."

Fantomo could see I was getting restless but carried on with questions, "I just want to ask a couple more questions then you two can go and enjoy yourselves again."

I sat up looking happier with this, "What do you want to know Fantomo?"

She again looked as though she wasn't sure how to word what she wanted to say, "Please don't take offence with this, but do you think your ghosts could use you as a vessel to get into Jardine?"

I raised an eyebrow shaking my head, "No Fantomo, I don't believe they would. I think if they really wanted to get in here, they would have done it a long time ago. Do you consider me a threat because of this?"

Fantomo and Morag looked worried with Morag speaking up, "No Hannah we don't. As you know we do take our security very seriously as there are always people trying to get into Jardine in anyway, they can. As we have told you there is a lot of dark magic around from the split many years ago. We just don't want that entering Jardine."

Alira looked at me with a sideways glance then back at Morag, "From what I have learned about Hannah's past, she would have turned bad a long time ago even without her magic, so I don't think you have anything to worry about there."

I leaned forward rubbing my hands in agitation, "Just remember Jardine invited me back, I didn't seek it out." Just as I said this, I could feel that distinct coolness in the room making me sit up thinking, '*Oh shit.*'

Morag could feel it as well, looking around the room, "Who is it, Hannah?"

I put my head down groaning, "I think one of my grandmothers is here?" Sure, enough a vision appeared of Matilda. Her outline became stronger moving over to me then turning to look at Morag, "Hello Morag."

Alira turned away groaning, "Oh Hannah, you and your ghosts."

Morag smiled, "Hello Matilda, what brings you here?"

Matilda looked annoyed, "Why are you questioning Hannah like this? She has not done anything wrong. This is why I did not remain in Jardine; you will only do the same to, Hannah."

Morag fidgeted with her hands looking down at them, "Sorry Matilda. You know we have to be careful."

I looked over at Fantomo and Gua who were sitting there opened mouthed with their instruments whirring away taking notes.

Matilda moved closer to Morag, "Maybe you should look at some of the people who have been in Jardine for a number of years assuming aliases, rather than Hannah who is new and has managed to keep a good heart."

Morag looked confused, "Can you tell me who these people might be Matilda?"

Matilda shook her head in disgust, "You know who Morag; you have had your suspicions for a long time. If you don't sort it out Hannah's ancestors will help her sort it out. No more Dragé women will die because of these people either. This charade has lasted long enough."

She then disappeared.

Morag looked uncomfortably at me as though she had just been told off, "Well that has sorted that question out Hannah along with why Matilda didn't come to Jardine very much."

I slumped back in my seat looking annoyed, "So, do you want me and my girls to leave Jardine and not come back?"

Morag got up looking apologetic, "No Hannah! Like we said, there are a lot of strange and new things happening, especially with you two. We want to be there for you all to help, not to restrict or alienate you."

Fantomo and Gua were putting things into their iPad madly exchanging notes quietly between themselves like excited professors discovering a new cure. Fantomo could feel we were getting ready to go putting her hand up to ask us something else "can I ask if you two one more personal question. Do you still get your periods? Only I have been told that women in your world go into sync."

I put my hand up to my implant on my arm, "I do a little bit but I have implant in so it is just light and I am due for it soon." I turned to look at Alira who had also put her hand up to her arm grinning, "I have one of those as well. Mum thought it would control my tempers, which it does most of the time. I'm due as well; it looks like we are in sync."

I looked over to Alira's arm noticing a dull white mark on her arm then turned back to Fantomo, "I played a lot of sport when I was younger and have experienced all of us going into sync together. The poor coach had some terrible times."

Fantomo looked as though she had won the noble prize, "Oh that is wonderful, thank you."

Morag smiled, "Come on I think you two have had enough. Go and enjoy the rest of your stay at Jardine. You know you can come back whenever you want, just let us know and we will bring you in."

I got up feeling a lot better with the backup I had, with Matilda appearing and Morag's change. I was curious as to who Matilda was talking about, but I thought I would leave that for another time as I wanted to get back to everyone.

Alira stood up looking pleased, "Well if that is all I'd like to go."

Fantomo and Gua got up looking grateful for all the things we had let them experience with Fantomo saying, "If you need any more help in researching your families, please let us know."

Morag came closer to me moving me aside talking quietly, "Can I ask you one more question, Hannah?"

I nodded smiling, "Yes Morag, what is it?"

She hesitated, "Har et av spøkelsene dine lært deg å snakke norsk (has one of your ghosts taught you how to speak Norwegian?)"

I grinned back at her, "Ja, men jeg vet ikke hva hun heter (yes, but I don't know her name)."

I knew she had one more question leaning in "What else do you want to know Morag?"

She grinned knowingly, "Can you let me know if anything happens with your ancestors when you are being intimate or meditating with Ferdinand?"

I looked puzzled not bothering to ask why, "Yes sure, Morag."

She patted my arm looking happier, "Thank you, Hannah. Do you want us to send you to your bungalows?"

I looked over to Alira noticing she was stretching herself out, as I felt a bit stiff as well, "No it's not far, I think we might walk back. Can you just point us in the right direction?"

Morag nodded walking over to the door looking back in the room, "Can you two take that off the walls as well before you go. It is pretty, but we prefer it to be plain. Are there any questions you would like to ask before you go?"

I grinned waving my hand over the walls with Alira following me to get rid of her part. I looked curiously at Morag, "Is it normal for your spirit animals to be able to speak a different language?"

Morag put her head on the side thinking about it, "No, not unless they have something to do with that nationality."

I shrugged it off, "Ok thanks."

Morag walked us to the door showing us which way to go, "I will catch up with you two later at the evening meal and if Ferdinand or Fia get grumpy send them to me to deal with. Try not to get into any more mischief."

Alira and I giggled as I said, "It appears to find us. See you later Morag."

Alira looked at me mischievously pushing me into one of the bushes then running off, "Come on Sister I'll race you."

I burst out laughing landing in the bush as I watched her with her skinny legs carrying her off. I called out to her, "I don't like running Alira." I managed to catch up to her, puffing then pushing her into a huge bush. The bush appeared to swallow her up with just her skinny ankles being the last thing I saw. I was bending over getting my breath back laughing at her struggling to get out of the bush when I felt someone behind me. I was still bending down getting my breath back when I turned my head to look noticing someone in a cloak with a hood over her (I presume) head. I tried to see who it was under there only able to see her pale mouth surrounded by pale skin.

I could feel the hairs on the back of my neck go up in warning getting ready to defend myself, but she beat me to it, waving her hand over me. I felt myself being teleported to an enclosed chamber. I looked around me taking deep breaths putting my hands up around the chamber which was clear all the way around so I could see out. I tried to open it thrashing around starting to panic with my heart rate raising.

--ooOoo--

Alira had managed to right herself in the bush just in time to see me being sent away sending a bolt towards the cloaked figure. It hit her leg emitting a low groan and bend in pain but she managed to retaliate and send something towards Alira, but missed. The cloaked figure then disappeared.

--ooOoo--

I was banging on it now yelling, "Let me out. Help, Ferdinand."

I could feel myself sweat with anxiety thrashing around the chamber but still managing to touch my tattoo, to call Ferdinand, when the hooded figure appeared again. I felt danger now watching the figure touch something on a control panel. I yelled at the person, "Who are you, let me out of here."

I tried to send some magic towards the person but it had no effect. I could feel a wispy stream coming from around the chamber getting angry thrashing around. A peel of thunder could be heard but the mist that was coming into the chamber must have been something to put me to sleep, as I felt myself dropping. I tried to fight it but it was too strong, finally succumbing to it.

Alira, looked to where the cloaked figure had sent a bolt, noticing a scorch mark, feeling relieved that didn't hit her.

She called out, "Hannah, where are you?" When I didn't reply she knew something was wrong and needed help, so magicae to the bungalow. She found Ferdinand there looking distressed, "I can hear Hannah calling from somewhere, where is she, Alira?"

She put her hands up in dismay, "I don't know. A hooded figure turned up when we were walking back and sent her away somewhere. I sent a bolt towards her hitting her in one of her legs."

Ferdinand then grabbed her hand, "She's touched her tattoo." Both Alira and Ferdinand magicae to the medical centre. Ferdinand tried to magicae into the room but couldn't get in. He then tried the door and eventually putting his shoulder to it, but couldn't get in getting distressed as he could he me yelling.

He was getting angry, "Alira call Fia. I'll try and get in another way."

Alira touched her tattoo with Fia appearing. Fia looked at them both, "What's happening?"

Morag appeared looking concerned, "What is going on here?"

Ferdinand was angry, "Hannah is in there; she's been calling me. Who put her in there?"

Morag tried the door, "We didn't put her in there."

Morag called a guard who appeared next to her. Morag told her to open the door, which she did, letting Ferdinand and the others come into the room.

I was quiet now just as the hooded figure was disappearing. Ferdinand made a dive for the figure but he wasn't quick enough.

Morag rushed over to the chamber finding me asleep looking at the indicators. She realised the sleep potion going into the chamber was dangerously strong. Morag tried to stop it but it had been tampered with.

Ferdinand was getting angry, "Get her out of there Morag, she doesn't like enclosed spaces."

Morag was panicking now, "The control panel is not responding to me and I think the sleep potion is too strong."

Ferdinand was looking around for something to smash the chamber with. He couldn't find anything so tried to force it open thumbing his fist down on it, but it didn't work.

The guard moved forward, "Let me try," pointing her staff at the chamber with it opening at last. Ferdinand reached in taking me out and over to a bed tapping my face, "Hannah come on wake up for me."

Morag told the guard, "There was someone in a hooded cloak who did this. Go and see if you can find that person and bring her to me." The guard acknowledged Morag and took off.

Morag, Alira and Fia came over to Ferdinand and me looking concerned. Alira rubbed my hand sending the white light around our hand, "Come on Hannah, we still have some fun to have yet."

I opened my eyes wildly taking a deep breath throwing out my arms and kicking my legs out with a look of horror on my face. Ferdinand held my hands leaning on me, "Hannah it's alright, you're safe."

I groped for air to go into my lungs taking deep breaths trying to get up. Ferdinand consoled me putting his head down to me cheek, "Relax honey, you're safe now."

I slowed my breathing down looking around me feeling Ferdinand close to me, "Where am I? Who was that?"

Morag moved closer looking worried, "Hannah take some deep breaths dear, you're safe now."

I turned to look at her, distressed, "Who was that Morag?"

Alira came into my view, "I couldn't see her face Hannah as she was wearing a cloak and a hood. I managed to get a bolt to her though and I'm sure I hit her leg."

I was breathing better now holding onto Ferdinand, "I want to sit up Ferdinand."

He helped me up looking angry, "Did you see who it was Hannah?"

I shook my head, "No. All I could see was her pale skin around her mouth. She didn't say anything to me but just threw me into that chamber."

The guard came back not looking very happy, "We haven't found anyone Morag."

She moved closer to Morag talking quietly then took off.

Ferdinand noticed this, glaring at Morag, "What did she say Morag?"

Morag looked distressed, "I need to investigate something first Ferdinand. Take Hannah back to your bungalow to let her recover."

Morag turned to Alira, "Thank goodness you two have that connection now."

Alira grinned, "It's come in handy. Whoever did this will have a sore leg or foot Morag, just remember that."

She moved closer to me, "Next time I'm in trouble you have to do that for me."

I looked confused, "What did you do, Alira?"

Alira took my hand watching the white light go over it again, "I gave you the spark to wake you up."

Ferdinand was putting his arm around my waist and under my legs to take me back, "I can stand up, Ferdinand." He didn't say anything but continued picking me up looking angry towards Morag, "I'll see you later Morag."

Ferdinand and I landed in the bungalow taking me to the bed. He lay me down with him lying down next to me moving a piece of hair off my forehead noticing the sweat. "Can you tell me what happened?"

I moved in closer to him feeling tears welling up eventually running down my cheeks. "I was just walking back with Alira after the meeting when this hooded figure appeared. I'm sure it was a woman but I couldn't see her face. She didn't say anything but just pointed at me before I thought about protecting myself. I landed in that chamber," wiping my eyes with Ferdinand giving me a tissue.

I wiped my eyes and blew my nose again, "She didn't come straight away. I started thrashing around in the chamber to try and get out but it also gave me time to call you. When she did come, she did something on the control panel sending that potion/gas stuff into the chamber knocking me out."

He gave me a little kiss on the cheek stroking my hair feeling a bit calmer now, "I want to go home Ferdinand." He looked disappointed, sighing, "Ok. Can we go after the evening meal at least."

I put my hand up to his hair stroking it, "I know you wanted it to be special here for me but I don't feel like staying at the moment."

He took my hand kissing it gently, "I understand. You're not supposed to be attacked in Jardine. If I get my hands on whoever it was, they will regret it."

We lay there not talking for a little while with Ferdinand putting me on his shoulder holding onto me. He then asked, "Did anything happen in the meeting?"

I rolled onto my side looking at him more, "We were discussing the connection between Alira and I along with ghosts."

I smiled briefly remembering, "Matilda came in and told Morag off."

He raised his eyebrow, "That must have hurt her pride?"

I nodded, "Yes and it also explained why she didn't come to Jardine very much. I threatened to not come back with the girls but Morag apologised and said we can come back any time. I must admit this is putting me off being attacked again."

I held his hand, "We also discussed how grandma has been coming into my visions and meditations and being able to speak Norwegian. They want me to do some more research on my family."

He lay there thinking about it bringing me onto his chest stroking my hair helping me to feel calmer. "Haben sie gefragt, ob Sie Deutsch sprechen? (Did they ask about you speaking German?)"

I felt weary and relaxed, "Ja, als wir intim waren (yes when we were being intimate)."

I realised what he did again slapping his arm, "Stop it, Ferdinand."

He chuckled rubbing my arm, "I got you smiling again at least. I wonder why they are so concerned about your grandma?"

I sat up looking at him again, "They think she is trying to get into Jardine through me and take over or something. I don't know what they're thinking. Matilda told them off about it."

He looked confused, "That is really odd." He rolled me onto my back, "How are you feeling now, do you want a drink of something?"

I sighed, "I'm feeling a lot better and yes, I'll have a glass of wine, thanks. I'll just go and wash my face."

He helped me up making sure I was alright then went and got a couple of drinks along with some chocolates on a plate.

I came back into the bedroom smiling at the sight of the chocolates, "You know the way to a woman's heart don't you." I sat next to him as he handed me a glass of wine then pointed to the chocolates elevating them in front of me, "Don't expect these all the time, it's just a treat." I took one off the plate then watched it go over to him. He took one then put the plate on the cabinet. I took a sip from the wine leaning on his shoulder, "You know some people have a fairy god mother I appear to have a fairy bad mother."

He looked at me confused, "What do you mean, Hannah?"

I took another sip of wine, "I go to a pub to have fun with my girls and friends and I get attacked by a leprechaun and witches. I come to magical Jardine and make love to a sexy guy, get closer to my girls and then I get attacked by someone who isn't supposed to do that here."

He smiled, "So you think I'm sexy?"

I groaned, "Did you hear any of the other stuff I said?" He put his hand on mine, "Yes, I did, but it made you smile at least. Do you still want to go home today?"

I looked at the glass of wine taking a sip, "Yes, I still want to go home Ferdinand. I want to see my Kimba and go to my boring job and try and forget some of this for a few days."

He looked disappointed, "Ok, but I'm getting a little voice in my head asking to see you and I really want to talk to her to see what that guard said."

He put his glass down taking my glass and putting it down, "Give me a hug."

I lay down letting him come over me kissing me gently. He stroked my hair, "I want to see what Morag has found out. We at least know that Alira has injured the person who did this. I'm not looking forward to your girls finding out."

We got up, going out to the lounge, telling Morag she can come and see us. I was sitting in the lounge when Morag and Cara arrived looking regretful. Morag came and sat next to me with Cara on the other side as Morag looked at me, "Would you like to go somewhere to talk Hannah?"

Ferdinand heard her from the kitchen, "I think it's best to stay here, Morag, as she is not safe here in Jardine either. It's taken me a while to calm Hannah down and now she wants to go home."

I looked at Ferdinand turning back to Morag, "Yes I think it's best to stay here Morag."

Morag looked down at her hands, "I'm sorry Hannah, this should never have happened in Jardine. Whoever has done this has broken a lot of rules and will be dealt with."

I felt I was getting annoyed but calmed myself, "I've just been telling Ferdinand it's like there is someone constantly putting something bad after I've had something good."

Cara patted my hand, "At least Alira managed to injure the person, so if she is still in Jardine, we will be able to seek her out."

I frowned, "I know if I had broken some rules and got injured, I would have taken off out of Jardine."

We continued to talk finally feeling better about things. Morag and Cara both got up and gave me a hug with Morag saying, "At least stay for the meal before you go. I want to be able to come and see you over the next few weeks, Hannah, to let you know of any progress of who it was that attacked you?"

I nodded, "Ok, Morag, I'll be happy to see you when you want. Like I said I want to go. I will check with my girls what they want to do."

They left after giving me another hug.

My girls came in not long after Morag and Cara had left, looking at my face, "What's happened Mum?"

Charlotte came over to me giving me a hug, "What happened in the meeting Mum?"

I sat down trying to hide my emotions, "The meeting went alright, although they have these strange ideas that the grandma who has been contacting me is trying to get into Jardine. I was lucky because grandma Matilda came in and sorted them out. I was also attacked after the meeting by some cloaked hooded figure and put into one of those medical chambers."

Amelia and Charlotte looked at Ferdinand then back at me in disgust. Charlotte started pacing in anger with her voice rising, "You mean to say you were attacked *again* in Jardine. Do they know who it was?"

I shook my head, "No, but Morag said the gas going into the chamber could have harmed me."

Amelia turned pale with anger, "This is just getting out of hand. You finally get your magic and you've got all these bloody idiots trying to get you. It better not have been that bloody Lilith after the bloody fuzzy wuzzy cake episode. So much for being safe in Jardine!"

Ferdinand grimaced, "Do you want something to drink, girls?"

Charlotte stood up going over to the kitchen area, "Do you know who it could have been Ferdinand?"

He looked annoyed at her, "No, but when I find out they will regret it. I've been trying to convince your mother to come here because it was safer, now she wants to go home."

Amelia went and got a glass of wine then sat opposite me, "I don't blame you, Mum. I might go as well. Did Morag have any idea who it was?"

I shook my head taking a sip of my wine, "No, although the guard said something to her but she won't tell us what she said. Alira injured the person's foot or leg with a bolt. That enabled me time to call Ferdinand thank goodness."

Alira and Fia came in looking sadly at me, "Morag has told me they haven't found anyone yet and that you're wanting to go home."

Ferdinand called out, "Do you two want a drink?"

Fia went over to talk to him and get some wine while Alira sat next to me, "Are you feeling alright now, Sister?"

I patted her hand, "yes, I am. I said I'd stay until after the evening meal. Thanks again for trying to protect me."

Alira gave me a hug, "That's what we are here for Sister. I'm sure you would have done the same for me."

We all sat around for a little while chatting about who we thought it could have been with most of us suspecting Lilith or someone like her.

Ferdinand was sitting next to me sulking a little because we had to go home. He called out to everyone, "The evening meal should be coming out now, so we better get going."

I got up putting my glass down going towards the bedroom. Ferdinand got up, "Where are you going Hannah, we need to go." I smiled, "I just need to go to the toilet; I won't be long." He hung around waiting for me as the others took off.

I came out finding him looking out the window, deep in thought. I went up to him putting my hand in his, "I'm ready now."

He took a few minutes to turn to look at me, "Sorry honey I was thinking about that attack."

I grinned, "You're getting as bad as me daydreaming."

He took my hand, "Come on let's go and get something to eat."

We were all looking around for someone who might be limping while we were sitting together enjoying our food, when Lilith came up behind us. Ferdinand took my hand looking at her, "What do you want, Lilith?"

Lilith rebuffed, "I just wanted to apologise to Hannah for the fuzzy wuzzy cake incident. I guess you two got me back in the end though, didn't you?"

I really didn't want to talk to her and said distantly, "Ok Lilith."

Ferdinand stood up still holding my hand, "We are going earlier than expected."

Lilith feigned surprise, "Oh really, what has brought that on?"

Amelia and Charlotte who had come to stand around us making Lilith look nervous.

Charlotte looked her up and down, "How's your leg Lilith?"

Lilith moved back getting agitated, "It's fine, thank you."

Amelia moved closer to her, looking deadly, "Why don't you just stay away from our family?"

Lilith looked at Ferdinand for support, "Ferdinand, why are they talking to me like this?"

Ferdinand didn't want to let her know that I had been attacked, "I don't know Lilith is there anything you can tell them?"

Lilith was showing her true colours now, "I think you all need to remember you are guests here, so just behave. I am a senior Jardine woman."

Charlotte grinned wickedly, "Just remember that when you are in our world. You are only a guest there and won't have Jardine to look after you."

Ferdinand got annoyed, "I was hoping they would come to live here; how would you feel about that Lilith?"

Lilith was getting agitated now with Ferdinand's attitude, "Well they would have to behave themselves wouldn't they and stop using their family magic."

She had had enough turning away, "Be careful in your world, won't you, Hannah?"

Amelia and Charlotte looked angrily at her ready to send something towards her. I put my hand up to stop them, "That's enough girls. We will deal with her if we have to."

I watched Lilith walk away trying to see if she was limping. I thought about it, she probably would have had it fixed if she had been hit anyway, so we couldn't get proof that way.

Ferdinand looked at my girls, "Come one let's get going."

Morag came over before we left looking at us all, "Can I ask what Lilith said, Hannah? She didn't look very happy."

I sighed, "She came to apologise for giving me the fuzzy wuzzy cake but then warned me to be careful in my world, after Ferdinand said he wanted us to come and live here."

Morag frowned sighing, "I really don't know what has come over her. She has done a lot of work for us in your world looking for magical people who were trying to recruit people for the wrong reasons. We may have to look at that role."

Ferdinand, who was still holding my hand, "Hannah thinks she has stronger feelings for me than I think. What do you think, Morag?"

Morag thought about it, raising her eyebrow, "That is quite possible. She has known you for a long time while Hannah wasn't around. You haven't been intimate with her, have you?"

Ferdinand looked shocked, "No Morag! We have just been friends all these years, but never got that close."

Morag nodded, "Alright. I will have to keep an eye on her. Are you all going home now?"

I nodded, "Yes Morag."

I put my wrist up showing her the bracelet, "Can I take this back with me?"

Morag smiled, "It is lovely. I have to touch it so it doesn't disappear once you go out of Jardine."

She leaned in, touching the bracelet, "There that should do it."

Amelia and Charlotte noticed her doing this coming closer with Amelia showing her a necklace and Charlotte a bracelet as well, "Can we take these back, Morag?"

Morag rolled her eyes, "Alright, but nothing else. If you try to sneak anything else through, it will disappear."

She touched those two items making the girls grin, "Thanks Morag."

I gave her a hug, "I'll see you through the week."

We went back to our accommodation tidying up and making sure we hadn't left anything personal behind. Ferdinand waved his hand around doing a cleaning spell. He took my hand, "Do you want to magicae or fly back?"

I looked around the sky that was getting dark now smiling at him, "I wouldn't mind flying back."

He grinned trying to get my mood up, "You just want me between our legs, don't you?"

I slapped his arm giggling, "Don't be naughty Ferdinand." I looked around one more time feeling a little sad that I was going, but I knew I didn't want to stay.

Ferdinand changed into dragon form as I magicae onto his back, "Ready when you are, honey."

Chapter 13

We flew part of the way back flying over the familiar sights of the beaches with a cool breeze coming off the water and the smell of pollution that I had never really noticed before. We magicae the rest of the way home, arriving in the unit just on dusk.

Kimba was pleased to see us rubbing herself against Ferdinand more than me getting him to pick her up and get her food. I looked at them both sighing, "I'm going to have a shower and get comfortable since she prefers you to me."

He put his arm around me before I went giving me a kiss, "I've just got that animal magnetism as you found out this morning."

I chuckled, "Yes dear." I looked at him smiling feeling a bit naughty, "Just curious, how many times can you make love Jardine style?"

He looked surprised, "Hannah you're not ready again, are you?"

I giggled at the look on his face, "No dear, but I might be in the near future."

He looked a little relieved, "No, there aren't any rules about how many times you can do it. Just remember though we aren't as young as we used to be," tapping my bum as I walked off, "Horny Dragĕ woman."

We went to bed having to set my alarm to get up for work groaning, "I'm not looking forward to going in, but then I am happy just to stop thinking about magic for a bit." He cuddled in, "Well you've had a taste of Jardine now and you know that is always an option."

I lay there in his arms in the darkened room thinking about everything that had happened the last few days trying to think positive about it 'well I suppose I'm getting my adventure like I asked for. I guess I didn't expect it to be so intense.' I eventually dropped off to sleep dreaming of big cats to cuddle into.

--ooOoo--

I woke to the alarm feeling a little dazed wondering where I was at first, then realising I had to get up to go to work.

I snuggled back down to Ferdinand who wasn't awake, thinking I'll lay here a bit longer. He moved rolling me over onto my back, "Come on time to get up to go to your boring job." I sighed, "You're going to keep rubbing that in, aren't you?"

He kissed me passionately on the lips, "This is what you would have been getting on a Jardine morning." He got up leaving me licking my lips sighing, "Oh well at least I get some of it."

I got up, getting dressed, as he fixed some breakfast for me and fed Kimba. We sat eating then having a cup of coffee feeling like I had been in a world that didn't really exist other than in my head for the last few days; with everything that had happened and now we were back to reality. As I was sipping my coffee, "What are you going to do for the rest of the day?"

He finished his toast, "Well I'm going to take you to work," making me roll my eyes, "Yes dear and what else?" He sipped on his coffee to make me wait for his answer, "Then I'll probably go to Jardine for a while and then I'll pick you up from work."

I thought about him going to Jardine, "Say hi to Omar for me, won't you?"

He smiled, "Yes I will, although you could say hi yourself."

I got up shaking my head, "I'm going to brush my teeth, then I'll be ready to go." I brushed my teeth going back into the bedroom to tidy up the bed with him coming in pulling me up, giving me a cuddle, "I'll fix that up. I'll come and spend some time with Kimba before I go to Jardine."

I smiled, "Oh you're a good house husband."

He thought about that, "I like that title," giving me a kiss on the lips, "Mm peppermint."

I smiled, "Come on we better get going I suppose. I'm expecting a big mess when I get there. Have you thought about where we are going to land?"

He smiled, "Yes just by the railway station should be good. There are lots of people there and they generally don't see someone just appear."

I went and got my bag and shut the balcony door taking his hand and magicaeing to Circular Quay railway station. Sure, enough there were a lot of people filing out of the entrance too busy to see us appear. I looked around at the familiar sights feeling a bit strange now, with the smell of the pollution from the expressway above us and the diesel smell coming from the ferries in the harbour, bringing people to work. I could only just smell the salt from the sea with all the other smells drowning out the sea air. Even the sound of the squawking seagulls and lots of people chatting felt horrible after the quietness of Jardine.

Ferdinand saw me looking around, "Are you alright?"

I nodded, "Yes just getting used to it again." He took my hand walking over to the building where I worked bumping into Alira as she smiled at the two of us, "Well Sister, back to the real world."

I groaned letting Ferdinand's hand go, "Don't remind me."

Alira waved to Ferdinand, "Come on we'll face this together."

I nodded, "Yes" turning to give Ferdinand a kiss, "I'll see you at the railway station tonight ok."

He kissed me back longingly, "Yes ok. Stay out of trouble."

I groaned, "Stop being naughty yourself," as I watched him turn to walk away then caught up with Alira to go into work. Alira stopped me before we got to the lifts "do you want to meet for lunch?"

I nodded, "Yes that will be good, where do you want to meet?"

She smiled, "I like to go down to Mrs Macquarie's Chair to do meditation; does that suit you?" The thought of being by the water and away from a lot people made me happy, "Yes that will be great. I'll see you there around 1.00p.m."

I got to my workstation finding papers and files all over the place, looking at Tom, my boss, who was an older guy going thin on the top with what used to be curly hair around the back. He had a kindly rounded face, wore glasses, who was fit but didn't have muscles. He was one of those guys who preferred to concentrate on his career, leaving having a family late, as he came out smiling, "Ah Hannah, thank goodness you're back."

I looked at him in disbelief, "Good grief Tom, did a storm come through here or something?"

Tom grinned, "We had a couple of temps who couldn't find things and I wasn't much help either, unfortunately."

I sighed, putting my bag away, "I'm going to get a coffee; do you want one?"

He tried to act as though the state of my desk was normal, "Oh yes that will be nice, then can you get started on some of the things I've dictated for you to type up for me."

I mumbled under my breath *'like I don't have anything else to do'* heading towards the small kitchen on our floor where we could make coffee. I realised I hadn't made any lunch for myself, as I normally put it in this fridge shaking my head, '*I'll just get something before I meet Alira.*'

I started to make the coffee for myself and Tom when Sarina came in smirking and flicking her hair, "Hi Hannah. Are you feeling better?"

I sighed thinking, '*Oh no just to make it even better to the start of the day with the office bully greeting me.*'

Sarina was a younger woman in her late 20s that thought she was beautiful wearing all the right name brand clothes, flicking her hair when she spoke to you and wore high heels to make sure she was taller than you. She wasn't ugly but I wouldn't call her stunning; she wasn't fat, but what I would call stocky and really didn't know much about life other than fashion and who was, "In" at the moment. This self-importance made her enjoy bossing people around or putting people down.

I tried to ignore her, looking busy making the coffee, so she repeated what she said in an annoyed voice, "Hannah I was asking if you are feeling better, or was it just an excuse to take time off work like a lot of other people around here. I saw you walking in with that Aboriginal woman Alira this morning, looking quite chummy; I'm sure she was just taking a sickie."

I turned to glare at Sarina, "Oh are you talking to me Sarina. I am feeling a lot better. I was sick, with snot and phlegm coming out of all my orifices everywhere, so I thought I better not share it with people like you! As for Alira that is her business where she was, not yours or mine."

Sarina screwed her face up, "Eeww Hannah you don't have to be so descriptive. Oh, I see you have a new chum now, sticking up for her. You want to be careful who you make friends with in this office Hannah, as you have always been considered the weird one."

I turned my back to her growling to myself trying to stay calm, pouring the water into the cups. I turned around to find her still there smirking at me. I didn't bother to say anything more to her, going out of the kitchen with our coffees when she stepped in front of me blocking my exit, making me look at her dangerously, "Get out of my way Sarina!"

She looked at me unsure now, stepping aside but moving to hit my shoulder with hers just as I went past her, making me spill the coffee over my hand. I ignored the coffee burning me, walking out with a chant coming into mind, saying it, "*Once I am away from you Sarina you will fall over those clumsy feet onto that face you think is pretty and neat giving you a taste of what you give just as a treat."*

I was back at my desk, when I heard a scream coming from the direction of the kitchen. I carried on putting the coffees down on my desk turning to watch, as I wiped my hands magically getting rid of the burn that was forming as I smiled.

Sarina had tripped over something making her fall flat on her face breaking her nose as she screamed, "Agghh my nose, not my nose."

Tom came out of his office hearing the commotion, "What's going on Hannah?"

I shook my head, not really caring, "Not sure Tom," turning to give him his coffee. I felt a little wriggle on my dragon tattoo, choosing to ignore it, sitting down to drink my coffee while sorting out the papers.

Tom came out once he had finished his coffee, "I'm in meetings most of the morning Hannah. There are a couple of reports I'd like done today then I'll let you sort out which ones can wait. Good to see you back."

I smiled nodding, "Ok Tom. Oh, how is your wife going with the pregnancy?"

He looked a little nervous, "Not long now, Hannah. No sleep after that event happens, I guess."

I nodded, "Yes, but it settles down soon enough."

He took off with a folder under his arm to his first meeting.

All of Tom's reports and letters were dictated digitally onto a computer program. I sat there thinking, *'I wonder if I can do some of it magically.'*

I visioned the book in my head opening the pages to an incantation I could use, pointing to one of the documents I needed to type saying the incantation, *"Type for me this document you see word perfect and correct to be seen for me."*

A document opened up with the words flashing in front of me and was done in 5 minutes. I looked around to make sure no one was looking clapping gleefully under the table.

I was thinking, *'I love this part of magic.'*

I went into the document and saved it into the right file and printed it out. I did it to another one I thought Tom would want, while I checked the one that I had just printed out. It looked perfect to me, knowing Tom, he will change it anyway, but otherwise there were no spelling mistakes and it sounded right. I was happy with that. I did this to four more documents that I thought Tom would need, saving them to a file and printing them out and checking them afterwards.

I felt satisfied, going to the ladies, then over to the kitchen to get a drink of water. Another secretary was in there getting a drink, whose name was Cheryl. I hadn't really had much to do with her before as she tended to keep to herself and was a quietly spoken woman with mousy brown wavy hair petite in stature and tended to dress about 5 years out of date.

I smiled at her saying, "Hi," when I went in there getting a drink of water and a biscuit. She stopped me, "Hannah did you hear about Sarina?"

I wasn't really concentrating so when she stopped me, I looked surprised, "Oh, no Cheryl, why what happened. I heard a bit of a commotion before but wasn't sure what happened."

She was trying to hide her smile, "I know this isn't very nice but she had a bit of an accident and broke her nose. They say it was quite a bad break and she will be off for a few days."

I shook my head, "Well I keep telling some of these younger ones not to wear such high shoes, which I am assuming she fell over on?"

Cheryl let out a burst of laughter putting her hand on my arm, "Sorry Hannah, I know it's nasty but she has been picking on me for a while. I did hear when she was being put onto the stretcher that she was blaming you."

I shook my head disgusted, "Well I was at my desk when it happened, so she has only her clumsy feet to blame." I took my water to go out of the kitchen with Cheryl putting her hand on mine again, "If it was you, thanks." I went out of the kitchen, back to my desk thinking about Sarina, "I'll have to be careful I guess." I did a few more documents magically then decided to go and sort out some of the filing.

There was a bit of filing to do in Tom's room so I decided to go and enjoy it while looking out his window which overlooked Sydney harbour. That was the annoying thing about this job all the bosses got the good views while all the secretaries had to sit in the middle without any view; so whenever Tom had meetings, I would go in there and daydream or just watch what was going on in the harbour.

I had tidied up my desk, then went into Tom's room shutting the door. I thought of a chant to help me tidy up the papers, *"I chant this chant for all the papers to gently fly like a butterfly to go where they belong in the filing cabinets in their right spots and belong so."*

I waved my hands saying the chant watching a pile of papers start to fly like a butterfly flapping its wings going into the filing cabinets making me relax and smile. I had brought my phone and ear buds in putting them in my ears and turning some music on with one of my favourites from Crowded House 'Don't Dream It's Over' while I stood in front of the window going into a daydream.

The sun was shining into the room making it feel warm and relaxed looking at the view outside, still wishing I was out there, but happy I was at least looking at it. The music was helping me to daydream while looking at the water and what was going on in the harbour.

As I stood there listening to the music, I felt someone come in behind me jumping as I felt some arms go around my waist as I giggled, "Ferdinand what are you doing here?"

He pulled one of the ear buds out listening to it, "Mm nice choice."

I pointed to my phone stopping the music, "I thought you would be in Jardine now?"

He cuddled me bringing my arm up with my watch on, "So it's just after 11.00a.m and you've dealt with a bully, used your magic to finish some of your work and are now daydreaming."

I turned to look at him smiling, "It's been a productive day, hasn't it?"

He looked at the papers flying to the cabinets, "I think you need to stop that before you get caught."

I gave him a long kiss on the lips bringing a smile to his lips, "You're being naughty, Hannah."

I gave him a cuddle, "It's nearly finished and then I'll finish the rest off by hand; does that sound alright?"

He sighed, "Yes, I guess so. I mainly came to bring you your lunch as you forgot it," handing me a container with my lunch in it. I took it from him opening it finding a salad in it and a chocolate brownie smiling, "Mm that looks nice. I thought I would have to go and buy something when I had lunch with Alira."

He turned to look at the view, "I remember watching you looking out here when we weren't together."

I looked at him wistfully, "It would have been nice if you had popped in then, but I probably would have gotten angry at you, I guess."

He put his arm around my waist, "So are you going to tell me what happened with the bully?"

I shook my head, "No not really. I'm not putting up with those type of people any more Ferdinand. It doesn't seem to matter what I do I still get in trouble, so I'll deal with them how I want now."

He looked a little worried, "Just don't do too much damage Hannah, that's all I ask."

I leaned onto his shoulder, "I won't kill anyone Ferdinand, if that's what you're worried about, but that stupid woman burned my hands and I wasn't going to let her get away with it."

He picked my hand up looking at it, "You did a good job at healing it" kissing it.

Tom's phone went, looking at Ferdinand, "I better answer that," and going over to his phone hitting the line button that was flashing. "Hello Tom Ferguson's phone, Hannah speaking."

Ferdinand smiled at my formal phone manner, as I turned away from him smiling, "Oh yes Tom, I'll send that to you in an email," and pausing with Tom saying something else with me replying looking at Ferdinand rolling my eyes, "No Tom I'm not in here daydreaming, I'm just filing."

I went back over to Ferdinand, "I have to go and send something to Tom in an email are you staying or going?"

He gave me a kiss on the lips, "No I'll go. Looks like your boss knows your habits as well. I'll see you tonight."

I sighed with his kiss, "Ok, see you then." I watched him disappear clapping my hands making the final papers find their place in the filing cabinet. I then went out to my computer and sent the report to Tom.

My desk was clear of papers at last and Tom's room was looking a lot tidier so I sat down to do some typing the normal way until it was time to meet Alira for lunch. Since Tom wasn't around, I decided to eat my lunch at my desk before I went out to meet Alira, hiding it away if someone came along. I saved my brownie for later to have a cup of tea with for afternoon tea.

It finally came to lunch time going out of the building getting some fresh air at last, walking part of the way amongst the crowds which were getting annoying; so, I magicae the rest of the way to Mrs Macquarie's Chair. Alira was there already standing near the water's edge watching the boats go past as the waves crashed up against the sandstone wall from the wake of the ferries going past.

I walked up carefully just in case she was somewhere else, but she turned looking at me as I got closer smiling, "Hi Hannah. I was just looking at a vision, not sure what it was about but I am sure it will sort itself out eventually."

I went over closer to the water watching it with the smell of the salt hitting me taking a deep breath, "I never realised how smelly this city was until I went to Jardine."

Alira frowned, "Yes it certainly hits you when you've had a different air quality."

She moved closer to me grinning, "So you're the talk of the office already."

I rolled my eyes, "What now? Not Sarina, I did have something to do with it but I wasn't around when it happened—I made sure of that."

Alira laughed, "You're wicked, Hannah Dragĕ."

I put my arm through Alira's, "She was spouting off about people taking sickies, especially you because you're Aboriginal and then she ran into me burning my bloody hands with my coffee. I'm not being nice any more Alira; it hasn't gotten me anywhere."

Alira sighed, "I know how you feel Hannah. As long as you can control it, that's all you have to worry about."

I squeezed her arm, "Maybe that is why I was denied the magic when I was younger because I probably wouldn't have been able to control it. (In a sophisticated voice) I'm considered more mature now!"

Alira laughed again, "Yes Hannah, whatever you say. Come Ms Sophistication, let's do some meditation. It's good to do it in different spaces, it makes you concentrate more and go deeper. Have you done meditation out in the open much before?"

I shook my head, "I must confess I haven't other than classes of course, but not much in the open."

We each pulled in a low chair, like you would use on the beach, to sit on, getting comfortable near the water but far enough away from the walking path.

Alira took a couple of deep breaths, "Do you want to try an Aboriginal form of meditation music?"

I looked curiously at her, "Yes sure I'll give it a go."

Alira showed me where to find it on my phone putting our ear buds in getting comfortable. I turned the music on with a digeridoo coming in almost like it was a vibrating wave going through my body, as I took deep breaths, concentrating on the music. I started to shut the sound of the boats and people walking past chatting, concentrating on the music, smelling the salt as I breathed, along with the trees and grass around me, hitting my senses.

I could feel myself going quite deep when I felt someone else was in my mediation with me. I saw myself standing in a green field looking around me smiling as I realised Alira was coming towards me.

We greeted each other with a hug feeling peaceful and calm holding hands. We turned to look behind us, finding a huge tree in the distance with branches that appeared to span for miles and its leaves glimmered in a gentle breeze, with it being framed by a brilliant blue sky.

Alira and I looked at each other, walking towards the tree, noticing as we got closer a group of people standing underneath it. As we moved closer some of the faces became recognisable making us smile realising, they were family members that had passed.

We got to the tree and were embraced by them, feeling the love. My mother came to me looking hesitant still, as I made the first move to give her a hug, not saying anything but just holding each other, as a mother and daughter do, not needing words to express how we felt with tears welling in my eyes, gently falling on my cheeks.

The music from the meditation along with hearing my breathing started to come back to me feeling it was time to go. Matilda came to me before I went, "We are proud of you, stay strong Hannah, but be careful."

I nodded walking back with Alira taking her hand as the scene faded and I could feel myself coming back to the park with its smells and noises hitting my senses. I took deep breaths opening my eyes turning to look at Alira smiling as she reached over to hold my hand, "Nice trip Sister."

I smiled, "It certainly was." We got up shaking ourselves out sending the chairs away as I went up to Alira taking her arm, "Wow that was a good meditation, thanks."

She leaned into me, "We are certainly connected Sister. It was nice to see you make peace with your mother as well."

I nodded, "Yes, no use holding a grudge is it. I suppose we have to get back now—unfortunately."

Alira nodded smiling, "Try and stay out of trouble Sister."

I shook my head, "It always seems to find me, no matter how hard I try to stay away from it."

Alira gave me a hug, "I've just got to duck into a shop before I go up, do you want to come with me or are you going back?"

I shook my head, "No I'll just walk back to stretch my legs a bit more. I'll see you later." I started to walk back going past the opera house looking at all the tourists milling around taking photos. I was thinking as I walked, *'It was a lovely day so the photos would come out nice'* feeling the warmth of the sun on me helping me to relax.

As I walked, I noticed a group of tourists being led by a tour guide who was speaking German, telling them about the opera house and the gardens, smiling to myself, 'Strange how I can understand them now.' One of the tourists who was trying to take a photo of himself and his wife came up to me, "Machst du bitte ein foto von uns (will you take a photo of us please)."

I stopped nodding, "Ja in ordnung (yes alright)."

They looked pleased that I could speak to them in German, gathering up in front of the opera house taking a couple of photos of them. I showed them the photos I had taken with them shaking my hand, "Danke (thank you)."

I walked on when another man came up to me, as I was nearing the station, not really concentrating, thinking it was another tourist, turning to see the priest walking along with me smiling, "So you speak German as well?"

I sighed, rolling my eyes, "Go away. Don't you have churchy things to do?" I started to walk faster as he caught up with me, "I can save you Hannah? Come to church at St Andrews in the city and I will save your soul."

I just shook my head walking faster when I noticed two men walking towards me looking at me with an unfriendly stare. I turned to look back at the priest who was looking smug at me realising they were with him. A chant came into my head deciding to use it, *"Those buffoons in front of me now are as stupid as can be. Deal with them as you please for the asses they are; breying like a donkey one two three to show how much of an ass they can be."*

I waved my hands, smiling a cunning grin, doing an elegant bow dipping like a lady as I said the chant, coming up to find the two men breying like donkeys. I checked behind me watching John Adams stop in his tracks with his mouth agape as I disappeared.

I landed back at work in the ladies' toilets in one of the cubicles, locking the door taking deep breaths, feeling my anger build up, doing little stomps like a little kid to get my frustration out. I finally calmed down, going out to wash my hands and fixing my hair. I got a text on my phone from Alira checking it as I went out of the toilets, "Are you alright, Sister?"

I got back to my desk ringing her on the work phone, "Hi, yes, I am now thanks Sister. I'm getting pissed off with some of these things happening but like Matilda said stay strong." I did some work, trying to focus on it, rather than what had happened, getting to afternoon tea time having a cup of tea with my brownie. Tom came back from his meeting just as I was doing this, "Oh that looks nice." I sighed, "it's quite big do you want half of it with a cup of tea or coffee."

He nodded, "Yes thanks that will be nice. Oh, HR rang me about what happened in the kitchen this morning; they checked to see where you were when it happened. I told them you were with me giving me my coffee; apparently Sarina is accusing you of doing some trick."

I put my hands up, "I don't know how she thinks I did anything, she's the one that wears those silly shoes; thanks for sticking up for me, Tom." I got up to get him a hot drink taking it in to him with half the brownie. I managed to finish the rest of my work with just one letter to do to take me to 5.00p.m.

Tom came out smiling, "You've done well Hannah to get through all that work, thanks for being a great help. I'm going now I'll see you tomorrow."

I smiled, "Sure Tom," feeling appreciated by someone for a change. I had the earphones in my ears just finishing off the letter when my work phone went, "Hannah it's Tracey, you have someone in the reception to see you."

I hesitated, "Oh who is it Tracey, I'm not expecting anyone."

She went to say who when the other phone went, "Sorry I have to answer this it's the big boss," hanging up.

I shook my head, 'Annoying, just when I'm about to go home.' I got up going out through the door that took me to the reception area, looking at Tracey who was still on the phone, with a big smile on her face, pointing over to the seats by the window.

I could feel my heart beat go up, as I turned to see Ferdinand stand up, looking dapper in a dark suit with an open white shirt smiling at me. I stood there surprised and annoyed all at the same time, as he came over giving me a hug and a kiss on the cheek, feeling myself blush.

I could hear a click behind me, turning to see Tracey take a photo of the two of us. I was going to say something when Ferdinand held onto me putting his hand up to my jaw, turning it back, "Leave it! Are you ready to go home?"

I knew I was going to be the latest gossip topic for work now for a couple of weeks, resigning myself to it, rolling my eyes, "I have to go and get my bag."

I went back through the door with people already staring at me who wouldn't acknowledge me in the past. feeling uncomfortable. I turned off my computer and got my bag and jacket putting it on, going out to face the music. Sure, enough other secretaries 'mysteriously' had to come out to the reception area to see Tracey, as Ferdinand put his hand out to take mine hearing an "aww." I took his hand pushing the button to the lift, hoping it wouldn't take too long to come, with Ferdinand grinning looking at me, as I continued to stare ahead.

Tracey came out from the desk, "Hannah are you going to introduce us to your 'friend.'" This made him worse, as we waited for the lift, putting his arm around my waist determined not to let go, turning to Tracey smiling, "Hi I'm Ferdinand, Hannah's boyfriend."

Tracey gushed, "Oh Hannah, you sly thing, you didn't tell us about Ferdinand."

I turned smiling at Tracey, "They tend not to last too long, so I don't usually say anything."

Ferdinand, not to be outdone, "Oh but I've known Hannah for a long time and we have finally got together at last, haven't we honey. So, I'll be around for a while."

The lift finally came, pinging its bell, as I let out a sigh of relief, "Bye Tracey."

She was all excited like a school girl, "See you, Ferdinand."

He turned putting on a charming grin, as we walked into the lift. I turned to say something to him, with him putting his finger up to his lips, "Shh" as the doors opened again letting some more people in. We got to the bottom walking out, as he took my hand getting outside the building feeling my anger build, "I ought to turn you into a toad, Ferdinand!"

He didn't say anything but just put his arm around my waist magicaeing home landing in the lounge. I went to go to my bedroom, when he held tight, turning me to face him as I put my hands up to his chest to push him away, "Stop it, Hannah! I didn't mean to embarrass you but I needed people to see you weren't alone anymore."

I tried to push away again, "Oh you didn't mean to embarrass me; I'm going to be the talk of the office for weeks now, as they know I don't have a lot of boyfriends. You could have at least warned me."

He grabbed my wrists with one hand holding onto me with the other, "Would you have come out if you knew I was there?"

I started to get annoyed knowing he was right as he looked at me determined, "Well, would you?" I relaxed a little, "No I guess I wouldn't have."

He relaxed as well letting go of my wrists, "I know you were attacked again on the way back to work. This is really starting to get me worried Hannah, I want you to seriously think about moving to Jardine with me."

I shook my head, "Huh! I got attacked there as well Ferdinand by your 'friend'." He looked away shaking his head, "That was just a prank Hannah, as you have done yourself and she is being dealt with. As for the other attack, we can't confirm who that was. These people are becoming more determined and still appear to know where you are."

I leaned into him putting my head on his chest, "I know this sounds nasty but why didn't you come and save me like a knight in shining scales when those men were coming towards me."

He held on to me, "I would have, but I was in a closed meeting with Morag. It wasn't until Cara came in who was keeping an eye on you that we found out. By that time, you had dealt with them and gone back to work. Morag and I were just talking about what was the best thing to do, both agreeing that there is something or someone who is monitoring you and that I am to be seen with you more so that they know you are not alone at least for now. She is also going to get together with you soon."

He let go, "Do you want a drink of wine?"

I nodded heading towards the sofa taking off my jacket first, putting it on the barstool and taking off my shoes then sitting down on the sofa with Kimba coming to sit on my lap. I stroked her ears hearing her purr and start to needle me with Ferdinand coming to sit next to me with a glass of wine giving it to me.

Kimba looked at him going over to his lap as soon as he got settled, shaking my head, "Typical. I know who she prefers now."

He looked a little uncertain at me, "Don't you want to be seen around me, Hannah."

I put my hand up stroking his face, "No it's not that Ferdinand; I guess it's just been so long since I have had anyone in my life, especially someone spunky like you."

He chuckled, "I could always change my hair colour to grey to make me look older."

I shook my head smiling, "No you don't need to do that. I've gotten used to you in my private life, now I have to get used to you in my public life I guess." I decided to turn on the TV to watch the news as we sipped on our wine. I laughed with him looking up from patting Kimba showing two guys down by the Quay breying like donkeys, that someone had obviously filmed.

Ferdinand shook his head, "Well they got what they deserved I guess." Another shot was taken from a different angle showing me bowing but not showing my face, then panning back over to the two guys breying still. I screwed my face up, "Mm that was a bit close."

He shook his head again, "Well you were graceful in your bow."

I sighed, "At least they didn't show me disappearing."

John Adams was then interviewed asking his opinion as to why these men were doing this stunt. He looked angry into the screen "it's not a stunt, we have evil women doing pranks on innocent people in this city and I intend to deal with them!"

Ferdinand turned it off, "I think we've seen enough" putting some music on.

I got up, "I might go and have a soak in the bath. I never really noticed the grime in the city before until I had been to Jardine. I had a good meditation experience at least with Alira. We went to a big tree and met some of our ancestors, including my mum. I think we've made peace with each other."

He looked up pleased, "Oh that's great Hannah. I forgot to ask you about that."

Just as I went into the bedroom my phone, which was still in the lounge, started to ping with messages coming in. Ferdinand called out, "Do you want me to have a look at them?"

I came out in my underwear going to the bathroom, "Yes you can, I'm not really interested."

He smiled at me, picking it up reading some of the messages as he heard me run the bath. He looked at them calling out, "Amelia and Charlotte are asking if that was you in the Quay and what is Ferdinand doing on FB."

I groaned coming out of the bathroom standing at the door, "Bloody Tracey is a pain in the bum. Well, you got your public outing now."

He got up reading some of the other messages on FB chuckling, "Well some of your friends appear to like me, asking where you've been hiding me. What do you feel like for dinner?"

He heard me coming up out of the water after washing my hair as he came into the bathroom, grinning, "Mm I know what I'd like."

I was looking for the towel as I had soap in my eyes, giving him the excuse to come in.

He put the phone down first stripping off handing me the towel moving me forward and getting into the bath behind me. I put the towel down looking at him get into the bath, laughing, "Don't be naughty Ferdinand," as he gingerly let himself down, "Ouch you've got it a bit hot, dear, no wonder your skin is nice and pink," as he finally got in leaning forward giving me a kiss on my shoulder.

I got the hose that was still running, I had been using for my hair, pointing at him wetting him, "I think you need hosing down, dear," as he grabbed it, sending water everywhere.

He put it back under the water kissing me again on the shoulder, "I think you missed some of the city grime," putting some soap in his hands moving my hair and rubbing it over my back then came over the front, as I grinned.

I leaned back on him putting the soap on his chest, "I think I've done those," as he moved down my breasts shaking his head, "No after close inspection, I've found them still dirty."

I giggled, "Ferdinand, you're being naughty," as he leaned forward over my shoulder, "No I'm just making sure you're nice and clean." He moved me forward rinsing the soap off my back and his chest moving his hand down to my touchy spot, "Mm isn't this where you get a little ticklish?"

I wriggled around, "Don't you start that there'll be water everywhere," trying to move out his reach, but he put his arm around my waist, "Mmm nowhere to go Hannah."

I giggled, "Stop it," leaning against him putting my head up, "Give me a kiss Ferdi" as he leaned down kissing me on the lips.

I sat up turning around on my knees as he watched me, smiling, "Now I want to wash your hair." He moved forward making the water splash as he brought his knees up to bring me in closer, putting the hose over his head as he closed his eyes.

I smiled kissing him, "Now who's being naughty."

He tried to grab me but I still had water going over his eyes, "No I have to wash your hair, be good." He chuckled, "Just don't drown me while you're doing it."

I put the hose down moving closer to put some shampoo in his hair soaping it up. He opened his eyes watching me as I concentrated on gently caressing his head with my fingers, letting out a groan. I got the hose before he could do anything else, washing off the soap. He grabbed the hose, "I don't need any more soap on my hair."

I started to struggle with him for the hose, sending water everywhere, as we were both laughing. I won putting my hand up, "No, I haven't finished yet."

I got some body soap and massaged it onto his chest and arms with a naughty grin appearing on his face, "Hannah," and going to grab me, but I got to the hose spraying it over his chest hitting up into his face as he yelled, "You little minx," fighting to get the hose off me this time magicaeing us out of the bath.

He grabbed some towels drying me, slowly, while kissing me on my neck as I groaned. He then magicae us into the bedroom being intimate; which was even better the second time around.

I lay there afterwards looking at him in the lamp light defining his muscles in his arms, "Well that was a nice way to end a crazy day." He leaned over kissing me, "It certainly was. Those baths are dangerous though, I think we'll keep those for special times."

I laughed, "I think you're just a horny dragon."

I heard his stomach grumble, "I think I need food now as you've depleted me Hannah Dragĕ; any special requests."

I shook my head, yawning, "No I'll leave it up to you."

He put some clothes on and went out to the kitchen as I got up getting dressed checking my phone with all the comments that had come on FB as well as messages from my daughters and friends.

I replied to my daughters telling them the story behind the news item and what a crappy day I had had.

Amelia and Charlotte ended up ringing me on a three-way call, so I closed the door talking to them. They were both pissed off saying we will have to think of a way to sort them out. I told them I was too tired for now, but we will chat about it later.

I came out to find Ferdinand dishing up some quiche and salad and small serve of chips putting my phone down having a big drink of water, "You've dried me out, Ferdinand."

He sat down next to me, "Get used to it honey. How were the girls?"

I started to eat slowly, "Oh they're annoyed about what happened once I told them the whole story. We're going to get together later and see if we can see how they are finding me." I started to yawn again, "That bath and the loving was nice, but it's worn me out."

He finished his meal, "Eat a bit more then we'll go to bed."

I managed to eat a bit more, "Sorry honey, it is lovely but I'm too tired."

He looked at me yawning, "That's alright I'll finish it off as I'm drained. You go to bed I'll be in soon."

I yawned again, "Ok, thanks."

I went and brushed my teeth cleaning up the bathroom that was wet, then went to bed. As I lay there checking my phone my eyes just wouldn't stay open falling asleep before he came in.

He came in to find me fast asleep, putting the phone on the cabinet beside me and turning off the light and cuddling in.

Chapter 14

We got up having breakfast while I checked my phone again smirking to myself, "Wow they like the look of you, Ferdinand." He grinned at me, "I'm not just your average dragon, Hannah. It's a shame you don't quite feel the same way."

I looked at him a little disappointed, "Ferdinand, I do love you otherwise I wouldn't have been intimate with you, it's just been a bit fast that is all," moving over to give him a hug. He relaxed, "I know, but like I said I'm not going anywhere, so you'll have to get used to me."

A text came in as I moved away to have a look at it, "Oh shit I forgot all about that wedding of Tania's you agreed to go to on my behalf. I'll send a message back saying I'm sick or something."

He grabbed my phone putting it up high so I couldn't reach it, "No I want to go still."

I tried to grab it as he moved away, "Something will happen Ferdinand. I just don't want to go."

He grabbed my hands, "Look there aren't any magic people there. I just want to go out and have a bit of fun with you in a normal way as a couple. If anything crops up or you just want to go, we'll come home. Come on just for me."

I flopped back down giving up, "Alright, but if anything happens, I'm leaving; besides I have the dress I may as well wear it now—I guess."

He smiled coming back to me kissing me on the forehead giving the phone back, "We'll give them something more to talk about."

I rolled my eyes as he came behind me watching what I text back, "See you then. Yes, I'll still use the makeup lady. Excited not," as he pointed, "Take that last word out, Hannah."

I groaned, "Alright" as I backspaced over the 'not' then sent it off.

She sent back a smiley face then, "Looking forward to seeing you *both*."

I turned to look at him, "I may as well just send you there, that's who they want to see."

He picked up the dishes, "I can't help my animal magnetism. Come on you better get going to work." He dropped me off close to work giving me a kiss on the cheek hearing a couple of giggles from secretaries from work, rolling my eyes, "I'll see you tonight."

The day went well, without any trouble feeling like a boring old day, giving me some time to go into Tom's room to daydream when he went to a meeting.

A couple of secretaries came up to my desk when I had returned, giggling, "Does your Ferdinand have any friends or brothers?"

I had to think quickly, "He does have some friends but they're not in NSW. He doesn't have any brothers I'm afraid."

They both looked disappointed, "Aww, well if any of his friends come here be sure to let us know won't you Hannah."

I rolled my eyes, "Yes sure." I thought about Ferdinand wondering if they have brothers or relatives in Jardine.

Tom came out at afternoon tea time, "You appear to be the talk of the office Hannah with your new man. I'd like to meet him; it's been a while since you've been serious with anyone hasn't it?"

I nodded, "Yes Tom. When he is in next and if you're around, I'll introduce you. I have a spare brownie do you want a cup of coffee and some brownie (changing the subject)."

He smiled, "Oh yes that would be nice, thanks."

Ferdinand picked me up from reception again, smiling, "Any dramas today, Hannah?"

I shook my head, "No thank goodness, although I got asked if you have a brother or friends that could be introduced to some of the women up there."

I looked at him, "Do you have any brothers in Jardine?"

He hesitated looking a bit distant then coming back, "Oh no Hannah, one of kind I am. Come on, let's go."

We went for a walk on the beach with the threat of rain coming in; looking to see a sheet of rain visible on the horizon, walking down the beach feeling the chill hitting us as we walked hand in hand.

I took a deep breath smiling, "I love the smell of the rain coming in like that."

He turned grinning, "Let's go for a ride," without waiting he grabbed me around the waist putting me onto his back as I squealed. His wings flapped hard taking us up quite high just below the clouds that were coming in, with the moisture making me feel damp, as I lay on his neck, "Oh this is wonderful."

The sea beneath us was starting to look dark and choppy, but it still looked glorious to me. He flew down the coast line watching people go in with the threat of rain coming and the wind picking up along with a clap of thunder sounding in the distance.

He looked up at me grinning a dragon grin, "That wasn't you, I hope?"

I shook my head, "No I'm too happy to bring that on." He dipped lower letting me smell the salt flicking up from the waves that were starting to crest with dirty smudges running through them. He looked back, "We better get back before we get too cold, especially those deadly weapons of your hands."

I slapped his neck, "Don't be naughty Ferdinand."

We magicae back to the lounge as he held my wrists out as I giggled, "Oh stop it," and putting one of my hands up to his cheek carefully, "Aww they're freezing."

He directed me into the bathroom still holding my hands, taking my clothes off before I had a chance to protest, "You go and have a shower and I'll put some dinner on."

I tried to turn to give him a cuddle, "Oh come on they're not that bad." He looked at me naked, "Go and have a shower or I'll have to warm you up another way."

I shook my head, "That's probably why you undressed me, you randy dragon."

He came up behind me giving me a kiss on the cheek, "Off you go. You're going to kill me at this rate," tapping my bum playfully, turning on the shower.

I came out to the smell of something nice cooking, sitting on the sofa with Kimba, "well, the idea of you being around me more appears to be working so far. Hopefully it'll last."

He came over taking Kimba off me to feed her then coming back with some food, "Yes it does. It's good to see you relaxed and smiling," giving me a little kiss, "Now eat up."

We went to bed ready for another day, feeling a bit like a married couple already, relaxing around each other chatting about different things. I lay there in the dark feeling content with the way things were going with him at least.

Friday started as usual, with Ferdinand taking me to work giving me a kiss, "I'll meet you in the reception area today."

I roll my eyes, "Can I ask why?"

He just looked at me, determined, "Because I want to."

I nodded, "Alright I'm getting used to being the subject of the gossip at work anyway."

He was about to walk away then remembered something, "I think Morag is going to meet you and Alira when you go to meditate today, so just be prepared."

I nodded, "Ok, I'll let Alira know."

He walked off as I watched him then turned to go to the office, "Wondering what Morag is going to talk about but then remembered she said she was going to catch up with us later in the week."

I telephoned Alira on the office phone telling her about Morag. She laughed, "Gee now you're the latest subject for the gossips about Ferdinand."

I sighed, "I know; I'm sure it will calm down. Why don't you get Fia in, that will give them something else to talk about?"

She chuckled, "No I'll leave it a bit longer before I do that. You two can have all the glory for now."

The day dragged to lunch time snacking on my lunch again when Tom went to a meeting so I didn't have to worry about it when I was out. I met Alira at Mrs Macquarie's Chair again not sure when Morag would turn up. We were just about to prepare for meditation when we saw a woman appear near the water's edge looking at the trees there.

Alira and I looked at each other realising it was Morag's familiar outline but she was dressed in our world clothes. I went over smiling, "Wow you look different in our clothes, Morag."

She looked down looking at the clothes, "Oh this is just something I threw on" laughing. Alira and I laughed with Alira joking with her, "Oh but it looks so new."

Morag gushed, "Why thank you, Alira."

She looked up at the trees and their leaves coated with salt and dirt, "I'm always amazed how the trees in your world survive but they seem to adapt, don't they?"

I nodded, "Yes we all have to adapt to that stuff."

Morag came away from the water, "Well so far our plan is working to lessen the attacks on you Hannah having Ferdinand be seen around you."

I nodded, feeling pleased about it, "Yes, but it's a typical male world, isn't it? A woman has to have a man around to be protected, not that I mind Ferdinand being around. We are getting on quite well apart from the odd difference of opinion."

Alira tried to supress a snicker, "Difference of opinion, you threatened to turn him into a toad when he arrived at work the other day," putting her hand up to her mouth, "Oops I don't think I should have said that."

I turned to her pulling a face, then turned back to Morag, "I wouldn't have turned him into a toad, Morag, he's bad enough as a dragon."

Morag just shook her head, "I think you better stop talking the pair of you."

I coughed to clear my throat, "Good idea. What did you want to talk to us about Morag?"

She looked at us, "Take my hand so we can talk freely."

We took her hand watching her produce a clear orb around us. Morag smiled they can't see us or the orb now and no one can hear us. Me, being curious, went to touch the side as Morag made a sound, "Buzz."

I jumped back with the sound of laughter coming from her and Alira, "Sorry Hannah I just can't resist. I know you're curious."

I tapped Alira, "You're not much better."

Morag sighed, "So let's get down to business. You probably know I have been having meetings with Ferdinand in Jardine, Hannah, about how things are going especially with regard to the attacks. He has made it quite clear he wants you to come to Jardine to live—how do you feel about that Hannah?"

I felt unsure, "I don't think I am ready yet Morag. I know he has said the same to me getting quite worried about the attacks. I'm just annoyed that this has started happening when I finally get my magic, plus I'm worried about leaving my girls. They might start on them next if I'm not here. Don't forget I was attacked in Jardine as well. Do you think it is the vibration thing with my magic getting stronger in this world?"

She sighed, "Yes, I have had people looking into it and they are of the same opinion."

Morag looked down at her feet feeling uncomfortable, "I also think we have what your world calls a '*beaver*' in Jardine."

Alira and I looked at each other smiling with Alira correcting her, "Oh you mean a '*mole*' Morag. They hide in the dark until they can strike basically."

Morag smiled vaguely, "Yes that is it. There may even be a couple of people who, for some reason, are trying to stop you reach your full potential and even stop you from coming to Jardine to be with Ferdinand fulltime."

Morag watched as some people walked past thinking, 'I'll be honest with you Hannah; it does worry me the strength you have gained so far. We really need 254 to look into your family tree a bit more closely to see if we can uncover anything. I remember Matilda wasn't this strong. Although that cousin you spoke about, Geraldine, who was killed in an accident, was getting quite strong. I don't want that to happen to you, Hannah.'

I put my suspicions to Morag, "Do you think one of them could be Lilith?"

She looked concerned, "Yes Lilith is a difficult one. We have questioned her about her interest in Ferdinand but denies anything other than friendship with Ferdinand. We are keeping an eye on her."

I took a deep breath, "You know I won't harm anyone in Jardine Morag, I just want to make that clear. I still feel I am being built up so my girls get the full benefit of the family magic before anything happens to me."

Morag nodded, "Yes, like I said before we don't feel threatened by your magic and Alira's for that matter."

I felt annoyed as Morag continued, "I know you are getting stronger as well Alira, I just keep getting this feeling that there is something behind it or that we are missing something."

Alira was thinking about what happened in Jardine, "Do you know what Hannah's grandmother spoke about in the meeting Morag?"

Morag's expression went blank the realisation came onto her face. Not sounding very convincing "I don't know Alira."

Alira and I looked at each other not feeling very confident at Morag's attitude. I looked out to the water trying to calm my emotions, "Well I guess the best thing is just to carry on as normal as possible and see what comes up."

Morag shook her head, "No I'm a bit worried about that Hannah. I want to protect you two as well as your girls, but I'm not sure Jardine will fix the problem. I know this sounds selfish as far as you two are concerned but it could put Jardine at risk if they try to get you two while you're in Jardine; something the elders are not happy with as well. We do have an idea though which we are putting together, and I don't want you telling anyone else about this," looking at the both of us seriously.

I shook my head, "No I won't tell anyone."

Alira shook her head, "No I won't either."

Morag put her hands up in prayer position to her mouth taking a deep breath thinking, "We would like to flush these people out, as well as the ones doing the attacks, but keep you two as safe as possible. To do this we have thought about setting up a boarding house for women with you living and working there. This will also help some women in your world but you two can do some undercover work for us while you're here in your world. What do you think about that?"

I looked at Alira with a faint grin appearing on her face as well as mine with me nodding, "I'm happy to think about it Morag."

Alira nodded, "yes, I am as well. Hannah and I can also be together magically. I do have my mum and daughter to consider, so once we can talk about it, I will have to put it to them before I make any decision."

I started to think about it, "What about Ferdinand and Fia though? You know Ferdinand won't stay in Jardine without me going to live there and I'm sure Fia won't either."

Morag nodded thinking, "Yes, we will have to sort all that out Hannah and Alira. For now, I would like you both to think about it, as we still have a lot of organising to do. If we manage to get a house lined up, which is quite difficult we believe in Sydney, that is when we will start talking seriously to you both, before we sign anything. How do you feel about that?"

I smiled at Alira, "It would mean we don't have to do these jobs anymore, I guess. We could become the female version of James Bond."

Alira cracked up laughing, "You're funny Hannah. We could be Jane and Jean Bond."

Morag looked a little confused then shook her head, "Anyway, please think about it. No talking to Ferdinand or Fia at this stage as nothing is finalised, plus we need to keep it quiet."

I nodded, "Well that is going to be hard given that Ferdinand can read my thoughts a lot of the time, but I will try. I also want to let you know, just in case something happens, Ferdinand and I are going to a friend's wedding tomorrow afternoon. I'm not expecting anything magical to happen, but that has proved me wrong before."

Morag looked at me, "Mm I didn't think of Ferdinand's ability to read your thoughts. Try and block it off as much as you can until we sort something out at least. Have fun at the wedding; just be on your guard."

Morag hesitated before she went to leave, "I have also been thinking about what you have said as though there is someone constantly sending attackers your way or just upsetting you. I want you both to be on your guard, especially you Hannah, no more daydreaming. Just look around you more to see if there is someone watching you, especially when something is happening. I know this could be hard because you're concentrating on what is happening, but just be aware of it."

I thought about it, "I certainly will, Morag."

Alira agreed, "It makes sense, they could just be the spectators to see how we react."

Morag gave us a hug as she evaporated the orb. I looked at the time making Morag apologise, "I suppose you don't have time to do your meditation now, sorry about that."

I shook my head, "That's alright, Morag, we can do it another time."

Alira waved, "See you later Morag," watching her disappear.

Alira and I walked back to work, not really wanting to go back, but thinking positive I looked at Alira, "Well at least it's not long until we knock off. Can Fia read your thoughts Alira?"

She nodded, "Yes, most of the time. I think it's a Jardine thing. We should think of an excuse if something pops into our minds like we were talking to someone about their new job or something. What do you think about that?"

I smiled, "Yes that's a good idea. I'll keep that in mind."

We got back to work giving each other a hug with Alira smiling, "Have a nice time at the wedding. If you need any help, call me."

I nodded, "Yes sure. I didn't really want to go but Ferdinand is still in his possessive mode from being intimate."

Alira laughed, "Yes Fia is to a degree, but not as bad as him. Good luck."

I got back to my work station trying to stay focused on work and not thinking about the information I had been told. I must also concentrate on the family tree to see if I can find anything else. I had some spare time before I finished work looking up Norwegian births, deaths and marriages again, to see if I could find anything on there.

I also had a thought about looking on the German side as well since I had started speaking it, which perplexed me, because I didn't know of any German connection in the family. I did a general search on Ingrid Dragĕ, coming up with a few different people with that name in Norway in different areas.

I was deep in thought and not watching the time when I got a phone call making me jump, with Tracey from reception ringing me, "Hannah, you have a visitor waiting for you."

I looked at the time, "Oh gosh I didn't realise the time. I'll be there shortly, thanks Tracey."

I shut my computer down, put my jacket on and got my bag. Tom was still in his office looking at paperwork, so I put my head in, "Tom I'm going now. Ferdinand is out in the reception area if you want to meet him otherwise, it can wait for another time (hoping it would be)."

He got up looking at me, "Oh yes that would be nice, thanks Hannah."

I quietly groaned to myself, waiting for him to come out of his office, following me towards the reception area. I took a deep breath smiling, finding Ferdinand there waiting for me in a dark shirt and dark jeans, looking sexy again, getting up, when he saw me come through the door. I waited for Tom to come through introducing him to Ferdinand. They shook hands, still feeling strange about this, as Ferdinand took my hand.

Tom smiled noticing this, "Well Ferdinand we were beginning to give up on Hannah meeting someone; nice to have finally met you. We know Hannah has a bit of a temper, so you have your work cut out for you. The office gossips have said you've known each other for a while but hadn't hooked up."

Ferdinand couldn't resist, "Yes well, we're working on the temper," smiling at me giving me a hug, "The gossips have it right, she kept saying no, but I kept annoying her until she said yes."

I looked at Tom annoyed, "I think you're exaggerating the temper, Tom."

This made Tom and Ferdinand laugh with Tom pointing at me, "Ah there she goes with the temper already."

I groaned calming down trying to ignore them, "I wasn't that bad, Ferdinand. We did lose touch for a few years when you went overseas—*remember*."

Tom shook his head, "Well I had better get going home to my wife. I don't know if Hannah has told you, but she is very pregnant. See you around Ferdinand; see you on Monday, Hannah."

I sighed in relief, "Come on let's get out of here."

Ferdinand looked over to Tracey who had a couple of friends with her smiling, "See you, Tracey."

Tracey smiled back in a dreamy voice, "See you, Ferdinand." Thank goodness the lift came quickly with Ferdinand putting his arm around my waist guiding me in making the women watch him, "Aww such a gentleman."

I got in the lift looking at him shaking my head, "You're enjoying this aren't you?"

He sighed, "Yes, but it's only a bit of fun Hannah, just relax. Did you want to go for a drink or get something to eat somewhere before we go home?"

I thought about it, "We can go to the Opera Bar if you like to have a drink. I haven't been there for a while so I'm not sure what their food is like. We can decide once we get there."

We walked up to the Opera Bar, that was part of the opera house, which was starting to get busy. We managed to get a table near the water, with Ferdinand going to get a couple of drinks and the menu to have a look at.

The rain had cleared from yesterday leaving a pink sky as the sun went down. I sat and watched the ferries churning up the water full of people either going home or coming into the city to go out. The bridge and the opera house were just starting to put their lights on as a gentle breeze came off the water with Ferdinand sitting down watching me, "What are you thinking, Hannah?"

I turned back to him, "I just feel really different from a few months ago. So much has happened since then; it's such a strange feeling, even sitting here with you. I wouldn't have been doing this a few months ago. Although on the downside, I've had some attacks, but being here with a sexy dragon, finally finding my magic along with my girls knowing it and being to Jardine. It's like I've been living in the wrong time line for so long and now I'm back on the right track."

He smiled putting his glass up, "I'll say cheers to that Hannah," as I put my glass up tapping his.

We both had a drink, "So you think I'm a sexy dragon?"

I laughed, "Yes dear." We ended up having something to eat then walked part of the way along the harbour watching all the people mill around, looking for somewhere to eat or drink. He turned to hug me, "Are you ready to go home?"

I nodded looking up at him, "Yes thanks." I had my shower first, telling Ferdinand I was going to do a bit of meditation on the balcony, while he had his shower. I lit some incense, put a sweatshirt on to keep warm and put the ear buds in listening to my meditation music, not intending to do a long session. I went into the usual scene of being in a boat floating along when everything stopped.

I knew who was around getting out of the boat walking onto the grass hearing it crunch under my feet, stopping when I saw a figure not far away, "Hallo bestemor (hello grandma)."

She didn't come straight over, getting the feeling she wasn't very happy with me, "Hva er galt bestemor (what is wrong grandma?)"

She eventually glided over closer to me with anger in her eyes, "Ikke se etter meg. Jeg skal fortelle deg hvem jeg er når jeg er klar! (Do not look for me. I will tell you when I am ready!)"

I growled with anger building, "Jeg trenger å vite siden vi er I fare (I need to know as we are in danger)."

Ferdinand came out of the bathroom, hearing me talk in Norwegian getting angry. He put a sweatshirt on and carefully sat behind me, putting me between his legs and joining us. I was still talking to grandma when he did this, as she was saying, "Du må konsentere deg om magien din (you need to concentrate on your magic)."

I growled again getting annoyed, when Ferdinand became visible, "Hannah hvem er dette (Hannah who is this?)"

Grandma looked angry at the intrusion, "Gå bort Ferdinand (go away Ferdinand)."

Ferdinand could see I was angry, "Hvorfor er Hannah sint (why is Hannah angry?)" A wicked grin appeared on her face, "Fordi hun har sin bestefars temperament (because she has her grandpa's temperament)."

I growled again, "Hva heter han (what is his name)?"

She floated up to Ferdinand playing with us now, "Se inn øynene til Ferdinand (look in Ferdinand's eyes)."

Ferdinand took my hand, "Slutte å snakke I gåter (stop talking in riddles)."

Grandma had had enough disappearing saying as she left, "Ikke bland Ferdinand (don't interfere Ferdinand)." We looked at each other hearing our breathing coming into our minds with the smell of the incense hitting my senses, coming back to the balcony.

I slowly opened my eyes finding Ferdinand behind me with his arms around my waist and his legs spread around me. I started to move and so did he, hugging me, "Hun er sta som en annen jeg kjenner (she is stubborn like someone else I know.)" I leaned into him thinking about what she said, "Og forvirrende (and confusing)."

He magicae us into the lounge turning me around to face him, "I guess you'll figure it out eventually."

I leaned into him, "Yes, I guess so. Morag was wanting me to do some more research so I did a bit at work. I think that is why she was annoyed; I was looking for her. I know you've been in my meditation before but I didn't think you could do that?"

He kissed me on the forehead, thinking about something, then came back to me, "Yes now that we have been intimate, we are joined a lot more."

I moved away, yawning, "Does that mean the more we do it the more we blend."

He laughed, "No it just means you make me age quicker."

I shook my head getting a drink of water, "Oh stop it. You're the one who started last time. I was just innocently taking a bath."

He shut the door to the balcony checking to see where Kimba was and locking the front door, "Oh yes, *innocently* walking around in your underwear."

I finished my drink, turned off the kitchen light, and went into the bedroom looking at him, "You'll just have to get used to it won't you because that is how I normally walked around."

He groaned going towards the bedroom, "I'm going to get very old, very quick; I think."

I lay there waiting for him to come in with Kimba jumping up to have a cuddle next to me. She knew Ferdinand would be coming on that side as well, so she could get a fuss from the both of us. I started to pat her, getting her purring "I know you are waiting for him; you rat."

Ferdinand came in laying down, "She knows who's the boss."

I shook my head, "Keep dreaming, Ferdinand."

Ferdinand was patting Kimba making me think about what grandma had said about his eyes, looking at them in the lamp light, as he played with Kimba. He had his lids lowered so I couldn't see his eyes fully. I knew they were yellow at times from being a dragon, but I could see a hint of dark pupil in them sometimes.

He smiled, "Stop looking at my eyes Hannah, she is just crazy," flicking his fingers to turn the light off.

I lay there still thinking, '*I notice you never shave, is that because of the dragon thing?*'

He rubbed his chin against mine, "Do you prefer whiskers?"

I kissed him quickly, "It doesn't bother me either way. I was just curious."

He cuddled in, "No I can't grow a beard because I don't have all the male hormones. Are you happy now?"

I patted his hand that was over my waist, "Yes, thank you dear."

Chapter 15

I woke with a small shaft of light filtering through the curtains and warmth in the bedroom already. I looked at Ferdinand who was still asleep watching his chest rise and fall, liking the familiarity of our relationship already.

In my other relationships, I would have been bored with them by now and would have started faking it in bed, bringing a smile to me, '*You can't do that Jardine style at least.*' I checked the time deciding it was too early to get up, rolling over to try and go back to sleep. Ferdinand rolled over putting his arm over my waist, "Good morning," giving me a little kiss on the neck.

I smiled, "Good morning. I thought you were asleep still."

He chuckled, "I was until I heard you thinking. Thank goodness for Jardine style."

I groaned, "Trust you to hear that."

Kimba jumped up on top of him rubbing herself up against the arm that was over me, "I think she is jealous of the attention you give me now."

He gave me a little kiss again and patted her, "I've got enough to go around for the both of you. I'll be going to Jardine for a couple hours earlier today so we'll have to get up soon."

I wriggled getting comfortable, "I'm not going to Jardine, so I don't have to get up yet." He chuckled, which made me nervous, "Oh yes you do. You have to get your hair done, don't you?"

I yawned, "Yes but that's not until 11.00am, so plenty of time for me to get up." I heard him putting Kimba down, but kept my eyes shut, trying to ignore him while feeling him move closer. He put his arm under the duvet, grabbing me, while holding my arms, "Maybe you need a bit of tickling to get you up," putting his other arm up my back to my ticklish spot.

I giggled, trying to wriggle away from him, "No Ferdinand don't be mean." I giggled harder now, "Don't Ferdinand I'll pee my pants."

He rolled me over, looking at me with tears coming down my face with laughter, "Or maybe we could get cosy to see if you are bored yet," kissing me on the lips. He still had my arms but I decided to play his game responding to his passion. He stopped looking at me, "You little minx," and going to kiss me again, when my phone rang looking up groaning, "Well that's a sign to get up."

I grabbed my phone answering it while he got up. It was Amelia wanting to catch up with me. I told her I would ring her back to see what we can arrange. I rolled over putting the phone back on the dresser deciding to just lie there and rest.

He came back in with a grin on his face as I turned to look at him, "No Ferdinand I'm having a lie in. I have to go to work normally, so this is my only chance," and rolling back over.

I knew it wouldn't work, but I tried to ignore him, as he pulled the duvet off me, "Come on Hannah time to get up, we'll go for a walk after breakfast. Besides if you were in Jardine, you wouldn't have to go work."

I curled up, trying to grab the sheet, "oh stop being mean, Ferdinand."

He leaned over, pulling the sheet off me and picking me up, "It's going to be a nice day; you can't waste it in bed."

I tried to wriggle out of his arms, but thought of something, putting my arms around his neck, kissing him around his neck, then up to his mouth, but he moved it away, "No you don't, that's not going to work."

He put me down on the sofa keeping my arms around his neck, trying to pull him down to me. He laughed, "You're a determined little minx today, aren't you?"

He grabbed my arms laying down on me, "Are you going to behave now?"

I was running out of energy, smiling at him, looking at his eyes again, "I can see two different eyes in you, your dragon ones and your male ones, is that normal?"

He groaned, "Your grandma is crazy Hannah, and yes that is normal. People don't need to see my dragon eyes only you do."

I could see it was starting to annoy him and I managed to get a hand free, as I stroked his hair, looking at his silver streak remembering something from when I was young, "oh dear you were the guy who stood on my feet in the dance class when I was young."

He chuckled, "Mmm and I'm looking forward to doing it all over again tonight at the wedding."

I groaned, "Oh I better take some boots with me then for protection."

He gave me a kiss getting up, "I have improved a bit since then, but you better have a good breakfast as you're going to need your energy for dancing tonight."

I smiled unsure, "Mm can't wait."

We had breakfast then went for a walk down the beach, feeling the warmth coming in off the land already. The waves looked inviting and clear, but I couldn't go for a swim because I had to get my hair done. He was getting ready to take off before we got back to the unit, "I'll see you around lunch time."

I gave him a kiss, "I'm not sure how long this will take as they usually do a few people at the same time, so I might not be there."

He nodded, "Ok, just as long as I know, so I don't get worried."

I went back to the unit phoning Amelia back deciding to meet in Miranda Fair shopping centre to get our nails done, plus I realised I needed some stockings. Ferdinand had done most of the cleaning, smiling to myself, 'He is a good guy, not many men would do that for me.'

I met Amelia in the shopping mall, having a coffee first, then going to get our nails done. While we were in the chair getting this done Amelia started chatting about the attacks but saying it so the ladies didn't know what we were talking about.

We picked our colours for our nails, when Amelia moved closer to talk, "Mum I've been talking with Charlotte and we would really like to do something to stir them up for attacking you. Nothing deadly just a prank like you used to do, just so they know that we know where some of them are and that we aren't going to take their shit."

I thought about it, "Ok, but leave it for a bit as they have left me alone since Ferdinand has been around me in public."

Amelia shook her head, "You shouldn't have to have a man around you to stop their nonsense. I know you like him around just like me and Charlotte like Shiro and Aetius, but we shouldn't have to feel we need to have them there."

I nodded, "I know I said the same thing to 'M' (not wanting to say her name just in case). M is also looking at what is going on with some people in J. I'll tell you what you have a look in the book, as I'm going to be a bit busy today and probably tired tomorrow. I'll have a look when I can, then we'll arrange when we want to do something."

Amelia smiled, "I knew you wouldn't want to let it go Mum. That's where we get our stirring from."

I grinned, "Yes, I've had plenty of practice at stirring people up. What did you think of the donkeys?" and winked at her.

She gasped, "That was fabulous. I'll have to have a go at that one."

Once we had our nails done, Amelia came with me to pick some pantyhose out. I was looking at the plain ones, when Amelia spotted some stockings that needed the garter belt, smiling cheekily at me, "Why don't you stir the old guy up with these, Mum?"

I chuckled, "I actually used to wear those when I was younger; just a phase I was going through."

I looked at the garter belts that look quite pretty with lace and satin feeling daring "I might try one on. Why don't you to give Shiro a bit of stir up?"

We giggled like teenagers going into the change room, trying a couple on, showing each other quickly. I came out deciding to buy a black one with some black stockings and I also got some ordinary pantyhose in case I decided not to wear them. Amelia got one as well feeling naughty, "This ought to stir them up, Mum."

I looked at the time, "I better get going it's getting close to the time I have to get my hair done."

We hugged, with Amelia looking at me, "We'll talk later. Be careful, won't you?"

I nodded, "yes, I will. The same goes for you and Charlotte, it won't be long before they will pick you two up as you're getting stronger."

I got back home, having a quick shower just to freshen up, then took off to the hair and makeup lady. It was at Tania's place out in a back room with all the women in their clucking around Tania, who had already had her makeup and hair done, sipping champagne.

I came into the room, with her making a big fuss, "Oh you're here. I'm so glad you decided to come, I really thought you would back out like you normally do."

I felt a little guilty because that's exactly what I was going to do, smiling, "Well I thought I may as well try out the new boyfriend see how he goes in amongst my friends."

Tania sat me down, "So tell me all about him," but the makeup lady came over, "You'll have to wait Tania. I need to do her hair. What do you want done Hannah?"

I thought to myself, '*Phew saved by the hair lady.*' I had my hair put up in a French roll which didn't take long, but had heaps of hair clips put in and enough hairspray to make sure not one strand of hair moved. I moved over to the makeup lady when Tania came and sat down next to me, "You still have to tell me about this guy, Hannah."

I groaned, "I can't really talk Tania; I'll tell you later." The woman doing the makeup was quite quick, asking me what colour dress I was wearing, putting subtle tones on, which suited me better than dark colours, feeling pleased once she had finished.

I got up hoping to go, but Tania came over with a glass of wine, "I know you don't like champagne so here's a glass of wine. You're not getting away yet until you tell me a little bit about this guy."

I sat down with her and told her the basics which I tended to tell other people, sipping on the wine. She smiled, "Well he sounds nice, Hannah, maybe he's the one that will put up with your temper."

I groaned, "Yes so everyone keeps telling me and him. Is Jonathon Hunter still coming to the wedding?"

She smiled cheekily, "Yes unfortunately for you."

I'm just preparing myself, "Hopefully he has matured a bit by now."

She laughed out loud, "You haven't seen him for a while have you, that would be a big 'NO'. I only invited him because I'm friends with his current girlfriend; just stay away from him and you'll be alright."

I got up, "Well I'll get going, I'll see you later."

She squealed, "Yes I feel good about this one."

I got home, not finding Ferdinand back yet so I put the stockings and garter belt in my draw starting to have doubts about wearing it. I had a look at the makeup and hair in the mirror feeling pleased with it. It was around 12.30p.m. so I sat out on the balcony having a drink of water thinking I couldn't do too much now that my hair and makeup was done, with Kimba jumping up on my lap. I was just thinking about what to have for lunch patting Kimba, when Ferdinand came into the lounge noticing me, coming out.

I looked up at him, not sure what he was going to think of it, looking at me surprised, "Wow you look different."

I wasn't sure if that was good or bad, "So you don't like it?"

He smiled, "I like it, it just makes you look different, I guess. I'll be honest I like you without so much makeup, but I'm sure it will settle down."

I stood, picking Kimba up, as he came up to me kissing me gently on the lips, "I knew your eyelashes were long but I didn't realise they were that long."

I chuckled, "Half a ton of mascara tends to do that to my eyelashes. I've got heaps of hairpins in my hair as well. I better not go through a metal detector; I'd set it off."

He went into the kitchen getting some things ready, "what do you feel like for lunch? I imagine it will be a while before we have something to eat, so we don't want empty stomachs to drink on."

I looked at him, "That reminds me Jonathon is going to be there, so please don't get sucked into his silliness. Apparently, he hasn't changed much." He looked at me, "Stop worrying Hannah, I'll be alright."

We had lunch feeling, he was a little quiet, but I told him about meeting Amelia to do our nails. We tidied up and started to get ready, "are you having a shower or wash?"

I shook my head, "No I had one earlier, you go ahead." I went in while he was in there, deciding to put the stockings and belt on, already having the dress on by the time, he came in. He looked at the stockings "oh you don't normally where those either," as I smiled, "It's only for one day Ferdinand."

I was starting to get a bit tense, so after I put my shoes on, I went and had a glass of wine. I wasn't going to get tipsy, as I didn't trust that Jonathon, "Do you want a glass of wine, Ferdinand?"

He called out from the bedroom, "Yes thanks."

I poured the wine and sat down for a little while getting the bracelet that he had given me, trying to put it on. Ferdinand came out with a suit and white shirt on and two ties in his hands, "I thought I'd wear a tie Hannah, which one do you think I should wear?"

I stood up, "Can you help me do up the bracelet first?" He came over to me doing it up looking at me with the dress on now, "You do look nice, Hannah."

"Thanks Ferdinand. Show me these ties."

I picked one, taking it before he had a chance to take it, putting it around his neck, lifting his collar, while he watched me with a smile on his face, "You remember doing ties from school don't you?"

I chuckled, "Yes I'm quite the expert after girls pulling them off you all the time."

He moved in closer putting his hands on my hips, as I was doing the knot on the tie. I could feel him moving his hands on my hips, "What do you have on?"

I just shrugged it off, "Just some pantyhose, why?"

Just as he was about to ask more questions and I was finishing off his tie, Morag popped in, "Oh hello you two. Are you all ready to go to your wedding?"

Ferdinand moved away from me, "Hi Morag, yes, all ready to go. Do you want a glass of wine with us?"

Morag smiled, "Yes thanks Ferdinand that will be nice?"

She looked at me as he walked away with a knowing grin, "He doesn't like your makeup, does he?"

I smiled, "No, but it's only for one night and he's the one that wanted to go, isn't that right Ferdinand?"

He handed Morag a glass of wine, "What's that Hannah?"

Morag looked at Ferdinand, "Oh you didn't want to go Hannah?"

I shook my head, "No not really, but if I'm going, I get dressed up for it."

Ferdinand looked at me, "Alright I told you I don't like your makeup, but you do look nice, don't get upset."

Morag changed the subject having a drink of wine, "Well you have a lovely day for it. Is it outside or in a church?"

I looked outside, "It's outside and it should be nice as it's in the gardens not far from here. We then go to a reception area near the water, so we aren't far from home, if anything happens."

Ferdinand sighed, "We are just going to have some fun, stop worrying, Hannah."

Morag came over to me, "Well that is why I am here actually. I have something from the people looking at your vibrations, attracting the people who have been attacking you."

She noticed the bracelet I had on from Jardine, "I see you have the bracelet on from Ferdinand that will be perfect."

I looked confused at her, "What do you mean, Morag?"

She came over to me, "Put your hand up," waving her hand over the bracelet with a light blue crystal called smithsonite quietly saying a chant with a blue vibration covering the bracelet, then going through me, making me shudder.

Ferdinand was watching looking concerned, "Are you alright, Hannah?"

I shook myself out, "Yes, it just gave me a bit of a buzz."

Morag looked pleased, "That should keep you safe for a little while until we sort something else out. Just make sure you wear the bracelet as I have attached it to that."

We finished our wine, "Well I will go now. Do you want me to take a photo of you two, as you do look lovely all dressed up?"

I smiled, "Oh yes that would be nice thank you."

I got my phone with Morag taking a photo near the curtains in the lounge "there you go I hope you like it?"

I had a look with Ferdinand looking at it, "Oh yes that is nice, thank you."

Ferdinand smiled, "Anyway, I suppose we had better get going Hannah?"

Morag took the hint, "I will catch up with you during the week Hannah, have a nice time and behave yourself Ferdinand."

He smiled, "Yes Morag I will."

We finished off our drinks, while Ferdinand fed Kimba and I closed the unit up. I got my little bag putting my phone in and taking off to the Camelia Gardens in Caringbah, landing near the carpark, feeling a bit nervous now.

He smiled, "Just relax, if you don't like it, we can go home. I do want one dance at least and by the way, you smell nice with that Chanel no. 5 on."

I nodded, "Ok, I feel a bit happier with that option plus the protection that Morag just gave me."

We went into the park finding the sign for the wedding, with Ferdinand stopping me, "Are you ready?"

I checked his tie looking at him nervously, "Yes I'm ready."

He gave me a kiss then took my hand, "Come on let's go in."

We went in finding white foldout seats all lined up in rows, going up half way to get a seat. I could feel eyes on me, as Ferdinand squeezed my hand, rubbing his thumb in my palm, looking a little nervous himself.

We sat down with a woman sitting in front of us, turning to look at Ferdinand and then at me, "Oh hello Hannah, I haven't seen you for a while. How are you?"

I squeezed Ferdinand's hand, putting a smile on, "Hi Angela how are you going? Yes, I thought I would come along since I had a boyfriend for a change."

I could hear Ferdinand, trying not to laugh, "Hi Angela. I'm Ferdinand, the boyfriend."

She chatted away with small talk with her husband Harold joining in when we heard the music start.

Angela got excited, "Oh well it's about to start, I suppose you will be next Hannah?"

I didn't get a chance to reply as we were asked to stand up for the bride to come, with Ferdinand smiling squeezing my hand, "Mmm maybe she's a fortune teller."

I shushed him, "Don't be naughty Ferdinand."

He leaned in saying quietly, "Your makeup looks plain compared to some of the others."

I looked at him smiling feeling a bit better about it now.

We got through the ceremony then got offered a lift to the reception area by another couple I knew Ella and Bill, not really wanting to, but felt obliged. Ella was chatting the whole way as we tried to concentrate but I just kept tuning out. Ferdinand could see I wasn't really listening, squeezing my hand again.

We got to the reception, walking out to the balcony area, having a glass of wine and getting some air, "Oh thank goodness some fresh air and no gossips."

Ferdinand had a drink, "Yes, they do go on a bit. I can see why you don't hang around them that much."

We stood out there for a while with Ferdinand having another drink, "I've seen wedding ceremonies from afar but never really been to one before, so I have found it interesting. Committing yourselves to each until death do you part. If I was from your world, would you do that for me?"

This took me by surprise, trying to think, "I thought I have in a way being intimate with you?"

He sighed, "Yes I suppose it is similar."

I moved in closer to him, giving him a gentle kiss, "The difference here is they don't stay together, even after they say it."

I then heard a click with Angela coming out, "Oh that has made a nice picture. Come on you two love birds we have to take our seats."

We went out and got seated, unfortunately near Angela and Ella, with them all chatting away. We got through the meal and the speeches with Ferdinand taking it all in, having a couple more drinks.

I could hear Jonathon, on another table, thank goodness, as loud as ever, making jokes that no one laughed at. I leaned in to Ferdinand, "That is Jonathon, the ex I told you about." He looked over to where he was sitting "ok, I'll stay away."

We finally got up to the bridal waltz watching Tania and Jack waltz around the floor. It was time for people to come on the floor and join them with Seal's 'Kiss from a Rose' coming on. Ferdinand stood up, putting his hand out, "Come on it's my turn."

A flash back came from when we were in the ballroom dancing lessons as I hesitated.

I put my hand in his getting up, "I haven't done this for a long time Ferdinand."

He pulled me into him, confidently holding me around the waist, starting to dance around the floor, bringing a huge smile on my face, "Oh Ferdinand this is wonderful." He looked down to me smiling, almost looking like a dashing prince in his suit and tie. Once it was finished, we walked back to the table, I could see people looking, then chatting to the person next to them. Ferdinand smiled at me, "Looks like we're going to be the gossips subject again."

We relaxed, finally with me saying, "Just about time to go," when Ferdinand got me up to dance a couple more dances, thoroughly enjoying ourselves.

I had to go to the ladies, "I won't be long," with a couple of women joining me chatting on the way, looking back at Ferdinand, as he shook his head. I was on my back with him pointing that he was going up to the bar to get a drink. I still had a glass of wine, so I sat down drinking that with a group of women, coming over like a gaggle of geese, chatting to me about where I met Ferdinand blah blah blah.

Ferdinand appeared to be taking a while to come back from the bar, so I looked over to see him sitting next to Jonathon making me groan.

Jonathon had his hand on Ferdinand's shoulder talking loudly with Ferdinand having another drink laughing.

I frowned thinking, *'Oh dear that bloody Jonathon has spiked his drink.'* I sat for a bit longer hoping Ferdinand would come over, but I could hear Jonathon getting louder so he was probably telling smart jokes about women and being a dick; which is why I left him in the end.

I excused myself from the women I was sitting with, going over to the bar with a chant entering my head, *"Whatever you have given Ferdinand to drink you will feel the benefit Jonathon times three by the end of this night you will as sick as can be."*

I went up to Jonathon and Ferdinand patting Jonathon on the shoulder as I said the chant in my head, smiling as he shook his head, "Oh Hannah, nice to see you. I've just been talking to Ferdinand or Ferdi, he's a nice guy. I hope your temper doesn't make him run away like the rest of us."

Ferdinand giggled drunkenly, "See Hannah I'm a nice guy. She does have a bit of temper you know, but I'm calming her down Jonathon."

I rolled my eyes looking away to stay calm, "Well I'm going Ferdinand are you staying with Jonathon or coming now?"

Jonathon laughed, "Aww see she's started to get that temper up again and boss you around, Ferdinand."

I pursed my lips trying to control myself, while I watched Ferdinand fall on the bar laughing then pushing Jonathon, "I know she thinks she's the boss but I'm the boss," pointing to his chest.

I had to just walk away, "See you Ferdinand," then looking at Jonathon saying louder "nice to see you haven't changed Jonathon, spiking people's drinks like you did mine to try and get me in bed, which didn't work."

Jonathon got annoyed trying to be smart, "Yeah but you enjoyed it in the end Hannah."

I laughed, starting to make the noises I used to do when I faked it, "Ah ah oh Jonathon yes!" I looked determined at him, "I faked it most of the time Jonathon before you fell asleep because you couldn't keep up."

Ferdinand had stopped laughing looking at me seriously, "Hannah, that's not very nice."

I just walked away having said enough, with a smirk on my face, noticing a few women laughing. Jonathon noticed them laughing, so he pushed Ferdinand, "Go and tell her off if you're a man, she's a rude bitch and always has been."

Ferdinand looked at Jonathon blurry eyed, getting up and catching up with me, when I was in the carpark, grabbing my arm, "Let go Ferdinand." He had a wicked grin on his face staggering as the fresh air hit him, putting his arm around my waist, "Come on Hannah time for a ride." My eyes went wide in anger, as I tried to get out of his grip, "No Ferdinand don't you dare!" He chuckled, with people coming out to see if I was alright, but we had gone.

They looked around, "Where did they go?"

Luckily, they couldn't hear me screaming at Ferdinand who had thrown me on his back, turning into a dragon. He held onto my leg making sure I didn't try to magicae off his back, "Hang on honey, it's time for a nice ride, because I'm the boss in this relationship."

I held on tightly as he flipped and dipped, while I yelled at him hitting his neck, "Let me go Ferdinand or take me home."

He kept flying, going over the sea and away from the lights, looking around worried.

The sea looked an inky black, with the sound of waves cresting beneath us.

The sea air must have started to sober him up a bit as he shook his head spouting flames from his mouth. I yelled at him again, "Take me home, Ferdinand, or I will turn you into a bloody toad."

He chuckled again going lower, hitting the tops of the waves as I screamed, "You rotten sod," putting my hands up trying to stop the water from hitting my face.

I growled, getting angry, "That bloody Jonathon is going to pay for this and so are you, Ferdinand," as a clap of thunder could be heard in the distance.

Ferdinand grumbled, "Oh alright keep your knickers on," (something Jonathon would have said) magicaeing home landing in the bedroom; flicking his fingers turning the bedroom light on.

He held onto my arm looking at me chuckling, "Your war paint has started to run dear."

I tried to shake him off, "Let go of me Ferdinand," watching him sway in front of me. I relaxed a little, pleased that we were at least home and this is the first time I've seen Ferdinand drunk, as I smirked. Ferdinand could see me smirking at him, "Oh so you think I'm funny now do you?"

I tried to pry his fingers off my wrist but he grabbed my other hand, pushing me against the wall, "Don't you try any magic Hannah, otherwise I'll tell Morag you zapped me. Like Jonathon said, I'm the boss."

I tried to push him away, "Ferdinand you're drunk let me go."

He staggered closer to me starting to kiss my neck, "You can't fake it with me Hannah," as I smelt whiskey on his breath, cursing Jonathon again.

I tried to push him away again, "I don't want to do it now Ferdinand and according to Jardine rules you aren't allowed too either." He was still kissing my neck pulling my dress off magically, looking down at the now ripped stockings and suspender belt. He grinned, "Oh so that's what you were hiding under there, you naughty witch."

I took a deep breath, as I didn't like that name, but I knew he wasn't himself.

He moved closer pushing himself against me, gyrating his hips like a man of our world would do, so I couldn't move. He was kissing my neck again, "Mmm a mixture of salt and Chanel no. 5, my favourite."

I stopped, resisting him hoping he would fall asleep, when I felt him starting to bite my neck. I got angry struggling against him, "Ferdinand what are you doing?"

He was sucking and biting my neck, as I pushed against his hands, "Ouch Ferdinand that is hurting, stop it!"

I had had enough, so I threw him over to the bed magically putting cuffs on him.

He looked around him realising where he was, struggling against the cuffs getting angry, "Hannah don't you dare put these on me, let me out of them now!"

I walked over to the mirror looking at my neck, while he struggled, watching me in my underwear, stockings and belt. I saw a bruise starting to form on my neck, "That bloody Jonathon and his stinking love bites. He thinks he's bloody funny, well I'll deal with him once I'm finished with you Ferdinand."

I looked at my hair that was sticking up everywhere, with so much hairspray it just stayed there. I had hairpins sticking out of it, looking like sticks, as I pulled some of them out.

My makeup was running over my face with black rings around my eyes where the water had made my mascara run.

Ferdinand was still struggling against the cuffs looking at me, "Hannah I'm the man you do as I say," which brought a naughty smirk to my face, "Oh are you, Ferdinand?"

He looked nervous as I approached him, with a wicked look in my eyes and an equally wicked smile on my lips. I had just my black bra, pants and garter belt on and what was left of my stockings, after being on his back.

I leaned down taking off my shoes not taking my eyes off him, still with this smile while he squirmed.

I went over to him, taking his shoes off, as he tried to lash out to me, to grab me around the waist with his feet. I moved up the bed a little sitting on his legs to stop him from moving, which wasn't hard because he was so drunk. He growled looking angry, "Hannah, cut this out let me go, you know I don't like this."

I leaned down with a smile on my face, saying in a sultry voice, "Ich bin für (I'm in charge)" making him stop struggling briefly, "Sprechen kein Deutsch (don't speak German)."

I sat up on his knees smiling at him taking his belt out of his pants "Ich werde tun, was ich will (I'll do what I want)."

I was still looking at him, watching him squirm with a wicked smile on my face, as I undid his pants leaning down putting my hand under his shirt, "Der Verantwortlicher ist Ferdinand (who is in charge, Ferdinand)." He tried to see what I was doing, looking worried, struggling to get me off his legs groaning then growling, "Hannah tut das nicht (Hannah don't do this)."

I started to move up, undoing his shirt running my hand up his chest as he tried his last attempt to try and stop me, with Jonathon's wise remarks, "Jonathon said you liked the love bite Hannah, he said it turned you on."

I kissed him gently on the chest looking at him with downcast eyes, hearing him groan, "Hannah ließ mich gehen (Hannah let me go)." I got his tie pulling on it, undoing it wrapping it in my hands going towards his mouth to gag him. It made him look quite fearful "nein Hannah (no Hannah)." I was still angry from his rough treatment of me, vowing that no man would ever treat me like that, so I went towards his mouth with the tie "warum sollte ich Ferdinand stoppen? (Why should I stop Ferdinand)?"

I ran the tie over his chin, going up to his mouth as he moved his head around violently with fear in his eyes, "I'm sorry Hannah, please!"

I hesitated realising I wasn't angry enough to watch him get that fearful and he was starting to beg, which isn't something I liked to see in a man. Besides, I was sure there was something magical being used in Ferdinand's behaviour, so I put the tie down calming him down by kissing his neck.

I deliberately moved up kissing him gently, looking like a lion with my hair sticking up so much like a lion's mane and my dark eyes.

He looked down at me worried, wondering what I was going to do next, as I smiled kissing him again gently on the neck, "I used to send Jonathon to sleep, did he tell you that Ferdinand?"

He started to struggle against the cuffs rattling them against the bed, "You wouldn't Hannah, let me out of these now!"

I kissed him again smiling, "I used to sing him a lullaby 'rock-a-bye Ferdinand it's time to stop.'"

Ferdinand tried to twist his hips to push me off him, to stop me from saying the sleep chant, getting angry yelling, "Hannah stop this now and take these off me!"

I had had enough now, so I just put my hand around his face, *"Rock-a-bye Ferdinand ist es Zeit aufzuhören, jetzt zu schlafen wie ein baby drop drop drop. (rock-a-bye Ferdinand it's time to stop, sleep now like a baby drop drop drop.)"*

He tried to struggle out of my grip, falling asleep, bringing a smile to my lips, "Huh still works after all these years."

I gave him a little kiss, hearing him drop into a deep sleep, getting off him sighing, "Well we did have a reasonably good night I suppose."

I watched as his chest rise up and down in sleep "I still think there was something magical causing this as well. I guess I'll have to see what he remembers."

I took his clothes off putting his shorts and t-shirt on him. I picked up his jacket that he had flung on the floor, looking at the brand inside around the pocket noticing it was a German brand name called 'Zalando'.

This made me curious as he normally flicks his clothes away magically, so I looked through his pockets not finding anything. I hung it on a coat hanger along with his other clothes I had taken off him.

I left him in the cuffs in case he woke up, putting a blanket over him, while I went and had a shower to get all the hairspray and makeup off me. I got out of the shower looking at the mark fully formed on my neck now, shaking my head, '*I can't believe that idiot still does that. How old is he 12!*' I went and checked on Ferdinand drying my hair putting on dark sweatshirt and sweatpants, deciding to go and see if they were still there. I landed near some cars, ducking down, as I heard some people coming out of the reception area. I put the hood of the sweatshirt up just in case someone saw me as I listened to see if I could hear Jonathon's voice.

I moved a bit closer smiling, hearing his drunk voice slurring louder than ever, making smart remarks about Ferdinand and I, with his partner holding him taking him towards a car, giggling at his stupid remarks. I put my hand on the love bite Ferdinand had given me flinging it towards Jonathon, *"Have your love bite back Jonathon multiplied by five showing around that scrawny neck."* I heard him yelp, "Ouch what the heck was that," with his partner just shaking her head, "I don't know dear come on I want to get home."

He stopped, getting angry, "Don't try to boss me around Melinda I had enough of that with that bitch Hannah. She thinks she can still boss men around. I sorted her out though giving that Ferdinand, I mean what sort of name is that, something extra than a spiked drink."

I was going to go, but after hearing that, I decided to do one more thing *"stumble stumble you fool over your feet until you fall on your face making that foul tongue of yours bleed and swell until you've seen the error of your ways."*

I hid down watching as he went to walk again, falling over his feet, hitting his jaw on the ground biting his tongue, with a loud scream coming from him.

I remembered what Morag had said about keeping an eye out for anyone looking on, so I quietly went around the cars looking around, still being able to hear Johnathon yelling in a gargled way. I hid behind a car that was nearer to the entrance of the reception area noticing an older woman standing there watching. I sat there quietly to see what she did.

She would have been able to see Jonathon fall and scream, but she just stood there, trying to look for someone else. She walked off in the end, not walking like an elderly woman would, making me wonder if she was in disguise.

I couldn't go after her as I still had Ferdinand in cuffs, so I took off, coming back to find Ferdinand still fast asleep with his hands still in the cuffs. I stood there deciding whether to leave them on him or not. I went and got a drink of water for myself as well as one for him and a bucket and towel, knowing he was going to be sick eventually.

I was still pissed off about what had happened, so I decided to leave the cuffs on him, but not tied to the bed, in case he tried something else on me. I still had the love bite on me, deciding to leave it there so Ferdinand could see what he had done. I picked up my dress putting it in the laundry to dry out until I decided what to do with it. My garter belt and stockings were in tatters in a pile on the floor deciding to just leave them there. I eventually got to sleep, when I was woken by Ferdinand, groaning sitting up and starting to heave. I jumped up, flicking the lamp on, pushing him over to the bucket.

A bit of spew landed on him but most of it got into the bucket, thank goodness; smelling disgusting. He sat on the edge of the bed hugging the bucket, still with the cuffs on, groaning as he heaved a couple more times into the bucket.

He looked up at me as I wiped his face. He screwed his face up trying to move his hands, "Aggh I thought it was a bad dream."

I rubbed his back, "No dear you were horrible, I left them on because you were getting rough."

He groaned again heaving into the bucket, with just water coming out now, spitting it out. I wiped his mouth again, "Do you want a drink of water?" He nodded sounding sorry for himself, "Take these off me first though—please!"

I hesitated then touched them, making them disappear, giving him the glass of water.

He sipped it looking at me sadly, "Did I hurt you?"

I moved away from him lying on the pillow "no, just pissed me off." I put my hand up to my neck, "Although you did a Jonathon special on me, obviously recommended by that idiot."

He put the bucket down and finished off the drink wiping his mouth moving over, looking at my neck, "Oh, I vaguely remember doing that—sorry."

I pushed him away, "Phew. I think you need to go and brush your teeth now, Ferdinand." He groaned getting back up brushing his hand through his hair, going out slowly flicking his fingers to turn the lights on going to the bathroom. I heard him be sick again in the toilet. I then heard the tap run as he brushed his teeth.

He came back in looking at me lying on my side facing the other way. He changed his top, sent the bucket away and got back into bed, flicking the lights off, coming over to me cuddling into my back not bothering to say anything more. I knew I couldn't stay mad at him and preferred to have him cuddling into me, so I just relaxed and went to sleep.

Chapter 16

I woke before Ferdinand, listening to him snore lightly and looking quite pale. I shook my head thinking, '*I told him so.*' I got up leaving him there to sleep opening up the lounge with the sun coming in to greet me.

Kimba came out looking for her breakfast, so I fed her, while I had a drink of water. I had had a few glasses of wine making me thirsty, but I had some water in between so I didn't get too drunk.

I felt like doing some meditation, so sat down in front of the balcony window putting my ear buds in, sitting in the warm sun. I put some elements around me to give me a boost and hoped my grandma wouldn't come in to disturb me this time.

I checked that I had water, earth, air (which was incense) and fire in the right places then went into my meditation. I could feel the elements joining me once I went deep enough helping me feel stronger within. It was just a relaxing meditation with a fleeting vision coming in of trouble in the world but I couldn't quite make it out. It soon passed, getting rid of some negative energy then I came back to the lounge. I got rid of the elements leaving the incense to burn out when I heard a noise behind me.

Ferdinand had gotten up, coming to sit behind me, putting his arms around me sounding a bit croaky "hi" as I leaned into him, "Hi, how are you feeling?"

He gave me a cuddle, "Like a truck has backed over me a few times, but I'll survive."

I smiled relaxing into him, "Well I told you so."

He sighed, "I was waiting for that." He looked down at my arms noticing some bruising on my wrists, "Did I do that?"

I looked at his wrists noticing the cuff marks, "Yes, just like I did that."

He touched my wrists making the bruising go and I touch his wrists making his bruising go.

He then pulled my hair around looking at my neck, "You left it there to show me, didn't you?"

I nodded, "Yes I did." He touched it, making it disappear then kissed the spot gently, "Sorry. Can I take you out to breakfast to make up for it?"

I shook my head, "No thanks."

He cuddled me again, "You're still angry with me then?"

I looked up at him, "Not so much angry but disappointed. I admit I was a bit scared there as well when we got home; you were quite determined and angry. If I didn't have the magic to rely on, I don't know what would have happened."

He looked regretful at me, "I thought I had it under control with those drinks but he just kept stirring me up and I was stupid enough to listen to him. Maybe I've spent too much time in your world, another reason for us to go to Jardine."

I turned to look at him, "He's always spiked people's drinks and he thinks it's funny. He even calls it his magic potion, maybe he's a witch but doesn't know it, I don't know. I think he did do something more than spike your drink as well. I got him back this time though."

He groaned, "What did you do?"

I smiled, "Just sent all the alcohol effects that you felt back to him and sent his love bite back to him." I didn't bother to tell him the other one, I was hoping that that just looked like an accident.

He shook his head, "I'm glad you control yourself with me—sometimes."

I smiled, "I'm open to you cooking me something for breakfast here, I've had enough of eating out for a few days."

This made him smile, "Anything in mind?"

I thought about it, "Some French toast would be nice, that's if your stomach can stand it?"

He got up, "Yes I'll be ok, I don't have much left in there and for some reason I'm craving something fatty."

I chuckled as I got up, "You have been spending too much time in our world, that's a classic hangover craving—something greasy. Do you want me to help you?" He shook his head looking unsteady still, "no you know I like to do my own thing; you can relax."

He went into the kitchen and started getting things ready while I went and sat on the sofa checking to see who had posted photos.

He came out after a short time, "I'll let that bread soak a little, where did you put my suit, Hannah?"

I looked up from my phone, "Oh it's in the wardrobe on a hanger."

He went into the bedroom getting his suit out of the wardrobe taking the shirt off the hanger and taking the sheets off the bed. He picked up some of my other washing including the stuff I had taken off last night being the garter belt, stockings, bra and panties.

As he picked up the garter belt, he felt funny having to sit on the bed with a vision of a woman in a garter belt and bra, laughing in front of a fire. He shook his head trying to make sense of it. He then remembered me climbing up him with my hair sticking up wearing the bra and garter belt and the tie in my hands speaking German. He wiped his face feeling a sweat come over him taking a couple of deep breaths.

I was laying there looking at my phone realising he hadn't come out of the bedroom calling to him, "Are you alright, Ferdinand?" I was just about to get up to check on him when he came out looking a little pale, carrying the sheets, his shirt and some other washing. I looked at him, "You don't need to worry about that I'm sure you're not feeling very well; I can do it later."

He shook his head, "No it's alright I just want to freshen up the sheets and I may as well wash my shirt at the same time."

I thought about my dress being in the laundry, "Don't worry about my dress I think it needs to be dry cleaned or handwashed, I'll sort it out later." I felt a bit guilty sitting there looking at photos of the wedding on FB so I got up to sort out the French toast, while he was doing that. I put the pan on to heat it up and got the butter out of the fridge when he came in, looking annoyed, "Lass es Hannah (leave it Hannah)." I got flustered putting my hands up saying, "Gut Ferdinand (alright Ferdinand)" putting my hands over my mouth then coughing, "Oh something got stuck in my throat."

He took my hands away from my mouth, "Du sprichst jetzt recht fließend Deutsch (you are quite fluent in German now.)"

I groaned, "Du hast mich reingelegt (you tricked me)." He gave me a kiss on the lips, "So much for just knowing little bits of German. Is this from your grandma again?"

I leaned into his chest hearing his heart beat in his chest, "Yes, she started flicking to speaking German. How come you can speak German, Ferdinand?"

He stroked my hair, "Most of us speak a couple of languages, Hannah."

I shook my head, "Oh ok (thinking about what Morag said). I know you looked surprised when I started speaking it last night. You also looked really fearful when I had the tie in my hand. You don't like that sort of thing, do you?"

He kept holding onto me so I couldn't see his face, "I don't really remember that part very well, but no I don't like anything like that."

He kissed me again, turning me around and tapping my bum playfully. "I'll sort this out before it burns, you go and lie back down."

I smiled, "I did have a nice time last night, Ferdinand, it was only Jonathon's silliness that made it annoying."

He took the pan off the heat. "I did too, Hannah. I'll sort this out and we can chat a bit more about it."

I went back and sat on the sofa not quite sure what to make of his reasoning behind knowing different languages but I just didn't want to analyse it right now. I looked through all the pictures from the wedding again, finding a couple of us including the one of us on the balcony when Ferdinand and I were kissing. I saved it as well as one when we were on the dance floor. I called out to Ferdinand, "There's a nice photo of us on the dance floor."

He smiled, "I'll have a look soon."

While I was there, I had a look for that elderly woman I saw last night in any of the photos. I couldn't see anyone like her, although I didn't have all the photos of all the people that were there. I made a mental note to ask Tania if she knew her.

We had breakfast laughing at the different photos that had been posted on FB. I got a text from Tania after we had finished telling me about Jonathon getting really drunk with heaps of love bites on his neck and then to top it off, he tripped over his feet and bit his tongue. It wasn't too bad but he will be a lot quieter for a while.

I giggled reading the text, with Ferdinand leaning over to see what I was laughing at.

He looked at me putting his arm around me, "I know you told me you put the drink on him and the love bites but did you do the last one?"

I shook my head still laughing, "No dear, he must have been really drunk and fell over, that is all."

He got up and put the washing in the dryer while I went and started the dishes. He came out still feeling a little ashamed of himself as well as hungover, "I'm going soon, what are you up to today?"

I thought about it, "Not sure. I might just sort some things out, maybe ring the girls and just relax basically."

We made the bed together with him being silly grabbing me and rolling onto the bed giving me a kiss, "We did have fun dancing and I enjoyed the ceremony. Did you?"

I smiled, "Yes, I really enjoyed the dancing. The ceremony was nice but I've seen that before."

He took off to Jardine leaving me sitting on the sofa, deciding what to do. I thought I had better go and handwash my dress to get any stains out from the flying last night, shaking my head, '*A few months ago, I would have thought I was nuts saying that.*'

I realised the washing was in the dryer still so I got that out folding up the sheets and put his shirt onto a hanger so it didn't have to be ironed, one of my 'only do if necessary' jobs. I looked at the label in the collar noticing it was a German brand as well, with the name 'Von Drachen' and two keys crossed.

I thought to myself, '*Haven't seen that brand before, it might be an old brand or something.*' I put it in the wardrobe realising his suit was still there with a nice feeling coming over me. He didn't have a lot of personal items in the unit because he generally brought them in magically. The only personal thing he really has here is a toothbrush but that doesn't really count. I put my dress out on the balcony to dry on a little line that I had out there, giving Kimba a pat who was sitting on a bed I had out there for her.

I decided to get the family book out locking the house up bringing it forward. I thought I would just sit and flick through the book to see if there was anything that could help me find out about my family a bit more.

I could see that there were different writing styles for spells and chants, which obviously was from different family members, but no one actually signed their names to any of them. I went to the back of the book again with the coat of arms still not fully filled in.

The shield looked familiar for some reason as I sat there thinking about it, deciding to get my phone out and search for family coat of arms and the name Dragĕ. I had done it before defining the search to Norway but this time I just did a general search for all over. Now that I had it in front of me, I could search it better as well.

A coat of arms came up that looked quite old with a similar dragon, shield and sword to mine, but it was facing another dragon in a different colour with flames coming out of its mouth.

As I looked closer at it, I realised it had a set of keys in between the dragons near their feet and then there were the usual scrolls that they usually embellished the coat of arms with in those days.

I expanded the picture a bit more, noticing in the four corners there were small diagrams of water, air, earth and fire. I decided to take a snapshot of it so I could show the girls to see if they might be able to find out any more information because they were really good at researching this stuff. I went back to the coat of arms in the book with the feeling the dragon was almost looking at me urging me to look at something. I hadn't noticed, but there appeared to be some pages added to the back of the book but I couldn't open them. I sat there puzzled trying to think of a chant or spell that might be able to help me, tapping a tune out on the book with my hand, which sometimes helped me because most of the chants were like songs or poems in some ways.

As I tapped my hand, I looked down at the signet ring my mother had given me all those years ago, bringing it up closer to look at. I remembered getting my initials put on the ring when I got it, but I hadn't noticed some of the other decoration on it above the initials.

Silly really, I had had it since I was 16 but I hadn't looked at that part very much. I brought in a magnifying glass as the decoration was quite fine, probably why I didn't bother to look at it. I sat there stunned when I got a good look at it finding a small dragon surrounded by scrolls which looked a bit like flames, but without a magnifying glass it just looked like a bunch of scrolls.

I took it off my hand and put it next to the coat of arms comparing the shield on it when it flicked out of my hand, as though pulled by a magnet, flipping itself over and going onto the picture with a flash of light coming out of it. The light sent a wave of vibration over me, throwing me backwards onto the sofa, with it convulsing through my body, sending pain in my back where I knew the tattoo was.

I groaned as I lay there holding my back, dazed and winded slowly getting up, pulling my top up to touch the tattoo, feeling moisture there. I brought my hand around to see blood on my hand grabbing a tissue to wipe it, then going into the bedroom to have a look at it.

It was fully done now, but with blood dripping down in little ribbons as though a tattooist had just done it with his needles.

I dabbed it gently with a tissue hearing a noise in the lounge that made me come out to find both Amelia and Charlotte standing there looking confused. Amelia came over to me, "Mum what's going on? I was in the middle of doing some exercise when I felt myself being pulled in and a pain in my back."

Charlotte was in her usual sweat pants and top with big socks on, shaking her head, "I was just doing some marking and felt myself being pulled as well with a pain in my back."

I went over to them holding the tissue on my back, "Oh I've been playing with the family book and I think I've completed our family crest. Check your backs to see if there is anything on them."

They turned around pulling their tops up revealing a small dragon on their hip whereas I turned around and had the full dragon, shield and sword just like the one in the book, on my back.

The girls began to laugh, with Charlotte coming over to me pulling the tissue away, "Wow it looks really fresh doesn't it, Mum? At least ours isn't bleeding like that. I'll go and get some tape to put on it."

Amelia went and looked at her tattoo in the mirror, "It looks nice, but I don't know what Shiro is going to say about it. I'll have to think of something to say."

Charlotte came out with some gauze and tape, "oh yeah, I didn't think of Aetius and his reaction. We'll have to think of something to say together that way it won't look as though Ferdinand is trying to put his mark on us or something."

I gasped, "I didn't think of that, luckily you girls did."

Charlotte taped up my back while Amelia got me a drink of water, "Are you alright Mum?"

I took a sip of water, "yes, I just got a big power hit from it. I have the unit locked, so I'm surprised you two could come in. I suppose being family and being connected to the book it's different."

Charlotte went over to the book, "I think the book wants us to do something else."

Amelia and I came over, looking at it noticing a blinking cursor there, as though it was a computer and was waiting for us to put a command into it. A thought came into my head, "Shall we hold hands and see what that does?"

The girls both nodded with Charlotte putting her hands out to me and Amelia, "May as well try."

We put our hands out looking a bit nervous, taking a deep breath, finally connecting when a white light sprung from me, back to the book then over to Amelia and Charlotte. I could hear the girls squeal in delight, "Yahoo!" It only lasted a few seconds but it was a big power hit turning to look at each other smiling with eyes glowing and the power slowly fading into our bodies.

We let go of our hands, starting to giggle with the sounds of other laughter coming into the room making us look around. White ghostly images faded in and out with some of them clapping then a voice I knew coming in, "Godt utført Dragĕ kvinner (well done Dragĕ women)."

Amelia and Charlotte still giggling looked at me telling them, "That was one of your grandmothers saying well done."

Amelia was curious now, "You understood her?"

I nodded trying to play it down a bit, "A little. She has spoken to me on the odd occasion giving me some magic to understand her, that is all."

Charlotte and Amelia just shrugged their shoulders, "Fair enough." We were still standing in a small circle when some words started to appear in the middle, almost like a hologram spinning, so that we could all read them. A big grin came over my girls with Amelia's eyes lighting up again, "This is so cool. I think it wants us to say that, Mum."

We held hands again looking at the words getting it into our heads then all together we started to recite them, "*My family is my bond; My ancestor's blood in my veins; Together we fight any enemy until they are all slain.*" This sent another wave of white light around us but it felt more like a protection as though a coat of armour had surrounded each of us.

I shook myself out, "Wow that felt good actually. Did it feel like protection to you two?"

They both shook their heads "yes it did."

I sighed contented, "Well I think we now have the family's protection on us. It might help if we are attacked at least."

Charlotte nodded, "Especially you, Mum."

I looked at them both, "You two still need to be careful. They might start on you two."

Amelia was annoyed, "Well we will have to sort that out won't we. I'm still interested in doing what I said to you before Mum."

I nodded, "Yes now that you are here, we may as well think of some things."

I went over to the book to close it when I noticed another cursor sitting there, "I think the book wants us to do something else."

Amelia and Charlotte came over, looking at it when some words came up on the page near the cursor, *"Do you wish to proceed to the next phase Dragĕ women?"* Two tabs appeared one green with the word 'Ja' underneath it, one red with the word 'Nei' underneath it, "Please press your selection."

I smiled, "Wow this is really getting like a computer, isn't it?" I looked at the girls, "So do we want to go to the next phase?"

They both giggled with Amelia putting her hand up, "I'm game if you two are?"

We smiled nodding, as I leaned forward pushing the green button, but nothing happened. I looked unsure, "Mm it didn't work."

Charlotte moved closer, "Maybe it wants all of us to do it together?"

I nodded, "Maybe you're right, are you ready?" We put our hands on top of each other pushing the green button when the pages that I had found locked, opened up with the sound of a lock being opened heard around us.

Before we could go any further though another message came up, *"A token of yourselves is required before you can go any further. A lock of the hair of a Dragĕ woman I think is fair. Please place it in the vessel provided."*

I smiled, "It looks like we need to get some scissors, girls."

I went over to the kitchen and got some scissors out cutting a small piece off my hair putting it into the vessel that appeared on the page. Both Amelia and Charlotte did the same thing watching a blue light appear around the rim of the vessel then disappear taking our hair with it. Another message came up, *"Thank you for your token it has been accepted and you are free to proceed."*

I turned the pages that were locked looking at all the different spells and incantations in gibberish, "I think I've had enough for one day. Do you girls want to have a look before I put it away?"

Amelia looked at Charlotte, "No I think we will have a break as well. Let's go and have some lunch."

I smiled, "Sounds like a great idea." I sent the book away and unlocked the unit.

I changed my clothes as they had blood on them, putting them in the washing machine to do later when I had enough clothes to do another load. I put the bracelet on that Ferdinand had given me and Morag had put the chant on to protect me just in case. The girls both changed their clothes into something a bit smarter with Charlotte giggling, "Wow I love this magic."

We went down to the Barefoot Café on the beach in Cronulla finding a good seat so we could see the water. We ordered some lunch and coffee with Amelia bringing up some ideas in a type of code so others couldn't tell what we were talking about and just in case our spirit animals were listening.

I chuckled, "We are getting clever, aren't we, girls?"

Charlotte high-fived me, "Dragĕ women power."

Amelia hi fived me as well, "Was it your ring that set that off, Mum?"

I nodded, "Yes it was. All the years I have worn it and I never really noticed the little dragon on it. I had to get a magnifying glass to look at it properly."

Amelia shook her head, "I wonder if Nanna knew that when she gave it to you?"

I shrugged my shoulders, "Who knows. If I get to see her again in my meditation, I might ask her."

We ordered some lunch and while we were waiting for it to come, I briefly told the girls what had happened last night with Ferdinand. Charlotte had a scowl on her face, "Well at least you dealt with him Mum, bloody cheek."

I calmed her down, "I know what he did wasn't right, but I do think there was a bit of magic in there as well as his drink being spiked. M has asked me to look around me a bit more to see if there is anyone hanging around watching. I would recommend you two do the same thing as I did see a woman who was supposed to be elderly but walked like a young woman."

Both Amelia and Charlotte agreed with Amelia thinking about it, "There is definitely someone stirring the pot I reckon."

While we were eating our lunch, Charlotte noticed the bracelet I had on, "Is that the one Ferdinand gave you from J, Mum?"

I nodded, "Yes and M put a thing on it to give me some protection. You two might need something as well now that we've had that bit of a buzz."

Amelia was just agreeing with me when she looked up smiling making me turn to see who she was looking at. Shiro, Aetius and Ferdinand were coming in the door towards us with grins on their faces.

We made some room as they grabbed another table giving each one a hug and a kiss, "Oh this is a nice surprise."

Ferdinand sat down next to me looking at me, "You look nice and bright, what have you three been up to?"

I smiled, "Oh nothing really, the girls just surprised me with a visit so we thought we would get some lunch. Are you all eating?"

Shiro already had a menu, "Too right Hannah, I'm starving."

They all ordered as we chatted away about what they had been doing in Jardine.

Amelia decided to have a little stir "the photos on FB looked nice of the wedding you two went to."

Charlotte scowled at Ferdinand, "So did anything else happen?"

Ferdinand put his head down moving his empty plate away about to say something but I spoke first, "We had a nice time but I'm glad it's over."

Ferdinand got up, "I'll be back in a minute," and went to pay for the meals then came back, "Come on let's go for a walk."

It was a glorious day with the sun shining and a hint of summer coming with warm air coming off the land. We decided to go for a walk along the beach with Ferdinand and I choosing just to wander holding hands walking along the shore line while Amelia, Charlotte, Shiro and Aetius were being silly having running races splashing each other.

Ferdinand noticed I had the bracelet on as we stopped to look at it shining in the sun, "Good to see you've got it on Hannah."

I nodded, "I would wear it even if Morag didn't put the chant on it as it looks nice."

Amelia and Charlotte saw us looking 'gooey' at each other, as they call it, signalling to Aetius and Shiro to have some fun and pull us in the water.

Before we knew it, the girls grabbed me and the guys grabbed Ferdinand, dragging us into the water laughing as we struggled against them, "No, you girls stop!"

I relaxed enough to trick them, pulling them in with me diving under the wave. My girls came up grinning like little girls, grabbing me as another wave came over us feeling a little vibration in the wave. I looked at them as we came up, "Shush" as they beamed at me feeling the strength of the water go through us.

I could see Ferdinand trying to put up a fight against the guys but they were just too strong and younger throwing, him in under the wave.

Shiro and Aetius came up triumphant putting their hands in the air, "Yahoo we got the dragon" appearing not to hear our little vibration. Ferdinand came up wiping his face grinning, "I'll get you two, just watch your backs."

I ducked under a couple more waves with Ferdinand coming over, "Come you water baby you'll catch a cold again." I came up smiling, "Oh it feels wonderful doesn't it."

He put his arm around my waist checking my hands, "Yes it does, but those weapons are turning cold again."

I slapped him playfully on the stomach, "Oh don't be mean, Ferdinand," as we walked out of the water.

The girls came over to me laughing and puffing after all their exercise with Charlotte getting her breath back, "I'll get going now Mum, I still have stuff to do. I'll chat through the week," coming up to give me a hug and a kiss.

She surprised me and Ferdinand going to give him a quick hug, "See you, Ferdinand." She took Aetius' hand and walked down the beach waving, then disappearing.

Amelia saw what Charlotte had done and decided not to be outdone, giving me a hug and a kiss, "I'll catch up later Mum," then went and gave Ferdinand a quick hug as well, "See you, Ferdinand."

Ferdinand was taken by surprise saying, "Bye girls" to both of the them. Amelia and Shiro disappeared with Amelia blowing me a little kiss, with a naughty smile on her face. Ferdinand stood looking at them with a grin appearing on his face, "Wow I didn't expect that, must be that animal magnetism working on them."

I laughed, "Of course it is dear."

He gave me a funny look, picking me up in his arms thinking we were going home, but he turned towards the water making me wriggle, "No, Ferdinand you said I shouldn't swim anymore."

I put my arms around his neck kissing him, "Come on honey let's go home."

He looked down at me grinning continuing to walk in the water, "That's not going to work dear." He saw a wave coming in dropping me in as I let out a scream, "Oh you rat."

I got up grabbing his legs pulling him down yelling, "Got you," as another wave went over us as we both giggled.

He picked me up wrapping my legs around his waist hugging him for his body warmth and putting my arms around his neck walking out of the water getting ready to go home when he stopped.

I wriggled holding on tight, "Hva er det honing (what is it honey) thinking he was going to drop me again."

He talked quietly to me, "Det er Lilith (it's Lilith)."

I turned to see where he was looking wriggling my legs to get down, "Bare bli der (just stay there)."

He started walking again looking at her unsure, "Lilith what brings you here?"

I tried to get down again as he held my legs turning to look at her, "Hi Lilith."

Lilith looked uncomfortable, "Sorry I didn't mean to intrude. I know I'm not supposed to just pop in but I thought I would come and say hi."

Ferdinand turned so I could look at her, "That's alright, Lilith, I was just trying to get Hannah out of the water as usual. If she's not sleeping with lions, she's in the water."

I looked at Ferdinand noting the little dig making Lilith look down, "Sorry about that Hannah. I didn't mean any harm. I might have said some things I shouldn't have when you were at Jardine. I'm sorry about that."

I sighed, "The prank I didn't worry about but what was said before we left Jardine has upset me a bit, I'm afraid."

Ferdinand looked at me shaking his head, "Well I better get Hannah home, she has hands that turn to ice very quickly." I smiled, "Oh stop it."

I tried to get down again but he held on tight looking at Lilith who was watching the two of us with a look of sadness on her face. I thought I had better make an effort to mend the fences, so to speak, "Do you want to come and have a drink at home with us?"

I could feel him squeeze my legs in disapproval but it was too late, Lilith knew she wasn't supposed to be with us, "No thanks Hannah, I'll get going. I just thought I would come and apologise and see how you were both doing."

She was about to go when she turned looking curious, "Did I hear you speak German Hannah?"

I thought to myself, 'Her hearing is good,' feeling a shiver coming over me as a light breeze started coming off the water cooling me down.

Ferdinand spoke up instead, "I'm teaching her some basic German for when we go on a trip to research her family. We best go. Hannah is starting to shiver. See you next time, Lilith."

I waved as I cuddled into Ferdinand, taking his body heat disappearing.

We got back to the unit landing in the bathroom letting me down turning on the shower, "I'll help you into the shower," and went to take my clothes off.

I suddenly remembered the tattoo, "No I'll be alright; can you make me some soup to warm me up," and going over to give him a hug. He gave me a little hug kissing the top of my head, "Are you sure, you'll be ok?"

I nodded feeling a little guilty because he was wet, "Unless you want to come in with me, are you cold?"

He shook his head, "No I'll dry myself off and make the soup." He went out, sighing to myself, taking my clothes off and getting into the shower gently peeling the tape and gauze off. I looked at it feeling pleased that it had at least stopped bleeding, the salt water must have sealed it.

I finished having a shower bringing in a nightie and drying off my hair. I put the wet things on top of the clothes that had blood on thinking I better tell him; he's going to find out eventually.

I went out feeling better smelling the soup that he was making and noticed he was all dry, "Mm that smells nice, is it French onion?"

He smiled pointed at me putting my dressing gown on, "I don't want you getting sick again."

I smiled at him, "Yes dear." I went out to the balcony to get my dress off the line finding it gone "oh you've brought it in, thanks. I put your shirt in the wardrobe, in case you're looking for it. Do you want to have a shower now I can look after that?"

He looked up, "No it's alright its finished now, come and sit down."

We had the soup with some toast warming me up nicely. I helped him clean up then he went and had a shower. I put the jug on for a hot chocolate, getting it ready for when he came out, then went to the sofa to relax turning on the television.

We had the hot chocolate, not really watching the TV, chatting about Lilith and the girls intending to tell him about the tattoo but he kept distracting me with other talk.

I leaned into him relaxing once I had finished the chocolate "come on let's go to bed, you've got work in the morning." I groaned, "I think I feel sick, cough, cough."

He chuckled, "Well, it's definitely time to go to bed," and picking me up, "No I was only joking, come on let's chat a bit longer. I need to tell you something." He shook his head, "We can chat in bed that way you will be comfortable and warm." He put me down near the bathroom, "There you go do your business and I'll check on Kimba."

Once I had finished in the bathroom, I went into the bedroom turning the lamp on getting comfortable in bed with him coming in with the jar of chest tub in his hand smiling, "Come on I'll rub you down with this, just in case."

I looked at it, "I don't think I need that I'm not sick."

He grinned wickedly, "Oh I think you do Hannah," and leaning over, as I giggled, "I'll just put a bit on my chest that is all I need."

He didn't bother answering going over my hips, "No Ferdi says you need it everywhere."

I tried to grab his arms, laughing, "Don't be naughty," as he put a big dob onto his fingers moving my hands away rubbing it onto my chest. I started coughing, "Phew I think you've put too much on, dear," as my eyes watered.

He raised himself up, "No now I'll put some on your back," rolling me over pulling my nightie up, "I need to tell you something first Ferdinand," trying to stop him. He started rubbing the rub on my back moving down then stopping as I lay there waiting for it, "Was haben wir hier Hannah (what do we have here Hannah)?"

I sighed, moving my head to look at him, "Ich habe versucht, es dir zu sagen (I've been trying to tell you dear)." I heard him sigh, "You've been playing with your family book again, haven't you?" I nodded trying to roll back over onto my back but he stayed where he was, "I'll finish rubbing your back, then you can tell me all about it."

He got off me, getting up to wash his hands then coming back, putting out his arm so I could cuddle into him, "Ok tell me about it."

I looked at him a little unsure, "I was just having a look at the coat of arms again when I realised that I had part of it on my hand all the time;" putting up my signet ring showing him. He looked at it, "Didn't your mother give you that?"

I nodded, "Yes when I turned 16. I brought in a magnifying glass finding a dragon in the scroll work. The book accepted it and finished off the tattoo."

He kissed the top of my head, "Is there anything else I need to know?"

I smirked, "It pulled the girls into me giving them a simple dragon tattoo on their hip, so you may need to let Aetius and Shiro know that it wasn't you doing anything."

He groaned, "Oh great, now they're going to think I'm putting my mark on the girls."

I cuddled into his side, "The girls said they would sort them out, so you may not have to worry. The book opened more pages of magic, so I'm not sure what that means, we decided to go to lunch instead of going through it."

A text came in on my phone leaning over to have a look at it reading it out to Ferdinand, "Oh Tom's wife has had a baby girl. He is officially on maternity leave only coming in the morning to do some work."

I smiled sending a text back, "Congratulations wish you all well, see you tomorrow."

Ferdinand yawned, turning off the light while I put the phone back on the dresser, rolling me over onto my side and cuddling into my back. A waft of air come up my nightie, hitting Ferdinand making him cough, "I think I put too much rub on you honey," as we both laughed.

He put his hand on my stomach saying sleepily, "I would have liked to have had a baby with you Hannah."

I lay there stunned at first, "Yes it would have been nice honey. We can't have babies though—can we?"

He chuckled, "That made you nervous, no dear only the elders can do that in Jardine. You're safe with our love making."

As we started to relax into sleep, I felt glad that I had at least told him about the tattoo. I knew I needed to talk to him about things rather than keeping things to myself; a habit of living alone for so long, I guess.

I could hear his breathing deepen for sleep making me feel relaxed when all of a sudden, I felt my tattoo tingle and Ferdinand jolt a little. Like you do when you're falling into sleep too fast.

I lay there waiting for him to say something but he was still breathing heavy feeling his heart beat on my back and with his arm over my waist. I shrugged it off 'not sure what that was' dropping off to sleep.

Chapter 17

I groaned with the thought of going to work when the alarm went off thinking well at least I will have some time to myself when Tom goes off.

I rolled over finding Ferdinand up already, which was unusual, so I got up to find him sitting on the balcony looking out to sea. I went up behind him putting my arms around his neck, "You were up early?"

He leaned onto my arms, "I thought I'd let you sleep until the alarm; I know how you love going to work."

I smiled giving him a kiss on the cheek noticing fine hairs growing there, "You're not angry about the tattoo, are you?"

He shook his head, "No, I'm glad you told me, but I do worry about that magic and those people out there trying to get to you."

I came around to face him sitting on his lap, "I'll be careful, Ferdinand, besides I still have my dragon to protect me," giving him a hug.

He got up picking me up, walking me over to the kitchen, "Well, we better get you started for the day."

I got into work having forgotten about the wedding photos being posted only to be met by Tracey on reception, saying dreamily "hi Hannah, your Ferdinand looked lovely in his suit at the wedding."

I sighed, "Thanks Tracey (no mention of me then, huh!)." I got to my work station finding Tom tired and panicking "Hannah, thank goodness you're here. I have sent you some reports and letters I need done today. Oh, and nice photos of you and Ferdinand."

I took a deep breath, "Tom take a deep breath, now do you want a coffee before you do anything else."

He took a deep breath, "Thanks Hannah, I know you've done it twice but its nerve wracking the first time, especially being older. Yes, I will have a coffee— I don't suppose you have any of those chocolate brownies, do you?"

I smiled, "Yes I do, go and sit down and I will get the coffee."

He managed to calm down eventually taking off just before lunch.

I told Alira I would meet her tomorrow for lunch as I had a bit of stuff to sort out for Tom. I had lunch in the tea room then got stuck into all the stuff Tom had given me deciding to do most of it magically.

Tom could access it at home to check, so I didn't have to do anything else once I had done it. I had it all done by 3.00p.m. sitting there thinking, '*Mm this could turn into quite an advantage*' going into Tom's room leaving the door ajar to do a little bit of filing but I knew that wouldn't take long.

I did a little bit of daydreaming as well because I didn't get outside, with some thoughts coming into my head about the family book. I didn't dwell on it too much though as I had a feeling someone was around; sure, enough Ferdinand popped in, coming in behind me, "Hi, how's your boss?"

I smiled leaning into him, "Oh he's a mess, but it will settle down."

He leaned down to kiss me on the cheek, "Daydreaming again?"

I nodded, "Yes, I didn't get out for lunch because I wasn't sure if I would finish everything. Tracey loves the photos of you at the wedding."

He gave me a little squeeze, "Of course she does. Maybe I should pick you up tonight just to give her a thrill."

I shook my head, "You're naughty. Just get her to ring me if you do come in as I may have to help another secretary if I don't look busy."

He kissed my neck getting a bit fresh, "Ferdinand don't wind me up now."

He turned me around smirking, "We could try it in a different spot."

I looked shocked putting my hands up to his cheeks feeling a light bit of hair there, "You're getting naughty Ferdi."

He put his hands down to my hips pushing them into him, which he hadn't done before, "we could pretend we're making a baby."

I started to feel flustered, "I'll see you later Ferdi."

He chuckled, "Ok. I'm looking forward to it," giving me a kiss on my lips lingering a bit longer than he should have.

He left, with me having to take a couple of deep breaths going to sit in Tom's chair, "wow he's getting a randy dragon."

To take my mind off Ferdinand, I started thinking about the magic that was in the locked section of the book that we had just opened, wondering what was in there.

I wanted to bring the book out but didn't want to risk it without locking the area up but I couldn't lock the office off in case someone tried to come in. I also needed to make it look like I wasn't just sitting in here doing my own personal stuff, otherwise one of the other bosses will give me extra work to do. I thought about it going to get a cup of tea coming back to my desk while eating my brownie. I sent a text to Amelia and Charlotte while on my break checking to see that everything was alright between them and Aetius and Shiro with regard to the tattoo. I had forgotten to ask Ferdinand because of he was being randy. They text back that everything was good.

I sat there looking at my computer trying to make it look as though I was still working while having my cup of tea. I was in google just flicking around when a news story came up about cloning and how scientists were doing it with sheep etc. That gave me an idea; if I could get a clone or a hologram which I had seen on some music shows to sit at the desk I could do some research into the family and the book. I went back into Tom's office, sitting to the side of the office, so I couldn't be seen from the door wondering how Morag brought that orb in so that no one could see or hear us.

The book sensed what I was thinking telling me what to do sending a chant, *"Orb to form to cover me now, no one can see or hear me now."*

I put my hands out from me as the orb formed around me, with a big grin coming onto my face doing a little clap 'yahoo'.

I called the book in on my hands going to the new area reading through some of the pages and putting my hand over some of the chants, finding some interesting ones there. I heard a noise come from the door with one of the secretaries putting her head in the doorway, "Hannah, are you here?"

I sat there frozen, shutting the book quickly and sending it away. It was Tracey from reception looking around the room then going back out leaving a note on my desk. I realised I was breathing lightly not sure if she could see or hear me but she obviously couldn't see me. I shut the orb down putting my hands out closing them in front of me. I got up looking at the time, *'Oh shit, Ferdinand must be in the reception area as it is 5.00p.m.'*

I went out to my desk looking at the note Tracey had left me, *'Hannah you have a visitor.'* I shut my computer down and got my bag going out to the reception area finding Tracey over by Ferdinand chatting away with her phone ringing away at her desk. I came out smiling, "Hi Tracey, sorry I was in the bathroom," grinning at Ferdinand, "Hello, are you ready to go?"

He got up with a cheesy grin on his face, "Yes Tracey was just saying how it's been so long since you've had a boyfriend."

I sighed, "Yes, we've been through that one before. See you, Tracey."

We got home putting my bag on the bed taking my shoes off with Ferdinand opening the balcony door then coming back into the bedroom as I was taking my jacket off, moving over to me helping me. I kept my head down a little but looked up at him hearing him groan, "Mm are you hungry Hannah?"

He took my hair out of the bun, running his hand through my hair, grinning at him, "Getting that way Ferdinand. A little kiss here," pointing to my neck, "Might stir it up a bit more."

That was enough to get us going, taking our clothes off. I noticed he was wanting to touch me a lot more in different places, so I followed suit, still a little unsure of Jardine ways, but feeling almost as though he was a man from our world. He responded well driving our passion up intensely being intimate.

Afterwards we lay on the bed feeling exhausted, lying in his arms with both of us feeling hot and sticky, "I think I'm going to get old a lot quicker as well Ferdinand."

He chuckled, "Well I have every intention of growing old with you Hannah," kissing me on the head getting up, "Phew, it's getting warm though, isn't it?" And going out to the kitchen to get a drink of water, "Do you want a drink of water?"

I called out, "Yes thanks." I noticed a bit of a sweat patch on the bed where he was 'wow he must have really heated up. It must be just that we are getting used to each other and more intense' smiling at the thought of it.

We had dinner, showers getting into bed turning off the light getting cuddly "I want to take you to Jardine again, Hannah?"

I hesitated, surprised he was asking, "Do you mean for good or for a couple of days?"

He cuddled in more, "You know I want to go for good but I'll be happy for a couple of days for now."

I thought about it, "Don't I need the elder's approval to go?"

He shook his head, "No Hannah, you need an elder to take you through, but all you need to do is ask."

I admit I hadn't thought about going for weekends but it would be a good idea to get used the place, as I would like to end up there with him, "I'll tell you what Morag will probably pop in through the week, I'll pass it by her when she does. There is a long weekend not this weekend but next, so can we leave it too, then? I can't take time off during the week at this stage because of Tom's maternity leave."

He must have been pleased with this because he started kissing me on the neck, "Yes that would be great, Hannah."

--ooOoo--

While at work, I started to get more knowledge from the book as I made time to study it. I went to meditation with Alira giving her a hug feeling a connection join us making her giggle, "What have you just given me Sister?"

I laughed, "I've opened another part of the book. It's really exciting, I must have given you some extra magic; have fun with it!" I was sitting after the meditation looking around me to see if there was anyone hanging around. I could see a young girl, probably around 16, sitting on a stone wall not far from us, eating an ice cream by herself. I tried to watch her without her noticing me but she got up, looking back briefly, walking away.

Alira was watching me, "What are you looking at Hannah?"

I was still watching the young girl walking away, "Just keeping an eye out for nosey people. There was one at the wedding as well dressed as an elderly woman but I'm sure was someone in disguise."

Alira looked annoyed, "Bloody annoying people. I wish they would bugger off and leave us alone. I'll have to look around a bit more as well."

Alira and I took off back to work, landing near the doors to the building. I gave her a hug, "I'll see you later." She grinned at me, "I might go and play with that gift you gave me."

I looked worried, "Don't you tell your mother I gave you an extra buzz."

She giggled, "Oooh are you scared Hannah?"

I looked at her worried, "Shit yes!"

Alira took off laughing.

I got back to my work station deciding to try out the hologram using a clear quartz crystal as a projector which was recommended by the book saying a chant over it, *"Scan me now to project it well showing me work and answer the phone as I command you during this work day until I tell you all is well."*

I ran the crystal over my body feeling it scan me, putting it under my desk as recommended by the book. I then pointed at it giving it some power from my body watching a fine white light go towards the crystal activating it and projecting an image on my chair, looking just like me. It was a little weak at first so I pointed at it again, making it stronger, feeling a satisfied smile come over my face.

I was lucky with my desk because it had privacy screens around it, with just a gap to the side so people would walk past just seeing me sitting there.

The next obstacle was to get it to do something for me. I stood behind it moving my arms as though I was typing or picking up the phone but it didn't do anything it just sat there.

I thought about it, '*I think I need a to put a movement chant into it.*' I put my head down thinking, connecting with the book, when a chant came into my mind, "*On my command you do as I say and say and I do whatever it is you must do.*"

I put my hands up as though answering the phone watching the hologram do the same, typing watching it do the same thing. I was getting excited as I watched it do the commands, I wanted it to do. The next thing I needed was to be able to watch it in case someone came around, so I turned my camera on the computer then connected it to my phone.

I could now sit in Tom's room in the orb to read or meditate, while leaving my phone open keeping an eye on the hologram. I did this for a couple of days, refining some things as I sat in the orb getting more knowledge out of the book.

By mid-week, I was sitting in the orb earlier because Tom was only in for a couple of hours, then had a couple of meetings to go to. I had done all the typing magically, then went into Tom's room doing some filing, watching the papers fly slowly to the cabinets.

I set up the hologram and was about to form the orb when I heard a woman's voice behind me making me jump "Hannah what are up to?" I looked around feeling like I was back in my teens being caught doing something, "Oh hi Morag, how are you?"

She came forward with a smirk on her face, "You are building up your knowledge quite quickly again."

I got up giving her a hug, "I've just had some extra time so thought I would read a bit more."

She shook her head looking at the pages flying into the cabinets, "I'm not sure you should be doing your filing like that Hannah; you might get caught."

I smiled, "You sound just like Ferdinand. I am being careful Morag."

She went and sat in Tom's chair, "Mm no wonder you get bored here, while the view isn't bad, I would feel quite trapped in here."

I checked my phone, with her noticing. She got up and came over to have a look with an impressed look on her face, "You've made a hologram of yourself and you have copied the orb I used. That is all very advanced magic, Hannah."

I felt good when she said that, "This part of the book is so interesting. I feel it is really challenging me."

She looked at the bracelet, "Just make sure you wear that protection. As you get stronger your vibrations get stronger and they will come and find you again."

I nodded, "Yes I will, Morag. I felt I also got some protection from the book when we were allowed to go further."

Morag looked curious, "We—did your girls get accepted as well?"

I grinned nervously, "Yes, they were pulled in when I worked out the ring that Mum had given me was the shield for the coat of arms. They also got a tattoo placed on their backs of just a dragon by itself."

Morag walked over to the window "that sounds like very old magic Hannah. I really think we need to do some more work on your family. Ferdinand has also asked that you be able to come and stay on weekends in Jardine from time to time. I'm happy with that as it will also give us a chance to catch up with matters that we have spoken about."

I nodded, "Yes, I know what you mean. Do I just get in touch with you or one of the others when I want to come through?"

Morag nodded coming back to me, "Yes, that is all you have to do, you are one of us now." That made me smile, "Thanks Morag, that makes me feel good, I have been the odd one out for a long time."

I thought about a couple of things I wanted to tell her, "I've been noticing people hanging around a little. They don't do anything just watch. The other day when Alira and I did some meditation at the park there was a teenage girl eating an ice cream just watching us. Do you think I should be worried?"

Morag looked concerned, "Yes Hannah, whoever it is, is just using disguises. Please be careful and keep watching."

I had another question pulling a bit of a face with Morag looking at me, "What is it, Hannah?"

I put my head down, "Have you had any luck of finding the person who attacked me, Morag?"

She looked disappointed, "No Hannah. Whoever it was is very clever."

The filing stopped flying over, having finished. Morag smiled, "Well that looks finished. I think I will call on your girls and give them something to wear for some added protection, just to keep them safe."

I smiled appreciatively at her, "Thanks Morag, that will put my mind at rest."

She gave me a hug, "Well I will go. Just stay on the right track Hannah, many people with magic have gone the wrong way with the knowledge you are learning."

I nodded, "I know, Morag. I may get angry but I don't get deadly and I have good support around me now to help me. I finally feel part of a community which makes me feel great and not weird."

I finished the day feeling happy after Morag's visit going home with Ferdinand telling him most of what we spoke about. He was happy that we could chat like this now, giving me a hug when I told him about going to Jardine, which also led to a bit more kissing resulting in being intimate again, not even making it to the bedroom this time.

We were lying on the mat in front of the TV panting as Ferdinand rolled off me, "Agghh I think you're going to kill me, Hannah."

I giggled, "I think we are going to die together with a smile on our faces at least."

This made him laugh moving over to give me another kiss, "Until death do us part as the wedding vow says."

I nodded stroking his hair that was damp with sweat, "Yes and the rate we are going it's not far away." I went and had a shower, thinking I would like to get a bit fitter plus get rid of some of the flabby bits that were appearing, deciding to do some swimming at lunch time when I could. I got to work the next day starting the work as quickly as possible but Tom was really agitated because of lack of sleep and stress from work. I got him a coffee and brownie putting a chant on the brownie before I gave it to him, *"Blessed be the birth of a baby, new to this world, new to see parents fresh as could be, let the baby relax and sleep to give Mum and Dad joy and peace so mote it be."*

He was sitting at his desk running his hands through his hair, "Gee Hannah I don't know how you did it on your own for so long? I'm struggling with lack of sleep and the CEO putting pressure on me still."

I patted his hand putting some calming light through him, "Just concentrate on one thing at a time Tom; while you are here, concentrate on that, while you are home concentrate on your baby and wife; don't try and think of everything together. Here have a coffee and a brownie with me."

I sat down on the chair opposite his desk with him nodding, "Thanks Hannah that's good advice." I sat back having a sip of coffee, "Take a couple of deep breaths relax and enjoy your coffee and brownie, that's all you have to concentrate at the moment."

He did as I asked with the calming light starting to take effect, leaning back in his chair sipping on his coffee and enjoying his brownie. A smile appeared on his face, "I'm feeling better already but I still don't know how you did it with two children on your own."

I chuckled, "It wasn't that easy Tom and I've made a few mistakes as there isn't any guide book with parenting, but as long as they don't harm anyone, get jobs or a lifestyle they enjoy and a nice partner, that is all your aim should be."

He shook his head, "I never realised you were a good listener."

I smiled, "I must be getting older, Tom. I'll go and do some more work and leave you to it," taking his plate and cup. I was typing away when he came out after an hour, "Well I have done everything I need to do and I'm ready to go home, thanks Hannah. I'll see you tomorrow."

It was getting close to lunch time, so I finished most of the work magically, setting the hologram up ready to go should I be running late. I went into Tom's room and took off from there to go to the Prince Alfred Park Pool not far from work. I had brought in my swimmers, a towel, some shampoo for my hair so it didn't smell of chlorine in a bag along with my phone to keep an eye on things and a little bit of money to get in.

I did 10 laps in the 50-metre pool feeling puffed '*I am out of shape.*' I had a quick shower washing my hair getting back to work without having to start up my hologram. I sat at my desk eating my lunch, noticing a woman I didn't know, going past me a couple of times. I made it look as though I was doing something on my computer when she walked past again, not looking at me. I was just about to get up and see where she went when I got a text from Amelia, "Mum can you come and see me I've got some trouble."

I sent one back, "Be there shortly." I sent Alira a text, 'can you get away for half an hour; if so meet me at this address.'

She sent back 'sure can see you there.'

I set up my hologram taking off to where Amelia was, going into a shop that she had to go in for her work. I met Alira out front pointing at my hair changing the colour and changing into some jeans. Alira smiled, "My turn" changing her hair colour and clothes. We magicae into the shop hiding behind some shelves to see what was happening.

Amelia knew we were there while she spoke to a guy who was pointing a wand to her, "I'm not giving you anything. I think it is time you went."

I could hear the guy chuckling, "Oh and what are you going to do about it if I don't."

She produced a wicked smile, "Mum will deal with you." His smile dropped spinning around to look for me, as a pool appeared on the floor. He turned back to Amelia who was gone now, with a sweat coming over him, "Get back here you little witch and stop playing these tricks."

I stepped forward grinning, putting my hand up with a crushing motion, which made his wand disintegrate in his hand. This burned his hand as it disintegrated, hearing him yelp and fall to the floor holding his hand.

Alira stepped forward producing a chair tying him to it. He looked around frantically, struggling against his bonds "who are you?"

I moved over to him, "I'm Mum and this is my sister and your worst nightmare."

Amelia came out looking smugly at him then looking at us two with our disguises, "Mm not bad you two."

Alira got cocky walking around him touching him gently, enough to give him a jolt off her, "So what's your name?"

Amelia pointed to the door, "Better lock it in case we get interrupted."

He looked even more nervous, "Come on I just wanted a bit of your spark ladies."

I sighed, "Sorry we don't give out freebies anymore. What is your name?"

He looked at the pool "why is there a pool here?"

Amelia moved forward looking curious but smiling, "Yes Mum why is there a pool here?"

I patted the guy's head feeling his hair, "My sister and I thought he needed a bath, he's a bit dirty."

The guy chuckled nervously, "Oh come on, do you think I'm some kid or something?"

I sighed, "Shall we Sister?"

Alira nodded smiling at me, "You can start, Sister."

I put my hands out in front of me picking him up chair and all putting him in the pool, watching him squeal and struggle, "Cut it out, let me out of this."

Alira then did a little twirl then bowed like a wave, making the chair lean back in the water ducking him under, until he started coughing, then pulled him up. She did this a couple of more times coming forward, "Are you going to tell us who you are now little man? You know in days of old lots of innocent women were tortured like this and even if they confessed, they were drowned. Is that what is going to happen to you?"

He was still coughing getting his breath back looking nervously at us, "Alright, my name is Toby Hunter. Now let me go." He was starting to shake with fear and cold, with the surname sounding familiar, "are you related to Jonathon Hunter?" He looked worried, which was enough to make me smirk at him, "You are related to him aren't you?"

Alira looked at me, "So you know the family Sister?"

Amelia also nodded, "Yes Mum knows *that* family more than she should have."

I looked at Amelia knowing she hated Jonathon, "Yes we all make mistakes don't we."

Alira started dunking him again enjoying herself, "Are you going to tell us who you are working for?"

He came up shaking the water off him struggling to get out, "I work alone. I share a bit of magic with Uncle Jonathon every now and then, but he is weak as piss so I work alone."

We were standing there deciding what to do next, when Cara arrived in the shop, "Ladies what are you up to?"

Alira and I grabbed each other's hands, "Oh shit!"

We turned to look at Cara making Alira squirm, "Oh come on we were just having a bit of fun." Ferdinand, Fia and Shiro arrived as well not looking very happy. I looked at Alira worried, "Oh shit now we are in trouble."

Toby started to cough again, "Let me out of here they were trying to drown me."

Cara moved forward freezing him telling Ferdinand to go over to me and Fia and Shiro to Alira and Amelia. Ferdinand gave Alira a look making her let go of my hand as he took mine squeezing it, "What were you planning on doing with him?"

Amelia was feeling bold now, "We were just making up our minds. He's related to Jonathon the dick that Mum dated briefly."

Ferdinand looked at me, "Oh that's a bit of coincidence, isn't it? What have you done with your hair?"

I flicked it feeling a bit more confident, "I thought I'd try something different."

Cara removed the pool then put a chant on him to make him forget what happened. She untied him drying him off as he stood there still frozen from her spell. Alira, who now had Fia holding onto her hand, "Oh come on, you're not going to let him go?"

Cara looked annoyed, "Well we're not going to kill him, Alira."

I looked at Alira then to Cara, "We weren't going to either, but we thought you might have an erasing spell or something so he would forget his magic all together?"

Cara sent him off landing him somewhere to unfreeze; she wouldn't tell us where, "We do but it tends to make them go mad in your world. You got rid of his wand and gave him a fright, that will have to do for now. I suggest you go back to work or whatever you were doing and forget about it. I don't want to see you going after him, unless he attacks you."

Morag and Lilith came in looking at everyone. Morag looked at me and Alira with different hair colouring, "What have you two been up to?"

Lilith just stood there quietly watching everyone. Cara filled her in from what she knew then Morag came over to Alira and myself, "So what is your version, Hannah?"

I smiled, "I got a request for help from my daughter so I came and helped. We wouldn't have harmed him, well not enough to kill him Morag."

Like petulant children Alira and I changed our appearance back to what we had on before. I went to move over to Amelia but Ferdinand kept hold of my hand as I gave her a hug, "I'll talk to you later, are you alright."

She didn't look happy with the outcome, "Yes I'm good, Mum, thanks for coming to help as well as you Alira."

Shiro was a bit offended, "You're supposed to call me when you want help Amelia."

She leaned into him, "I did touch the tattoo but you didn't come, so that is why I called Mum."

Cara and Morag came forward with Morag looking at her tattoo, "That shouldn't have happened. We will have to look into that. I wonder if that other thing is interfering with it, Hannah?"

I shrugged my shoulders, "It's quite possible, Morag."

Lilith looked at me then back to Morag wondering what we were talking about but didn't have the courage to ask.

I checked my phone, "I better go. I'll talk to you all later."

Ferdinand stopped me, "What have you got on your phone?"

I put it away, "It's just telling me when someone is looking for me at the office that is all."

He grabbed my waist looking at the others, "I'll see you all later," landing in Tom's office still holding onto my waist, "No you don't what have you got as a warning."

I tried to hide a grin, "It's just a little bell thing, don't worry about it."

He leaned down to give me a kiss grabbing my phone off me, walking away as he had a look at it noticing the hologram. I tried to get it off him getting annoyed, "Ferdinand, give it back."

He turned to look at me surprised and annoyed at the same time, "Why do you have a hologram at your desk?"

I was getting annoyed, "I have to go and sort it out, I'll explain later, give me the phone."

He shook his head, "No, you go and sort it out I'll wait here for you."

I groaned going over to the doorway saying a quick chant so the secretary froze briefly giving me a chance to turn the hologram off and sit in the chair and putting my headphones on.

I released her smiling at her, "Hi Diane, sorry I had my headphones on and didn't hear you, what can I do for you?"

She looked a little confused, "Oh sorry I didn't realise you had your headphones on. We are just having some cake for Crystal's birthday and you're welcome to some."

I nodded, "Oh thanks. I'll just finish this and then I'll come over."

Once she had gone, I went back into Tom's office with Ferdinand sitting in Tom's chair, "This is not a bad chair, do you think it was expensive?"

I sighed, "Yes it was because he quite often bragged about how expensive it was." I noticed my phone on the desk quickly pulling it into my hand smiling at Ferdinand, getting slow dear.

A cunning look came on his face as he came towards me, "Start telling me what's going on Hannah. You said you would be upfront with me, but it appears you haven't. Why do you need a hologram at your desk?"

I started backing up, "Don't get angry Ferdinand. I was going to tell you things, but I was refining them until they worked properly that is all. Morag knows what I've been doing."

He still kept walking towards me looking annoyed, "That still doesn't answer my question, Hannah. Why do you need a hologram at your desk?"

I looked behind me realising I was running out of space to move, "I just wanted it there so I could come in here and daydream a little, you know what I am like," putting on a little smile. I could see he was trying to suppress both frustration and a smile, "You've been daydreaming for years Hannah and haven't needed a hologram, what else did you need it for?"

I was now up against the wall, "I wanted to read the family book without being interrupted, that is all."

He was really close to me now, as I wondered if I should magicae around the room, when he took hold of my arms, "No magic madam. You wouldn't bring in the book without it being secure and I know you wouldn't be able to lock this room up because people would ask why it was locked."

I tried the puppy dog eyes look as he shook his head, "Don't you look at me like that Hannah. Tell me what else you have learned."

I gave up sighing, producing an orb around us both, as he looked up smiling, "Mm you are getting clever then, aren't you?" Moving in closer, looking dangerous now. I did a nervous chuckle, "Ferdinand I was going to tell you, but like I said I was refining things; you know what I'm like, it has to be right before I show anyone things."

He groaned, "You're driving me nuts Hannah, especially when you get me annoyed all this lust comes up. Are you sure you haven't put a spell on me?"

I shook my head, "You know I'm not allowed to do that Ferdinand, I'm afraid it's all you *mein Liebling* (my love)."

He put his hand behind my head kissing me on the lips pushing himself against me, making me groan. He was just putting his arm around my waist kissing me when we heard a noise at the door stopping to look.

Diane and Lidia had come back to see where I was, "Hannah are you in here?" We stood there looking at her with Ferdinand grinning, "They can't hear or see us, can they?"

I smiled back, "No but I should go, you randy dragon, they'll wonder where I am."

Lidia shrugged her shoulders, "Well she isn't in here. Have you seen her new boyfriend Diane he's quite a catch? I'll be keeping an eye on Hannah. If she does her usual thing of dumping him soon, I'll be moving in on that one."

They went out with Diane saying, "She might be in the toilet."

I looked at Ferdinand aghast, "What a bitch!"

Ferdinand chuckled, "Don't worry dear she's not my type. I've calmed down for now, I'll pick you up from reception, so you don't get into any more mischief madam."

I fanned myself, "I'll have to go to the ladies to cool myself down you naughty Ferdi."

He moved in again, "Well we could finish it off."

I pushed him away, "No I better go in case they come back."

I took the orb down as he watched me, amazed, "I really can't get over how fast you are learning things. I am proud of you honey, it just worries me when you don't tell me what you are learning and what I need to protect you against."

He put his hand up to my chin looking earnestly at me, "That is what I am here for, you know, not just your lover boy."

I giggled, "I know honey, I'll try to keep you informed better."

He gave me another kiss taking off, letting me magicae to the ladies toilet, to tidy myself up and calm my heart down, fanning myself in the cubicle shaking my head, "I think he is going to age me quite fast at this rate."

Diane smiled when I came into the tea room, "Oh there you are, Hannah, we came looking for you."

I nodded, "Yes I went to the ladies," giving Lidia a funny look making her feel uncomfortable.

Ferdinand came and picked me up as promised, having a surprise for me when we got home. He put his hands over my eyes leading me along, when the smell of roses came up to me as I grinned, "What have you done Ferdinand?"

He gave me a kiss on the cheek, "Are you ready?"

I nodded in anticipation, "Yes come on."

He took his hands off my eyes to see the bath full of water with candles, crystals and rose petals leading up to the bath and in it. I turned to look at him smiling putting on my sexy eyes, "Now you *are* going to kill me, aren't you?"

He groaned getting ready to point to us to take our clothes off, when I stopped him, "No, I want to do it my world way." He looked at me curious, "Oh what do you mean by that Hannah?"

I stood back from him, "No touching until I say," slowly taking off my clothes, then I went over to him trying to help me, "No just leave your hands where you are." I slowly took off his shirt and then pants kissing him gently on the neck and chest as I was doing it. I then got him to touch me in different places listening to him groan and kiss me, "Oh god Hannah, you're driving me nuts."

We were lying in the bath afterwards exhausted, finally moving when the water got cold. He moved, "Come on, otherwise they'll find two old people frozen to death in the bath."

I giggled, "Yes dear. I think I've used a few muscles I didn't realise I had. Getting up stretching my back out."

He came up behind me with a towel, "I could give you a massage if you like."

I looked at him tiredly, "I would love that honey, but when I've recovered," giving him a kiss.

He went and got something for us to eat while I tidied things up (magically of course), then we sat out on the balcony in robes having a glass of wine. I had some things running through my mind, "Are we supposed to be this randy, dear?"

He choked on his wine a little, "I don't think so. I haven't really asked many people about this; I could though it you want me to. I do love it when you orgasm, I don't remember anyone telling me about that." A little embarrassed, "Oh am I not supposed to do that?"

He took my hand, "You do whatever you want dear."

I yawned, "I thought I better mention, because I know you like to know, that I've decided to do some lengths in some of my lunch times at the local pool. It might help me keep up with your love making as well," looking at him grinning. He smiled back at me, "Actually that sounds like a good idea, I should do something as well."

I got up, "I'll just give the girls a quick ring before I go to bed to make sure they keep an eye out for bad magic people." I left him on the balcony, going into the bedroom to speak to both girls. Charlotte was a bit annoyed about the attack on Amelia saying, "I've been looking at something to deal with those people who are attacking us."

I was curious, "Oh what is that, Charlotte?"

She laughed, "I'll come for brunch on Sunday and show you Mum. I think it's quite cool."

I smiled, "Well it sounds intriguing. I'm about to ring Amelia so I'll get her to come as well." I rang Amelia, "Are you alright after the attack, Amelia?"

I heard her sigh, "Yes Mum, he was just a dick. I've spoken to Charlotte about having brunch on Sunday with her new invention. I'll see you then." I went and brushed my teeth finding Ferdinand in there already, brushing his, "Are the girls alright?"

I nodded, "Yes, they want to have brunch on Sunday, apparently Charlotte has made a new invention she wants us to have a look at."

He shook his head, "You Dragĕ women are real thinkers, aren't you?"

Chapter 18

We managed to get to Sunday without any other magical problems and to calm ourselves down in the bedroom as well. Ferdinand got up, "I suppose you don't want anything to eat since you're meeting the girls?"

I shook my head, "No thanks."

He was in a playful mood, coming over and putting his hand up my back, "Mm nice and ticklish up there."

I moved away, "Ferdinand don't be naughty."

He put his arm around the duvet holding my arms in place, "Ah got you now."

I giggled, "Don't I need to pee, your silly dragon."

He stopped, giving me a kiss, "Come on let's go for a walk before I go."

I got up, "Ok but you behave yourself."

We got up going down to the beach with a warm but cloudy day to greet us. You could feel the warmth coming from inland but the clouds were coming from the sea with the threat of rain. As we walked down the beach holding hands, "What do you do in Jardine while you're there?"

He looked at me grinning, "I took you over to where the dragons hang out and you met Omar. We have races and sleep there. Sometimes the elders ask us to help out in the community in our human form or animal form depending on what they want done or on how long we spend in Jardine."

He gave me a kiss, "Does that satisfy you?"

I nodded, "So you don't hang out with any of the women there?"

He chuckled, "Are you getting jealous?" He came over, giving me a hug being silly, "Hannah's jealous."

I slapped him, "I'm just checking on you like you check on me Ferdi."

He put his arm around my shoulders, "Well you wouldn't have to if you came to live in Jardine. Besides the women there are not like that, they have their own spirit animals to be content with."

I shook my head, "You're determined I'll give you that. We wouldn't be able spend all our time together there either, would we?"

He shook his head, "No we would both have to contribute to the community, that is how it works there. The good thing is that we wouldn't have any people chasing your magic there, which would make me a lot happier."

I leaned into him, "Just remember I was attacked there, Ferdinand."

He looked annoyed, "That was a rare event, Hannah. I assure you it won't happen again. They are looking for that person as well. She or he will get caught eventually."

We walked a little further as I thought about things, "I know you love Jardine and magically I would be safer there, but it has put a bit of doubt in my mind what happened there. I also know my grandmother Matilda didn't want to stay or have much to do with Jardine. I wonder if it was because she was strong as well and didn't like to be controlled by them?"

He looked disappointed at me, "Like I said, that shouldn't have happened to you but it won't happen again. Let's just take one day at a time and see what happens."

We went back to the unit giving each other a kiss and a cuddle with him looking down at me, "Now you behave with those girls, won't you?"

I sighed, "Yes dear. I'm only having a brunch with them. They did say they might see if Alira, Sophie and Hine want to come as well, so it will be a real chat fest."

He rolled his eyes, "Oh dear I'm glad I'm not going then with all those gossiping women." He took off, giving me a chance to get changed, when Amelia and Charlotte popped in calling me from the lounge.

I came out putting some shoes on, "I was just getting changed."

Charlotte grinned at me, "I made it Mum."

I looked a bit confused, "What was that?"

Charlotte went and sat on the sofa, "Have a look Mum, I'm thinking of calling it a 'magitrap mk1' bringing out a compact mirror."

I looked bewildered, "What does it do Charlotte?"

She looked a little annoyed, "Remember I was telling you I was looking at inventing something to trap the *bad people's* magic. Well, this is it. I got the idea off a ghost busters movie I was watching a few days ago."

I sat down next to her with Amelia on the other side, "I'm going to be the one who sells it to Jardine."

Charlotte pulled a face at her, "Yeah, yeah. You open it just like a normal compact mirror and it looks just like a mirror to the average person, but it has a couple of features. Firstly, it has a pointer which is in the holder here." Bringing it out, "Which if you point it at the person you are dealing with stuns them, long enough for you to do this," and holding the compact up facing away from us pushing two buttons on either side of it. It sounded like a snapshot on a phone, hearing a click along with a circle appearing that went inward towards the mirror.

I looked amazed, "So have you tested it on anyone yet?"

Amelia formed an orb over us as I laughed, "Oh you picked that one up as well."

She smiled, "Yes you must have taken it off, Morag, and when you used it for your own use, it stored it in the book; a bit like a computer hard drive."

I looked at them both, "So what is so secret that we need to get the orb out?"

Charlotte and Amelia looked at each other grinning as Amelia started to giggle, "Do you remember Toby?"

I nodded, "Yes what about him?"

Amelia fidgeted a bit, "We found him and tested it on him. He is no longer a threat to us, put it that way. No harm done as well, but no magic anymore."

I jumped with joy, "Oh that's wonderful. I'm so proud of you two." Both of them beamed as I gave them a hug, "So when are you going to present it to Jardine?"

Charlotte closed the mirror, "Well you said you were going to Jardine next weekend; we thought we might come along as well and show them it then."

Amelia put her hand on mine, "There is something else we want to do today as well Mum, but we didn't tell you because we know you are getting quite close to Ferdinand plus, we don't want you blamed."

I looked unsure how to take this, "Oh and what were you planning?"

Charlotte smiled, "We want to go and stir the priest up in that church that keeps annoying you. It will just be a bit of harmless fun. Besides if any magic people turn up, we can zap them with my magitrap. I've made you both one, by the way."

She handed us both one, opening it with a thought coming to me, "It won't do anything to me if I use it just as a mirror will it?"

She shook her head, "No Mum you have to push the buttons like on a phone. I'm hoping to play with the settings a bit so it can't be used on us as well."

I shook my head, "Wow you two are amazing."

Amelia put her hand on mine, "There is one more thing before we take the orb off, I've been doing a bit more research into the family and have found a couple of churches that might have the information we want. They are in Norway, but we will have to get over there to check it out. I did try to ring but I don't think I got the information quite right or there was something lost in the translation. There is also one more thing; there was another sealed section in the new area we have been allowed into but I couldn't get into it."

I looked confused, "Oh I've been going into it at work and didn't see that. I'll have a look next week."

Charlotte looked around, "I think the others are coming, we better get rid of the orb."

Amelia closed it up just in time for Hine, Sophie and Alira to arrive in the unit. We got up to greet them with Charlotte showing them her new invention. They all looked impressed grinning looking over to me with Hine saying, "You Dragé women don't stop thinking."

I spoke quietly to Alira, "So do you know what they are planning?"

She chuckled, "They just told me, cunning little buggers. It should be fun; I'm starting to get a bit bored."

I nudged her laughing, "Oh dear we are sisters, aren't we?"

We took off going to a little café called *"The Black and Bronze Café"* in the city not far from the church. It was only 9.00am so we had plenty of time to go to the service which was at 10.30am.

We went in ordering breakfast chatting away about what was planned in a type of code just in case anyone was listening to us either around us or in our heads.

I could feel the excitement of being naughty again, building up in me, which hadn't happened for a while. The girls were all chatting about other things, so I pulled Alira aside, "Can I ask you something Alira?"

She nodded, "Yeah sure Sister, what?"

I looked a little uncomfortable, "Do you and Fia do it a lot?"

Alira chuckled, "We have our moments, but I imagine you two are making up for lost time. How long has it been that you've known each other—50 years isn't it? Mind you, I think you two are just randy buggers as well." It dawned on me, "Oh yeah, I didn't think about the 50 years, not being randy buggers."

I thought I would ask her one more thing while I had her attention, "Ferdinand has been pestering me about going to live in Jardine. I'm still not sure, especially with what happened last time, plus they have made me feel as though we are a threat because of our magic; how do you feel about it?"

Alira thought about it playing with her lip, "I don't feel comfortable going either Hannah because of what happened. That's why I'm interested in the other thing M said. As for the strength of our magic, I think you're right, they do feel a bit threatened. This is why Mum doesn't do much with them. She isn't really strong but she feels as though she is being a bit controlled."

I gave her a hug, "Thanks Sister it's nice to have someone to talk to about things."

It was time to go, with big grins appearing on our faces, as we paid for our breakfast. We found a public toilet, deciding to change our appearance in there knowing there wouldn't be any cameras around, just in case.

We came out looking at each other laughing. Amelia gave us all a sprig of lavender putting it somewhere visible so we knew who we were in case we got into trouble or got separated.

Alira and I changed to little old ladies with grey hair, floral dresses, a jacket to cover our arms and support shoes with big handbags. We took each other's arms magicaeing near the church walking the rest of the way. We looked around with the others coming up behind us, as though they were just joining the crowd.

We had sorted out different chants, having one each to do, it just depended on how things went as to which ones would be done. I started to get nervous moving up into the church putting my head down to Alira saying quietly, "I hope I don't cast a dark shadow or anything when I go in there."

She slapped me smiling, "Don't be silly dear," in an elderly woman's voice.

We went into the pews, finding seats together with our sisters but spread out with a pew behind and ahead keeping our heads down because we knew there were cameras in there. I got some glasses out of my bag to wipe them, putting them up in the light of the church. While doing this I changed one of the hymns to 'When the Saints Go Marching In'.

As I brought them back down, I saw a woman's head that looked familiar, with raven black hair pulled up in a messy bun. I put my glasses on digging into my bag to get my phone out sending a quick text to everyone, "Is that Lilith?"

The lady next to me growled, "Can't you leave those phones alone for 5 minutes, put it away dear" as she pointed up to a sign *"Please turn off all phones."*

I smiled putting my hands up to my cheeks, "oh sorry dear." I looked around the church briefly, as a big crowd came in, feeling a bit nervous now putting my hand on Alira's, "Mm getting nervous dear."

She chuckled, "Just think of your school days dear." That made me smile.

The service started with the Deacon coming out saying the prayer as everyone knelt on the board in front of us, following what everyone else did.

I heard a little shriek go through the church making us look up to see some of the candles start to flicker, then flare up, like someone had turned the gas up on them.

The people in the front row were getting nervous, watching as the candles were now bouncing in their holders, almost to a tune. The Deacon tried to ignore it, carrying on with the prayer but saying it a lot faster.

We were all asked to stand now for the first hymn when an eerie noise blew through the pipes of the organ. It started off sounding like wind going through a deep sounding wind chime. People shuffled in their seats looking around them.

I looked up noticing some faces I had seen before in different meditation meetings and even a couple from my work.

The organ player tried to start playing the hymn when a gust of wind blew through the pipes making the tune unrecognisable with a deep howl, almost like a banshee screaming, going through the huge pipes.

The Deacon started singing loudly to distract the worried people in the church with the howling pipes saying words now. His eyes widened with fright as words like *"evil lives within"* and *"you are the demons in disguise."*

I looked up over to Alira, playing along looking nervous, "Oh dear what have we come into here, dear Sister."

The rude woman next to me, looking nervous, but trying to sound confident, "They are old pipes, I am sure it is just some wind or something."

It calmed down briefly, allowing the organ player to play some of her tune, when a huge blast of wind howled through the pipes, almost as though they were laughing. I watched the dark headed woman in front of me who was looking to the side of the church, as I followed her stare to see John Adams standing there in his robes with an angry look on his face. She then turned back looking at the pipes and around the church.

Alira had her head down briefly putting it up tapping my hand, "I think it is who you think dear."

John Adams came out to the alter singing out loud and waving his hands to distract the parishioners from the noise coming from the organ. He stood up at the podium with a large Bible sitting on it, turned to the pages that he was going to read from.

In the front of the podium was a huge carved wooden eagle, sitting there proudly looking over the people in the pews. The pipes settled down making everyone quieten down, waiting for the reading of a prayer from John Adams.

John cleared his throat, "It appears that we have some pranksters in the church today."

He was very expressive with his hands gesticulating to emphasise that these events should be ignored as they are all safe within these historic walls.

He then started to read from the Bible, when I noticed the eagle's eyes started to flicker, then the beak twitched. I could hear some of the people starting to mumble not sure if their eyes were playing tricks on them.

The eagle then moved its head emitting a loud *squawk* echoing around the church. It looked as though it was trying to take off, with the podium start to sway left and right.

John's eyes widened in disbelief, holding the Bible, talking louder as he read a part from the Bible *"any woman who is compassionate in her life will be rewarded in heaven, while those who act in anger will be punished. All the virtues she practices are aimed at making her husband's life better teaching her children and serving God."*

The eagle started flapping its wings now, trying to escape the podium, squawking and turning to try and peck the Bible that John was holding onto.

I started my acting again saying loudly, "Oh dear Sister look, at that bird trying to escape the podium," sending ripples through the crowd.

Alira caught on, "Oh yes Sister; is this church possessed with evil spirits?" This was enough to start the muttering amongst the people crossing themselves putting their heads down.

John Adams tried to distract the people again, signalling to the organ player to play the next hymn, making me smile, as I dropped my head, thinking this was my cue.

The eagle was still trying to escape, as the Deacon came over with a walking stick he had taken off one of the parishioners, hitting it to stop it from moving.

The organ player found the hymn at last cranking up the organ, starting the tune of 'The Saints Come Marching Home'. John who was now holding his Bible in his hands heard the tune, looking confused, while the Deacon continued to try and control the bird. The congregation stood up, getting their song books out as I flicked the words to *'The Saints Go Marching Home'* noticing the faces that I had recognised, look around them to see where it was coming from.

Everyone started to sing the words feeling a bit more confident with the eagle settling back down into its position—you could almost hear the sigh of relief.

When the hymn was just about up to the chorus, I mumbled a chant while holding Alira's hand for extra strength, *"Ghosts of the past of this church come to thee come and see this priest and congregation full of glee. Arise from the pictures on the windows in blue, red, yellow and green to dance with such gait and glee around us for all to see dancu kaj movu, dancu kaj movu, dancu kaj movu."*

Once the congregation started the chorus the figures in the stained-glass windows started to move out of their surrounds, hearing bits of lead fall from the windows. A woman cried out as she fainted, falling to the floor, which could just be heard above the noise of the organ.

Red, yellow, green and blue figures started marching away from the windows as people were singing, hearing John and the Deacon sing louder, encouraging people on. The saints from the windows were marching around the people. I yawned allowing me to put my head down, whirling my finger.

The pictures of the saints started to dive bomb the people in the pews, knocking peoples hats off or stopping in front of them pulling faces.

I could hear people scream in horror, with a few diehard people singing along with John and the Deacon. The louder John and the Deacon got, the more things came to life, with the candles flaring again to the tune, along with eerie noises booming out from the pipes as the organ player tried to play. The eagle came to life again trying to escape the confines of the podium.

Alira, who still had her hand on mine said, "Oh dear I don't like this church Sister; I want to go."

I nodded my head, "Oh yes Sister this is a wicked place."

The people on either side of us heard what we said looking petrified, as the pictures were attacking people, deciding to get up and go as well.

We stood up with them while I put my hands on my head as though protecting myself and Alira was flaying her handbag around as though trying to hit them. The pictures weren't hitting us, but we had to make it look as though they were.

We started to shuffle out from the pew, hearing John and the Deacon trying to calm everyone down, "Please take your seats this will settle down; they are just pranks from some evil people."

I squealed loud enough for other people to hear, "Yes evil people in this church. I'm getting out of here."

I could see the others from our group starting to move now, causing a wave of people to get up, while still being hit by the pictures dive bombing them, trying to protect themselves.

We kept our heads down noticing some people take videos on their phones. I thought our disguises were good, but we weren't sure if someone would recognise something on us. We started to make our way to the door holding onto Alira's arm as though we were supporting each other. Some people were crying in fear, pushing through the crowd to get out the door first.

I kept looking around, putting a look of fear on my face, but I was making sure we all got out. I couldn't see the others as the crowd was panicking and getting quite thick, so I guided Alira to go towards a large public seat that was just outside the church, going to sit on it looking upset. I started to get worried because I couldn't see the others while we sat on the seat, fanning ourselves.

Hine and Amelia saw us as they came out, sitting down next to us shaking their heads putting them down to hide their uncontrollable laughter.

One face that came out of the church, I hadn't noticed before was that of Sarina, still with plaster on her nose, squealing with a saint hanging onto her hair, pulling it up like reins of a horse.

There were still younger people videoing the scene before us, so we kept our heads down.

I finally saw Charlotte and Sophie come out, putting an act on, looking as though they were about to faint.

Lilith came out quite calm, looking around to see if she could see anyone who would be doing this. She put some sunglasses on, moving to the side of the church scanning around the area. I looked down and mumbled to Alira and Amelia, "Watch out, Lilith is looking around."

A film crew from the local TV station had pulled up out front of the church setting up their cameras and a reporter getting her microphone ready to try and talk to some of the people who were wailing in distress.

Some of the younger people were yelling, "Wow cool service."

I got up signalling to the others to make a move as we didn't want to be seen on the news. I helped Alira up moving towards the park, which was on the other side of the church, when Alira stumbled on her shoes. As I moved to catch her my jacket sleeve moved up revealing the dragon tattoo on it. I saw Lilith looking at me putting my head down quickly covering my tattoo and helping Alira up.

Lilith was moving towards us, so I put my arm through Alira's to support her. I then put my hand out whirling my finger in my hand, while Alira watched me. A small whirlwind formed near the church picking up and throwing dirt and leaves around, the now terrified people standing in front of the church. The reporter and the cameraman were being buffeted around by the wind still trying to report the events unfolding as they held onto their gear. Alira and I then moved off as I supported her with her injured ankle.

The others from our group (who were becoming good actors) saw Alira hobbling putting their hands up in disbelief, wailing encouraging other people to follow us, to get away from the wind.

We knew we couldn't magicae out of there yet because there were faces scanning the crowd and not enough people around us; so we continued to walk towards the park and Town Hall, which wasn't far away.

There was a flock of pigeons pecking on the grass being fed seed by a woman giving Amelia an idea. She turned around briefly, pointing to the ground, producing some seed which led towards the church. She then turned back to scare enough of them to follow the seed.

Once a few of them took off the rest followed cooing madly around the seed. This sent people towards us more, allowing us to take off to our designated spot to meet.

Chapter 19

We had arranged to meet at the Fortunes of War, in the Rocks landing in different places not far from it and meeting at the bar.

We had all changed back to ourselves by the time we landed. I helped Alira hobble over to a seat near where we landed, "Are you alright Sister?"

She screwed up her face, "It looks as though I've sprained it."

I put my hand on it to see if I could help it heal, looking up at Alira, "Does it feel any better?"

She smiled, "Yes it does," and getting up still a bit wobbly, "I may need to strap it though just to give it a bit of support."

I told her to sit down, "Here I'll do it now bringing in some strapping and putting it around her ankle." We looked around us then magicae the rest of the way to the pub walking into the bar, finding the others standing there with a drink already, laughing.

I helped Alira to sit down on a chair and went and got her a drink. We decided it was a little crowded to talk about things there so we went into the beer garden and sat under a big old jacaranda tree. Relaxing at last.

Hine came up to me, "That was definitely Lilith, Hannah. I think we should do a couple of extra things as she will have the elders here soon, asking all sorts of questions."

I nodded, "What did you have in mind?"

Hine called the others over, "Put your hands on Alira's ankle and take the strapping off, as that is a bit of a giveaway."

We all did it making a bright light form over Alira's ankle bringing a big smile on her face, "Wow that feels good."

I looked at Hine, "I think Lilith saw my tattoo when I was helping Alira up. I'm worried she is going to try and get me into trouble again with Jardine."

Hine patted my shoulder, "We'll see how it goes Hannah. Just relax."

Sophie looked around us, "We should bring in a little bit of shopping as well. That way we can say we had breakfast down that way but went shopping and then came here." Everyone agreed bringing in an item of shopping putting the bags under the table.

We sat down getting comfortable with our drinks feeling satisfied we had done enough when I got a vibration, "I think we have visitors coming ladies."

They all acknowledged me continuing to chat, when Morag came in smiling at us all, "Hello all of you. You look as though you've been having a nice time."

She came around and gave us all a hug, with Amelia asking if she wanted a drink. Morag shook her head producing a glass of her own, "Thanks Amelia. I think I will just have something of my own."

Morag smiled, "So what have you all been doing; oh, looks like some shopping at least?"

Amelia and Charlotte went and sat near her like excited children bringing out the magitrap. Morag looked over to me looking impressed as Charlotte showed her how it worked.

I could feel others coming in looking at Alira, "I think the men are coming in."

Alira took another sip of wine chuckling, "It's like being back at school, isn't it?"

I looked away, trying not to laugh, when I saw Ferdinand, Shiro, Aetius, Fia and two others come from the bar area. Sophie went and greeted a woman who had soft red hair, that was pulled up in a bun with fine sharp features and large round eyes. She was dressed casually in light jeans and a striped top, bringing her over to us, "This is Renee, my spirit animal."

I got up to give her a hug, "Hi Renee nice to meet you."

Ferdinand came over smiling, giving me a kiss, "Wow you've got a good crowd here by the looks. Hi Renee, nice to see you could join us."

Another guy came forward looking at Ferdinand, "Hi Ferdinand, is this Hannah?"

Hine came up behind him, "Hello I wasn't sure if you were going to come?"

He turned around giving her a big hug, "Of course I would come."

Hine held onto him around his waist, "This is Manu my spirit animal." He was a tall man with a beefy build but not fat, along with long hair that was pulled up into a 'man bun' wearing jeans, checked shirt and a waist jacket over top. Ferdinand shook his hand, "Yes this is, Hannah."

Manu looked at me, "You don't look that bad tempered, Hannah," laughing when he saw me pull a face. I looked at Ferdinand annoyed, putting his arm around me, "I didn't say anything. I'll go and get some drinks before I get into any more trouble."

Manu and Aetius went as well to help, while Renee and Sophie came up to us smiling with Renee saying, "Nice to finally meet everyone. You do have a bit of a name for your temper Hannah, but that's nothing to be ashamed of."

I smiled, "I have calmed down a little," hearing Alira coughing in the background, turning to pull a face at her.

Sophie moved in closer, "You looked a little surprised that I had a female spirit animal Hannah?"

I nodded, "I must admit I was. I didn't realise there was female spirit animals."

Sophie looked at Renee lovingly, "Yes, they don't discriminate in Jardine. Not everyone is the same."

I smiled, "It's good to hear Sophie. As long as we are happy, that is what is important."

I looked over to Morag who was still chatting to Amelia and Charlotte nodding looking impressed at the compact. I shook my head, "Poor Morag, she will be hearing all the facts and figures from Charlotte about her invention."

Hine came close to me talking quietly, "Just watch that Lilith Hannah, there's just something about her I don't trust. If I could put a truth spell on her I would."

I looked thoughtfully, "I know how you feel Hine. I just feel that she is hiding something from me, especially about Ferdinand. I would like to put a truth spell on her as well, do you think we could?"

Hine shook her head, "No it's not allowed unless the elders approve of it."

I looked disappointed, "I wonder what her excuse is for being at the church."

Hine looked down so she couldn't be seen talking, "Oh probably some rubbish about being there investigating for the elders."

I groaned, "I will certainly keep an eye on her. I always feel she is trying to get me into trouble or cause trouble between Ferdinand and I. She was really annoying in Jardine popping in all the time. Morag had to tell her to stay away."

Hine turned again, "I heard you were attacked Hannah. I feel she has something to do with it. I just don't trust her."

Alira came up just as I was saying this, smiling, "Did you hear about the lions, Hine?"

I chuckled, "Oh come on Alira they were safe."

Hine smiled, "No I haven't heard that story, tell me."

Sophie and Renee came up to listen as Alira started to narrate with her flair, "We had been walking around Jardine when we first got there getting used to having lions and different animals walking around us; which is a bit nerve wracking at first when you're not used to it. This sister went pale a couple of times in fright."

I started to yawn, "Come on Alira get to the story."

Ferdinand came up with drinks "what are we talking about?"

Alira put her hands up, "Shush I'm telling the story. As I was saying, this Sister was going pale, watching all the lions walk around. Lilith decided Hannah needed a sleep after the big meal in Jardine so gave Hannah a fuzzy wuzzy cake—only a small one mind you!"

Ferdinand groaned, "Oh not this again."

Alira gave him a look, continuing, "Hannah having a bit of a sweet tooth and not knowing that it helps promote sleep, rather than being a dessert, ate it then wandered off into the bush." Sophie, Renee and Hine started to smile shaking their heads with Manu coming in to listen to the story.

Alira was in her element now with this audience, starting to act out what happened, putting her hands up to her face, "Ferdinand came over to us looking frantic because he couldn't find, Hannah."

Ferdinand put his arm around me and groaned, "Alira."

Alira put her hand up to stop him again, as she continued, "He couldn't feel where she was because she was naughty and had turned her thoughts off again!" Alira shook her head looking at me, "He set up a search party to go and look for her, because she didn't know her way around Jardine and could get lost." She put her hands up to her eyes as though searching with a concentrated look on her face, in the deep jungle, "We all went out into the bush in different directions searching for Hannah and calling her name."

She pointed to her chest looking confident, "With my indigenous background for tracking people I chose a path that looked like somewhere Hannah would go; so, I set off finding some tracks of little feet. Have you ever noticed how small her feet are; I mean how does she walk on them?"

I giggled, "Good grief Alira, we'll be drunk by the time you finish."

Alira put her hands up to her eyes again as though searching, "Now with great bravery, because I could still hear lions all around me, I continued to search for my sister. I looked down at the ground following these little footprints, when I came to a bush area that had big tall trees just beyond them. I saw something in the distance making me stop." This is where she was really dramatic now putting her hand up to her mouth. I rolled my eyes looking at Ferdinand who was pulling a face.

Alira played it out, "I bent down to find a shoe of a really small foot, then moved on finding another small shoe, then a pair of pants, which looked similar to the ones Hannah had been wearing, starting to get scared now." She put her hands up to her mouth as though biting her fingernails, "I then found a top. Now I had been hearing the sounds of lions all this time, hoping they would stay away from me as I had to find my sister!"

Sophie and Renee sighed, "Aww you're a very good sister."

Alira nodded, "That's right. Anyway, I carefully moved forward looking at a tree, only to see a pack of lions laying underneath it, sleeping. I crept back to a bush, as they started to stir and I'm not very good with lions, as I said."

Ferdinand had had enough and came in then, "You came running back to us screaming and as pale as white sheet saying that she had been eaten by lions."

Everyone that was listening burst out laughing including Morag who had joined the conversation, shaking her head.

Alira looked annoyed at Ferdinand, "I didn't come back screaming and I already told them I went pale. I thought perhaps with Hannah being from our world they might like the taste of something different and thought she had been eaten by them."

This made some of them shake their heads again laughing with Morag coming in now, "Our lions wouldn't eat anyone. Hannah was naked and fast asleep in amongst the lions, which made it a little difficult to get her out without disturbing them too much as they tend to get grumpy. I might add here to that she used to do that all the time when she was little."

I felt a blush coming on, "Oh dear."

My girls were standing listening as well with Charlotte commenting, "We had to cover all the men's eyes, except for Ferdinand's of course because he had already been there; if you know what I mean."

I looked away embarrassed, "Charlotte do you have to."

Amelia came in now, "Luckily Morag lifted her out of the lions, putting her gently into a blanket for Ferdinand to take back to their bungalow. We had to comfort Alira and bring her colour back to normal."

Alira shook her head, "I was worried for my sister, what do you expect."

Ferdinand shook his head, "After that dramatic story, I'll go and get some food to snack on."

I nodded giving him a little kiss, "Ok honey."

Hine came up to me after he had left, "With that story and how you thought Lilith is trying to get you into trouble, I think we might change our plan if Lilith comes in. I am sure she will, so just follow us, Hannah."

I looked confused at Hine, "What do you mean?"

Hine nudged me, "Speak of the devil," noticing Lilith and Cara walking in with Ferdinand who was carrying some food. Lilith who was helping to carry some of the food was chatting away to him, when he looked up to me with an annoyed look on his face. Hine smiled, "Ah there you go. She couldn't wait to get her bit in. Just do as I ask, Hannah."

Once Lilith and Cara reached the group, Sophie and Renee went up to Cara greeting her while Hine and Amelia went over to Lilith greeting her, making her look surprised.

Hine was laughing now, "Alira was just telling us of the prank you played on Hannah in Jardine Lilith," nudging her (perhaps a little harder than she should have). "It looks like you're one of us after all."

Lilith looked confused, "What do you mean, Hine?"

Ferdinand came over to me not looking very happy, going to say something when Hine interrupted, "We just want to say something before the wrong people get blamed."

Morag looked at Cara then at the rest of us not sure what was going on. Ferdinand was holding my hand, "Is there something you need to tell me?"

I got annoyed, letting his hand go but he took it back, noticing Lilith was starting to smirk.

Hine could see this happening, carrying on to get everyone's attention, "We played a little prank on some of the people in the church today."

She turned to look at Morag whose smile had faded, "It was our idea not Hannah's or Alira's; they were just bystanders. We saw Lilith there at the church realising she had got the message to come and have some fun as well. There was no harm done, but it did get a bit of attention and we are sorry for that."

Morag shook her head chuckling, "Well you are all a bit naughty doing this, but it is done now. I am surprised you were there Lilith, as I thought you had other things to do?"

Lilith was stumbling now, realising she couldn't get out of it, "I didn't know what they were actually going to do, Morag?"

Hine put her hands around her shoulders, "Oh don't be so modest, Lilith, you had some good ideas there," and laughed.

Sophie joined in, "Gee Lilith you played the part well. That priest didn't even suspect you, even though you didn't have a disguise on, like the rest of us."

Cara was standing there quietly listening to all the comments made then moved over to Lilith glowering, "I'm glad I came to check it out before you got anyone into real trouble, Lilith."

Amelia went up to Cara, "Would you like something to drink Cara, we're having one more for the road?"

Cara nodded, relieved, "Yes I think I will, thanks Amelia."

Ferdinand pulled me aside looking regretful, "I'm sorry."

I put my head down, "It's alright. I guess we shouldn't have done it really, but I had no idea they were going to do it until it happened. I was going to tell you later when we were alone."

He gave me a cuddle, "Come on we'll have one more drink and go home."

Amelia got a drink for Lilith putting a little bit of sparkle in it, coming back from the bar handing it to her, "Here you go Lilith you may as well have one with us before we go."

She looked frustrated but accepted it, "Thanks Amelia. I didn't get a message that you were doing anything in the church today. I don't know where Hine got that from?"

Amelia shrugged her shoulders looking curious, "Well why were you there then?"

Lilith looked nervous, "I was doing some work for the elders that was all."

Morag and Cara came over to Lilith talking to her quietly, while Lilith sipped on her drink not looking very happy.

Morag and Cara took off first giving everyone a hug, telling everyone to behave themselves. Lilith was starting to get a bit happier now with the special wine Amelia had given her.

I went over to Alira, Hine, Sophie, Amelia and Charlotte to thank them for the way they dealt with it all. Hine grinned indicating to look at something, as I turned to find Lilith, smiling making her way over to Ferdinand, who was talking to Aetius and Shiro.

Lilith put her hand on his arm to get his attention; he stopped talking to Shiro not looking very happy, "Yes Lilith?"

She giggled, "I wasn't there as part of their group, you know."

He just shook his head, "So you keep saying Lilith. I don't know what to believe from you at the moment."

Shiro looked at her, "I thought you were spending time with Pardus today?"

She giggled again, "I suppose I should bring him in" rubbing her tattoo with Pardus appearing.

Ferdinand smiled at Pardus, "Hi there, I haven't seen you for a while."

I looked at Hine, "He looks like a nice guy I don't know why she doesn't want him around."

Hine chuckled, "Well if Ferdinand wasn't around, he probably would be."

It disappointed me, "Oh you noticed it as well."

Hine nodded putting her arm through mine, "Yes, but don't worry, Ferdinand only has eyes for you."

I leaned into her smiling, "Thanks Hine."

Alira came up happy, "Come on you lot I think it's time to go home."

We all took off taking our shopping with us. Ferdinand and I landed in the unit with him holding me around the waist.

I went to move away when he pulled me into him giving me a passionate kiss then moving to my neck, "Ferdinand wait. I've bought something to show you."

He continued to kiss my neck hungrily making me groan, "You don't need anything else," picking me up taking me to the bedroom kissing my lips.

Afterwards he lay there, looking at me, "What did you buy?"

I turned to look at him exhausted, sighing, "Well it was supposed to be something to turn you on." I got up to get it, coming back in with a black teddy negligee with skimpy knickers on going over to the bed trying to look sexy, but not getting the reaction I hoped.

He went quiet, as though he had something come into his thoughts, then pulled me into him taking it off, "You don't need to buy those things to excite me honey."

I felt a bit confused with his reaction as he threw it to the side of the room giving me a cuddle, "Do you not like those type of things, Ferdinand?"

He looked at me seriously, "No, especially on you. I like you just the way you are."

He must have realised he'd upset me, smiling giving me a kiss on the neck calming down, "Don't be upset. I just don't like those type of things that is all. Come on we'll have some dinner and have an early night."

I resigned myself thinking, '*I guess everyone doesn't like those type of things and he's one of them.*'

I had a shower watching a bit the news while he cooked dinner with the report from the church coming on. I went to flick it over with him calling out, "Leave it there I want to see what you all got up to."

I groaned getting up to go and do something else but he came over grabbing me around the waist, "I want you to tell me which one was you?"

I giggled trying to take his hands off me but he wasn't letting go, so I gave up, "Alright see if you can guess?"

He moved over to the sofa, putting me on his lap, "Stay there and show me which one was you."

I leaned into him, "I'm probably not there I was careful to stay away from the cameras." It wasn't until we were outside the church and I had put a whirlwind up, holding Alira that I saw us, giggling.

He wrapped his arms around me pointing to us, "Those two old ladies are you and Alira?"

I nodded, "She fell over her old lady shoes and I was helping her up."

I looked at it closely thinking there was something odd in there but I just couldn't work it out. The whirlwind came up with Ferdinand tapping my leg, "I know that is your trick madam, I've seen you do that before."

I nodded, "I thought it would take the cameras off us but obviously it didn't work that well."

He laughed, "You both look funny; I don't think I would have recognised you."

I turned changing into the disguise I had on, saying in an elderly voice, "See dear this is what you have to expect when I grow old."

He burst out laughing, "You silly woman, change back."

Ferdinand stood up turning me around, "No more though, otherwise you'll get yourself into trouble."

I got a little annoyed, "Come on Ferdinand if they attack us, I'm not just sitting back or running away and hiding."

He looked at me seriously now, "You call me if anything else happens, do you hear me. I know you are getting stronger in your magic but that is why I am here."

I sighed a bit frustrated with him looking at me again, "Hannah do you understand?"

I nodded, "Ja liebes (yes dear)."

He pulled me into him, "Come on dinner is ready."

We got into bed having a cuddle, "Can we take Kimba to Jardine on the weekend? I feel guilty leaving her on her on her own all the time."

He was starting to drop off sounding sleepy, "Yes she can come in with me," and yawning, "I'm sure she will love it there."

I lay there in the dark listening to his breathing change thinking about that news article I had watched with him. There was something odd about it but I just couldn't put my finger on it. I might see if I can bring it up on my phone tomorrow and have another look at it.

Chapter 20

I got to work ready for another day. At least with all the things I had put into place I could do some interesting things rather than sit there and type boring letters and reports.

Tom was in a great mood for a Monday, saying he and his wife had had a great sleep because the baby was starting to settle down nicely now. He smiled at me, "I told my wife about the little talk we had had and she thought it made very good sense; so we have decided to follow your advice and just think in the moment. It certainly seems to be working as far as the baby is concerned, sleeping a lot better."

I felt a little embarrassed, "Thanks Tom, it's good to see that things are settling down for you both."

He finished his work by 11.00a.m feeling pleased with himself, "I'll see you tomorrow, Hannah."

I was already typing some of his letters, "See you, Tom." I finished the one I had started then I completed the rest magically waiting a couple of hours to send them to him otherwise he would start asking questions.

I went into his office to do some of the filing, doing it magically, giving me a moment to daydream out the window thinking of that news report while playing with a mini whirlwind in my hand. Alira stood at the door shaking her head, making me jump. "You're naughty, Hannah, with your flying filing and a whirlwind."

I chuckled, "I know it just gives me time to think."

She came into the office, "Do you want to do some meditation today?"

I nodded a little distracted still, "Yes that will be great. Do you want to go to the same place?"

She came over to me, "What's on your mind?"

I turned to look at her, "I was watching the news report on our little activity yesterday and I noticed something unusual when I watched it. It was almost as though I saw someone, I knew but then they were gone. I mean they can't do that on the TV."

Alira looked confused, "I don't understand what you mean."

I thought about it, "You know how you might see something out of the corner of your eye, for me it is usually a ghost, but I know you don't like those, but this wasn't a ghost."

Alira nodded, "yes, I know what you mean. Who do you think you saw?"

I came over to her, "That's just it, I can't quite work it out. It was almost a mixture of two people, one I wasn't sure who but the other one was similar to Ferdinand, but it wasn't him. I don't know it was weird. I noticed it also appeared to be when Lilith was around."

Alira shook her head, "Well see if you can pull the news broadcast up again and have a look at it. I had better get back to my desk. I'll see you at our usual spot."

I went back out to my computer once the filing had been finished deciding to bring the news report up on the bigger screen to see if I could see it better. I put the incident into the search engine with the headline coming up. I clicked on it getting ready to watch it when a message came up, *"This news broadcast is no longer available."*

I tried to search it another way with the same message coming up. A thought came to my head, *'Maybe work has put a firewall up and doesn't allow those type of things to come in.'* I got my phone out searching it on a couple of sites with the same message coming up. I shook my head, *'That's strange.'*

I decided not to dwell on it for now, putting my hologram up so I could go and do some work on the family book in Tom's room. I sat in my usual spot away from the door putting the orb up then bringing in the book. I thought about the protection Morag had given me on the bracelet that Ferdinand had given me.

I might see if the book can duplicate it and strengthen it giving not only me but my girls some extra protection. I took the bracelet off placing it on top of the unopened book to see if anything happened. I sat there waiting to see if anything happened and was about to pick it up when a dazzling light flashed around the bracelet.

The bracelet then floated in the air with the pages of the book flipping to a spell *"this bracelet from another land is now stronger in the protection of Hannah on her hand. Wear it always to keep her safe from those who wish to harm her being foe or evil in air, water, fire and earth their spells will now be repelled and dispersed."*

I put it on the page saying the spell seeing another dazzling light form around the bracelet. I put it back on feeling a jolt go through me with a white light form around me then disappear. I felt happy with that, intending to tell my girls to do it with their piece of jewellery they had for protection.

I then went to see if I could find the sealed section that Amelia had spoken about. I strolled through the pages looking at them finally coming to a small old-fashioned envelope sitting in the middle of the page with a wax seal on it. I felt a little confused that I hadn't noticed it before, putting my hand on the seal when a message came up, *"The Dragĕ woman requires a password and cannot enter without the one who has put this here to permit entry."*

I sat back, "Oh good grief, a password. I'm not very good at working those out." I sighed, *'Well I might have to leave that one for the girls to play with or find the one who put it in there to let me go in. Mmm that's going to be difficult because the family history is missing.'*

I heard a noise making me look at my phone first to see if someone was around my desk but then I realised Ferdinand had arrived in the room saying quietly, "Hannah, are you in here?"

I smiled putting the book away then closing down the orb allowing him to see me sitting in the chair. He came over to me with my lunch in his hand, "I thought you might be in here somewhere with your hologram out there. You forgot your lunch again." I stood up, giving him a kiss, "Oh I did too, thanks for bringing it in. It's nearly lunch time as well; so just in time."

He looked at me, "You've been playing with your magic again, haven't you? I can see you're glowing a little."

I put my arm up, "I just strengthened the protection on the bracelet that you gave me, that's probably why I'm glowing."

He came closer looking at the bracelet then putting his arm around my waist, "Mm it makes you look appetising, maybe I should have you for my lunch."

I slapped him playfully on the arm, "Ferdinand, I think you need to go on a diet," not listening, he started to kiss me moving to my lips. He was working both of us up, "Put the orb around us, Hannah."

I groaned, "I shouldn't," then I thought, *'Oh heck'* putting the orb around us.

We stood in the orb naked and depleted, "Ferdinand, you're a naughty boy. I have to go and do meditation with Alira now."

He chuckled as he pushed some hair away from my face, "It takes two to tango, isn't that the saying? You could have said 'no'."

I got dressed, "Well, I did say you needed to go on a diet but you didn't listen. Maybe you should join me doing some swimming to get rid of some of that energy."

I rubbed my hands over his chest noticing some hairs growing there, "Mmm your muscle tone is still good for an old guy though."

He grinned taking my hand off his chest giving it a little kiss, "Thank you— I think?" He got dressed, "I'll see how I feel, just let me know when you go to the pool next. I'll see you tonight in the usual spot."

I took the orb down, "Ok" going over to the mirror in Tom's office straightening myself out so I could go to meditation with Alira. I took the hologram down and took my lunch with me to Mrs Macquarie's Chair meeting Alira there. She looked at my lunch, "You usually eat it before you come, did you get busy with your magic or something?" I smiled, "In a way. Ferdinand dropped in because I had forgotten it, deciding he wanted me for lunch."

Alira burst out laughing, "That'll teach you for learning to do those orbs. Gee he is getting randy though, I don't know how you keep up."

I sat down, "He's starting to exhaust me. You know I have noticed every time I do a bit of family magic it appears to stir him up. Do you think there is a connection there?"

Alira sat down thinking about it, "Well that is quite possible. You have connected both of us to you, just don't expect me to be intimate with you that is all."

It was my turn to burst out laughing now, "Don't worry Sister. I am happy with the way our relationship is."

Alira looked at me, "What were you doing when he came in?"

I showed her the bracelet as I ate some of my lunch, "I was strengthening the protection on this bracelet, which did put a white glow around me. He reckons he could see me glowing, so maybe that's what he could see and it turns him on. I was looking at a section that the girls had mentioned but I couldn't get into it anyway, that's when he came in."

Alira shook her head, "I don't know Hannah, maybe you need to talk to Morag or another elder about it. Did you manage to get to have a look at that news article again?"

I shook my head finishing off my lunch, "No I couldn't get into it. I tried a couple of different ways but it kept saying it wasn't available anymore. I won't worry about it for now. Well, I've finished that are you ready to do some meditation?"

Alira nodded bringing in something to sit on, "Ok let's do this."

I don't like feeling rushed so it took me a little longer to settle into my meditation eventually going deep, in the boat floating along the stream relaxed and feeling carefree. I started to hear a noise that was upsetting me making me sit up to look around me. I couldn't see anything within my meditation that was happening but my breathing was coming back to me taking me out of the meditation quite quickly, when the noise became more recognisable.

It was Alira's voice trying to bring me out of the meditation as I opened my eyes breathing heavily, looking around me frantically for Alira, only to see a man holding Alira with a wand to her neck, backing away. I touched my tattoo, then slowly got up with my hands up, "What do you want?"

A tall Aboriginal man with a black track suit and runners on said, "Just this one will do me fine, thanks."

I smiled, "She's my sister. I can't let you do that."

He looked nervous treading carefully because there were large fig tree roots sticking out from the ground, making it uneven.

Ferdinand arrived behind him looking at me putting his finger up to his mouth to be quiet. I shook my head, "You know she isn't going to give you anything, so you may as well let her go and be on your way."

Alira was looking scared, "Hannah just be careful he has something dark in him."

Ferdinand moved in quickly grabbing his arms so he would lose his grip on Alira.

The guy struggled to try and hold onto Alira, who was trying to break free, turning enough to point the wand at Ferdinand. It sent a bolt of magic towards him, hitting him in the leg, making him fall to the ground in pain.

He put his wand up again about to send another bolt towards Ferdinand which allowed me to get closer to him. I put my hand up crushing his wand in his hand, which sent the spell he was about to send to Ferdinand go down his arm through his body and into Alira.

I lunged forward, getting Alira's hand tapping her tattoo to get Fia in, who came instantly. The attacker was laying there unconscious telling Fia to help

Alira while I checked on Ferdinand. I went over to him with my heart racing "Ferdinand are you alright?"

He groaned holding his leg, "Oh shit," pulling his trouser leg up to have a look at it.

There was a big gash on it with blood seeping out. I put my hand over it stemming the bleeding magically as much as I could. He nodded, "That will do, go and check on Alira."

I got up with Ferdinand's blood on my hands getting angry, while Fia was holding Alira who wasn't looking too good. The attacker was starting to stir, making my anger flair. I pointed to him with all my anger binding him in a red laser light around his body picking him up in the air, "What have you put on my sister?"

He started to struggle and scream, "I don't know what you're talking about."

Ferdinand sat up, "Hannah calm down."

I didn't listen to him looking deadly at the attacker twisting my hand which made the bonds tighten saying in a deep voice, "Tell me now!"

Fia was looking at Ferdinand then back to Alira who was coming around now, "Hannah Alira is coming around."

I was too angry staring at the attacker who was laughing hysterically now, "You white fellas don't know our ways."

I smiled wickedly, "That's where you're mistaken, Alira has taught me some of your ways."

He looked nervously at me as I tightened the bonds one more notch which made him scream.

Alira started to talk, "Hannah I need to call Mum, don't do anything else."

I turned to look at her, calming myself enough but still holding the attacker where he was, "Ok Alira do it now."

Morag and Cara came in along with Alira's mother Yindi looking at the scene. Yindi went straight over to Alira checking her, while Morag came over to me and Cara went over to Ferdinand.

Morag calmly came over to me putting her hand on my shoulder sending a calming spell through me, "Feeling better, Hannah?"

I smiled, "A little Morag. I suppose you want me to put him down now."

She smiled, "Yes please."

I lowered him to the grown dropping him the last half metre hearing him groan as he hit the ground.

Yindi came over to me, "You must be Hannah, nice to finally meet you."

She shook her head, "I'm glad I'm not on the end of that anger." Yindi went over to the attacker speaking Aboriginal to him, finding out he had tried to put a curse through his wand which went back through him when I crushed his wand.

He was laughing weakly, "I've probably just killed myself."

Yindi knew what she was dealing with now, coming up to me and Morag, "I'll take Alira home, I know how to deal with this, she will feel a bit off for a couple of days. You may as well let him go; he won't last much longer. He's sent a deadly curse through to himself. You were lucky it didn't hit Ferdinand."

Ferdinand got up with Cara helping him, hobbling over to me and Morag, "What was that?"

I turned to look at him, "You were just about cursed dear."

He sighed, "Luckily that didn't hit then. Is Alira alright?"

She was being helped up by Fia and Yindi, "yes, I'm alright for now thanks, Ferdinand." She turned to look at me then the attacker who still had the laser binding on him, "You may as well let him go Sister, he's a goner."

I was feeling calmer now, "Alright, you go first I don't want him trying anything else on you."

She chuckled, "You're a stubborn woman, but I love you. Can you let work know I won't be back and I'll talk to you later."

I went over and gave her a hug, "Ok see you later. I'll tell them at work you went home sick." Yindi, Fia and Alira took off. I hadn't thought about the people walking past us with a small group gathering over by the footpath. Morag turned to look, "Don't worry, we will sort them out. Just get rid of that off him and don't do anything else, Hannah."

I could feel a bit of anger flaring again, "Can't I try Charlotte's magitrap on him?"

Morag gave me a look my mother used to give me, "No Hannah, you heard Yindi, he's cursed himself."

I took a deep breath, "Fine!" I turned taking the binding off him, hearing him sigh with relief, "Agghh you bitch I was after you but I couldn't touch you." That was enough to stir me up again, growling at him, sending a bolt to him which made him fly into the water screaming. He was floundering in the water as the waves from the ferries buffeted him trying to get back to the shore.

I could hear Morag groan, "Hannah that's enough! Ferdinand, can you take Hannah where she needs to go and make sure she is alright."

I smiled, "Well that feels better."

He hobbled over to me looking weary, "Come here, Hannah. Do you want to go back to work?"

I looked at him, "Yes I better go and sort things out then I might go home early."

He held my hand landing in Tom's office pulling me up to him, "Why can't you do as you're told."

I grinned wickedly, "Because that's not me and you know it. How is your leg?"

He walked over to Tom's chair, sitting down, "It's alright now, Cara did some more healing on it."

I still had his blood on my hands, "I'll go and wash this off and call into HR and let them know about Alira and that I'm going home early. The only other thing I have to do is send the work to Tom and then I'll go. Do you want to meet me at home?"

He shook his head, "No I'll go out to the reception area and wait for you there."

I went up to him, "I'll be alright Ferdinand you are looking a bit tired, why don't you go home and have a rest and I'll meet you there."

He was getting irritated, "I said I will meet you out in the reception area, now go, so we can get going."

I backed off, "Alright, I was just asking."

I went and washed my hands dropping into HR and then sending the documents off to Tom. I was just turning everything off when I got a call from Tracey telling me that Ferdinand was there.

I went out noticing he looked a bit pale sitting quietly on the sofa, getting up when I came out, "See you, Tracey." Tracey looked a little unsure what was going on between us two, "See you later, Hannah."

We got home with Ferdinand looking down at me giving me a hug, "I'm going to have a shower. I might order pizza for dinner."

I hugged him, "I can cook something if you want?"

He chuckled, "No I'm happy to have pizza."

I knew he was a little grumpy so I didn't annoy him too much "alright I'm happy with that." I went and opened the balcony door and put some track pants and a t-shirt on getting comfortable on the sofa with Kimba. He came out in his shorts and t-shirt coming to sit on the sofa with me. I pulled him down putting his head on my lap, "Are you alright?"

He still didn't look very happy, "Yes, I'm alright. This is just another reason to go to Jardine, Hannah."

I sat there stroking his hair, "Let's just have a nice time on the weekend and see what we can sort out while we are there."

He sat up looking at me a bit happier, "Do you mean that?"

I nodded, "Yes, but I can't say I'll be going next week or anything."

He smiled laying back down, "That gives me something to look forward to at least, Hannah."

He looked at the bracelet I had on, "At least that worked for you today. Just as well you increased the protection on it."

I sighed, "Yes. I must let the girls know as well to increase their protection."

Kimba jumped onto his chest making a fuss of him while I text the girls letting them know what had happened today and about the protection.

I continued to stroke his hair relaxing him and eventually falling asleep. I smiled as I watched his chest rise and fall. *'I still find it hard to believe a few months ago there wasn't anyone here for me other my cat Kimba.'* I put a blanket on Ferdinand as he dropped off to a deeper sleep. I turned the TV on leaving the sound down low, thinking about that news report from yesterday and how I thought I had seen someone similar to Ferdinand.

This also brought thoughts on my brother for some reason. I went onto my phone looking at FB to do a search on my brother to see what he was up to. I hadn't seen him for a long time, basically because we don't agree on anything, especially after Mum and Dad passed.

I thought I might go and see him, to see if he knew anything more about the family. I searched on FB looking at his profile on there but he had closed it off to only certain friends and I was obviously not one of them. I decided to message him, to see if I could go and have a chat one day at lunch time. I didn't want to go to his house or him to come here as I don't get on with his wife Deirdre. I dozed off while sitting there, waking at the sound of a text coming in on my phone, looking around to find the room starting to darken as the sun went down.

Ferdinand started to move, as well getting up to sit next to me, smiling at me giving me a kiss, "Did you drop off as well?"

I nodded, "Yes, must have been all the excitement of today."

Ferdinand frowned, "yes, the kind of excitement I don't want any more. I'm hungry I'll order the pizza, anything in particular?"

I shook my head, "No you can choose."

"I looked at my phone finding a message from my brother saying he can meet either tomorrow or Thursday for lunch for just half an hour."

Ferdinand shut the door and came back sitting near me pulling the blanket around us, "Mm it's cooled down, give me a cuddle."

I leaned into him, "I've decided to go and see my brother to ask him a couple of things about the family. Do you want to come and meet him?"

He looked surprised, "Oh what's brought this on?"

I looked at him, "I just thought he might know something else about the family that I wasn't told. Morag as has asked me to research it. I'll warn you though it may not be pleasant as we don't get on."

He thought about it, "Yes I'll come, but I'll warn you, he has seen me before."

I turned to look at him surprised, "When?"

He smiled, "When you were a normal little girl."

I slapped him, "Stop being nasty."

He gave me a kiss, "He caught me dropping you off once when we had been flying and he has also seen me around when you were playing hockey or doing other stuff that your parents made you do, to keep you busy and out of trouble."

I sat there stunned "the mongrel never said anything to me either. You can see whose side he was on then."

Ferdinand looked at me seriously, "It's no use going to see him if you're going to be angry about that, it will just make it worse. He might not like me around either as I was the *bad* guy."

I sighed, "yes, I know. I will try to be good and I don't care if he doesn't like you around, I don't like his wife either so we'll be even."

I sat there still shocked getting up, "I'm just going to have a shower before the food comes, keep this spot warm for me."

As I was eating the pizza, I got my phone, "Which day suits you, tomorrow or Thursday to go and see Christian."

Ferdinand was watching TV enjoying his pizza and not concentrating, "What oh, any day suits me. I can make the time."

I thought about it, "I think I might get it over and done with tomorrow, that way if anything goes horrible it won't spoil my weekend."

He shook his head, "Don't go there angry, Hannah."

I sighed, "No I won't."

I text back saying tomorrow suited me better. He got back reasonably quickly saying, "See you at 1.00p.m." Humph, "No looking forward to seeing you then or anything."

Ferdinand got up shaking his head, "This is going to be interesting; do you want a drink of anything?"

I screwed my face up thinking about the meeting, "I think I'll have a wine thanks." I sent Alira a text to see how she was, getting a reply saying, "She was alright, just sleeping it off."

We got into bed with Ferdinand looking a bit happier about Jardine at least. I checked his leg to make sure it was alright, "Cara did a good job on it, you were lucky. I might get something for you for protection."

He pulled me into him, "Stop fussing, besides you won't need it soon."

I smiled, "Yes I know, but until we get there, I'd like to think you were safe as well."

He gave me a kiss, "we'll have a look at something in Jardine for me to wear."

Ferdinand fell asleep quite quickly considering he had had that nap earlier, but I started thinking about the meeting with my brother making me feel a bit restless. I eventually fell asleep dreaming of when we were growing up, how he always used to be horrible to me until I went marching and had all the girls around; he was a bit friendlier then—well until he met Deirdre.

I woke about 3.00a.m. needing to go to the toilet deciding to magicae out of the bed so I wouldn't disturb Ferdinand landing near the toilet. I never put the light on because I didn't like it hitting my eyes when I was going back to sleep, plus the bathroom was light enough to see what I needed to see.

I did what I had to coming back out to the lounge feeling a cold draft go past me with the hairs on my neck go up.

I stood still waiting to hear a voice, "Hallo Hannah (hello Hannah)." I looked around but couldn't see anything, "Hallo Oma (hi grandma)."

I could feel a coolness move closer to me, "Es ist eine Tante (it's your aunt)."

I hesitated, "Ich wusste nicht, dass ich einen hatte, der Deutsch sprach (I didn't know I had one that spoke German)." A light chuckle came out of the darkness of the room, "Wir sin uns sehr ähnlich, die seltsamen deshalb (we are very much alike, the weird ones that is why)." I looked confused, "Wie heißen sie (what is your name)?"

I could see a shadowy form starting to appear, "Mein name ist Adalinda (my name is Adalinda)."

I moved closer to the shadow, "Ich war ein uneheliches baby, deshalb has du noch nichts von mir gehört (I was an illegitimate baby that is why you haven't heard of me)."

I couldn't remember being told about anyone being born out of wedlock, "Wer war deine mutter (who was your mother)?"

I heard Ferdinand move, who must have been standing there listening to some of it, "Mit wem redest du mit Hannah (who are you talking to Hannah)?"

I saw her move, "Sei vorsichtig Hannah (be careful Hannah)" then she disappeared.

He came out to me worried, "Who were you talking to?"

I looked up into his eyes that I could just see in the dim light, noticing they were worried with a little bit of anger in there, "An aunt apparently. I didn't know I had one."

He rubbed his face taking my hand leading me back to bed, "Come back to bed, did she say her name?"

I followed him back to the bedroom, "Yes. Adalinda."

He stopped as though he had heard that name before then groaned trying to make light of it, "I wish your relatives would pick better times to chat."

He snuggled into my back, "I woke up finding you gone and I got worried."

I yawned, "Never a dull moment with this family, isn't it?"

He chuckled, "No."

I woke to the alarm finding Ferdinand up already making some breakfast. I got up going out to him, "Did you have a good sleep?"

He nodded, "Yes apart from the little interruption from your ghost."

I moved over to the barstool sitting down, "Yes there are some strange things coming through at the moment. I guess they'll make sense in the end," going to the bathroom.

We had breakfast, noticing Ferdinand was a little quiet. I didn't really feel like talking too much either with the impending visit to my brother on my mind. I got ready to go, "Are you still coming to meet my brother today?"

He nodded, "Yes I'll meet you downstairs and we can take off from there."

I got to work with Tom excited at how things were settling down for him and his new baby. He had heard about what had happened with Alira asking if I was alright.

I nodded, "I'm fine, Tom. It looks as though you can't go and do some meditation in the park anymore these days."

He looked surprised, "Oh I didn't realise that is what you were doing there. Do you do that quite often Hannah?"

I looked a bit distant, "Yes, I've done it for years Tom. It's a good relaxation method, you should try it."

I got through the rest of the work ready to go and meet Ferdinand and then my brother, starting to feel a little anxious. I got downstairs meeting Ferdinand, who looked nice in a blue shirt and jeans, giving him a kiss. He took my hand, "Are you ready?"

I nodded, "Yes let's get it over and done with."

We landed near Christian's work, which was a small office in the west of the city, for a construction firm. We walked up holding hands going up to his office in the lift with Ferdinand looking at me smiling, "It'll be alright. Just don't get angry that is all."

I looked downcast at him, "I'll try Ferdinand."

We got to his floor going out to let the receptionist know who I was, with an odd look coming over her face, "Oh you're his sister?"

I nodded with a tight smile, "Yes, just let him know I am here thanks."

She picked up the phone a bit annoyed, "Apparently your sister and a friend are here Christian."

I stood there waiting, starting to fidget because he was taking his time, when he finally came out. He came out looking at me then at Ferdinand, not smiling, showing us into a small office to the side of the reception area.

His hair had gone quite white from age and his face was red and puffy from overeating and stress. His suit looked ill-fitting because of his weight. He was a lot taller than me with different coloured eyes, making we wonder how I was his sister a lot of the time. He indicated to take a seat not bothering to introduce himself to Ferdinand. We sat down, as I said to him, "I'd like you to meet Ferdinand, my boyfriend, Christian."

He put his head on the side with a sarcastic look on his face, "I know who he is Hannah and I know he's *not* your boyfriend."

I looked at Ferdinand who was trying to hold his tongue, but couldn't, calmly saying, "I am actually Christian. I see you haven't changed much." This made Christian look uncomfortable, shifting in his chair, ignoring Ferdinand, "What do you want Hannah?"

I took a deep breath to calm myself, 'I am doing some family research and was wanting to know if you knew anything?'

He rolled his eyes, "Oh not this rubbish again! I suppose you're trying to work out where the *'magic'* came from. I told Mum she should have kept you on that medication that you were on when you were younger."

Ferdinand squeezed my hand as I felt myself burr up, trying to stay calm, "I was trying to work out for my daughter's sake and also to see how I ended up with an arsehole of a brother like you?"

I could hear a low groan come from Ferdinand, as he leaned back in his chair.

Christian shook his head, getting up, "You haven't changed, Hannah. If I was you, I would check on your parentage because you are still weird?"

That was it! I stood up, pushing my hand out, sending him up in the air with a laser light going around him, with a terrified look on his face. He was struggling against it, "You bitch, put me down."

Ferdinand just sat there calmly, "Hannah put him down."

I shook my head calming myself but kept Christian where he was, "Now brother dear, what is it you need to tell me, or should I float you out the window to get a better view."

He looked at Ferdinand for support, "Can't you control her?"

Ferdinand shook his head, "Sometimes, but according to you I'm not her boyfriend, so I'll just make sure she doesn't kill you at this stage."

I tightened the laser a bit more as he squealed, "Hannah let me go or I'll get you committed."

I chuckled, "Oh like you tried when I was younger dear brother. No, you don't have any power over me anymore. Just tell me what I want to know and I'll say goodbye."

He struggled a bit more looking at Ferdinand, who just sat there smiling, "Alright I'll tell you what I know then you can both bugger off. All I know is that Dad isn't your father that is why you were a lot different to us. That some of the family came from Norway and Germany on Mum's side."

I sat there shocked, "So do you know who my father was?"

He was struggling trying not to answer out of pleasure, "Tell me Christian."

He relented, "All I know is it happened when Mum and Dad went on holiday overseas and that Mum came back pregnant with you."

I sat down confused, "But Dad was on my birth certificate as my father. It was there when I applied for my passport."

He chuckled cruelly, "That is easily fixed and Mum didn't want her precious daughter being called a *bastard*!"

I growled, "You're the only bastard in this family," moving my hand up and down watching him hit the roof and then the floor, like a bouncing ball.

Ferdinand stood up calmly still, "Come on Hannah that's enough. Let him go and we'll get out of here." The receptionist, who could hear the commotion coming from the office, opened the door looking in horror. Her mouth fell open as she watched Christian being bounced around the room, "What is going on it here? I'll call the police."

I sent a chant to her, freezing her in her tracks, smiling at Christian who looked in horror, "What have you done to her?"

I realised that they were more than co-workers by the look on his face, "Oh she's your latest conquest I see Christian. I haven't hurt her, something you will do later no doubt. Send Deirdre my regards." I let him down with a flop onto the seat, "I bet you wish you had learned the *magic* now, Christian." I flicked a chant over the receptionist, so she didn't remember anything that had happened. I took Ferdinand's hand smiling at Christian disappearing in front of him, watching as a stunned look came over his face as we disappeared.

We got back to Circular Quay with Ferdinand hugging me, "You did quite well considering."

I hugged him, "I was surprised you didn't try to stop me actually."

He pulled back from me, "I know what he is like and he doesn't appear to have changed. He was part of the problem between you and I, so I thought I would let you have some fun. Like I said, as long as you didn't kill him, that was all I was worried about."

I gave him a kiss, "Thanks for being there for me. Another question with regard to the family to think about now I guess."

He looked at me thoughtfully, "Try not to overthink it too much, I am sure it will come to light eventually."

He gave me a kiss, "I'll see you tonight."

He took off as I turned to look at the building where I worked, not wanting to go up just yet because I was still a bit wound up.

I checked the time, thinking I have a little time, I might go for a walk around the Rocks as I had a ghost that I would bump into from time to time. I magicae over to the nurses walk, going down the alley way, trying to relax myself.

There weren't many people around so I just took my time walking, when I heard a quiet voice, "Hi Hannah."

I smiled stopping to look around, "Hi Martha, how are you?"

I followed the voice noticing a shadowy figure at the end of the alleyway appearing "I am good Hannah. There has been a bit of gossip going on that you are a witch."

I chuckled, "Wow I'm the subject of gossip in a lot of places by the look of it. I have magic in me, but I don't call myself a witch."

Martha chuckled moving closer, turning her head to make sure no one else was coming down the alleyway, "Well as long as you're not harming anyone that is all that is important Hannah. There was a man here by the name of Stefan who wanted to talk to you, but he has gone again."

I shook my head, "This is turning out to be a strange week with a lot people turning up I didn't know about. Well, I had better get back to work Martha, thanks for the chat."

Martha disappeared into the walls of the alleyway, "Take care, Hannah."

I looked around to see if anyone was around then magicae back to the Quay walking up to the office. I took a deep breath, still not really wanting to go up, but I forced myself, thinking I could at least do some research once I had sent off the work to Tom.

I managed to calm down, sorting out Tom's work. I rang the girls telling them what happened at the meeting with Christian along with the information he had given me. Both of them were pissed off saying, they were glad they didn't have much to do with him. Amelia tried to comfort me, "Well at least you know why you were always different to them, Mum."

I chuckled, "Yes, it certainly explains some of it."

I was feeling a bit weary now, so I put the hologram up and went and did some meditation in Tom's office. Nothing came up just a relaxing time to calm me down thank goodness.

I came out of the office still having half an hour until I went home. I took the hologram off sitting at the computer fiddling around with the computer when a woman came up to my desk. I looked up at her frowning thinking, '*I know you from somewhere*' when she smiled a tight grin, "Are you Hannah Dragé?"

I looked at her still thinking, '*Where have I seen you before?*'

I smiled back, "Yes, I am."

She stood there looking at me as though she was scanning me, raising an eyebrow, "I am Korvin Smada's Secretary Jacinta Tampler. He would like to see you next week in his office."

I realised who she was then, looking mystified, "Why does he want to see me?"

She shrugged her shoulders looking at what I was wearing, "Who knows. I will send you a meeting time, please just accept it," then walked off. I watched her go shaking my head, "A weird day."

Chapter 21

I managed to get to Thursday without any other problems. I told Ferdinand about the proposed meeting with the CEO next week. He frowned, "Why would he want to have a meeting with you?"

I shrugged my shoulders, "I don't know. If I have any trouble, I'll call you in."

I tried to do some research on the family but nothing else really came up. I also did some work on the family book increasing my knowledge with different spells encouraging the girls to increase their protection.

Alira had decided to take the week off, so she could recover properly. I sent her the spell to put some more protection on her. Yindi sent a text back, "Thanks, Hannah."

I didn't bother to go down to the park to meditate preferring to meditate in the office. I also went to the pool a couple of times to do some laps. Ferdinand joined me once coming up behind me, giving me a fright, then making me laugh as he tried to get fresh in the pool. He was still a little tired from the attack and kept saying he was looking forward to going to Jardine to relax a lot more.

To get some fresh air, I went down to the Rocks a couple of times to talk to Martha to see if the other ghost had returned, but she said he hadn't.

I was sitting at my desk after lunch doing some research on the family when I got a text from Charlotte, *"Mum I need to see you."*

I knew she would only message me if it was urgent.

I put the hologram up magicaeing down to Charlotte, who was in the park by the water near the Mersey Bluff lighthouse.

It was a windy day, with dark clouds blowing in from the sea, making the waves crash against the rocks along the shoreline. I put a jacket on, looking around to see if I could see Charlotte, putting my hand up to my eyes to protect them against the fine rain that was starting to come in.

I saw someone moving around by the lighthouse, then running into the bush that was close to the lighthouse. I magicae up there calling Charlotte's name quietly, when she stood up quickly, then ducked down back in the bush, "Mum come here quick."

I crouched down going over, "What's happening Charlotte?"

She was bending down, looking to see if there was any movement. "I was getting some fresh air in the park when this man approached me, pressing me for information about our family. I was calm at first telling him I didn't know anything, but he started to get angry. I'm sure he has magic in him but he didn't use any against me; but his angry attitude started to worry me so that's why I called you."

I continued to crouch down with her, looking around to see if I could see anyone. A man appeared near the lighthouse with ash blonde hair, a rounded face, probably not much taller than me wearing dark pants and a thick dark woollen jacket.

I pointed to him, "Is that him Charlotte?"

She nodded, "Yes that's him."

I looked at him, "Do you want to call Aetius?"

She shook her head, "No I'll see how things go with you."

I changed my appearance a little making my hair black, putting jeans and a thick jacket on, "I'll go and see if he talks to me."

Charlotte nodded, "Ok, be careful I don't like the look of him."

I went around the other side of the lighthouse, walking around to where he was, looking at him from a distance at first.

He saw me looking at him and started moving in the opposite direction. I put my hands in my pocket (keeping them warm) walking along slowly to follow him.

He went down towards the water, stopping to watch the waves as they crashed against the rocks. I felt sure I could deal with him if I needed to, so I walked towards him, when he disappeared turning up behind me. I jumped as he held onto my arms with my hands still in my pockets so I couldn't do anything with them.

I tried to shrug him off, as he leaned closer saying against the wind, "Hello Hannah."

I pushed him off turning around, "Who are you?"

He grinned looking at me waving his hand over my hair changing it back to the proper colour, "Ah that's better."

Charlotte came up behind him putting him in a binding spell, as he struggled then relaxed smiling, "Mmm not bad for novices," making it disappear.

I looked at Charlotte and she looked at me deciding to take off, as he grabbed me just as we disappeared, landing near the Poseidon statute with him still hanging on.

He put up his hand, "Hör auf, Hannah, ich muss reden (stop Hannah I need to talk.)"

This made me hesitate looking at Charlotte, "Wait Charlotte we'll see what he wants to say."

Charlotte was ready to send him something, "Are you sure Mum?"

I moved away from him, "Wer bist du (who are you?)"

Charlotte looked at me, "You've got to be kidding you're speaking German now."

I looked at her in a motherly way, "We'll talk about it later, Charlotte." The guy looked at the two of us smiling, "Sie sind gleich (you are alike)."

Charlotte was getting annoyed, "Can you speak English for me as I haven't caught up with my mother's ability to speak German yet."

The guy had a cocky grin on his face introducing himself, "My name is Olwen Drachen."

I thought for a few minutes. *'I've seen that name somewhere before, but I had done so much research it was getting a bit jumbled.'*

He smiled, "You recognise my last name Hannah."

I kept thinking, *'I have been trying to research the family and have come across that name, that is why it sounds familiar.'*

A large gust of wind blew up, making him yell, "Can we go to a coffee shop to talk."

I nodded, indicating to Charlotte where we wanted to go, as she took my hand and Olwen looked at me nervously, as I took his hand magicaeing to the nearest coffee shop.

As soon as we got there, we dropped hands, walking into the warm coffee shop and got a seat. I sat down, "I can't stay too long as I am supposed to be at work" getting my phone out to have look at the hologram to make sure there wasn't anyone around my desk.

He leaned over, looking impressed, "Ah a hologram, impressive."

Charlotte looked at it, "It's a great idea, although I could tweak it a little for you if you like. Do you want coffee?"

Olwen got up, "I will get it, what do you want?"

I shook my head, "Like I said I don't want anything."

Charlotte asked for a latte no sugar.

While he was gone, I looked at Charlotte, "So who do you think he is?"

Charlotte shrugged her shoulders, "I don't have a clue. I'm still getting over the fact that you speak German now."

I chuckled, "It's to do with the grandma who comes to visit, she keeps flicking from Norwegian to German for some reason."

Charlotte leaned back surprised, "So you speak Norwegian as well?"

I screwed up my face, "Yes. I think it was a spell or something she put on me."

Charlotte rubbed her eyes, "Good grief what a strange day."

I nodded, "Tell me about it. I've had one of those weeks."

Olwen came back with the coffees and a cake for each of us, "If you are anything like the rest of the family you like your sweet things." This made me look, "Oh so you think we are part of the family?"

He nodded, "Looking at your colouring and your ability to do magic, I'm quite sure. I have been doing some research as well on the family. I had heard stories of a sister being born to another woman, but did not hear anything else. I then saw Charlotte's post on a family research website requesting information about the Dragĕ family from Norway. You see Dragĕ, which is Norwegian and Drachen which is German both mean dragon. I went on a hunch that the two are connected somehow, as I knew that there were both nationalities in the family."

I put my hand up scratching my head, "This is quite strange because I have just had a conversation with my brother, that didn't go very well. He decided to inform me that my father I grew up with was not my father."

Charlotte looked at me shaking her head, "Naughty Nanna."

He chuckled, "Well if I'm correct I could be your brother."

I sat back in the chair taking it all in, "Well you look nicer than my other brother."

Charlotte sipped on her coffee looking at the two of us, "We could do a DNA test to see if you like?"

I smiled, "Charlotte is a bit of a scientist and knows about all these things."

He thought about it, "I suppose it is one way to see for sure rather than guessing. Can you organise it, Charlotte?"

She nodded, "Yes sure. How long are you going to be around as I can't do it until tomorrow and then we are going away for the weekend."

He nodded, "Yes that will be fine with me. Is that good for you Hannah?"

I looked over to Charlotte, "I can pop down in the afternoon only, so just let me know. I'm afraid I have to go as I can see someone walking around my desk."

I got up and shook his hand, "Nice to meet you Olwen." As we shook hands, I could feel that magical tingle making me smile, "I'll see you tomorrow Charlotte."

I walked out of the coffee shop magicaeing to work and going into the ladies toilets to change and tidy my hair up.

I looked in the mirror, '*It's strange how everything is popping in at the same time. It's like something is needing to be cleared up for some reason. I guess I will have to relax and see how things go.*'

I was walking back to my desk with a secretary just about to go into my cubicle, so I called out to her, "Hi Molly I'm here did you want something?"

--ooOoo--

I went and met Ferdinand once I had finished work, going home and changing into something comfortable.

I got a glass of wine, "Do you want a glass of wine?"

He appeared a bit grumpy again, "Yes I will thanks going to sit on the balcony."

I sighed going over and sitting next to him, "Is everything alright?"

He took a big sip, "I believe you had trouble with some guy and didn't bother to call me in."

I took a sip groaning, "That's because I didn't need any help."

He looked a little agitated, "I'm getting tired of all these attacks Hannah."

I put my hand on his, "I was with Charlotte."

He took my hand, "She should have called Aetius as well, but no you Dragĕ women don't need us spirit animals, do you?"

I was tired and getting annoyed, "I was going to tell you what happened, Ferdinand, when I got home, but if you're going to get silly about it, I won't bother."

I got up going into the lounge to sit on the sofa, with him coming up behind me, magicaeing out of the room putting me on his back, "It's time for a ride I think, Hannah."

I scrambled for the harness as he flew erratically, thinking I'll magicae off, but he grabbed my leg, "Ferdinand let me go!"

He chuckled, "No Hannah. I want to have some fun without your magic."

He flew high, going up through the clouds, making me laugh, holding onto his neck, "You silly bugger, stop it!"

He then went out to sea, flying over the beautiful ocean with its vast blue expanse appearing to go on forever. I sighed, "Oh I have missed this, Ferdinand." We flew over dolphins jumping and whales breaching with me, wishing I could go and swim with them.

He flew back towards the land going over some of the golden beaches of the north shore, landing on a quiet beach at West Head Beach. He spread his wings fully, landing on the beach with his huge talons digging into the sand, then changing into male form holding me.

He looked at me with my hair windblown and messy along with my cheeks flushed from the wind that had whipped past me as he flew. He put his hand around the back of my neck kissing me, "I miss these simple times."

I leaned into him, "Yes, I do to. I guess I'm getting too caught up with all the family stuff."

He kissed me again, "Come on we'll go back home. I'm looking forward to going to Jardine to be a normal couple again."

I smiled, "Yes so am I, honey."

We got back home, kissing me again leading to becoming intimate. We lay there quietly talking as I play with the hairs on his chest that were appearing quite rapidly. I told him about meeting my proposed brother, making him roll over to look at me, "Really, where is he from?"

I looked at him, "You'll never guess, but Germany. That is why I didn't call you in honey. We sorted it out in the end without too much trouble."

I got up, "Look he might not be my brother, but Charlotte said she will do a DNA test to check. We will just have to wait and see."

Ferdinand got up, "I'd like to go to Jardine tomorrow after you finish work."

I thought about it, "Yes that will be fine with me. I'll let the girls know."

We got through the evening going to bed laying there as he cuddled into my back, "I do love you, Ferdinand."

He kissed me on the cheek, "I love you too, honey."

The next day went well, doing the usual work load and doing some meditation in Tom's office, then going out for a walk to get some fresh air.

Charlotte rang me, "Can you come soon, so I can get a sample off you for the DNA test."

I went down straight away to Charlotte to do the test before I had to go back to work.

Olwen was there as well, doing the test "I'm looking forward to getting this result Hannah."

I looked at him, "I just realised I didn't ask what your father's name is."

He grinned, "Do you want to know now or wait until the test is done?"

I shook my head, "No I think I'll leave it until we've done the test."

It finally got to home time with Ferdinand coming to the reception area to pick me up.

He was joking with Tracey when I came out, "Have you two finished? I'm ready to go home."

Tracey was a bit more relaxed now with me and Ferdinand, "Have a great weekend you two."

I nodded, "Thanks Tracey, you too."

We went downstairs walking over to the Quay, "Do you want a drink or anything?"

Ferdinand shook his head, "No I want to get out of here. I've arranged with Cara to take you through to Jardine at 7.00p.m. as well."

I chuckled stroking his face, "Ok Ferdi let's get going."

We got home as I flopped onto the sofa. Ferdinand went and got Kimba's travel cage putting it on the barstool. He then came over to me from behind giving me a kiss on top of my head, "Come on honey get changed then you can relax."

I yawned, "We have plenty of time Ferdi."

He went and got Kimba giving her a bit of food before she is due to go into the cage. I still hadn't moved making him annoyed, so he came over and picked me up in a fireman's lift, "Come on honey get changed for me then I'll be happy."

I struggled hitting his back, "Ferdi there isn't any rush give me a chance to wind down."

He put me down in the bedroom giving me a kiss, looking like a boy in a sweet shop, "Can you get changed, then we will be ready to go?"

I started to strip, "Alright I'm doing it now," yawning again.

He made us a light meal that we sat and ate in front of the TV watching the news. I went and cleaned up while he was putting Kimba into her cage chuckling, "Poor Kimba doesn't know what's going on."

He had the unit all locked up and Kimba ready to go quite quickly, getting me up off the sofa, "Come on its time to go."

I put a jacket on, "Ok I'm ready. I'll just check the doors."

He took my hand, "No I have done all that."

We took off meeting at the Blue Mountains path near the Hydro Hotel. Alira, Charlotte, Amelia, Hine and Sophie were all there. All the spirit animals had already gone through.

Cara came forward smiling when we arrived, "Hi you two. We're all ready to go."

Ferdinand growled, "I told you we should have left earlier."

I smiled, "Alright. Be careful with Kimba."

He gave me a kiss taking off.

Alira came up smiling, "He looked excited to be going to Jardine."

I nodded, "yes, he's a bit uptight about the attacks and things going on with my family. How are you feeling now?"

She smiled, "Oh I'm great now, thanks Hannah. Mum couldn't stop talking about your temper. I told her that was mild to what you are normally like."

I looked shocked at her, "Oh thanks Alira."

Cara called us, "Come on ladies, let's go." We went down the track going through to the stone then going under the waterfall. We got to Seneca the gatekeeper, telling her the password moving forward to my turn, telling Seneca the word.

She put her hand up to stop me, "Hannah Dragĕ isn't it?"

I nodded feeling a bit nervous, "Yes why."

She smiled, "Oh just getting your face in my memory as I've heard you can be" as she hesitated thinking of the right word 'naughty'.

I smiled, "Oh I thought I was getting better—obviously not."

She smiled letting me past, "Just try a bit harder."

We went through the cleansing area getting into the Jardine clothes sighing as I came out, "Ah that feels better." We all met together going towards the meal area where people were still mingling eating and drinking. I wasn't really hungry so I grabbed a glass of wine going to find Ferdinand.

He was talking to Aetius and Shiro still holding onto Kimba's cage. I came up to him taking the cage, "I'll take her if you want to chat with them."

He held onto the cage, "No it's alright. Come on we'll go over to the bungalow now if you like and get her settled."

I looked around, "Don't you want to mingle a little first?"

Shiro and Aetius did a little wave moving over to talk to someone else with him putting his arm around my shoulders, "Come on we can settle her in then come back if you like."

We went over to the bungalow that we had before opening it up putting Kimba on the bed. Ferdinand shut the door letting her out as I lay on the bed watching her slowly come out sniffing around giving me a nudge, pleased that I was there.

I looked at Ferdinand smiling, "See she will be alright."

I patted her to comfort her, "Oh I forgot a kitty litter tray."

He smiled, "It's all sorted don't worry about it." Kimba jumped off the bed sniffing around the room while I lay there watching her.

I looked at Ferdinand with that hungry look on his face deciding to get up, when he grabbed me making me laugh, "Ferdinand we're supposed to be socialising don't be naughty."

He lay on top of me, "We have to wait for Kimba to get used to the room."

I giggled, "Any excuse."

We did go out near the end of the meal to catch up with those who were left. Alira and Fia were still there with Alira smiling, "What have you two been doing?"

I grinned, "We had to settle Kimba in."

Alira burst out laughing, "Oh I'll have to remember that one."

We went back to the bungalow to relax having an early night. Ferdinand was cuddling in, "Agghh it's so nice to be here again."

I patted his hand, "Yes dear."

We woke feeling refreshed, with Ferdinand getting up to make some breakfast, as I came out with Kimba making a fuss of her and giving her some food.

Ferdinand was smiling, "See she is settling in nicely."

I sat down, "I'd like to do some things in the community, who do I see about that?"

He thought about it bringing some food over, "Cara should be able to help you or tell you who to speak to at least."

I started to eat breakfast, "I might do some meditation first. What are you up to today?"

He sat next to me, "I'll go and do my dragon thing but I'll come and see how you are doing or if you want to go somewhere I can take you."

We had our breakfast then Ferdinand went off for half an hour to let me do some meditation. Nothing much came in for a change, giving my mind a good rest.

Ferdinand came back to pick me up making sure Kimba couldn't get out for now so she would get used to the place, then going to see Cara.

Cara was pleased that I was interested in helping in the community, "What do you like to do Hannah? There are cooking duties."

Ferdinand chuckled, looking at me, "You don't really want to do that, do you, Hannah?"

I slapped him, "Don't be nasty Ferdinand." I looked at Cara, "No I prefer to do some gardening or something like that if I could."

Cara took me over to a big area where fruit and vegetables were grown, some of them were hydroponic and some were grown outside. My job was to pack the fruit into special containers so that they could be kept for later. I looked at them, "So do you freeze them?"

Cara shook her head, "No Hannah. I don't fully understand it myself; you will have to ask the experts for that. All I know is, that it keeps them long enough for us to use them so we don't have any waste. The longest you can stay here is four hours Hannah. Someone else will take over then."

I started packing some blackberries into the special containers, sampling them as I went. I was chatting to the other people around me who were nibbling on the fruit as well.

There were strawberries and blueberries being packed, so we were having our own little feast.

Ferdinand popped in after an hour catching me eating some blueberries, laughing, "You're going to get a belly ache if you eat too much of that."

He gave me a kiss on the lips, "Mmm makes your lips nice and sweet."

One of the ladies that was working near me whose name was Sam, put strawberry all over her lips puckering up, "Come on Ferdinand it's my turn."

There was a big eruption of laughter from everyone around making Ferdinand get embarrassed giving me a quick kiss, "I think it's time I went."

I was just about finished when Morag came in smiling at me, "Are you enjoying yourself, Hannah?" I smiled back at her, "Yes I don't mind this sort of thing."

Morag tasted a couple of blackberries I was packing, "Mm they're nice and sweet. I hope you haven't eaten too much; you'll get a sore stomach."

I rolled my eyes, "You sound just like Ferdinand. I've had some of the other fruit as well, so if I'm going to get a sore stomach it's going to be worth it."

Morag smiled, "After lunch can you and Alira come and see, me so we can talk about a couple of things?"

I nodded, "Sure Morag. I'll let Alira know."

Morag patted me on the shoulder, "You're doing a good job. Your girls are over at the science block promoting their magitrap at the moment."

I nodded, "Oh I had forgotten about that. Hopefully they'll like it?"

Morag came back shaking her head, "They did let it slip that they've tested it on someone. You Dragĕ women are naughty."

I chuckled, "At least I'm passing something onto them."

Morag left, waving to everyone and it wasn't long after I had finished my time there. I walked out after washing my hands to be met by Alira, on a pony holding the reins of another horse, "Come on Sister, time for some fun."

I looked at the pony with no saddle on, pulling a face, making Alira look, "You can ride, can't you?" I nodded, "It's been a while but I haven't ridden bareback before."

The horse came forward nudging me, "You'll be alright, Hannah, I won't be too rough on you."

I giggled shaking my head, "I still can't get used to these talking animals." I moved around to get onto the pony, not sure how to get up without a saddle on, hearing Alira laugh, "Sister, just magicae onto Dropsy."

I looked curious, "What's his name?" The horse turned his head towards me, "Dropsy. Just get on and let's get going."

I pulled a face thinking, '*Odd name*' magicaeing onto his back and grabbing the reins.

It felt a bit strange at first not having a saddle but as promised Dropsy was good with me, just doing a gentle trot. We went through some bush trails at first then Alira led us over to the beach area, just walking along the edge of the water with the horses.

It was magical making me feel so relaxed. I felt someone coming, with Ferdinand hoping on behind me, wrapping his arms around my waist and giving me a kiss, "Who said you could ride someone else, Hannah?"

I leaned back into him, "Are you jealous?"

He kissed my neck groaning a little, "Don't be naughty, Hannah."

Dropsy stopped looking back, "I hope you're not getting frisky back there Ferdinand."

This made Ferdinand look up, "Oh hi Dropsy, no just checking Hannah isn't getting used to another animal between her legs."

I was shocked slapping him, "Ferdinand don't be naughty."

He leaned in talking quietly, "Just watch Dropsy he's been given that name for a reason."

I looked confused, "Oh why?"

He just gave me another kiss, "I'll see you at lunch," disappearing with a big grin on his face.

We started to head back going towards a river bank, to let the horses have a drink. We dropped their reins so they could dip their heads to drink, when Dropsy leaned over, dropping to the ground landing on his side, throwing me off.

I screamed out, "Oh no what's happened? Have I killed him?"

Alira slipped off her horse laughing so much she was buckling over with tears streaming from her face, "That's why he's called Dropsy."

Dropsy put his head up, doing a whinny then laughing with the look on my face. I shook my head, "You little bugger Alira Kingy," going towards the river throwing up some water magically wetting her.

This made her scream, "Oh so that's how it's going to be," and sending some back to me.

Dropsy got up, "Humans are strange creatures, aren't they?"

Alira and I were still throwing water at each other when Fia and Ferdinand popped in, getting a full blast of the water that was being thrown. Alira and I looked at each other trying not to laugh, but throwing one more at them, with Ferdinand grabbing me and Fia grabbing her, taking us into the river laughing and screaming sitting us down in the water until we were thoroughly wet.

We got out of the water soaked sitting on the bank to get our breaths back and dry off.

Alira pointed at the horses taking their reins off so they could just wander off on their own. The sun shone down on the patch where we were sitting. Ferdinand lay down pulling me on his shoulder giving me a kiss, "It's great here isn't it, Hannah?"

I looked up at him, "Yes dear as you keep saying. Alira and I have a meeting with Morag after lunch, I'm not sure what it is about."

He looked at me curious, "Well maybe you could mention that you are interested in coming to live here with me."

I smiled, "I'll see what she wants first. It might be just to see who has attacked us and what progress we are making on the family history."

Ferdinand sat up looking patiently at me, "Ok, we'll wait and see. Let's go and have some lunch."

We got back to the bungalow changing into something dry feeling my stomach lurch a bit. I groaned, "Oh dear. I think that horse riding has made my stomach shake up the contents a bit."

Ferdinand shook his head smiling, "I told you not to eat too much of that fruit. Have a drink of water and some bread to see if that settles it down."

I got the water and bread and sat on the sofa playing with Kimba, slowly sipping on the water and nibbling on the bread. Ferdinand came and sat next to me eating some hot chips, at first smelling alright, but then the smell of the grease started to make my stomach turn. I quickly got up running to the bathroom with the sound of Ferdinand laughing, as I threw up in the toilet.

It eventually stopped, as I came back in laying down on the sofa, groaning looking at Ferdinand who was behind the kitchen counter smirking tidying up. Kimba jumped up on my chest giving me a nudge and a little meow "Yes, I know Kimba at least you aren't mean to me."

Ferdinand came back over sitting me up, "Drink the water at least, you have that meeting with Morag, don't forget."

I groaned, "Oh yes."

I managed to feel a bit better by the time I was due to go and see Morag. I met Alira just outside the meeting room we had been in before, going in to find Cara and Morag waiting for us. Morag smiled, shaking her head, "I told you not eat too much fruit, Hannah."

Alira looked closely at me sniggering, "oh yes you are a bit pale."

We sat down waiting for Morag to talk, "Well ladies how are you both feeling now after your attacks?"

I looked at Alira then back to Morag, "I am ok, Morag."

Alira nodded, "yes, I am a lot better now. Hannah has given me something to wear for a bit of protection as well."

Morag nodded, "Oh that's good, thanks Hannah."

She looked at my wrist, "You haven't been wearing yours here, Hannah?"

I shook my head, "No I didn't think I would need it here—should I?"

Morag pulled a face, "I have mentioned that we might have a problem here but are not sure who it is. I would probably put it on just to be safe."

Morag put up an orb around us making Alira and I look at each other, "I'm a little worried that there are listening devices somewhere that is why I have put this up. We are still looking at the possibility of setting up the boarding house with you two going into it to do some undercover work for us—that is if you're still interested."

I sighed, "The only thing I worry about is Ferdinand and his reaction. He is getting a bit grumpy with all these attacks lately, pushing for me to come to Jardine to live."

Alira nodded, "Mum and Fia are similar in their attitude."

I heard my stomach groan a little patting it, "Sorry about that. I will be happy to do it for a couple of months to help you out until you find the ones you are looking for or find someone else to take over from me."

Morag nodded, "I know what you mean Hannah but you would be safer in the boarding house than at your work and home because it will be a Jardine house. The only thing we want you to do is find out where the attackers are and that is all. We would set up a system that you alert us straight away so we can deal with them, not you."

I looked pleased, "Oh well that sounds reasonable. As long as Ferdinand can be included in some way and I am sure Alira would like Fia there as well."

Alira looked at me nodding, "Yes with the possibility of my mother and daughter."

I looked at Morag, "You sound as though you are going ahead with it, Morag?"

She sighed, "It hasn't been fully decided yet. There are some people who are not interested in doing it because it could bring too much fighting with magic in your world. Just look at the prank you all did at the church, there were cameras everywhere, which is happening all the time now, so we can't hush it up or use an excuse to make it look to be something else. As for Ferdinand and Fia we have thought about just making them your husbands or partner, whatever you call them, for the sake of your world rules. It would mean just wearing rings around the house that is all, nothing official. Ferdinand can cook, so he could do some of the meals and Fia can help out in the yard or something. We will let you know if we get any closer, for now just think on it."

I looked at Alira pulling a face, "Wow husbands, that'll be a shock to the system after so many years."

Alira nudged me, "Tell me about it, Sister. We certainly won't tell them that one until we have to, they'll get all big headed."

I laughed, "Yes for sure Sister."

Cara smiled shaking her head, "Have you two finished? Have you found any more information on your family, Hannah?"

I nodded looking pleased, "Yes apparently the father I grew up with wasn't my father. Charlotte then had a visit from a guy, who she thought was attacking her, but could end up being my half-brother. We are getting a DNA test done."

Morag and Cara looked at each other confused, "What test is that?"

I smiled, "It tests your DNA to see if you are from the same family. I don't know all the ins and outs but Charlotte is doing it for us. We should know in a couple of weeks. The interesting thing is he has magic in him as well."

Morag looked surprised, "Oh really, that might be why you are quite strong in your magic having two lines in your family."

I thought about it, "Oh I didn't think of that."

Morag looked down at her hands not sure how to say something, "So what happened with your other brother, Hannah?"

My smile faded, "Oh you heard about that did you?"

Alira looked at me, curious, "Oh what happened Sister?"

I cleared my throat, "I threatened to throw him out the window but decided to just bounce him around the office like a ball instead."

Alira starting laughing turning to look at Morag and Cara, "That's not funny, is it?" Trying to supress her giggles.

Morag sighed, "Ferdinand did say that you managed to stay reasonably calm."

I looked proud of myself, "Yes, I did actually. He was very rude and nasty but I still managed to stay calm."

I could hear Alira's muffled giggles still, as I tried not to smile.

Morag looked seriously at us now, "There is one more important thing we would like to tell you both but must be kept to yourselves."

Alira and I looked at each other looking curiously, "What is it Morag?"

Morag looked at Cara, "We believe there is a group in Jardine wanting to join your world back to Jardine. They feel it is time to join together again, but you know as well as I do there is still too much conflict and greed in your world to even consider it. These people believe that they can join together with people like you two controlling it with strong magic lines to keep those type of people in line. The frightening thing is if you don't join them, they intend to take what they can."

I sat back, "Wow that's a lot to take in. Do you have any idea who is behind this?"

Morag nodded, "We have our suspicions but nothing concrete. You won't know this but we do have discussion groups about these types of things, that way we can air our views and deal with them. It has served us well for many years; but it appears this group are more serious about it than talking. I'm telling you this as a warning to be careful."

Both Alira and I nodded, "Thanks for letting us know Morag. At least, we know why they are attacking us now."

Morag put her hands up to her face in prayer position, "This is why we have been trying to stem your anger as well, especially Hannah at the moment. It is not to control you but to guide you. If you can't control your anger, they might be able to manipulate you to turn to them and help them."

I looked solemnly at them, "I'll be honest Morag and Cara, I know I have a temper but I do feel as though I am being controlled by Jardine, especially when I or we" as I looked at Alira, "Get attacked. I've told you before I wouldn't kill anyone, but I will defend myself."

Morag sighed, "You are a stubborn woman Hannah, just like your ancestors. We know that is why Matilda didn't stay in Jardine for very long preferring to go on her own. I also know she didn't harm anyone, but then again, she wasn't as strong as you. We need to meet in the middle, Hannah and work together."

I nodded, "I will make a better effort, Morag. There is one more thing I need to ask and that is I be able to tell Ferdinand about the proposed plan of the boarding house once we are back home. Like I said, he is getting angry about the attacks, so if I can tell him some of the basic details about your idea, it might settle him down a bit. He will think I'm hiding things from him otherwise."

Morag didn't look happy about it but said, "Alright Hannah, but he better not tell anyone else. The same goes for you Alira, if you want to tell Fia you can, but only basic details and he must not tell anyone else." We both nodded in agreement making me smile, "It's hard to shut things down from him sometimes, so this will make that a bit easier at least. Thanks Morag."

Morag took the orb off now, "Well that is about all the news I have for you two. Please think about things and stay on guard. Have some fun while you are here at least," smiling at us both, "I hear you have met Dropsy, Hannah."

I laughed nudging Alira, "Yes Sister here set me up really good. I guess it's payback for the lions."

We ended our meeting going out to the fresh air walking back towards our bungalows stopping just before we got there. I turned to look at Alira, "What do you think about all of that?"

She looked thoughtfully, "I think we have a bit of thinking to do. Let's just relax and enjoy ourselves for now and talk about it later."

I nodded, "Yep sounds like a great idea."

We saw a group of people walking towards the sounds of shouting and cheering with both of us deciding to follow them.

Ferdinand and Fia joined us just as we approached a large stadium where the noise was coming from. I looked at Ferdinand, "What's going on here?"

He gave me a kiss, "There is a game going on, do you want to have a look?"

I nodded, "Yeah sure it sounds exciting."

Fia gave Alira a kiss, "Did the meeting go alright, Alira?"

Alira smiled, "Yes it did, but I'm curious to see what's going on in there."

Ferdinand and Fia took us into the stadium getting some seats in a dimly lit arena. I looked to the side of me saying, "Hi" to the people sitting there.

A huge cheer went up making me look to see what was happening. Ferdinand pointed to a woman who was on a hologram horse that was lit up with bright blue illumination wearing a type of armour wielding a bat with an orb in it towards a goal.

The goal was an ornate box that had a lid that opened and closed, so it looked a very complex game.

There were four women to a team one in red and one in blue trying to control an orb and a hologram horse while getting the orb into a box that is opening and closing. I shook my head, "Wow I don't think I could do that type of game."

I looked at Ferdinand who was watching the game intently leaning over to him, "What's the name of this game?"

He put his arm around me, "Hang on we'll see if she gets it into the goal."

He was getting excited yelling, "Come on."

I watched as the woman in the blue team finally got it into the goal sending up a cheer from some of the audience. Ferdinand looked back down to me, "It's called Holustix. Do you like it?"

I yelled over the roar of the audience, "Yeah I love it."

I looked around the stadium to see if my girls were here, finally spotting them further on down, yelling and cheering at the teams. I smiled as I watched them enjoying themselves with Shiro and Aetius next to them.

Someone came around with food, with it feeling strange that you didn't have to pay for it. We sat there until the end of the game really getting into the excitement of it all. We came out ribbing each other, because Ferdinand and I backed the blues, who was also the winning team.

We walked towards our bungalows looking at the sun that was slowly lowering.

Ferdinand put his arm around me looking at Alira and Fia, "We're just going to have a rest before the main meal time. We'll catch you two later."

I looked up to him about to say something but he magicae us to the bungalow before I had a chance to say anything. We landed in the bungalow with his arm still around my waist, "I didn't know we needed a rest before meal time."

He grinned, "You looked a little weary, so I made the decision for you."

I looked at him with a curious look, "Oh you think I'm tired, but I'm not dear."

He picked me up, "Oh yes I think you are," going towards the bedroom as I giggled, "You know you're going to wear me out before we go home." His smile faded a little, but he carried on, laying down on the bed, "well, we could stay here."

I smiled again, "I'll be dead in a month or a haggled old woman because you've loved me to death."

He started to kiss me on my neck, lying on top of me, moving up to my lips getting passionate. We were working each other up when he opened my legs lying in between them, which felt nice, but it wasn't his usual move.

I thought, '*Oh well he's trying our world things maybe he's heard about this.*' I decided to do what I would normally do with a man from our world putting my legs around his hips. This certainly excited him letting out a groan, working us both up. He slowed it down looking at me with love in his eyes, "You know I can't do anything more like in your world, honey."

I nodded, "I know I'm happy with the Jardine method."

He took our clothes off continuing in the Jardine method.

I lay on his shoulder afterwards playing with his chest hair again, "What made you go between my legs like that honey."

He played with my hair, "I don't know it just felt right. You liked it didn't you?"

I nodded, "Yes, I guess I wasn't expecting it, that is all. I've noticed your chest hair growing a bit more, is that normal for a Jardine man?"

He shrugged his shoulders not really caring, "Yes, I think so. You're probably stirring me up a bit after so many years, that things are growing where they weren't before."

I guffawed, "me, stirring you up! Who was coming to have a *rest*?"

He hugged me smiling giving me a kiss on the top of my head, "How did your meeting go with Morag?"

I was dreading this question, "It went well. She was just catching up to see how we were feeling after the attacks, how the research was going and she commented on what happened with my brother," pulling lightly on his chest hair.

He grabbed my hand, "Ouch you little minx, what did you do that for."

I tried to move my hand to pull his hair a bit more but he held onto my hand, "Because you told her what happened between me and Christian."

He chuckled, "Oh yes I did."

He rolled over on top of me to stop me pulling his hair taking my arms above my head, "Don't be naughty, Hannah."

I relaxed looking at him going to move my hands but he stopped me, "Come on the meal will just about be due to come out now."

He wasn't going to move, "Did you ask about coming to Jardine?"

I tried to move my arms again sighing, "Yes, I did. We are just sorting out when the best time would be to come in. Are you going to let me up now?"

He put his head down near mine kissing me gently letting out a sigh, "I don't know what you have to work out, but I guess I will have to be satisfied with that." Before he let my hands go, he raised himself up looking at me seriously, "If there are any more attacks though, we will be coming back straight away, without any delays."

I decided he was getting too bossy, pushing him off with a bit of magic behind it. He landed on the edge of the bed then fell off, giving me a chance to get up and get dressed. I looked at him annoyed, "Don't try to boss me around Ferdinand. I told you I was organising it with Morag. I'm going for a walk before the meal—by myself."

I walked out getting to the balcony door hearing him get up, "Hannah wait," landing in front of me still naked putting his arms around me, "I'm sorry. I just don't want you to get hurt, there's a lot of rumours going around about people in your world trying to build up a type of army or something; I don't know, but it's worrying me."

I put my arms around him, "We will sort it out Ferdinand just be patient."

I looked past him noticing a couple of people walking past looking at Ferdinand's bum in the window. I pulled away from him, "I think you better get dressed dear you have an audience."

He turned to see some people waving and smiling at him. He grinned a little embarrassed and put some clothes on. I gave him a kiss, "I'll just go for a little walk and meet you at the meal area."

He stopped me, "You're not angry still, are you?"

I shook my head, "No, I just need some space that is all. It's been a busy day. I won't go far, so don't worry."

I went out of the bungalow with him watching me, go down one of the paths not far from the bungalow. I didn't really know where I was going but after a short walk, I heard a stream running, so I headed towards that going to sit next to it.

I felt a little annoyed at both Ferdinand and Morag in some ways with their expectations of me and Alira. I was also annoyed that the people who were attacking us were in my life as well, when all I wanted to do was to learn my magic, have some fun with Ferdinand and my girls, but now I have to make major decisions just to stay safe.

I did a big sigh thinking about Ferdinand's behaviour as well. He appears to be acting more and more like a man in our world. I closed my eyes listening to the gentle flow of the stream turning my thoughts off, so I could relax. There was a filtered stream of sun light coming through the trees hitting the spot where I was sitting, making me feel warm but not hot. I could smell the bush around bringing different smells into my senses helping me to relax even more.

I heard a movement near me, making me open my eyes, noticing a big black panther softly padding her huge feet towards me. Her fur glimmered in the sunlight looking sleek and beautiful. She turned her head towards me emitting a small growl with big yellow eyes. I smiled not feeling scared or anything, "Hi I'm, Hannah."

She sauntered over to the water near me, licking it then turning to look at me, "Hi my name is Tendua. You look a little tense."

I nodded, "Yes I don't like being an adult sometimes."

She chuckled with a bit of cat growl mixed in, "Ah yes, I don't think I would like to be a human being. You manage to make everything so complex."

She walked into the water stopping to turn and look at me, "Come for a swim in the pool just over there. I find it helps with a lot of things."

I smiled taking my clothes off walking carefully over the stones so they didn't hurt my feet. She stopped to look at me, "Lay on my back, I will take you the rest of the way."

I did as she asked laying on her back, feeling the soft fur beneath me, putting my arms around her neck. We got to the pool she had spoken about when Tendua said, "Hold on I'll take you in the pool."

I held on feeling excited when she dived into the pool, while I held on tight making a huge grin come over my face, as the cool water hit my body making it tingle with goose bumps going over it. I squealed in delight as she took me down with small fish coming to meet us then flitting away.

I let go of her neck as she went back up while I floated a bit longer feeling like I was in space with my hair swirling around me. There were beams of sunlight coming through the clear water enabling me to see around me.

I went back up taking a breath of air then going straight back down again loving the sensation, wishing I could stay down for longer.

--ooOoo--

The meal was starting to be served with Ferdinand walking over to meet me but not finding me there. He found Alira, "Have you seen Hannah arrive yet Alira?"

She shook her head, "No not yet. She's not missing again, is she?"

He looked worried, "We had a bit of a disagreement that is all and she went for a walk. I'm sure she will be back soon."

Alira could see he was getting worried, "Do you want both of us to go and look for her?"

He nodded, "Yes just in case she is still annoyed at me, she might stay a bit calmer with you around."

Alira groaned telling Fia where she was going, walking off with Ferdinand going down the path he had seen me go down.

Alira heard the stream, "I bet she has headed that way; you know she loves the water."

He agreed, "Yes she's always been drawn to it."

They walked over to the stream seeing my clothes sitting near a rock making Alira groan, "Oh no, now what?"

A big black panther came strolling out of the water shaking herself and looking at both of them. She smiled showing her big teeth which made Alira jump up Ferdinand's back, "Aggh is that a black panther?"

Ferdinand tried to get Alira off his back, "Alira cut it out it's just Tendua."

Tendua sauntered out, "Hi Ferdinand how are you and who's the scaredy cat on your back?"

He pulled Alira off his back, "This is Alira, she's from the other world and not quite used to big cats. Is Hannah in the water?"

She went up to Alira rubbing herself against her, "Hi Alira, you smell nice," making Alira pull a face and wail, "Ferdinand, don't you leave me here."

He ignored her stripping down to his shorts going into the water, noticing me take a breath and going down again into the water like a dolphin. Alira went and sat on the rock hugging her legs, "Ferdinand she will be alright come back here."

I was floating in space again watching the fish swim around me and through my hair grinning, when I saw someone coming towards me. I recognised Ferdinand who wrapped his arms around me, taking me up to the surface. He shook the water off his hair and wiped his face, "We thought you would be in the water somewhere."

I had a big grin on my face, "Doesn't it make you feel wonderful."

Alira yelled out, "Hannah, get back here please!"

I looked over to see Alira sitting on a rock hugging her legs with Tendua sitting near her, licking her fur.

Ferdinand smiled, "Come on we better get over to Alira, she thinks she's going to be eaten by Tendua."

I giggled pushing away from him, going under one more time, as he groaned, "Hannah come on its meal time."

Tendua looked over to Ferdinand, "Do you want me to get her for you?"

Alira was sitting there nervously waving to her, "Yes you go and get her, Tendua."

Ferdinand shook his head, "No she'll be up again so I'll grab her then."

I decided to play a trick on him moving over to the other side of the pond then coming up.

He was wading in the water waiting for me to come up for air but I didn't. This made him start to look around and put his head under the water to see where I was.

He dived down but couldn't see me; coming back up then looking around hearing me giggle. He swam over to me, "Come here Hannah," grabbing my arm before I could swim away again magicaeing out of the water, holding onto me. I put my legs around his hips as he walked out, laughing, "Oh that was delightful thanks Tendua."

Alira looked at the tattoo on my back, "Oh I didn't realise the tattoo was fully formed now."

Ferdinand brought in a towel putting me down and drying me off, "Yes I thought I had told you."

Goose bumps came over my skin again, shivering a little, "Oh that was lovely and cool."

Ferdinand was drying my hair off then put my clothes back on, "You better not get a cold Hannah."

I pointed to my hair drying it off properly "I'll be alright, stop fussing Ferdinand. See you later, Tendua, thanks for the swim."

We magicae back to the meal area with a vast array of food on the tables and people helping themselves.

Alira squeezed me, "Will you leave those blasted cats alone."

I chuckled, "Oh stop it; Tendua wouldn't hurt you."

Ferdinand kept hold of my hand leading me over to a spare spot to sit down to eat. Fia came up to Alira, "You look a bit pale dear what's the matter?"

She sat next to us mumbling, "Oh Hannah, and those cats again."

I ate a little bit not feeling really hungry because of my stomach upset before, so I sat and watched everyone chat and eat.

Amelia and Charlotte came up to me with Amelia playing with my hair, "Have you been swimming again, Mum?"

Ferdinand nodded, "Yes and with a panther."

Charlotte laughed turning to Alira, "I thought you looked a bit pale Alira."

Alira sarcastically laughed, "Yes very funny. She was a big black hairy panther and Hannah was swimming with her for crying out loud."

Morag was wandering around as well coming over to us, "Amelia and Charlotte you did well presenting your invention, great job."

She looked at Alira who was still mumbling, "What's the matter, Alira?" As she said this Hine and Sophie came over with Hine looking at Alira, "You're looking a bit pale again Sister?"

Alira was annoyed now, "Hannah has been swimming and playing with a black panther and we had to go and find her. Well, actually I found her."

Ferdinand scoffed, "No you didn't Alira you jumped on my back as soon as you saw the cat." Everyone was laughing making Alira annoyed more turning to me, "If you go near those cats again, I'm not coming to get you Sister, no matter what."

I leaned over giving her a hug, "Ok Sister it's a deal."

Morag shook her head chuckling away moving on, while the girls went and got us some wine to drink. Ferdinand looked at my plate, "You haven't eaten very much Hannah?"

I shook my head, "No my stomach is still a bit funny. I'll have something later if I feel like it." The girls came back with the wine as we all relaxed, mingling with the others until it was time to go.

Ferdinand took my hand, "Come on you look a little tipsy now."

I smiled, "Yes I feel nice and relaxed especially after that swim."

We walked back to the bungalow holding hands bumping into Lilith and Pantera, who were just on their way back to their place, "Hi Lilith and Pardus, how are you?"

She looked away as though she didn't really want to talk, but felt she had to in front of Pardus "I'm good thanks Hannah. I hear you've been swimming with cats again."

I groaned, "Wow that didn't take long to get around."

She raised her eyebrows, "Alira was telling a good story after a couple of wines."

Ferdinand squeezed my hand, "Well it was good to see you both maybe we'll catch up tomorrow."

Lilith nodded, "Are you going to the mudfest tomorrow?"

I looked at Ferdinand, "What is that?"

He looked at Lilith, "I was going to surprise Hannah with it."

Lilith's face dropped, "Oh sorry Ferdinand. Anyway, we'll see you there." We wandered back to the bungalow, "So what's the mudfest?"

He just grinned, "You'll have to wait until tomorrow, it's a surprise."

We got back to the bungalow going and sitting on the sofa while Ferdinand went into the kitchen. He came back out sitting next to me, putting a plate of food on the coffee table, picking me up onto his lap and getting the food, "Come eat a little bit more for me."

I put my arms around his neck snuggling in kissing him gently, "Nein Ferdinand ich habe keinen hunger (no Ferdinand I'm not hungry.)"

He chuckled, "Komm schon, Hannah, nur ein bisschen (come on Hannah just a little bit)."

He looked at me lovingly, "I'll tell you about mudfest if you have a little bit for me. I just worry that you will get sick, especially with all that swimming."

I kissed him on the cheek, "Ok, just to make you happy. My stomach is a bit squeamish from the fruit, but I'll try a little bit for you."

He turned me around on his lap giving me the food watching me eat a bit of it. I put the plate down on the table, "There are you happy now."

He nodded, "Yes I am, thanks."

I got up putting my legs over his hips and my arms around his neck smiling at him, "Now what's this mudfest?"

He chuckled, "Oh I forget now."

I pulled a face at him, "Ferdinand, you said you would tell me."

He grinned magicaeing out of the room putting me on his back yelling to me, "I can't remember."

I slapped his neck laughing, "You're a naughty dragon, Ferdinand."

We flew over the bush looking at animals wandering along then flew over towards the ocean that was looking clear and clean, showing various fish, dolphins and whales swimming in the waters. I pointed to some of them squealing, "oh look at that one."

We flew back to the bungalow landing just in front of it feeling good that we didn't have to worry about being seen or anything.

I jumped off giving him a kiss before he changed, "Thanks for the ride honey."

He changed in front of me putting his arm around my waist walking into the bungalow.

Chapter 22

I woke early listening to the slow chatter of birds and animals starting to move around as the sun began to rise along with listening to Ferdinand breathing deeply in sleep. I got up to go to the toilet feeling restless, with all the things going through my head. I had some strange dreams that didn't make me feel happy, along with everything that was going on and with the decisions I had to make.

After going to the toilet, I looked in to see if Ferdinand was still sleeping as he has a knack of looking asleep and then he would surprise me. This time he did appear to be asleep, so I went out onto the balcony to sit and watch the sun come up.

I decided to do a bit of meditation, not bothering with my usual CD, but just listening to the sounds of the bush waking up. I relaxed going deep into my meditation listening to my breathing, bringing in my usual vision of a boat that was floating down a river, lying in it relaxing when instead of gentle lull of the boat it started to rock with me having to hold on to the sides.

I finally managed to sit up looking around me to see dark figures throwing rocks in the water trying to hit the boat. This was also causing the water to become rough. I was trying to use my magic to stop them but it wasn't working so I tried to call Ferdinand but he couldn't come because they were holding him somewhere.

I could feel my heart racing in my chest as I was trying to work out what to do, when I felt something rub itself up against me, calming me. My breathing started to return to normal bringing me out of my meditation. I took some deep breaths, opening my eyes to see a couple of the lions I had been sleeping with in the pack last time, sitting near me, panting.

I calmed myself when one of the lions came and rubbed itself up against my arm, "Hi Hannah, are you alright now?"

I nodded, "Yes, thanks Aslan. It wasn't a very nice vision unfortunately. I think trouble is coming my way—again!"

The other lion came in closer lying down on the balcony, "maybe you should lie with us until you calm down enough."

I nodded, "Thank you Leoa, I think I will." Aslan lay down letting me lie between them, as we talked about what I had seen.

Aslan panted giving a little growl, "That certainly doesn't sound very good Hannah. Make sure you have some sort of protection." The sun was coming around to the balcony warming us all, making us sleepy. I fell asleep listening to the steady rhythm of the lions' hearts and breathing, stopping any more thoughts of danger.

Ferdinand woke up finding me gone and Kimba sitting in my spot, "Where has you mother gone now Kimba?"

She let out a little meow going over to give him a kiss as he got up to pat her.

He listened to see if he could hear me moving around, deciding to get up to have a look to see where I was. He looked around the bungalow finding I wasn't there feeling his heart rate rise a bit, deciding to look on the balcony.

A smile spread across his face, shaking his head, "Good grief Hannah, what next. At least you're not naked this time."

He put Kimba up to the window to show her mother asleep in amongst the two lions. Kimba was sniffing, looking through the window, not sure what to make of the two big cats on the balcony.

Ferdinand put Kimba down going out to the balcony, just as Amelia and Charlotte arrived, stopping dead in their tracks. Amelia tiptoed towards the lions noticing me in the middle of them, then turning to look at Ferdinand, who was just coming out.

Ferdinand smiled, "She is really getting into those cats, isn't she?"

Charlotte just shook her head, "No one at home would believe this."

She took a photo on her phone with Ferdinand frowning, "Don't worry I won't show anyone at home. I might use it to scare Alira."

Amelia laughed, "Yeah that would be funny."

Ferdinand shook his head, "You two have your mother's sense of humour."

Shiro and Aetius came in just as Ferdinand was leaning down patting Aslan on the head to wake her up gently saying quietly, "You have to wake them up quietly otherwise they get a bit grumpy."

Shiro looked shocked, "Whoa your mother likes her cats."

Amelia giggled, "Now I know where Mum gets the grumpy mood in the morning from and I thought it was from you Ferdinand."

Ferdinand turned to look at Amelia while stroking Aslan's head pulling a face at her.

Aslan put a big paw up to knock Ferdinand's hand away, letting out a quiet roar, opening her eyes, "Oh hi Ferdinand it's you. I thought it was an annoying insect or something."

She looked around to see everyone standing there, "I suppose you want Hannah, do you?"

Ferdinand nodded, "Yes thanks."

She let out a roar waking Leoa, "What Aslan?"

She put her head up panting, looking around, "Oh hi Ferdinand. Hannah was meditating but didn't look very happy, so we came to comfort her."

She looked around to the others, "You must be her daughters, hi."

Amelia and Charlotte looked nervously at them both saying, "Hi" together.

I yawned and stretched feeling the movement along with people talking, sitting up wiping my eyes. I looked around me to see everyone there, "Oh I was just having a chat and we fell asleep."

Both the cats got up shaking themselves out and having a bit of stretch, "See you later Hannah," as they sauntered off.

Ferdinand came over smiling shaking his head, "What am I going to do you with Hannah?"

He helped me up, "Well at least, I wasn't naked this time."

Amelia and Charlotte came over to give me a hug with Charlotte showing me the photo she had taken. I giggled, "Show Alira that, it will make her go pale again."

Charlotte grinned, "That's what I said. It's no use showing anyone at home, they would never believe it."

Ferdinand took my hand looking at the others, "Have you had breakfast yet?"

Shiro came straight up on the balcony, "No and I'm starving."

Amelia looked at him, "You did so have some."

He rubbed his stomach, "There's always room for more."

We had breakfast discussing what we were going to do today. Ferdinand stopped everyone talking, "We are going to do the mudfest."

Shiro and Aetius grinned wickedly with realisation coming over Shiro's face, "Oh yeah I had forgotten about that."

Amelia, Charlotte and I looked at them with me saying, "I tried to get it out of Ferdinand but he just tricked me and said nothing. So, what's it about?"

Ferdinand came up to me getting my plate, "You'll have to wait and see. We will have to go soon to get to it."

We got up and helped to clean up listening to Amelia and Charlotte have Shiro and Aetius on, trying to get information out of them about mudfest.

I also tried putting my arm around Ferdinand's waist, "So is this mudfest fun."

He put his hand up to my chin kissing me lightly on the lips, "You'll have to wait and see dear."

I groaned, "You're stubborn."

He chuckled shaking his head, "You can talk madam. That reminds me what happened in the meditation?"

My smile faded, "Oh that! It wasn't very nice. A vision came through that I had lost my magic and you had been taken away from me. I must have come over upset when the lions came along and brought me out of it."

He looked a little worried at me, "Mm that doesn't sound very good. No one can take me away from you, Hannah."

He finished what he was doing putting his arm around me, "Come on we'll make our way to the mudfest, that will cheer you up."

The girls took off with Aetius and Shiro while Ferdinand decided he wanted to fly there for a change. I stood on the balcony watching him change into a dragon, noticing he was crouched down on all fours with a small groan coming from him.

I was worried, "Are you alright, Ferdinand?"

He shrugged it off, "Yes, I just got a funny feeling when I changed. I'm sure it's nothing to worry about, probably getting jealous of your lions or something," trying to make light of it.

I went up to him kissing his scaley cheek, "You'll always be my number one dragon honey."

I climbed onto his back, taking off doing a full circle of the bungalow first then flying towards a bush area that was partly cleared with a large group of people standing around talking.

He landed a little way away from everyone letting me get off changing into male form turning as he squinted his eyes, as though in pain. I moved over to him, "Are you sure you are alright Ferdinand?"

He nodded, "Yes I think it's just a bit of heart burn of something."

I looked surprise, "Oh I didn't think dragons got heart burn."

He was getting annoyed, "Don't worry about it, Hannah it will pass."

He looked at me because I had a concerned look on my face, "It's alright honey, come on let's go and have some fun."

He took my hand and led me over to the group of people we had seen, bumping into Alira and Fia as well as a younger version of Alira smiling at her, "You must be Alira's daughter?"

She turned to smile at me with Alira's cheeky smile but just a younger version, "Hi Hannah, I'm Poppy. I thought I would come and see what this mudfest was all about. Mum wanted me to come the whole weekend but I had things to do with my friends."

I gave her a hug, "Well it's nice to finally meet you."

Amelia, Shiro, Charlotte and Aetius came over, looking excited with Charlotte producing her phone, "Alira I have something to show you."

Ferdinand shook his head, "She just couldn't wait could she."

Alira squealed, "Hannah you've been at it again with those blasted cats." Poppy leaned in to have a look laughing, "Oh Mum has been telling me about some of this. It looks hilarious, I don't know what she is going on about."

Alira scowled at her, "They are big and scary and also have big teeth."

Poppy chuckled, "So were some of your boyfriends, but you weren't scared of them." This made us all laugh with me going up to give her a hug, "Poppy has a wonderful sense of humour Alira."

She just shook her head mumbling, "There's always a smartass in the family, isn't there?"

A loud trumpet sounded then a voice came over the crowd telling everyone to move in closer. Ferdinand took my hand moving in closer with a large clap of thunder going overhead making me look up, "That wasn't me."

He smiled, "I know dear just wait." A burst of rain started to fall as I looked over to Ferdinand and then over to my girls who were also looking around wondering what was going to happen next.

Ferdinand held onto my hand not saying anything, so I turned to look at him again, "Ferdinand it's raining."

He was trying not to grin, "I know dear, just wait for it."

Another trumpet went, when Ferdinand pointed to my feet removing my shoes and his starting to move forward, thinking, '*Ok this is strange.*' Ferdinand pulled me along with everyone else picking up the pace to a light jog when the people in front of us hit a huge mud patch, slipping and sliding.

I tried to stop but Ferdinand was holding on to my hand tightly, plus the people behind us were moving closer, squealing in delight. As we moved into the mud patch, the mud was getting thicker but the rain also got heavier making it really squishy. I squealed, "You rotten sod, you knew what this was."

He picked up a handful of mud and threw it at me, before I had a chance to duck, getting the whole amount down the front of me. I let go of his hand getting a handful in both hands throwing it back but he dodged it.

Amelia and Charlotte came up behind him, putting handfuls of mud over his hair as he groaned, "Agghh you Dragĕ women are going to pay for that."

He turned around grabbing their legs as they tried to get away, watching them fall, face first into the mud.

I stood there laughing with tears running down my face, going over to Ferdinand trying to push him over, but he just picked me up, as I screamed and put me back first into a big pile of mud. The rain was pouring down now, causing rivets of water to run down our faces through the mud.

I tried to get up, still laughing, but my feet were slipping underneath me, so Ferdinand relented and came over to help me up. I decided to cheat a little and used some magic to push him over on his back, landing on top of him, putting a handful of mud all over his face.

He managed to grab my hands laughing, "You'll pay for that Hannah," flipping me over, sitting on my hips and smearing mud all through my hair. I couldn't stop laughing, with some of the mud going into my mouth, spitting it out.

The rain kept falling cleaning our faces enough to see at least, as I pushed him off again getting up. I was running out of energy now, leaning over to get my breath back watching the others throw mud at each other.

Ferdinand got up to take a break as well, putting his arm around me, "Well that's a good bit of exercise," panting as he said it.

I looked at him smiling, "Just as well you didn't tell me I guess; I probably wouldn't have come."

He flicked some muddy hair away from my face, "That's exactly why I didn't tell you."

I rubbed the mud on his stomach in a bit more. He took my hand, "Come on we'll move forward, there are showers at the end of the mud patch."

I was laughing as we walked forward watching everyone throw mud at each other, just like a giant snow fight, but with mud. The rain was making it nice and gooey allowing the mud to fly further. A few handfuls were hitting us as we moved along, giggling at all the antics going on.

Lilith and Pardus were throwing mud at each other as we passed them laughing and joking together. I looked at Ferdinand who was watching them smiling, turning to me, "Looks like they are getting on better now, thank goodness."

I nodded, "Yes it's good to see."

We made our way forward through the mud and rain which was starting to ease now. I could see large pipes with shower heads hanging down from them and people going under them to clean off. We were just about at the showers when Aetius and Shiro came up to us grinning making Ferdinand hold onto me, "No you two, I'm helping Hannah to the showers."

They grabbed his arms pulling them off me and dragging him back into the mud, throwing him down and pouring mud all over him.

He was trying to fight them off yelling at them, but they were too strong for him. I stood there buckling over with laughter when Lilith came up to me, "Are you having a good time Hannah?"

I nodded, "yes, it's a great idea this. It's sort of like a giant snow fight but with mud."

She smiled, "Oh yes, it is. We have big snow fights as well in winter, you should come to that. It looks like Aetius and Shiro got their revenge for your girls."

I nodded, "Yes it's certainly been a lot of fun."

Pardus came up behind Lilith with handfuls of mud putting them on her front. She turned with a wicked grin coming over her, "Pardus you brat. I'll get you for that."

Ferdinand finally managed to get up coming back over to me putting some mud down my back, "Thanks for helping me, dear." This made me scream, "Oh you …" turning around quicker than he thought putting some mud down his trouser front then squishing it. He gave me a hug squishing the mud on my back making it worse, looking at Lilith and Pardus who were out of breath now, "Great mudfest wasn't it?"

Lilith hesitated looking at Ferdinand as though she could see something different about him but then put on a smile, "Yes, I was just telling Hannah that we have a snow fight as well and that she should come back for that one."

Ferdinand smiled, "We should be living here by then, so she won't miss that."

Lilith looked at us both surprised with a flicker of annoyance going through her face, "Oh are you coming to live here Hannah?"

I sighed, "We are talking about it, just not sure when though."

This annoyed Ferdinand taking my hand turning to Lilith, "It won't be far away Lilith" moving off towards the showers.

I was trying to stay on my feet, with Ferdinand still holding onto my hand, pulling me along, "Ferdinand, slow down its too slippery for me."

He stopped and picked me up putting me in front of him, "Put your legs around my hips and I'll take you to the showers."

I did as he asked looking at his face, "Don't be angry Ferdinand. I'm going to come here, I'm just not ready yet."

He didn't say anything more but just put his arms around me as I put my head on his shoulder until we got to the showers.

People were lining up going under the water that was flowing quite fast, washing off as much mud as they could. I watched quietly as we moved slowly forward while everyone laughed at the state of their clothes, faces and hair.

It came to our turn to go under the showers with Ferdinand putting me down on the ground helping me wash the mud off my hair, face and then as much as we could off the clothes. I watched him wash his hair and face under the shower pulling his pants out to let the water run down there, trying to get him smiling again. He managed a smile, "Don't be naughty, Hannah."

We moved off the matting under the shower to another dry matting area bringing in towels to wipe our faces and hair. Ferdinand got the towel and wiped under my chin and down my neck, "You missed a bit here, dear."

I put my face up to let him wipe it while I watched him, "This should make my skin nice and smooth at least."

He smiled, "Yes it will."

I turned myself off to his thoughts as I was beginning to wish I was able to tell him Morag's idea now, rather than have to wait until we got home. If he doesn't come right, I will do it regardless and just get into trouble with Morag. I can always put an orb up and tell him, that way we can make sure no one is listening to us.

He looked at me giving me a little kiss, jolting me back, "You were daydreaming again, weren't you?"

I smiled briefly still getting my breath back, "Yes, I'm feeling a little weary though."

He took my hand and magicae back to the bungalow straight into the bathroom taking our clothes off and turning on the shower. He washed my hair for me and then I washed his to make sure we got all the mud out. We then wash ourselves checking each other that we had gotten all the mud.

We dried ourselves, getting dressed and sitting on the sofa together after he had got us something to eat and drink. I ate a little bit and had a big drink of water, being thirsty after all that exertion, "Can we go to that little market so I can get you something to wear for protection?"

He nodded, "Yes sure. Do you want a rest first though?"

I nodded, "Yes I think I do."

He got up taking my hand, "I think I need one to, that has worn me out." We lay down cuddling, slowly dropping off feeling a little sad that we have this between us.

I woke to find Ferdinand gone from the bed, looking around for him but couldn't find him. It was no use going to look for him, as I didn't know Jardine well enough to do that. He has probably gone to the dragon lair or something anyway.

I sat on the sofa playing with Kimba having a drink of water thinking about what Morag was proposing again, but also making sure I was blocking off thoughts. I just couldn't make up my mind without talking to him about it first anyway. I was also worried about him getting some pains, not sure what that was about. He was also quite moody and growing hair, that really confused me. Maybe he needs a check-up from the doctor or whatever they have here. I might suggest it to him before we go home, that might be why he is quite grumpy at times.

I thought about the bracelet with the protection on wondering where I had put it. I'm sure I had brought it with me but I just couldn't think where it was. I tried to pull it in but it just wouldn't appear, feeling annoyed.

Ferdinand came in while I was thinking this, looking a bit happier, "Oh good you're up. Do you want to go and look at that market now?"

I nodded, "Yes that will be great. I was just wondering where I had put my bracelet, have you seen it?"

He thought about it, "No, we'll have a look when we come back because the markets will close soon."

I shrugged my shoulders, "Ok" getting up and putting Kimba down. He took my hand and we magicae out to the market strolling around looking at the stalls.

The sun had come out warming us, helping to relax me as we looked at all the lovely things people had made. We came across a jewellery stand that had some more masculine items in it.

I saw a necklace on a black strap with a dragon encased in an unusual design done in silver. I asked to look at it, showing Ferdinand, "Do you like this?"

He had a look at it closer, "Yes it's nice."

He put it on around his neck, "How does it look?"

The lady brought a mirror out so he could look at it as well, "I think it looks nice on you."

He smiled, "Well this looks like the one then," bending down giving me a kiss, "Thanks honey."

The lady in the stall smiled, "It does look nice on you Ferdinand," looking pleased with himself. We strolled along a bit more looking at different things, "There are some lovely things here, Ferdinand."

He was busy looking at things turning to me with an annoying grin, "Yes and you can look to your heart's desire when you are here."

I didn't bother to answer this time as I was getting annoyed.

We got back to the bungalow, "Can you take it off and I'll put some protection on it for you?"

He nodded taking it off, "I'll just go and do some things with the dragons. I'll meet you back here for the meal," giving me a kiss and taking off.

I went into the bathroom and cleansed the necklace first under the water saying a chant asking the elements earth, air, wind and fire to cleanse it. I then went into the bedroom taking Kimba with me, shutting the door and putting an orb around us bringing in the family book.

I put the necklace on top of the book letting it analyse it when the dazzling light went around the necklace just as it had done on my bracelet, watching it float in the air and turning to a page in the book and stopping. A spell came up, *"This necklace from another land is now stronger in the protection of the dragon Ferdinand. Wear it always to keep him safe from those who wish to harm him* being foe or evil in air, water, fire and earth their spells will now be repelled and dispersed."

I said the spell putting my hand over the necklace watching a bright light form around it giving it the protection it needed.

While I was there in the book, I thought I would have a little flick through going to the sealed section again. It was still closed touching the seal with the words coming up again that I needed a password to enter into it and the one who put it there's permission.

I thought of a couple of passwords it could possibly be one being *'Drage'* nope that didn't work. I thought of my possible new brother's name *'Drachen'*.

"No that wasn't it." I thought about my grandmother's names, *'Matilda'* no *'Ingrid'* no.

I was getting annoyed *'I need a clue book'* thinking nothing was going to happen when words came out of it wavering like on a screen, *'The password you seek is the one that this is about.'*

I thought, *'Well if I knew who it was about, I wouldn't be asking'* groaning not feeling patient enough to work it out right now, closing the book and sending it away.

I closed the orb and lay down on the bed with Kimba talking to her, "This is turning into a bit of a mess Kimba. I feel like running away, in some ways, so I don't have to make a decision. Either way I'm going to piss one of them off." Kimba got up rubbing herself against me giving me a little meow.

Charlotte knocked on the door, "Anybody home?"

I got up taking Kimba with me, "Yes I'm here, Charlotte."

She came in smiling, "I've just got the result back from the DNA test. I know somebody who knows somebody sort of thing, so they did it a bit quicker than normal."

I smiled nervously, "Oh yes, so what's the verdict?"

She smiled, "Looks like you've got another brother."

I grinned at the thought of it, "Wow this is good but scary news. I just hope he turns out better than the ones I have now."

She came in and sat down, "Where's Ferdinand, I thought he'd be here by now getting ready to go to the meal?"

I shrugged my shoulders, "I don't know he's in a funny mood again, so I thought I'd give him some space. I've just got a necklace for him and put some protection on it. Have you girls got something for yourselves?"

Charlotte nodded showing me a bracelet with blue crystals on it shaped into dolphins "aww that's nice did Aetius pick that?"

She looked affectionately at it, "yes, it's lovely, isn't it? There're a few things I would like to get from there but we aren't allowed to take them home."

I smiled, "Yes I know."

Charlotte looked around, "Is Ferdinand getting moody because he wants you to come and live here?"

I went and got a drink of water, "yes, I think that is part of it. I think he is in a little bit of pain as well, as he looked as though he was in pain last time, he changed into a dragon in front of me."

Charlotte got a glass as well and had a drink, "Are you going to come and live here?"

I shrugged my shoulders, "I'm not sure at this stage I'm a bit torn. I don't want to leave you two unprotected, even though I know you have Aetius and Shiro and I'm not that far away, but I feel a little controlled with my magic here. Not that I'm going to be doing anything bad with it. I've finally got to play with it and I keep getting told not to do certain things with it. Morag wasn't really happy with you two using that magitrap on that guy, but as far as I'm concerned, he deserved it and it takes him away from us."

Charlotte sighed, "I know how you feel with regards to the magic. They appear to be quite happy to tell you off for just defending us but nothing really gets done about the ones doing the attacks. I mean they say they are dealing with them but it's not deterring the others from coming forward and attacking us."

I sat on the chair, "I love being here in Jardine, it is the dream life, with magic being normal and everything being free and community-based work, but our family magic appears to be different in a lot of ways and I feel I haven't discovered it all yet, that's why I say I'm torn."

I needed to talk to someone about the other option so I leaned in talking quietly, "M has an idea of doing something with Alira and I, but I'm not allowed to say anything yet."

Charlotte looked curious, "I hope it's nothing dangerous, I mean you're not getting any younger Mum."

I smirked, "No it's not dangerous, but thanks for reminding me I'm getting old."

Charlotte got up, "Well I'll get going to the meal, do you want to come with me?"

I sighed, "yes, I may as well. I'll leave a note for Ferdinand telling him I'll meet him there. What time are you all going tomorrow?"

Charlotte thought about it, "I think just after breakfast as I have some things to sort out before I go to work on Tuesday. It will give me a chance to relax as well."

I wrote the note out, "Yes, I might do the same. Knowing Ferdinand though he will probably want to stay as long as possible."

Charlotte put her arm through mine, "Just remember he's not in charge, you both have a right to do things your own way and try and meet in the middle."

I appreciated her to talk to, "yes, I know I get a bit soft around men sometimes. I think that is from watching my mother being bossed around by men and assume it is the way it should be. All the other times it was my temper that stopped me from being bossed around," chuckling, "It came in handy then."

Charlotte smiled, "It's got you in and out of trouble, Mum."

We went out and down to the meal area mingling with the people there. I was chatting away to a woman called Malus who was asking about our world when Ferdinand came up looking a little tired, "Hi sorry I lost track of time."

Malus looked at Ferdinand, "Hi Ferdinand what have you been up to lately?"

He looked at Malus as though he didn't really want to talk to her but felt he had to "oh just showing Hannah Jardine hoping she will come and live here with me."

Malus looked at me questioningly, "Oh are you thinking of coming here to live Hannah. Wouldn't you miss your world and the way they do things?"

I felt awkward with the way they were both looking at me, "It's still being decided at the moment. I think the food is out, nice to have met you Malus."

Ferdinand said goodbye to her as well, talking quietly as we walked, "She is an elder but isn't very nice, just watch what you say to her."

"Yes alright. Did you have a nice time?"

He smiled, "Yes just doing some stuff for the elders, you don't mind do you?"

I shook my head, "No I was just doing the protection for your necklace and talking to Charlotte. She got the result back from the test, by the way; it looks like I have another brother. Hopefully this one turns out nicer than the others."

He smiled, "Oh that's good, I suppose. Like you said you don't know him so you'll have to wait and see."

We had the meal and a couple of drinks, going around chatting to people. I caught up with Morag and Cara making them laugh when they heard about the lions again. Morag looked at my wrist, "Where is your bracelet, Hannah?"

I put my hand on my wrist, "Oh I was looking for it before but couldn't find it. I tried to pull it in as well, but it didn't come in. I'll have another look when I get back. We are leaving tomorrow and just in case I don't see you, thanks for a nice time here I've enjoyed it."

Morag and Cara gave me a hug, "We'll see you later and let you know how things are going."

Morag frowned, "It's unusual it didn't come in when you tried to bring it in. I wonder where it could have gotten to? Try to find it, Hannah, I don't like you unprotected. As for tomorrow, if I don't see you then I'll catch up next week."

I watched Ferdinand chatting to some people, "I think Ferdinand might need a check-up next time we come. He has been quite grumpy along with mood swings."

Morag looked over to him pursing her lips, "He does look different somehow. Just remind me either when he comes in or when you are both here next."

I gave her and Cara a hug, "See you later then."

I went back over to Ferdinand who was still not quite himself, but was quietly listening to people who were chatting away. I went over to see how he was, taking my hand, walking around with me.

After a couple of hours, "Can we go home now I've had enough?"

I nodded, "Yes sure. What time were you looking at going tomorrow; the girls were wanting to know. They are leaving just after breakfast."

He thought about it being careful what he said, "I was thinking just after lunch, is that alright with you?"

I looked at him, "Do you have something you need to do only I wouldn't mind going a bit earlier as well."

He grumbled, "Yes I do have something I want to do and it will save me coming back to Jardine."

I put my hands up, "Alright I was just asking. I'll go and let the girls know. I can meet you at the bungalow if you like?"

He shook his head looking determined, "No I'll wait here for you and we can walk back together. That way you won't wander off with lions."

I could see he was trying to lighten the conversation, so I carried on, "Oh come on I'm not that bad."

He gave me a quick kiss, "Go and tell the girls and we'll get going."

I went and told them and Alira what time we were going. They all said they would pop in before they went to say goodbye. I gave them all a hug, "You could always come and have a drink with us tonight if you like?" All of them said they will see when they were finished here.

I got back to Ferdinand, with him taking my hand, walking towards the bungalow "are you alright Ferdinand? Do you need a check-up or something?"

He put a smile on, "No I'm alright just not looking forward to going back. You've had a good time here, haven't you?"

I smiled, "Yes but I have things to do still."

He sighed frustratedly, "Yes I know."

We got back to the bungalow going to sit on the sofa and Ferdinand going into the kitchen, "Do you want a drink or anything, Hannah?"

I was checking my phone, "Yes a glass of wine would be nice, thanks."

He came over with the wine and some snacks while I was still checking my phone.

He had a drink and a snack then lay down putting his head on my lap as I put my phone down. I stroked his hair, feeling I should talk to him about what I felt but I wasn't sure if he was in the right mood to talk about it. I had a couple more sips of my drink stroking his hair as he lay there with his eyes closed, "Ferdinand you know I like Jardine."

He didn't reply so I looked down and realised he was asleep, 'well there goes that idea.'

I left him there stroking his hair occasionally looking at my phone and drinking my wine. The others messaged me that they were coming by, so I put Ferdinand to bed magically changing his clothes and shutting the door. I thought if he wakes up, he can join us, otherwise I'll just have a couple of drinks with the others.

They came around asking where Ferdinand was, telling them that he was tired from the mudfest, so he went to bed. They of course, made jokes that he's getting old and can't hack it anymore.

They left saying they would come around tomorrow for breakfast. I went in and had a shower going in to find Ferdinand still fast asleep. I gently got in trying not to disturb him, lying there listening to his breathing. He woke briefly putting his arm over me giving me a cuddle and going back to sleep.

Chapter 23

I woke to find Ferdinand up, hearing a noise coming from the kitchen presuming he was cooking breakfast. I came out to find him busy making pancakes and toast looking up and smiling, "Good morning. Did you have a good sleep?"

I smiled, "Good morning, yes, I did. It looks as though you did as well."

He nodded, "Yes I was exhausted from that mudfest, I think."

The others came around for breakfast having Ferdinand on about getting old then they all took off for home.

We tidied up the bungalow cleaning things as we went. Once we had finished, I went up to Ferdinand, "Are you ready to go home now?"

He shook his head, "No I just have a couple of things to do and then I'll come and take you home."

I was a bit disappointed, "Oh come on Ferdinand I'm ready to go now."

He came up giving me a cuddle, "I won't be long. Just give me an hour and I'll be back."

I agreed, not really happy about it, going to sit on the sofa, "I still can't find my bracelet; do you know where it is?"

He shook his head, "No I thought you had found it. Have a look around while I'm gone."

I noticed he had his necklace on which I was pleased about. He took off letting me get up and have a look for my bracelet. I looked under the sofa, around the kitchen area and in the bedroom.

I stood there thinking where I had it last been, being sure it was on the bedside cabinet. I thought I could bring the book out and put the protection out on something else while I am waiting for him. I decided to go for a walk first to get a bit of fresh air and possibly a swim down at the pond where I was yesterday. I left him a note in case he came back early and was looking for me. I went out following the path, finding the river and the swimming area just over from it. Tendua was there sunning herself again on a rock watching the water glide over the rocks half asleep. I went up to her carefully so I didn't give her a fright, "Hi Tendua, how are you today?"

She opened her eyes turning to look at me, "Oh hi Hannah I am good. Just sunning myself. Are you here for another swim?"

I grinned, "Yes now that I am here, I may as well go in. We are going home soon and I'm not sure when I will be back again."

Tendua yawned, "I won't join you this time, I'm too sleepy. Enjoy yourself."

I took my clothes off and carefully walked over the stones through the river to the swimming area.

I dived in feeling the rush of the cool water over my body making me feel alive. I don't know if it was just all the natural minerals in the water or not having any pollution but the water here just made my skin tingle. I was swimming around going down as deep as I could floating in the water feeling the joy of being suspended there with a clear view around me, when I saw a movement near me and Ferdinand swimming down to me. I smiled at him going to move away but he caught me and took me up to the surface.

He held me around my waist as we surfaced, "Trust you to be here, Hannah."

I giggled, "I will miss this when I'm back home so I thought I'd have a quick swim while I waited for you."

He magicae out of the water walking the last part as I wrapped my legs around his hips. I looked at him, "You were quicker than I thought. I couldn't find my bracelet so I was going to put a protection on something else when I got back."

He looked distracted and not listening to me, "What is it?"

He kept walking towards my clothes, "It's Lilith and Tina."

I turned around to see them standing there looking at us as we walked out of the water, realising Lilith was staring at my back with the dragon tattoo on. I brought a towel in to cover myself, "Let me down, Ferdinand."

He shook his head, "No stay there. Hi Lilith and Tina what brings you two here?"

Tina smiled briefly looking at me, "Oh this must be Hannah?"

I was trying to hold onto the towel and Ferdinand, "Hi Tina, yes nice to meet you. Ferdinand put me down."

Ferdinand smiled, "Hannah was just having a quick swim before we went, so we must get going. Is there anything you wanted to talk to either of us about?"

Lilith and Tina shook their heads with Lilith saying, "No we are looking for something but it obviously isn't here. Have a nice trip home, Hannah."

I turned again, "Thanks." Then Ferdinand took me back to the bungalow.

He let me down drying me off with the towel walking me towards the bed with a naughty look in his eyes.

I smiled, "Ferdinand don't be naughty you can do that when we get home."

He didn't listen still drying me with the towel walking me backwards towards the bed starting to kiss me on the neck.

We got to the bed, "Ferdinand I want to do a protection spell" kissing me on the mouth stopping me talking and laying me down on the bed.

He straddled my hips, still kissing me, leaning forward to get something when all of a sudden, he took my wrist in his hand and put something around it. I felt like there was a drain on my powers while I tried to move my hand, "Ferdinand what are you doing?"

He kept his head down kissing me, when he took my other wrist and I realised what he was doing as I struggled yelling at him, "No Ferdinand!"

He bound them together as I tried to get free, at first under my own way, but then using magic. Once the rope was closed, I felt my power drain from me, "What have you done?"

Ferdinand smiled kindly at me, "We are staying here Hannah. I'm not going back to see you get attacked anymore. This rope is one of the guard's ropes that stops you using your powers, so don't fight them."

He got off me putting my clothes on, "Ferdinand, you'll get into trouble for stealing a guard's rope, please what is going on?"

He was looking around the room not listening to me, "Where is Kimba I want to get going?"

I was starting to panic struggling against the rope, "Ferdinand lässt darüber reden (Ferdinand let's talk about it.)"

He looked at me angry, "Don't think you can get around me that way Hannah. You keep saying that you have wasted 50 years not knowing me as well as your magic. Well, *I've* missed you for 50 years also and I am not going to stand by while you volunteer to go out hunting for bad people with magic. I didn't steal the rope, a guard let me use it."

I looked shocked at him, "How did you find out about that? Ferdinand this was supposed to be confidential, please listen to me."

He growled getting angry, moving towards me. I felt I had a little bit of strength left so I put my feet under him pushing him away from me, throwing him off the bed.

I rolled over, getting off the bed to try and get away from him, but because I was weakening, he caught me as I was heading towards the door, putting me back on the bed. I started hitting him with my hands and legs and screaming, "Ferdinand stop; this is a trap! No one is supposed to know about that, who told you? I was going to tell you when we got home."

He put his hand over my mouth stopping me from yelling. He said a chant putting a magical gag on, as I tried to struggle against him, with no strength physically or magically.

He looked worried, "I'm sorry honey but these ropes normally knock people out but as usual a stubborn Dragĕ woman has to have the full effect."

He pulled the rope from my wrists out like a rubber band with a white glow on it, like those glow sticks you see at events. He stretched it down to my feet, "This should make you sleep Hannah until we get to where I want to go."

He wound the rope around my feet feeling the effects of it, as I slowly succumbed to the rope, going to sleep.

He found Kimba putting her in her cage, wrapped a blanket around me and took off to a remote part of Jardine.

We landed in an older style bungalow that no one had lived in for a long time. It had an old wood fire place, a bit like what you would see in a log cabin in a western movie.

He put me on the bed placing Kimba down on the floor until he sorted me out. He looked at me worried about what I had said, about it being a trap shaking his head, *'No I am sure she is wrong. She just didn't want me to find out, that is what I was told by a reliable source.'*

He opened the blanket and undid the binding on my feet tapping my face to wake me up. I slowly opened my eyes, wildly looking at him, starting to struggle. I still had the gag on and my wrists were still bound.

He held onto my arms, "Stop struggling and I will take them off and that goes for the gag as well."

He looked at me determined as I struggled against him when a vision came into his head of a past time, he couldn't remember where from, of a woman laughing and he was there on a huge bed with her.

He shook his head confused about the vision clearing his head and coming back to me taking the gag off, "Hannah, stop it! Look around this is our new home; they won't find us here. When you have come to accept that we will be living in Jardine, we can go back to the main area."

I could feel the ropes sapping my energy and powers so I decided to stop struggling, "Where are we Ferdinand?"

He looked around, "This used to be a community many years ago but the houses are not used anymore because they were hard to heat and had building materials that weren't ecological anymore."

I tried to sit up, with him putting his hand on my shoulder, pushing me back down, "Hannah just relax and when I feel you are going to behave, I'll take those ropes off you."

I looked at him worried, "Won't they find us Ferdinand? Do you realise if they do, they'll take you away from me?"

He leaned down and kissed me trying to relax me, "I didn't take the ropes and I intend to send them back once you behave. Besides no one knows we are here and it is a long way out of the main area."

I started to get angry, "Ferdinand this doesn't feel right. Can we go home so I can at least leave my job and sort my place out. I promise I will come back then."

He shook his head, "No Hannah, I know you will try and talk me out of it or get one of the elders to order me around. I'm not doing that any more. There are two people in this relationship and I want to live here."

He got up to get a drink of water coming back and sitting me up giving me a drink. I looked at him, "I was going to tell you what Morag was proposing Ferdinand once we got home. I hadn't said yes to it, you have to understand that. I told Morag I wouldn't do anything without talking to you about it, you have to believe me."

He was getting annoyed, "It doesn't matter Hannah. I have made a decision to be together with you as a couple until we die of natural causes not if someone kills us."

He got off the bed moving towards the fire, "I want to get the fire going as this house isn't very warm and I don't want you getting sick. You can scream as much as you like here no one will hear you."

I rolled over onto my side not wanting to look at him while I tried to fiddle with the ropes. I could hear him putting some wood into the grate getting ready to light it, "You won't be able to get them off you Hannah, they only work for me."

I lay there thinking about who could have told him and given him these ropes.

Ferdinand came back over to me, "I'll get you comfortable and then I'll let Kimba out."

I looked at him angrily, "Go away Ferdinand and leave me alone. You're turning out just like the stupid men in my world. You have also forgotten I got attacked here as well!"

This made him scowl at me trying to make me turn to look at him, "You'll get used to being here Hannah, so the quicker you get out of your bad mood the quicker you'll get more freedom."

I still had enough magic in me to feel a vibration coming in. I turned to look at him with contempt "well someone has found us Ferdinand because I can feel someone coming in."

He hesitated not sure whether to believe me, then wrapped the blanket around me so my hands were hidden, with two guards appearing either side of him pointing their staffs at him.

The woman Malus, we had met at the main meal, came in along with another dark woman by the name of Ziller. Both Malus and Ziller didn't look very happy at the scene, "What is going on here, Ferdinand? What are you two doing in this area?"

I spoke up trying to get them to go, "I wanted to see some more of Jardine before we went home. Ferdinand knows I get cold easily so lit the fire for me. We were going to have a little picnic then go home, are we not allowed here?"

Malus grinned slyly nodding to one of the guards who pulled the blanket off me revealing the ropes on my wrists.

Ferdinand picked me up, "I didn't steal them, one of the guards let me use them until Hannah agreed to come and live here."

Ziller smirked, "You can't force a woman to come and live here Ferdinand, I think you have overstepped your role as spirit animal. We will have to confine you until we get to the bottom of this."

I put my arms around Ferdinand's neck, "No don't do that. He was tricked into doing this and he's hasn't been feeling well lately."

Malus shook her head annoyed, "Hannah, you have let him become too controlling with you, he needs to be dealt with. He has stolen ropes and used them to force you to do something you didn't want to do. He will be confined to Jardine until we sort this out."

Ziller nodded at the guards, "Put Hannah down, Ferdinand. The guards will take you away."

I tried to hang on to Ferdinand, "No he is my spirit animal and I will deal with him."

One of the guards took the ropes off me, pointing a staff at Ferdinand's neck, "Put her down Ferdinand."

He reluctantly put me down onto the bed looking worried, "I didn't steal the ropes." The guard put bracelets on his wrists like handcuffs but were made to control him more turning it on, "This will confine you to Jardine and restrict your magic."

I tried to grab Ferdinand but the guard pulled me off him, "You will be taken to your home Hannah until this is dealt with."

I tried to shake the guard's hand off, "Where is Morag or Cara, I want to speak to them."

Ziller looked annoyed, "They are on other business and have obviously been too soft with you two as well."

Ferdinand got angry struggling against the guard, "You can't send Hannah back without any protection they are still attacking her."

Ziller nodded to the guard knocking him out as he slumped, with the guard holding him up, "Take him away."

Malus turned to the other guard, "Get Hannah's things and take her back to her house and come straight back," with the guard nodding. I tried to plead again keeping my temper in, "Malus please, can you at least let me talk to Morag or Cara before I go back." Malus shook her head, "No, Hannah."

She signalled to the guard to go; I put up my hand, "Wait I want to take my cat."

I got off the bed and picked up Kimba, who was still in her cage, as the guard put her hand around my arm and magicaeing back to the unit. I felt sick as I moved forward to sit on the sofa, "How long does the effects of those ropes take to wear off?"

The guard came forward, "Should only be a couple of hours and you will feel better. I have never been in your world can I take a look around?"

I didn't really care leaning over to let Kimba out of her cage, "Yes do what you like."

I sat there numb, "I didn't think Jardine was so strict with their rules."

The guard whose name was Jeneca, came out of my bedroom looking out at the view from the window, "wow you have a lot of crystals there, you could almost form your own vortex. They are getting quite strict with some rules because we are getting women from your world who are not strong enough with their spirit animals or men generally. I better go otherwise they'll be wondering where I am. Take care, Hannah."

I got up feeling a bit giddy, "Can you tell me where Morag or Cara are at least Jeneca?"

She shook her head, "No Hannah. She did make me laugh though saying how you like to be with the lions even in your world. Bye for now."

She disappeared out of the room giving a little wave, looking sadly at me.

I found my phone in my jeans which were automatically changed when I entered our world. I needed to talk to someone, so I tried to call Amelia finding I had no reception. I tried Alira, again with a message coming up that my phone was out of order.

I sat there rubbing my head that was starting to ache, '*So I have no spirit animal and no phone reception and limited magic. I'm cut off. I could drive to Amelia's but I'll have to wait, until this wears off.*'

I was trying not to panic and get angry all at the same time. I got up carefully to go and feed Kimba and took some painkillers for my head, having a big drink of water. I took a deep breath moving slowly over to my bedroom with my head still spinning when I tripped and fell onto the floor landing on my left arm, feeling a pain shoot up my arm.

I yelled out in pain bringing my wrist up to my chest holding it, '*Oh shit not again. Is anything going to go right today.*' I got up on my knees, with my head still spinning and my wrist aching and crawled to the bathroom to get some strapping I had there. I then crawled back to the bedroom and lay down on the bed, strapping my wrist up. I pulled the duvet over me feeling hot angry tears start to fall, groaning in pain and anger, pulling my wrist up to my chest, '*I'll get those bastards who have done this. If I find out Lilith has something to do with this she better look out. I'm not going to be nice anymore.*'

I could hear a rumbling outside in the distance of thunder as I yelled, "You wait I'll get you." I eventually calmed down enough to fall asleep.

I woke to find my bedroom with late afternoon shadows around it and Kimba on Ferdinand's pillow feeling miserable. I moved the strapping touching the tattoo to see if I could get him in, but it didn't work.

I checked the time to see I had slept for four hours, getting up slowly to see how my head was. I sat there feeling sore and dishevelled trying to think what to do next as the anger started to build again.

I got up carefully, deciding I needed to see how strong my powers were first as they may have put something extra in those ropes. I went out to the bathroom first and washed my face, looking at my hair that was knotty from a restless sleep, just patting it down not really caring.

I then went to the kitchen going to get some wine then going to sit on the balcony. I decided to do the elements to see how strong they came in, taking a sip of wine first. I put the glass on the table beside me, then opened my hand out twirling my finger in my palm to bring up a little whirlwind. A small one appeared but I couldn't make it any stronger feeling something deep within stopping it.

I let out a groan, '*Agghh you bloody mongrels I'll get you for this!*' I sat there thinking while I sipped on my wine looking at the sea trying to calm myself down.

After I had finished my wine, I looked down at the clothes I had on wondering if they could be tainted in any way, because they would have been stored somewhere in Jardine. I got up not feeling so clogged in my head at least, going into my bedroom, taking off all of my clothes and putting them in a plastic bag.

I started to feel better, so I decided to go down to the sea and cleanse myself and some crystals while I was there, putting my swimmers on, that were in the wardrobe. I found Ferdinand's suit and shirt in there with my stomach dropping, '*I hope they're not hurting him.*'

I thought I had better not use my magic too much, at this stage, so I got a towel and my key putting my crystals in my swimmers and walked down to the beach, not far from my unit. I threw the bag of clothes in the big bins outside not wanting them anymore. I wrapped the towel around me, keeping an eye out for anyone I might suspect that might be there to attack or anything, quickly dropping my towel on the beach and putting my key in it.

The waves weren't too big, but they looked as though there was a strong pull to them, so I carefully went in feeling the coolness, as the waves started to hit my body. I called out to the water to cleanse me to take any evil or spell that is within or around me as I dived under the water feeling something leave me.

A chant came into my head, *"Cleanse me now from this evil and foe that has been placed from Jardine and is now to go. Water take it away let the salt within absorb it, cleanse it and deal with in anyway."* A black stain went from me floating out through the waves and out to sea. I felt cleansed now knowing that the chant was from my book and it was able to get deep within.

I ducked under a couple of times cleansing my crystals as well, then got out, as I was starting to feel cold. I went and grabbed my towel wrapping it around me starting to shiver, when I saw that priest looking at me grinning. I knew I had to conserve my magic so I put my head down and walked towards my unit. He started to taunt me, "Oh has Hannah hurt herself. Where's your friend Hannah? Come on Hannah it's time to come with me," putting his hand on my arm.

His hand ricocheted off me with a look of surprise coming over his face and a deadly look coming over mine, *"Get away from me now you annoying man and go swimming with the seagulls 'peto'."*

He flung off into the sea hitting a flock of seagulls quite a way out, that were sitting in the water looking for fish. I didn't even bother to look, smiling as I heard him scream, while he was thrown into the water as the birds squawked, when he landed in amongst them.

I got back into my unit feeling a lot better, but cold so I took the strapping off and had a hot shower, putting my nightie and dressing gown on to get warm.

I wasn't hungry, so I just had some toast and cuppa soup, sitting there thinking still in the quiet without any TV or music on. Kimba came and sat next to me while I sipped on my soup trying my phone again with "no service" still coming up.

I could feel myself getting stronger with the cleansing but I wanted to get full strength back before I did anything else. I dried the strapping out in the dryer then put it back on my arm noticing it was starting to swell. I shook my head, "I think I've broken something in it again!" I had a thought, I'll try and bring in a brace which will help it a lot better than strapping. I visualised one that I had seen in the chemist, with one coming in next to me. I took the strapping off and rubbed it down with deep heat, then put the brace on. It was starting to feel better at least. I felt the need to meditate with the elements, so I got everything ready putting my crystals and a candle with me trying not to think of Ferdinand and what was happening to him. It took a bit longer because of this, but I finally started going deep feeling the elements around me. I drew them up, visualising the earth bringing it within me, the air, the water and then lastly the fire groaning, feeling my full magic return, along with my anger, fuelling it even more.

I could feel myself lift off the ground and went out of my body to look, seeing myself float in the air with the elements swirling around me, sending bolts of themselves to me. A white glow formed around as protection sighing with the strength of it. I started to come back down from that plain of my higher-self sitting on the floor, along with the elements settling down. I was still meditating sitting within the strength of the elements when a cold shiver came over me, "Hei bestemor (hello grandma)."

She came within my vision of the meditation in her ghostly appearance, "Hei Hannah. Du er for sint (hi Hannah. You are too angry.)"

I chuckled, "Jeg trodde de ville bli fornøyd bestemor (I thought you would be pleased grandma)."

She must have been quite close because I thought I could feel her cold hand stroking my hair, "Ikke gjør noe dumt nå (don't do anything silly now.)"

I just growled, "Gå bort bestemor (go away grandma). Jeg har fått nok (I've had enough.)" I started to bring myself out of the meditation not wanting to talk to her anymore listening to my breathing. I felt a cold rush of air go over me hearing her growl at me.

I came out of my meditation looking around me in the darkness of my unit now, with just the candle going, flickering soft light around the room. It felt so empty without Ferdinand there, just like it used to be before he came into my life. I tried to touch the tattoo again to see if my magic coming back would help, but he didn't come. I closed the balcony door, cleansing the unit one more time and checking the guard did not leave any surprises. I found an extra crystal down by my bed that I was sure wasn't mine. I picked it up and growled at it angrily destroying it in my hand, watching as a small puff of black smoke rise from it.

I then locked up the unit securely, only letting my family members in, from now on and brought the book out, feeling sure nothing was around to try and get into it.

I put my hand over the front of the book closing my eyes, "*I wish to see who they that have done this to me. Bring them forward as a vision to me so I can deal with them one by one with your permission.*"

A bright glittery light in the shape of a cone came up from the middle of the book opening up to a small wavering screen with some pictures showing on it.

I looked at the pictures before me coming up through the screen making me leer at the sight of Hildegard, Allegra, Suzannah, Lilith and a surprise one of Cara. I shook my head in disappointment with the sight of Cara's picture coming up. I asked the book, "Are you sure that Cara is the one who has done this." The book just kept showing her picture spinning around in the little screen.

I shut the book down sending it away leaving the unit locked for family only.

The vision of this had stirred me up a bit and I wasn't feeling so tired now. It was still early anyway, so I got changed into a dark track suit, going to the meditation centre in Newtown, not sure what I was going to do or find, but all I knew is that I was getting angry and had to do something.

I landed in King Street, which is the main street of Newtown, feeling my anger build as I approached Dickinson Street where the old church was and where they did the meditation. I still wasn't sure what I was going to do, getting closer to the church to see some lights on in the building. I changed my appearance to a younger woman with jeans and a jacket, on walking closer to the church.

I knew there wasn't a meditation meeting on because of the long weekend so I crept around the side of the building to see who was in there. I also knew other groups used it for different classes, so I didn't want to hurt anyone else. I got to a window on the side where the servery was, when I saw them standing at the opening having a drink and talking. The three women Hildegard, Suzannah and Allegra appeared to be discussing something important with serious looks on their faces. I also noticed that they had wands sitting on the servery, just near their hands.

I stood there thinking when the book started to put ideas into my head lock the doors, crush the wands, send a whole lot of snakes in, take their pictures. I chuckled to myself, '*Looks like I have the books permission.*' I moved around to where I knew there was a door that led out to the little courtyard stepping inside as quietly as possible, starting the suggestions the book made. I put my hands out blowing on them moving around in a circle locking the church up with the sound of loud clicking going around the church then the door I had just come through banging shut.

I then put my hands up to crush their wands before they had a chance to grab them. I could hear them yelling at each other, "Quick grab your wand," hearing them scream as they disintegrated in front of them. I heard Suzannah walking out into the middle of the floor sounding angry, "Who is there?"

I thought to myself, '*She doesn't look quite so old now*' as I sent a whole lot of snakes, like a fountain, coming up from the middle of the floor, hearing them scream. I saw an old straw broom against the wall from Halloween, bringing it to me sitting on it and flying into the room.

Suzannah looked at me screaming, "Get her." Hildegard and Allegra were too busy trying to avoid the snakes that were piling into the room, slithering along the old wooden floor boards towards them.

Hildegard and Allegra looked angrily at me, "Hannah, change back to yourself before we deal with you."

I smugly smiled changing myself back, leaning on the broom, "Don't you like my little tricks ladies?"

Suzannah was starting to panic with my relaxed attitude and the number of snakes that were piling up in the room, as she tried to get up on the servery, to get away from them.

She was squealing looking at me, "Hannah stop this now, we need to talk."

I continued to float in the air leaning on the broom watching them trying to climb whatever they could to get away from the snakes. I put on an elderly voice, "Oh dear what would you like to talk about now."

Suzannah angrily said, "I opened you up with that dagger, you little bitch."

I chuckled, "I had already opened up. You might have felt my magic but it was a lot stronger than you realised. You just gave me part of a puzzle that is all. Thanks for that by the way."

Hildegard was standing on the servery petrified, "Come on Hannah we didn't mean any harm. You'll get your dragon back."

Suzannah growled at her, "Shut up Hildegard."

Allegra who was next to her on the servery whacked her arm, "Yes Hildegard shut up."

I yawned, "Oh I have it on good authority you were involved in the little incident in Jardine. Cara and Lilith aren't as loyal as you thought."

Suzannah looked worried trying to act dumb, "Who are you talking about Hannah?"

I was getting tired of their bullshit, flying around the room on the broom, "Oh to be a witch, isn't it fun ladies." I started to go around in a circle, "Oh did you hear what happened to Jonas and Harriet?"

Allegra giggled, "Oh yes, the washing machine. Nice, Hannah."

It was Hildegard's turn now to whack Allegra, "Will you shut up!"

As I went around in a circle it was stirring the snakes up making them raise their heads in the air trying to get them all. The women couldn't go any higher so they took their shoes off trying to hit them.

I stopped close to Hildegard and Allegra, "Have you seen my new phone ladies, it's a mirror and phone in one." Hildegard and Allegra were busy trying to stop the snakes come up to their feet in a high-pitched voice, "We don't care about your bloody phone Hannah, take these away from us."

I stopped the broom close to them steadying myself in front of Hildegard and Allegra, "If you let me take your picture, I'll stop the snakes from getting you; how about that?"

They looked up at me with a glimmer of hope on their faces and Hildegard looking suspicious, "How do we know we can trust you, Hannah?"

I chuckled, "Well you don't, but I am a bit more honourable than you two. Take it or leave it."

Allegra had a snake crawling up her leg now as she screamed, "All right Hannah do it, but stop the snakes first."

I waved my hand near them making the snakes settle down, "Now say cheese."

They both looked at the mirror as I clicked it with a dark vortex coming from them and into the mirror. They stood there stunned smiling like idiots who had seen something nice.

Suzannah started to panic, "Don't you point that thing at me, Hannah." She had a little bit of magic within her sending a bolt towards me, knocking the broom.

I held on tight dropping the mirror into the snakes watching them sliver over it. I looked at it then looked at her furiously, "Now look what you've made me do Suzannah," as I put my hand up lifting her up, sending the laser lighting around her body squeezing her.

Hildegard and Allegra were watching still with stunned smiles on their faces then looking down at the snakes, "Oh look at the pretty snakes."

Suzannah was screaming, "Let me down you bitch or you'll never see your dragon again."

I tried to hide my fear which made her cackle, "If anything happens to me, they'll deal with him." I moved closer to her, "Well they're going to have trouble on their hands aren't they because he was the only one that calmed me down you old hag. If he goes a lot more of you go." I forced her face up to look at me taking the snakes away pulling the mirror up and opening it.

Suzannah tried to struggle again, "Hannah please you could be so useful in our organisation with your strength and family lines."

I hesitated, "What do you know about my family?"

She cackled again, "You don't know do you? I believe you have a dragon tattoo on your back, there is still more to come once you have got your full strength. Just think, we could help you and get rid of some of these stupid old men who are running this world and slowly killing it with their pollution, greed and wars. We could make it great again like Jardine, if not better than Jardine."

I continued to hesitate, "And what would be in it for me, dear Suzannah?"

An ugly smile formed on her thin pale lips, "Whatever you want, Hannah."

I felt a vibration, which meant someone was trying to get in, "You bitch—you're just delaying me because you've called someone."

She screamed, "No I didn't, stop."

I pulled the mirror out of the snakes and took her magic, watching her slump. I knew it wouldn't take them long to get in so I put Suzannah over with the others taking the binding off her, sitting her down as they smiled like idiots while looking around at the snakes.

I went over to a corner jumping off the broom and putting an orb over me to see who came in. Three figures appeared not far from me looking at the snakes slither around the floor then over at Hildegard, Allegra and Suzannah, sitting on the servery smiling at the each other.

I stood there trying to control my anger as I watched Lilith, Malus and a guard from Jardine look around at the scene hearing Lilith say, "It must have been Hannah because she's used that magitrap that her daughter invented."

Malus growled, "Well we need to deal with her she has been told about doing this without going through us first. Get rid of the snakes and do something with those women."

Lilith went towards the three women, getting rid of some of the snakes, talking quietly to Hildegard, "Are you in there Hildegard?"

Hildegard giggled, "We've angered the witch Lilith; your plan is working. Not long before they will deal with her and she'll be gone once and for all hehehehehe."

Lilith turned to watch Malus and the guard look around the church and getting rid of any other snakes. They both went over to Lilith with Malus saying, "Did she say anything, Lilith?"

Lilith looked disappointed, "No just garbled talk. That thing must be quite strong."

I stood there listening and watching in disgust wondering why Lilith is so bent of getting rid of me, when Suzannah giggled and clapped her hands, "The witch is still around do dah do dah."

I realised she must have seen me disappear because the others went quiet looking around the room. The guard started scanning the room with her staff, so I quickly magicae out of the church and onto the broom, flying over the harbour letting things sink in.

Unfortunately, I flew a little low hearing some squeals below me and some flashes of light of people taking photos. I quickly changed my appearance to a witch with a long nose and black hair. I flew for a couple of minutes then disappeared hearing gasps, hoping they thought they were just seeing a prank.

I decided to go to Amelia's in the end just in case they did come after her and Charlotte. I needed to tell someone what was going on.

I landed on Amelia's balcony looking in the door to see her and Shiro sitting on the sofa, feeling relieved that they were alright. I knocked on the door making Amelia look up surprised to see me coming over and opening the door, "Mum what are you doing here?"

I gave her a hug, breaking down as I went inside, "I can't stay too long. There's been a horrible thing happen in Jardine." I sat down and told her the story in brief along with my phone not working and what I found in the church in Newtown.

Amelia and Shiro were horrified, "What are we going to do Mum?"

Shiro was fuming, "I'll go to Jardine and see what they've done with Ferdinand."

I got up stopping him, "No, as much as I want him back, there's something not right. I don't know where Morag is either."

Amelia called Alira asking her to come to her place as quick as possible. While we waited for her to come, she also called Charlotte and Aetius to come as there is an emergency.

Alira, Yindi, Charlotte and Aetius all came in looking worried at the sight of me upset. Yindi stood watching me hug Alira and Charlotte then came over to me, "Now tell us what has happened, Hannah."

I sat down calming myself telling them all what had happened as they sat there quietly listening.

Charlotte got up fuming, "We should storm bloody Jardine and give them what they deserve, especially that bloody Lilith."

Yindi put up her hands, "Now stop right there, all of you. I know you're all angry at what has happened, but sit and think about it for a moment." Yindi came and sat next to me, "You said you heard Lilith talking to Hildegard saying they wanted to anger you. Well, it looks like they've succeeded, not only with you but all of you. Don't you see, this is exactly what they want, they know you are strong in your magic and it will set Jardine against you and you against Jardine."

I could feel my frustrations building with the sense of this calming me a bit, "What do you suggest we do then Yindi?"

She thought about it, "I know this is going to be hard, but I think you should just go about your normal daily life until we can sort something out. I also think you had better get home in case they come to see where you are, especially since you were flying."

I grinned, "They can't get into my place it's locked up really well now."

Yindi didn't look so sure, "They might not be able to get in Hannah but they will look for signs of you around."

I flopped back on the sofa knowing that Yindi made sense "alright Yindi, we will do it your way" looking at the girls, "Don't you two try anything—alright!"

Charlotte was pacing the room, "We can't just let them hold Ferdinand in Jardine when he was obviously framed."

I got up and hugged her, "I'm just as frustrated as you Charlotte," turning to Amelia who was getting upset now, "But we need to work a few things out first."

Aetius and Shiro were quiet with Aetius saying, "They can't kill him Hannah, that is against Jardine law. He is probably safer there than what he would be here because they could harm him here."

I felt a bit better with that knowledge at least, going to Amelia and Charlotte, "I better get going just in case they are watching my place, something I'm used to anyway."

I gave them all a hug looking seriously at Amelia and Charlotte, "Don't you do anything without talking to me first or Yindi and Alira."

They nodded not looking very happy about it with Amelia saying, "Are you going to be alright though Mum. Is your phone working yet?"

Alira had been reasonably quiet getting up, "To think they even knocked your phone out of action. They're all heart, aren't they? No spirit animal, no communication with your family until your magic came back and just dumped you in the unit weak and ended up hurting yourself. I tell you what, when we do get to talk to someone about this, I'll be chewing a few ears off."

Yindi looked worried at her daughter, "Don't you get your temper up now Alira."

Yindi turned back to me, "Get going Hannah and no more flying tonight."

I smirked, "It certainly gave them something to talk about. I'll get going, we'll talk later. I'll see you at work Alira."

I landed back at my unit in my bedroom not turning the bedroom light on and looking out the window. Sure enough, there was a woman in dark clothing walking around looking up to my place every now and then.

I got angry again mocking what Malus said, "We'll have to deal with her."

I'm going to do what Yindi said for now, but if I can think of a way to get Ferdinand out of Jardine I will. I got changed into my nightie getting a drink of water turning off the lights. I looked at my bed noticing Kimba on Ferdinand's pillow, feeling my mood drop again saying to Kimba, "I'm not up to sleeping there tonight Kimba without him there."

I brought my pillow and duvet onto the sofa getting comfortable and trying to go to sleep. I lay there looking at the ceiling trying to will myself to sleep but I couldn't. I got up going back into the bedroom, leaving the lights off, but putting up a small orb, looking in the wardrobe at Ferdinand's clothes there bringing a tear to my eye.

I pulled out his pants to see if I could smell him on them but I couldn't. I hugged them hoping he was alright visualising when he wore them last at the wedding dancing around the floor, especially when we did a waltz. I went to put them back deciding I was getting too emotional, when I dropped them. I picked them up noticing something bright, that caught my eye in the hemline in his pants sticking out. I pulled it closer looking to see very fine stitching with something metal sticking out in between the stitches. I went and got some nail scissors I had in the drawer, carefully cutting the stitching.

I opened the material tipping it up to let whatever was in there fall into my hand. I watched as a small key fell into my hand, wondering what it could be for as it was quite small.

I had a rose quartz necklace on so I put the key on with that, feeling it would be safe there until I could work out what it might be for. I stitched the pants back up magically putting them back on the hanger and putting it in the wardrobe. I saw his shirt hanging in there taking it off the hanger deciding to put it under my pillow, hoping it would help me to sleep.

I lay down, with the orb following me, checking my phone again, still not getting any reception, so I put it on charge, thinking I will deal with that tomorrow. I checked my wrist, taking off the brace to see how it was looking, noticing it was puffy and bruised still. I put my hand over it, trying to send some healing to it. This worked a little, taking some of the pain away.

I sighed putting the brace back on sending the orb away, lying on the sofa trying to stem my anger down to relax for sleep. I had a restless sleep with people popping in and out of my dreams telling me off or yelling at me groaning, when the alarm finally went off, "Oh shit I don't know if I want to go to work now."

I checked my phone again still without any reception, *'Well I can't ring the boss or anyone so I may as well go at least for today.'* I dragged myself up leaving the duvet there putting the jug and some toast on while I went and got dressed. As I was getting dressed, I could smell something burning, realising it was the toast groaning, *'Oh for crying out loud.'*

I decided to go down to Nulla Nulla and get a hash brown and coffee there. I might even catch the train; I'll see who is around. I went into the bathroom brushing my hair which was a mess with knots in it as I tried to get them out, without hurting myself. I put my makeup on and brushed my teeth looking at the key around my neck as I did this; I wonder what it could be for?'

Kimba was winding herself around my legs meowing, "Yes I'm going to feed you now picking her up once I had finished and taking her over to the kitchen to give her some food." I threw the toast in the bin not bothering to clean up, 'I'll do that when I get home.'

I got my phone to check the reception but it was still coming up with 'no reception'. I turned it off for a little while to see if it would reboot it, grabbing my bag and took off down towards the mall.

Just before I went downstairs, I heard Jessica and Todd arguing again rolling my eyes as they did this quite a bit. I was going to continue when I heard a slap and Jessica begging him to stop it.

I took a deep breath feeling my anger burr up again. I heard another slap deciding I can't stand by and ignore it, so I changed my appearance to an old lady magicaeing into their unit.

I found Todd standing over Jessica yelling at her that she was a lazy bitch and swearing. Jessica was cowering on the floor near the kitchen with a fat lip and bruising starting to appear around her face.

They both looked up as I appeared in my floral dress, comfortable shoes and grey hair looking confused.

Todd turned to me with a murderous look on his face, "Who the fuck are you? Get out!"

I just walked up to him shaking my head, "Dear, dear, what a terrible mouth you have on you Todd."

He looked at Jessica, "Is this one of your nutty relatives or something because she is going to get a belt as well?"

Jessica shook her head terrified, "No Todd I don't know who she is, just let her be."

He took a step closer, "Get out of here, you old bitch, if you know what's good for you."

I smiled sarcastically, "No Todd, I can't do that. Now I think you need a good slap to stop being a bully."

He laughed menacingly, "Oh yeah and who is going to …"

I just walked straight up to him before he had time to react, slapping him hard across the face adding some magic. I watched him fly across the room, hitting the wall and knocking the wind out of him. I went up to him with an angry look now, "A couple more times to see what you do to Jessica, I think," as I hit him in the face a couple more times. His lip started to bleed as he groaned with the wind knocked out of him.

I then grabbed his, "Man bits," squeezing them as he let out a very high pitched scream, *"Too much testosterone in these balls I think I will drain them and make them small,"* as he looked at me in horror, trying to throw a punch at me or take my hands off his balls.

I looked at him angrily, "Are you going to hit Jessica any more Todd because I will dry these out like raisins if you do?"

He shook his head screwing up his face in pain still with a high-pitched voice pleading "no no no I won't please don't do any more."

I let him go watching him as he fell down the wall going unconscious. I then went over to Jessica to help her up, "Where's your phone Jessica?"

She pointed over to the table looking at me and then Todd, "who are you?"

I put my hand up as I rang 000 asking for the police telling them there has been a domestic violence assault and to come straight away, giving them address and hanging up. I smiled at her, "Let's just say I'm your fairy bad mother."

I went back over to Jessica looking at her sternly "now I don't want you saying he didn't hit you; do you understand Jessica? He needs to learn not to do this. If I hear you aren't going to let the police deal with this, I will come after you. Do you understand?"

Jessica looked worried but shook her head, "Yes alright."

Chapter 24

I magicae out of there, changing my appearance to black hair, jeans and a jacket so I could walk faster and not be recognised. I went down to Nulla Nulla getting my hashbrowns and coffee with Cecilia not recognising me, bringing a smile to my face.

I caught the train without any problems feeling funny sitting on there again as I drank my coffee, day dreaming out the window, thinking of everything that had happened.

It gave me time to think as well, turning my phone back on, to see if I finally had reception shaking my head, "Bloody mongrels," it's back at least. I sent the girls a text telling them I was safe and was on my way to work.

Both Amelia and Charlotte met me at the Quay giving me a hug, as I changed myself back to normal. Amelia looked worried, "Mum you look worn out. Maybe you should have stayed at home?"

I shook my head, "No I'm too angry, Amelia, to stay there and I'm worried about Ferdinand. I thought I'd come in today at least to try and straighten my head out a bit plus like Yindi said I need to try and do my usual things. If Aetius and Shiro manage to see Ferdinand, can they let him know I love him?"

Charlotte was looking furious, "They have no right to leave you unguarded without even a phone to protect you. Just as well we have the family magic to rely on otherwise you would have been in real trouble. Where is Morag at least?"

A sudden dawning came over me, "The guard that brought me back said something about Morag telling her about me being with the lions even in our world. I haven't been to see the lions here for a long time. I wonder if that is where she might be?"

Amelia and Charlotte were too worked up to think about Morag being with lions with Amelia saying, "You call us if you need help Mum, don't hesitate, do you hear me."

I felt a lot better with their help and protection, "I will girls. Just make sure you watch out for yourselves as well."

I got up to work going to my office meeting Tom who looked at me, "Hannah what have you done to your arm?"

I rubbed it, "Oh I've just sprained it badly and had to put this on."

Tom moved closer, "I don't think you should be here with that Hannah maybe you should go home?"

I frowned, "My phone wasn't working last night, so I couldn't ring you. I'm sure I will be alright and just take my time on the typing."

Tom didn't look happy, "I'll check with HR to see what they say. I don't think they'll be very happy about it. Wasn't Ferdinand's phone working, or have you two had a fight already?"

I rolled my eyes trying not to show my sadness at the mention of Ferdinand's name, "No Tom, we haven't had a fight. He had business to do away from Sydney and doesn't know about my wrist yet. I can stay at least long enough to get today's work done if HR don't want me to stay; that way you can arrange to get another temp in."

He smiled appreciatively, "Thanks Hannah. Did you have a nice weekend at least before that happened?"

I nodded, "Yes it was wonderful," going a bit daydreamy thinking of the fun we had before everything went sour. I came back, "How about yourself?"

He smiled bringing out his phone showing me the latest photos of the baby and her mother.

I smiled at the lovely photos then asked Tom if he wanted a coffee? He must have been thinking of something else not really concentrating, "Yes, thanks Hannah," going into the office and picking up his phone.

I put my bag down going over to the kitchen to get our coffees. Alira met me there looking at my arm, "How's your arm, Hannah?" I put it up scratching around my palm "it's a bit sore. I'll just keep taking some painkillers and keep an eye on it. Tom is checking with HR to see if I can stay; he doesn't think I will be able to."

Alira put her arm around my shoulders, "Well you just keep talking to all of us and try not to get angry, like Mum said. It might be a good time to do some more research on that family of yours."

I smiled appreciatively, "yes, you're probably right. It's just horrible without Ferdinand there now. I've become so used to him being around, it just goes to show how lonely I was before."

Alira sighed, "I'll try and see if Fia can get any information for you about him. I'm sure he is alright, just angry like you, that he can't get out of Jardine."

I thought about it, "I bet he is. I did manage to get some of my anger out this morning, just in case you find out about it."

Alira looked at me while getting a drink of water looking curious, "Oh what have you done now Hannah Dragé?"

I looked around to see if anyone was listening, luckily, we had the kitchen to ourselves. "My next-door neighbour was beating up his girlfriend and I was just in the right mood to deal with him, threatening to turn his man bits turn into raisins."

Alira was chuckling now trying not to be so obvious, in case someone came in, "Oh Hannah, you are hilarious. I'm just glad I'm your sister and not on the end of that temper."

I looked down at the coffee seeing the funny side of it grinning. I thought again about Morag and the lion thing "what do you think about Morag being with the lions at the zoo? Do you think I should go and check it out?"

Alira looked at me in horror, "Oh no not those bloody lions again, Hannah."

I put my hand on hers, "You don't have to come; Alira I don't want to put you in danger anyway."

She shook her head, "No I want to be there to help you, Hannah. You've been left unguarded all night. By the way, talking about that you didn't go flying last night did you by any chance?"

I smiled uneasily at her, "Why do you ask?"

She slapped me, "You silly bugger it's all over FB that people have seen a real witch."

I looked at her phone chuckling, "Oh dear. Jardine are going to be pissed with that."

She just shook her head, "Mum wasn't very impressed either. You better lay low for now and see what happens. Let me know if you have to go home?"

I put my arm through hers giving her a hug, "Thanks Alira, you're a great sister."

Alira went back to her desk as I walked back quickly with the coffees producing a brownie before I took Tom's into him. He was just putting the phone down not looking happy, "I'm afraid you will have to go home, Hannah. HR said you might do more damage to your arm here and will need a medical certificate to come back."

I let out a big sigh, "I can stay until I've finished some of your work can't I Tom?"

He could see I was disappointed hesitating, "I won't say anything if you don't. Just be careful, you need to look after yourself."

I smiled wanly, "Thanks Tom. I'll take it easy. Here's a brownie for you."

Tom grinned, "I will miss these while you're away."

I went back out to my desk starting up the computer feeling my stomach drop at the thought of being stuck at home without Ferdinand. It's no use asking Jardine to fix it at the moment as I know they'll be pissed off with me. I'm surprised I haven't heard from them to be honest, with the attack on those three women and my flying.

I got into my computer finding a couple of emails waiting for me looking puzzled as they weren't for Tom. I opened one finding a meeting acceptance email with the CEO as the posh secretary had mentioned before I went away. It was for Friday, feeling a bit relieved not really wanting to go anyway, so I pushed declined and sending it off.

I opened the other email, not recognising the address with a bold statement coming up saying, *"Hannah Dragé you are to desist from using the magitrap on people without the permission of Jardine. You are also to desist flying around Sydney as a witch causing problems with non-magic people. THIS IS AN OFFICIAL WARNING!"*

I sat there stunned at first with a big grin coming over me, "What a load of crap!"

Saying in a sarcastic voice, *"You should desist!"*

I sat back thinking about it, '*If Ferdinand wasn't stuck in there, I would give you your desist and shove it somewhere.*' I forwarded it to Alira to see what she would say about it. I also told her I had to go home once I had finished my work.

I stored the email into a personal folder in case I needed it for any reason going into the program I used for Tom's work. I got an email back from Alira with a video of a person laughing hysterically. I couldn't stop chuckling with tears coming to my eyes. She put on the bottom of it, "Come and see me before you go."

I closed her email and started my work. I had just finished a report when I got a phone call from an internal phone number; not sure who it was. I answered formally with Jacinta's voice on the other end sounding annoyed, "Hannah why have you declined the meeting invite I sent you?" I put my formal voice on, "Hello Jacinta, I have declined it because I have hurt my wrist and HR has demanded I go home soon and rest it until it is better. I don't envisage it being better by Friday."

She let out a loud sigh, "When are you going home?"

I hesitated not wanting to go to see him, "As soon as I have finished Tom's work, which won't take long."

She let out another loud sigh, "I will let Mr Smada know and get back to you. Can you telephone me before you leave."

I cringed, "yes, I will. Can you tell me why he wants to see me?"

She was getting inpatient now, "No I don't know Hannah," and hanging up.

The click of her phone going down, appeared really loud, as I put my finger in my ear rubbing it, 'Gee she slammed that one down.'

I managed to get quite a bit of Tom's work done with the help of a little magic before he left to go home. I hadn't heard back from Jacinta, hoping I would go before I did.

Tom came out just as I was finishing the last report smiling, "Wow you've done a good job Hannah, thanks."

I looked up at him, "I'll just do a little bit of filing and then I'll go home, that way you'll be up to date with everything."

He put his hand on my shoulder patting it, "That'll be great. Let me know how you go with your wrist when you get it x-rayed?"

I nodded nervously, thinking, *'Oh crap, I'll have to go to the hospital or doctor for that.'*

I rubbed my arm, "I'm sure it's only a sprain Tom and won't need an x-ray."

Tom looked kindly at me, "They won't let you back until it is healed, Hannah. I know you don't like doctors but you need a medical certificate." His mobile phone rang with him quickly saying, "I'll see you later Hannah, let me know how you go."

I groaned, doing a little wave, "See you." I finished off the report feeling annoyed that I have to go to the bloody doctor now or the stupid hospital to get an x-ray.

It was coming up to lunch time and I finished the report so I went to the ladies before I went out to get some lunch sitting in the cubicle feeling tired and upset still, when two secretaries came in to fix their faces. I recognised their voices being Lidia and Diane who came in looking for me when I was in the office with Ferdinand that time. I knew they were gossips so I put my feet up carefully as they started chatting about different people in the office, checking under the doors to see if anyone was listening.

Lidia started on about me, "Well did you see Hannah had hurt her arm. I wonder if she tried to belt her lovely Ferdinand with that bad temper she has. I think it might be time to move in soon; oh he's dreamy."

I mouthed to myself, '*Bloody bitch*' pointing in the direction of the tap making it spout out water everywhere, with a smile coming over me as I heard screams coming from them. I was trying not to giggle as I sat there, listening to them yelling, "Turn the bloody taps off."

I magicae out, going to my desk feeling pleased with myself. I saw Diane walk past drying herself with a towel, "Oh Diane what's happened?"

She was soaking wet, looking angry, "Those taps just went berserk in the toilets. I swear this place is just falling to bits."

I rang Alira to see if she wanted to go and get some lunch. She said she would meet me in the reception area and we would go down together. I closed off the program I had been working on checking my email to see if there was anything else from Jacinta or the CEO feeling relieved there wasn't.

I went out to the reception area thinking of all the times I had met Ferdinand there feeling annoyed because I was the latest gossip with him doing that. I felt sad thinking, '*I would rather have him there and being on the gossip list now, instead of missing him so much and wondering what was happening to him.*'

Alira saw my face getting close to me, "I know you're missing him still Sister, but just stay strong. We'll sort this out."

I smiled affectionately at her, "Thanks Alira."

The lift came quite quickly with us getting in noticing two other women who were in there selecting the ground floor. Alira and I stood there not wanting to say too much in front of them when I started to get a strange feeling off the women.

I looked at Alira as the lights started to flicker in the lift. I handed her some ear plugs, with her looking at me curiously, putting them in. I put some in my ears when the lift came to a stop in between floors. I clapped my hands loudly, causing a loud bang to go around the lift, causing the lift to vibrate and shake. The women screamed in pain holding their ears buckling up with the pain.

They had their wands in their hands allowing Alira and I to take them and destroy them. Alira grinned at me pointing to herself, mouthing "my turn."

She pointed to the women turning them upside down while they were still struggling with their hands on their ears, hanging them from the roof of the lift.

I high fived her, then stopped the vibration going around the lift, looking at the women as we both took the ear plugs out of ears. We both sighed, "Now I wonder who these two are Alira?"

Alira smirked, "They look like a couple of bats at the moment."

I couldn't help myself laughing, "Tell me now you two, who you are and who you're working for, otherwise I'll get angry and make sure you don't speak again."

One woman who was a redhead with fair skin turned red with the blood running to her head, "We heard what you did to Suzannah and the others. We're here on our own to try and get you two to help us become stronger."

Alira looked at me rubbing her chin, "I really don't know if I believe you, but to be honest, I can't be bothered."

She put her thumbs together, doing a flapping motion with her hands, watching them disappear.

I grinned, "Can I ask where you sent them, Sister?"

Alira pointed to the lift getting it going again, "I thought I would give them a brief flying lesson over the sea to see how long they lasted."

I shook my finger at Alira, "Ooohh you're going to get a naughty email now."

The lift got to the ground floor as we walked out linking arms, "I really don't bloody care. I'm finally starting to enjoy myself to be honest, how about you?"

I walked along, "Yes, I am too. I would feel better if Ferdinand was here, but then he would probably be telling me off for doing this."

Alira giggled, "Don't you tell Fia, although he'll probably find out and so will Mum, I'll probably get it when I get home."

We went and bought some lunch from a takeaway shop under the railway station going over to the First Fleet Park sitting on one of the seats as we sat and watched the ferries coming in. It was quite warm with clouds starting to come in off the sea, "I think we are going to have a storm soon."

Alira giggled, "As long as it's not the Dragé thunder, I don't mind. I'll come with you, by the way, if you want to go to the zoo. I'll just have to suck it up."

I took a bite of my sandwich thinking, *"I'll let you know more about that later."*

I could feel a vibration of someone magical coming in, "I think we have a visitor coming. Do you think we should change, Sister?"

She waved her hand over herself changing to a man and I changed to a man as well continuing to eat our lunch looking around us. I put my head down, "Over by the railing, mate," making Alira look over towards the Commissioner's steps, near where the cruise liners birth.

We sat there watching as Lilith appeared walking along looking around her. I spoke quietly, sounding angry, "Gee I'd like to grab hold of that one."

Alira put her hand on mine, "It's not the right time mate."

I calmed myself down having to be satisfied to watch what she was doing. A small boat docked at the steps with the two women who had attacked us in the lift getting off it, wrapped in a thin blanket, looking very wet and angry.

I coughed, "Oh dear, their flying lesson didn't last very long by the look of it."

Alira sounded disappointed, "I'll have to practice that one a bit more, I think."

I recollected something, "I forgot to tell you I did something similar with the priest yesterday. I saw a flock of seagulls quite a way out and that is where he landed. Maybe focus on a certain distance."

Alira was chuckling looking down shaking her head, "You crack me up mate."

As I sat there watching, I couldn't help myself, I put my hand up with my palm facing up blowing on it gently, sending dust and debris towards them all. I watched Lilith, the women and a man that had come off the boat, getting buffeted by dust and debris.

After waiting for a few minutes, I then put my finger in my palm making a circle as the dust and debris swirled around them all. A few tourists were caught up in it hearing them squeal, trying to stop dresses and hats going flying.

Lilith was being buffeted by the wind looking around angrily to see who was doing this. I sat still drinking the water I had, "just sit still mate, otherwise she will see us."

Alira looked down at her phone, "Don't worry mate I'm enjoying it too much to go anywhere."

She brought up a tissue in her hand doing a loud sneeze in it, sending the wind towards the water carrying Lilith and the two women with it. They tried to grab something to stop themselves, but it was too strong as they tumbled along like tumble weed on a TV western, hitting the steps then landing in the water, yelling.

A crowd started to form near the railing as I calmed the wind down, "I suppose we better get back to work mate."

Alira looked over to the water watching Lilith and the two women bobbing in it, when a wave went over them from a ferry that had come in. It sent its wash over all of them as they went under the water, coming up coughing and spluttering.

I looked at Alira, "Oh dear, they are having some troubles, aren't they?"

We walked a little way then took off to the toilets on my floor changing our appearance back to ourselves. We came out of the cubicles trying to hold back the laughter as a secretary came in. It was Cheryl who came in looking at my arm, "Hannah what have you done to your arm?"

I washed my hands, "Just badly sprained, Cheryl. I have to go home soon as they're worried, I'll hurt it more by typing for some reason." Cheryl screwed up her face, "Sounds a bit silly to me, but take care. I'll see you when you get back."

She went to walk away then remembered something, "Oh that (saying quietly) *snooty* secretary of the CEO came looking for you while you were at lunch. She said she will give you a ring when you get back."

I rolled my eyes, "Thanks Cheryl. I don't know what she wants. I might try and sneak out before she gets back to me."

Alira was drying her hands, "I'll come with you if you're worried about anything Hannah."

I looked pleased, "Thanks Alira, I'll let you know." I walked Alira over to the lift saying to her, "I really don't know what he wants, but I don't feel good about it."

Alira was thinking about it as we neared the lift, about to say something, when the lift opened and Fia came out.

Alira looked up at him frowning, "Oh hello dear."

Fia wasn't looking very happy but leaned forward giving her a kiss talking quietly, "Is there somewhere we can go to talk?"

Tracey on reception shot up from her desk in surprise coming around her desk ignoring the phone that was ringing smiling, "Alira, who is this?"

Alira groaned, but put a smile on her face, "This is Fia, my boyfriend Tracey."

Tracey came forward putting her hand out to shake his hand, "Well you ladies know how to pick your men. I will have to start hanging out with you two."

Fia shook her hand smiling at her, "Nice to meet you, Tracey. I'm afraid I can't stay too long, I just needed to speak to Alira with some urgent news. I'll come and say hello next time I'm in."

Tracey was disappointed but her spirits lifted when he said he will come and say hello next time he was in. Tracey pointed to a small meeting room just off the reception area, "You can use that room if you like, it's not being used at the moment."

I was getting nervous with Fia's expression going into the meeting room, "Come on, you two."

Alira and Fia followed with Fia smiling sweetly at Tracey, "Thank you Tracey, I really appreciate it."

I could hear her gushing as I shut the door after Fia coming in. Fia looked at both of us, "It's alright Hannah, nothing has happened to Ferdinand, although he has been told about you two playing up and is getting angry about being trapped there."

He looked at my arm, "I told him about your arm as well. He wished you could go to Jardine to get it fixed."

I felt, relieved, "Thanks Fia, I think. Don't worry about my arm I'm sure it is alright."

Alira rolled her eyes, "So what is the other important news you have?"

Fia took her hand, "Your mother has asked me to come and tell you to stop playing your pranks you two. All you're going to do is upset Jardine."

I looked at Alira and burst out laughing, with us both high fiving again and saying in unison, "Good!"

Fia took Alira by the waist looking annoyed, "Alira and Hannah you're just making people angry."

Alira turned Fia's jaw towards her looking determined, "They have attacked us Fia and we are just defending ourselves. We have been attacked in the lift and that crazy bitch Lilith is helping them. Don't worry, I will sort Mum out when I get home."

Fia sighed deeply, "Hey I'm only the messenger, but I am worried about you getting into trouble, Alira."

I patted his arm, "We will try to behave Fia, but if we get attacked, we're not going to stand by and let them have the upper hand." Looking earnestly at him now, "How is Ferdinand?"

He looked sadly at me, "He is alright Hannah just really angry and frustrated. I have heard that Lilith has been trying to get to see him but the elders, especially Malus, won't let her. He has been ordered to stay with the other dragons."

I sighed, "I wonder what she is up to, that cunning little bitch. She has been like a thorn in our side. Is he still showing pain when he changes into a dragon?"

Fia, who was a soft caring man, looked at me worried, "yes, I have seen him groan when he changes. I'm not sure what is going on there."

There was a knock on the door with Tracey's voice coming through it, "I'm afraid you will have to go now, as that room is going to be used soon."

We filed out thanking Tracey. I gave Fia a hug, "Thanks for the news Fia. Tell him I love him, won't you?"

He smiled kindly at me, "I will, Hannah."

I left them to say goodbye, going towards my desk thinking about what Fia had said feeling a little better about Ferdinand at least. I found a note on my desk from Jacinta saying she had been to see me asking me to call her when I got back. I really didn't want to go to see the CEO as I didn't feel comfortable about it. I went into Tom's room quickly doing the filing magically.

I shut my computer down and tidied up my desk thinking I better make an effort to ring her at least, otherwise she might get the shits. I dialled the number hearing it ring but she didn't pick up and it went to her answering service. I felt a bit relieved leaving a message, *"Hi Jacinta it's Hannah Dragé, just ringing to see if you're available, but it doesn't appear you are. I'm on my way home now. I'll catch up when I come back from my injury."*

I put the phone down going towards the reception area being stopped by Lidia "hi Hannah. I hear Alira's new boyfriend came in to see her and is a dreamboat as well. We may have to get together some time and see where you meet these guys."

I smiled, "Yes, we will. I'm afraid I'm on my way home now with my bad arm. See you next time." I thought as I walked away, *'I won't be going out with that bitch.'* I went towards the reception area noticing the lift opening through the glass doors and Jacinta coming out. I ducked behind a large pot plant that was near the door looking around to see if anyone was watching me.

The coast was clear so I magicae out of there, just as Jacinta came through the doors heading towards my desk.

I landed near the Caringbah medical centre to see if I could get an x-ray done there on my wrist. I walked into the reception area looking around with people everywhere. I groaned, '*I don't think I'm going to get this done here today.*'

I finally got up to the receptionist who was looking frazzled "it's a 2 hour wait I'm afraid. You could go to the hospital and get it done quicker there." Disappointed, I smiled briefly, "Thanks, I'll go there then."

I went to the hospital emergency department feeling my heart rate go up looking around me nervously. That distinct smell of hospitals didn't help either, as I walked up to the receptionist, who wasn't busy. She was tapping away on her computer not looking up at me as I patiently waited for her to acknowledge me.

I was getting annoyed, so I flicked my fingers with a little spark coming up from her keyboard, making her jolt up turning to look at me. I smiled tightly putting my arm up, "I'd like to get this x-rayed to see if it is broken."

She sighed deeply as though I was holding her up, "What's your name and date of birth?"

I forgot about this part hesitating, with her turning to look at me ready to type it into the computer, "I need it for our records."

I told her my name and date of birth as she typed it in with her face changing as the screen came up. I leaned around the screen that was in between us noticing a red banner coming up on my file.

She saw me looking, turning her screen towards her more, "Can you go and wait around the corner, so a triage nurse can see you first, Mrs Dragé?"

I put my head on the side looking snidely at her, "It's Ms Dragé. Where abouts did you say to go again?"

She looked annoyed at me pointing to the ground, "just follow the line around to the triage nurse *Ms Dragé.*"

I looked at the line going around the corner to another window finding a nurse sitting there tapping away on the computer, looking up at me, "I'll be with you in a minute." I sat down on the chair near her window getting my phone out to take my mind off things. She finally finished what she was doing calling me over, "You must be Ms Dragé? Can I confirm your date of birth and address."

I told her the information, then she asked me how I sustained the injury. I told her I tripped on a mat in the unit. I mean I wasn't going to tell her my magic was coming back making me giddy, was I.

She typed it into the computer, "We aren't very busy at the moment, so you're lucky. A radiologist will be out shortly to take an x-ray for you. Please take a seat."

I waited about 10 minutes, when a young guy came out showing me into the room where the x-ray was to be done. He took the scans at different angles then asked me to wait back in the waiting area.

I put my brace back on noticing the bruising coming out a bit more now, thinking, '*I should have tried some healing on it so it didn't look so bad.*'

I was called into another room by a male doctor with my x-ray on a lit-up board. I looked at it noticing a small break in the bone. He looked annoyed at me, "Can you sit down, Ms Dragé and I'll explain what you have done."

I raised my eyebrows at him, "I can see I have a small break doctor, I'm not stupid."

I sat down looking annoyed at him, as he sat nervously typing something into the computer. Again, I saw that red banner appear on his screen leaning forward, "What is that banner on my file doctor?"

He reduced the page, "It's just some extra information on your file from your past. I will need to put a cast on your wrist as the brace will not support it enough, plus you may be tempted to take it off, which will slow the healing down."

I sat back annoyed, "Alright let's do this then."

He got up leading me into another small room with plaster on a trolly and a bucket with different size bandages.

I sat down and watched him mix the plaster up. He then asked what colour I wanted the plaster to be and put that in the mix. He then wrapped my wrist, hand and a little way up my arm not saying much.

I was thinking about that banner on my file waiting until he finished. He still looked a bit nervous, so as soon as he had finished, I said a chant, "*Doctor doctor tell me the truth, what is on my file as I am sure it is nothing but vile.*"

He was taking off his gloves picking up a kidney dish with a loaded needle in it when the chant kicked in, turning to me with a dazed look on his face.

I looked angrily at him, waiting for him to say what I wanted. I could see he was fighting against it, so I said it again with anger behind it. He was starting to sweat trying to fight the chant, "It's a warning that you have a bad temper,

Hannah. Your brother, Christian, is to be contacted should you get abusive with the possibility of being confined as he has an order allowing him to do that."

I growled standing up, as he went towards the syringe, but I threw a freezing spell at him stopping him, looking like a statue. I stood there thinking about it, "Bloody Christian, I'll deal with him later." A spell came into my head from the book, "*Like a robot you will be, go into the computer and wipe away all of the rubbish you see, setting me free, from Christian and anyone else who wishes to control me.*"

I took the needle off the doctor then told him to go into the other room following him in there. There was a security guard at the end of the hallway, so I hid the needle following the doctor as though everything was alright.

The doctor went to the computer, sitting down and opening up my file again. He looked to be fighting my spell again, so I repeated it while touching his shoulder. He did as I asked deleting all the notes about Christian and my temper.

I then got the needle and stuck it in his hand in between his fingers, seeing him flinch as it went in. I injected the contents into him watching him drop off to sleep and slump in his chair.

I touched the little hole in between his finger healing it up then put the needle into the safe disposal container. I double checked he had deleted everything I wanted off my file. I put in the notes that my behaviour was exceptional and that he didn't have any problem with me.

I also wound my finger around his head, "*Hannah Dragé was a good patient, just getting her arm in plaster and having a joke. You felt tired afterwards having a rest but will awake happy and refreshed*" flicking my fingers watching it take effect.

I went to go, when I noticed something sticking out of his pocket, pulling it out groaning, "A bloody wand. They're everywhere lately." I disintegrated it watching a puff of smoke rise from it and putting the debris in the bin.

I replaced it with a fake one, putting it back into his pocket and made sure he was comfortable in the chair. I looked out the little window in the door to see where the security guard was, then went out smiling calling out to the doctor, "See you later. Thanks for your help."

The guard watched me go, as I went out of the hospital, taking off as soon as I could, landing back in my unit. I felt exhausted and angry, stomping my foot just because it made me feel better, with poor Kimba diving for cover thinking she had done something wrong.

I opened the balcony door taking some deep breaths to calm myself down looking over the balcony at the people walking past. I noticed the priest walking past feeling annoyed again, so I threw a spell at him, *"Show yourself to be the chicken you are cluck cluck clucking like a chook from a farm along the path, for half past the hour this will occur."*

As I walked away, I could hear a loud, "Cluck cluck" grinning as he put his hands up to his armpits, flapping his wings and pecking like a chicken.

I sighed deeply, "That feels better," going into the bedroom getting changed and letting my hair out thinking I must get a haircut. I sat down on the balcony sitting back, so no one could see me, but I could see them, bringing in a glass of wine watching the priest cluck like a chook.

Kimba finally felt safe to come out, sitting on my lap purring away and sniffing the cast I had on my wrist as I looked down at her, "Yes my baby, Mum has been in the wars."

I looked over to the other chair missing Ferdinand again, feeling sorry for myself, taking a big gulp of the wine with hot tears starting to run down my face.

I brought in a tissue blowing my nose and wiping my eyes looking at Kimba who was now sitting up putting her head into my stomach, wanting me to pat her neck. This made me smile through the tears, "At least you're the same Kimba, always there for me, well except when Ferdinand is here."

I sat on the balcony patting Kimba, finishing my glass of wine with the chant slowly wearing off the priest. I could just see a small crowd gathering around him making me smile at last. I sent a text to Amelia and Charlotte to ring when they were free, with them sending one back, "Will do."

I stood up taking Kimba with me laying down on the sofa putting Kimba beside me. I lay there thinking, playing with the necklace around my neck as well as the little key I had found in Ferdinand's pants. I put my good hand back touching Ferdinand's shirt getting some comfort from it slowing dropping off to sleep.

Chapter 25

I woke to my phone ringing with Kimba jumping off as I rolled to grab it off the floor. The room was getting dark with some storm clouds coming in, from the sea and a change in direction of the breeze, making things blow around in the unit.

I answered the phone waking myself up a bit more with Amelia sounding concerned, "Mum, are you alright?"

I yawned, "Yes, I'm good, Amelia. I just fell asleep on the sofa."

She sounded relieved asking how it went at the doctors with my arm. I told her everything that happened making her angry, "If you we don't get crazy witches going after us, we get crazy strangers after us."

We chatted away about work and how the CEO was wanting to see me, making her curious as well.

Just as I hung up from her Charlotte called me telling her the same things that had happened today. I could hear the anger in her voice, "This is just getting stupid now Mum. We need to find Morag or someone who isn't stupid and sort this stuff out."

I yawned again, "I know Charlotte. I'll be home tomorrow so I will go and check out the zoo to see about the lions. Alira said she will come with me."

Charlotte didn't sound very convinced "I don't see why she would be there, but I suppose you may as well check it out. You know I can see why Matilda didn't get too involved in Jardine now."

I agreed with her, "I'm beginning to feel the same way, Charlotte. Even once I get Ferdinand out of there, I'm not sure if I would want to live there with all this rubbish going on, which is a shame, because it's the ideal world. Have you heard anything from Olwen?"

She hesitated, "I sent him the results. He just sent back that he would be in touch."

"Oh well, he's the least of my problems at the moment. There is one thing I'd like to know, was there a feature on your magitrap that could reverse the trapping of their magic?"

Charlotte thought about it, "It probably isn't as strong as it could be. Any smart person in Jardine will probably be able to work something out how to reverse it."

I felt disappointed, "I've just got this feeling that someone will try to do that. Anyway, we'll see how things go. I'm just going to concentrate on my research of the family and the spells for now."

We hung up getting up off the sofa watching the dark clouds swirl around over the sea coming into land. I looked over towards the kitchen thinking, *'I suppose I should cook something hesitating. Nah! I'll just bring something in. I wasn't hungry still so I brought in a vegetable chowmein and went and sat on the balcony watching the storm come in with a glass of wine.'*

Once I had finished my meal, I looked over to the seat where Ferdinand would normally sit feeling down. I scolded myself, I will have to work out how to get him out and concentrate on spells and the family. I could feel my anger build up again adding to the lightening that was coming in over the sea.

I went back into the lounge bringing out the book looking at the family tree. I decided to put a live copy of it on the wall over by the balcony doors, watching as a tree appeared with its branches slowly growing out and a picture of each member of the female side of the family appear in a circle. Their male partners appeared next to them as still pictures, including Ferdinand, Shiro and Aetius, as technically they were our partners now.

All the females were smiling looking over to me as the tree grew with the different members of the family appearing on it. It stopped, unfortunately after Ingrid, like in the book.

I sat there drinking my wine going over to the sealed section of the book still not letting me in. I got frustrated so I left the family search deciding to have a look at another spell. I thought about what I wanted, deciding to learn an invisibility spell.

I studied and practiced it until I felt sleepy having a quick shower, shutting the door with the storm still throwing strikes around the water area but not producing any rain. I couldn't be bothered drying my hair properly and my hand was getting sore.

I eventually dropped off holding onto Ferdinand's shirt having a dream of flying high with him. I woke with Kimba on my chest touching my face with her cool nose wanting to be fed. I groaned as I got up rubbing my arm thinking, '*Bloody thing. I must have a weakness there now,*' feeling it ache.

It was still quite early with the sun peeking through the clouds that were blowing out to sea. I fed Kimba, deciding to go for a walk along the beach, while it was quiet. I changed my appearance walking along the shoreline coming back feeling refreshed.

I still wasn't hungry so I just had some yoghurt and fruit and a cup of coffee looking at my family tree on the wall. I had worked out the invisibility spell deciding to test it later.

My relatives were smiling at me from the family tree as I sat there watching them while drinking my coffee. I put my dishes in the sink sighing, "I better tidy up a little" magically doing the dishes. I decided to do some meditation first then practicing the spell later.

I sat in front of the window bringing in the elements putting my ear buds in. I went into my meditation travelling along on the boat with it stopping, feeling a coolness around me. I knew someone was there as I sat up looking over to the green field. I got out of the boat walking over to a woman sitting on a rock watching me come over to her with a faint smile on her face.

I sighed sitting down, "Hei bestemor (Hello grandma)."

She had blonde hair, a rounded face, quite slim and an old-fashioned lace dress on, turning to look at me calmy, "du har roet deg ned I det minste (you have calmed down at least)."

I felt depleted, "Ja til de rører meg opp igjen (yes until they stir me up again)."

She looked at me sadly, "Ferdinand kommer tilbake. Prøv å ikke miste fokus på magien din (Ferdinand will be back. Try not to lose focus on your magic)."

I got up to go. "Jeg går. Jeg vil vite hvem du er neste gang. (I'll go. I want to know who you are next time)."

I heard her chuckle, "Du er definitivt en Drage kvinne (you really are a Dragé woman)."

I went back to the room, feeling frustrated that she wouldn't tell me who she was again, but feeling a bit better that she said Ferdinand would be back. I got up looking at the time realising Alira would be at work, so I decided to go and try the invisibility spell on her. I smiled to myself, '*she will get a nice surprise.*'

I shut the doors to the unit magicaeing to her level near the entry doors, quickly putting the spell on me. I opened the doors walking in confidently towards Alira's desk when all of a sudden, I heard a scream from a woman who was at her desk. I turned to look at her puzzled thinking, *'I'm sure I'm invisible, what is she going on about?'*

She continued to scream then fainted as other women came to her aid pointing towards me looking horrified. I was heading towards Alira thinking my bloody spell can't have worked, when Alira whispered, "Hannah is that you?"

I looked at her then down at me knowing I was invisible speaking quietly, "Yes Alira. Is something the matter?"

Alira looked around her trying not to show that she was talking to me, hiding her smile, "We can still see your cast on your arm."

I groaned, putting it up saying quietly, "Oh shit! I'll see you tonight," disappearing hearing Alira trying to stifle her laughter.

I got back to the unit feeling frustrated looking at the cast, 'Bloody thing.'

I sat down deciding to have a cup of herbal tea and turning on the television with Kimba joining me on my lap. I turned it over to the news channel to see what was going on in the world. There were reports of a man who had killed his wife pleading innocence, even though he had been having an affair. I was feeling annoyed, thinking of something as I knew it was a live feed, pointing to the television, "*One two three four make the man spout it all out in the court. Time to tell the truth that's for sure.*"

I turned it over watching a bit of a movie turning it back after a couple of hours to find the guy had pleaded guilty to all the charges. I smiled feeling pleased with myself.

I kept myself busy working on spells, just having a snack for lunch falling asleep on the sofa again then waking to feed Kimba. I had a couple of glasses of wine watching a small shower come in over the sea bringing in some vegetables again until it was time to go and meet Alira at the zoo changing into a dark tracksuit.

I met Alira at the zoo, who was wearing a dark track suit on as well, giggling at me, "You silly bugger coming to work like that."

I grinned, "I forgot about this bloody thing. I'll have to remember that next time I use the spell." She took my arm, "Come on, Sister, let's get this over and done with. I still can't believe it's lions again, but I'm going to be there for you, Sister."

I gave her a hug smiling, "Come on then." We had researched the map where everything was before coming, so we landed close to the lions.

Alira took my hand quietly walking towards the sound of the lions, who would roar every now and then. The rain was holding off, but you could feel the dampness coming again threatening to rain.

There was enough light around the zoo to see where we were going, I just hoped there weren't too many cameras. We both put our hoods up to cover our faces as much as possible finding the lion enclosure.

We didn't know what we were going to be looking for exactly, so we went up to the railing wall, which fell into a deep pit with water in it and the lion's enclosure beyond that with rocks and trees for them to sit on or under. All of the lions were in their cages by the look of it, making Alira a bit happier, while we stood there looking to see for any sign that Morag might be there.

I leaned over to her saying quietly, "Can you see anything?"

She was scanning the area when she noticed a little light coming from inside the enclosure not far from a platform where the lions would sun themselves. Just beyond that platform was what looked like a cave made to give the lions somewhere cool to sleep during hot days.

Alira pointed to the small flickering light saying quietly, "Hannah there's a light over there in that cave."

I squinted my eyes to see, "Oh yes I can see it."

The rain started to fall again looking at each other nervously saying, "Do want to go with me or not? I won't force you."

She sighed, "yes, I'll go with you. Just promise me if she isn't there we'll come straight back out."

I smiled, "It's a deal. I don't trust these lions like I do the Jardine ones. I'll be running as fast as you Sister."

We took a deep breath holding hands and magicaeing over to the cave, landing just near the entrance. I saw the light that was flickering ahead of us pointing to it, "Come on, I think it wants us to follow."

Alira squeezed my hand, "Are you sure Hannah?"

I nodded, "I don't think this is very deep, Alira, so we won't be going far."

We walked carefully along watching out for rocks and sticks on the ground following the small light that almost looked like a firefly. My eyes were adjusting to the darkness as I was scanning the area when a woman came forward with a light on her hand. We both jumped with Alira grabbing me.

Morag smiled, "Hello you two."

I walked forward to give her a hug noticing she looked tired and withdrawn. Alira gave her a hug, "There aren't any lions with you here are there, Morag?"

Morag chuckled, "No Alira. I can't stay too long. I was hoping you would remember this place, Hannah. I came last night but you didn't come. I have heard you went and dealt with other things instead."

I put my head down, "I've been left with no choice, Morag, so please don't lecture me."

Morag sighed walking away to sit down on a chair she had brought in for us, "Come and sit down and tell me what's been going on." We sat down as the rain started to fall heavier now telling her everything that had happened in Jardine and here.

She was very worried, "Oh Hannah, that is terrible." Tears started to form in my eyes as I looked away, getting up to walk around feeling the anger burn in me again, "I'm so angry Morag. I know you don't like it when I'm angry but it is just building in me with these attacks, which is probably exactly what they want. I'm going to stay home for a few days and just relax and get this better," putting up my arm.

She came over to look at it touching it, "Oh dear that is broken again Hannah. Jardine would fix it but that isn't going to happen at the moment."

Morag paced, "I think it's a good idea you stay home. I imagine you have secured it very well?"

I nodded, "Yes only family can get in. So, if you need to talk to me, you'll have to use another method. Don't use my phone I think that has something on it, I'll have to sort that out when I get back home."

She nodded, "Ok I'll think of something."

I looked at her, "I did a spell on my book to see who was involved in the Jardine thing with regard to what happened with Ferdinand and myself with Cara coming up as one of the culprits. Is this correct?"

She turned looking surprised, "I don't know Hannah. Oh, dear that is terrible if that is true, she knows a lot of things. I've never heard her say anything about wanting to change things."

Alira stood up, "Where have you been Morag?"

Morag looked at Alira, "I'm afraid I can't tell you Alira, they may be trying to read people's minds."

The light that had guided us in came up to Morag sitting on her shoulder, "This is Vila she is known as a fairy in your world. She has been helping me with various things."

I smiled going over to her, "Wow I thought it was a firefly or something. She is lovely." This made Vila smile and send a little fairy kiss over to me.

Morag heard a noise looking nervous making Vila fly out towards the entrance of the cave then come back in. She spoke into Morag's ear noticing Morag's expression changed, "It is time to go you two. It appears we have been tracked. I will get back to you when I can Hannah, I'm not sure how long this will take though, so please be patient and try not to get on the TV too much, especially when you're flying on a broom," shaking her head at me. I grinned, "I'll try Morag."

Morag passed the flame over to me putting it in my cupped hand taking off with Vila.

Alira looked at me, "We better go Sister."

I nodded, "I don't have a very good feeling either." We heard a growl come from the entrance with a huge male lion coming towards us wet from the rain with its mane all messy and matted.

Alira hugged me, "Let's go Hannah, now!" We held hands but nothing happened, with Alira looking terrified at me, "Hannah what's going on?"

I shook my head, "I don't know Alira but it's not looking good. Just stand behind me and I'll keep this flame up to try and distract the lion, while we slowly walk out." I moved slowly up with the flame in my hand and Alira hanging onto me around my waist saying quietly, "Don't try and run Alira or he'll go for us."

She squeezed my waist in recognition too afraid to say anything. I moved closer to the wall but was still heading for the entrance when the lion roared towards us, making Alira scream. I yelled at it throwing the flame towards it making it back off.

I tried to summon something in from the book but nothing was coming, saying quietly, "There must be a big block on this cave." I thought, *'I'll try and talk to the lion like I did in Jardine.'*

"Hi I'm Hannah and this is Alira. Have you been to Jardine they have lions there and I like to sleep with them?" The lion looked as though it was thinking about what I said giving a roar, while we were still edging towards the entrance. I had an idea how to get rid of the block, "Alira, just stay behind me I'm going to try something."

I carefully bent down and took my shoes off, watching the lion as it followed our movements panting. I continued to talk to it, "The lions in Jardine are allowed to roam free I bet you wish you could do that." The lion roared again as though it was trying to talk to me. Once I had taken my shoes off, I planted my feet in the dirt putting my arm around Alira holding her tight, "Just hold tight Alira, I'm not sure if this going to work."

I planted my feet in the dry dirt, trying to summon the element of earth, I had fire and there was a breeze coming in through the entrance.

Unfortunately, I didn't have water but there was plenty of it outside now with the rain coming down. I looked at Alira, "I need to move outside a little to get to the water. Just slowly move with me." I could see she was terrified so I held onto her tightly, "Come on just little steps."

We slowly edged our way to the entrance feeling the rain hit us as I tried to make sure my hand was still in the cave to keep dry. It was like the lion could see that we were trying to escape, edging its way towards us, looking menacing now, *"Earth air wind and fire I summon thee to help us flee to beyond that fence that I can see."*

We flew over to the boundary fence, just as the lion made a dive for us, getting my shoes in frustration and ripping them to bits. Alira screamed then jumped up and down in the rain, "Oh thank goodness, Sister. Let's get out of here before anything else happens."

I put out the flame noticing a figure move over by some bushes, "Yes I think we have company coming," taking off before they got to us. We landed back at Alira's place soaked from the downpour of rain as we escaped the cave.

Yindi looking worried, "Why are you two so wet. Alira, what is the matter?"

Alira went over to her mother, "We had trouble Mum. They blocked our magic to get out of a cave where we met Morag and then a lion came to eat us. Luckily Hannah had a trick up her sleeve with the elements, otherwise we would have been lion fodder."

Yindi was furious getting a towel for us both "wipe yourselves down. This has really gotten out of hand. Did Morag get away alright?" We nodded making me feel undecided, "yes, she did actually. The block happened after she left."

Yindi looked at me, "You're suspicious aren't you, Hannah?"

I nodded, "Yes, which is sad because I really like Morag. I guess we will have to wait and see." I gave her the towel back, "I'll get going just in case they have planted something on me again." I gave Alira a hug looking sad, "Thanks for coming with me Alira. Keep in touch."

Yindi came over, "We are here if you need to talk to someone, Hannah."

I nodded, "Thanks Yindi." I took off deciding to fly in the rain a bit covering my cast with a plastic bag bringing in a broom, enjoying feeling the water hit my face then went home.

I landed in the bathroom stripping off getting ready to have a shower, looking at the plastic bag on my arm. I noticed something just near my thumb on the cast what looked like a little dot of plaster, but it was slightly different to the rest of the plaster on it. I went into my bedroom and got a clear quartz crystal cupping my hands around the crystal and holding it over the dot, *'Tell me what this is and make it go with a fizz.'* I took a deep breath as I could feel the book kicking in scanning it with some words coming up *'tracking bug'* then the crystal sent a bolt of white light through it burning a hole right through it. This made me cough, as a small cloud of smoke wafted up from the cast, shaking my head, *'So that's how they did it.'*

I could feel my anger burr up again, not only with what happened tonight but as well as the tracking device on me. I stood there thinking while listening to the rain come down and thunder building around me, partly from me and partly from the weather. *'There's just something not right here and when I get to the bottom of it, they better watch out.'*

I decided to go and have a shower not doing anything else tonight. I had a couple of wines playing with the news reports again enjoying myself that way at least, eventually dropping off on the sofa.

After a restless sleep, I woke with my arm aching and Kimba looking at me wondering when I was getting up. I groaned getting up rubbing my eyes, giving her some food. I went and opened the curtains to see clouds hanging around but the rain had stopped.

I could feel a bit of a cold coming on again after being out in the rain last night. I shook my head, *'I really don't know who to trust any more. Did Morag have something to do with us being trapped in that cave? Who put the tracer on my cast? Was it really Morag?'* I went to the bathroom looking at my hair in a mess after my restless sleep giving it a quick brush still looking a mess, but I couldn't be bothered.

I had a look in the fridge and pantry to see what to have for breakfast deciding on just some toast again. I better watch it, putting it in the toaster and putting the jug on while taking some painkillers. I managed not to burn it this time going to watch the news while I ate my toast and drank my coffee.

The usual problems in the world came on making me wonder why I watch it sometimes, as it only gets me down and angry. A story came on about two guys driving madly in a stolen car down the highway hitting cars, with police cars chasing them. I shook my head sighing pointing at the TV watching the car go into a ditch and the police dragging them out of the car; giggling to myself. I blew on my finger, like they used to the westerns with their guns, "this is a deadly weapon."

I changed my appearance deciding to go down to the beach for a walk again. I was never a very good runner with my lungs, but I just felt like running a little way along the sand. I started off only going a little way leaning down on my knees getting my breath back thinking, *'I'm definitely not fit and my lungs haven't gotten any stronger.'*

I could see a couple of women walking along the beach towards me not getting very good vibrations off them, so I walked towards the roadway noticing them following me. I ducked between a couple of cars and magicae back to the unit.

I decided to do another meditation trying to stay focused on my magic rather than the idiots trying to get to me. I did the meditation with my crystals on my chakras to see if it made me any stronger.

I lay down putting my ear buds in and certain crystals on the right spots for the particular chakra, doing the guided meditation. As I lay there, getting into my meditation, I could feel each chakra pulse releasing the tension from my body. I got down to my sacral chakra with a vision of Ferdinand floating around me, being intimate; making my mood drop briefly at the thought of him. I then carried on down to my root chakra clearing it with another pulse.

I floated in the boat hearing the birds sing around me and the smell of the water and plants come to my senses, as I listened to my breathing relaxing me. The boat stopped once again making me sit up to see the woman I had seen yesterday sitting on the rock.

I felt annoyed deciding whether to go over and talk to her, deciding in the end to go over and sit near her waiting for her to speak.

She glanced at me frowning, "Du er sta Hannah. Jeg er bestemor Wilhemenia Drage (you're a stubborn woman Hannah. I am Wilhemenia Dragé)."

I looked up at her curious, "Hvorfor er du så mystisk? (Why are you being so mysterious)?"

She got up agitated, "Det er alt jeg skal fortelle deg for nå (that is all I am going to tell you for now)."

She looked as though she was going to disappear but turned to look at me, "Bare bli sterkere i magien din og slutt å feste for Ferdinand. Du trenger det snart (just get stronger in your magic and stop pining for Ferdinand. You will need it soon)."

She disappeared after that, as I watched her, shaking my head, yelling after her annoyed, "Thanks!"

I got back in the boat listening to my breathing feeling the warmth from the crystals that were lit up, seep through my body. I lay there for a few minutes thinking about what she had said and how I felt with the crystals; feeling a light sea breeze blow over me, getting up eventually. I went to get a drink of water noticing another picture appear on the wall of grandma Wilhemenia Dragé, bringing a smile to me. *'Slowly getting there.'*

I found another spell I was interested in, of changing into an animal deciding to practice that. I ended up taking some painkillers after a while laying down to have a sleep to be woken by Kimba sitting on my chest looking at me again.

I patted her ears smiling at her, then looking at the time groaning, *'Dinner time already. I missed lunch again, feeling a little grumble come from my stomach. I suppose I better eat something.'* I got up getting Kimba her dinner and a drink of water for me, going out to look over the balcony to see what was happening outside. I couldn't see anyone I thought looked suspicious around, so it felt safe to go down and have a walk.

I decided to practice the spell I had been working on taking the cast off first then changing into a seagull, getting onto the balcony wall and flying down to the beach. I landed a bit roughly hitting my beak on the sand. A wave came in as well hitting me in the head making me squawk. I flew down to the quieter end of the beach landing near the water again looking around noticing there weren't many people around. I quickly changed into myself but then changing into a male form, feeling annoyed I have to go to these lengths just for a walk on the beach.

I sauntered down the beach, feeling pleased with the bird spell at least. I hadn't put the cast back on, feeling like going for a paddle in the water. It was a little cool, but it was inviting watching the sun lower over it going in up to my knees, feeling goosebumps appear on my legs.

A wave came in a little higher than I expected wetting me up to my waist, as I giggled, 'I may as well go for a quick dip then go home.' I dived under the next wave, making me gasp as I came up, with the cool water hitting me. I turned to walk back out of the water noticing a woman walking down the beach recognising her. It was Hildegard looking quite well. I could feel my anger build, *'They obviously had found a way to get their magic back.'*

I ignored her keeping my head down because I was in disguise, walking out of the water wiping my face. She slowed her pace down looking at me deciding to talk to me, "It's a bit cool to go swimming." I knew she was checking me out deciding just to nod saying, "Yeah," but not looking at her. I had a feeling she was going to try something to reveal who I was, so I turned and dived back into the water.

While I was under the wave, I put a swirling water wheel in my hand and sent it out towards her, hearing her scream as it hit her, knocking her off her feet.

I came up grinning, watching her being buffeted around with the water wheel. I stopped it, watching her flounder on the sand like a fish out of water magicaeing back home.

I got back to the unit angry, changing back to myself. I growled as I dried myself off going towards the fridge to get a glass of wine, *'That bloody bitch is back. That means the others are as well.'*

I downed a couple of glasses of wine a bit quicker than I should have, while standing out on the balcony watching the sun go down. I didn't feel hungry, so I had another glass of wine feeling the calming effects of the alcohol seep through me. I started to get the giggles thinking of something to do to lift my mood. I changed into a suit like the super heroes wear on TV looking down at my chest, *'What can I call myself.'* A thought came into my head, 'SW' for Super Witch. I giggled to myself as I put the letters in silver on my chest. I looked in the mirror at the suit and the letters pushing my chest out, 'All I need now is tits and muscles.'

I went and had another glass of wine feeling a bit light headed now, putting to the book that I wanted tits and muscles, with a chant coming to me.

I went into my bedroom putting the glass down, "*Now I see bigger tits and muscles for thee, just while I wear this suit you see.*"

I watched, giggling as the muscles in my arms and legs became bigger and my tits grew. This made the letters on my chest stand out better. Kimba came in looking at me giving me a little meow.

I got the giggles deciding to put a cape on the back and a little mask over my eyes. I then took a photo of myself sending it to my girls, falling on the bed afterwards laughing.

I didn't wait for a reply getting on a broom and flying out the balcony window thinking I'll go and see Alira. I decided to go over Newtown first to see if there was anyone there, finding the lights were on in the old church where we did the meditation. I flew over the church landing in the little courtyard with the light spilling out onto the courtyard. I sneaked up to the doorway sending the broom away, hearing voices echoing around the hall. I could feel a sneeze coming on trying to stifle it putting my finger up to my nose.

The urge went away so I put my invisible spell on me walking into the church remembering I didn't have the cast on this time, feeling safe. I moved closer to see Lilith, Allegra, Hildegard and Suzannah talking as though they were old friends and looking quite well.

I noticed wands in their hands so they definitely had their magic back. They must have been getting ready for a meditation meeting because incense was burning along with a candle in the middle of the floor with dried flowers around it. I thought to myself, *'They must be doing a spring equinox ceremony or something.'*

I could hear them talking quietly but couldn't quite make out what they were saying. Lilith was quite happy laughing at whatever Hildegard was saying stirring my anger up with the wine in me. I felt like going over to them and belting them but I stopped myself deciding to point towards the candle, watching it tip and fall onto the dried leaves that were surrounding it.

I then pointed to the incense making the smoke that was coming from it, get worse, filling the hall with it. I blew on my hand towards the smoke, as it swirled around the hall more, with the flames taking hold, not only to the dried plants but the floor of the church.

I slammed the front door shut with a gust of wind being produced, fanning the flames on the floor more. Lilith and the others stood there stunned at first but looked around the church.

Lilith put her finger up to quieten the others, "I think it's Hannah, she's getting very clever."

Suzannah and Hildegard brought their wands out looking around for me, deciding to send bolts around the room. Allegra and Hildegard looked at the flames taking hold in the church pointing towards it to put it out, but I blew again sending it towards them watching them scream.

I smiled as I watched them getting angry looking around the church for me as well as planning their escape, which the only way out was passed me. I put out an invisible rope just as they went running past me, all falling over it making me giggle.

Lilith was getting angry, getting up off the floor rubbing her arm, "Hannah Dragé show your bloody self."

I moved quietly, noticing she was about to send a bolt towards me, hitting the servery setting it on fire. I wasn't going to give her the satisfaction of seeing me plus I could feel another sneeze coming on. I magicae out to the street bringing the broom back in and taking off.

I was still invisible but the broom wasn't, deciding to fly around the church a couple of times fanning the flames that had now spread to the front door and up to the roof. Lilith and the others came running out looking at the church in horror then looking up noticing the broom flying around.

Lilith growled throwing a bolt at me, missing, as I threw one back throwing her down the street. I heard her groan as she scraped her knees and arms along the footpath.

I thought about my broken wrist as I watched her falling, '*I think it's time you got something broken as this was done because of you.*' I pointed to her as she sat up looking at her elbows and knees all bloody. I picked her up to a good height and then dumped her on the ground. She screamed and flayed her arms and legs when she felt herself being lifted, then a look of horror went over her face as she was dumped on the ground. Her arm was underneath her when she landed, hearing a loud crack.

Again, she let out a scream with the pain of her arm being broken. I had enough taking off, over to Alira's place feeling satisfied, I had got them back a bit at least.

I could see her in her bedroom reading, so I tapped on the window taking the invisible spell off me, making her jump. She looked wide eyed at me with a grin coming over her face opening the window "Hannah, what are you doing now?"

I started to giggle standing on the broom with my hands on my hips, "What do you think?"

She shook her head, "Get in here you crazy woman."

Yindi went out onto the balcony to see who Alira was talking to, "Hannah, get in here now."

Alira pulled a face at me, "You better get in, Mum's seen you."

I groaned magicaeing into their unit, sneezing just as I did. I brought in a tissue lifting my mask and blowing my nose then putting it back, "So what do you think?"

Alira came into the lounge trying to stifle her laughter in front of her mother, "So what are you now super woman?"

I looked at her sarcastically, "No … I'm Super Witch!"

Alira burst out laughing with Fia coming out of the bedroom looking at me.

Yindi turned away trying not to laugh, but turning back to me, "You're being very naughty Hannah. What have you done to your hair?"

Fia took a photo of me shaking his head, "Ferdinand won't believe this."

I looked at him, "Don't you show him Fia, otherwise I'll come after you."

He pretended to look worried, "Alright I won't."

I went to look in the mirror, "What's wrong with my hair … oh I think it's become a bit knotty. Maybe I should change my name to Phyllis Diller the Super Witch."

Alira burst out laughing again turning to look at Fia, who didn't understand who I was talking about. She turned to him trying to explain to him who Phyllis Diller was.

Yindi came over to me taking me by the shoulders, "Come and sit down and I'll give it a brush at least. Phew you smell like a winery, how much have you drunken? Have you had anything to eat?"

I sat down on the sofa grinning at her, "Yep I've had grapes to eat," sneezing again.

Alira was giggling again saying to Fia, "Grapes."

Yindi could smell the sea in my hair, "You've been bloody swimming as well. You're going to get a cold again and you've taken the cast off."

I rolled my eyes trying to stand up, "Super Witch doesn't care because she has the power," as I started singing "She Has the Power" putting my finger up, making it echo.

Yindi pushed me back down, "Sit down and let me fix your hair up at least. Alira, can you get something to eat for Hannah?"

She was still laughing with tears running down her face with Fia trying not to giggle now going to help her.

Poppy came out to see what all the noise was hearing the song I was singing, rolling her eyes, "Hannah what are you up to now?"

I tried to get up to sing again but Yindi pushed me back down, "Hannah, stay still while I get these knots out."

I flexed my muscles and put my chest out as Alira came out with some lasagne and salad, "Here muscle witch, have something to eat."

I was screwing my face up now with Yindi trying to get the knots out of my hair, "Yindi stop! I'll have a go at it when I get home in the shower."

She growled, "You better Hannah. Now eat your food. What else have you been up to tonight?"

I went and sat at the table slipping on my cape and falling off the chair, "Oops, slippery little bugger," hearing Alira start to giggle again, looking at her mother, trying to stop.

She helped me up saying quietly, "Behave yourself."

I whispered back, "Why is the headmaster here?"

She wrapped her hands around my arms, "Where did you get those muscles from you silly woman."

I stood up suddenly hitting her in the chin, knocking her over, flexing my muscles.

She yelled, "Hannah!"

She was rubbing her chin, watching me flex my muscles and my chest, "Do you like them, I ordered them on magic.com.au."

She was stifling her laughter again, putting her hand up, "I'll be back in a minute" as she went into her bedroom shutting the door with a loud burst of laughter coming from there.

Yindi came over, "Sit down Hannah and have something to eat. I hope you haven't done anything else while you were flying around."

I started to eat the lasagne "I was invisible, Yindi, so I *won't get into trouble with Jardine* (sarcastically). Although I forgot to hide my broom, so some people might have seen a broom flying around. Oh, and I think I burned the church down in Newtown."

Poppy was still listening from the door giggling, "You did what?"

Yindi also came and sat down next to me looking serious, "Hannah what did you do?"

I got halfway through the food feeling full, "thanks that was lovely, but I'm full now."

Yindi told Poppy to put the news on the television. Sure enough, it showed the church on fire at Newtown where I had been. Yindi put her hand on mine, "Hannah you could get into trouble for that."

I patted hers, "They didn't see me Yindi, stop fussing. Lilith, Hildegard, Allegra and Suzannah were all there laughing and joking with wands. I accidently knocked over a candle that was on the floor and they let it burn, deciding to chase after me instead."

Yindi shook her head, "So they knew it was you though?"

I wiped my mouth, "They were guessing it was me. They couldn't see me, like I said. They sent a bolt towards me while I was hidden, which hit the servery and set another fire, so they were to blame as well. They didn't even attempt to put it out."

I got up doing a big burp, while holding my stomach, "Thanks for the food, Yindi. I better get back just in case they are patrolling around my unit. I left the lights on so they should think I'm still in there. They can't get in, only family can do that."

Yindi looked worried, "Do you want one of us to come back with you?"

The alcohol was wearing off a little now, but I still flexed my muscles, "No Super Witch can deal with it."

I brought out the broom with Yindi taking it off me, "Just magicae back you silly bugger and put your cast back on once you've had a shower."

I giggled, "Ok Yindi" giving her a hug. I gave Alira, Fia and Poppy a hug with Poppy screwing her nose up, "Lay off the wine a bit, Hannah." I stood in the middle of the lounge saluting them all doing a loud cackle like a witch in the movies, hearing Alira being told off for laughing again.

I landed back in the unit near my bedroom door, just in case they were looking in the balcony window, finding Amelia, Charlotte, Shiro and Aetius standing near the balcony door talking loudly to someone.

Amelia saw me first, trying to stop smiling at the suit I had on, putting her finger up to her mouth, "Sshh Mum, it's Hildegard and Allegra on brooms out by your balcony. They're looking for you for some reason. We've told them that you are sick in bed."

I smiled, "They can't get in."

Charlotte noticed me arrive telling them, "She's up now I'll go and see if she wants to talk to you."

Charlotte came over to me smirking, "Mum what have you been up to now?"

I looked over to Shiro and Aetius looking a bit guilty, "I was attacked on the beach again so I came and had some wine," looking over to the empty bottle on the table. "I then got the shits with them so I made this suit, deciding to go for a ride on the trusty old broom."

Shiro came over, looking at me, "So what does SW stand for?"

I grinned, "Super Witch. I decided to go and see if anyone was around at the old church, finding those four there laughing and joking as though they were the innocent ones." I was about to continue when we heard a voice coming from outside. Charlotte stopped me, "Get changed into your nightie, Mum and come and talk to these stupid bitches."

I did that, putting the cast back on, as well and put tissues in my hand. I didn't need to act being blocked up as that was happening anyway. I moved over to the balcony looking at Hildegard and Allegra sitting on their brooms just off my balcony.

I sighed, "What do you two want?" Hildegard sat up on her broom with her wand in her hand, "We know you were responsible for the fire at the church Hannah, don't act all innocent with us."

I groaned, "I have been here in bed because I was sick you stupid bitches. Maybe it was one of your other friends looking for you."

Amelia had taken a photo of them both without them realising, for evidence, just in case, then came out to me, "So you can go away and play somewhere else."

Allegra's face turned to a scowl "you think you're so clever. Lilith will deal with Ferdinand then you won't be so cocky, little, Hannah."

I could feel my anger burr up with Aetius coming over to me talking quietly, "She's bluffing Hannah. Lilith isn't allowed near him and she has restricted places she can go in Jardine."

I took a deep breath calming myself calling out to them, "You can go now; you're disturbing my rest." Hildegard knew their bluff didn't work, talking quietly, "Come on Allegra let's see if we can get her."

Charlotte and Amelia came beside me with Charlotte saying, "Mum I think they're going to try and get on the balcony."

I grinned, "Just watch girls." Hildegard was too angry to see my grin as they both flew off but circled around coming straight towards me with their brooms hitting the shield, I had put around the balcony, bouncing off like they had hit a rubber screen. Their faces screwed up in horror as they screamed, falling off their brooms, going towards the ground.

I pointed at them sending a magical net towards them, stopping them from falling. I then threw them out to sea far enough, so it would take a while to swim in. The only thing that landed on the ground was their wands and brooms, which I crushed.

Both my girls, Shiro and Aetius stood there laughing as they watched it unfold.

Amelia shook her head, "That's a great shield Mum. I might have to do that one as well."

Charlotte looked a little annoyed, "Why did you stop them falling Mum? They deserved to get hurt."

I shrugged my shoulders, "I don't want to have to explain how two people got badly hurt or died underneath my unit. That's not me. I'm sure they'll piss someone off enough one day to meet that fate, but I don't want that to be on my conscience."

Amelia gave me a hug noticing I had lost some weight but didn't say anything about it, "Do you want to have something to eat?"

I shook my head, "I had something at Alira's, which I was getting to when they rudely interrupted. They didn't even try to put the fire out, but just kept looking for me. Stupid women."

They all looked at the family tree I had put up on the wall noticing Wilhemenia up there now with Charlotte saying, "Why did you put the family tree up on the wall, Mum?"

I moved over to it, "I was doing some research and got annoyed having to go into the book all the time, so I put it up there. I finally got the Norwegian grandmother's name being Wilhemenia. She wouldn't give me any more information."

Charlotte could hear I was blocked up, "Do you want to go to the medical centre to get something for your cold?"

I looked at the time, "Oh yes I may as well just so it doesn't get worse."

Amelia came forward, "Shiro and I will come with you, so Charlotte can go back home."

I got changed shutting the balcony door but leaving the lights on. We took off to the medical centre in Caringbah, managing to get in quite quickly, as they weren't too busy. The doctor asked a few questions how I hurt my arm but Amelia and Shiro came in with me so he didn't say too much else.

He gave me some antibiotics for my cold only if it got worse and some stronger painkillers for my arm, which we managed to pick up from a chemist, that was open late.

We got back to the unit with Amelia and Shiro checking if everything was alright cleaning up a little as she went. She noticed the blanket on the sofa, "Have you been sleeping out here Mum?"

I sat on the sofa, "Yes, it's not the same with Ferdinand not being here. Kimba likes me here as well."

Amelia looked at the time, "Well we will get going. Please call if you need to talk or come and have a meal with me if you don't feel like getting anything?"

I knew what she was getting at, looking at the painkillers I had been given "I will. Stop worrying."

I watched them go, getting up to take a painkiller then having a shower trying to get some of the knots out of my hair with the conditioner in it. I managed to get some of them out of it but got frustrated. I could also feel the painkillers kicking in feeling tired.

I got dressed and turned off the lights lying in the dark with a bit of light coming through the curtains as I hadn't shut them fully, eventually dropping off.

Chapter 26

The painkillers knocked me out for quite a while, waking early with a glimpse of light coming through the curtains. I tried to go back to sleep but I couldn't, so I got up opening the curtains, blowing my nose again, going to the bathroom then coming out to feed Kimba.

I didn't feel hungry again, so I just had some coffee and a banana that had seen better days, but it filled a gap in my stomach. I sat there drinking my coffee turning on the TV watching the news again while coughing. A breaking news report came on about the church that had totally burned down in Newtown. I thought, 'Wow I thought they would have stopped most of it with their magic. Obviously not!'

I decided to go for a walk along another beach this time hoping I wouldn't be bothered. I got changed and looked on a map of Sydney deciding to go to the northern beaches, walking along the white sand to get some exercise with the smell of the sea calming me.

I was just about to go when two women approached me, deciding to put a clear orb up so they could see me, but couldn't harm me. I realised it was Malus and a guard from Jardine in our world clothes which made them look quite different.

Malus didn't look very happy coming up to me, "You've been causing trouble again Hannah."

I sneezed into a tissue, "And what would that be Malus?"

Malus moved back a little, not wanting my bugs, telling the guard not to get too close as well, "You set fire to the church in Newtown and flew around on a broom again."

I rolled my eyes, "No I didn't set fire to the church. I did have a little fly around because I was attacked again, while I was innocently walking along a beach to calm down. Are you going to do something about them or am I the only one you pick on?"

Malus looked annoyed, "You know the rules, Hannah. I'm sorry you have been attacked but that doesn't give you the right to frighten the non-magic people. They're not used to seeing that."

I blew my nose again moving closer because I knew it annoyed them, "Well maybe I don't want to be a part of Jardine anymore, so give me my spirit animal back then we won't have to worry about me breaking any rules."

Malus moved back again getting agitated, "If it were up to me, I would eject you from Jardine but I can't make that decision. As for Ferdinand, there are questions that need to be answered and he is not behaving either. He will not be returned to you until we get to the bottom of some things."

I had enough "well that ends our chat. Goodbye," taking off as I heard her yelling at me to come back. I got back to my unit stomping my foot again, '*Who does she think she is? She obviously knows she can't get into my unit otherwise she would have followed me.*'

I lay down trying to stem my temper again, eating some chocolate and putting some loud music on, looking at the family tree. I pointed to the ceiling putting more branches over it just for something to do. I sat up liking the look of it, so I pointed over to another wall putting some painted trees and bushes around, with some big cats in amongst them and a purple dragon, smiling affectionately at it.

I lay back down with Kimba coming to lay near me dozing off again after taking some more painkillers. My cold was just at the chest stage so I left the antibiotics to see how I went.

I woke again around 1.00p.m. looking out the balcony window with a beautiful sunny day outside not really feeling like going out just now, after all the attacks and people approaching me no matter where I go. I brushed down my hair, knowing it was messy again. I turned the radio up listening to the music with a Crowded House song coming on bringing out a glass of wine sitting there listening to it. I looked over to the kitchen thinking I should eat something when I felt a vibration of someone coming in. I knew it had to be one of the girls as no one else could get in, when Olwen appeared looking at me. I had a glass of wine in my hand, "Hi Hannah. I hear you've been having troubles and aren't taking it too well."

I groaned looking at him, "How did you get in here?"

He came and sat next to me, "You set your security for family only. I'm family—remember."

I grabbed a tissue blowing my nose that started running again sounding clogged, "I'm not really in the mood for visitors at the moment Olwen can you come another day."

He looked at the paintings on the walls and ceilings, "It feels like a jungle in this place."

He then noticed the family tree getting up to have a look at it, "So this is the Dragé family. Amelia and Charlotte said you were doing some research on them."

He was too bright for my mood, "What do you want Olwen?"

He came back over sitting next to me, "I think you should come and stay with me for a few days to give you a break from here."

He made the mistake of taking my glass off me, that I was slowly sipping on, feeling my temper build up, pointing at him, putting him in a binding spell. I floated him up off the ground looking deadly at him, "I don't know you Olwen. You're probably just like all the rest and after something."

His face was screwing up with the pain of the binding, "Gee you're a lot stronger now Hannah," struggling against the spell.

I picked up my glass taking another drink, "Are you going to go away?"

He shook his head groaning, "No! I want you to come with me. The girls have said you're getting up to mischief and are sick."

I groaned, "I can look after myself Olwen, I'm just going through a phase getting stuff out of my system. I suppose you're like those goody two shoes Jardine people trying to get me to conform?"

He was in real pain now, "Hannah let me go. I want to talk to you. I'm not a part of Jardine. I'm a loner."

Amelia came in looking at Olwen in the air in pain, "Mum let him go."

She looked at Olwen, "Sorry, I got held up. I knew I should have come in with you."

I looked at Amelia, "What's going on Amelia?"

Charlotte came in as well looking at Olwen then the paintings around the lounge, "Mum let Olwen go."

Amelia sat next to me, "We want you to go to Olwen's for a few days. He may have a way to get Ferdinand out of Jardine. He doesn't like Jardine either but his partner is still part of it. Come on let him go and we can talk properly."

I sighed, letting him go, watching him drop to the ground, then getting up rubbing his arms, "You're definitely a Drachen and Dragé, stubborn as anything."

Charlotte came and sat next to me on the other side, "Come on we'll go to Germany with Olwen and see what we can sort out, plus give you a break from these attacks."

I blew my nose again looking angry, "I went to a different beach today only to be approached by that bloody elder Malus and a guard saying (sarcastically), *'You've been a naughty girl again, Hannah blah blah blah.'*"

Amelia took the glass from me putting it on the coffee table, "Come on Mum let's get going. You can take Kimba with you as well."

I sat there still not sure about this, "How do you propose to get to Germany? Do we have to hop over 10 countries to get there?"

He grinned a cocky grin, "No I have a special way of getting there. Come on go and have a wash and we'll get going."

Charlotte pulled up my hair, "I know it's clean but it's still knotty. I think you might need to brush your teeth before we go," waving her hand in front of her face, "Phew wine breath."

I looked at her sarcastically, "You know how to cheer me up, don't you Charlotte."

I got up reluctantly going to the bathroom hearing someone tip the wine down the sink and getting Kimba's carry case and putting her in it. I put the brush through my hair again cringing as the knots were being annoying and not wanting to come out. I ended up just rolling it up putting it into a clip at the back of my head. I put a little bit of makeup on making my face look a bit better, hiding the dark circles under my eyes at least.

I came out looking at everyone who had tidied up, shutting the door and had Kimba sitting in her carry case, "Do I need to change now or should I wait?"

Olwen raised an eyebrow, "I've heard your hands are deadly," pointing to me putting some jeans and a jumper on, along with some gloves.

I grimaced, "There's always a wise guy in the group isn't there."

I looked over to the pictures of my grandmothers who were looking at the girls smiling. The picture of my mother was just staring at Olwen.

Olwen shook himself out when he saw that, going over to me, "Is that your mother?"

I looked at her staring at Olwen, "Yes, she probably recognises you from your father."

He took my hand along with Amelia's who took Charlotte's who was holding onto Kimba as well, "Let's get going."

Olwen took us to an area just out of Sutherland to a place in the national park called Winifred Falls, landing just near the waterfall.

I looked around me hearing the water rushing over the falls with all the rain we had just had and the distinct smells of the Australian bush of tea trees and eucalyptus trees. A kookaburra started laughing, with Olwen going towards a huge gum tree, waving at us to follow him. The gum tree had a hollowed area where the tree had split and the roots were sticking out from the ground.

The opening was high enough for us to go in and not hit our heads as Olwen encouraged us to follow him in. I looked at the girls' knowing snakes and spiders live in these things, with Olwen coming back out looking perplexed, "What's the matter?"

I looked worried, "We've lived here long enough to know that snakes and spiders live in those things."

He smiled, "They won't bother you this is a magical tree to us. Come on before someone comes along."

We all went into the gum tree flicking his fingers with a small orb coming up to give us some light in there. He then brought out a huge old-fashioned black key as I watched him intrigued.

He grinned, feeling clever, waving his hand over the back of the gum with a lock appearing; then he put the key in turning it. The back of the gum tree where the lock was, split in two like the doors of a lift, opening and letting us look inside. He put his arms out, "Don't go in yet ladies this has to recognise my voice."

He then said, "Dieser Baum ist unser Portal nach Deutschland an diesem Tag, bringen Sie uns postbesorgt dorthin (this tree is our portal to Germany this day, take us there post haste with care.)"

He looked at us pleased with himself again when a whooshing noise came over us and a clear lift with an ornate top and a big ball on the top of it, appeared opening its doors to let us in. We all walked in, with the doors for the tree shutting first, while Olwen leaned back on the wall looking pleased with himself, "Are you ready ladies?"

We all looked at each other not sure what to expect.

The tree opened up above us letting a filtered light in from the branches above then a multicoloured mist formed around us, starting to spin like a whirlwind. We put our hands out in front of us watching them disintegrate as we all squealed.

Olwen laughed heartedly, "Just relax, it'll put you back together."

I felt like I was in one of the science fiction movies when all the people's molecules disintegrated in one place, then reassembled in another.

The next thing we remembered was landing in a round room that had brick white painted walls. We could see ourselves coming back together, giggling at the sight of it.

I looked at Olwen, who was just casually standing there watching us, waving over the doors as they opened. We stepped out onto a concrete floor looking around us. Charlotte worked it out before us, "We're in a lighthouse. Wow that's clever."

Olwen leaned over to her grinning, "Germans make a lot of good things."

Amelia coughed, "Yes sure Olwen."

He turned around to the lift putting his hand up, sending it away then bringing the key out again, when a lock appeared, turning it and disappearing.

Amelia and Charlotte took my hands walking down some stairs carefully looking at them both, "I can walk down the stairs girls."

They shook their heads with Amelia squeezing my hand gently, "No you've been through enough Mum, we don't need you falling down the stairs," putting up my hand with the cast on.

We got to the bottom, going outside, being met by a cool sea breeze and the gentle sounds of the waves hitting the shore. I felt a bit of a shiver going down me.

We looked around us taking it all in, when Charlotte said, "Where are we, Olwen?"

He came up behind us, "We are in a small place called Strande, which is not far from the Danish border. Take my hand, Amelia, while holding onto your mother you two and I will take you to my place."

We magicae out of the lighthouse landing in a large foyer with black and white tiles and an ornate wooden staircase with pictures on the walls that were painted in dark reds or crimson with white borders.

I looked up at the ceiling that also had ornate white plaster designs going around the edges but was plain in the middle until you got to a chandelier in the centre, which had a dome with a flower design around it. There were big wooden doors on the entrance with a large old-fashioned black lock.

Olwen took us into an elaborate room to the side with big windows that let in the light with more paintings, but modern furnishings and a woman sitting on one of the sofas near a fire that was burning.

She stood up as we entered smiling, "Well hello you must be the Dragĕ family Olwen has been telling me about."

Olwen came in taking off his jacket, "This is Monika my partner. Monika this is Charlotte, Amelia and, Hannah."

We all moved forward shaking her hand and smiling, with me saying, "I hope we aren't putting you to any trouble. Olwen was quite insistent that we come here."

She smiled going over to him putting her arm around him, "No he told me of his plan to bring you all back here as he felt things weren't going right for you. Looking at your arm and how pale you are Hannah; I think he was right."

Olwen moved away from Monika, "I'll take you up to your rooms so you can get comfortable. Hannah you are looking tired again, do you want a rest before we eat?"

I nodded, "Yes that would be nice, thanks Olwen." We followed Olwen out of the room up the staircase, looking at the pictures of men and women on the walls stopping at a handsome man in German uniform with the same eyes as us, "Is this your father Olwen?"

He came up behind me putting his hands on my shoulders, "Yes that is *our* father. His name is Stefan Drachen and was a good man. Come, I will show you to your rooms. You can have a look around at your own leisure afterwards."

I was shown mine first going into a deep blue room with large windows encased by light curtains and a large four poster bed with an elaborate bedspread on it. The roof was similar to the one downstairs with an ornate ceiling around the edges and a large round light in the middle with ornate flowers surrounding it. The carpet was a deep blue with what looked like small gold star bursts scattered throughout the carpet. It had a writing desk near the window and a large white ornate fireplace to the side of the room that was burning making the room warm.

I smiled at Olwen, "Oh this is lovely Olwen. It is a very calming room."

Olwen guided me over to the bed, "Go and have a rest, Hannah. I will send one of the girls in to get you when we are ready to eat."

I was feeling quite tired with everything that had gone on and not eaten properly. I sat on the bed taking my shoes off as I watched them go out giving me a little wave.

The girls were taken to similar rooms along the corridor just different colour schemes. By the time they came back to see me, I was asleep, pulling the blanket over me looking at the dark rings under my eyes.

They went outside shutting the door quietly with Amelia shaking her head, "She looks worn out. We should have checked on her more."

Charlotte nodded, "You know she is stubborn about these things, look what she did to Olwen. We've got her now and should have a good rest."

I was woken by Amelia after a couple of hours sleep feeling a bit dazed at first, trying to remember where I was, "Mum, you're in Olwen's house, remember."

I stretched out yawning, "Oh yes that's right. It feels a bit like a dream, doesn't it; being in this lovely house."

Amelia agreed, "Yes and they are both so nice. We have been looking at all the relatives while looking around the house. It's not a huge house but it's bigger than your and my flat, put it that way."

I chuckled, "Anything would be bigger than our flats dear."

I looked at Amelia who had changed her clothes to a dress, "Do we have to change for dinner Amelia?"

She nodded, "Yes. It's not formal but put a dress on, just to fit in. I have to tell you also that Aetius and Shiro will be there."

I looked a little sad, but put a smile on for her, "That's good Amelia, they should be with you two."

I looked over to the fire that was burning noticing Kimba sitting there in front of it, going over to her and giving her a cuddle. I brought some food in for her, "There you go baby girl; you've been through a lot to."

She started purring as I put her down to have something to eat.

I went and had a wash in the little ensuite just off the room, fixing up my makeup trying to hide the dark rings under my eyes and putting a dress and shoes on feeling strange after wearing track pants and my nightie for a few days.

We went downstairs to be greeted by Ingrid who was in a dress as well, "Hallo Hannah Ich bin Ingrid und ich helfe Monika und Olwen im Haus. Schön, dich kennenzulernen (hi Hannah I help Monika and Olwen around the house. Nice to meet you.)"

I shook her hand, "Schön, dich kennenzulernen, Ingrid. Es war so schön von Olwen und Monika, uns bleiben zu lassen. (Nice to meet you, Ingrid. It was so nice of Olwen and Monika to let us stay.)"

Amelia looked at me shaking her head, "Charlotte said you were speaking German. Don't tell me—grandma?"

I nodded, "Yes, she started to flick from German to Norwegian I think it was a spell or something."

Ingrid looked from Amelia to me, "Oh, deine Oma hat dir beigebracht, dass das gut ist (Oh your grandma taught you, that is good.)."

Amelia chuckled at Ingrid, "Grandma is a ghost though."

Ingrid looked surprised answering in stilted English for her benefit, "Oh dear. I don't like them much."

Amelia started to walk towards the dining room which was on the other side of the staircase, "I don't mind them, but I would rather they left me alone."

We all went into the dining room, with a fire burning in the large fireplace. The walls were painted an off white with a deep red carpet and similar ornate ceilings and a chandelier hanging over a large wooden table seating 8 people. It wasn't a huge ornate one but more a modern contemporary design, which was more to my taste.

Monika, who was standing near the fire place, "Come and have a glass of wine with me Hannah so we can talk."

I smiled, "Yes sure Monika," as she gave me a glass of wine. I hadn't seen Aetius and Shiro at first, but when they heard my name being mentioned, they came over and gave me a hug with Aetius saying, "It's good to see you again, Hannah."

I looked at both of them, as Monika gave me a glass of wine worried, "Have you seen Ferdinand at all?"

Shiro looked down at his feet, "We saw him yesterday Hannah but they have made him stay over in the grotto with the other dragons."

I sighed, "I still haven't heard anything about any investigation of anything even after speaking with that Malus today. 'She just keeps saying we are investigating things.' Have either of you seen Morag at all?" The both looked at me disappointed, "No, Hannah."

Olwen came over putting his arm around my shoulders, "Try not to worry, Hannah, I am sure he will be alright for now. Monika and I have been talking to the girls about your mother's side of the family and we think, if you are up to it, we should go to Norway tomorrow."

That cheered me up, "Oh yes, I would like to do that. It will take my mind off things, especially now that I know grandma's name."

Olwen smiled, "We thought so. We will leave around 9.00am so we can get back to have a rest."

We were called to the table by Ingrid, who put some food on the table magically to have dinner. We enjoyed chatting about other things going on in the world. I noticed Olwen was eating meat and the rest of us were eating vegetarian not saying anything.

I just couldn't eat too much apologising to Monika, "Sorry Monika, I think my stomach has shrunk. I hope you didn't slave away over all this lovely food."

Monika chuckled, "Hannah I don't cook, I hate it. Ingrid gets it in magically and Olwen likes meat, which both Ingrid and I can't stand cooking as well. So don't feel guilty about it."

We had a nice evening, going into the lounge to have a couple more drinks while I watched Aetius and Shiro making a fuss of Amelia and Charlotte, feeling a bit down that Ferdinand wasn't here. I stayed as long as I could saying, "I think I'll go up now and make sure I'm well rested for tomorrow."

They all gave me a hug saying, "Have a good rest."

I went upstairs, looking at the painting of Stefan almost as though his eyes were following me, just like you would see in scary movies, but it didn't scare me. I smiled thinking, "Well, at least I look like him and not the milkman."

I went into my room relieved to be away from the chatter. I went and had a shower trying to get some more knots out thinking of doing some meditation but I decided to do some tomorrow when I would be fresher. I went to bed bringing Kimba in with me, giving her a cuddle in the big bed falling asleep eventually.

I woke early, having a really sound sleep in the end, feeling a lot more refreshed. Having some food in my stomach would have helped, I guess. I got up feeling a bit of a chill in the air as the fire had gone out and it was quite early in the morning. I started the fire up again magically, then put some jeans on and a jumper and went into the bathroom to put some makeup on so I was ready to go when the others got up. I sent a quick text to Alira telling her where I was, just in case she got worried.

I opened the curtains to a dull day and the sun just starting to rise behind the clouds, trying to shed its rays over the land.

I decided I would go outside and go for a walk to get some fresh air, putting a jacket on and magicaeing outside, landing on a gravel footpath near the house. There was a large lawn in front with trees and bushes close to the fence line that backed onto a road. I walked over to one of the big trees, which I think was an oak tree, deciding to do some meditation under it. I brought a blanket in sitting down on it. I sat down looking back to the house noticing the flicker of a curtain, not worried about it. The front of the house was in the style of a traditional German nobleman's house done with the bottom half in stone and the top half done in the unique timber designs that were well known in Germany along with a tiled roof. It looked big but homely with a gravel path going around it then a long gravel drive leading up to the road.

I turned back around taking in the smells of the countryside, fresh air with a hint of the sea coming in through with it. I brought in the elements around me to strengthen me. I started to meditate closing out the noises around me bringing in the water, air, earth and fire feeling their strength within me build me up, helping to heal my thoughts.

I went out of myself looking to see myself raise off the ground with the elements raise with me. A fine mist like light was going from the elements to me encircling me sending a wonderful feeling through me. I looked back up at the house to see Olwen looking out the window while I did my meditation. I went back into my body concentrating on the elements again feeling the strength build and help my mental health. I went back down onto the blanket sitting peacefully and breathing deep when a vision came in of a man, I recognised, making me smile.

He fully formed in my vision, "Hallo Hannah. Schön, Sie im Haus der Familie und mit Olwen zu sehen. (Hello Hannah. Nice to see you in the family home and with Olwen.)"

I came out of myself again going into my vision to give him a hug, "Es ist schön, dich Papa zu sehen und endlich rein zu passen. (It is nice to see you Dad and finally fit in.)"

He pulled away from me, "Deine Mutter war eine feine Frau (Your mother was a fine woman.)"

I sighed, "Wir sind verschiedene Menschen Papa. Ich will nicht darüber reden (We are different people Dad. I don't want to talk about it.)"

He chuckled, "Du bist stur wie sie. Pass auf Hannah auf. (You are stubborn like her. Take care Hannah.)"

I felt someone sitting next to me joining me in my vision. I looked to see Olwen come in, "Hallo Papa (Hello Papa)." Stefan smiled a loving smile, "Hallo Sohn. Es ist schön zu sehen, dass du Hannah endlich hier hast. (Hello son. It is good to see you finally got Hannah here.)"

Olwen put his arm around me, "Wir warden für Sie über sie wachen. (We will watch over her for you.)"

He disappeared leaving me to return to my body hearing myself breath slowly coming back to the lawn with the sound of birds singing their morning songs, the distant sound of the sea and Olwen sitting next to me. I turned to smile at him leaning into his shoulder, "That was nice Olwen thank you."

He hugged me, "I haven't done that before, so it was a new and nice experience for me, thank you."

I took a deep breath, "I've always had this thing with ghosts of ancestors. It has come in handy at times. It was nice to have you join me as well to see Dad."

He stood up helping me up, touching my cold hands, "Aww heck Hannah, your hands are freezing."

I got up laughing, "I know I've shocked a few people with them. I drive Ferdinand nuts with them."

He pointed at them putting gloves on my hands, making me laugh again, "You're just like Ferdinand, he keeps doing that."

I sent the elements away and the blanket, walking back inside with Olwen joking about my hands.

We went inside to be greeted by the others in the dining room starting to have breakfast. I took my jacket and gloves off sending them away, having Olwen joke with me, "You keep those things away from me, Hannah."

Amelia and Shiro chuckled, "Oh you've discovered Mum's hands, have you Olwen?"

He went over to the fireplace lighting it, "Here Hannah, come and put your hands over here for a little while to warm them up."

I shook my head, "They're not that bad, Olwen."

He pointed to me bringing me over to him, "No arguing. Those things are a deadly weapon."

Monika giggled, "Don't be mean, Olwen, leave Hannah alone."

Chapter 27

We had breakfast and got ready to go to Norway. Amelia, Shiro, Charlotte, Aetius, Olwen and me went back to the lighthouse with Olwen explaining, "it will be faster to go this way. We could magicae there, but we would have to stop a couple of times."

I nodded, "Yes that is fine. I'd like to do this as quickly as possible."

He brought out the key he had used before summoning the lock putting the key in bringing forward the lift that we had used before. We got into the lift, "Bringen Sie uns jetzt nach Norwegen mit dem Ziel Ostfold poste eilete (take us now to Norway with the destination being Ostfold post haste)."

Shiro and Aetius were looking around intrigued holding the girls' hands.

We landed in Ostfold, Norway in a park within a cluster of trees. We reformed looking at all the trees that were very dense around us.

Olwen opened the doors letting us out, sending it away going over to Charlotte, "Where was that church you thought had the best possibility of finding your family Charlotte?"

She brought it up on her phone showing us where to go. She brought up a picture of a simple wooden church we were going to, which was painted white with a steeple on the roof and a bell hanging in it.

We all held hands magicaeing to the church, looking around to see what was around us. There was a large cemetery to the side of the church with all of us deciding to have a look around to see if we could find any Dragĕ gravestones.

I went over towards the church more, while the others all spread out to make it a faster search. There were some really old gravestones, quite close to the church with the names barely visible.

I bent down to have a closer look to see if I could see the surname at least. I was going over to the next one when a priest came out of the church noticing me, looking at the grave stones, so he came over to me.

I looked up smiling as he stood there looking at me, becoming a little uncomfortable asking, "hie ikan du hjelpe meg? (Hi can you help me?)"

The priest was looking at me intently, "Ja, hvis jeg kan (yes if I can.)"

I stood up, "Jeg har en slektning fra denne regionen som vi prøver ä finne med etternavnet Dragĕ. (I am trying to find a relative from this region with the surname Dragĕ)." He went quiet hesitating, "Følg meg (follow me)."

He opened the church door that he had come out from, taking me into the church to a small area that looked like an older part of the church. He went to a doorway that had a curtain across it, opening it and going down some stairs to a crypt. There were large marble slabs up on the walls with different family names and the date of birth and deaths on them.

There was one at the back of the crypt that the priest took me over to, with two wooden plaques on a dark marble slab, showing the name of Von Dragĕ. It showed the names of the people who were buried there were Wilhelmenia and Ritter Von Dragĕ (Ritter took his wife's name). Ritter died first in 1729 and Wilhelmenia dying 1756.

I put my hand up to the plaques running my hand over their names feeling relieved that we had found them, as I felt something when I touched the plaque from Ritter, like a shiver running down me as I shook it off. I noticed on Ritter's plaque a little key underneath his name similar to the one I had around my neck.

The priest introduced himself properly with his name being Father Daniel, telling me that there was a folklore story about them. Wilhelmenia met Ritter when he was over here in Norway for business when Ritter fell madly in love with Wilhelmenia, asking her to marry him very quickly.

They announced the marriage with Ritter taking Wilhelmenia back to meet his family. He had a brother Friedrich Ziegler who was a bit of a playboy in Germany. He always had various women around him sometimes getting them pregnant. Ritter often had to sort things out by paying the women to go away and have their babies, to avoid scandal so he wouldn't tarnish the name of Von Dragĕ.

When Friedrich met Wilhelmenia he fell madly in love with her wanting her to marry him instead of his brother. Ritter found out what Friedrich was wanting but he also knew that Wilhelmenia was from a long line of witches. He threatened to expose her and her family, which in those days was to be hung or burned at the stake, if she did not marry him and kill Friedrich.

She had no choice but to agree, only asking to live in Norway rather than Germany. She could not kill Friedrich as she loved him dearly, so she secretly bewitched him somehow never to be seen again.

Wilhelmenia and Ritter had two children. He went over to a big book of names finding theirs being Erik Von Dragĕ and a daughter Elese Von Dragĕ. It has been said that Elese never married but did have a daughter Marit dropping the Von from her name just calling herself Dragĕ, when she moved away from the area.

Father Daniel looked at me as I had tears running down my face, but I was trying to stop them as he comforted me, saying, "We are not sure if it is true, like I said it has been passed down and could be wrong."

He put his hand on mine, "Du er I slekt er ikke deg? (you're related, aren't you?)"

I nodded, "Mitt navn er Hannah Dragĕ. (yes, my name is Hannah Dragĕ)"

I could hear my girls coming over so I pleaded, "Snakker du engelsk (do you speak English)."

He nodded, "Ja. (yes)"

I turned to see them coming, "Døtrene mine snakker ikke norsk (my daughters don't speak Norwegian)."

He nodded, "Of course, I will speak English in front of them."

I grabbed his hand, "One more thing, can you not tell them the story I will do that. I just want to show them their grandparents names. That will make them happy."

Amelia and Charlotte came in with Amelia saying, "Here you are Mum, did you find something?"

I quickly pulled myself together, "yes, I think we have found them. There is a plaque on the wall here that Father Daniel has confirmed the children's names."

Father Daniel looked at my girls, "Well, you all look alike, don't you. I will show you one more thing that you can look up on google. I will bring it up for you now on my computer," as he started it up with us watching.

Aetius, Shiro and Olwen came in looking for us with Olwen saying, "Oh here you are. Have you found something, Hannah?"

I introduced Olwen, Shiro and Aetius to Father Daniel shaking their hands, "I was just bringing up a photo of the Von Dragĕ's."

He went into a site bringing up a picture of Wilhelmenia and Ritter Von Dragĕ showing Wilhelmenia with long blonde hair that was swept up on top of her head with braids going around in a circle. She had piercing dark blue eyes with a sadness in them looking like me and my girls. Charlotte was shocked, "Wow talk about family resemblance."

I then looked at Ritter who had the same colouring as Ferdinand but had a rounded face and wasn't as handsome as Ferdinand.

I moved aside while Daniel printed out the pictures of Wilhelmenia and Ritter going back over to the plaque looking at the key. I ran my finger over it when a copy of the key fell into my hand leaving a copy there. I quickly put it on my necklace I had on under my jumper, when Olwen came over to me putting his arm around my shoulders, "Well it looks like we have found them Hannah."

I smiled, "Yes, it's a great relief. I have been told before I have two lines of magic in my family and it has been proven correct now." I went back over to where the others were getting the printout of the pictures of Wilhelmenia and Ritter to take home with them. I smiled at Father Daniel, "Takk fader Daniel for hjelpen (thank you Father Daniel for your help.)"

Olwen looked at me impressed and shook Father Daniel's hand, "Kan du anbefale en kaffebar far (can you recommend a coffee shop, Father?)"

Father Daniel smiled at Olwen nodding going over to a map and showing him where to go.

Olwen came back to us, "Come on, Father Daniel has recommended a coffee shop not far from here. You may as well have a little look around before we go back, since it didn't take as long as we thought."

Amelia and Charlotte looked excited with Amelia saying, "Can we have a browse around the shops as well?"

Shiro took her hand, "You don't need any more clothes, Amelia."

Olwen shook his head, "We'll go and get a coffee first and see how we go."

He signalled for everyone to start filing out of the church putting his arm through mine, "Er du klar til å dra til Hannah? (Are you ready to go, Hannah?)"

I nodded without thinking, "Ja, jeg er glad det ikke tok så lang tid (Yes I'm glad it didn't take so long)."

Olwen grinned, "Jeg visste ikke at du snakket norsk. (I didn't know you spoke Norwegian.)"

I shook my head, "Du er like ille som Ferdinand lurer meg (you're as bad as Ferdinand tricking me)."

We caught up to Amelia by this stage, who heard us speaking Norwegian, "Mum what are you saying now?"

I giggled, "Your uncle has just found out I speak Norwegian."

Amelia groaned, "Oh yes grandma has taught her both Norwegian and German. We didn't know until it slipped out one time."

Olwen squeezed my arm, "It's a good gift from your grandma."

We walked a little way, coming into a shopping area with the girls getting excited. Shiro and Aetius were moaning "we're not here to shop you two."

Olwen called to them, "There is a bakery just down the main street that Father Daniel recommended come this way."

We made our way down the main street listening to Amelia and Charlotte finding things in shops that they would like to go and have a look at while Shiro and Aetius were holding tightly onto their hands.

We came across a bakery called Indre Olsford Bakery showing a display of lovely looking pastries and cakes in the window; smelling the delicious smells of them and coffee when someone came out of the shop. Amelia and Charlotte were pointing to different cakes and pastries, "Oh look at that one."

Shiro came closer, "I'm quite hungry now, come on let's go in."

We all filed into the bakery that was softly lit, finding a table to sit down at. Amelia groaned saying quietly, "Oh we don't have any Norwegian money."

Shiro stood up, "Don't worry I have some, just tell me what you want."

Olwen looked at Shiro, "I am happy to pay for them Shiro."

Shiro shook his head, "No it's the least we can do Olwen. Just let me know what you want and I'll get it." We went up and had a look at different cakes and pastries. I picked a lovely pastry and a coffee sitting back down while the others decided what they wanted.

An old man was sitting at a table with his wife looking at me. He had thin wispy grey hair a rounded face, blue eyes and a moustache the same colour as his hair.

He spoke to his wife quietly ending up coming over to me, "Hei er du en Von Dragĕ. (Are you a Von Dragĕ?)"

I hesitated whether to say yes, then I nodded, "Ja only Dragĕ nä skjønt (only Dragĕ now though?)"

He smiled broadly, shaking my hand, "Velkommen tilbake jeg heter Leif (welcome back my name is Leif)" looking over to his wife, "Ja, hun er en Von Dragĕ (yes she is a Von Dragĕ)." The others came back, with the old man looking at my girls, "Ah ja de er definitivt Von Dragĕ (ah yes, they are definitely Von Dragĕ)."

He shook their hands saying, "Velkommen tilbake (welcome back)."

My girls looked at me, "He is saying welcome back."

I turned to the old man, "De snakker ikke norsk (they don't speak Norwegian.)"

He put up his hand saying in pidgin English, "It is good to see Von Drage back. Velcome." The girls smiled both saying, "Thank you."

He looked back at me, "Blir du lenge (are you staying long?)"

I shook my head, "Nei, vi skal ha kaffe, er jeg redd. (No, we are having coffee then have to go I'm afraid.)"

Olwen stood up shaking the old man's hand, "Jeg er Hannah's stebror Olwen, jeg skal bringe henne tilbake en dag. (I am Hannah's stepbrother Olwen; I will bring her back again someday.)"

He nodded still smiling broadly "Ja, det blir vidunderlig. Jeg lar deg ta kaffen din. (Yes, yes that will be wonderful. I will leave you to have your coffee.)" He sat back down with his wife talking quietly to her. His wife got her phone out coming over, "Kan jeg ta et bilde av dere alle? (Can I take a photo of your all?)"

Amelia and Charlotte looked at me as I smiled, "She is asking to take a photo of us all."

I nodded getting up going over to the girls, "Ja, det går bra. (yes, that will be ok)." She got Olwen, Shiro and Aetius in there as well, then got a waitress to take a photo of us, with her and Leif. They thanked us all sitting back down talking quietly and still looking at us.

We got our coffee, pastries or cakes taking our jackets off, as it was starting to get warm in the shop, with other people filling the shop, looking at us. It was starting to get a bit stuffy after having my hot coffee and the shop being quite warm so I got up, "I'm just going out to get some fresh air, it's a bit stuffy in here, plus we appear to be drawing a crowd."

Olwen smiled, "Yes we won't be long, Hannah."

Amelia and Charlotte came out with me wandering down the street looking at the shoe shops and dress shops not far away. They disappeared in one of the shops shaking my head, *'Shiro and Aetius aren't going to be happy.'*

The others came out not long after with Olwen following, "where are the girls?"

I pointed down to a shop, "They're down there."

Shiro and Aetius grumbled, "We'll go and get them."

Olwen and I stood waiting by the bakery while they went and got the girls, "You speak quite well in Norwegian Hannah. Who did you say taught you?"

I smiled, "It was Wilhelmenia. She just started appearing in my meditations, I suppose putting a spell or something on me, to speak Norwegian and then German."

He smiled shaking his head, "I think you may have known it before with the ease you speak both languages Hannah. I haven't met anyone with so much contact with ghosts."

I looked at him sadly, "I have always spoken to them, especially when Mum wouldn't let me talk about magic or any of my dreams or visions; I would talk to them instead."

While we waited, I started thinking about Ferdinand, "Do you or Monika have spirit animals, Olwen?"

He nodded, "Yes, I have a lion and Monika has a bear. We hide our tattoos like the Jardine people though, as it tends to give you away too easily. Like I said, we are a bit of loners. You don't need to belong to Jardine to have magic and spirit animals."

I was surprised at this, "I did realise about the magic but I wasn't sure about the spirit animals."

The girls came out with a bag each looking pleased with themselves. I walked up to them, "Where did you get the money to pay for those?"

Amelia looked pleased with herself, "They were happy to take our credit cards, so we used them."

Olwen looked at what they had bought commenting, "Oh they are a good brand and look nice. Well, are you ready to go now?"

I nodded noticing another elderly couple making their way towards us, "Yes I'm not sure I like this celebrity status."

We started to make our way out of the main street with the elderly couple calling, "Wait Von Dragĕ familie kan vi ha et bilde (wait Von Dragĕ family can we have a photo?)"

Amelia looked at me, "What did they say?"

I sighed, "They want a photo."

Charlotte was happy to oblige "oh come on one more wouldn't hurt."

We had a photo taken, then walked quickly out of the main street to a quiet one so we could take off. Charlotte stopped us, "We should have asked where they used to live?"

I hesitated, "Oh yes, I didn't think of that. I suppose there isn't anything left anyway."

Olwen looked at us all questioningly, "Well do you want to ask or not?" It was starting to get cold, "No we will have to come back another time and stay to have a good look around."

The girls thought about it, "Yes, I would prefer not to rush as well. Let's go."

We went back to the park area to the trees that were quite thick, watching Olwen bring back the lift with the key from a small opening in a tree.

We got in and took off going back to the lighthouse. Once we got out of the lighthouse, I looked at the water, "Do you mind if I go for a walk along the beach just to get some sea air?"

He shook his head, "No, do you want some company?"

I shrugged my shoulders already looking out to sea thinking about things, "You please yourselves. I will find my way back otherwise."

He asked the girls, "Do you want to go for a walk along the beach girls?"

Charlotte and Amelia looked at Olwen grinning with Amelia saying, "No but are there any shops here in Strande?"

He looked over to me standing there looking out to sea, "I will take you. I think your mother wants some thinking time by the water." He came over to me, "Hannah, I'll take the girls to the shops. I'll see you back home."

I nodded giving him a hug, "Thank you for taking us to Norway, it was good of you."

He returned the hug, "That's what family are for. I'll see you at home."

I watched them go, then turned back to the water, walking towards it breathing in the fresh sea air. I took off my shoes and socks pulling my jeans up so I could just touch the water to let me ground myself.

As the water ebbed and flowed it finally touched my feet making me jump with the coolness of it. I stood there a little longer getting used to it, feeling calmer.

I thought about the key I had just retrieved off the plaque, deciding to cleanse both of them in the water while I was here. I took the necklace off looking around to see if there was anyone around, feeling a little nervous again, because I was alone. I put the keys and my crystal into the water saying a cleansing chant over them.

Once I started the chant the two keys fused together crossing the shafts, which made them look similar to the coat of arms I had seen, when I did a search on the different coat of arms.

I put it back on the necklace, then around my neck feeling the coolness on my skin from the water. I went out of the water collecting my shoes and walking a little way down the beach, which was quite empty, except for the odd person walking their dog or just meandering down by the water's edge. I turned back around going towards a rock to sit down and put my shoes and socks back on, noticing a woman in a long cream dress walking along the water's edge with long flowing blonde hair smiling at me, as she got closer.

I recognised her, standing once I had finished putting my shoes on, "Hallo Wilhemenia (hello Wilhemenia)."

Her hair and dress were softly blowing in the light breeze that was coming off the land, her face was pale but her eyes looked happy, "Hei Hannah likte du Norge (did you like Norway?)"

I nodded, "Yeah vi må gå tilbake og utforske litt mer (yes we will have to go back and explore a bit more)."

Wilhemenia came closer with a look of urgency, "Du må gjøre noe for meg nå (I need you to do something for me now!)"

I looked at her shocked, "Kan du fortelle meg om legenden først? (Can you tell me about the legend first?)"

Wilhemenia looked annoyed at me, "Ingen Hannah som bare er sladder. Jeg møter opp på toppen av fyret. (No Hannah that is just gossip. I will meet up on top of the lighthouse.)"

She disappeared making me feel confused and annoyed, but I reluctantly did as she asked, going up to the top of the lighthouse.

She was there waiting for me, looking out to sea, almost like something you would see on a romantic movie, with her hair billowing out from her and her cream dress showing her full figure.

I went up to her, "Jeg er her (I'm here)."

She turned with her pale face not showing any emotion, "Kall deg jenter inn (call your girls in.)"

I was getting annoyed, "Hvorfor hva som skjer. Hvis jeg får dem, må du snakke engelsk (why, what is going on. You will have to speak English if I do.)"

I could see where I got my temper from because she came right up to my face, looking angry, "Just get them in Hannah." I shook my head, "Alright. I haven't done this much so it may take a few minutes."

I took a deep breath, closed my eyes and visioned both my girls standing here with me. It took a couple of goes but I finally got them to me, opening my eyes with both girls standing there, looking surprised and then annoyed, with Amelia saying, "Mum what the heck is going on. We were shopping with Olwen."

Charlotte looked at Wilhemenia, "Is that grandma Wilhemenia?"

I nodded, "Yes. She wants us to do something urgently, that is why I have called you in."

She came over to the girls, "I need you all to do something for me, as we are running out of time."

Charlotte smiled, "Well at least we can understand you this time, what is it you want us to do?"

Wilhemenia was trying to move us closer but her hands were going through us, "I need you to go into a circle and hold hands then call in the book."

I looked at her unsure as to why, but I did what she wanted, hesitating, "I need to put us in an orb first to protect us."

She was looking agitated, "Yes alright do it!"

I put us all in an orb standing in a circle, then called in the book looking at Wilhemenia for the next instruction. She smiled with delight, "Oh you have upgraded it wonderfully Hannah. Your magic is certainly getting nice and strong."

I was getting agitated now, "Yes Wilhemenia what do you want us to do? Olwen will be looking for the girls, soon."

She tapped it watching it open to the sealed section we had been trying to get into, "Get the keys you have Hannah and put them on the seal."

I pulled up the chain taking the joined keys off and went to put them on the seal.

She put her hand up, "Wait, you must join hands before you do that." She looked behind her, "Come on it is your time to come out and play."

I looked at her thinking, '*Ok she has gone a bit cuckoo*' when Ritter appeared next to her faintly at first, then becoming more visible with a big smile on his face, "Why did you wake me, Wilhemenia?"

He looked around at us first then out to sea, "Ah Germany it still looks lovely. What am I doing here Wilhemenia?"

Wilhemenia turned Ritter around, "You can look on your own time. We need to do this now as we are running out of time."

He turned around, "Hello, are you my granddaughters?" We nodded, with me going to talk to him, when Wilhemenia interrupted us, "Enough of the chitchat it is time to get this done. Now hold hands the three of you and Hannah put the keys onto the seal."

We did as she asked, holding hands and putting the keys on the seal. Both Wilhemenia and Ritter put their ghostly hands over the seal with a message appearing *"you have the key and the permission of those who did this please stand by."*

Ritter looked amazed, "Hannah you have upgraded the book, well done."

A blinking *cursor* appeared above the seal with the keys disappearing into the seal and then a funnel of starry light along with a miniature dragon flying out from the middle of the funnel, screeching. It flew up to Wilhemenia and Ritter going through their ghostly bodies then flew around me and my girls screeching with a flame coming from its mouth putting the starry light around us. This sent gasps of power reverberating through us, as we writhed with the power flowing within us.

It felt like I had gone into another space but came back down feeling my heart racing taking deep breaths, opening my eyes, looking at my girls. They two were breathing heavily taking in everything that had happened.

I looked down at the book to see the sealed section come up with a notice *"initiation complete. This area will no longer exist. Goodbye."*

I shook my head, '*I think I went overboard with the computer dialogue.*' I turned to look at Wilhemenia and Ritter who were hugging each other smiling.

Wilhemenia clapped her hands, "Very good girls. Now go and get Ferdinand."

I gave her a funny look, "That's easier said than done." Wilhemenia came closer to me, "You must get him Hannah. He will be in trouble otherwise. You set the pattern in motion by getting the other key. You must get him."

I started to get annoyed, "You're talking in riddles again. Tell me about the legend."

She too was getting annoyed, "Just go and get him then everything will make sense."

Ritter came up to me giving me a ghostly kiss, "You look so much like your grandmother. If he doesn't come back call me, I am sure we can work something out."

Wilhemenia growled, "You randy ghost, leave her alone. We are going now Hannah, work it out!"

They both left leaving us confused and unsure how we were going to get Ferdinand out of Jardine. I sent the book away and took the orb down feeling someone come in, turning to see Olwen come in next to us looking worried, "What is going on, Hannah?"

I turned looking out to the sea, "Our grandma and grandfather came insisting we deal with a special area in the family book right now. Sorry, I had to pull the girls in to do it."

Amelia came up behind me, "What are we going to do Mum?"

Charlotte, who had obviously been thinking of things, "We need to go back to Olwen's as I have an idea."

Olwen looked perplexed "can someone tell me what is going on here?"

I took Charlotte's hand, "Ok let's go back to Olwen's place."

Olwen just shook his head, "Well it looks like we are going back home."

We all went back to Olwen's place landing in the foyer. Olwen looked annoyed, "What is happening here, Hannah? I was worried sick when the girls disappeared thinking some lunatic from Australia had grabbed them."

I looked at him apologetic, "I'm sorry Olwen, my grandma insisted I call them in to do something straight away to do with Ferdinand. She said that I had started a sequence or something and it had to be finished."

He grumbled, "You and your blasted ghosts, come and sit in the lounge so we can talk about it."

I looked at the girls squirming, "Oh dear, looks like I've pissed him off."

Amelia and Charlotte took my hand walking into the lounge taking our jackets off and sitting down.

Olwen went and got a drink of whisky, "Do you want anything?"

I nodded, "Yes I'll have a gin and soda thanks." The girls had a vodka, bringing them over to us.

He sat down looking annoyed still having a good mouthful of his drink, "So tell me what has happened?"

I told him what had happened on the beach with Wilhemenia and Ritter along with having to pull the girls in and then dealing with a special section in our family book.

He looked at me, "So you have a family book? You never mentioned that before."

I hesitated, "It didn't seem necessary at the time; besides I don't really know you to share that. It's great that you have let us stay here but we are still getting to know each other."

He shook it off, "Don't worry I'm not trying to get information from you. We have our own family book, which I probably won't share with you either."

I looked at Charlotte, "So you said you had some ideas about how I can get Ferdinand out of Jardine?"

Olwen looked over to me annoyed, "You are not doing it by yourself, Hannah."

I looked at him determined, "I will have to go in by myself. If anything happens, my girls can carry on the family magic."

Amelia growled, "You can't just go in by yourself Mum."

I looked lovingly at them, "This is to do with Ferdinand and me. If anything happens, then we will go together. Jardine is still under a black cloud at the moment and we don't know what we are dealing with, so I would rather use my strength to get him out and I'm not arguing about it anymore. I have done so much in the last few months that makes up for the 50 years I didn't do anything along with you girls learning the magic and meeting Olwen. Now tell me what ideas you have, Charlotte."

Charlotte was sipping on her drink thinking, "Well I think the only way you can get in and out of Jardine is to assume a different DNA signature. I am sure that is how the guards determine who you are. You can't just change your identity like we have been."

I nodded, "Ok so how would I do that?"

Charlotte smiled, "You will have to take a piece of hair or skin (yuck) and cast a spell over it so your body receives it. A little like they did in Harry Potter when Hermine changed into a cat by mistake."

I thought of that movie, "ok, that makes sense."

Olwen got up and got another drink, "What are you going to do once you get in there Hannah. They will pick you up and I believe after talking to Shiro and Aetius, he has a tracking bracelet on, that won't let him out of Jardine."

Charlotte interrupted then, "If you have a DNA signature of a person who is an elder or high up you should be able to release it and take him out."

Monika came into the room looking at us, "Well you look as though you are all serious. Did something go wrong in Norway?"

Olwen got up to give her a kiss, "Do you want a drink honey?"

She looked at all of us, "Yes it looks as though I will need it."

We discussed all the possibilities that could go wrong and came to a conclusion that we needed to use old school techniques because Jardine ran on vibrations.

Monika also added into the plan, "My spirit animal may be able to help you. He is a bear and goes there to rest."

I was a bit nervous, "I'm just a bit worried having spirit animals and others helping me because whoever is causing trouble in Jardine at the moment may take it out of them. The less people or animals I get involved, the happier I will be."

Shiro and Aetius came in as we were talking not looking very happy. Amelia and Charlotte got up going over to them with Charlotte saying, "What is the matter, Aetius?"

He looked at her lovingly and then back to me, "Ferdinand has been placed in the medical area into a chamber. We don't know why."

Monika got up calling Ingrid in who appeared at the door, "You called me Monika?"

Monika smiled wanly, "I think we will have our meal soon Ingrid as we have some work to do." Ingrid looked at all of us having a drink and chatting earnestly, "Ok, I'll be back soon."

She laid some food on the table calling us when it was ready "ok the food is ready."

We changed ourselves magically going into the dining room having something to eat. We sat quietly enjoying the food thinking about things. Once we had finished, I looked at Olwen having thought about it while I was eating, "I want to go in tonight, Olwen."

He sat back in his chair, "I had a feeling you were going to say that. I think you should go in tomorrow morning early."

I shook my head looking determined, "No Wilhemenia said I don't have a lot of time. Aetius' news has worried me as well."

Monika shook her head looking at me, "You've made up your mind, haven't you, Hannah?"

I smiled nervously, "Yes Monika."

Olwen was a bit agitated, "Alright, but you will need to go through the Norwegian gate to deflect from us."

I smiled, "You have been thinking about it to."

We cleared the table mapping out a plan of what I could do to get into Jardine and getting Ferdinand out.

Chapter 28

We had realised the only way I could get in by myself without an elder was to go in with one of the spirit animals taking their DNA; Aetius being an eagle was the best option.

After that, I would be on my own as I didn't want them to get into trouble. Olwen, Aetius and I went to the lighthouse then to Norway, landing in Oslo.

We magicae to the gate which was in a large park that had a river called Sarabräten River. Olwen was looking worried, "Hannah, I'm not happy about this."

I was nervous and getting annoyed, "Look Olwen I have to do this now. I know you are worried for me and I thank you."

I looked at Aetius letting him change into an eagle plucking a feather off him saying the spell *"with this feather I do change taking the DNA whole heartedly to rearrange, 'Allege'."*

I changed into a small eagle allowing Aetius to pick me up in his talons taking one last look at Olwen before we took off.

Aetius flew in going through a type of forcefield which scanned him on entry, rather than actually looked at him.

He flew over mountains and bush land in the dark, making it hard to get my bearings, until he felt it was safe to land, letting me go then changing into his male form.

I reversed the spell changing back into myself, looking at Aetius who had a determined look on his face, "I'm not going until you come back Hannah, so don't try and change my mind."

I started to pace, "Aetius, you will get into trouble helping me, please just go back to Charlotte, she needs you there."

He was determined, "I will be near the gate to go out. Ferdinand knows where it is." He took off before I had any further chance to argue with him making me growl, *'Stubborn man.'*

The girls and I knew that Jardine worked on vibrations, something Ferdinand had said before, which was how some of the others knew where I was at times. I had decided to bring in an old method of getting around, which was the broom.

It only emitted low vibrations and under cover of darkness I should be able to get around alright.

Aetius and Shiro had told me which direction to go in, bringing the broom out getting on and taking off. The air was cool and the area was quite dark feeling worried I wasn't going to find the place as there was very little lighting around, unlike our cities.

I did have a compass on me, heading west on the advice of Aetius. I had pulled the hood up over my hair and put some dark shoe polish on my face just in case someone looked up and saw me, feeling like I was going into a war zone.

After flying for a little while, I started to fly over some bungalows with lights on, going, higher just in case they could see me. It made me sad thinking of the time I had spent in one of those with Ferdinand.

I took a deep breath, building positive thoughts up and kept going, coming across the meal area, that was quiet now, with just low lighting in case anyone wanted to walk around. I saw animals ambling through there looking around in the cool of the night.

I flew on recognising, the meeting rooms I had been in with Morag, Cara and Alira turning to the left which is where I thought the medical area was. I finally found a building that had lights on around it, noticing a sign saying, "Medical Centre."

It was quiet around the building, remembering that they don't get that busy because people aren't sick that often, not like our hospitals, who are always busy.

I saw a bush area just near it, landing quietly down there, sending the broom away hoping, I wouldn't bump into any animals wandering around.

I noticed some windows, sneaking up to one of them to see if I could see anything, finding a woman sitting at a desk with a lamp on it, reading something. I moved around to another window to see if I could see Ferdinand or a chamber at least. It wasn't until I got to another window that I saw the chamber with Ferdinand lying in it. I could hear my heart racing looking at him pale and motionless in the chamber without anything on other than a loincloth over the lower part of his body. I knew I had to keep my magic down to the bare minimum to stop people becoming aware that I was around, so I stood there thinking for a moment.

There was a balcony going around the front of the building near the entrance so I crept up there carefully opening the door sneaking in and shutting it quietly, without disturbing the medic.

It was dark near the door so I had a reasonable amount of cover, deciding to use some magic putting an orb around me. I felt myself breath a bit more, realising I must have been holding my breath, walking slowly in the orb towards the medic. I couldn't see anyone else around in the room with just a dim light over Ferdinand and the light that the medic had on over her desk.

I got as close as I could to the medic sending a sleep spell towards her watching her drop to sleep on the desk in front of her. I did another check to see if there was anyone else around, feeling confident there wasn't, so I took the orb off me. I moved closer to the medic to see if there was anything to open the chamber on the table, not finding anything. I walked over to Ferdinand, feeling nervous now, as it felt like a lifetime since I had seen him.

I looked at the chamber, noticing some buttons just underneath it, feeling tears prick my eyes in frustration as they didn't appear to make sense. I took some deep breaths thinking, '*You're not going to get him out getting frustrated.*' I was just about to try one of the buttons when something made me hesitate, what if they are operated by finger print detection from the medic. I went back over to the medic, sitting her up in the chair and moving her over to the chamber. I took her hand touching one of the buttons with her finger I thought would open the chamber.

Sure enough, I heard a noise indicating that the glass chamber was opening, taking the medic quickly back to the desk and laying her over the desk to let her sleep.

I came back to the chamber that was fully opened now touching Ferdinand's face to see if I could wake him. I noticed he had a beard growing and his hair had a few more streaks of grey going through it. He still had the bracelet on his wrist that meant he couldn't leave Jardine; but I thought I will deal with that when the time comes.

I touched his face again tapping it gently, "Ferdinand, wake up honey." I didn't get any response feeling those tears prick my eyes again, "Ferdinand weckt meine Liebling auf (Ferdinand wake up my love)."

I could see his breathing changing, so I kissed him on the lips, to see if that would wake him faster when I heard someone moving from the shadows. I looked to see if the medic had woken up, but she was still fast asleep on the desk.

I strained my eyes to see who it was moving forward, when Lilith appeared with a sneer on her face, "I knew you would come eventually Hannah, especially after I told Aetius and Shiro that Ferdinand was in here."

I tried to act calmly, "I was worried about him and I wanted to see him."

She noticed the plaster on my arm starting to mock me, "Oh poor little Hannah, you're always hurting yourself. Oh, poor little Hannah couldn't get to use her magic for 50 years. Oh, poor little Hannah couldn't ride her dragon. You just wouldn't go away would you Hannah or even top yourself, which I know you thought of doing a couple of times. Geraldine got too close and she had that unfortunate accident."

She put a fake sad face on saying, "*Oh poor Geraldine.*"

I looked at my plaster, "How is your arm now Lilith? It's a shame Jardine fixed your one."

Lilith scoffed, "Something you won't be able to do Hannah especially once I've finished with you."

I could feel myself getting angry saying in a terse voice, "What do you want Lilith? Oh, don't tell me you love Ferdinand and was trying to keep him to yourself."

She chuckled wickedly, "No Hannah, this is how stupid you are, I've got the honourable job of being his keeper, making sure he stays as a dragon. Unknown to me your stupid mother gave you the book and like she predicted you picked it up quickly, but we can fix that. I even fooled Jardine, as my predecessor did, saying that he was a spirit animal and changing his name to Ferdinand."

My anger was building now, "You little bitch," making Lilith nervous throwing a spell at me binding my hands with the ropes similar to what Ferdinand had used on me previously, as I struggled against them.

She looked ugly in the dimmed light as she moved forward putting her finger up to her face in thought, "I know I could say you had to go into the chamber because you had hurt yourself badly but you died of a heart attack because (as she pouted her mouth) poor little Hannah gets claustrophobic."

I put on an act looking scared, because I knew the ropes weren't as strong as the guards' ones, but I wanted to hear her story, nervously looking at the chamber then back to her, "So you were the woman who told my mother not to let Ferdinand near me or to come back to Jardine?"

She chuckled wickedly, "Oh the dumb blonde has worked it out, has she? I was sure after all the stupid pranks you did you would go to bigger things and get put into prison or even better die!"

She turned scornfully now, "I was the one who was put in charge of Ferdinand looking after him all this time until you came along. We were happy doing things together but then (mouthing it off) *Hannah came along.* At least one thing will make me happy with you taking the curse off Ferdinand, he will die soon so you won't have him either."

I'd had enough with her smart mouth remarks feeling the anger build within me, smiling wickedly at her, which she noticed. I threw a binding spell at her, with a look of surprise coming onto her face, "You know Lilith, I've just found out I come from two lines of witches and these trinkets you put on my wrists don't work," making them disappear.

She screamed so I put a gag on her as she struggled against the bindings. I went closer to her, "Now I'm going to put a truth spell on you to see what else you are hiding you little bitch!"

I heard a movement behind me and a croaky voice saying, "Hannah." I looked over to see Ferdinand getting out of the chamber looking weak. I went over to help him and helped him out of the chamber. He looked at Lilith shaking his head in disappointment, "I heard everything she said Hannah. Let's get out of here."

I could see Lilith was getting upset with me saying, "No Ferdinand I need to know what else she knows," going to say a spell when he hugged me from behind putting his hand over my mouth, "No Hannah we have to go. She might have notified someone you are here."

I looked at him angrily shaking his hand off my mouth, "Alright but I'm putting her in the chamber so we have plenty of time to get away."

He nodded his head standing there weakly, "Alright, but be quick."

Lilith was struggling looking at Ferdinand with pleading eyes. I picked Lilith up magically putting her in the chamber, taking the gag off her when she yelled, "Ferdinand don't go."

She then turned back to me looking angry, "You won't get out of Jardine anyway you still have the bracelet on and only I can take it off you." She put a wicked grin on for me, "See how you get around that one, *Hannah.*"

I slapped her across the face making her whimper, then put a sleep spell on her, taking the binding off. I cut some of her hair off putting it into a bag. I was still determined she would tell someone the truth so I quickly put a spell on it, *"No more lies will come out of this mouth only the truth will be what you say from this day on."*

I shut the chamber with my finger print knowing they wouldn't be able to open it straight away.

I went back over to Ferdinand putting my arm around him as he looked at me giving me a quick kiss, "Can you put some clothes on me honey this is a bit revealing and I am too weak to do it."

I had forgotten about that, "Oh yes that would probably help wouldn't it. So, you're a man now" as I let go lifting up the loin cloth making him pull it down getting annoyed, "Hannah cut it out." I turned away trying not show the smile on my face, putting a dark Jardine outfit on him, then put my arm around his waist again to help him.

He shook his head, "You're terrible. What have you done to your arm?"

As we moved to the door, I sighed, "I'll tell you later once we are out of Jardine," going to the door checking to see if anyone was around. I waved Ferdinand to come out going down the balcony then over to the bush area.

He looked at me in the dark, "How are we going to get to the gate I can't fly now, plus they will stop you at the gate because they didn't see you come in and I have this on," putting his arm up, showing the bracelet.

I brought out the broom with him looking at it, "You've got to be joking?" I smiled at him, "I can't use too much magic otherwise they'll find me, plus we are going to the Norwegian gate, you may have to guide me a little as I'm not very good in the dark."

Ferdinand looked puzzled, "Why are we going to the Norwegian gate?"

I put the broom up floating, "Just get on. I'll explain on the way."

I headed off in the direction I had come, going as high as I could, with the two of us on the broom. He was looking nervous as he hadn't been on one before, hanging onto my waist (which felt nice).

We managed to get past the meal area and bungalows with all their lights, going into darkness hearing birds fly around us. I looked behind, "Are you alright Ferdinand?"

He nodded, "Yes, why are we going to the Norwegian gate?"

I looked at him in the darkness, "Aetius or Shiro told you about my new brother I have come to know about, didn't they?"

He leaned closer to my ear, "Yes."

I rubbed my cheek on his, "Well I've been staying with him in Germany."

He squeezed me coming closer, "Why have you been staying with Olwen?"

I patted his hands, "It's a long story. My girls are there also and Olwen has a partner."

I could feel him relax pointing to change direction a little to head towards some mountains. I heard some flapping near me and I could feel Ferdinand looking around, finally to see Aetius come towards us, looking at Ferdinand on the back of the broom, "Good to see you, Ferdinand. Hannah didn't want me to hang around but I said I wouldn't go until I knew you two were alright."

He smiled at Aetius, "Thanks Aetius, she is a stubborn woman so thanks for ignoring her."

I chuckled, "Don't be mean, Ferdinand. I needed to make sure he was safe."

We flew together going towards the mountains, feeling the cool air hit us sending a shiver down me. Ferdinand held on tighter, "are you getting cold, Hannah?"

I nodded, "Yes, but I'll be alright."

Ferdinand pointed to a lake area with a single light near it, "Go down there Hannah just away from the light. That is where the gate is."

I looked around to see if there was some sort of gate there thinking, '*He must know what he is doing.*'

Aetius followed us landing in a darkened area, so we could get rid of the broom and change. Ferdinand fiddled with the bracelet, "I don't know how you are going to get it off Hannah? You may have to leave me here. I can hide out somewhere in the forest until you sort something out."

I shook my head, "No Lilith gave me the answer to that, so don't worry."

I got the little bag out with Lilith's hair in it, putting it in my hand and saying, "*With this hair I do change taking the DNA wholeheartedly to rearrange, 'Allege'.*"

I changed into Lilith in front of Ferdinand, who looked shocked, "Whoa that's a different one." Aetius who had changed into male form smiled, "Those Dragĕ women worked it all out Ferdinand."

I touched the bracelet on his wrist hearing a click and the little light that was flashing on it go out. He took it off throwing it into the lake "good riddance." I took a deep breath, "Now let's see if we can get you and I through here."

Ferdinand stopped me, "Wait what are you going to say why you are taking me out. They know I have been restricted at all the gates."

I thought about it, "Oh heck I didn't think of that part."

Aetius came over, "Maybe you should say you have had to move him because of a threat from Australia or something like that."

I paced for a little bit, "Yes, I think that will have to do. I will put these on you to make it look as though you are my prisoner," and pointing to him putting cuffs on him.

He put his hands up, annoyed, "No Hannah, take these off."

I pulled his arm, "it's only until we get through the gate, now stop it."

He came along reluctantly, "This better work and if it doesn't you take them straight off me."

I nodded, "Yes alright."

Aetius smiled, "Good luck. I'll see you on the other side. I wish I could carry you both out."

I gave Aetius a quick hug, "Thanks for staying around Aetius."

My hand touched his neck, "Agghh good grief, Hannah, those bloody hands."

Ferdinand laughed, "Now you know what I have to put up with. You better put a glove on actually because that cast hasn't disappeared."

I looked down, "Oh shit it hasn't either."

I pointed to my hands putting gloves on, "Better now."

He grinned, "Yes at least I won't get touched by them."

I shook my head, "Come on I want to get out of here."

We started to move towards the light when Aetius came back looking worried, "They have turned a lot of lights on around the medical centre, so you better move as fast as you can."

He took off, "Be careful you two."

I took Ferdinand's arm leading him over to the light with Ferdinand saying, "There is a cat who guards this gate and his name is Gaupe. He's a bit of a charmer and I am sure that Lilith didn't like him, so just play it calmly."

I nodded, "I'm actually getting some of her thoughts through in my head. She certainly has some strange thoughts about you."

He looked at me annoyed, "You know you're the one I want to be with Hannah. Come on you'll have to take the glove off and touch the lamp post to bring Gaupe out faster."

I nodded moving over to the lamp post taking my glove off and touching it. I heard a noise to the right of me in the darkness looking at Ferdinand nervously, when a lynx cat came sauntering towards me with big pointy ears and a brown/black coat with spots on it.

His big feet just seem to pad their way over to me not making much of a dent in the ground, when a lazy voice came from him saying, "Well who do we have here at this time of night at Oddlief?"

He looked at me then at Ferdinand and his cuffs on, sounding like the Cheshire cat of Alice in Wonderland, "Oh Ferdinand, I had heard you had your wings clipped and now it looks like you've got your paws clipped as well," chuckling.

Ferdinand frowned, "Very funny Gaupe. Why don't you help me out of these and away from her, then I'll be able to make jokes like you."

He rubbed himself up against me, "Mmm Lilith still madly in love with Ferdinand and you have him in cuffs, just the way you like him."

I looked annoyed, "I have been given orders to take him out of Jardine. Can we get going, Gaupe?"

He sighed, "Well it looks like I'm not going to have much fun with you two tonight," changing into male form with brown hair a rounded face that looked like it had been touched by the sun, stocky built with Jardine clothes on and not much taller than me.

He moved over to stand in front of the lake putting his hands up saying a chant. I could hear the water starting to move with a huge vortex forming not far from the shore line going down into a funnel shape with stairs appearing on one side.

I looked at Ferdinand surprised giving me a wink, indicating to move forward. A woman appeared at the top of the stairs that was dressed similar to Seneca at the other gate, looking at Gaupe "who is coming out this late Gaupe?"

He turned to look at Ferdinand and I, "These two. One of them obviously a prisoner. You're welcome to them, they're not much fun tonight."

The woman came over to us as we moved forward, "Lilith what is going on?"

I had to think quickly, "I have been told to move Ferdinand out of Jardine to a safe house in Europe, that is all I know. Can we get going?"

Ferdinand put an act on as I took his arm, "Portvakt can you help me."

I knew Ferdinand was saying this because I didn't know her name, giving him a knowing look, then getting annoyed, "Just do as you're told Ferdinand. Portvakt, can you help me get him down the stairs?"

She nodded taking Ferdinand by the other arm, "Come on Lilith has to follow orders."

He put up a bit of resistance, going down a couple of stairs shaking us off annoyed, "I'll go down on my own thank you."

Portvakt shook her head, "You men are annoying," going down the stairs. I carefully walked down the stairs looking at the water spinning around the stairs with Ferdinand saying quietly, "Don't touch the water it has dangerous fish in it."

I kept my hands close to my body deciding to take Ferdinand's arm again just in case I fell over. He acted indifferent but was pleased I was holding onto him.

I saw this really strange fish come to the side of the water that looked like a frog and fish all rolled into one opening a huge mouth as though it was going to bite me. I held tight onto Ferdinand talking quietly, "Eww that one looks horrible."

We got down to the bottom, walking along a short tunnel that had what looked like a glass dome over top, something like we have in our aquariums with fish floating over top of us. There were a lot more different varieties than in our world, opening big mouths showing a lot of teeth.

We got to the end of the tunnel where a single boulder stood in an area similar to the one at the other gate.

Ferdinand said quietly, "You have to take your glove off and put your hand on the rock."

I nodded looking as though I knew what to do taking my glove off my good hand.

Portvakt watched me, "Are your hands cold, Lilith?"

I nodded, "yes, I think I am in for a cold. Once I get this job done, I might go and have a rest in Jardine. That's what you get for being in their world too much," sneezing to make it look better.

Portvakt nodded, "Yes, I'm glad I don't have to be up there. Ferdinand you will have to put your hand on the rock as well because you normally fly out of here, we need to identify you."

He groaned, "Alright" leaning forward putting his hand on the rock begrudgingly with me following.

Portvakt put some water over our hands with blue symbols appearing underneath our hands, scanning us. I held my breath hoping the spell had worked alright when the sound of being sucked out of there and into another cave happened. Ferdinand looked at me briefly saying quietly, "So far so good."

Portvakt was already walking down a tunnel well ahead of us, "Follow me you two. I don't want your cold, Lilith."

I looked at Ferdinand grinning briefly, taking his arm walking down the tunnel. We walked along a dimly lit tunnel with drawings on the walls similar to the other gates of the history of Jardine hearing the sound of a waterfall in the distance.

Ferdinand mouthed, "Not far now."

I nodded, quickening our pace to catch up to Portvakt and to get out of here. I could hear my heart beat quicken with the anxiety of getting to the end of the tunnel. It appeared to take forever to get to the end of the tunnel with a sheet of water going over the entrance covering it.

Portvakt put her hand on a symbol near the entrance, which stopped the water running enough to allow a path to form with small blue lights coming on, to show us the way.

She waved us on, "There you go. Good luck Lilith and make sure you come back to get rid of your cold. You don't want that world's bugs in you."

We moved forward giving her a wave, "thanks Portvakt," treading carefully along the path so I didn't slip, trying to remember to breath, with my heart racing. We moved past the waterfall coming out to a thick wooded area quickening our pace down the path hearing the waterfall start flowing again, where we had just come through. We had just got off the path when we heard a voice call out, "Lilith come back here they are shutting the gates down."

I looked at Ferdinand in the darkness putting an orb around us taking the cuffs off him, hearing the voice call out again, "Lilith, are you there?"

Ferdinand held my hands, "Just wait and see what happens, don't send anything out unless you have to."

I nodded, listening to see what was going on around us hearing Portvakt come out just past the waterfall looking around. She couldn't see us, hearing her talk to someone, "She has already gone. She said she was taking Ferdinand to a safe house or something. She didn't say where."

I couldn't hear the other voice properly and what they were saying but Portvakt got the waterfall flowing again, breathing a sigh of relief.

Ferdinand looked at me, "Can you change yourself back now? I don't like you like that."

I nodded, "Yes sure. I'll tell you what she has a lot of things going through her head, especially about you."

He looked annoyed, "I don't care, she has really pissed me off this time and I intend to find out what she meant by being my keeper. You did warn me, didn't you?"

I nodded reversing the spell coming back to myself with my tracksuit on, "I didn't think she was that dangerous though."

Ferdinand smiled, pulling the hood off my hair running his hand along my pony tail, "I've missed you," and giving me a kiss.

I kissed him back holding there for a few minutes, "We better get moving in case they come looking. Olwen said he will put a signal up so we can find him. We'll walk a little in the orb, just in case."

Ferdinand put his arm around my waist, slowly walking in the orb towards some trees and a small clearing. I saw a small light in the shape of a lion in the distance pointing to it, "Ferdinand there is his light."

He looked where I was pointing, "do you want to stay in this orb or just magicae there?"

I looked around us to make sure there wasn't anyone around, "I think it's safe to take this off us." I took the orb off when a flash of light struck on the ground just near us. I grabbed Ferdinand and magicae near Olwen's light that had gone out now.

Another flash hit the tree as we started to move, ducking down, "Olwen should just be over there," moving along quietly. Another flash of light hit near us, but I couldn't see who was sending them. I saw a flash of light come from the direction of where Olwen was. I waved my finger around the palm of my hand putting a whirlwind up around us sending leaves and branches everywhere, with Ferdinand holding on.

I encouraged him to walk slowly bringing the whirlwind with us hearing a yell from the outer part of the wind sending someone flying off. I heard my name called being sure it was Olwen, so I flicked my fingers stopping the whirlwind letting Olwen and Aetius land near us with Olwen saying, "Come on Sister let's get going." I nodded, taking Ferdinand's hand in one hand and Olwen's in the other. We magicae to Oslo within the dense bush area, watching Olwen take his key out and summoning the lift.

Ferdinand looked in surprise not saying anything, walking into the lift letting Olwen send us back to Germany. Olwen relaxed then smiled at Ferdinand, "You must be Ferdinand, nice to meet you at last," shaking his hand.

Ferdinand smiled looking tired, "Yes it has been a very dramatic time. Nice to meet you too Olwen."

I looked at Aetius and Olwen, "Did either of you see who was firing at us?"

Olwen shook his head, "No all I saw was a figure. How about you Aetius?"

Aetius nodded, "Yes it was a woman, and I think it might have been Cara, I can't be sure though as it was quite dark."

I sighed, "That is disappointing if it was her."

We landed back into the lighthouse with the doors opening and we filed out letting Olwen lock the doors and close it off.

I took Ferdinand's hand squeezing it, feeling happier we were at least here in Germany together, "You're looking tired, let's go."

We all magicae back to Olwen's place, being greeted by everyone, lying on the sofas with blankets on them dozing waiting for us.

The girls heard us enter first jumping up, "Oh thank goodness, they're here." Both Amelia and Charlotte came over and gave me a big hug and then hugged Ferdinand. Monika got up as well giving me and Ferdinand a hug, "Thank goodness you are safe. Nice to meet you Ferdinand, I'm Monika."

He gave her a hug, "It's nice to meet you as well and good to be back with Hannah."

She ushered him to a sofa moving the blankets and stirring the fire up, "Come and sit down you look worn out."

He looked at me smiling, wiping the black off my face noticing the dark circles under my eyes, taking my hand, sitting down together to have a rest.

Olwen rubbed his hands together, "A nightcap before we go to bed anyone?"

I smiled, "Yes thanks a gin and soda would do for me."

Ferdinand nodded, "Yes I'll have the same, but just the one."

I went to get up with Ferdinand taking my hand, "Where are you going?" I patted his hand, "I'm just going to the bathroom to wash my face. I won't be long dear."

He looked quite tired and confused, "Ok, don't be long."

I got up giving him a quick kiss going out to the bathroom off the main foyer.

Monika sat down next to Ferdinand getting a drink from Olwen, "You look a little worried, Ferdinand?"

He looked at Monika taking a drink from Olwen, "I feel as though I've been in a different time zone and I've just popped out. Hannah seems to be the only thing that is the same although she is looking tired."

Monika leaned forward talking quietly, "She was a bit of a mess when Olwen encouraged her to come here and stay. They were constantly attacking her. She was doing a lot of pranks as well as learning a lot of magic to combat it. Just be patient with her she has a strong love for you."

Ferdinand looked sadly, "Thanks Monika, I will."

I came back feeling a bit better with my face washed and a thinner top on getting a drink from Olwen as I walked in looking at Ferdinand talking to Monika. I decided to go and talk to Aetius and the girls to let them talk when I felt Ferdinand behind me putting his arm around my waist.

He gave me a little kiss, "That looks better I can see your face better now."

I smiled leaning into him, "I thought you were still talking to Monika."

He looked wearily at me, "I was but I'd much rather be with you. Are you ready to go to bed soon, I'm quite tired?"

I had only had a little bit of my drink, "I won't be long honey. Do you want anything to eat, I imagine you haven't eaten for a while after being in the chamber?"

He shook his head, "No I think I'd prefer sleep first."

I could see he was getting a little agitated so I finished my drink, saying good night to everyone. I took his hand, "Come on we'll go to bed. There's also a little lady who is looking forward to see you."

He looked at me not sure who I was talking about, going out into the foyer looking around at the paintings on the walls. We stopped at the top of the staircase, "This is my father, Stefan Drachen."

He smiled looking at him then me, "Now I can see the resemblance." We carried on up to the room I was in with the fire going to warm it up and Kimba sitting on the rug in front of the fire. She gave a little meow when we walked in getting up and doing a big stretch making him smile and go to pick her up.

She purred rubbing herself around his face realising that he needed a shave. He rubbed his chin coming up to me and rubbing his chin on mine, "How do you like me with a beard?"

I tried to push him away but he was determined to rub his chin on my face, "Mm not sure about that." I got away from him, "I'm going to have a shower and go to bed."

He put Kimba down going to sit on the bed, "Mm feels nice and comfortable."

I went into the bathroom taking my clothes off putting a bag onto my arm, turning the shower on, when he came up behind me naked, "I want to have a shower with you."

I got in the shower with him following, turning me around and giving me a hug under the water. I put my arms around his waist leaning into his chest and cried. We stood there holding each other when he kissed my head, "Come on let's get washed and go to bed."

We washed each other noticing that I had lost weight and I noticed that he had a lot more hair on him and was greying more than I remembered. We dried each other with me putting some clothes on him and drying our hair smiling, "It feels funny doing this for you since you were the one who had taught me to do it."

He gave me a little kiss, "Hopefully when I get my strength back, I might get some magic back."

We went to bed, just happy to lay in each other's arms with the fire flickering its dancing light across the room and Kimba at the bottom of the bed on his side.

Chapter 29

I woke to find him lying there watching me sleep with a worried look on his face. I moved over to him lying on his shoulder as he put his arm around me, "Good morning honey."

He kissed me on the cheek, "Good morning. Did you have a good sleep?"

I nodded, "Yes, a couple of strange dreams but otherwise I feel a lot better. How about you? You looked a little worried, did you have some visions of your past?"

He sighed, "Monika told me how they found you Hannah and I feel responsible for that. I shouldn't have forced you to go with me to that area. You could see it was a trap but I was too blind to see it."

He stroked my hair, "No I didn't have any visions yet."

I leaned up on my elbow looking at him earnestly now, "I admit I was really angry at you and Jardine for leaving me alone and I did go off the rails a bit; but we are together again and that is all that matters to me. Remember when you said to me about the anger and how we can't turn back time," grinning a little.

He chuckled, "You're thinking of that bloody song Hannah Dragĕ," sitting up pushing me down on the bed and kissing me. I giggled singing in a squeaky voice, "If I could turn back time."

He kissed me on the mouth stopping me from singing, eventually moving my mouth away, "There's always a critic isn't there." He started to kiss my neck feeling the old feelings starting to rise stopping him, "Ich denke, Sie müssen vielleicht ein bisschen mehr Honig zurückgewinnen (I think you may need to recover a bit more honey.)" He looked at me with hunger in his eyes, "Mal sehen, was passiert. Es funktioniert möglicherweise nicht (let's see what happens it might not work)."

I smiled, trying to push him away, "Don't be naughty Ferdinand, you haven't been well."

He kissed me on the mouth again lying over me as I sighed, "Oh Ferdinand come on we can wait a …" as he kissed me again on the mouth. He moved down to my neck pulling his clothes off and then mine while he was on top of me, looking a bit nervous now, "I haven't done this for a long time, Hannah you may need to guide me."

I looked coyly at him, "Oh so I'm the teacher now?"

He started kissing my neck, "Yes so be kind to me."

I chuckled, "Well you keep doing that then you can start to move down to here."

He did as I asked while I put my hand in his hair hearing him groan.

We were getting quite passionate and he was laying between my legs when I felt things moving, making me grin.

I reached down to touch him there, hearing him groan, "Oh Hannah."

He wanted to go inside me but I slowed him down, "Just a little longer honey."

I eventually let him join with me, both of us groaning in orgasm and a white light forming around us.

He lay on top of me still as we panted with the exertion and I ran my fingers through his damp hair, "Bist du in Ordnung, Schatz? (Are you alright honey?)" He rolled off me "Ja mein Liebling (yes my love)" pulling me to him falling asleep again, holding each other.

I woke to a quiet tapping on the door, "Mum are you awake yet?"

I sat up putting my nightie back on waking him, "Where are you going Hannah?" I gave him a little kiss, "Amelia is at the door wanting to know if we are getting up."

He smiled, "Tell her we did."

I slapped him, "Don't be naughty Ferdinand."

He was playing with me trying to stop me getting up, but I managed to get away from him.

I looked at the time on the clock on the mantel piece being 8.30am then going over to the door opening it a little, "Hi Amelia we just woke up."

She smiled a cheeky smile, "Well I know you've been kissing now; you have a beard rash."

I rubbed my face feeling the prickly rash, "Oh heck. Are you having breakfast?"

She nodded, "Yes, do you think you will be down soon?"

I could hear Ferdinand groan turning back to her, "Yes, we will just get dressed and come down. I'll see you there."

I shut the door going back over to the bed, "Come on you it's time to get up."

He tried to grab me as I giggled, "No Ferdinand, behave yourself."

He flopped down after the exertion of doing that, "See you're still a little tired. Do you want me to put some clothes on you?"

He gave up, getting up, as I looked at him admiringly, putting his hands in front of himself, "Do you like what you see Hannah?"

I nodded smiling smugly, "Yes I do."

He turned around to get his pants when I noticed something on his back, going over to him to look. He grabbed me being playful slapping him on the arm, "Stop Ferdinand, you have something on your back."

He let go of me going into the bathroom to look in the mirror finding a tattoo on his back similar to mine, "Oh shit. Do you think that was from our love making?"

I came up to him nodding, "I think so. There was a white light after we connected."

He gave me a hug, "You might have given me some magic in more ways than you thought."

I stood back, "Have a go at doing something."

He tried putting some clothes on himself, with it working. A big smile came upon his face giving me a hug, "Oh this is great." He kept holding on kissing me, "No Ferdinand don't you dare." He picked me up, "I'm all excited now just a little longer."

I looked at him seriously, "We need to go downstairs. Come on we have plenty of time."

He nodded a little disappointed, "Alright honey. Before we go how did you hurt your arm?"

I looked at him a little sheepishly, "I tripped over in the kitchen and landed wrongly that is all."

He looked at me suspiciously, "Now this is a worry you being in the kitchen for a start. You either got angry because you were trying to cook something or you were drunk."

I looked shocked at him, "No I was just going out of the kitchen and I tripped."

He chuckled, "I know you better than you think Hannah Dragě."

We got dressed and went downstairs with everyone sitting at the table just finishing their breakfast. I looked a little embarrassed, "Sorry we are so late Olwen and Monika."

Olwen smiled, "That is quite alright Hannah, after what you two have been through. Just tell Ingrid what you would like to eat and she will bring it in for you."

We took our time eating with the others staying around to chat while we ate.

Ferdinand was quite hungry now, eating a couple of serves of things. I still didn't have a big appetite picking at my food. I was sitting there sipping my coffee when he looked at me picking at my food knowing he was wanting to say something, but kept it in.

Olwen got up leaning on the back of his chair, "So what do you want to do today everyone?"

I looked over at the girls, "Did you two have anything in mind?"

Amelia got up putting her plate on the tray that was for the dirty dishes, "Well I wouldn't mind going shopping, since we got interrupted yesterday."

Charlotte jumped up smiling at Ferdinand, "Oh yes because we had to save someone's butt."

Ferdinand started to smile putting his eyes down trying to ignore them finishing off his food.

He then looked up, "I'll take you shopping if you like, to make up for it?"

I rolled my eyes, "Good grief."

Olwen looked pleased, "That is great, then I don't have to go."

Monika got up, "Yes you do, I want to go as well."

He groaned, "Oh come on."

We all took off going to Kiel, doing some shopping and having some lunch while we were there. I walked down the street holding Ferdinand's hand, enjoying just relaxing not thinking about anything in particular.

Olwen came up behind us with Monika, "Ferdinand, do you remember much yet? I was just wondering if you remember what area your family came from that is all?"

He shook his head, "No nothing has come back to me yet. I have got some magic back though, thanks to Hannah."

Olwen looked at me raising his eyebrow smiling, "Oh really! How did you do that?"

I looked at him sheepishly which made Olwen laugh, "Oh ok."

Monika also giggled, "Good to see you have the same family drive."

We got to a supermarket looking at Ferdinand and Olwen, "I just need a couple of things in here. Do you want to come in?" Both Ferdinand and Olwen shook their heads with Ferdinand saying, "No I'll wait out here. Just don't get into any trouble."

I shook my head, "Like I would do that."

Amelia, Charlotte and Monika came with me, leaving the men to wait outside for us.

Olwen moved closer to Ferdinand, "You still look worried Ferdinand, what's on your mind?"

Ferdinand was slowly walking down towards a jeweller turning to look seriously, "With this spell or curse off me I think I'm could die soon."

Olwen sighed, "Charlotte was talking about that at breakfast before you two came down. She is looking into it. You need to talk to Hannah about it as well."

He nodded looking sad, "Yes, I know. I am sure the only reason I am here now is because I was put in that chamber in Jardine and Hannah has given me some magic. I want to marry her before anything happens."

Olwen looked surprised, "What! Ferdinand, I know I haven't known her for very long but I am sure she has similar feelings to me about marriage. You can always try but I would put a suit or armour on or something if I was you."

Ferdinand smiled, "You're probably right, she has spoken about it before and would get quite angry about it, swearing she would never do it again. I'm just a bit old-fashioned I guess and would like some sort of ceremony to celebrate our love."

Olwen turned to look at the jewellers he was looking at, "I am sure she is happy with the love you have for each other." As they were standing there Shiro and Aetius came back from Jardine not looking very happy.

Olwen smiled, "Oh hello you two."

He looked at their serious faces, "What's the matter?"

Ferdinand turned to looked at them, "Has something happened in Jardine?"

Aetius nodded, hesitating, "yes, they've put a rumour around to bad mouth Hannah saying she has killed you. You know that is not a good thing in Jardine. We have been denying it but they don't believe us."

Ferdinand growled, "Was that bloody Lilith?"

Shiro shook his head, "No it was someone else, we don't know who. Lilith has apparently told the truth to the elders about everything that happened with you, her and Hannah. She has now been confined to Jardine until they decide what to do about it."

Ferdinand sighed smiling briefly, "Hannah must have put that truth spell on her after all. I don't know what is going on in Jardine."

Olwen looked annoyed, "Now you know why I don't go there."

Another man came walking up to them with sandy coloured hair a rounded face and muscular body dressed in jeans and a mustard shirt smiling.

Olwen smiled shaking his hand, "Hi Leon, I haven't seen you for a few days."

Olwen turned to Ferdinand, Shiro and Aetius, "This is Leon, my spirit animal, although he just turns up when he feels like it."

Leon smiled looking at everyone, "Well you really don't need me that much, do you?"

He moved over to Ferdinand shaking his hand, "Ah you're the one they are saying has been killed by Hannah. Well, they got that one wrong then."

Ferdinand looked annoyed, "Yes something we will have to straighten out. They are just trying to discredit Hannah now."

Shiro and Aetius shook his hand when we all came out of the supermarket looking for them. Charlotte noticed Aetius, "There they are. Shiro and Aetius are back from Jardine."

We all walked up to them being introduced to Leon. When he came up to me, he shook my hand, "Well you don't look like a trouble maker, Hannah."

Amelia coughed looking away trying to not show her mirth.

Ferdinand came up and took my hand, "She has her moments but she is going to be good now aren't you, Hannah?"

I smiled, "I'll try dear. You look a little tired do you want to go back and have a rest?"

He nodded, "Yes, I think I will. Have you finished shopping because I'd like to go now?"

I turned to Olwen, "We might go back if that's alright. Ferdinand's getting a bit weary."

That was a good excuse for him wanting to go as well, "Sure Hannah. I am sure everyone has had enough shopping now." The girls nodded with Amelia saying, "yes, I have to stop anyway I'm starting to get messages from work wanting to know when I'm coming back. I'll have to go back tomorrow by the look of it."

Charlotte went over to Aetius, "Are you alright?"

He nodded putting a smile on, "yeah, I'm ok. Are you going back tomorrow as well?"

She nodded, "yes, I better get back. Mum is good now, so I can't use her as an excuse."

Olwen looked disappointed, "Well you know you can always come back any time."

We started to walk down to an area without too many people around and took off from there. We landed back in the foyer at Olwen's place still holding hands with Ferdinand, who was walking towards the stairs, "We'll see you later. Thanks for a lovely day."

Everyone went in different directions with Monika calling out, "Come down for afternoon tea in the drawing room when you've had a rest."

I turned nodding, "Looking forward to it."

Ferdinand and I got into the bedroom putting my purchases down on the chair by the window looking out. He came up behind me giving me a hug, "Aetius came back with some news Hannah from Jardine."

I leaned back, "Oh yes, what are they saying now?"

He leaned in, "They're saying that you've killed me, which, as you know is considered a bad crime there."

I put my hand on his arms, "They just keep playing dirty, don't they? Was it Lilith?"

He kissed me on the cheek, "No and you know she didn't because you put that truth spell on her. She's apparently been telling the elders everything."

I chuckled, "Well at least that one worked out alright."

He turned me around giving me a kiss, "Come on let's have a rest. I'm starting to feel a little tired again," taking my hand and leading me over to the bed. We lay down cuddling, "There's something else you're not telling me, isn't there, Ferdinand?"

He sighed, "Yes, I think with the spell or curse off me I will die soon. I'm just getting all these odd feelings in my body along with aches and pains."

I lay over his chest, "Oh Ferdinand if I had known it would do that, I wouldn't have done it. Grandma kept pushing me for some reason. I don't want to lose you again."

I sat up looking at his face seriously now, "I'll find a way to keep you with me Ferdinand; I'm not losing you again and I will die with you."

He looked annoyed, "Don't say that, Hannah. You have your girls to consider. You don't know how to keep me alive yet, I'm only preparing you should anything happen."

I looked determined at him, "I know either I or the girls will find a way to keep you alive. I don't want to be alone anymore," starting to cry as I lay into his chest.

He stroked my hair, "Come on, it might not happen. Charlotte and Amelia have said they are looking into it; they're bright girls and will find something."

He got me a tissue so I could wipe my eyes, "I would like to ask one more thing just in case something does happen, Hannah."

I looked up at him, "What is it?"

He looked a little nervous, getting up putting me on the pillow, taking my hand and looking into my eyes, "I want to marry you?"

I was shocked sitting there stunned "Ferdinand you know how I feel about that. We love each other surely; we don't need to do that?"

He looked sadly, "It doesn't have to be your world marriage just some sort of ceremony."

I shook my head, "I'm sorry Ferdinand I just can't do that. I love you and I'll tell you until anything happens, but I don't want to do that again."

He relented, giving me a kiss, "Ok Hannah. I love you to and always have. I will ask again though."

I smiled shaking my head, "It will still be the same answer."

He rolled over pulling me into him, "Well that will be my challenge. For now, let's have a rest."

I rolled my eyes, "Sweet dreams."

I woke to shadows coming in through the windows wondering what the time was looking at my phone, "Oh heck it's 3.30p.m." I looked over to Ferdinand who was just starting to wake up, "Did you have a good sleep?"

He rubbed his eyes, "Yes, I did. A couple of strange dreams but otherwise it was good." He sat up waking himself up properly, watching me get up off the bed and having a stretch, "Do you want to go home tomorrow? I guess we have to face it eventually."

I nodded, "yes, I was thinking about it after the girls said they were going. We have to get back to reality. It has been nice here, hasn't it?"

He nodded looking around, "Yes I was getting flash backs every now and then even before you lifted the spell with the visions looking similar to this."

We went downstairs with the girls coming out of their rooms as well. I smiled at Amelia, "What have you done with your hair Amelia; it looks like you've been through a wind tunnel."

She shook her head, "I don't know it just keeps going crazy."

Shiro came up behind her wrapping his arms around her kissing her on the neck, looking at me a little guilty. I looked at Ferdinand smiling, going downstairs saying to Stefan's painting, "Hi Papa."

We had afternoon tea sitting around chatting. Charlotte looked at me and Ferdinand, "So if Ferdinand wasn't really your spirit animal who do you think was supposed to be?"

I nodded, "I thought of that myself actually. I suppose it is still a dragon?" I looked at Ferdinand, "I don't suppose you know anything?"

He shook his head, "No I'm in the dark just like you."

Amelia was looking at her phone, "Charlotte and I have been doing some research on your family Ferdinand. It appears that where we were today is probably where your brother Ritter set off for Norway either landing in Gottenberg or Oslo; we would have to get shipping logs for that. Ships still go that way today. We have also established your surname is (hesitating) Ziegler which Father Daniel in the Church in Norway said as well. There was a Frederick and Ritter Ziegler in the Kiel area around those dates, so I am assuming it is you two. There is a property just out of Kiel in a district called Kirchbarkau and there is a mansion there that was called …"

Ferdinand butted in looking distantly "Herrenhaus Ziegler."

I looked at Ferdinand, "Do you remember the name honey?"

He nodded, "Yes, but that is all."

Amelia looked sadly, "The property has been sold a few times and it is now called Herrenhaus Bothkamp. I do think though, that they use if for venues like weddings etc."

He sighed, "It doesn't matter about the name as I will go like all the other men in the Dragĕ women's life and take their name; especially when Hannah finally agrees to marry me."

He looked at me cheekily, "We could get married there, dear."

I got up growling walking out, making the cups and plates shake around on the tables.

Olwen shook his head, "I did warn you, Ferdinand."

Ferdinand chuckled, "I'm up for the challenge."

Charlotte and Amelia looked at each other with Charlotte looking squarely at Ferdinand, "Have you proposed to Mum and didn't bother to ask us?"

Ferdinand was looking nervous, "It was a spur of the moment thing, in case I didn't survive the spell being taken off me."

Charlotte got up looking deadly, "Aggh it's always about something happening to you!"

Ferdinand looked annoyed, "Well I could die, Charlotte, is that not a good enough reason?"

She walked out of the room growling, making the cups and saucers rattle again.

Ferdinand looked at Amelia waving his hand, "Well are you going to add to it?"

Amelia grinned, "No, I'd be happy for you to marry Mum, but you know it won't happen unless you're on your death bed or she is."

Ferdinand smiled, "Well at least I've got one on my side and hopefully I won't have to die to get there."

Monika was putting on a sarcastic smile, "Well if it does happen you are welcome to have it here if you don't have it in Herrenhaus Bothkamp. At least one member of the family will have a wedding here."

Amelia sighed, "Perhaps if you do get a chance to ask again and she hasn't maimed you in any way, just say a, 'Ceremony of love' or perhaps what they used to call it being a, 'Handfasting' not a wedding or marriage. It sounds too much like ownership to Mum rather than love."

Ferdinand nodded, "Thanks Amelia, I'll keep that in mind."

Amelia got up, "I better go and try and calm Charlotte and Mum down before they destroy something."

Olwen chuckled not picking up on Monika's remark, "Do you want me to show you some family armour, Ferdinand? You might need it."

Ferdinand was just about to say something when Monika got up annoyed, "Oh yes Olwen you just continue joking about this. If Ferdinand wants to get married or have some sort of ceremony you should be encouraging him not discouraging him or making jokes. You are so insensitive sometimes you, you … dragon!"

She too got up walking out of the room sending the cups and saucers flying this time, making them both duck.

Olwen looked after her as she slammed the door and the cups and saucers were breaking. Ferdinand, Olwen, Shiro, Aetius and Leon were now trying to protect themselves from the cups and saucers flying in the air. Olwen got up, "Good grief, bloody women. This is your fault Ferdinand and your 300-year-old ways. I think I need a drink."

Ferdinand got up moving some of the broken cups and saucers out of the way, "Yes I'll have one as well."

Shiro, Aetius and Leon went and joined them sitting there dazed as to what had happened.

I went outside calming myself down in the fresh air that was turning cooler now. I saw Charlotte come out the front door and coming over to me not looking very happy, "Are you alright Charlotte?"

She growled, "He has no right to ask you to marry him without speaking with us first."

I nodded, "I know, plus he knows how I feel about marriage."

We stood there grumbling for about 5 minutes when we saw Monika and Amelia come out joining us to have a grumble looking up at the windows. I could see Olwen and Ferdinand looking down at us having a drink.

I said to Monika, "They're up there getting drunk now and we are out here in the cold. I think it's time to get back up there before they get too bad."

We all agreed to go and get changed first ready for the evening meal. I decided to do a bit of meditation, hoping that my grandma would come in and tell me what to do about keeping Ferdinand alive.

I might have been annoyed with him about the, 'Marriage' thing but I wanted him to live. I got upstairs to our bedroom taking some deep breaths, while walking around to clear my head of the anger.

I finally felt calm enough to do the meditation sitting in front of the window, putting my ear buds in, relaxing into the meditation. I visualised myself in the boat going down the stream hearing the sound of the water hitting the boat as I floated along listening to my breathing when the visions stopped. I sat up in the boat looking around me to see who was around. The boat stopped on the shore letting me get out when I saw Wilhemenia sitting on a seat near the water, looking in the distance with a relaxed smile on her face. I walked over to her feeling happy that I at least I know her name now and she has come to me when I had hoped she would.

I sat next to her on the seat "Hei bestemor. (Hi Grandma)."

She turned to me looking at me, "Hei Hannah Jeg er litt skuffet over at du sier at du vil bli med Ferdinand hvis han dør. (Hi Hannah I am a little disappointed with you saying you will go with Ferdinand if he dies.)"

I looked down at my hands, "Jeg har gjort det du ville, og hvis jeg ikke kan være sammen med ham, vil jeg dra. (I've done what you wanted and if I can't be with him, I want to go)."

She chuckled, "Du har alltid sagt at du ikke trengte en mann da du var yngre. (You always said you didn't need a man when you were younger.)"

I got up agitated pacing, "Jeg vet det, men jeg er eldre nå, og jeg vil ikke være alene. Kan du hjelpe ham å holde seg i live? (I know but I'm older now and I don't want to be alone any more. Can you help him stay alive?)"

She got up coming over to me looking in my eyes seeing the determination there, "Du har fortsatt mye å gjøre Hannah, men jeg vil gi deg ditt ønske. Selv jeg likte en mann. (You still have a lot to do Hannah but I will grant you your wish. Even I liked a man around.)"

She took my hand in her ghostly one cupping it and sending a magical pulse through me, "Introduser ham til boken som vil gi ham hans levetid. Han er en heks Hannah akkurat som du er, men han kan bli drept nå som han ikke har forbannelsen på seg (Introduce him to the book which will give him his life span. He is a witch Hannah just as you are but he can be killed now that he doesn't have the spell on him just like you.)"

I hugged her ghostly form with tears welling up, "Takk bestemor. Kan du fortelle meg historien en dag? (Thank you, grandma. Will you tell me the story one day?)"

She stroked my hair, "Han vil huske det en dag og fortelle deg det selv. (He will remember it himself one day and tell you himself.)" She moved away from me starting to fade "Jeg vil ikke se deg i ånden før din tid, Hannah. (I don't want to see you in spirit before your time Hannah)."

I went back to the boat feeling happier, getting in and floating away hearing my breathing come through. I sat there breathing wondering when I could get him to look at the book, when I heard the door open. I looked around to see him worried and coming over to me, "The others are downstairs and said you were coming up to get dressed. I got worried so I came looking for you."

He helped me up giving me a hug, "I thought I would do some meditation first to calm down." He wrapped his arms around me, "I'm sorry I didn't mean to upset you. I won't talk about, 'Marriage' again."

I looked up to him surprised, "Really, you're giving up that easily?"

He smiled, "I can't guarantee if I've been drinking or anything, but yes."

I moved away taking his hand to come and sit on the bed as a cheeky smile came over him, "No we are not having cuddles. I need to show you something."

That made him look naughty still raising an eyebrow, "Ferdinand, I need you to do something for me. Grandma has told me how to keep you alive, unless you get run over by a bus or something then that is your problem."

He chuckled, "Ok. So, what do we have to do, make love again?"

I pulled a face, "Will you stop thinking of your new talent and concentrate. I need to show you the book. Grandma has given me something that will activate something in the book. Do you want to do it now?"

He got onto the bed moving over to the middle "yes just in case you kill me if I say the 'm' word again."

I slapped him on the arm, "Behave!"

I put an orb over us bringing in the family book. I put my hands over it not quite sure what to do as grandma didn't give any instructions. Nothing happened, looking at him and then the book, "Mmm she didn't really tell me what to do." I thought about it, then something came into my head, taking his hands in mine and laying them on the book. A pulsating vibration ran through us both from the book making Ferdinand quiver and shake. It then stopped letting go of his hands, "Are you alright?"

He nodded shaking himself out a bit, "Wow that was a big buzz." The book then opened with words coming up, *Hannah Dragĕ, do you wish Frederick Ziegler to have access to the book?* A yes and no button came up making me hesitate, looking at his name different from what I've known him for all this time. I looked at him, "Do you want to join with us?"

He nodded, "Yes Hannah. I do."

I pushed the yes button with the ink well coming up and the feather coming on top of the page.

Ferdinand looked at it picking up the feather, "What do I have to do with this?"

I took his hand opening it, "Prick the feather into a finger. It wants your blood so it can tell who you are."

He looked impressed, "Wow you have made some modern changes."

I thought about that comment shaking it off, watching him prick his finger and putting the blood into the inkwell. We both sat there watching the inkwell fill with the blood then the book analysing it.

A confirmation came up, *"The witch Frederick Ziegler has now been given access to the family book. Welcome back."*

I looked at the words confused, "Welcome back?"

He looked at me confused as well, "I don't know what that is about Hannah?" The book sent a white light over him again as I watched his hair grow longer and more flecks of grey turning it salt and pepper, (as they call it), and a full beard appear.

I sat there with my mouth open, "Wow I wasn't expecting that."

He put his hand up to his hair and then felt the beard on his face. He smiled nervously, "Do you still like what you see, Hannah?"

I nodded smiling, "yes, I do. Has anything else come back to you in your memory?"

He shook his head, "No."

We heard a noise at the door of someone tapping "Mum are you coming downstairs we are having some drinks before dinner."

I looked at Ferdinand in the dim light that was shining off the book and onto his face, "We will have to revisit this later. I'll show you how to bring the book in and everything then."

He nodded, "Ok."

I shut the book sending it away and taking the orb off us calling out to Amelia, "We'll be down soon Amelia, thanks." I heard her walking away getting off the bed looking at Ferdinand, putting my head on the side, "Mm very different but nice."

He got off the bed smiling, "Should I try to shave this off before we go down?"

I shook my head, "No I like it. Besides they're waiting for us. You don't mind it do you?"

He came up rubbing his chin on mine, "Do you like it?"

I squealed as the course hair hit my face laughing, "Yes I like it." I moved away going to wash my face, get changed and put some makeup on. He came in behind me putting his shirt on looking at his beard and hair, "I might need a haircut at least. Do you still cut hair like you used to?"

I pulled a face, "Good grief. I haven't done that for years. Maybe a hairdresser the first time, then I can trim it."

He wrapped his arms around my waist, getting frisky, "Stop it Ferdinand or should I say Frederick?" He stopped and thought about it, "No, I prefer Ferdinand for now, even though that was Lilith's choice. One thing at a time."

We went downstairs feeling a bit nervous now, with Ferdinand in his suit, shirt and pants and me in a dress feeling like we were going out to a restaurant as different people. We went into the dining room with the room going quiet when they looked at Ferdinand.

Olwen came over, looking at him, "Wow you must have a good love making routine you two."

I slapped him, "Olwen we didn't make love. Grandma has helped me keep him alive and this is what happened."

He grinned, "I want to talk to you about that later. Come over and have a drink."

We had a couple of drinks, starting to feel relaxed. Monika called in her spirit animal Lacis, who was a bear in animal form, to introduce him to everyone. He was a big burly guy with dark brown hair and brown eyes but with a gentle nature.

I was mingling around talking to Aetius and Shiro getting the gossip from Jardine who still hadn't been able to find Morag. Ingrid also joined us having a couple of drinks and obviously not used to drinking that much, getting tipsy quite quickly, speaking in German to my girls who didn't understand her.

I ended up pointing to my girls putting a translation spell on them so that they could understand her, looking over to me putting their thumbs up.

We went and had dinner, which was a bit back to front, because Ingrid was tipsy and brought it in in the wrong order. No one complained as we were all getting that way as well. We all got together afterwards sending the dishes away magically having a great laugh doing it. We went into the lounge room relaxing with the fire going having another drink.

Monika was saying, "We don't normally have the fires going this time of year but it is still a bit cool and with you all being from Australia, we thought you might catch cold."

I smiled chatting to her when I heard Amelia and Charlotte laughing at something with me looking up to see Ferdinand grin a tight grin, looking over to me with downcast eyes.

Charlotte was laughing hard now, "And this is when the priest started clucking like a chicken."

I looked at Monika, "Did Ferdinand say we were leaving tomorrow?"

She looked at me trying to stay calm then over to Ferdinand who was looking at something else not looking very happy, "yes, he did. You know you are quite welcome to stay."

I patted her hand, "We have to get back eventually unfortunately. I think I might go to the bathroom," putting my drink down when I heard another bought of laughter coming from Olwen now because Amelia had showed him something I had done.

I made my way to the door when I heard "Hannah I need to talk to you." I quickened my pace, "I just have to go to the bathroom," but he got to the door before me, wrapping his arm around my waist, putting me over his shoulder.

I started to shriek, "Ferdinand put me down," hitting his back. I could hear Olwen laughing saying loudly, "No they'll be alright. She has enough magic in her to deal with him."

He went out the door before anyone could stop us, taking me into the dining room sitting down on one of the chairs in there. He put me on his lap wrapping his arms around me so I couldn't get away, "What have you been doing in Sydney Hannah?"

I tried to get my hands free saying, "Meine Liebe, ich habe dich so sehr vermisst (my love I missed you so much.)"

He growled, "Sie haben also eine Kirche niedergebrannt" (so you burned a church down).

I was getting annoyed now, "No I didn't burn it down. Your friend Lilith didn't bother to put it out."

He put his hand up to my jaw while still holding my hands, "And?"

I stopped struggling looking innocent, "I just fanned it a bit. I thought they would put it out but they didn't. So, it was their fault it burned down!"

He was still holding my jaw and hands when he kissed me holding it there until I stopped struggling. I heard the door open a little then shut. He let my hands go, "What am I going to do with you Hannah?"

I smiled brushing his hair back off his face, "Come on, let's go and have some fun on our last night."

He put me down, "There aren't any other pranks I need to know about is there, before we go back?"

I shrugged, "I don't think so. I don't know what the girls have shown you?"

He took my hand and went back to the lounge being greeted by more laughter.

Olwen was being shown a picture of something else. I froze not sure if I wanted to go in. Ferdinand looked at me grimacing, "I suppose that is something else you have done?"

I took a deep breath, "I may as well face it and get it over and done with."

Charlotte looked at us coming back in, grinning like a little girl, "Did Fia show you this picture, Ferdinand?"

Ferdinand still holding my hand moved closer to have a look at the phone with a picture of me in the Super Witch outfit and my hair sticking up like I had a shock. He turned to me shaking his head, "Good grief, Hannah, what brought that one on?"

Olwen stood up, a bit tipsy now, "Come on, Hannah, put it on for us so we can have a look at it."

I felt a little embarrassed, "I was getting the shits with everything so I made that."

Olwen came up putting his arm around my shoulders, "Come on show us the suit, this is hilarious."

Ferdinand raised his eyebrows, "You may as well do it, otherwise they'll keep pestering you for it."

I let go of his hand standing back waving a hand over me, producing the Super Witch outfit with a mask over my eyes.

Olwen and my girls, who were quite drunk now, burst out laughing with tears running down their faces and buckling up in laughter.

I stood there getting into the spirit flexing my muscles, "Super Witch strikes again!"

Ferdinand came over to me laughing with the rest of them now, taking me in his arms, "You silly woman."

Charlotte got up now excited, "Mum show them how you frightened a woman at Alira's work, as well as Alira."

I grinned looking at Ferdinand, "I didn't do it intentionally."

Ferdinand moved away from me shaking his head, "Go on show us what you did."

I did the invisible spell with just my cast showing walking around. This sent them all into fits of laughter again. I brought a broom out getting on it and flying around the room with just the cast and the broom showing.

Charlotte was telling the rest of the story, "Mum went in to surprise Alira doing the invisible spell, walking into her work area with just the cast showing. A co-worker of Alira's screamed and fainted."

I came back re-appearing still with the Super Witch suit on pointing to Charlotte, Amelia and Monika, putting one on them each in different colours.

They all looked at themselves getting up flexing their muscles and putting their chests out to show their 'SW' on their chests.

I went up to Ferdinand who had sat down on the chair now, pushing my chest out to him. He pulled me into him sitting me on his lap, "Mmm they look nice Hannah; we might have to try that out later."

He was rubbing his beard on my cheek making me squeal and laughing sending tears down my cheeks.

We all ran out of energy sitting down on the sofas getting our breaths back feeling a little weary.

Olwen got up, "One more drink before bed everyone?" We all agreed telling him what we wanted. Olwen brought Ferdinand and my drink over talking quietly to us, "I really want you two to stay a couple more days. I have a business idea for you Ferdinand, and Hannah is looking a lot better."

I looked at Ferdinand, "I aren't really in a hurry to get back. Do you want to stay for a couple more days."

Ferdinand had a sip of his drink, "I suppose you're right. There's nothing to rush back for, as you're off work. It was just a familiarity thing for me getting back to something I was used to. Sure, we'll stay a couple more days then."

Olwen grinned, "I'll tell Monika, we really enjoy your company."

We were all relaxing with our last drink as it was getting late, when Olwen came up to me, "Hannah I need to ask you to do something before you go."

I looked at him starting to feel tired, "What is it, Olwen?"

He took my hand helping me off Ferdinand's lap, "I just want to ask Hannah something, Ferdinand," leading me away from everyone, "Can you bring out Papa again. I really enjoyed talking to him. Should we use Ouija board or something?"

I giggled with the drink hitting me, "No they usually just come to me. I don't really have any control over them when they want to come."

He looked disappointed, "Can you try?"

I nodded, "Ok, ich werde es nur für dich versuchen, Bruder, Lieber (ok I'll try just for you brother dear.)"

He put his arm around my shoulders leading me back, "Oh wunderbar (oh wonderful)."

Olwen clapped to get everyone's attention, "Hannah is going to try and bring Papa in before she goes to bed."

Ferdinand looked worried, "She's not a medium Olwen, they normally just come to her."

Olwen patted Ferdinand on the shoulder, "It's alright she said she will just give it a go. If he doesn't come, we will leave it."

I clicked my fingers dimming the lights with just a couple on and the fire light flickering around the room. I could hear Ferdinand groan not liking it.

Everyone sat quietly as I opened the curtains letting in the light of the full moon sitting down on the floor in the moon light which was shining off my hair.

I started to breath loudly swaying my body, "Come to me Papa."

Ferdinand started to grumble, "Hannah for goodness' sake."

Olwen was getting annoyed, "Shush Ferdinand."

I giggled, "Sorry, Ferdinand knew I was being silly."

Olwen sighed, "Do you think you can do it or not?"

I was serious now, "Ok I'll try now. Just don't try to interrupt me." I started to do my meditation breathing with just the sound of the fire crackling, then all I could hear was my breathing. I knew I was starting to rise off the floor, going quite deep, being relaxed from the drink.

After a short time, I could feel myself out of body looking around at the faces watching me, when I felt someone next to me. I smiled, "Hallo Papa Olwen wollte dich wiedersehen (hello Dad Olwen wanted to see you again.)"

I looked over to Olwen who could hear me talking wanting to join with me but I said, "Kannst du dich ihnen allen zeigen? (Can you show yourself to them all?)"

He smiled at me fondly, "Hallo meine Tochter, ja, das werde ich. Ich möchte meinen Enkelinnen Hallo sagen (Hello my daughter, yes, I will. I want to say hello to my granddaughters)."

I grinned, "Danke Papa (thank you Dad.)"

He appeared thinly at first with just the firelight going through him then coming through more solidly looking at Olwen, "Hallo mein sohn (hello my son)."

Olwen grinned like a little kid, "Hallo Papa. Es ist schön, dich zu sehen. Kannst du Englisch sprechen, damit ich dir deine Enkelinnen vorstellen kann (Hello Papa. It's good to see you. Can you speak English so I can introduce you to your granddaughters.)"

He smiled warmly, "Yes of course Olwen." He floated over to Amelia and Charlotte, "Ah you are the spitting image of your mother. I wish I could have met you when I was alive, we could have had some fun."

Amelia smiled, "Nice to meet you grandpa. It sounds like we have a real mischievous streak in our family. I wish we could have met as well."

Charlotte looked at him, "You are so different from our other grandpa. I think I would have really liked to have known you in the flesh."

While this was going on, I could see Ferdinand keeping an eye on me worried that I was staying this way too long.

I floated over to Papa hearing them gasp and Ferdinand getting up looking worried. I put my hand up, "It's alright I have done this before. I'm not dead yet. I have just come to get Papa it is time for me to come back."

Papa looked at me kindly, "Thank you Hannah. I will see you all again some time."

He walked back with me, both of us fading away from their sight. I gave him a hug and before he left, "Take care Hannah. You are strong in your magic but there a lot who would dearly like to take it. Olwen will help you as much as he can, he's a good boy."

I nodded, "Thank you Papa. I had better go. I love you."

He disappeared letting me concentrate on my breathing taking a little longer this time, but finally settling down and sitting on the floor.

I took some deep breaths opening my eyes to find Ferdinand there to help me up, "Come on Hannah. I think you have done enough for tonight."

He flicked his fingers putting the lights back on, holding onto my hand. Olwen came over giving me a hug, "Thank you so much, Hannah, that was great. I will have to try that."

Ferdinand put a smile on, but I knew he didn't like me doing that, starting to walk away with my hand in his, "Are you tired?"

I was nice and relaxed, "Not too bad but I'm ready for bed." I went and gave everyone a hug, "See you in the morning," hearing Aetius and Shiro encouraging the girls to go to bed as well.

Chapter 30

We got to our room sighing kicking off my shoes in the corner "that was a nice evening, except for you being bossy."

He came over giving me a hug, "You're a naughty girl doing all those pranks, but I understand why you did them. I don't mean to come over bossy. I just worry about you."

I gave him a kiss, "I suppose this is the, 'Man' hormones coming out of you as well. I'm going to have a shower."

He let me go taking off his jacket waiting for me to finish sitting on the chair that overlooked the window thinking about things, getting up occasionally poking the fire that was burning well and warming the room.

I came out feeling a lot better "it's all yours."

He went and had his shower while I waited in bed getting nice and warm, listening to him spraying something, then he called out to me, "Hannah can you come here please. I need your help with something."

I got up going into the bathroom, "What's the matter, Ferdinand?"

He had foam all over his beard and was looking at the razor I had bought him, "This doesn't seem to be working properly, can you have a look at it."

I nodded feeling tired, "Alright let's see."

He picked me up putting me on the vanity so I was high enough for me to help him. He just had a towel wrapped around his waist, smelling nice after the shower, "Don't you get any frisky ideas now, Ferdinand."

He smiled through the foam, "I can't guarantee anything dear. Show me how to use this blade at least."

I looked at the razor, "Oh you've left the safety shield on," taking it off moving closer to start to shave him.

He was grinning again moving closer opening my legs, "Just remember I have blade in my hand dear." His smile dropped a little, "Just be careful then won't you."

I kept shaving him going around his face doing his upper lip as he watched me in the mirror. I put his chin up looking at him, smiling as I went down his neck, "I think you need some more foam on there, it's a little dry." I picked up the can squirting some in my hand rubbing it into his neck when he grabbed my hand, putting some over my face. I was giggling as I fought him off, "Stop it, you silly man," as foam started going everywhere.

He was laughing while grabbing both my hands rubbing his chin up against my face putting more foam on me then kissing me. I was trying to move away from his mouth with the taste of the foam around my mouth, trying to slap him. He took the blade out of my hand wrapping his arms around me getting the washer to wipe his face.

I giggled, "You said you wouldn't get frisky," he didn't bother to answer but just kept kissing me. I was trying not to get passionate but he smelt so nice, I just couldn't help it. He pulled my nightie off kissing me around my neck when he noticed my back in the mirror.

I said to him in between kisses, "I thought you were tired?"

He kissed me hungrily, "I'm still in training so I need as much practice as I can."

I thought to myself, 'Thank goodness I have an implant for protection.'

--ooOoo--

I woke to find him out of bed standing next to one of the big windows with the curtain open, staring out deep in thought. I lay there watching him deciding to let him think, perhaps getting some memories back.

He must have heard me move, coming over to me getting back in to bed to give me a cuddle, "Good morning."

I kissed him realising his beard was back, "I see magic likes you with a beard."

He laughed, "Yes it was fun shaving it off though. Before the girls go back to Sydney, I'd like to go and have a look at the house I was supposed to have lived in."

I ran my hand down his beard "yes sure. Do you want me to go with you?"

He looked at me surprised, "Yes of course. I had a bit of a dream last night with this long driveway lined with trees and a big brick building at the end of the driveway. I didn't see the pictures that the girls were looking at, so I'm presuming it was the house they were talking about."

I smiled at him pushing his hair off his forehead, "I didn't see it either so we will soon find out."

He put his arm under my back holding me close when he pulled it back up noticing blood on his hand, "Hannah why is there blood on your back?"

I got up suddenly hitting him in the forehead, "Oops sorry."

He held his head, "Agghh," showing me his hand with blood on.

I got off the bed pulling my nightie up concerned, "Where is it, Ferdinand?"

He slid over, looking at it, "It's the tattoo again. It appears to have changed."

He flicked his fingers putting the lights on, "It now has two dragons looking at each other with a shield, a sword and some keys at the bottom of it."

I looked surprised, "Oh I saw that one time when I was doing some research on our family. Do you have anything?"

He lifted his t-shirt feeling where his was "oh yes, I can feel dry blood there. Looks like the book has branded us again." He turned to show me, "Oh well we're a matching pair I guess."

I looked at the sheet noticing blood on it, "Oh dear I'll just fix that up," pointing to it removing the blood off the sheet. We both went into the bathroom wiping each other's back cleaning it off and putting some tape over it to stop the bleeding.

I pulled my nightie down, "Well that got us up. Do you want to look at the house before breakfast?"

He looked at the time, "Yes I don't think they will be up yet, we may as well."

We got dressed bringing the address up on my phone as well as sending Amelia a message telling her where we were going and magicaeing to the property. We landed just down from the driveway walking up to it hand in hand, when a horse and buggy came slowly out of the driveway. The driver did a double take looking at Ferdinand then waved his hand, "Guten morgen (good morning)."

Ferdinand nodded, "Guten morgen (good morning)."

The driver slowed down stopping, "Sind Sie aus dieser Gegend? (Are you from this area?)"

Ferdinand shook his head, "Nein, aber meine Familie war (no, but my family was.)" The driver scratched his head lifting his cap when he did it thinking, "Wie hieß Ihr Familienname? (What was your family name?)"

Ferdinand hesitated, "Mein Familienname war Ziegler (my family name was Ziegler)."

This made the driver look surprised, "Sind Sie mit Ritter Ziegler verwandt? (Are you related to Ritter Ziegler.)"

Ferdinand nodded, "Ja."

I looked at him seeing a lot of emotions passing over his face squeezing his hand, turning to look at me unsure. The driver shook his head, "Möchten Sie hereinkommen und sich umsehen (would you like to come in and have a look around?)"

Ferdinand looked unsure turning to look at me, "Möchten Sie hingehen und einen Blick darauf werfen? (Do you want to go in and have a look?)"

I nodded, "Ja (yes)."

He smiled nervously, "Ja, wenn Sie die Zeit haben (yes if you have the time.)"

The driver patted the seat next to him, "Hop on Ich nehme Sie auf (hop on I will take you in.)" We jumped up onto the hard seat of the buggy with the driver introducing himself, "Mein Name ist Karl Ich besitze das Anwesen jetzt. (My name is Karl I own the property now.)"

Ferdinand shook his hand and so did I "Schön, dich kennenzulernen, Karl. Mein Name ist Ferdinand Ziegler und das ist Hannah Dragĕ. (Nice to meet you Karl my name is Ferdinand Ziegler and this is Hannah Dragĕ)"

Karl turned the buggy around going back to the house, entering into the driveway just as Ferdinand described it, with trees that were starting to shed their leaves ready for autumn lining the driveway with a big red brick building at the top of the driveway.

Karl clicked his tongue getting the horses to go a bit faster, rocking us around on the hard springs of the seat and flicking up leaves as we went along, reaching the top of the driveway.

Karl got out and so did Ferdinand helping me down, looking a little nervous. Karl called to someone, when a young man came out, "Beobachten Sie einfach die Pferde, ich werde nicht lange sein (just watch the horses I won't be long.)"

He nodded watching Ferdinand and I follow Karl into the house with his mouth open. We went into a foyer that was painted white with marble tiles on the floor, a staircase that wound in a spiral upstairs that had a black wrought iron railing with marble steps with a black carpet runner going up the middle.

I looked around at the different paintings on the walls looking up at the ceiling to a lovely chandelier swaying lightly when the door was opened.

Karl waved at us to go into a room which was the lounge, with big windows along one wall similar to Olwen's. The walls were painted in light shades of blue with white trims and cream sofas, making the room nice and bright when the sun came out.

Karl pointed to a picture on the wall over the far side, "Vielleicht interessieren Sie sich für dieses Gemälde (you might be interested in that painting.)" We walked over, looking at the other paintings as we went, coming to the one that Karl had pointed out to us.

It was Ferdinand (or Frederick) and Ritter with Ritter standing behind Ferdinand who was sitting on a chair and his brother's arm was leaning on Ferdinand's shoulder looking sternly, which they tended to in those days. They had dark waist coats, britches and stockings on with white shirts underneath. The Ferdinand in that picture had similar long hair with a silver streak in the front and a beard just like Ferdinand had now but minus the salt and pepper greying. I looked at it then at Ferdinand smiling, "Du könntest Zwillinge sein, lieb (You could be twins dear.)"

Ferdinand raised his eyebrows with a tight smile staring at it. I took a photo of it with my phone then wandered around looking at the other photos hearing Karl start to talk to Ferdinand; I think about the legend that the priest had told me.

I didn't want to hear it again, so I was just wandering around looking at the different paintings then I went over to one of the big windows looking out to a garden, that was full of rose bushes. Further back down the lawn was a big arch with roses growing over it. I shook my head thinking to myself, *'That must be where they have the weddings.'*

Ferdinand came back over to me following my gaze as to what I was looking at "oh schau lieber ein Hochzeitsbogen (oh look dear a wedding arch.)"

Karl came over, "Ja, wir machen Hochzeiten hier (yes we do weddings here.)"

I smiled at Ferdinand, "Wir sollten besser zu meinen Brüdern zurückkehren, liebe (we better get back to my brother's dear)." Karl thought for a bit, "Hast du gesagt, dass dein Name Drage war? Das war der Name in der Legende. (Did you say your name was Dragĕ? That was the name in the legend.)"

I looked surprised, "Oh was für eine Legende? (oh, what legend?)"

Ferdinand squeezed my hand, "Ich werde es dir auf dem Heimweg erzählen. (I'll tell you on the way home)"

He turned to look at Karl, "Danke Karl, vielleicht bekomme ich Hannah eines Tages wieder hierher, um eine Zeremonie zu machen. (Thank you, Karl, maybe I'll get Hannah back here one day to do a ceremony.)" Karl smiled, "Hier ist meine Karte. (here's my card)."

I groaned quietly starting to walk out with Ferdinand following me, looking at Karl "Danke Karl. Wir werden gehen, wenn es Ihnen nichts ausmacht. (Thank you, Karl. We will walk if you don't mind?)"

Karl nodded, "Sicher hoffe ich, Sie wiederzusehen. (Sure, I hope to see you again)."

Ferdinand and I followed Karl out of the house watching him get back into his buggy taking off down the driveway, with the young man staring at Ferdinand, as we walked down the driveway.

I looked at him, "So any memories come back?"

He looked a little confused, "I get little bits and pieces. Once I looked at that painting, I remember sitting for it for some reason. Ritter and I were actually being silly when that was done, so I think we had a good relationship."

We walked to the end of the driveway, looking back at the house "so you're not curious as to what the legend is?"

I looked surprised, "Oh yes, I had meant to ask you. What was all that about?"

He hugged me, "You've heard it before, haven't you?"

I groaned, "Yes, but grandma said it is just gossip that is why I didn't bother to say anything. She said you will remember when it's time and tell me all about it."

He kissed the top of my head, "She is probably right. Those legends tend to get exaggerated through the years. Let's go back to Olwen's."

We magicae back, going inside to find everyone sitting down for breakfast. We took our jackets off sending them upstairs and going in to have breakfast.

I put some scrambled eggs and a piece of toast on a plate while I watched Ferdinand looking at the sausages that were there. I moved closer to him, "Do you feel like meat?"

He sighed, "I don't know they look tempting."

I pointed to the smaller one "try one and if you don't like it they won't mind."

He picked it up putting it on his plate with a few other things.

We were sitting there chatting over coffee when Ferdinand looked at my plate, "You haven't eaten very much Hannah. Aren't you hungry still?"

I shook my head, "No I'll work up to it though, don't worry."

Olwen could see he was annoyed, "You would think with the all the funny business you two do, you would be starving."

I grinned, "I can see where I get my sense of humour from."

Amelia, Shiro, Charlotte and Aetius all got up with Charlotte saying, "Well we had better get going."

I got up and gave them all a hug, "I'll let you know when we get back ourselves."

Amelia looked seriously at me, "Just relax and eat better, do you hear me."

I nodded, "I will, stop worrying."

Ferdinand came up behind Amelia, "Don't worry Amelia, I'll get her sorted out."

Olwen came over, "I will as well, so she is out numbered."

I rolled my eyes, "Maybe I should go back to Sydney then, if you two are going to pick on me."

Olwen came up giving me a hug, "No you stay here with your brother, I'm only teasing you." Olwen went off with the girls to take them back, with Ferdinand coming up wrapping his arms around me, "Come and finish your breakfast. I think Olwen wants to go riding later, so that will be nice."

I leaned back on him, "I haven't ridden very much, so I might need to take it slowly."

Monika, who was still finishing her breakfast, "Come and sit next to me Hannah while you eat. I will take you out on one of my older horses and remind you what to do. I'm sure the men will race or something silly like that."

I took the hint of going to finish my breakfast sitting down with her as I picked at it, then drank my coffee. Ferdinand sat next to me having his coffee looking at some things on his phone. He leaned over putting some food on my fork, "come on, eat a little more, Hannah, you're a bit thin."

I took another sip of my coffee, "No I've had enough, Ferdinand. I'm drinking my coffee now. What are you looking at?"

He put his phone in front of me showing me a sight about handfasting ceremonies with a big grin coming over his face, "What do you think of something like this for us rather than the 'm' thing?"

I groaned, "You said you weren't going to go on about that?"

He put his hand on mine, "I'm not, this is something totally different, we join together with our love."

I put my cup down having a look at it, "I have heard of this, but haven't really looked at it properly."

Monika leaned over having a look, "Oh that looks interesting. Maybe I should show Olwen that as well, it might not make him so nervous."

I giggled, "We are alike in some ways, aren't we?"

I read the information on it thinking, *'I could probably incorporate something magical into it if Ferdinand did continue to pursue it. I won't make it easy for him though.'*

I gave him his phone back, "That looks interesting dear."

He was just about to say something when Olwen came in rubbing his hands, "Are you ready to go for a ride in the beautiful German countryside?"

Monika groaned, "They know it's pretty dear. Is it raining yet?"

I got up putting my plate and cup on the tray "I haven't ridden very much, other than the brief ride I had in Jardine on Dropsy, so I'll be a bit slower than you two, but Monika has said she will give me some pointers."

Ferdinand looked disappointed at my response about the handfasting but looked forward to riding a horse again. He took my hand, "I'll help you as well, I'm sure you will enjoy it again."

We went out to the stables with some cloud cover coming over cooling the temperature down. I put a jacket on with Olwen pointing to me, putting some riding boots and pants on along with a hard hat, "That should keep you safe and warm. Maybe you should put some gloves on as well?"

Ferdinand came over to me already dressed, "I'll help you onto the horse, Hannah," putting some gloves on me before I had a chance to say anything.

I turned to look at him, "I don't think I really need these."

He gave me a kiss, "They're deadly weapons dear, best to keep them warm."

A stable hand brought out a horse for me all saddled up. It was a lovely looking mare that was dark brown with a white blaze in the front down her nose. I patted her nose as it let out a small whinny. Ferdinand lifted me up giving me the reins, "Are you alright?"

I wriggled around on the saddle, "It's different from a dragon," making him grin. I watched as he mounted his horse along with Olwen and Monika getting onto theirs walking out of the stables with a low cloud starting to drop over the fields.

Olwen breathed in the fresh air, "Doesn't it smell wonderful, even with the threat of rain."

Monika came up beside me, "He loves it here, as you can tell. We would both love it if you two came to stay here, we have plenty of room."

I watched Ferdinand and Olwen ahead of us chatting away, "Thanks Monika. It is lovely here, but we need to sort a few things out in Australia. We will certainly keep it as an option."

Monika told me a few pointers on riding saying, "Do you want a bit of a race."

I grinned, "Yes sure, I like a bit of a challenge."

We raced past the men going down to the end of the paddock which had a large hedge at the bottom of it. The men came racing up behind us with tufts of green coming off their horses' hooves. Monika leaned over to me smiling, "You can see Ferdinand came from a noble family by the way he rides."

I watched him with his straight back and the way he controlled the horse expertly feeling proud of him, "At least I can keep him alive a bit longer to enjoy these things."

Ferdinand grinned coming up beside me, "Who won the race?"

I looked away, "Oh I'm not sure, it's not important."

He leaned over giving me a kiss, "I'm jealous of you having another animal between your legs."

I slapped him, "That's enough. You've had your fair share already as a man."

Olwen groaned, "Can't you two keep your hands off each other for five minutes. Come on Ferdinand, let's see if I can beat you back," looking up at the sky "I think it's going to rain, so we better all get back."

Monika looked at me, "I'm just happy to canter back, how about you?"

I nodded, "Yes, I'm not used to riding now and it's showing on my legs."

We watched the men take off back towards the stables, allowing Monika and I to just take it easy and chat on the way back. Monika took me via a small cluster of trees showing me the different trees they had in Germany.

I looked up at them with a mixture of oak and birch trees taking a deep breath, "They smell divine and so different to the Australian bush." We were just near the end of the line of trees when two women appeared in front of us.

I recognised them straight away getting angry, "What are you two doing here?"

The guard pointed to me putting ropes around my body and arms making me feel drained. I struggled against them, "Get these off me Malus, you have no right to do this."

The guard pointed to me again so I couldn't talk. Malus looked annoyed at me, "You need to come with us Hannah, you have broken a few rules and need to go before the elders."

Ferdinand and Olwen were looking for us then realised we had been stopped by some women. Ferdinand growled, "Olwen they are Jardine women, we need to get over to them."

Olwen looked angry, "Come on, they have no right to be here."

They both spurred on their mounts getting to Monika and I just in time to see me struggling against the guard's ropes unable to talk.

Olwen called out to Malus, "Stop that now you two, you have no right to be here."

Ferdinand pulled up beside me getting off his mount and taking me off the horse before I fell off. He looked menacingly at Malus, "Take this off Hannah now and go back to Jardine."

The guard watched Ferdinand as he put me on the ground against a tree. He turned to look at the guard menacingly about to say something, when she pointed to him binding his arms and silencing him as well, watching him fall to the ground.

Olwen got off his horse helping Monika off her horse then checking on us two, "Take those off them now. You're not taking them anywhere."

Olwen could see the guard was about to do something so he called in his spirit animal and about to send something back to the guard, but he wasn't quick enough with her binding his hands and throwing him down next to Ferdinand.

The guard looked over to Monika, who I had taught to do the invisibility spell, disappearing before the guard could do anything towards her. This gave Monika a chance to call in her spirit animal Bacchus the bear. She instructed him by thought to take the staff off the guard and give her a bear hug.

Leon, Olwen's spirit animal, came in taking the staff and pointed it at both the guard and Malus.

Monika reappeared looking menacing at the guard, who was struggling against Bacchus' bear hug, and Malus, "What are you doing here Malus?"

Malus had been quietly watching everything unfold "I'm here to take Hannah back to Jardine to answer some questions on how she got in to take Ferdinand out. You know as well as I do that is against the rules."

Monika scoffed, "You have to be joking Malus. Jardine has done nothing but accuse Ferdinand of stealing ropes that were given to him, with no chance to stand up for himself. Even in our world we get that opportunity."

Malus sighed, "He was trying to control Hannah; he knew he wasn't allowed to do that Monika. Let Jeneca go and tell Leon to put that staff down."

She looked at Jeneca then back at Malus, "No Malus, Hannah was dumped back into the unit without any powers, the guard that dropped her back left a dark crystal there and told her some jumped up story about Morag wanting to see her within the lion enclosure at the zoo only to be attacked again."

Malus looked curious, "I didn't know about that. Why would the guard tell her to go and see Morag at the lion enclosure?" Malus looked over at Jeneca, "It was you who took Hannah back to her unit wasn't it Jeneca?"

Jeneca was struggling against Monika's bear looking at Leon who was holding the staff at her ready to pounce if he needed to "I didn't tell Hannah that. She's making up lies."

Monika looked deadly at her, "Hannah was also left, still under the effects of the ropes with no magic, falling and hurting her wrist. She also didn't have any phone reception so couldn't call any family or friends in to help her. She has also been attacked by various people. So where is the protection from Jardine she was promised at the ceremony?"

She moved closer to Malus asking Leon to move closer, "And you're worried about how Hannah got into Jardine to get her spirit animal back, which you had no right to take off her! She didn't do anything else while in Jardine but get Ferdinand out of there."

Malus looked uncomfortable now, "I didn't know about any of this Monika. All I know is that Hannah was causing problems in your world acting up again."

Monika was angry now pointing at Malus, "You take those ropes off all them and start sorting out Lilith, who appears to be behind a lot of this rubbish. She killed one of Hannah's relatives and was getting close to doing it to Hannah and probably going for her daughters after that to get rid of the Dragé family once and for all. This is all because of some bloody curse that happened 300 years ago!"

Monika turned to Jeneca, "You've shut them up because you were the guard that gave Ferdinand the ropes and took Hannah back, you traitor!"

Jeneca got angry, "Malus she can't talk to me like that. Tell this bear to get his paws off me, I am here on official business to deal with Hannah who is breaking the Jardine rules."

Malus had called another guard in who appeared near Jeneca. Jeneca looked at the guard looking pleased, "Can you help me with this bear Ciara?"

Malus moved closer to Jeneca, "She is here to take you away. We thought you were in with Lilith, but didn't have any proof."

Ferdinand and Olwen had been listening to all of this getting angry, with Olwen turning to look at Malus, "Take these bloody things all of us now! You need to see how Lilith tricked Jardine for nearly 300 years with Ferdinand; I bet you're a bit embarrassed about that!"

Malus looked angrily at Olwen, "There's no need for that tone, Olwen. We were investigating that, especially after Lilith started talking."

Olwen jeered at her, "Oh you mean the truth spell that Hannah put on her, that's the only reason she started spouting the truth, you silly woman. You're lucky Hannah didn't turn dark because she has become strong quite quickly and could have done some damage to your precious Jardine."

Malus looked shocked, "Are you threatening us, Olwen?"

Monika stepped forward with Leon, "Take those ropes off them Malus and get off our property. You've done enough damage to those two."

Malus pouted her lips pointing to everyone taking the ropes off us all along with the silencing spell. Ferdinand got up going over to me helping me up, "Hannah, come on honey."

I grabbed him with a look of horror coming over me, "You're not taking him away again Malus."

Ferdinand held me calming me down, "It's alright Hannah Monika has sorted it out with her, she is going now."

Angry tears came to my eyes as I watched a guard about to take Jeneca, "You bitch, you were the one who left me unarmed and that black crystal in my room."

Ferdinand helped me up holding onto me, "She was also the one that gave me the ropes Hannah. She's been helping Lilith by the sounds of it."

Olwen and Monika came over to me to see if I was alright with Olwen turning to, Malus saying in a dismissive way, "You can go now Malus."

Malus looked offended at the way Olwen spoke to her turning to me, "I didn't know those things were happening to you Hannah, they were very clever. We still haven't found Morag, so I don't know who it was that met you in the lion's den."

Ferdinand held on tightly to me looking sarcastically at Malus, "Looks like you found out a lot of things from the truth spell that Hannah put on Lilith. I bet there's a lot of red faces in Jardine at the moment?"

Malus nodded at the guard to take Jeneca away turning to me, "Hannah I am sorry for all the trouble you have had, but we will like to talk to you when you feel better so we can strengthen our security."

I didn't get a chance to speak with Olwen walking in front of me, "That will be when she is ready to talk to you and not before. Now go!"

Malus reluctantly went, leaving us to get the horses and go back to the house.

Ferdinand put us both on my horse with him sitting behind me spurring it on as we felt a few drops starting to fall.

We got to the stables with Ferdinand telling Monika and Olwen, "I'll take Hannah to our room to have a rest, I think those ropes have knocked her around again."

Olwen gestured with his hands, "Yes of course go. We will sort out the horses."

Ferdinand and I magicae to the room laying me on the bed, then going to stir up the fire. I felt drained taking the gloves off my hands and slowly undoing the jacket I had on.

Ferdinand came back over to me looking worried at me, "You didn't say you hurt your hand from the effects of the ropes, why didn't you tell me that and all those other things."

I could feel myself getting emotional as tears started to run down my cheeks, "I didn't want to think about it anymore, I was just relieved to have you back."

He took off his things putting a t-shirt and shorts on and changing my clothes pulling the blankets over us, "Komm schon, meine Liebe, wir werden uns ausruhen (come on my love, we will have a rest)" as he pulled me into him giving me a cuddle.

I lay there feeling his warmth and his heart beat, which helped to calm me, along with the crackle of the fire and the flicker of the flames from the fire going around the room. The rain started to fall hitting the windows as I slowly drifted off to sleep.

I woke to hear the crackling of the fire in a darkened room. I could hear the rain still falling outside as I cuddled up against Ferdinand, feeling like I had a bad dream of him being sent back to Jardine without me.

He felt me moving leaning down giving me a kiss on the lips, "How are you feeling honey?"

I put my hand up to his face looking at his concerned eyes shining in the dark, "I'm a lot better, thanks honey."

Ferdinand rolled onto his back pulling me to his chest, "You should have told me what had been going on Hannah. No wonder you did so many pranks, that appears to be your way of coping with things."

I lay there playing with his chest hair, "I was going to talk to you once we got back to Sydney, I just wanted to have a nice time here and not think about it."

He stroked my hair listening to the rain, "Come on we'll get up and join Monika and Olwen and have something to eat. I'm sure they are a bit shaken with all this happening as well."

I got up reluctantly with him getting dressed. I went to the bathroom freshening myself up coming out, "Can you plait my hair dear?"

He smiled lovingly at me, "Yes sure."

He plaited my hair and we went downstairs to find Monika and Olwen in the lounge.

They were both sitting on the sofas talking and looking up as we entered. Olwen came over to me giving me a hug, "How are you, Hannah?"

I looked at him lovingly, "I'm a lot better, thanks Olwen." I looked over to Monika smiling at her, "You handled that very well, Monika. I really appreciate it."

Monika got up coming over to give me a hug, "I'm just glad you showed me that spell as well, as told me everything. That silly woman Malus certainly didn't like being told, did she?"

We went into the dining room, having something to eat then moved back to the lounge relaxing or reading listening to the fire crackle and the rain hit the windows.

Ferdinand and Olwen ended up playing a game of chess while Monika and I chatted about different things until it was time for our evening meal.

Ferdinand and I went and got changed, teasing each other to lighten our moods. I could see Ferdinand was still concerned about what had happened while he was trapped in Jardine. I ended up asking him what he had to do when he was in Jardine.

He wrapped his arms around my waist, "I was mainly in the dragon grotto but I was finding it hard to change into a dragon by that stage. They ended up finding me things to do in the fields and community, feeling a bit ostracised."

I looked down not sure how to say it, "Is it true Lilith wasn't allowed around you?"

He put his hand under my chin looking at me seriously, "yes, it is true."

"She did try to get to see me, especially when I was in the community but they were keeping an eye on her thank goodness. I think she had seen the changes starting to happen, that is why she wanted to see me."

I looked at him frustrated, "She has caused a lot of trouble with our families; do you remember anything?"

He shook his head, "No I'm afraid not. I'm sorry honey, once I do, I will certainly let you know. I still can't believe all of this is happening."

We went downstairs to have our evening meal with Monika and Olwen having a drink afterwards.

Olwen called me over to his piano, "Come here Hannah, I'll give you a piano lesson."

I had a couple of drinks by now chuckling at him, "I can't play the piano Olwen."

He grinned, "Well, now it's time to learn. You've picked up magic and a couple of languages easily enough, you should be smart enough to play the piano."

I groaned going over to him reluctantly sitting next to him, "Ok teacher, show me what to do."

We tinkled around on the piano with him showing me the basics giggling together learning chopsticks. I ended up getting frustrated saying a little chant to myself, *"Time to play on this piano a little tune to impress my brother and all around us play play play."*

I started playing American Pie on the piano with Olwen wrapping his arms around my shoulders laughing, "You're cheating now, Hannah."

We went up to the bedroom feeling relaxed at last and happy to go to bed. I sat with Ferdinand next to the fire having a last drink in the wing back chairs, with just the fire's light in the room. I went and sat on his lap kissing him gently, stirring our passions up.

He took my hair out of its plait running his hands through my hair kissing me gently on the lips, "Are you sure you feel like it, Hannah?"

I got off his lap taking his hand and pulling him onto the mat in front of the fire, "Yes honey I do."

Chapter 31

We spent the next day relaxing and then going to a local market, having a look at homemade items unique to Germany. We had a lovely lunch there, frustrating Ferdinand still with my lack of appetite. Monika pulled him aside, "Just be patient with her Ferdinand, she will pick up with her appetite."

He sighed, "I just remember seeing her when she was younger doing something like this getting very thin."

Monika smiled, "I'm sure she will sort it out, she's not that young girl anymore."

We spent the rest of the day relaxing and going for another ride with the sun coming out warming us as we rode.

--ooOoo--

It came to the time when we decided to go back to Sydney. Monika and Olwen tried to convince us to stay a bit longer, but we wanted to get back and sort some things out.

Monika gave us a big hug looking at me sincerely "you come back to us if you have any other troubles, Hannah."

I looked at her fondly, "You're like a sister to me Monika, thank you. I will return if anything else happens."

Olwen didn't look happy about taking us home, but put a brave face on, "Come on you two let's get you back to your little unit, Hannah."

I gave him a cuddle, "I do love you Olwen and will come back if we have any trouble."

He pulled away from me, "Don't you stand any nonsense from Jardine. If they come back annoying you again you ring me."

I smiled, "I will, thank you."

We got to the lift with Olwen and Ferdinand talking about the business proposition and how Olwen was going to do some research on Ferdinand's family with regard to bank accounts. We arrived back in the national park with the doors opening being greeted by the familiar smells and sounds of the Australian bush. I gave Olwen a hug, "We'll keep in touch."

Ferdinand and I landed back in the unit letting Kimba out of her cage. Ferdinand looked around at the paintings I had put up, along with the family tree on the wall.

He walked over to it looking at me with a photo of him next to me, smiling turning to look at me, "Why did you put this up here Hannah?"

I sat down picking Kimba up and patting her, "I was doing some research and got sick of pulling out the book. It also felt nice having the family watching over me."

He looked at the paintings on the wall of bush and animals, "It looks a little like Jardine this one."

I looked up at it, "As much as the people annoy me there at the moment, I do love the bush and animals."

He opened the balcony door letting some sea air in looking at the empty bottle of wine on the table picking it up and putting it in the bin with the others. He came back over noticing the duvet and pillow on the sofa, "Why were you sleeping on the sofa," as he sat down playing with Kimba's ears.

I sighed, "It wasn't the same with you not there, so I slept out here with the family."

He smiled getting up taking the pillow back to the bedroom noticing the shirt under there picking it up, "You really missed me didn't you."

He leaned over teasing me putting his arms around me, "I think you need to do a ceremony with me."

I chuckled, "I admit I missed you, but I don't need to go to those extremes."

He kissed me on the forehead, "I'll keep trying Hannah. Come on we'll clean up a little and go for a walk along the beach."

I groaned, "Can't we just do it magically?"

He pulled me up, "It'll be good for you to tidy up and get it back to normal, come on."

I got up reluctantly helping him tidy up. I ended up taking the paintings away as I could see he didn't really like them. I took the family tree away as well as it was a bit unnerving with the family watching us, especially when we cuddled.

We went down to the beach for a walk afterwards heading towards the café we enjoyed going to. I kept looking around me wondering if someone was going to appear and harass us.

We sat at a table with him taking my hand looking worried at me, "Do you want to go home?"

I took a deep breath, "No I'll have some lunch and then we can go. I shouldn't let them get to me."

Ferdinand tried to relax me, "Olwen has offered me a job with his company Hannah."

I focused on what he was talking about, "That sounds wonderful dear. What will you be doing?"

He looked a little worried, "Mainly reports. That is something else I needed to talk to you about, I will need your help to show me around a computer. I mean, I know how to use a phone, but a computer might be a bit more difficult."

I smiled, "I like being the teacher for a change. I look forward to it."

We had some lunch slowly walking back to the unit. It was a warm day, which was a bit of a shock after the cool days we had been having in Germany. I could feel the heat draining me a bit of my energy.

We got back to the unit with Ferdinand coming up to me, "I think you should have a lie down honey, you look a little tired."

I yawned, "Yes I think I will."

I was just about to go and lie down when there was a knock at the door.

I looked at Ferdinand, "Who could that be?"

He hesitated, "Just wait and see if anyone calls out."

I heard a voice calling my name feeling, relieved, "It's Jessica from next door."

I went over to the door looking through the peep hole with Ferdinand behind me, "Is it her?"

I nodded, "Yes, it is."

I opened the door carefully "hi Jessica, how are you?"

She looked at me then Ferdinand, "I hadn't seen you around lately so I thought I would check on you Hannah."

She noticed my arm, "Oh you hurt your arm, are you alright?"

I put it up looking at it, "I slipped on the kitchen floor—not drunk, by the way."

She smiled looking at Ferdinand hesitating. I noticed her look, "This is Ferdinand my boyfriend Jessica and no he didn't do it to me. I did actually fall."

Jessica felt awkward, "Sorry Hannah, you know what sort of stuff I've been through. I got help from an old woman, who just popped out of nowhere, telling my boyfriend that if he didn't stop hitting me, she would turn his," coughing nervously, "You know what's to raisins."

I tried not to laugh, "Oh that's a direct way of dealing with him; did it work?"

She smiled happily "yes it did. He is getting counselling and we are getting on a lot better. I promised her I wouldn't put up with it any longer as well."

I gave her a hug, "That is great to hear, Jessica."

She hugged me back, "I just wanted to return the favour to someone else, as I know how it feels to be treated badly by a man."

I looked proudly at her, "That's wonderful, Jessica."

She moved away from the door looking at Ferdinand, "I hope you treat her well Ferdinand?"

He moved forward putting his arm around my waist, "I will, don't worry, Jessica."

She waved goodbye, "See you later Hannah and Ferdinand."

I shut the door with Ferdinand taking my hand, "That was nice. You did that didn't you?"

I gave him a hug, "Yes, he was beating her up again. I just couldn't stand it anymore, so I dressed as an old woman."

He pulled away from me, "I'll have to keep in mind you threatening to make his private bits like raisins."

I giggled, "It worked."

He walked me over to the bedroom, "Come on I'll lie down with you until you go to sleep."

We kicked off our shoes and lay down together rolling me over on my side cuddling into my back stroking my hair. I heard him talk quietly, *"Rest now my sweet to regain your strength and when you wake to feel your best."*

I could feel myself dropping off to a sound sleep, feeling content with him lying next to me.

Ferdinand heard my breathing changing, going into a deep sleep, gently getting up watching me as I slept. He put a light throw over me, picking Kimba up and going out to the lounge.

Ferdinand went out to the balcony sitting down with a glass of wine thinking about what I had been through, feeling angry that I had been abandoned by Jardine. He brought in the phone Olwen had given him, deciding to take his mind off things looking to see if he could find anything about his family and the possibility of bank accounts still open.

He was looking on the phone when Olwen popped in, coming over to Ferdinand looking briefly over to the bedroom, then going out to the balcony "is Hannah having a rest?"

Ferdinand looked up, "Yes, she was a bit tired after we went for lunch and a walk. Do you want a drink?"

Olwen sat down, "Yes that will be nice."

He put his finger around his collar, "it's a bit warmer here, that's for sure."

Ferdinand gave him a wine, "That was another thing making Hannah tired."

Olwen took a sip of wine, "Were you looking for anything in particular on the phone?"

Ferdinand put his phone on the table next to him, "I was just looking to see if there were any bank accounts or property in my family's name still. I know you've offered me a job but I thought if I could get some extra funds from family bank accounts or property, it will help Hannah and I decide what to do next."

Olwen nodded thinking, "Yes, I know what you mean. I will certainly have a look around for you. Sometimes, it's better as to who you know than what you know."

He turned looking out to sea, "I don't mean to come over heavy handed Ferdinand but I feel quite protective of Hannah, even though we have only known each other for a short time. I have heard the rumours about you being a bit of a playboy in your younger days. I will be very angry if you hurt, Hannah."

Ferdinand pushed his hand through his hair looking uncomfortable, "I don't remember any of those times Olwen. I love Hannah and I assure you I won't be doing that to her."

He took a sip of wine grimacing, "I'm sure she would do something to me magically if I tried anything like that as well. The next-door neighbour came earlier telling us of a woman threatening her boyfriend, who had been beating her up, to turn his man bits into raisins."

Olwen chuckled choking on his wine, "That sounds like Hannah. She's a clever witch; we will have to keep an eye on her. I'm just doing my brotherly duty Ferdinand, no hard feelings."

Ferdinand tapped Olwen's glass, "No hard feelings, Olwen; at least I know where I stand. Thanks again for the job offer; Hannah has said she'll help me with the computer."

Olwen sat back relaxing with his wine, "That's great."

Ferdinand grinned, "I wonder what she would have been like if she had the family magic when she was younger?"

Olwen raised an eyebrow turning to look at him, "You know I never thought about that. She's picked up so much already, I could feel the strength when she put me in a binding spell when I came to pick her up."

It was Ferdinand's turn to choke on his drink now, "She did what?"

Olwen chuckled, "Yes, she wasn't in a good mood, as we have said. I arrived before Amelia and Charlotte surprising her. I tell you what I couldn't get out of it, she was very strong."

Ferdinand took another sip of his wine thinking, "As you know Hannah gave me access to her family book to keep me alive. It welcomed me back, so I'm not sure what that was about."

Olwen sighed, "It's a shame we don't know what else that Lilith said under the truth spell. Do you think the Jardine women will tell either you or her?"

Ferdinand shrugged his shoulders, "I don't know. I'm sure if Morag was there, she would have told Hannah, but no one knows where she is. You never know Hannah might convince them when she goes to visit."

Olwen grumbled, "'if' she goes to visit. If I had my way she wouldn't be going back, but it's up to her in the end I guess."

A thought came to Ferdinand, "I just remembered something that happened before I was captured. I had been left a note saying that Hannah was going to do some work for Jardine to help catch the dark magical people. We might have to talk to her about that?"

Olwen rolled his eyes, "I will be encouraging her not to do it. Again, it's up to you two." Olwen got up, finishing his wine, "I better get back to Monika. I'll call in after a couple of days to see how you are all going and let you know about the job."

Ferdinand got up shaking his hand, "You've been a great help to Hannah and me, thanks Olwen. It's a shame you weren't around when she was younger as well."

Olwen leaned in, hugging him. "We'll just have to make up for lost time. I see you later. Send my love to Hannah."

He walked out to the lounge going into the bedroom to check on me still fast asleep blowing a kiss to me. He came back out, "She's fast asleep. Did you use a little magic?"

Ferdinand grinned. "Just an old chant that came into my mind. She'll probably get annoyed with me, but she needed the sleep."

Olwen patted his arm. "I've still got that suit of armour there if you need it. I'll see you later."

Ferdinand watched him disappear going to check on me as well. He turned on the fan as it was quite warm in the room, shutting the door.

Ferdinand had a lot of emotions running through him, feeling a little annoyed about Olwen worrying about him hurting Hannah. He stood looking out to sea leaning against the door frame, *'I wouldn't hurt Hannah, especially with another woman. I've waited a long time to be with her and I'm not sure how long I have got with her, so I definitely wouldn't be looking at another woman.'*

He decided to do some meditation to see if it would open his mind up hopefully bringing back some memories as well. He wasn't very good at it, but anything is worth a try. He lit some incense and put the CD on that I used, sitting in front of the balcony window with a gentle breeze floating over him as he relaxed himself, listening to his breathing. He felt himself going quite deep, visualising himself floating along in a boat when everything stopped making him look up from the boat getting out to a grassy area in front of him. He saw a woman he knew walking over to her, "Hallo Wilhemenia (hello Wilhemenia)."

She smiled at him as he approached, "Hallo Frederick, du siehst aus wie dein altes Ich (hello Frederick you are looking like your old self)."

He pushed his hand through his hair, "Ich erinnere mich immer noch nicht an vieles. Können Sie mir das sagen? (I still don't remember a lot. Can you tell me?)"

She looked at him admiringly, "Nein Friedrich, es wird zu dir kommen. Stellen Sie nur sicher, dass Sie meine Enkelin nicht verletzen. (No Frederick, it will come to you. Just make sure you don't hurt my granddaughter.)"

He smiled, "Das ist die zweite Warnung, die ich heute erhalten habe. Sie sagte, sie würde für mich sterben. (that's the second warning I've had today. She said she would die for me.)"

Wilhemenia shook her head, "Du magst im Moment ihr Herz haben, aber sie ist stark genug, um dich zu zerquetschen, wenn du sie verletzt. (You might have her heart now but she is strong enough to squash you if you hurt her.)"

He looked at her earnestly. "Ich werde sie nicht verletzen. Ich liebe sie sehr und möchte genießen, welche Zeit ich mit ihr habe. (I won't hurt her. I love her dearly and want to enjoy what time I have with her)."

Wilhemenia looked sadly at him. "Das haben Sie schon einmal zu einer anderen Frau gesagt. (You have said that before to another woman)."

Ferdinand was getting frustrated. "Ich erinnere mich nicht daran und ich nehme an, Sie werden mir nicht sagen, wer. Ich habe Hannah gebeten, mich zu heiraten. (I don't remember that and I suppose you won't tell me who. I've asked Hannah to marry me.)"

Wilhemenia chuckled, getting up and walking away. "Viel Glück mit diesem Frederick, Sie wissen, wie sie über die Ehe denkt. (Good luck with that, Frederick, you know how she feels about marriage.)" Wilhemenia faded away, leaving him to go back to the boat.

He came out of the meditation, sitting there and wondering what he had done in his past life, feeling frustrated and angry not knowing who put this bloody curse on him and why. It was obvious, Wilhemenia wasn't going to tell him.

He got up, shaking himself out, bringing in another glass of wine and sitting on the balcony, waiting for me to wake up while trying to recall some of the visions he had.

He sipped on his wine with thoughts running through his head, 'I'm definitely going to have to get hold of Lilith somehow and see why she was his guardian or keeper, whatever she bloody called herself,' feeling his anger burn up at the thought of her.